Fay Sampson was born in Exmouth and grew up in the fishing and farming village of Lympstone. She had her first children's novel published in 1975 and since then has had a further eighteen published, as well as two educational books, and the sequence of five novels, DAUGHTER OF TINTAGEL (also available from Headline). She has taught adult education classes in writing and visits schools and other groups as 'writer in the community'. She divides her time between Tedburn St Mary and Birmingham, is married and has two grown-up children.

*Also by Fay Sampson*

Daughter of Tintagel
Wise Woman's Telling
White Nun's Telling
Black Smith's Telling
Taliesin's Telling
Herself

# Star Dancer

Fay Sampson

Copyright © 1993 Fay Sampson

The right of Fay Sampson to be identified as the Author of the work has been asserted by her in accordance with the Copyright, Designs and Patents Act 1988

First published in 1993
by HEADLINE BOOK PUBLISHING PLC

First published in paperback in 1993
by HEADLINE BOOK PUBLISHING PLC

A HEADLINE FEATURE paperback

10 9 8 7 6 5 4 3 2 1

All rights reserved. No part of this publication may be reproduced, stored in a retrieval system, or transmitted in any form or by any means without the prior written permission of the publisher, nor be otherwise circulated in any form of binding or cover other than that in which it is published and without a similar condition being imposed on the subsequent purchaser.

All characters in this publication are fictitious and any resemblance to real persons, living or dead, is purely coincidental.

ISBN 0 7472 4150 3

Typeset by Avon Dataset Ltd, Bidford-on-Avon

Printed and bound in Great Britain by
HarperCollins Manufacturing, Glasgow

HEADLINE BOOK PUBLISHING PLC
Headline House
79 Great Titchfield Street
London W1P 7FN

To Diana and Harry

# Author's Note

The ancient land of Sumer occupied the flood plain of the Tigris and Euphrates, now southern Iraq, some four thousand years ago. Cities that once housed hundreds of thousands of people are today sand-covered mounds. Gardens and cornfields, watered through irrigation channels with the fertile overflow of those great rivers, have fallen victim to the desert. Some of the marshes remain, for a while at least. Sumer was a land with little stone and few trees. Clay and reeds were its natural resources.

In this land flowered one of the earliest civilisations. Luckily for us, these people wrote with reed styluses on clay tablets. Thousands of pieces of their writing have survived, though often in fragments. We have an enormous number of economic and legal documents, but also hymns, poems, history, science, and a handful of myths, legends and epics.

To those brought up on the Book of Genesis, many of the myths bring a start of recognition. We find life brought into being by the Word, images of tree and snake, the Flood, the confusion of human languages. We should not be surprised. Abraham is said to have set out on his journey to the land of Canaan from Ur, the city of the Sumerian Moon Lord, Inanna's father. Yet, while the outward details of some of the stories are familiar, the concepts behind them are very different. It is hard to imagine the Yahweh of Genesis being put on trial for rape! For this reason, I have avoided using the words 'god' and 'goddess', even with a small 'g'. They carry a meaning for us which would be inappropriate here.

I wanted first to tell the story of Inanna, who descends to the Netherworld to meet its queen, Ereshkigal. Then, as I read more of the myths, I realised that my understanding of this central story was changed and deepened by knowing what had happened to earlier generations of her family, some of whom were still carrying the pain of their own

Netherworld experiences. Even small parts in Inanna's story took on a new significance now.

Somewhere under those sands there are probably many more stories, unknown to us or alluded to only in tantalising references. We have no reason to believe that the stories we do know ever formed part of a continuous saga. The choice in joining them together in this novel has been my own. Many other ways of connecting them up are possible. Different versions of the stories exist. There are inconsistencies over the relationships between the characters. The principal figures are known by a multitude of titles, but sometimes these same names are used for separate people. The Sumerian language is still imperfectly known, so that eminent scholars who have devoted a lifetime to the texts may differ radically over the translation of a crucial sentence. I have relied on my own instinct to choose the version which seems to me the most convincing in the context. I have elaborated freely on the stories. I have invented to fill the gaps. But within my necessarily limited knowledge I have tried not to contradict the known sources. Every chapter has its foundation in an original text, though I am sometimes building on a single sentence.

I have had to make one arbitrary decision. Who was Ereshkigal? Some texts call her Inanna's 'sister'. But the Sumerians used this word for a wide range of kinship or association. She seems to me to belong to an older generation, where the first characters were closely related. The answer I find most convincing to explain the stories which follow is that she was the twin of Enki, Inanna's grandfather.

Wherever I could, I have used the earliest Sumerian sources. I find their tone more democratic, less violent, more respectful to women than some of the later stories. But I have felt free to turn to Akkadian or other versions where these would fill a gap or provide an additional insight. I have endeavoured to be faithful to the spirit of the texts, as they communicated themselves to me. Many of the poems, both of joy and sorrow, express the woman's point of view. There are songs dedicated to Inanna which celebrate an uninhibited pleasure in the sexual act, especially the rite of marriage. There are other hymns which address her more fearfully in her battle aspect, as protector of her people. She is both Lover and Lion.

One problem I found in reading the stories is that very

many of the names begin with 'Nin', meaning 'Lady' or 'Lord'. These names are usually written as a single word, but if they are separated into two parts it becomes no more difficult than an Arthurian romance where many of the characters have names beginning with 'Sir'. To make identification still easier, I have separated the women's names, for example Nin Shubur, but left the smaller number of men's names as a single word, for example Ninurta. This introduces a gender distinction which is not present in the original, but the Sumerian reader had the advantage of knowing already which of the names were female and which male.

I am indebted to the great number of scholars who have excavated, conserved, catalogued, transcribed, translated, published and commented upon these clay tablets, sometimes with a leap of insight that connects a fragment in, say, Istanbul with another in Chicago and sees that they are part of the same story. I particularly express my gratitude to Samuel Noah Kramer for decades of work on the language, literature and life of the Sumerian people, to Thorkild Jacobsen, who has in addition sought to explore deeper into the beliefs behind the stories, and to Françoise Bruschweiter for her detailed study of the many-faceted character of Inanna and the difficult question of what the Sumerians understood by Kur. For those who would like to read the central Inanna stories in a translation faithful to the originals and learn more of their background, I recommend Diane Wolkstein and Samuel Noah Kramer's book *Inanna, Queen of Heaven and Earth*. I have tried not to quote directly from any of these translators, but I could not remain uninfluenced by their language, nor would I have wished to.

I am aware that a few happy years researching and writing this book are not enough to avoid many mistakes and oversights which must be apparent to those who have devoted their lives to the subject. This is a work of fiction, not of scholarship. It tells what the texts say for me.

Fay Sampson
1993

# Prologue

A little girl wanders through the dust at the parched end of the year. A last dog moves weakly in the shadow of the wall, his starveling ribs like slatted reeds. The girl clutches a belly that is unnaturally swollen and always painful. Hunger gnaws obsessively, dulling her mind to the beauty of the vivid blue sky, the fronded date palms, the gold and purple reaches of the desert. The air is still, save for the buzz of flies. No one is stirring. Her people lie, exhausted by pain and fear, in the darkness of their huts. They would work, weak though they are, if there were work to do. But what is there to be won in fields where no crops grow? What use to clear and mend channels whose beds are sun-cracked and waterless? Slowly the huge and gorgeous bud of the date palm will still unfold, but it is long yet to harvest.

The storehouse stands on its platform above the flood plain, like a communal temple. Two pillars of reed bundles tower above its doorway, their tops scrolled like the prow of a ship. Its walls are plaited in an intricate latticework that lets in the wandering breeze to cool and refresh. The door stands open. The matting curtain, rolled up, dangles unevenly, half-secured. No one is guarding it.

That open, empty doorway shocks the girl. It is a thing she has not seen before. This should be a busy place, where streams of sweating villagers shoulder the heavy baskets of grain to their resting-place, where the sweet sticky mass of the date clusters takes pride of place, where slaughtered sheep and goats, having dripped their last blood, are now strips of flesh drying on racks to last till winter lambing. Or else the doors are shut, and an elder, too old to work, crouches with bony knees in the shadow of the rustling wall. From time to time he clambers to his feet, and ducks inside, inspects for marching ants, brushes away the maggot-laying flies, asserts his self-importance. Or, on a feast day, the whole village comes with ritual pipes and tambourines. The women shake spears, their right limbs clad like men; the men ululate, their left side dressed like women. Summer and winter meet, male and female, the Anunnaki are married. And out of their storehouse pours what the people need. Meat, grain, cheese, beer, the dates that know no taint of decay.

Today the doorway is empty. The mound deserted. The Guardians have gone.

The child, frightened but enormously daring, crosses that threshold. The chamber is vast. Buttresses of lashed reeds arch together over her head. The sky glints through the fretted walls like chips of lapis lazuli. The dusty floor is dappled with sunlight like the hide of gazelles.

The sweet smell of barley, the savour of beer, the fragrance of date honey are missing. A faintly rancid smell of cheese still hangs on the air. And from the farthest end comes an insistent buzzing.

It is hard for the girl to enter this place. Harder still to make herself walk to the far, dim end under the patterned circle of the window. But she must do it, though there seems no reason why. Past seven pillars, under seven archeo, and with each step she seems to shrink and lose a little more of her infant self-possession.

The last vault now, and though the window lights her, a cloud, hostile without rain, shadows the floor, strips all the jewels of sunshine from it. The shade that had seemed welcome at first strikes now with the chill of death.

The storehouse is empty, every bay, every rack, every vat, every basket. It has all been eaten. Even the flour dust in the straw has been gleaned by mice. The rains have failed. The famished sheep have given up their bones. The corn has withered. There is nothing left.

Nothing but this, pendant from a hook on the wall, swaying now to the touch of a mocking gust of wind. It releases its putrid stench as it swings, and the mat of flies that covers it rises in front of her face, making her shriek and cover her eyes.

A green and rotting side of meat, festering with maggots. All that is left of a ewe lamb.

The girl stares at it with a fascinated horror. And as she watches, the cloud shifts across the sun and the cruel light strikes in again. The flies are settling, like a curtain of blue-black hair. Those crawling maggots gleam like features of pale skin. She has seen those features, looking up at her out of palm-hung pools in the years when there was rain. Through a long and terrible moment she is gazing at her slaughtered self.

A voice strikes through sleep, hauling the Star Princess in her soft bed back to life.

'Wake up! Inanna!'

# BOOK ONE

Star-Rise

# Chapter One

Inanna opened her eyes.

A face that was not Lama her nurse bent over her. These unfamiliar features and voice had never woken her before. They would be with her now every morning for eternity.

A high-boned, slightly yellow face, marked with the threads and pinpoints of tattoos. The dark, tip-tilted eyes, sympathetic but wise. The slightly teasing smile that promised playfulness for the child Inanna, held within bounds by official respect for the eldest daughter of Lord Moon. Creases between the eyes that hinted at a private sadness.

Nin Shubur. The Lady of the East, a shaman. Inanna's *sukkal*, since yesterday.

At the pain of loss and fear, Inanna rolled over and buried her head in the softly-looped wool of her coverlet.

A small, perceptive hand rested on her head, dry, where Inanna's skin was already sweating. A song crooned from the young woman in a tongue foreign to Sumer. Inanna felt soothed, the hurt already receding.

But not for long.

'Sit up, my young lady. Breakfast is ready.'

'It's not morning, is it?' The chamber was windowless, the lamps softly shadowing.

'So much the better. The sun will be up to bully us soon. Out on the roof the light is coming already. Wash and eat, and come out to see it with me. The whole world is waiting for you, Inanna, between night and sunrise. It's the best time of day.'

Fresh bread, with date syrup and cream. Copper pitchers of lukewarm water sluicing the sweat of the night away in the tiled bathroom. Palace servants whose names she did not yet know waiting upon her as others had done at her mother's house in Ur.

'Will I have to see An?' Great-grandfather, whose house, E-Anna, this was. Inanna's home, now.

Nin Shubur's hand rested on her shoulder, over the fleecy towel, with understanding. 'Not yet. The old are allowed to live life more slowly.'

Inanna watched the soap-grey water running away through the drain. A shiver of remembered fear passed over her. 'There was a terrible storm in the night. It woke me up.'

'It is over now, and the sky will be all the sweeter for it.'

'I heard the Thunderbird roaring. I could see the lightning through the door curtain. The rain sounded terrible. I thought . . . if An and Enlil were so angry with me . . . Could it happen again? The Flood?'

Again that playful smile, the arch of the eyebrows.

'For you? Never again, Inanna. Not like that. We promised, remember? But a serious flood, for all that. There was much damage done. Come and look.'

Inanna came walking through the roof garden of the E-Anna into a morning as new as herself. Dawn was breaking. The violent overnight storm had drowned in a vast, golden calm. Every canal and distributary of the broad Buranun River had overflowed its banks across the level land. The feathered heads of date palms inclined to see their reflections in lakes as infinitely deep as the cloudless sky above, as shallow as children's footsteps.

The pools were serene, but the torrent of the rivers still forced a turbulence of brown waters rushing towards the sea like tawny lions after their prey. Banks had been broken down, reed clumps seized and swirled away, dead sheep and cattle eddied like inflated skin rafts out of control. Even whole precious trees had been uprooted and tossed into the hungry flood.

It was as if Enlil was threatening. 'Beware, little humans, you black-headed people of Sumer, so fragile upon the Earth. We formed you out of clay. We blew the breath of life into you. We made you to be our servants. Do not grow too proud. Do not forget. We could overwhelm you in a moment with another deluge.'

Inanna tried not to be afraid of Enlil. She did not entirely succeed. Great-grandfather An was older, more remote. But when he bellowed at her, she trembled too. Now, in the sweet, soft peace before sunrise, she walked wide-eyed as if she felt the shadow of her violent destiny. Her own silver star shone luminous through a rising mist, mirrored in lagoons, before the sun was fully awake.

Then she shook her hair and smiled. Wasn't she Inanna, daughter of the Moon Lord Nanna, granddaughter of Enlil, who came from both Earth and Sky? Inanna, daughter of the Reed Lady Nin Gal, granddaughter on that side of Enki, made from both Sky and Water? In her sweet person, morning and night, light and darkness, solid and shifting met in a promise of perfection.

She walked on feet ringed with gold and lapis lazuli, over the terrace of the Sky House that was lofty enough to keep even the rearing Buranun at bay. It was paved for rulership, paved for reverence. Black bitumen tiles sealed themselves against the parapet. Inner bands of terracotta red made two walks on which her retinue could attend her. Nin Shubur preceded her. Inanna walked alone along a central path of celestial blue. She was too young to need any dress save her silver and gold ornaments. But the many white tiers of Nin Shubur's tasselled skirt brushed rain-heavy sprays of fruit bushes that grew in earthenware pots, releasing the fragrance of well-watered blossoms all around them. Inanna fondled their leaves, and they seemed to swell for her with new growth between her fingertips. The blue-veined marble of her breasts, as yet unformed and innocent, moved against the cool sway of her silver and coral necklaces. Her fresh-washed, blue-black hair lifted very slightly to the last touch of the night breeze.

She brushed it away from her eyes, and stood looking east, leaning on the kiln-fired bricks of the boundary wall.

Houses had crumbled. The waters were thick with the dissolving clay of their sun-baked walls. Roofs, that frail human hands had painfully cut and lashed together from reed bundles, had been torn apart in moments. A baby, nursed in its mother's womb for nine hot and heavy months, floated face downwards, drowned more swiftly than it was born.

Inanna watched, a little awed. 'Did we do this? We, the Anunnaki? I didn't like that storm. It reminded me too much of the other one. Even in the middle of the house my bedroom felt as if it was shaking with the fury of it.'

Nin Shubur drew her eyes back from the far horizon. Too far away, even in daylight, to see the mountains of her own childhood. Too far away to guess the snows, the high blue peaks, the precipices, the smoke-hung huts of home, the house over the abyss where she had been a princess, Lady of the East, before Enlil called her to serve Inanna.

'No ordinary tempest that, my lady. The waves were like the ones they say flooded the coast when your grandfather Enki was fighting for his life... But yes. We have that power. We all come from water.'

Inanna seated herself on a bull-headed clay bench by the parapet. 'Tell me!' she demanded, suddenly the imperious young mistress to her *sukkal*.

Awareness of rank flashed in her minister's eyes. She bowed an obedient head.

The first shell-pink of dawn was creeping up the sky. The planet Dilibad still shone among the paling stars. Far below them, the flood tide girdled the base of the Mound of Uruk. The *sukkal* squatted at Inanna's feet.

# Chapter Two

*Before the first day, before the very first day, there was only water. Nammu, the Great Deep, the mother of us all, wrapped herself round in an endless embrace, without colour, without sound, without form, in utter darkness.*

'What did she do?' breathed Inanna.

*What did she do? What did she not do? Nammu made herself very small. She made herself very great. Her oceans writhed and squeezed and coiled and rushed. She hugged, she longed, she loved, she gave herself. The primal waters opened. An-Ki was born.*

*An-Ki, the Mountain of Heaven and Earth.*

*Dark yet, all wrapped around with the blood-warm, liquid body of Mother Nammu. No light, no pain, no knowledge, except of themselves. There was no beyond. An was an empty Sky, Ki was a stony Earth. They hardly knew that each was an other. They had only each other. Close was their embrace, while Mother Nammu swirled round them, holding them blindly in the moist vortex of her creating.*

*How long were they one, An-Ki? There was no Sun to measure the day, no Moon to dance the months, no Morning and Evening Star to mark the threshold of total night. No immortal or human observed that holding together, that infinite moment of meeting. Twins, still barren and unfulfilled, within the infinitely fecund fluid of their mother.*

*Love, of themselves in the other.*

*And then a sigh.*

*A breath, a wind. Enlil. Lord Air.*

*Their firstborn.*

'Enlil!' Inanna's tone was sharp with bitterness, but Nin Shubur silenced her with a finger.

*An-Ki rejoiced! The mighty Bull of Heaven impregnated the willing Cow of Earth again and again. Fifty times and more the cosmic mountain heaved with their coupling. Ki grew great with An's seed multiplying within her. In the dark of her womb teemed the first generation of the Anunnaki, as yet unborn, unnamed, not yet assigned to their particular tasks. Life throbbed within Mother Ki as the blood of her own mother beat around her.*

*Yet time was not, and space was not, and there was no room for anything to burst forth. Only the weightless, formless breath of Enlil puffed and struggled to expand. The closeness of An-Ki smothered his infant voice, would not let his more solid brothers and sisters be born. No grass clothed the limbs of Ki in jewel-green. No stones of lapis lazuli or carnelian, no metal of silver or antimony beaded her neck. No wool hung from fat sheep. No milk spurted from cattle. Canals could not be dug, cities could not be built, no hoe could till the soil.*

*There was only the thought of all this in the mind of Enlil. 'I must make room for us!'*

*A movement now, an energy, a direction. Troubling the dusty surface of his mother Ki. Stirring the calm space of his father An. Still they are bonded, An-Ki, the cosmic Mountain. They will not let each other go.*

*Enlil is restless, growing. In him there is a vast possibility for change. He is impatient for time to begin. His own seed stirs within him with a latent luminosity, touching his grandmother's liquid breasts with a first dim sheen.*

*Nammu is drawing away from them, creating more space for her offspring, defining herself into a primordial circle of ocean, under Ki, above An, surrounding Enlil. Still she yearns towards the dry body of her daughter, arches the weight of her watery belly over her tearless son.*

*And then that wind. Like the point of a knife, not yet fashioned, from metal not yet forged, with fire as yet unknown, from ore not yet dug. But it penetrates his parents' common body. He severs the unity to which Nammu has given birth. Once they cleaved together, now they are cleft. A vast distance opens between An and Ki, and through it a rushing, unstoppable wind sweeps and howls and whoops. When it has passed, An-Ki is no more.*

*It was Enlil, their own son, who separated them, moved Sky away from Earth.*

Again that start, which Inanna could not control.

Nin Shubur's hand was swiftly on the girl's knee. 'Joy came of it, as well as hurt. We need both to grow.'

'He did it to me too! Enlil! He's taken me away from Mother, and Father Nanna, and Ur, and everything!'

Dangerously close to tears, she ran to the reed fence that topped the parapet and clutched the canes with small, fierce hands. Nin Shubur's voice pursued her, with the incantation of old griefs.

'Let the tears come, Inanna. The laughter will follow.'

*Who can say the pain of that first breaking apart? The Mountain of Heaven and Earth, the Father–Mother, the wholeness that was the universe split in two. Ki lay prostrate. An was flung reeling upwards, loosed from her loving hold, against the warm embrace of his mother. Young Enlil, Lord Air, shimmering with the first, faint, created light, danced in triumph between them. Vast Nammu cradled her son in her arms, nursed her daughter in her lap. She waited to hear the very first words, spoken by the Breath of the Universe.*

'*I will have the Earth!*'

*And that is how it was. An became Lord of the Sky. Enlil was Governor of the Earth. You see, Ki is already dispossessed.*

'He would!'

*And Ki? What will she give us? What will she not give, Ki the Earth, Urash the Tilth, Nin Tu the Lady of Birth? The good, the warped. The wholesome, the dangerous. The brave, the weak. All must come out of her now. She lies in her dry-eyed, desolate isolation, great with An's children, unclothed, solitary save for her son's wandering touch on her stony skin.*

*From the new-formed, almost limitless distance, An looks down and can no longer see his sister-spouse in this twilight cosmos. Like a little boy, he would weep for his lost love, the great Lord of Above, but he has no tears. He buries his head in the breast of his mother Nammu and her waters heave against the still-expanding air. Her waves sound in An's ears. In the quivering of his son's element, the vast soundbox of his separation from his wife, An hears for the first time his mother's voice, a shushing without words, and the beat of her great heart.*

*An loses himself in his mother. He finds no comfort for the lost contours of Ki, but he learns to weep. And from the mingling fluids of their bodies, mother and son, twins are born, a boy of fresh face and flowing hair. Enki, they call him. And a dark and lovely daughter, Ereshkigal. What is there left for them to inherit? An has the Sky. Enlil has taken the Earth. These two must seek their destiny deeper still.*

Inanna muttered, her thoughts still on her own grief. 'What's happened to me, that was Enki's fault, too. He didn't give me enough.'

A spasm passed over Nin Shubur's face as her spirit was recalled to the present.

'Child! You think you can have anything you want. And I fear we shall all of us give you more than we should.' She stood behind Inanna. The woman's hands played with the younger girl's hair.

The sun leaped up with a blinding suddenness, turning the turbulence of the flood from tawny brown to flashing gold. Almost at once the storm-washed sky deepened to an intense blue.

Inanna bit her lip. The memory of the childish anger that had brought her here frightened even herself.

'My lady,' said Nin Shubur gently. 'The sun is up. It is time for you to pay your respects to Lord An.'

# Chapter Three

An's quarters occupied the highest buildings of the Sky House, as far from the teeming city of Uruk as hands could raise it. The huge artificial mound was lifted above the totally flat river plain, a mountain fit for the Father of all the Anunnaki. Just below in the district of Kullab, many of the Children of An had their houses, set amidst dark-shadowed gardens, ringed by brick walls. The E-Anna of Father An was the largest and loftiest of all, white limestone dazzling at its base, blue-enamelled tiles mirroring the sky.

Inanna climbed the hot, high stair ramp, feeling sweat trickling down her body.

The entrance was dark, like the blessed relief of nightfall. Palm-leaf fans stroked the air. She felt the coolness of basalt under her feet after the warmth of beaten earth and kiln-baked bricks.

Nin Shubur had resumed the formality of a princess's *sukkal*, walking before her mistress with her silver wand, no longer the shaman storyteller, or the sympathetic older sister. Linen-clad eunuchs bowed as she passed. The pluck of harps and the tap of finger drums continued as unobtrusively as birdsong. The blind musicians could not see the small procession.

At the inner door, Nin Shubur's small, clear voice announced, 'Inanna, First Daughter of Lord Moon, Lady Morning Star.'

The Lady of the East was a small woman. Between one narrow shoulder and the bronze-bound doorposts, Inanna could glimpse the chamber beyond where lamps still burned even in the hot morning. There was a tumble of striped blankets. There was a tumble of bodies, too, as two naked girls, one golden, one black, slipped off to kneel beside the couch, faces turned curiously to her. Another woman rose more slowly from where she had been sitting beside An's pillow. Sharp, canine features, like a jackal. Alert, golden eyes, black-rimmed with kohl. Teeth bared as she smiled. Nin Isinna, in the lick of whose tongue, they said, was healing.

Now Nin Isinna bent to help An rise a little against the cushions like heaped clouds. An old man, his hair thin and white without the ceremonial blue-black wig in which Inanna was used to seeing him at Councils and feasts. Even to the child, he seemed oddly vulnerable, less fearsome in the flesh than her dread had been imagining him.

For his part, An gazed across the windowless chamber, hazed by the aromatic incense burners. Blue eyes, that had pierced space from high Angal above the Sky, blinked uncertainly.

Nin Shubur moved aside. An saw a girl-child was standing in his doorway facing him. Not yet a woman. Slender, yet with no angularity on her sweetly-rounded, blue-white limbs. Jewellery of silver and gold, lapis lazuli and coral clasped wrists and ankles, throat and navel. Otherwise, she was as naked as the summer sky. Why did he tremble with a far-off passion that was not the lust he had felt for the concubines a minute before? A cloud of blue-black hair, so soft it seemed to float even in this windless chamber. Tendrils of it caught in the hollows of her neck; the fall of it shadowed her barely budding breasts. She was too young for pubic hair.

His voice breathed out an age-old pain, barely a sigh, but with all the baffled longing of a groan.

'*Ereshkigal?*'

# Chapter Four

*Ki's time is near. Her body swells and heaves. So little light, so few to see her, yet An, her twin, who covered her from the moment of their birth, has been stripped from her, and she lies naked to the curious gaze of her son. She tells Enlil to help her build the first birth hut, the Duku, creation chamber of the world.*

*He gathers stones; she plasters the mound with clay. On her mountainous belly, between the raised peaks of her knees, it stands, covering the dark portal of her vagina. Form has appeared on Earth. She will be called Nin Dim, Lady Fashioner; Nagarshaga, Carpenter of the Insides; Ama-Dugbad, Mother Spreading the Knees; Aruru, Foetus-Loosener.*

*And so her babies come, tumbling from their mother, groping for shape and destiny. The Anunnaki.*

*The Children of An and Ki. Most are the offspring of great love. Inside this Duku are all the things that Enlil dreamed of. Brothers and sisters of the soil and sky, living things and things that are made. Crawling blindly like maggots still, unaware yet of their multiple usefulness. Ki feels them squirm against her and smiles at last. She can nurse them ages yet. They will grow to bless the world with gladness. They will come out with the joy of the Earth in their hearts and the wonder of the Sky in their eyes.*

*She is Ama-Ududa, Mother Who Has Given Birth.*

*There was no pain in bearing, for the Lady of Childbirth. But an earlier anguish has left its mark on some. They have been scarred in the womb by that terrible moment of loss and agony when An was torn from Ki. These babies bring an ambivalent benediction. They will seize and hurt. They will strike fear and desolation. They can also renew life. They are the Dark Guardians.*

*Now something darker still is slipping from Ki. A power seemingly inappropriate to the birth hut, yet necessary for it. Those little squealing beings, not yet seen, have drawn their vital blood through this. Life in all its variety is coming into being. Death is its other face.*

*Kur. Slipping over the edge of the world into the nether darkness between Ki's Earth and Nammu's Water. No eye to see the shape of his malevolence. Ki feels his serpent coldness slick beneath her back and buttocks. Nammu senses him come. In the eternal rush and tumble of her waters around all things, she does not judge. Kur is. He will always be here now. As she is, and was, and will be.*

*But loss bites at the heart of Kur. His mother has been robbed, and he must have his compensation. He writhes and fumes, under the supine bulk of the exhausted Ki. He grows, matures, takes hideous shape beneath her shadow. A creature huge as Earth itself, this Netherworld, yet dangerously unconfined. His scaly coils rear up into a monstrous neck. His spiked tail lashes. At each stroke the waves of Nammu rise and crash against the cosmos. Space fills with flying spray. A fearsome, horned head, whose breath smokes like the exhalation of a rotting marsh and flickers with noxious gases, creeps swaying up above Earth's horizon. Slowly his baleful eyes peer round the gloom of sunless air. All this is An's or Enlil's. What is there left for him?*

*The Sky Lord looks fondly down but sees only the Duku hiding the babies he has fathered. He has not perceived this unlovable afterbirth. Kur clambers upwards into Enlil's element. Clawed talons, tipped with stone and dripping venom, thrust aside the shifting breakers of Nammu, rake gashes in Ki's sides. He does not feel for others. There is no pity in his heart, only an unfulfilled hunger vast as the distance that has separated his parents.*

*His eyes in the snuffling, questing snout are almost blind, this worm of darkness. But his body stiffens, turns. His fangs are streaked with saliva. He has smelt sweet, living flesh.*

*Young, virginal, dancing in the dark sky of that original night. Blacker still, her hair swings out behind her in a great fan of cloud, not quite silvered at the edges by the far-off light of Enlil's eyes. Pale limbs no sun has touched, gleaming faintly as they weave in careless freedom through all the space of heaven. Ereshkigal, the Sky Princess, chasing her brother Enki.*

*He, like a river, dives and tumbles, twists and evades, and doubles back to rise and overarch her. She slips through his reaching hands, turns her face and laughs with the music of sweet pipes.*

*Far below, too dark and distant for them to see, stands the Duku, where the Anunnaki still crouch waiting for their names and destinies. Enlil, unusually still, watches the darting of his brother and sister above him. He guards the Earth. This is his prize. He has plans for it. Words of creation are beginning to shape in his heart. He watches thoughtfully that frivolous pair who race through their father's realm with no thought of time or boundaries, as though infinity and eternity were enough. How long will they be incurious about their destiny? Will these beings of Sky and Water ever try to seize back the Earth?*

*His mother's eyes are on her birth hut. Her arms are round it, cradling her young. She guides her nipple in to find the questing mouths of the Anunnaki. She is the Great Mother. She can nourish them all.*

*The Duku is too small a thing to concern young Enki and Ereshkigal as they dash across a sky that is unencumbered with stars. Nor have they noticed Kur. He is too large to comprehend. Only Enlil has seen the monstrous shadow spreading across space. Enlil narrows his eyes, lest he should leak too much of that inner brilliance waiting to be engendered in a child. Better no one but he sees what is coming. Better no shriek sets the air waves trembling. Better that the grace and abandon of the game that the brother and sister are playing should vault and spiral and somersault unconfined by fear or caution to its dreadful conclusion.*

*What will he do with her, her awful brother Kur, who has grown so great he fills the Netherworld and more? Will he want Enki too, or has he eyes only for the girl? Does Enlil see or only imagine the dimly-glistening fangs gape wider, the throat yawn huge and lightless, those eyes, vast lakes of bitterness, roll upward to the loving, unconcerned face of Father An, watching and smiling as his children play? Does Kur hate him for that calm benevolence, who let Ki go only at Enlil's Word?*

*Enlil shifts a little, like a cool breeze. He does not fear Kur's fangs. He thinks the Air Lord cannot be bound or wounded.*

*The monster is threatening half the sky now, an eclipse of its almost-nothingness, as black as Ereshkigal's hair. Enki races away, dives into his Mother Nammu's waves with a gurgle of laughter. Ereshkigal speeds after him, spins, baffled at his total disappearance, darts earthwards, checks, comes face to face with Enlil. The wind eddies around her limbs. Enlil shifts, points.*

'*Try that way, sister.*'

*Her face glimmers through the cascades of her hair. Her eyes are dark. He sees only reflected star points of his light dancing with mischief.*

*'You would not trick me, Windy One? I thought I lost him in the waters. But, since he has vanished, see if you can catch me!'*

*She slips beguilingly out of reach, turning her head to see if Enlil will follow. Earth is slipping away, under her pale, bare feet. She does not heed it. She has had no vision of its riches to come. The dark Greater Earth beneath it is still unknown. It is enough to race, and laugh, and whistle through her small, soft lips and tease her brothers.*

*Enlil chuckles, takes a few mocking strides towards her, and she is off. Can Ereshkigal outrun the wind?*

*It seems she can. At all events, she is alone when she is aware that in front of her an unnatural blackness blanks out the perpetual twilight of the sky. A hooded horror is towering over her, lowering, looming. Huge claws on colossal stumps of arms spread wide to claim her. Higher than that, mercifully, she cannot see.*

*Ereshkigal has not known fear in her brief life. Why should she? She, child of her father's sorrow, has been given only love and laughter. She and Enki were the twin blessings who lightened An's grief. These two are the tricksters who are difficult to catch, cannot be bound, have made the universe their playground.*

*A drop of blood, unconsidered, slides warmly down her leg. Apart from that her flesh is cold.*

*A chilly dampness breathes towards her out of Kur. His breast heaves with a gigantic pain he cannot recognise. He knows no name for love. His serpent head, that could swallow mountain ranges, stoops over her. A drop of gall, bitterer than any tear, falls from his fang and touches Ereshkigal's shoulder.*

*She shrieks then. All heaven rocks with her anguish. Even Enlil is shaken. Ki heaves and tries to rise. The Sky Lord is mute and immobile with horror. Enki, parting the spray of his mother's waters to peer out, glimpses the sudden pallor of his sister's slim figure in the flash of Enlil's eyes, then sees the darkness overwhelm her in its enormous embrace. Ereshkigal screams and screams again. Taut-muscled limbs that flew her tirelessly across the skies thrash vainly against the slowly crushing scales that are tightening around her. Her small throat, made for music, retches at the stench that smothers her.*

*'Enlil!' As the half-light of her world vanishes, her last shriek for help is to her half-brother.*

*Enlil closes his eyes. Primordial night descends again on the universe.*

*'Ereshkigal!' An's despairing cry echoes round Angal's vault.*

*The boy Enki halts halfway in his rush across the sky, overcome by darkness, terrified.*

*There are no weapons, no wisdom, no ritual yet to grapple with evil fate. They can only listen appalled to the slither of that unimaginable deformity lowering itself over the rim of the Earth into the Netherworld, and the sound of Ereshkigal weeping.*

*Then there is stillness in the upper regions, save for the shushing of Mother Nammu's primeval waves. Ereshkigal, the Sky Lord's daughter, will dance no more.*

*Kur has taken her.*

# Chapter Five

'No. I'm Inanna.'

To her surprise, her voice sang clear and true. She was afraid of her great-grandfather, but she must not let him know it. And the fear was not as great as she had thought it would be. This slightly fusty chamber was not the great Council Court in Nippur. An was not enthroned in the President's chair on the highest dais.

Above all, Enlil was not here in Uruk.

Nin Isinna was helping An knot a long net kilt about him, a formality only. Her hierodule's practised hands tied the padded sash.

Inanna made herself walk forward, tall as she could hold herself. She forced her lips to smile. It was harder to command her eyes to obey. She had practised this dancing smile for Nin Gal her mother, for Father Nanna, for Grandfather Enki, and seen it triumph, like sun melting butter. Would its power work over An?

She had already passed the crouching concubines before her great-grandfather lifted his white head from watching Nin Isinna's movements and said gruffly, 'Well, come closer then, girl. Let me see you.'

She was less prepared than she had thought for the piercing stare of his pale-blue eyes. He studied her from head to foot without speaking, without smiling. Waves of cold, then heat, passed over Inanna's body under his scrutiny. Would she be able to hide nothing from him, after all? Something of her hard-held dignity crumpled. She felt her lips tremble.

'Charming,' An said at last. He shook his head. 'Wilful, but lovely. You, we shall keep carefully. And teach you wisdom.'

She could not be sure whether the twitch of his lips was an old man's irritation or the ghost of a smile.

She renewed her own smile for him, lips parted over perfect teeth. To her alarm, she saw his member leap beneath the kilt, and Nin Isinna make a swift movement to disguise it. A pulse was beating hard in her own throat. Nin Isinna was angry. The gold eyes snapped. Inanna almost expected the pointed jaws to growl. The child, standing before the grown woman and the aged Lord, felt without fully understanding that power was in dispute, that she had a strength which this hierodule suddenly feared.

Inanna's smile grew wider still, relaxing her body into a soft flowering. She dropped with an easy grace to sit at An's feet and turned up her face to him. The smile was truly in her eyes for him now.

An cupped her face in hands that were dry with age but tender.

'Well, little jewel of the stars, it seems I am the one who must guard you from others' hands. And from yourself.'

# Chapter Six

*Enlil shuddered and opened his eyes. The half-light had returned to the upper air. Now his face was clouded with doubt. Within the Duku the Anunnaki howled with the shock and fear of a calamity they could not understand.*

*He started. Enki was standing before him. The younger brother's limbs trembled with pent-up rage and helplessness.*

*'Do it!' he roared with the sound of crashing surf.*

*Enlil's eyes widened. The light within him flashed like spear points. 'Do what, brother?'*

*Enki gestured furiously at the waiting Earth, the birth hut, the empty sky. 'Whatever you have to do! Bring them out, name them, empower them. Fill the universe if you must. Create anything we need to rescue her.'*

*'I? How?'*

*'As you separated our father from your mother. With your breath, with your Word!'*

*Enlil looked at his brother for a long moment, lifted his eyes to the dark horizon where Ereshkigal had vanished, considered. 'You think I can do it alone?'*

*'If you want me to organise it for you, give me the authority. But get things started!'*

*Enlil walked towards the birth hut, stooped his head, and looked in. With his breath he summoned the Anunnaki. By his great Word he brought them into life. And as each one emerged into the world, Enki placed in their hands the* me, *their particular powers, gave each a task.*

*He called forth Nin Gikuga of the Pure Reed and Sumugan of the Wild Plain.*

*He called forth Gibil, the Cleansing Fire.*

*He summoned Enbilulu of the Sparkling Waters.*

*Nin Kilim of Mice and Vermin came at his bidding.*

*He breathed life into Lisina, Guardian of Onagers.*

*Like smoke from a fire that has taken hold, the Anunnaki*

*poured out of the Duku. They stood upright, opened their blind eyes, wiped the milk of Ki from their lips and looked about them.*

*On and on the naming went, as Lord Air brought into the space he had created between Sky and Earth his sisters and brothers. Wild beast Lords of the steppe, fish Ladies of the canebrakes, powers of the vegetation of the riverbanks and the wilderness. All these and many more Enlil brought out.*

*United for a moment in amazement and triumph, the two brothers sprang forward and embraced each other.*

*The Earth was resplendent. Grass clothed its golden skin like a fine linen garment. Tassels of reeds lined its watercourses with luxuriant fringes. Thick foliage of trees made a covering for the mountains. Its rocks were braceleted with silver. Diorite clasped its cliffs. The leaping fire of Gibil flashed on carnelian and lapis lazuli stones. The good rain showered over it. Seeing the beauty which he had once embraced in darkness, An hurried down from high Angal to stand beside his twin. They smiled gravely at each other. Their hands touched again. But there was space between them now. Enlil eddied past. And in that space the wild things grew and flourished. The heavy-seeded grasses, the sticky-budded palms, the onager braying for her mate on the steppe, the heron rising from the canebrake with a fish in his beak.*

*The Anunnaki wandered over the lands, where no cities had yet been built, no irrigation canals dug. They stumbled against each other, quarrelled, copulated. There was no wisdom, no civilisation. The Children of An and Ki went down on their knees like brutes, ate plants with their mouths, drank water from the ditch.*

*'Is this the best you can do?' said Enki angrily, looking at the wild things that were his half-sisters and -brothers. 'We can't fight Kur with such simpletons. How can we rescue Ereshkigal with these?'*

*Enlil shrugged and spun in a half-circle, making the new leaves flutter. 'What more do you want? We have clothed the stony hills, we have brought life to the marshes. Lightning brightens the sky. Rain falls.'*

*'We need wisdom,' said Enki. 'We need order. We need things made. We need skills.'*

*He snapped a reed growing beside him and pressed its broken end into the damp clay at his feet. Images began to appear. One of Enlil's younger sisters stepped out of the reed thicket and peered thoughtfully down at the pictures.*

*'What is it meant to be? I don't know these things.'*

*'A plant to cut for food, so that you needn't spend your lives endlessly munching grass. A beast that will yield abundance of milk and drag heavy loads.'*

*'That's clever,'* the girl said. *'You have a vision of things that are not. And so there is born the possibility that one day they will be.'*

Enki smiled and handed her his reed stylus. *'Nidaba, Lady of the Reed, for you shall be the* me *of knowledge. I am giving you the power of the pen. Well?'* he challenged Enlil. *'What are you waiting for? I have imagined them. Can you call them out?'*

Enlil sighed, a little impatiently. *'Of course I can. Is it not enough for you? Thunderstorms, fire, running streams, anemone flowers, mice, kingfishers, cedar forests. Must you stamp order on this chaos, like your signs in clay?'*

*'Kur is the greatest chaos of all. He has seized my sister.'*

*'I have peopled the Earth with Guardians. Should the Netherworld not have its wardens too? Shouldn't we leave Ereshkigal to be a great princess there?'*

*'You don't care, do you? You tore your parents apart. But you never stirred a breath to snatch Ereshkigal out of the arms of Kur! I ask you a second time. Will you bring these to life?'* He pointed to the pictures at his feet.

Enlil's mouth turned down in an abrupt annoyance. Then, swiftly, he moved to the dark door of the Duku. The last of the Anunnaki children babbled inside, without names, empty-handed still. Two girls lifted their heads expectantly to meet the light of his eyes.

*'Ashnan!'* His voice rustled through the chinks in the birth hut like the wind through a field of grass.

The girl stood up, swaying under the power of his voice. She stepped towards him, and with each pace she seemed to grow. Her golden hair, thick and abundant, curled over honey-coloured shoulders. Her green eyes shone with the moist brilliance of lettuce and cucumbers. The savour of leeks and bean flowers rose under her feet.

As she came out of the Duku into the verdant, watered world, Enki opened his arms in delight. He hugged and kissed her.

*'You've come at last, sister! Here's grain and goodness, vegetables and vegetation of the farms. Multiply them for us!'*

Ashnan coloured warmly. *'The land is dry, my lord. You must water it generously.'*

*'Oh, I shall, my honey, I shall. Ask your elder sisters!'*

*Behind her, Enlil's voice bellowed louder. 'Lahar! Come forth!'*

*Ashnan's sister pushed out of the creation chamber, almost knocking Enlil aside. She was strong of shoulders, massive-faced. But for all her strength and bulk, her eyes were brown and gentle. Generous breasts swung low, already dripping milk.*

*Enki released golden Ashnan and hurried to bow himself respectfully before Lahar. Her soft lips nudged him. The fragrance of milk was warm about her.*

*'Lahar, my love. Take cattle, sheep and goats for yours. Take the byre and the sheepfold. Take the churn and the cheese press. Take the shearing of wool and the skinning of hides. I'll give you helpers.'*

*He raised his voice in a great shout.*

*'I give to Enkimdu the plough and the furrow.*

*'I give to Nunbarshegunu the fields of mottled barley.*

*'I give to Nin Kasi the secrets of brewing.*

*'I give to Haia the keeping of stores.*

*'I give to Nindub the plans of the architect.*

*'I give to Gugun the builder's tools.*

*'I give to Mushdamma the laying of foundations.*

*'I give to Kulla the brickmould.'*

*The world changed. Enlil himself took gold and made a handle. He shaped lapis lazuli into a cutting blade and brought the two together. He broke the ground at the centre of the world with the very first hoe.*

*Then he handed the tool to others.*

*When Enki saw that civilisation had begun, that fields could be farmed and orchards planted, that metals could be mined and tools fashioned, that houses and cities could be built with reeds and clay, and canals dug to water the furrows, his heart warmed.*

*He reared up, like a great wild bull over the land. He raised himself over the newly-dug riverbed of the Buranun. He lifted up his penis. In the flash of the lightning his life-giving seed sparkled. He filled the Idiglat with his fluid; he brought joy to all the rivers. The first harvest came.*

*The date palm blossomed hugely. The barley swelled with goodness. The ewes dropped twin lambs, the goats triple kids. The udders of the fertile cows ran richly with milk.*

*Enlil, whose Word had brought it all into being from his mother's birth hut, watched with a faintly mocking smile.*

*'Very nice, brother. But what good will all this do you? The girl is gone.'*

*Enki swung round, eyes blazing with the reflection of Gibil's fire. 'Where there is prosperity, there will be craftsmanship and the making of instruments. When all is ready, reed and knife, wood and adze, bitumen and cord, the arts of seamanship and the skill of navigation, I shall build a boat. I shall embark upon the great adventure. I shall set sail for the bitter waters of the Kur, to rescue Ereshkigal.'*

*'Will you indeed?' Still that maddening smile teased Enlil's changeable features. 'Will you bring back the Princess from the Netherworld? But what for? Have you not understood? Father An has chosen the Sky, and I am keeping the Earth for myself.'*

*'What is that to Ereshkigal, or me?'*

*'To you, I allow the fresh waters springing from the Deep under the Earth. So what is there left for Ereshkigal, the last of Nammu's children? I might as well give her what she already has, wouldn't you say? The Great Below.'*

*A flash in Enki's eyes, between horror and understanding. 'Is that yours to give?'*

*'Oh, yes, brother. It is all mine.' He turned to where the birth hut stood, mounded over with clay and roofed with reed mats, the first harvest storehouse now. 'I think I shall take the Duku as my seat. All the Anunnaki came from it. Here I shall have them build me my house, E-Kur.'*

*The creases of wisdom deepened round Enki's eyes. 'The House of Kur. Oh yes, I begin to see.'*

# Chapter Seven

'Why do I need a Guardian? Enki is giving me the Battle Spear. I can look after myself, can't I?' Inanna tilted up her face with a confident smile.

'Enki is a fool! Enki, Enlil, you! Have you learned *nothing*? Must the same folly be repeated in every generation? Why do you think you were brought here?'

He crashed his fist down, splintering an ivory table by his couch. Nin Isinna moved to soothe him, but his snarl drove her back. Inanna was kneeling, terrified, like the concubines. The calm, white-haired old man had gone. It was as though a wild black bull was loose in the room.

'There!' He was struggling to subdue his rage. 'I frightened you. Good! I have seen too much pride, ambition, cruelty in this family. I have lost too much. But you, our little Star Princess, don't go the way of the rest. Dance for us. Be sweet and loving. Let others love you.'

Inanna's lips trembled mutinously. It was on the tip of her tongue to say, 'That is not enough!' But she saw his eyes were still veined with red. He could hardly control the violence of his hands.

From the doorway, Nin Shubur moved her head warningly. Inanna bowed her face, so that her hair hid it.

'Yes, Great-grandfather. I will try to please you.'

Dull, obedient. Words forced from her lips, but not from her rebellious heart.

'Inanna, look at me!'

She raised her troubled eyes and saw through the tears of fear a grey, stern face frowning down at her.

'Enki and Enlil were fools. The Lord of Earth, the Lord of Wisdom? I will not let Kur have you too. Obey me.'

# Chapter Eight

*When the arts of civilisation were coming into being, when the Anunnaki had developed the craft of making boats, Enki withdrew to the lagoon at Eridu. The moment had come. The materials and skills were ready. There was nothing now to stop him challenging Kur.*

*Out in the marshes, where the great river left its overspill, where the cattle did not graze, and the Anunnaki had not cut reeds for huts and fences, where the huge wild boar with savage eyes lay hidden at noonday, and the goliath heron flapped her slow way across still lagoons, Enki, the brave young Water Man, found Nin Gikuga, the Reed Woman. She started away when she saw him, and for an instant he thought of Ereshkigal's fleeting form glimpsed between rainclouds. But she stayed for him, swaying restlessly, the wind troubling her pale hair. Her limbs were rounded, ringed with bracelets, her voice like a deep-tuned, true pipe. He told her the plan that obsessed his soul, to find his sister and bring her back into the upper air.*

*'The world is sad without her,' said Nin Gikuga. 'If I can help, take anything you want. Cut the stoutest reeds in my canebrakes. Make yourself a strong boat. Let it be so long that seventy rowers could sit in it. Let the prow rear up and curve like the head of a swan; let the stem sweep over and coil like the neck of a crane. It will hold whatever provisions and weapons you need to take.'*

*Enki caressed the stiff, hollow stems of the stand of reeds. The biggest of them were as thick as his arm. With narrowed eyes he watched the Fisherman Nindara poling his deft way across the lagoon, saw how he eyed the dark sky, watching for the darker cloud that would signal a coming storm, saw him judging the distance between his slender craft and the sheltering fringes of the swamp.*

*'Even Nindara in a high-prowed canoe is afraid to be caught in the open water when the storm strikes,' he observed. 'You're*

*generous, my sweet. But how could a mere craft of reeds and bitumen hold out against the savagery of Kur?'*

'I would help you if I could,' Nin Gikuga said wistfully. 'There should be a girl-child to dance in the Sky again, as once you say your sister played.' The feathery fronds of her hair leaned towards him. Her voice thrilled like the music of an elegy. Enki felt a longing well up within him. And not for Ereshkigal, this time. Then the wind blew between them, making the waves leap and splash against the canes, sending Nindara poling for shallow water.

A pause. Tiny frogs shrilled in the cresses at their feet. The water purled along the channel, steadily spilling its way from the river through the marsh. Bats darted through the air in the continual twilight.

A cold determination returned to Enki. 'For this, I need something stronger than you can offer.'

Still, there was some regret in his heart as he went away from her. Nin Gikuga followed him for a little way until the wild canebrakes ran out into the long rows of reeds that lined the straight canals the work parties had dug and banked.

'There's Ningishzida,' she called after him. 'Perhaps it is possible to make a boat from trees.'

He left the marshes for the hills.

Ningishzida was one of the dark Lords and a power to be feared. As his trees grew mighty, their roots became more and more like serpents, thickening, twining, arching over and under each other, burrowing deep into the earth. More than most other Anunnaki, Ningishzida understood the pull of the Below.

The journey was long and lonely across the lowland wilderness. Enki climbed the foothills and found the Lord of the Good Tree at last on the slopes of the Cedar Mountain. The Guardian sat, as though meditating, his knotted fingers clasped round gnarled knees, leaves caught in his uncombed hair like a tiara cunningly crafted by a goldsmith. His deep green eyes, flecked with tawny copper, stared down at the dim-lit plain where willows marked the watercourses and date palms studded the oases. The heights above him were thickly clothed with cedars and fir, making the shadowy world darker still, a night through which ranged wolves and bears with shining eyes.

'Brother,' said Enki, sitting down beside him. 'For Ereshkigal's sake, may I set axe to bark, cut down a single tree, fashion myself a magur boat of cedarwood to assault the Netherworld?'

*Ningishzida did not turn to look at him. His gaze withdrew a little, fell to his bare, splayed feet planted in the sandy soil where ants ran to and fro. He picked up a fallen twig. He made no signs such as Enki had once drawn in clay with Nidaba's stylus. He dug thoughtfully around the roots of a cedar tree, and the scent of needles disturbed perfumed the air. The surface was dry, but as he delved, a rich, moist loam became revealed. Still he dug on. A tiny trickle of peaty water seeped in to fill the bottom of the hole. The crumbly sides shivered, a shower of earth tumbled into the bottom of the pit. Water closed over it. A piece of bark fell from Ningishzida's hair, floated on the water.*

'Enlil has already given you the axe.' His voice boomed like a strong wind through fir boughs. 'Can a mere Tree Guardian withstand the Air Lord and the Water Lord? Take one. Kur may recognise it. My leaves drink life from the Sky; my trunk is a wall on Earth. My roots strike down to the Netherworld. If anything can stand against him, it must be things born of lower darkness: heartwood and stone.'

So, for his sister's sake, Enki built the very first magur ship. He borrowed from Enlil the primordial pickaxe which the Air Lord had fashioned, a powerful, magical tool. Its head was of lapis lazuli, darkly blue, ground to a gleaming edge. Its haft was burnished gold, smooth to the hand. The mountain rang with the blows as the tooth bit through bark, cut the soft new wood, entered the heart. Ningishzida sat with his back to the felling. At each stroke, he shuddered. Blood crept, thick and slow as sap, from his mouth where teeth had bitten through lip. Crooked fingers gripped the soil, could not hold on. The cedar tree creaked, screeched, roared as it crashed to earth and the mountain shook with the massive weight of trunk and branches. The split stump stood, some splintered spikes still appealing to the sky. An angry red suffused the raw surface. The roots deep in the earth fell still, nursing within their serpent shapes an inexpressible scream.

Once it was done, the Anunnaki set to work busily. Mushdamma laid the keel. Gugun brought boat-building tools. The carpenters and cord spinsters set about their business. The sides of the ship were curved and planked, the gunwale pegged in place. The mast soared like the very first tree linking the waters to the sky. Mushdamma's keel, weightier than the surface-skimming reed canoes, reached for the depths. Bitumen, bubbling from the ground, was gathered and heated, smeared on the sides, caulking the joints, proofing the wood. Enki was a boy no more.

The Lord of Wisdom turned himself into a man of war to fight with Kur.

They rigged a wide sail to carry the ship as long as air lasted. Nin Gikuga came shyly to the quay bringing her stoutest canes for punting poles. Lahar and Ashnan filled the boat with provisions for the journey.

Enki took hunting tools for weapons of war. Stone-tipped arrows, shaped like leaves, but sharper than any willow. A huge net that could hold a mighty suhur fish. A mace of brown-veined diorite, massive, bone-crushing. A spear of copper, a shield of stiffened hide.

'And for yourself?' asked Nidaba the wise Reed Scribe, with a lift of her brown-fringed eyebrows. 'A leather cloak, perhaps, with studs of copper? A helmet of gold, moulded to resemble the braids of hair it covers? A corselet of silver plates?'

Shamefaced but resolute, Enki had the craftsmen make all these things. He, the man of the free-moving waters, bound himself in the stiff armour of a warrior.

'Ereshkigal will hardly recognise you,' said Enlil, drifting lazily around the scene of activity with that seemingly supercilious smile of detachment.

Enki rounded, swung the spear menacingly. But what good is copper and flint against the shifting breeze?

What good against Kur?

'How will you find her?' asked Nidaba.

'I saw Kur once,' maintained Enki. 'He was like a mighty land, a mountain. He reared up from the western horizon, towered towards heaven, blotted out half the sky. He brought a darkness from the Netherworld blacker than the night sky of An. He disappeared with Ereshkigal over that rim of the world.'

'And this your boat,' said Nidaba, laying her hand on it in blessing, 'and these your arms are all you have to fight against a mountain of darkness, an ocean of bitter waters? Go if you must, Enki, Lord of the Sweet Waters here. Go well, Lord of Wisdom, and find more wisdom yet. Come back to us.'

Two tears fell from her eyes like raindrops trickling down reed stems. They flowed away to join the uncharted morass of Sumer's marshes, on past Eridu to where the tides of the Idiglat and Buranun mingled and lost themselves in the salt seas of the Great Gulf.

There was no crew for the sturdy magur boat but one. No other of the Anunnaki dared make that descent. Only the son of

*Nammu himself would risk this perilous voyage over the edge of the world. And even he sailed stoutly protected and inwardly fearful. The friendly Guardians of farms and fisheries gathered on the wharf at Eridu to wave farewell. Their wilder sisters and brothers peered across perpetual dusk from desert or marsh to watch him pass. Nin Gikuga stood forlorn among the cane clumps, raising her hand in mute farewell.*

*The* magur *boat with its lone helmsman Enki was launched into the muddy swirl of the Buranun, poled out into the current, swept southward, a dwindling speck upon the vast, grey reach of waterway, was swallowed up in twilight. It followed the tears of Nidaba down into the salt waters and the unknown sea road to the west.*

# Chapter Nine

An stood up. She had not realised how alarmingly tall he would be, even with his shoulders slightly stooped. She scrambled to her feet.

'That's enough. They will be waiting for me in the Porch of the Rising Sun to hear their lawsuits. It is a tiresome business to be a Great Guardian.'

Nin Isinna signalled. Attendants came hurrying forward with preparations to wash An and dress him in his regalia. Inanna was not sure if she had been dismissed. Nor was she certain that she wanted to be. Fearsome An was, yes. But what was there for her in the E-Anna, except what he could give her?

'Shall I help you?' She tried to charm her smile for him again.

'No. Go away now. Spin, play or whatever it is little girls do. But come back. Towards the end of the siesta hour. I should be rested then. That will be the time to begin your education.' This time his own smile shone clear for a moment as his gaze travelled over her again. Nin Isinna clicked her teeth and began to walk towards the bathroom.

As his eyes turned from her, Inanna felt herself at once grow small and unimportant. The whole E-Anna complex, this private chamber, the huge audience halls, the close-stacked lodgings of its personnel, the workshops, offices, kitchens, stables, all centred around this one tall, tired old man. The estates of his family on the slopes of Kullab, the houses of Uruk crowding as close as they could get to their Lord, all spoke of their dependence on An's authority. In him supremely was power and blessing.

And Inanna? Born in the high mountains beyond Aratta, raised in the E-Kishnugal of the Moon on the plain at Ur, she now followed Nin Shubur disconsolately out to the dim antechambers, like a petal blown from its stem and washed up on a strange shore.

'One day,' she whispered after An's retreating back, '*I* shall have a house as grand as this.'

They came out on to the highest terrace and Inanna gave a startled gasp. The blue and golden morning had gone. Banks of mist had rolled up from the surrounding water, like the smoke of innumerable sacrifices. Grey wraiths wandered past her face. She looked up in dismay and could not find the darkened disc of the sun through the fog. Nin Shubur was walking steadily towards the head of the great stairway. Inanna ran after her, forgetful of dignity now, and clutched her hand.

'What is it? Where's the world gone? What's happened to Uruk? Where are we?'

The face that turned to her was young, but the creases of wisdom round the eyes looked ancient.

'You feel it, do you, Inanna? The shadow approaching? Be brave. The light Above is struggling with the water Below. It will pass.'

'What if it doesn't? What if the water is too big, and the light can't ever get through? I'll be lost, in the mist and the dark for always, won't I?' There was an edge of panic in her voice.

'This shadow will lift, my lady. But when the light shines again you may wish it had not. Have you forgotten the things the flood had washed up at our gates?'

And she led the way down into the blindfolding, humid gloom.

# Chapter Ten

*On, past the sterile shores of desert still waiting for the sun. On, past the coconut-hung beaches of the south. Out into the grey adventure of the open ocean. The ship's prow soared to the sky, then, too heavy to take flight, plunged down the back of the still-climbing waves. At first, Enki sat huddled in his cloak, dreading the wild, cold tumble of the salt waters. Then, as his* magur *boat proved seaworthy, he took courage. He loosed his cloak from his neck, let the wind play over his young limbs, moved the steering oar, felt the ship respond and learned the power of helmsmanship. As the sail flapped and filled and the wind strengthened, he wondered if Enlil, his brother, were invisibly present, his wind hurrying Enki on to the rim of knowledge. From high Angal, Father An looked down. There was nothing he could do to help his son and daughter. Mother Ki was out of sight.*

*There was no sun to mark the days, no moon to light the night, no stars to steer by. A faint suggestion of illumination at the centre of the world, the Land of the Two Rivers. Ahead, a wall of darkness.*

*'It doesn't matter where I go,' said Enki, through gritted teeth. 'In all directions the world must end and the floods will sweep down beneath me into the void below.'*

*The ship strained and tossed in the strong wind. Planks creaked and bowed, moving against the bond of bitumen. Spray splashed over the bows. The sail protested at the crash of the wind. For as long as he could, Enki, Lord of the Sweet Waters, sat shivering in his leather kilt, lashed by salt spume. At last, with a little whimper, like an otter cub that finds his dam has left him and he is alone in the river, he burrowed back into his felt-lined cloak, shielded himself from the elements.*

*After a run before the wind so long it numbed both body and mind, there came a time when the gale died. A stillness fell upon the waters. The boat slowed. Enki found himself watching the pure blackness of the sky expectantly. His eyes would not accept the void. Time and again he peopled it with a young girl, light as silver, stepping up over the horizon, shining down on him.*

*It was only a trick of his baffled pupils, a flaring of his creative imagination. Enlil was not there to pronounce the Word. The sky stayed blank.*

*And then he heard it. From far away, like rain drumming on the roof in a thunderstorm. There were no shores to judge the swiftness of his passage. The boat lay level, no longer driving through the pitch and toss of rollers. And yet the water began to hiss along the sides. The limply hanging sail quivered, seemed to belly back rather than forward. Enki moved the oar. The ship did not respond. A force more powerful now was gathering her up, sweeping her forward. Like a woman in the paroxysms of desire past all control, she surged now towards the force that was waiting for her.*

*Enki was not Lord here. All the skill that had built his well-found* magur *ship, all the art that had managed steering oar and rigging, all the vision of mind that had led him out from Sumer to where he believed the entrance to the Great Below must lie, all was wiped away. He was a fly, perched on the streaming woodwork. He was an ant when the landslide tears away the mountainside.*

*As the salt waters ended and he tumbled, gasping, through the bitter, plunging roar, he heard a voice boom, as though the Netherworld were one vast cavern.*

*'Welcome to my realm, Nammu's son!'*

*Light now. A reddish phosphorescence that gleamed on smoothly dripping surfaces and left the hollows blacker still. The rage of waters was still in Enki's ears and the Netherworld shuddered with its force. But here, for a moment, was an enclosed stillness. A sluggish trickle of liquid bore the* magur *boat, barely moving forward. He sensed, and partly saw, an arched roof over him, its vaults slick as gums between indented bone. The air breathed a foul-smelling mist.*

*'Kur,' his own voice trembled, like a loose mat rattling in a doorway. 'Where is my sister?'*

*The answer seemed to come from before him, as though this tunnel were one vast throat. 'She sits enthroned where none who worship her may ever leave. What you did not give her on Earth, I have given her in Kur.'*

*Now the tunnel was narrowing above another rapid. The walls were closing in. The mist was thickening in an intolerable stench.*

*Too late already to turn the heavy ship round. He seized one of Nin Gikuga's punting poles.*

*Kur laughed. The walls of the cavern shook bitter saliva over Enki. The* magur *boat rocked.*

*'Would you go back, little Lord?'*

*Enki turned his head and saw the gleam of arrow-sharp teeth that crashed together. Spray flew around him with the shock. Before he could put his fear to the test against his willpower, the boat had made her own decision. The mast of pinewood snapped like a piece of straw against the roof, though great Kur yelped and cursed. The bows dipped sharply down an incline. Enki gripped the gunwales. No thought of steering now. Hopeless to think he could pole his way back up this enormous, slippery, winding ramp down which the ship coasted like a runaway sledge on a mountainside. His flesh shrank from the gall that showered on him from the walls. He tried not to breathe the noisome gases. His heart quailed at the laughter.*

*A jarring explosion of spray. A spreading of thick and sluggish ripples. A deeper, danker pool.*

*He was not alone. Across the brown, bile-tasting lagoon were seven small figures, bearing torches that flared with a blue-white, comfortless flame. The slopes on which they stood were slippery, faintly pink-tinged, blotched with a dull purple. The galla had snouts fanged like jackals, hands sharp and clever as bats, feet clawed like vultures. Their red and lidless eyes were restless, pitiless, and their voices buzzed incessantly like flies over rotting meat. They swarmed towards Enki.*

*A shudder took him, the chill that comes before sickness. How had they come here? What had called these demons into being? Hard to imagine that they had ever had a mother.*

*No! Not her!*

*He crouched, paralysed with terror, clutching the wood of the cedar tree from the Land of the Living. He knew no spells of magic that would serve him here. His was the power to create, to bring into being both good and bad. He could not unmake what already was. Out of the pain that had forced An and Ki apart had come a bitter separation. Above was love and learning, mating, birth . . . and, for the animals, death. What was waiting Below? Stagnation? The ending of all hope?*

*The galla were the executioners of sentiment. They knew no pity, never yielded to persuasion, obeyed Kur's orders without feeling, loved no one, knew not how to mourn, had no hearts.*

*They never slept, and so they had never dreamed.*

*Yet, for a waiting moment, the* magur *ship hung in the centre of that brackish pool and the* galla *did not move to seize it. There was no need. Enki had entered the Netherworld of his own free will.*

*He rose to his feet, with a brave attempt at dignity. The light of torches flickered on his wet limbs like waterfalls.*

*'Take me to Ereshkigal.'*

*A multitude of mocking laughter greeted him.*

*'Where else?'*

*'There is one road in Kur.'*

*'All who enter here must come to her.'*

*'She is the core of Kur.'*

*Hard for Enki to leave that trusty boat, Ningishzida's cedarwood that even Kur respected. Hard for the Lord of the Sweet Waters to step down into that vile fluid.*

*And yet . . . Kur is closer than a half-brother. This monster's father was also An, though he has lost sight of the Sky. His mother was Enki's sister Ki. Nammu gave them all life. And Ereshkigal is, it seems after all, alive, in some sense.*

*He drew his mailed clothing tight about him, grasped his shield, checked the weight of all his weapons. The* galla *watched in the sawing hum that passed for silence. He stepped one foot over the side.*

*The brown pool made him gasp. It stung every cut and blister on his skin.*

*But a louder hiss forbade him. 'Aah! No!'*

*He raised bewildered eyes. The* galla *were lined on the brink, pointing threateningly at him.*

*'Not like that!'*

*'Take it off!'*

*'Put it down!'*

*'Leave it behind you.'*

*Enki looked down at himself knee-deep in slime. The oily surface showed him a distorted reflection. A young and handsome Lord crowned with a golden helmet, shaped artfully to echo his hair. His copper-studded cloak he had hung round his shoulders again, stiff bull's hide that could deflect a spear thrust. The silver-plated belt protected his vital organs. He had grasped his spear and shield, slung his arrow and bow ready at his side. The mace was heavy against his thigh, the net looped over his shoulder.*

'You must enter the Netherworld as you were born into the Great Above.'

'Naked as a baby.'

'Carrying nothing.'

Enki raised despairing eyes. 'I am a Son of An. How can I die?'

A furious chattering, like infuriated monkeys, broke out around him.

'Die?'

'Are we dead?'

'Isn't Kur alive with demons as the Earth above teems with Anunnaki?'

'We have a queen. Soon we shall have a palace, and governors and judges.'

'And constables and scribes and servants, as you have.'

'All life will be here.'

Could it be so? Across his mind, under the unfeeling gaze of the galla, there wandered through Enki's mind a vision of Ereshkigal when he was younger still. His twin, a girl with limbs like mesu blossom, hair darkly swinging as a mare's tail, dancing as though her bones were moths and all the night of space was free to her.

The roof of Kur's belly shut him in. Outside he heard the roaring of Nammu's waters.

For Ereshkigal he had built his magur boat. For Ereshkigal he had come this far. For Ereshkigal Enki now laid down his shield and spear, cast off the weight of threatening weapons, stone and metal. He raised his skilful hands, unclasped the armoured cloak and let it fall, loosened the plated belt, and the leather kilt slipped away from his loins. He stood naked before the forces of the Netherworld.

As he took the first, slow step through the turbid lagoon, a hiss broke out, claws fought to claim him.

'Let me alone,' he croaked. 'I have come willingly.'

But their hands clawed and clasped, and hooked and pulled. The strongest hauled him through the little pushing crowd. And yet an indignant order imposed itself upon the procession. Two went in front, holding their torches aloft to flare on the fleshy, black-fringed passageway. Two more marched close behind, with breath like hot draughts. Two jostled him at the sides, the rough scales of their arms scratching his unprotected flanks. They filled the tunnel, that became so low Enki had to stoop, though the surging galla *allowed him no chance to slow his pace. The floor was slick but ridged, yielding unpleasantly between the spars of gristly bone. It dipped and coiled, confused his senses, till he stumbled on unthinkingly, breathing as shallowly as he might in the fetid atmosphere.*

*At last the excited chatter dropped to a more reverent murmur. The rush of their passage slowed. The quality of the light had changed. The stark blue-white was giving place to a pulsating rose. It had the colour of blood, but not its warmth. The air was dank, chiller than the humid passages. Even before the wet tunnel opened out into a vast courtyard, Enki felt the overturning of his mind, the conflicting evidence of his senses, the clash of reason with the horror of reality.*

*The red light beat from a mound across the black-paved square. Where the airy space round the Duku at Nippur would be full of the Anunnaki coming to hold council before An and Enlil and Ki and Enki, this yard was almost empty. Bleached bones of dead animals laid out a shocking roadway across it.*

*The* galla *pushed him forward roughly, let go of him.*

*'I didn't think about death,' Enki said to himself. 'I knew it happened to the beasts. I didn't consider it important till now.'*

*Almost empty, this courtyard, but not quite. A creature stood at the foot of the mound. Where the attendants of the great ones Above wore linen or tufted sheep's fleece, this official Below was girdled with entrails. His staff was tipped with a lamb's skull. No woollen turban graced his hair, but a cap of lungs and lights. Before humans had been created, in the time of the deathless Anunnaki, Kur held already the menace of mortality.*

*The mound on which the palace was being built reared like a mountain. In the crimson heart-light, its lapis lazuli was almost indigo. No silver or gold flashed in the distant torch glare. Only the darker, harder stones: obsidian, jasper, basalt, swallowed the illumination and gave back no more than a dim sheen. Its level top was floored with skulls.*

*She sat on a great bull throne set high on the mound. Naked as the day she was snatched from the Sky. It must be she, as all the* galla *prostrated themselves before her and the name whispered up like the hiss of sap when green wood is consumed on the fire.*

*'Great Queen of all the Below. Ereshkigal!'*

*'Sister!' he started forward, stopped.*

*No word from the throne. No movement to guide him. Across that distance, she seemed to lean forward on one horn of her Bull, watching him through her fall of hair.*

*The skull-staff beckoned him on.*

*The* galla *fell back from him, would not enter Ereshkigal's court without her bidding. Still Enki hesitated.*

*The chief* galla *prodded him insolently. 'Don't you want to meet her, after all?'*

*No visible gate. Only a step from the hot and hostile channels of Kur into this chill, black void that was not yet a palace.*

*'Ereshkigal!' he tried. 'It's Enki. I've come to take you home.'*

*No answer helped him. No cry of delight sang across the yard. The* magur *boat was far behind him, the entry from the Great Above inaccessible. The seven demons huddled at his back were observing his hesitation with a curious glee.*

*As well go on as back. He was Enki. He had given the Earth life, civilisation, craft, sex. For love of Ereshkigal he must try the Great Below.*

*One step he took, past the clawed hands of the* galla. *The flesh of Kur gave way to colder stone under his feet. Still he walked on, leaving the light. He stopped at the base of Ereshkigal's throne, looked up at his lost sister.*

# Chapter Eleven

*No wind blew through these buried caverns and tunnels of Kur. But her hair was tangled like a nest of snakes. Her once-taut body arched towards him, slack and swollen. White limbs that had clasped him joyfully from behind, in a game of catch, had now the shrivelled pallor of old fungus. The nails dripped black. Her feet, that lightly walked on clouds, were splayed and yellowed, with sinewy talons like some bird of prey. Her face was mercifully hidden behind her hair.*

Enki halted, refusing still to accept what his heart knew. 'Where is she? What have you done with Ereshkigal?' A small boy's wail.

Then her voice howled at him, desolate as the wind through a sheepfold that wolves have ravaged. 'You let Kur have me.'

For an instant, searing pity for the girl who had been transcended horror of the Lady who was. Then self-justification asserted itself.

'I? What could I do? I was a boy. What could I do against the might of Kur?'

'Who made Kur what he is? You and Enlil.'

'It wasn't me! You and I were not yet born when Kur was conceived.'

'Enlil called the Anunnaki out of the Duku. You gave them the me.'

'But Kur was gone, long since.'

'When the power was already there, ungiven.'

He felt himself trembling with a vast possibility let slip. 'Can't it be redeemed?'

Hair parted slightly then. Yellowed skull-teeth smiled, like a little girl trying to please. A horrible incongruity.

'Oh, you have done better since, brother. Stillbirth, disease, death. They are all in the world now, though only for the beasts, yet.'

He shuddered, thinking of animal carcases, his leather kilt.

*Her hag-mouth grew serious, almost tender. She picked up a serpent skull and played with it. 'But life comes out of the darkest places.'*

*He could not bear the darkness of her veiled eyes.*

'Life?' he said. 'Out of the Below? You! Will you come back with me, then?'

*Trying to imagine it. Leading this monstrosity in front of Enlil's assembly. Having An look down from Angal to see this lost daughter.*

'Would you restore me?'

'My boat is here. It's still sound.' *He spoke in a whisper, as though Kur was not all round them, nor listening to them.* 'I'll prove how much I love you. Step down from your throne. Bid your sukkal clear the path, order the galla to stand aside and let us pass. Return to the Great Above with me.'

'Fool! A ship! What is your boat? A thing of rotting wood. What are clothes? Moth and mildew. What use are weapons here? Nothing can go back the way you came.'

'Then let's sail on! As far as the mouth of Kur is to the west, let's journey to the east, under the Earth. We'll rise together on the other side. Dance in the Sky for me again, Ereshkigal!' *The tears were running down his cheeks, blinding him now to the hideous hag-face glimpsed behind her hair.*

*One hawk-like foot descended a basalt step. One black-nailed hand reached down towards his. She bent and swung her head over her brother, her hair wild as the unkempt fronds of leeks.*

'How great is your love for me now, my brother? Enki – Lord from Earth! Will you take the Great Below in my place, and become as I am? I think not!'

*She swung the snaking hair back from her cadaverous face. It was not the ageing of her loveliness, not the brown mottling of her sunken cheeks, not the sprouting of black bristles that horrified him. The mouth was hard and bitter. The narrowed eyes burned red, without pity. She looked at the twin whom she had once trusted to swing her laughing across the sky and in her grimace now was only a cold contempt.*

*How easy the words of courage in the heat of the moment. The galla quailed before Ereshkigal, hid their own red eyes. One glance towards them and they flinched, though she carried no whip. How bitter her wrath must be that even the demons were terrified of her. She was indeed Kur's mistress. Enki's hand slid away from hers. So vivid his vision of his erstwhile twin, this Lord of Imagination. So alike they had been in gaiety, in speed, in beauty. He could see her now, tumbling among the cumulus clouds, merry as a lark, whistling to fill the sky with song. He could, he must, believe she could be so again, that she might be reborn.*

*But he, her twin? Could he grow old like this, and hard, and hateful? In Eridu more sacred* me *were waiting. The* me *of priesthood, the* me *of lovemaking, the* me *of scholarship, the* me *of beauty. If Enki, Lord of all these, gave himself over to the black soul of Kur, what would that mean for the future of the Earth?*

*'Ereshkigal . . . sister. Enlil has taken the Rulership of Earth for himself. But I have filled it with life. Yes, the rough with the easy, yet always rich with possibility. If . . . if I must stay in the Great Below for you, could you take all this in your hands? Would you guard the* me*? Can you make the Earth abound with life?'*

*'I do! And I shall make Kur abound with the dead, too!'*

*She shook her hair round her face, peered out at him again with that terrible face, smiled widely at him with her stretched grey mouth. Around him the great black vault of Kur shook with laughter.*

*With a growing horror that even yet he would not allow himself to admit, Enki took a step backward. The galla hissed and snarled, uncovering their eyes, swarming forward to the edge of the courtyard.*

*'Let me go,' begged Enki in a whisper. 'I should not have come. It's too late.'*

*'No,' said Ereshkigal, taking his hand firmly in her cold, scaled grasp. 'You did well to come. It pleases me to see you here in Kur. Are we not twins, you and I? Born of the same blood in the same moment. There is a bond between us. The Deep, the Abzu. Look at me well. Do not shudder and turn your eyes away. You see the other half of yourself, Enki. Remember me well, as I truly am. Remember. When Kur took me, he could have seized you instead. You live Above, because I rule Below. If I were there, you must be here. Think well on that. You have what you want, you, Enlil, Ki, An. I have chosen and cherished what you despised. All that was left.'*

*A treacherous silence. He cannot say he will not pay that price. 'It's not for myself. The ordering of the Earth . . . The* me *. . .'*

*Her eyes, like two pulsating hearts, burned into him, seemed to push him away.*

*'Wait! Take this.' Her hand groped in the hollow of the serpent*

skull. She drew out a small, pale oval and laid it in his palm. Then she let him go.

A shock to the touch. He had expected cold stone. This thing was faintly warm. Smooth-skinned, with a tuft of silky hairs. A living seed.

He raised his troubled, puzzled eyes to hers. But the dishevelled hair was over her face again. He could imagine anything behind it now.

'And . . . Kur would let me leave?'

'Plant it.' Only a whisper. Too low to call it harsh. 'And watch what comes of it. Now, go.'

He felt himself move back, unresisting across the courtyard. The buzzing of the *galla* sounded distant now, like a field of sleepy bees. His unprotected body seemed washed through their yielding ranks as if he floated in a shallow sea among clumps of rotten reeds.

A rushing in his ears. A mightier river, the current catching him, swirling him onwards. Thick darkness yet.

A painful bump recalled him to reality . . . if this was real. A wall of hard wood, curving above his head. A smell of tar and scented wood. A stirring of memory, then a fierce longing for the Earth he had left. His *magur* ship!

Was he alone? The river was quieter here. Above its suck and gurgle he heard no squeal or hiss of *galla*. With difficulty, he clambered up the outswung side, hauled himself over the gunwale, stood beside the upswept prow, caressing the gooseneck coil of the carving. His heart was beating fast. The river had left him wet and stinking. He found the stout reed punting poles and the homely strength of cane spoke to him sweetly of Nin Gikuga. He thrust the ship forward.

'My work is too important,' he muttered to excuse himself, heaving the heavy ship along the now sluggish channel. 'The world needs me.'

With each push of the pole, with each shove of his hand upon the low roof, the tunnel seemed to groan, a low reluctant growl, as if of anger hardly kept in check.

Cold gripped him, even in the oppressive heat of the tunnel. Ereshkigal had cheated him! Kur would never let him go. He had no one to substitute for him, no one to pay the price of his release.

The noxious air was thinning, scarcely a lightening, only a weakening of the darkness. A distant round appeared ahead. He urged the ship towards it. And the sides of the tunnel seemed to heave, contract, force him forward and then bar his exit with a *tight constriction. He hammered on the walls, picked up his copper spear, pierced the sides in fury. The mouth of the channel shot open again. He seized a pole and snapped it instantly in a great heave that thrust him towards escape. Once more the opening shut. He swung his mace, and the massive diorite head thudded against the imprisoning roof, brought out a roar of rage.*

*The Netherworld exploded. Shot him out into a chaos of blue-black water.*

*The boat was totally submerged. Enki clung on now desperately to the splintered stump of mast. The boat raced upward. He gasped for air, found none. His lungs were choked with bitter fluid. Was this his mother Nammu? Was he drowning in the ocean that gave him birth? A huge dark tail lashed across the paling depth of the water, whipping it into a fury that thudded round his head. His eyes were darkening. He did not see the ship, like a dead leaf, flung upon the surface of the water, tossed like a toy. Rollers mightier yet were sweeping towards him. He retched a stomachful of foulness, coughed up the vile excrement of Kur. He shook his wet head, saw all his armour and weapons washed overboard. Only the stout cedarwood of Ningishzida stood between him and the fury of the sea. The last of the plain cane stems of Nin Gikuga's gift was trapped under his all but unconscious foot.*

*One glance over his shoulder cleared his brain. Kur was pursuing him.*

*The monstrous horned head loomed over the breakers now, mouth gaping to savage him. The taloned hands, broad as volcanoes, spouted missiles at him. Rocks, torn from the seabed, huger than giant turtles, thundered against his keel. Enki seized the last reed cane. The ocean floor was far out of reach. He paddled for his life.*

*Kur bellowed like an earthquake. Another furious hail of stones assaulted the stem like a merciless pack of wolves. Enki drove the boat through the water with all his strength. For the me, for the order and arts of the world ... away from Ereshkigal, despair and chaos.*

*His last look behind showed him an annihilation of water coming. A tidal wave, unimaginably high, sweeping down upon him.*

*Like a lioness felling her prey, the vast green nemesis swept over the boat, under it, tossed it, overwhelmed it, smashed it. It tore Enki from the wreckage, raced him across the sea, bore him into the Great Gulf, still clutching his floating reed pole. Cradled him in moist arms like a mother, rocked him gently, carried him home, laid him to rest on the sands of Eridu.*

*Enki was released. His sister was left Below.*

*In the hollow of his unconscious hand he grasped that small, pale seed with a tuft of silken hair.*

# Chapter Twelve

Nin Shubur was wise. By the time they had reached the lowest terrace of the E-Anna, overlooking An's pleasure park, the fog was thinning. The sun strode up the sky, strong, proud, lusty, fading the light of the morning star to a pale fleck that the sky swallowed. Out of the vapour smoking from the watery world around them emerged the tallest palm fronds. Quickly the last mist trails disappeared, revealing the flooded plain.

Now the sound of keening rose more clearly from the levels beneath them. Mothers wailing for their lost children, flooded homes. Men lamenting for beasts swept away, crops devastated. The Buranun River was still swirling its dark debris past. Some of the sad flotsam of wood and cloth and leaf and flesh had come to rest in quieter eddies lapping the base of the city mound.

Inanna gazed down solemnly. 'Enlil and Enki made us Lords and Ladies of Sky and Storm, didn't they? Poor little humans! It must be terrible to live such a little time and have to die.'

The merest inclination of Nin Shubur's truthful, respectful head. 'Even so, my lady. Humans do violence to themselves in their small quarrels. And in our name and for our sake much larger devastations tear their world apart. For city states and their Anunnaki, children die, and others lose their freedom to work and love in their own homes.'

Inanna darted a sharp glance at her *sukkal*. 'What do you mean? Are you sorry you came here to serve me, Nin Shubur? Would you rather have stayed a priestess-princess in some icy wilderness no one's ever heard of? Don't you want to be the chief minister of Inanna? I am the Lady of the Morning and Evening Star.'

'I am the handmaiden of the great Children of An,' Nin

Shubur answered peaceably. 'Enlil gave me breath. He spoke my destiny as well.'

'That's not very grateful.' Inanna put out a hand coaxingly on Nin Shubur's wrist. She had discovered early the winning power of her touch. 'I'm only young yet. But one day, you'll see, I'll be the greatest Lady in all the Four Quarters. They shall fear my name in the mountains where the Idiglat and the Buranun spring. Prisoners will come to build my palaces. People will heap my treasury with grain and gold. And you know *my* destiny? When a man and woman lie down in bed together, mine is to be the name whispered between them!'

Nin Shubur laughed. 'Slowly, my little lady! Yes. But you are still a long way off the marriage bed yourself. And Uruk is the city of Sky Father An. Lady Morning Star is only the smallest maiden here among the Children of An.'

'I *will* be the greatest.'

'Hush, my lady. Remember that it was to humble that pride that you have been sent here.'

The terrace was vast, the buildings strange. As the sun marched higher, the heat was intensifying, till the sky itself grew pale and weary and the fruit bushes between the paving tiles hung waterless, no wind to rustle their dry leaves. Inanna leaned against the parapet, suddenly limp and lonely.

'Oh, the poor thing!'

It was not a human corpse, nor a dead dog, not even a sodden buffalo with blind, bulging eyes that had caught Inanna's pity.

A tree was floating past. Short of trunk, not fully grown to have yielded yet its promise of wide, smooth timber. Its crown sprouted sharp shoots, half-opened buds. Roots clawed like desperate fingers that had lost their hold, and in their skinned and broken yellow clutch they waved the pitiful remnant of the clay that had been scoured from beneath them.

'A *huluppu* tree,' observed Nin Shubur.

The small dark mountain woman remembered shade by upland torrents, where goats grazed. Inanna saw royal groves of timber, the woodmen with their axes, the benches of palace craftsmen more skilled than any other artists in the land.

'I want it.'

'My lady?'

'That tree. I want it for my own. Get it for me. Quick!'

'Child! The whole land's awash this morning. There's hardly a foothold to stand on. The waves are lapping at our very doors.'

'I want that *huluppu* tree. Enki has sent it out of the great thunderstorm for me. I know it! It's because it's young and beautiful and royal, like me! I'm going to rescue it and plant it down there in the garden. An wouldn't mind, would he? In summer I shall water it myself. I shall sit and sing to it. It will grow into the greatest and most handsome tree in all the world. Then I shall cut it down and make it into . . . Oh, hurry up! Before it's gone!'

The uprooted tree was indeed hurrying its unsteady course past the mound of Uruk on a cresting current. Sun was bringing the turbid brown waters back to flashing gold. The small, silver-green leaves of the *huluppu* tree seemed patterned with gilt dust. Nin Shubur signed to the file of slaves behind her.

'You and you! A boat at the Water Gate. As if every threshold in the town wasn't a landing stage this morning! Go after that *huluppu* tree. Catch it with ropes. Bring it back, with no more damage, even to a single twig. Run! You four. Get hoes. Prepare ground in the lower park. Dig a deep hole. Find a *nindingir* priestess to sing prayers for fruitfulness over it, as though it were a marriage bed. You, Ummana, go to the treasury. Find for my lady a trowel of pure silver. Girls! Bring boots for your mistress, the soft ones of gazelle skin, her apron of spotted cheetah hide. Inanna the gardener has work to do!'

A strangely mocking smile tilted the lines of Nin Shubur's eastern face, usually so carefully controlled. The servants ran on silent, unshod feet, as if a second storm had swept them from the terrace.

Soon a small, tarred boat was sculling away from the city walls, pursuing the skewed but stately progress of the *huluppu* tree. The rings on Inanna's fingers ground against the bricks of the parapet. Her small feet stamped in impatience on the bitumen black that sealed the terrace. She peered down over the roofs of the town at the turbulent river far below.

A rope weighted with a wooden peg darted through the brilliant air, swift as a black and white kingfisher, and dived across the trunk. The tree hardly slowed. The boat strained to keep level with it.

Another line meshed in the forked branches. The tree

swirled across the current, tugging angrily.

A third rope knotted itself around the roots. The *huluppu* tree was caught.

# Chapter Thirteen

*The Anunnaki of Eridu came rushing down to the water's edge to find Enki. Nanshe, his daughter, in her shimmering fish-scale dress. The two-faced Isimud, his counsellor and messenger. Asalluhe, his loud-voiced son. Nindara, the Fisherman. Nin Sun, Lady of Wild Cows, was with them. Even shy Nin Gikuga came running out of the canebrakes that the salt wave had flooded. They knelt over his poor, bruised body, mottled white and purple by the battering of the stones that Kur had hurled and the frenzy of the ocean. They gathered up the shattered fragments of the* magur *boat that came ashore, looked at the splintering of the stout timbers with horror.*

*When Enki opened his eyes, he saw a still lagoon, with a hint of deep jade and a dark, calm blue, fringed with palms that leaned their slender, supple stems over the water. It seemed to him that the air was lighter than he remembered, a suggestion of colour in these shadows, waiting to be born.*

*Isimud bent over him, one face creased in a smile of relief, the other still watchful.* 'My lord! We feared that Kur had captured you.'

'Then we saw, deep out in the night of the east, that huge eruption,' Nanshe said, *gliding her sure hands over his beaten body.*

'We feared the end had come for all of us. We thought that all the order Enlil has been establishing while you were gone . . .'

'The wolves and scorpions banished to the desert and the mountains . . .'

'Our children playing in the sand unharmed. The sheep grazing safely on the inland steppe. All the security and peace of the world,' Nindara explained eagerly.

'We thought all that was going to be lost in the coming chaos.'

'We feared our world was ending.'

'And then we saw you,' said Isimud, *helping his master to sit up, while Nin Sun unwound the fleecy cloth from her shoulders and breasts to dry his shivering flesh. 'You looked a great Lord indeed! You came riding the tidal wave in your* magur *ship like a charioteer breasting a mountain pass.'*

*'Your bounding ship was like an ibex from the Deep.'*
*'We saw you galloping down a great dark hill of water.'*
*'Saw the monstrous horned head reared behind you!'*
*'Saw boulders fly, like poppy seed exploding.'*
*'Watched stones rain down on you, vicious as hail.'*
*'Saw the raging ocean crash over you.'*
*'Saw nothing more.'*
*'We wept, we mourned for you.'*
*'And then . . .'*
*Isimud knelt, and all the Guardians of Eridu prostrated themselves before Enki.*

*'You are indeed Ruler of all the Waters, Son of An. The sweet waters own you, Lord. When you are with us, you make the land glad. Even the salt ocean could not overcome you. You are stronger than Kur. You are cleverer than your mother Nammu. You are Enki, Lord of the Deep. Let us build a great house to honour you, here by the lagoon of Eridu.'*

*'Where the sweet water runs down towards the salt.'*
*'Let us make your Sea House.'*
*'We will build you the Abzu.'*
*'Blue shall be its colour.'*
*'Water shall lap its walls.'*
*'Silver and gold will sparkle in its secret places.'*
*'There should be a deep, deep well in it, down into the depths.'*
*'It must have a high house on its terrace to touch the clouds.'*
*'A noble mountain.'*
*'A sacred pit.'*
*'The Abzu of Enki.'*
*'Lord of the Deep.'*

*The words beat round Enki's ears like waves on stone. He hardly heard their sense. Their praise meant nothing to him.*

*'Look!' cried Nanshe. 'The sky is turning darker still. The clouds are massing. It's starting to rain again!'*

*This time it was a deluge of pure water that crashed down on them. In moments the salt and slime of Kur was washed from Enki's skin by streaming rivulets. The air was filled with the music of fresh and running water. Frogs croaked ecstatically. The* hamah *fish jumped in the filling marshes, where the rainwater cleansed the salt. The canes hissed with the steady torrents pouring through their dried fronds.*

*The drumming rain brought no joy to Enki's soul. He had returned from Kur. He was safe. He had failed. He had left Ereshkigal behind, in his place.*

*He let Isimud and the women do with him what they wanted. They brought a canoe and poled him across the lagoon, carried him to a reed house in Eridu.*

*He lay in his chamber, hardly speaking, while his wounds healed and the rain fell hour after hour. When it stopped, he heard the sounds of many workers labouring.*

*A great pit was dug, filling with water, dark, unstoppable. A mound was walled around it. A platform raised. Mud bricks were shaped and fired. Walls were rising, with buttresses and recesses to pattern their faces. A block of veined stone, costly, was ordered to be brought from the mountains down to this land without rocks. A clay offering table would stand in front of it. A niche for a statue of Enki himself. Later, there would be rooms for all the officials of his household, courtyards for craftworkers. It would be a house to make even a great Lord envious.*

*Far above, wind moved the wide banks of clouds across the heavens. Down here, at sea level, no breeze shook the palms in the humid dusk around Eridu. No cooling draught eased Enki's aching head.*

*At last he tied a net skirt about him and walked outdoors.*

*The dull waters of the lagoon were muddied with the activity of building. The air was loud with the thud of bricks from the moulds, with the singing of labourers as they shouldered their loads up the ramps. They looked at him hopefully for approval. Enki scowled at them all, and called for Isimud.*

*'Get me a boat ready. We have a journey to make.'*

*Just for a moment, Isimud looked startled. 'What sort of boat, my lord?'*

*Enki grinned like a wolf. 'No need to wet yourself. I'm not going against Kur again. Just a river journey. A* shagan *canoe will do.'*

*The small, light craft of lashed reed bundles skimmed its way north up the vast spread of the Buranun. The wandering channels and lakes of the delta merged into one immense river flowing through a land of total flatness that reached away beyond sight in the dim light. It was rich with orchards and date groves.*

*Past Kiabrig and Ur, clusters of reed huts by the river. Cow pastures, where the cattle waded in muddy channels and browsed the edges of scattered marshes.*

*Upstream to Uruk, and the river still broad and gentle. Enki bent forward suddenly, peering ahead.*

*'Have I been away so long the face of the Earth has changed? What is that mountain doing in the plain of Uruk?'*

*'Other households than yours have been busy. They are building the Sky House here, for Father An.'*

*'Are they indeed? If they raise that mound much higher, my father won't even need to stir himself. It'll break through the clouds into Angal itself!'*

*'Twenty-four cubits, my lord, the mound alone. And his house to go on top of that.'*

*Enki sank back on the thwart, as if suddenly tired. Then he grinned. 'Does Enlil know about it?'*

*'I am sure he does, my lord.'*

*'And he will . . . ?'*

*'Just so, my lord. I fancy the Children of An are going to be very busy building in Nippur.'*

*The smile lingered a while longer in the creases round Enki's mouth.*

*Sheep country now, the grassy runs of the steppe, lost in the twilight. A jackal howled mournfully. The note came back from fifty throats. Far off still, the ploughlands around Nippur, where the Buranun bent east towards the Idiglat and the broken ground yielded the Anunnaki corn.*

*Wilderness between. Wild barley, growing ghostly grey. Vetches tumbling over the gravelly clay. Onagers kicked their heels and broke into a mad gallop, testing their freedom.*

*'The Edin,' said Enlil. 'The untouched garden, at the heart of Sumer. This should do.'*

*Isimud paddled to the shore and made the canoe fast. He watched his master attentively, waiting for his command. But Enki sprang ashore. The blue-black hair rippled down his back. The shadows hid his face. In his hand he held a copper hoe. Isimud watched him walk a little further up the river. He was no more than a shadow now, in a shadowed world. Then he bent and began to dig in the moist earth.*

*A deep, dark hole, filling with water welling from underground. A dark, deep place to hide the small, pale seed that Ereshkigal had taken from the serpent's skull and laid in Enki's hand.*

*A pain, as if a scab had been wrenched from a wound, to let it go. All he had left of her. But he must. The seed of life, out of the Great Below. Cover it now with earth. It would not stay hidden.*

*He must watch what came from it.*

# Chapter Fourteen

*Enki took his father's hand, lightly but firmly, and led him across the dark tracts of Angal. Far beneath, near a bend in the Buranun River, one of the new-built cities gleamed palely up at them.*

*'Uruk,' said Enki, savouring the name on his tongue, as though, like Enlil, to pronounce its syllables was to bring it into being. 'Raised for you, Father.'*

*'And that is E-Anna?'*

*It stood proud on the crest of its artificial mountain, above the cluster of mud-walled dwellings and reed-mat storehouses and byres. A house fit for the Father of them all. A statement in clay. A mighty staircase soared to the summit of the mound, whose upper surface had been levelled. An open courtyard spread wide to the air across this base. Rising from it, a single white-washed dwelling, almost windowless. But inside, it was alive with colour in the lamplight. Tens of thousands of small clay cones, dipped in red or black or buff, studded the walls and pillars in a geometrical fantasy of triangles, lozenges, zigzags and chevrons. A secret beauty.*

*'Step down. Honour this house. Be welcome.'*

*A crowd of Anunnaki was gathered on the terrace, gazing up. An stood, a giant figure on the topmost roof, acknowledging them. Then with an amused dignity he allowed Enki to lead him down the first lordly-sized step, and so they descended to meet their lesser family.*

*'Very good, very good,' said An, bending his head to inspect the house's interior. 'Yes, I could be contented here for a while.'*

When Enki sailed back to Eridu, the Abzu was finished. The sanctuary rose before him. His household was ranged on the water-steps to greet him. The Enkum and Ninkum holding their magic staves; his sons and daughters born of many mothers; Nanshe, whom he had installed to rule in his absence. Fifty lahamu, *young lion-like men with long curled sidelocks, waded in the water towards him holding nets full of leaping fish. Nimgirsig, the captain of the* magur *ship, steered across the lagoon. The Children of An watched the changeable face of their Lord.*

*In the calm dusk he saw two Sea Houses. One reached towards the still unlit heavens; its twin seemed to lie beneath the dark, mysterious waters of the lagoon. Enki looked down in silence. He too seemed to meet his twin in the depths, the fair face twisted by some slight commotion of the waters. The figure shivered, shook with suppressed emotion, looked about to strike.*

*'It is splendid, is it not, Lord Enki?' Isimud was standing at his elbow as the ship docked. 'Come and see.' He led the still mute Water Lord forward, preceded him proudly up the wide staircase carrying his staff, on to the walled terrace. The high rectangular doorways of the house loomed dark. Fire burned in sparks of rushlight flame, flickered on gold in abundance. The panels of lapis lazuli gleamed darkly blue as water. Threads of silver glinted like spray.*

*'Listen,' requested Isimud.*

*Under the brickwork, from a dark mouth at its centre, was a steady sibilant shushing, like a mother over a restless child. Enki listened, and it seemed that longing and rage welled up in his heart at the sound. Then, shocking the vast, echoing vault of the enclosed chamber, came a roar from the depths like a cow's bellow. The walls of the Abzu shook with it, and something broke loose in Enki with the shuddering echoes. He lifted his head and howled too, a shout of shame, rebellion, despair and loss.*

*'Oh, Ereshkigal!'*

*The roar in the deep abyss echoed away into a mourning throb, and the Lord was sobbing now. The walls took up both voices, tossed them back in oracular murmurs and whispers.*

*'Ereshkigal!'*
*'She is lost.'*
*'An unborn girl is rising.'*
*'She must go.'*
*'She is the light.'*
*'The dark is waiting for her.'*
*'She will go.'*
*'To Ereshkigal.'*
*'The Below.'*

*Enki clapped his hands over his ears. His attendant Anunnaki watched with awe and drew back a little.*

'*Your house speaks, my lord.*'

But Enki could not speak. The abyss was in his soul, and its waters were bitter.

At last he walked out into the open air. After the darkness the glimmer of the sky seemed almost radiant.

He said, not turning his head to see if Isimud was listening, '*It seems there is more light now than there ever was. Where does it come from?*'

'*From Nippur, Lord. Enlil is active there.*'

The Anunnaki all made an obeisance. Enki let his eyes range over their black, bowed heads, the covering folds of the women's dress lengths.

'*He is only the Air Lord,*' he said sharply. '*He cannot light the sky.*'

'*He is Enlil, the Kurgal.*'

'*Without him, no cities would be built.*'

'*No sheepfold erected.*'

'*The fish of the sea would lay no eggs in the canebrake.*'

'*The fields and meadows would not be filled with rich grain . . .*'

'*Don't I control the me?*' shouted Enki angrily. '*Enlil called out the Anunnaki from the Duku, gave them their names. But I have ordered the cosmos. I gave to every one of you your allotted tasks. I filled the Idiglat and the Buranun. I made the Earth sprout life.*'

'*Enki is wise beyond all the Anunnaki,*' said Isimud soothingly. '*But the first Word was with Enlil, young Lord of All.*'

'*Are not there four Great Guardians? An for the Sky, Ki for the Earth, Enlil for Air and I for . . . Water.*' A gulp still caught his throat. There was a fifth, whose name and dark domain he found he could not pronounce a second time outside the Abzu.

Nanshe was on his other side, the fish scales of her dress and sandals rustling. '*Yes, Father An keeps the Sky. But our Exalted Lady submits to Enlil. The son has become greater than his mother. He says it would be disrespectful now to name her Ki, since Enlil is Governor of the Earth. Nin Tu, Lady of Birth, becomes her better; Nin Mah, the Noble Lady.*'

'*So we are all losers,*' said Enki bitterly. '*An, Ki. . . . Ereshkigal . . . I.*' The word had come and gone. The abyss had not thundered in the Abzu. The scar was hardening. '*We have all had something taken away, except Enlil. He would like it all, wouldn't he?*'

'He does not have the Abzu,' Isimud pointed out. 'No Anunnaki will ever have a Sea House like yours. Sail to Nippur, my lord. Heap a nisag boat with gifts for your brother. Tell him the Abzu is completed. Invite him to rejoice with you.'

'And pay him tribute?'

Again that sibilance, as though he were a stranger unversed in their language, hard to communicate with.

'Lord Enlil is . . .'

'You should visit him, my lord.'

'You will see why all the Children of An bow down in reverence before him now.'

'Great Enlil is . . . He seems . . . There is that within him . . .'

'This universe will grow brighter because of him,' said Nanshe with a calm certainty. 'He will illuminate the world.'

'And all creatures will give him thanks.'

'And I, should I invite myself to a feast with him? Will he thank me for news of this shining Abzu you have built for me? I, who came from the Netherworld, dragging the stench of darkness? I, shall I be welcome in Nippur where the Air Lord sits high?'

'You must go,' encouraged Nanshe. 'Soften his heart with gifts of the south. Fish, reeds, the dates of your palms and their sweet honey, the wine of your grapes and the wood of the willows by your watercourses. For the oneness and peace of the Earth, be courteous to Enlil.'

'For you, my dear, I will try to behave myself.'

So Enki ordered a big nisag boat, flat-bottomed, built for cargo. He heaped the bounty of his orchards, the abundance of the marshes, the wood of its thickets, the flesh of its game. The lesser Anunnaki laboured willingly for him. Nin Gikuga came herself with arms full of her biggest reed canes.

'Take these to my Lord Enlil,' she said shyly, 'with my love and duty . . . And come back to us.'

He gazed at her golden face, her pale brown arms and feathery hair. Something quickened in his eyes. But he seemed to see through her beauty a more awful memory, of grace distorted, gaiety soured. His body pulsed with a suddenly roused yearning for comfort.

He raised a crooked, difficult smile for her. 'Don't go away, my lubi. I shall be back.'

Then he stepped down into the wide-bellied nisag boat. The kara boatmen poled away from the shore, across the lagoon where *a mist hung darkly on the water, away from the Abzu with its high, flat roof rising above the fog towards heaven. They started up the broad Buranun and headed through the narrowing lanes of reed beds towards the city of Nippur.*

*As they passed one spot far from any town, where the river curved through the steppe, Enki craned his neck to peer at the bank ahead. When at last he saw what he had been watching for, he gave a little start, hardly enough to disturb the boat.*

*Not far from the water's edge, a shoot of leaves had broken through the ground. A single* huluppu *tree.*

# Chapter Fifteen

When she saw the uprooted *huluppu* tree dragged from the river, a private tear crept from Nin Shubur's eye and travelled coolly down her sun-bathed cheek. She was still a young woman, as the Anunnaki reckon. Yet for her too, one lifetime was over. Nin Shubur, once a princess in the East herself, was from yesterday *sukkal-mah* to the Young Lady of the Morning Star. She was wise. She had accepted her destiny, Enlil's decision. She knew that already she loved this wilful, charming child. There was not a Lady of the Anunnaki would have served her better.

The two men in the boat were hidden from them now. They had towed their booty under the lee of the wall, out of the ripping current.

'Come on!' urged Inanna, tugging Nin Shubur's hand.

Slave girls hurried before her, flinging open the bronze-leaved doors, scenting the shadowed air with petals, brushing the dust from the steps where she would tread. Inanna ran out through the last high gates into the dazzle of the lower park.

The overnight waters had scarcely seeped away from their trespassing. Blue frogs hopped like professional acrobats. The fertile, alluvial earth bubbled like a well-fed baby. Bulbul birds flashed among the flowering almond trees.

Halfway between the river boundary and the base of the mound, gardeners had already been hard at work. Overtaking Nin Shubur, Inanna raced ahead. Drops of water flew round her bare legs making miniature rainbows. Petals of pomegranate blossom showered sunset-red on her hair. It was the first morning of her new life in An's house. This was her very first order to the E-Anna servants. She stopped, in a half-frightened wonder, and looked down to see what she had done.

A new hole gaped like a pit shaft into the Netherworld. A pool had gathered blackly at the bottom, and swift rivulets ran from the piled clay round its sides, falling in tinkling cascades to meet the rising groundwater.

'We had better be careful, or the flood may overtake us even here,' observed Nin Shubur.

'I am a child of the Moon. I'm not afraid of water,' said Inanna, tossing her tumbling, blue-black hair. 'My great-grandmothers were Ki, the Earth Lady, and Nammu, Mother of the Deeps. I can hold them together.'

'We all come from those two,' said Nin Shubur drily.

Like a darker sun, rising above the steps from the Water Gate, the first spiked rays of the *huluppu* tree were appearing. The stained and sweating men bore it triumphantly aloft.

Inanna drew a long, shaking breath. The thing that was approaching her looked very different from the gilt-covered trophy glimpsed from high above.

The bark was sodden, sprouting strange, spongy growths, as though it had lain submerged far longer than a single night. Mud dripped from its branches. The green slime of disturbed canal beds drooped sourly from its trunk. The roots had been snapped, long before the careful slaves' hands could catch them.

They lifted its wounded flesh over the paving and carried it like a gigantic first fruit of harvest to the Lady Inanna. The sun still shone on it, but more cruelly now. It was no longer a lovely thing, close to. Sinister, rather. Only the uncurling leaves, their silvered undersides like new moons, offered promise.

If Inanna felt the cold hand of disappointment or revulsion she did not show it. She looked at the damaged *huluppu* tree steadfastly.

'Set it in the hole,' she said. 'Here at my feet.'

The men lowered the tree. Its splintered crown shadowed the sky. Rich, black earth was tumbled into the hole to hide the fractured roots.

Girded now, with laughing solemnity, in a spotted hide apron and soft boots, Inanna herself knelt before it, carefully pressing the soil over those roots to make a smooth, close covering. She straightened up, and licked one muddy finger, almost as if she was tasting the milk of her mothers. She trod down the dark circle she had made, with small, firm feet. Then she reached up a hand and touched the branches, one by one.

Nin Shubur handed her a copper jug, and Inanna stepped

in a ring around the half-grown tree, scattering the water of life in a brilliant shower.

The palace girls began to sing:

> My Lady, the Morning Star, is radiant on the horizon.
> My Lady, the brightest star in heaven, shines on the Earth.
> This tree will take root for her, the leaves will unfold for her.
> The heart of the *huluppu* tree will drink in the sunshine of Utu.
> The feet of the *huluppu* tree will bathe in the waters of Enki.
> The touch of Inanna, young Lady of Life, will restore the tree to life.
> The people of Sumer celebrate her goodness with joy.

As the hymn caressed her ears, Inanna seemed to grow taller, smiling, confident in Ladyship. She reached out one small, eager hand, creamy as new-drawn milk, the nails stained red. She pressed the touch of her vitality on the trunk of the *huluppu* tree, and the wet, grey bark thrilled back to her with the hope of strength.

'Tree,' she vowed, 'you are my own tree. My *huluppu* tree. The south wind has uprooted you from the soil. The Copper River has carried you to my gate. You are mine now. I have set the hand of my Ladyship upon you.'

Nin Shubur was still studying the tree, with a crease in the pattern of her tattooed forehead. 'This tree is not fully grown, yet I feel it is ancient.'

Inanna turned to her with a dazzling smile. 'It will be fully grown when I am.'

# Chapter Sixteen

*There was a gleam ahead. The primeval dusk that had hung over Sumer since its creation seemed to shimmer with an expectancy of light. Enki felt, though he said nothing to the others, a sense of awe. In spite of rage and rivalry, he felt himself drawn to that sheen of mist above the waters. His eyes ached for something more.*

*Cut channels were branching away, straight-sided, hacked by hoes. The current slackened and they were carried through fields of barley springing dimly green. The plain seemed awash with silver. Not sparkling, but brighter than Enki's indigo lagoon.*

*Enki allowed himself a flash of jealousy.* 'Who filled the Idiglat and the Buranun, then? Whose semen made the great rivers run, gave life to all Sumer?'

'My Lord of the Abyss is mighty indeed. The Abzu honours him,' *said Isimud prudently.*

'But not Enlil's E-Kur? Damn you for a two-faced diplomat, Isimud!'

*Wharves were reaching down to the waterfront now, under mud-brick walls. The piled* nisag *boat was punted out of the current of the broad, pale river. The city of Nippur rose above them. Houses of clay, walls of fired bricks. Glimpsed over all this was the high terrace on which the builders were hard at work.*

'The E-Kur is still not finished,' *announced Isimud.* 'Enlil's great dwelling. Here the Fifty will meet in council. Here the Seven will pronounce wise judgment.'

*Another canal, the finest and most strongly-banked of all, angled under the north-west side of Enlil's capital, reared on its mound above the reach of floods.*

'The Id-Nunbirdu,' *said Isimud.*

*In the distance, young, slender girls were wading waist-deep in its water, washing themselves and their families' garments. Some bent and let their hair flow in the stream like trailing cresses. Others, just come to womanhood, cried out when they saw the* nisag *boat approaching, turned their fair backs, drew lengths of dripping cloth round their nether parts. But still their faces watched the newcomers with curiosity.*

*The Eridu men did not turn their eyes away. Enki watched the young women, felt his maleness stirring.*

*The boat drew up and moored at the broad Karkurunna quay. It was busy with cargo canoes, laden* magur *boats, while gangs of workers went up and down its steps, unloading, portering, smeared with brickdust, streaked with clay, hands tarry with bitumen.*

'Should the Children of An labour like beasts of burden?' *wondered Enki.*

'It's true, the work is very heavy here. There have been complaints.'

*A stillness fell on the swift-moving tide of porters. All heads were raised to gaze up at the top of the stepped ramp.*

'Hail, Enlil! Young Lord of Air and Wind!'

*The Anunnaki all bowed their foreheads to the ground. Even the Water Lord himself, always supple of body and quick to catch the current of mood, felt himself bending. Then he resisted, shot a look upward from his sea-blue eyes, to find his half-brother standing tall on the terrace above. Wind stirred Enlil's long hair. He seemed to carry an aura of freshness with him. His clothes were light, a net skirt, a scarf of almost transparent linen. He carried himself easily, moved forward on feet that hardly seemed to need the ground.*

'Brother!' *He flung his arms wide.* 'You have returned safely from your voyage! I hear that you could not fetch back your lovely sister. But you have still brought me a fine cargo.'

*Enki began to ascend the steps, menacing as a rising flood.* 'Don't speak her name! You haven't seen it. You haven't felt the terrors of the Netherworld. Don't presume! Lord of Air, you may be. You have taken the Earth from Ki. All the Four Quarters are yours because you seized them. But Kur, the Great Below, you don't know yet. Ereshkigal is Queen of Kur, not you!'

*Enlil's answer sounded easy.* 'Then let her keep it, by our will. What is darkness to us? What is death and decay when we have air and . . . light?'

*Again that troubled lust in Enki, for something not yet born. He knew – who could avoid acknowledging it? – that light was contained within Enlil already. It did not blaze from him. It was not yet made manifest. But all eyes turned to the veiled radiance of his presence. When darkness still draped the Sky, when the*

*Earth was always shadowed, when the crops struggled for fruitfulness in perpetual twilight, how could they not? He was their hope, their future.*

*Enlil seemed to surge down the steps to meet his brother, extended a swift, cool hand. Enki felt himself being drawn up, away from the river into the higher atmosphere of the Air Lord's city.*

*They passed through streets and squares, over Id-Shauru, the central canal. Gardens were being planted, courtyards enclosed. The unfinished E-Kur was looming ahead, a complex of buildings far more elaborate than the Abzu.*

*Enlil moved quickly, guiding Enki round baskets of rubble waiting to be poured into the cavities of the walls, past stack upon stack of clay bricks. In the brickyards outside the city tens of thousands of them were laid out to dry in the restless wind. Kulla, the Brick Lord, straightened his back and wiped his sweating brow.*

*'We must wait for Gibil to do his work. I need fired bricks for the outer walls to throw off the rain . . . especially if Lord Enki's back!' He grinned at the Water Lord briefly.*

*'Hurry! Hurry!' Enlil clapped his hands like an impatient child. 'You can surely use these others for something. Is there not more interior work waiting to be done? What about the donkey stables? The lamp room? The cupboards for my concubines' cosmetics?'*

*Kulla raised his eyes to the unmoved sky, then bowed circumspectly. 'As my lord says. There is always more work to be done. You there! Get across to the back corner. Has Mushdamma laid the foundations of the* giparu *residence yet?'*

*A sudden growl burst from the group of porters who had been squatting beside their empty baskets.*

*'Is there no end to work?'*

*'Someone should be signalling: this is the time for labour and that for rest.'*

*'When do we sleep?'*

*'When can we play?'*

*'When do we eat?'*

*'When can we make love?'*

*'Is it only when* he *says?'*

*Enlil whipped round and started to stride towards them. At the sight of his swinging skirt, his billowing scarf, the builders sprang to their feet, touched their foreheads respectfully, covered their lips, murmured apologies, filled their baskets with dried bricks, went back to work.*

*'An ass is more willing than these!' said Enlil impetuously.*

*'The work is heavy. The Children of An were meant for play and talk and the care of creation,' said Enki, not displeased to see the rumblings of rebellion in Enlil's Nippur.*

*'Has an ox hands? Has a monkey brains enough? Who could work for me if these did not?'*

*Enki punched him sideways, with a grinning savagery. 'Take that cross look off your face. Haven't I more to be solemn about than you have? I'm the one who's escaped from the Netherworld, not you. Get yourself a girl! Didn't I hear something about concubines?'*

*Then with a wild abandon he lifted his penis over the wall, directed a spray of semen towards the moat below and sent the young women walking past shrieking for cover.*

# Chapter Seventeen

*Sud, Princess of the Winnowing Pan, sped on her light, white feet up the steps from the Karkurunna quay on the river, carrying her basket of washing. Even though the E-Kur was far from finished, her parents had business here in Nippur. They had been given quarters in the Kiur, next to the E-Kur. It was sweet with the warm smell of grain and wool and dates. She passed her father Haia, Lord of Stores, on the wide steps as he went down to supervise the unloading of Enki's nisag boat. She threw him a breathless kiss.*

*'Steady on, my lass! A Daughter of An has all the time in the world ahead of her. You're not a thing of a few years, like a ewe lamb, that has to pack all her living in while she can.'*

*'I love it! I love it!' Sud gestured at the rising glory of the E-Kur, its buttressed walls, the paving of its terrace in shades of grey and red and blue, the white stone reinforcing the quay at Karassara, the blue at Karkurunna. She had never felt so happy as she did here at Nippur, so light, so free.*

*'It's a good place for a great Lord who still seems young,' agreed Haia.*

*'Who . . . ?' began Sud. But she was already past her father on a higher step as she turned her head to ask. He did not hear her. He was going on down to the waterfront with that steady, slightly bow-legged walk of one accustomed to shift heavy weights with those wide, square shoulders. She watched him fondly. But the strange, southern boat quickened her blood too. Enki and the sukkal Isimud had long since left it for the E-Kur. Only the* kara *boatmen remained, overseeing the bounty of the marshes and orchards of Eridu that was Enki's tribute to his brother, his invitation to rejoice at the completion of the Abzu. If Sud had heard of this, the memory had blown easily out of her girlish mind. But that someone had come to disturb the purposeful work of building she had clearly seen. One glimpse from the moat, one shocking, funny, unsettling moment had left her both repelled*

70

*and curious, eager to learn something about its perpetrator.*

*She whisked past Enlil's gatekeeper, Kalkal, who smiled appreciatively at the pretty princess, across the city and through the door of the Kiur.*

*What light there was in Nippur, and it held more than most cities, had a silvery sheen. Lord Enlil himself seemed almost to carry no colour and yet to be the opposite of darkness. But somehow, here at home, in the place of her father Haia and her mother, the Barley Woman Nunbarshegunu, it seemed that colour was wanted. Gold gleamed dully from its shadows, waiting to burst into glory. Great heaps of grain mounded their courtyard. There seemed always more than could possibly be needed, except for that heartstopping time when Enki had descended to Kur and the rains had ceased. Yet all the barley was fresh, running like rivers when she touched it. Plump, hard, sweet kernels. Mice feasted in it. Cats chased them. Sparrows flew down to peck and grow fat. She knew that on threshing floors oxen trampled unmuzzled, gorging on their own labours. And still there was more. Now that Enki had returned to Eridu the fields were packed with harvest again. Sud threw her arms wide as if to embrace the cornfields all around. She tossed her head back and laughed, a light, silvery peal of gaiety.*

*'Are you clean and sweet, my girl?' asked Nunbarshegunu, hurrying forward laughing herself, with her arms full of a fine, tasselled woollen robe. 'Here, put this on. Pick out your best jewellery. The tiara with the golden flowers and the little lapis lazuli dogs and cats swinging from it. Paint your eyes with kohl. Make yourself beautiful for the feast.'*

*'What feast? Is it the strangers? There was a big boat at the Karkurunna quay. Father was going to unload it. Where has it come from? Who are they?'*

*'Steady, steady. You're right to be curious, though. It's Lord Enki. That's who.'*

*'Enki of the Waters? Who went to the Netherworld . . . and came back!' Awe and eagerness wrestled in Sud's still-childish face.*

*'The same. And has a big house of his own now, in Eridu, he wants to celebrate. The deep-blue Abzu.'*

*'Oh, but Nippur is better, isn't it? So high on its platform. So light, so airy! I feel marvellous here. I feel as if I could fly. As if I could touch the sky.'*

*'That's Lord Enlil,' said Nunbarshegunu, starting to arrange her daughter's dress length around her hips and over her left*

*shoulder, being careful to leave one small, white breast exposed. There was no reason for Sud to cover her sweet flesh modestly yet. More reason not to.*

*Sud twisted impatiently inside the light but imprisoning cloth. 'Then . . . was that Lord Enki himself, walking round the walls with Lord Enlil?'*

*'You saw him?'*

*'Yes.' A wave of giggles overcame Sud and the very pale gold of her face blushed fiery red. 'Mother, he . . . he watered the moat, when we were all bathing just beyond in the Id-Nunbirdu. He did! We saw him.'*

*'Did you indeed? And I have no doubt he meant you to. Well, didn't he fill the Idiglat and the Buranun at the time of creation? Didn't he bring the rain to make the barley grow? What would Enlil's own Duku throne of wool and grain be without Enki's water? You tell me that.'*

*'But in public. With all of us girls bathing and washing our clothes. It wasn't proper . . . He shouldn't, should he?' And yet through her blushes, her eyes were bright and her breath came in little rushes of excitement.*

*'Stand still, girl. A stalk of barley? You're more like Lady Air!'*

*'How do I look? I must paint my fingernails again. Do you think he noticed me?'*

*'How should I know? What's in your mind, girl? Would you leave Nippur after all? Go and live in Eridu? Be the wife of the Lord of the Abyss?'*

*The laughter left Sud instantly. She drew back. 'Leave Nippur? I didn't think! Couldn't I still live here, under Lord Enlil? What is it like to be married to a Lord?' She looked intently at her mother, as though the reality had only just occurred to her.*

*'You'll find out soon enough,' Nunbarshegunu told her. 'It's a pity your hips are so slim. You don't look like the mother of plenty. But with your frivolous ways, you'd be better married as soon as not.'*

*'And you really believe . . . ?' Her wide, gold-flecked eyes appealed to her mother for confirmation.*

*'Lord Enki?' Nunbarshegunu snorted a little. 'I think a princess like you should be married to a great Lord, yes. But we shall see.'*

*The feast was awe-inspiring. An had been invited to sit in the place of honour, with Nin Mah beside him, while their children served them. It was as though the two great Lords of Air and Water were vying with each other for pre-eminence in generosity. All the riches from the south that Enki had brought were heaped on Enlil's table. The flesh of gazelles, enormous barbel fish, fresh grapes and wine in abundance, great heaps of dates. Enlil himself piled in front of the guests mountains of new-baked loaves, cakes of honey and flour, big, hard cheeses of cows' milk, soft, small cheeses of ewes' milk, fragrant cheeses of herb-fed goats, much cream and butter. He had commanded the Beer Woman Nin Kasi to brew vast bappir vats and the servants poured copiously from two-spouted* lahtan *jugs. The banqueting hall was full of food and merriment, and the light of palm-oil lamps. Outside was the ever-present, starless night.*

*But though she sat at the side of the highest dais, pretty Sud felt herself ignored. There were greater Ladies than she. Nidaba the wise Reed Scribe. Her own mother, ample provider of grain. Ashnan, Lady of all Growing Crops. Lahar the Cattle Princess. What was the little, light Seed Girl among so many, when the great Lord Air himself was giving the feast?*

*She thought Enki was magnificent. His blue-black beard rippled over his broad chest. His unbound hair tumbled in waves. The blue veins threaded his arms like tributaries from the mountains. She thought of him battling with Kur, and her heart seemed to miss a beat. Licking sticky date honey from her fingertips, she tried to imagine what it would be like to be held in those mighty arms, to be crushed against that chest, to press her face into that thick, dark hair. She felt her body tightening in panic. She seemed to herself so light, so small. What would it mean to be invaded by a power like that? Would she remain herself, Sud, the Seed Girl, afterwards?*

*The pluck of lyres, the roar of talk and laughter all round bemused her senses. She heard her own name with a start.*

*'My lord desires the Lady Sud should taste this. It is a wine fit for an Anunnaki princess.'*

*Nusku, Enlil's* sukkal, *was standing behind her. From a red-veined, chalcedony pitcher he filled her fluted cup. The wine was golden, faintly perfumed. A gift from Eridu. She tasted it and fire seemed to warm her small body. She looked up over the edge of the beaker and found Enlil himself smiling at her from his couch of cushions. He raised his own goblet to her. Enki was laughing beside him, more than half-drunk.*

*'You do me honour, my lord. The wine of Eridu is exceedingly good,' she said in her small, rustling voice. She did not think*

*either of them could hear her across the noisy room. Her smile must thank them instead.*

*'Well,' said Nunbarshegunu undressing her afterwards. 'You will be a greater Lady soon, it seems.'*

*'Why? I don't think Lord Enki even noticed me.' She hung dejected over her jewel box, heavy with too much food and barley beer and wine, and too little sleep. Had she wanted him to, when the thought of his embraces frightened her? Did she really want to be a woman and lay herself open to that hurt?*

*'Lord Enki? Not him! There was another hardly took his eyes off you all evening.'*

*Sud turned to stare at her mother sleepily, almost too tired to be curious.*

*'Who?'*

*'Who, child? Who but the greatest prize of all! Lord Enlil, of course.'*

*Suddenly it was as if a flock of butterflies had been panicked into flight inside her chest. Lord Enlil? Still dumb, she stared at her mother with eyes round and childish now.*

*'Lord Air?' she whispered at last. 'At me?' Her voice was almost a squeak.*

*'There,' Nunbarshegunu soothed her. 'There's nothing to be done about it till tomorrow. Then we must see. He's a busy man. There are Ladies in plenty hanging round him. But tonight . . . I think he noticed your looks for the first time.' She combed her daughter's fine gold hair with vigorous strokes. 'There. Sleep on it. It's fully dark now. Enlil must be asleep. When the light in him wakes and he brings the gleam of morning over the Id-Nunbirdu . . . Well, get your beauty sleep, girl. Let me think how to manage it.'*

*Sud woke sooner than she wished to. To her relief the world outside her window was dark. Enlil must be sleeping yet. That she should be afraid of what little veiled light they had made her more frightened still. Lord Enlil! She rolled swiftly over in her woollen blankets and hid her face deeper, trying to bury her imagination. She was trembling now, whimpering softly. Lord of the Air and Wind? All that force, that energy, that might. She felt herself too frail, too small, too much a child. And yet . . . The Lord of Nippur!*

*Like a shadow, even in the darkness, her mother was standing over her. And indeed when Sud slowly lifted her head she thought the night was faintly greyed by twilight. Her heart seemed to drop into the pit of her stomach.*

*'Come along, child. Hurry. There's no one about.'* The familiar smell of corn came from her mother. The girl wanted to bury her face in the fullness of that belly, hold Nunbarshegunu's warm strength in her own cold, thin arms. But this same big, generous, fruitful mother was the Lady who was sending her out into the growing pallor of the day.

*'What shall I wear?'* she shivered.

*'Wear? What should you wear but the beauty I gave you, Miss Grain! Sweet as a swan in the time of her first fullness, when her cygnet feathers have turned pure white. Fresh as the morning of creation when the Anunnaki came out of the Duku and rubbed their eyes. What should you want with clothes this morning?'*

*'What then must I do?'* Sud was standing beside her bed now, her arms wrapped round herself, defensively.

*'What you have done hundreds of times before. Go down the steps to the Nunbirdu Canal. Wash yourself in the stream. Dance, if you like, as you often do. Yes, I've watched you.'*

Sud coloured softly, but turned pale again. *'Now? Alone?'*

*'This very instant, before the city is stirring. And yes, of course, alone.'*

*'What if the city gate is locked?'*

*'It will be open.'*

Sud raised slow, comprehending eyes. She was powerless. This day was planned. And all her life would be changed because of it. It was happening so fast, she did not know whether she ought to rejoice.

*'And he . . . will marry me? Because he sees me dancing naked on the canal bank?'*

*'The moment is ripe. Like the day the ears of barley stand proud and full, before the stalk begins to bend, and the farmer knows it is time to put in the sickle. The light is trapped within him. He must find the right woman to release his seed. You are that Lady. You will sit beside him on the Duku. I shall lead him to your marriage bed.'* Then, as if relenting, she handed her daughter a tasselled shawl. *'Here, child, you're shivering. Wrap that about you while you go. The world is not warm yet. Bring us good luck!'* She kissed the cold brow of her daughter, then pushed her towards the door.

No lamps burned. Sud threaded her way out through the Kiur, so close to Enlil's own house. She was guided by her fingertips on the smooth walls of plaster, the rougher brick of the outer courts, the scent of the grain stores, the hasps of the gate. The street that led down to the Water Gate of the city seemed deserted. Her own *soft, bare feet made hardly a sound. She peered for Enlil's friendly gatekeeper, hoped for a spark of flame in the gatehouse. There was none. The Water Gate, guarded by its two stone dragons, was the smallest fraction ajar. No need to clatter with bolts and latches, to call for help. She stepped through, like a small breeze that leaves no trace of its passing, tiptoed down the ramp to the empty quay, began to walk along the canal.*

# Chapter Eighteen

It seemed impossible that the vast E-Anna could hold such total silence. To tiptoe through it was to feel that you were the only being left alive. It was hard not to tiptoe. Nin Shubur glided in front on small, bare feet that made no sound. Inanna found herself torn between a felt need to move with caution, not to wake these hundreds of sleepers from their afternoon siesta, and the desire to run to catch up with that one, sure, known figure moving ahead.

Strange that already Nin Shubur should seem like a signal of safety, an oasis in the desert.

They went by the inner staircases this time, away from the pounding heat of afternoon. Huge flights rose before her, the painted figures on the walls towering in the dimness, a shadowed underworld.

What did An want her for? Why now, before the end of this silent double-hour? The careful Nin Shubur had overseen an even more particular bathing and grooming and ornamenting than this morning's for Inanna's second visit. She looked down thoughtfully at her white body, still childish, but growing taller with that slow unfolding of the Children of An over thousands of years.

'I beg your pardon!'

Someone had stepped from behind a half-pillar of studded mosaic and almost cannoned into Nin Shubur.

It was a shock to see someone else alive, moving, as Inanna was. And what she saw and smelt was strange too, in this scented palace of linen-clad servants.

This was a boy, older than Inanna herself, but still not fully grown. A sun-browned face, dark in the half-light that sheltered the E-Anna halls from the brilliant afternoon sun. Hair bleached to the curly paleness of sheep's fleece. Brown eyes that danced. He wore a sheepskin kilt too. He was carrying a basket.

Seizing the excuse, Inanna let herself run forward. It occurred to her that in this house of soft-footed eunuchs and beautiful women she had met few men yet, certainly no boys. After the boisterous rough-and-tumble of her brothers Utu and Ishkur, this feminine world was strange to her. Yet it seemed Great-grandfather An liked it so.

Close to, the boy smelt warmly of cheese and goats, but something worse than that too. The sheepskin kilt and the body above, as well as his legs and arms, were fouled with mud.

'I know you, don't I?' she cried with sudden recognition. 'You're . . .'

'Dumuzi Ama-Ushumgalanna . . . *my lady*.'

Yes, the eyes crinkled at the corners with the same laughter with which he had greeted her before. Dumuzi, her mother's young half-brother.

Enki's son. Dumuzi Abzu.

'It was you. In Nippur. You came to fetch me back to the Ubshu-ukkinna court . . .'

'To hear the Council's verdict.'

This boy had been a witness to her humiliation. She could not stop the blood from flaming in her cheeks at the memory. She felt the warmth travelling down her body. Dumuzi's eyes followed it. There was an embarrassed silence.

'How . . . has it been?' he said, a trifle huskily. 'Is An very angry? How is he treating you?'

She tossed her fragrant hair. 'I am a princess of the House that Brings Light, in Ur. How should Father An treat me but well? I'm on my way to see him now.' She wrinkled her nose. 'You smell.'

He laughed loudly, with his own quick flash of pride. 'So would you if you'd done what I have. Haven't you noticed there was a great flood last night? I had to paddle across the swamp from our farm on the edge of the steppe, over the top of what should have been a good road. It wasn't easy. The storm has stirred up all sorts of things that would have been better left undisturbed on the bottom.' He flicked pellets of drying mud from his arm. 'It took longer than I expected.'

'The flood brought *me* a tree. I've planted it. What have you got in that basket?'

'Butter, cream, cheese, fermented milk. I bring An some of these every week. The human farmers can't get the same bite in the cow's cheese, the same creaminess in the ewe's cheese.

They don't catch the same flavour of herbs from the steppe. And my sister Geshtinanna's sent him a bunch of late grapes. No one else can grow grapes like Geshtin.'

Inanna's finger stole out as he lifted the cloth and parted the cool palm leaves. One small, scarlet nail bored into the heart of a soft, round cheese and carried the sample to her mouth. Her eyes were fixed on his, as if to challenge him. She saw a flash in his own she did not understand. Then he was holding up the grapes to tease her while she reached to steal one. His brown eyes gazed back at her now in smiling pleasure, uncritical as a sheepdog's.

'I'll take them for you. I'm on my way to see him.' She seized the basket from his arm before he knew what was happening.

'But—'

'I'm sure he'll be *very* pleased with your present. Thank you!'

'My lady . . .'

Inanna was already heading for the foot of the staircase that led to the third level. For a moment, Nin Shubur hesitated, as if uncertain whether to reprove her mistress with a diplomatic demurral. Then she too seemed to yield to the eagerness of Inanna's smile.

'Lord An wished to see Inanna alone.'

She led her mistress unprotesting up the stairs.

When they were out of earshot and crossing the floor towards the highest ascent, she ventured to say, 'Was that quite kind to the lad, my lady? He's risked a long, hard journey to bring his gift today. Shouldn't you have let him have the reward of An's gratitude himself?'

Inanna swung her face round, laughing now, her fears forgotten. 'He doesn't mind. I think he likes me. Did you know that Enki said he could marry me one day?'

She was enjoying a sense of importance, the heaviness of the basket pressing into her bare arm, the rich, farm smell of the goodness it contained. It smelt like Dumuzi. Not today's foul stink of mud but as he had smelt before, coming for her in the E-Kur where she waited for the Anunnaki's verdict. She needed that small victory, to turn the tables, to be the one in control, to wipe out the memory of the powerlessness Dumuzi had witnessed.

# Chapter Nineteen

*It was dark, it was cold, it was lonely, it was threatening. As a child, Sud had come to bathe here, to play and gossip with other young Daughters of An. The herons had taken flight far down the channels, the frogs had hidden in the mud. Now she walked alone on her slight, light feet and nothing fled from her. Toads croaked; the sharp-billed geese loomed out of the canal's misty surface, hissed at her.*

*What if I should meet a scorpion, a cobra?*

*But Enlil had banished all harmful things from the cities of Sumer. A small sob of gratitude that was also fear choked Sud's throat. They were all so dependent on him. He had given them everything. An presided over the Council, but surely the Anunnaki could refuse Enlil nothing he wanted? Like a small, white kid to an altar she stumbled forward, clutching her fleecy shawl about her.*

*Here, where the reeds grew tall on the bank and had gained a footing in the water, here, where the faintest sheen of pearl lay over dew-wet gardens, here, where those comforting walls of Nippur were still close above and some other girl's mother might be looking down, Sud halted.*

*She unwound the cloth from her newly mature limbs, clutched it longingly in cold fingers, let it fall. She stepped reluctantly down the smooth, damp clay, met the shock of the water. It was warmer than she expected. She thought of young, laughing Enki spraying them all from that corner of the wall beyond the lofty Eshmah tower. Did she wish she had not run from him and escaped?*

*She was a virgin, a child yet. No, not quite. She remembered the fright, the blushing surprise, the troubled secrecy with which she had confessed to Nunbarshegunu, the awe with which she learned what little of the truth her mother had thought it fit to tell her. That blood, more dark than bright on her white legs in the shadows of her chamber, her own* itima, *in the heart of the*

Kiur. That blood was gone, but she bent to wash her thighs and the soft silk of her pudendum vigorously in the sandy water. Feeling relieved and cleansed, forgetting for the moment why she was here, she plunged into the deeper water. The stream received her, welcomed her, covered her over. She turned and let her hair float loose. The current played with it, tugged it gently.

Then Sud remembered the awful, awkward purpose of her coming. How could she dance in this hush before the energy and activity of the work time? She waded towards the reeds, and it seemed to her the currant bushes in the gardens stood out more clearly than before, the bluebirds were singing more loudly, the unseen cattle beginning to low.

A faint luminosity was growing over Nippur. The air seemed to ache for light. The small waves she left behind her caught a faint gleam at the rippled edges. Slowly but irresistibly, Sud turned.

Enlil was coming along the towpath. It could only be he. No other Son of An was so tall, so fair, moved with such swift but weightless energy. No other Lord but he shimmered with a power caught inside him, like a beautiful, caged animal waiting to break out.

Every nerve in her body wanted to fling herself before him, kneel on the footpath, bow her dripping head to the dust. But she must pretend she had not seen his coming. She turned her back, lifted her hand and shook the water from her hair. Bent, as if carelessly, scooped fresh handfuls over her pale legs to wash the mud away. Plucked a feathery reed head, teased her skin, began to laugh, to sing in a little shaking treble, and to dance.

The pallor of morning was in front of her now. Not bright enough to cast a hard-edged shadow from her feet. But, softly outlined, she saw her shape immensely tall, stretching away towards the unploughed desert lands. No heat warmed her. Rather, she felt a cold breath on her back.

'Sud? I find the fields of early morning are sweeter than I knew!'

A finger touched her spine. She started like a gazelle. Arms went round her, turned her.

'A kiss now? From lips tastier than bread and honey! Your song was much more enchanting than the nightingale, but I shall expect a deeper magic in the stopping of your mouth.'

His leaping breath fanned waves of blood into her cheeks. His lips were cool and moist, his tongue was strong. She struggled like a netted bird.

'Yes! Now! It must be now!' His eagerness was like the wind. It hardly let him speak. Like a gale flattening a barley field he was forcing her down into the grass. His huge, hard member pressed against her shivering flesh. She was imprisoned by him. Yet in his blind, single-centred abandon, Enlil missed his mark. They rolled sideways off the raised levee, tumbled down the bank. Enlil was laughing, groping for her, cursing colourfully, as the mud smeared his fair skin. Sud, like a flake of chaff, spun out of his loosened arms, darted into the clumps of reeds.

He stood up then and bellowed after her, 'Come back, you little coot! Don't be afraid! I'm going to fill you with the seed of the greatest of the Sons of An. You'll love it! I promise. Let me teach you. Come here, little Miss Barley Ear.'

From the canes she called in her quivering voice, 'You are too great for me. I am too young. I have never known a man. My vagina is too little for what you want to fill it with. My mouth is too small for someone like you, my lord. Choose someone else!'

The tears were running down her face. This was not what her mother had told her. This was not the warm, corn-smelling comfort of her father with his arm round his wife. This was not the marriage bed of the Queen of the E-Kur. She was as helpless as a small silver fish beneath the hunter's spear.

He was coming towards her. The reeds bent and swished before his eager advance. Sud fled towards the water, dived once more into the tepid shelter of the canal. That hint of light was spreading over the surface towards her, hunting her out. She ducked her head, held her breath, swam on.

A curse now, a shout. Rising to breathe in a more distant patch of twilight, she heard him call, 'Nusku! Where in the name of Kur are you hiding?'

'Coming, my lord. What's upsetting you? You told me to keep out of sight. What's wrong?'

'The girl, damn her! She's given me the slip.'

'They're all like that, sir. Well, half of them at least. There's one lot that'll chase after you, and hang out all they've got in front of your nose. The others run a mile, but you can bet they're looking over their shoulder hoping you're still coming after them.'

'I'll come after her, deceitful bitch! Dancing on the towpath, showing me everything! She must have known I was watching. Then she says she's too little. Her mother wouldn't like it. Not today, thank you. To Enlil!'

'Which way did she go, sir?'

'Into the water, curse her. She's as tricky as an air bubble. I should have let Enki have her. But I'll not be made a fool of by a chit like her. Get me a boat!'

'At once, my lord. Keep an eye out for her while I'm gone. See if you can see her . . . bubbles.' With a roar of coarse laughter the sukkal dashed away back to the not too distant Karkurunna quay.

The water, that had seemed so friendly, was not Sud's element. She could not hide in it for ever. As she raised her head she found herself bathed in that pearl-like prelude to radiance that Enlil carried with him now wherever he moved. She ducked again, but the startled ripples betrayed her. She glided downstream. He was beside her on the bank. She fought her way back against the current. He kept pace easily. She swam to the farther bank, but the sides rose steep, unclimbable. Behind her, across the moat, Enlil's uncompleted walls of Nippur rose high to the shadowed sky. The city was full of his people, the gates kept by his men. Who would befriend the Princess Sud once Enlil had uttered his Word?

The boat was coming. Nusku had grabbed the first craft that came to hand. It was no more than a raft of reed bundles lashed together, its prow spiked upwards in imitation of the shagan canoe; its stern was unprotected. Nusku was poling this floating basket fast. Sud turned in terror, but the bow cut across to the shore where Enlil was running. He hardly waited for the nose to ground. He leaped across the intervening water with a bound that almost swamped the fragile craft. But for all his great size and strength, Enlil was light and agile. He swiftly crouched and settled his balance, urged Nusku to punt on.

'There! She can't stay underwater long. Do you see her? Foolish as a nanny-goat kid! Why is she running from me? What woman have I offered myself to before her? I must have her! I must have someone! Before I spill the light that is in me and make the powers of chaos laugh.'

'You shall have her, my lord. Trust me.'

The men bore down on Sud, struggling in the water. The raft almost covered her. Nusku leaped out, diving to catch and hold her. He heaved her to Enlil, who dragged her aboard. The raft rocked madly, almost submerged, as Enlil threw himself across her. Without another word he forced himself through and into her, tore away the husk of her virginity.

They let her go at last. She tumbled, racked with tears, back *into the water. And Enlil rose up alone on the rocking raft, flung his arms to the sleeping sky, cried out, 'I have done it! I have made the Light! Praise me!'*

*No answer yet from the city.*

*Still sobbing and choking, Sud floated in the water, drifting faster than the raft that was making its way towards the bank. Her pale, slender limbs were bruised, her shawl was lost, her vagina torn. Around her, shining, beaded bubbles of Enlil's semen pearled the surface of the Id Nunbirdu like infant moons. Threads of her own red blood sank, unnoticed. Suddenly she was out in the wide river, in sight of the Water Gate.*

*The weeping maiden, maid no longer, staggered out. The day had begun. The Anunnaki were busy on the quay and in the town. Sobbing harder now for humiliation as well as hurt, Sud ran past them up the steps, shutting her ears to their cries of concern. Kalkal at the gate looked her over with pity, shook his head, threw her his rain cloak from the hook on the wall.*

*'Too early for bathing, missy,' he said. 'Wait till there's more light next time, so that you can see what's coming.'*

*'It* was *the Light!' she screamed at him, shocking herself with the sudden gust of her own voice.*

*She had the whole city to traverse, in a stumbling run between staring crowds.*

*The door of the Kiur was already open. Her father was standing there, grim-faced. Nunbarshegunu hovered behind him, her golden countenance now drawn and grey.*

*'What is this? Where have you been? What has been done to you?'*

*A pale pink thread of blood, diluted by the canal water, crept down Sud's leg. She bent her streaming face to hide it from her father, looked down at her soiled self, let the gatekeeper's cloak slip from her shoulders, revealed her bruises.*

*Her cut and swollen lips staggered on the words as her legs swayed.*

*'Enlil has raped me.' Then, 'I am going to be the mother of his Light.'*

# Chapter Twenty

Inanna and Nin Shubur climbed the last steps to An's private chambers on the loftiest platform. Lifted so high above the flood plain they caught the light spring breeze. No sounds rose to them on it. Even the cattle were resting.

'What if An is asleep too?' Inanna whispered.

'The time for siesta will soon be over,' murmured Nin Shubur. 'But poor Dumuzi will only now be lying down to rest.'

There were attendants here in the columned antechamber, squatting on cushions against the wall, hands idle, eyelids drooping, or curled, their faces flushed with sleep, resting on sweating arms. The long wooden drums and the harps festooned with bells and finger cymbals stood silent. But the servants roused warningly, like sunning snakes, at Inanna's and Nin Shubur's approach.

'Lady Morning Star to see the Sky Father,' announced Nin Shubur. 'He asked for her to return towards the end of his siesta.'

The women exchanged glances. One of them half rose and uncertainly moved a hand towards the door curtain. Two naked little girls, younger than Inanna, reached sleepily for palm-leaf fans and stumbled upright.

'I've brought him a present from Dumuzi Ushumgalanna,' Inanna said importantly, showing the basket.

The doorkeeper shrugged, and lifted the curtain partly aside. 'Lady Inanna, my lord!'

The Eldest Daughter of the Moon prepared her brightest smile to disguise the thudding of her heart and stepped into the heavy-scented sanctum.

She checked. Her first sight of the tumble of bodies on the couch made her feel alarmed and a little sick. Nin Isinna seemed to be wrestling with An fiercely, mounting him, forcing herself on to him. Her golden, pointed face was panting like a bitch, her pink tongue licking him. Old An lay on his back, uttering little bleats of ecstasy and welcome. The sheets were crumpled, the bodies glistened with sweat.

Inanna's head swam. She had believed that what was done in great Sky Father An's house must be things of majesty and glory, fit for the first of all the Lords.

Nin Shubur had withdrawn.

'I am one of the Daughters of An too,' Inanna told herself. 'I have come here to learn their ways.'

She nerved herself to walk boldly to the head of the couch. An hardly seemed to recognise her presence. But Nin Isinna recoiled like a rabid dog from water.

'Get out!' she hissed. Inanna took no notice. She seated herself by An's head cushion, leant over him, held up the bunch of rare, ripe, end-of-season grapes like jewels over his mouth, a wrinkled pledge of the next harvest, still on the far side of summer. It was silly to be trembling.

The willing struggle between the Lord and the Lady seemed to be over. An lay back perspiring and breathing heavily. His hand moved to his collapsing member. Nin Isinna, glaring at Inanna, nevertheless moved her hands and tongue as if in a ritual she hardly needed to think about, stroking, smoothing, settling flesh and clothing, licking eyes and face with her health-giving kiss.

An opened his eyes, saw the vine fruit.

'Fresh grapes!' He was still panting. 'Are they for me?'

Inanna's whole, sweet body smiled for him. 'Yes. They're a present from Dumuzi. His sister Geshtinanna grew them in her vineyard on the other side of the flood. He paddled all the way here to bring them to you. You should have seen how dirty he was!'

The old, exhausted, satisfied face of An wavered before her eyes, became the boyish and eager golden-brown features of Dumuzi, the young Shepherd of the steppe. His firm, warm fingers were lifting the grapes from the basket, showing her his treasures proudly. She remembered how she had laughed and reached for them. He had pulled them back too slowly and his hand had brushed hers. Those dark brown eyes had flashed with a brilliant intensity. She had felt the thrill of power.

Then her eyes cleared and it was An's face beneath hers again, intent on her now. She plucked one grape from the bunch, held it over him tantalisingly. Smiling impishly, she took it between her teeth, saw that same flash in the old man's eyes. She bent over him, with the fruit still unbitten, let its sweetness brush his lips. He opened his teeth, yellowed, but still complete. His breath smelt like smoke and ashes. His sere lips reached towards hers, enclosed the fruit. Skin, juice and tongues became confusingly intertwined. She felt her heart beating against his shoulder.

'I shall call your *sukkal*,' Nin Isinna gasped.

'Why?' murmured Inanna, twining her arms round her great-grandfather. 'I'm only sharing with Father An the gift Dumuzi gave us. I think I shall send Nin Shubur to Geshtinanna with a thank-you present. What should I give her? My little mother-of-pearl shell, with some green eye-paint?'

Nin Isinna drew a sharp breath, hesitated, then sat down with a flounce on a stool and refused to move. Inanna did not mind. Better to have a witness to this first, small victory. It was a victory, wasn't it? Still, she was not sure what to do next. An's lids were closing. He looked very tired. She fed him the grapes one by one, ate a few herself. His arm reached up and pulled her down to snuggle against him on the damp couch. He was hot and sweating.

An's eyes opened again. His mouth smiled, the eyes did not. Her heart was beating much too fast. But he only lifted her small hands to caress his shoulders.

'Ah, yes,' he murmured. 'That's it. Massage the muscles, my dear. Nin Isinna, show her the way I like it done.'

The Healing Woman's claws scraped on the post of the bed as she hauled herself to her feet.

'Here.' A soft growl. 'Like this. Harder. Stronger!'

Nothing more was required of the child that first day.

# Chapter Twenty-one

*That little Lady Seed, running weeping through Enlil's city, aroused a tornado. Great Father An in Angal was woken by the sound of her whimper. Nin Mah, Exalted Lady, felt her motherly bosom stir with wrath.*

Enki, in the privacy of his guest room, grinned at Isimud. 'Lord Air has puffed himself up too much this time. It will be interesting to see if a grateful creation lets him get away with this one.'

Isimud toyed with the stem of his electrum wine goblet. 'It was perhaps imprudent of the Wind Lord to choose the daughter of Haia for this . . . escapade.'

Enki's eyes narrowed in thought, then widened suddenly. 'By Kur! One of the Lords of Judgment! Who stands beside Nanshe and Nidaba and brings injustices to harvest, puts the sickle in, plucks the thistles out of the corn, burns up the weeds.'

'Just so, my lord. Not a man to see his child violated and not exact redress.'

'Exact? Can they . . . can *we* do that? Call even Enlil to judgment?'

'They say in the E-Kur that Father An means to do precisely that. Nippur is the centre of the world. The Lord of this city, above all, must be pure. Word has been sent to Eridu to summon Nanshe the Just.'

'My lordly brother on trial? For rape?' Enki leaned forward, savouring the meaning in all its fullness. Then he threw himself back on the embroidered cushions and laughed uproariously.

'They say *I'm* randy. But my women are always willing. Oh, Isimud, I'm enjoying this! But Enlil will marry the girl, won't he?' Enki was serious now. 'Isimud. It is no joke, what Enlil has done. Perhaps the how, but not the why, was questionable. You've seen him. How could any of us help but see that he has . . . he had . . . One way or another, his seed is now in little Sud.

*She's a slim-hipped thing to bear what she must. But bear it she will, for all of us.'*

One corner of the E-Kur's vast concourse had been set aside as the meeting place for divine assemblies, the Ubshu-ukkinna. Not since it was made had such a grave conference met there. Wine and food was spread before the Anunnaki, but it was a solemn feast.

An presided. Nin Mah sat at his right hand, Enki on his left. The setting of those three chairs was in itself shocking. There should have been a fourth. Enlil, one of the four Great Guardians, was himself on trial. His father, flanked by his mother and his brother, must pronounce the sentence of the Anunnaki, if the court should find him guilty.

The judges were ranged on a lower step, below the greatest three. Nanshe at the centre, her calm face grave with the responsibility of this day's case. If it frightened her to be trying Enlil, she did not let it appear. Nidaba, with tablet and stylus ready, supported her. Sataran would assess the case with them. Again that menacing disruption of the normal order. Haia, whose place should have been with them, must lead the prosecution. His tawny eyes burned, twin fires of righteous indignation, for his daughter abused and justice violated.

Enlil towered, larger than them all, and the waiting, murmuring Anunnaki drew back from the wind of his restless movements. The Air Lord seemed a thing that should not be pent there, hardly a prisoner, yet summoned, compelled to attend, held here by the court's authority. How easy it would be for him to sweep them all aside, surge over that wall, bound away across the desert in a swirl of sandstorm, smoke up into the mountains and disappear. Yet a desire for order, law, common consent held greater and lesser Guardians together obedient to the forms of this court.

Nanshe's sukkal Hendursag read the charge. The evidence was brief. Sud, still weeping, told her story. She dared not lift her eyes to Enlil's face. Even his feet, on which she kept her gaze while she confronted him, seemed to hurt her eyes with the dazzle of light, though the child was not born yet.

Nunbarshegunu kept a prudent silence about her own part in the affair. She confirmed her daughter was with child. Gula, a Lady of Healing, led Sud away, back to the Kiur.

There remained the question: could it be proved that the

*maiden was unwilling? No one, not even Enlil, disputed the act had taken place. Least of all, Enlil. His whole body had seemed to leap when he heard the mother's confirmation that his seed had taken root. Out of Sud his child would be born. He threw an almost exultant look at his father An, at his mother Nin Mah. They gazed reproachfully back.*

*Nusku, Enlil's sukkal, was called as witness. His voice was hoarse, unwilling.*

'How did it happen?' Nanshe urged. 'Was it as the young woman said?'

'The girl was dancing!' he protested. 'Dancing on the towpath with not a stitch on her.'

'She is a child!' burst out Haia. Hendursag silenced him.

'Not so much of a child as all that,' Nusku retorted. 'Not too much a child to be got with one of her own. She knew what she was doing.'

'No, she did not!' growled Haia. 'She went to the Id-Nunbirdu with no thought in her head of meeting a man.'

*Nunbarshegunu lowered her eyes, hung her head.*

'So Enlil came upon her, followed her, persuaded her? She consented?' Nanshe prompted.

'Not exactly like that. Well, they never do, do they? He got a hold of her. But they lost their balance, and then she ran away a bit. You'd expect her to, wouldn't you? She meant him to follow her.'

'Ran where?'

'Into the reeds by the canal.'

'And then he followed her and she consented.'

'Well no, not just then. She dived into the canal. She'd got him excited by then with her teasing. His blood was up . . . And the other thing too.'

'He followed her into the water, and there she consented. Gave herself to him?'

'Not straightaway. I had to fetch him a raft to go after her.'

'And she consented to come aboard and lie with him?'

'There was a bit of . . . difficulty, first.'

'How then?'

'I . . . well, I had to jump out and hold her, help push her aboard.'

'And there, on the raft, at last she consented?'

*The sukkal's eyes went to his master, apologetically. But for all his rough, knowing masculinity, the first minister of Enlil had sworn by Nin Ki's snakes. He could say in open court nothing but the truth he had seen.*

*A low sigh, like the wind in a hollow reed. 'N-no-o. In the end he had to take her by force.'*

*Haia raised his hands, appealing to the sky, tore his hair. Nidaba wrote purposefully with lowered eyes. Nanshe's round, sad face gazed for a long while at Nusku's darkened countenance. The Guardians of Justice conferred briefly, while all the Anunnaki murmured their fears, squatting in a comfortless pallor that was not yet daylight. What would it mean if the Lord Enlil himself was threatened with retribution?*

*The task of the judges was the less difficult one. Nanshe rose, and all the court stood for her.*

*'Hear me, brothers and sisters of the Anunnaki. Your judges have taken counsel. We can speak no other than the truth. We find the plaintiff guilty.'*

*'Heam. Heam. So it is.' The affirmation from the other judges confirmed her verdict.*

*All eyes, including Enlil's, swung then to the higher platform where the presiding Great Three sat. Only they could pronounce sentence on one of their own number. An rose and all the Anunnaki bowed their heads to the ground.*

*'My children. . .' His calm, old face seemed already to have lived vast ages even then, before the name of the first human had been spoken. Now this his son, his firstborn, stood before him a criminal.*

*'Allow us time. A grave injustice has been done, a deed of violence masquerading as love. The voice of the weak appealed in vain; strength overcame it. This is not an easy matter to settle among ourselves. Yet we must show what kind of world we mean to make.'*

*'The Light!' shouted Enlil. 'You forget the Light! It was for that, and nothing else. I am bringing you Light!'*

*'Silence!' Thunder rocked the E-Kur. Thick darkness clouded them. Even Enlil trembled. Rarely was Father An moved these days to interfere in the doings of his busy children. It was a long time since the Bull of the Sky had bellowed. Enki lifted unruly eyebrows and smiled a little, savage grin.*

*'Go, Lord of Air. Leave the court. Walk outside the E-Kur for a while. Your mother and brother and I will confer about your sentence. This is no light thing.'*

'They made me do that too! I had to wait,' Inanna cried out.

★ ★ ★

*Sud lay on her mattress in the heart of the Kiur. Her home was only a few steps from the E-Kur, looking towards the northern wall of the city. Tumults of emotion swept through her. Her carefree childhood had catastrophically ended. She shook with the terror of being again in Enlil's presence. From that fateful morning, its full meaning understood only too late, she carried now a legacy. Yet, try though she would, she could not bring herself to hate or even to regret the thing that was growing in her. The knowledge of its presence filled her with such wonder she felt herself to be growing lighter rather than otherwise. Her pregnancy was not at all what Nunbarshegunu, fussing over her, concerned and guilty, had prepared her to expect. It felt like the first stage of an intoxication. A slowing yet enriching of her senses. A feeling of well being, of tolerance to all the world, fanned out around her, so that she caught herself sometimes smiling for no reason, between her bursts of tears. How could that storm of violence have given rise to this love?*

*'Sud!'*

*Like a hammer to a gong, her heart pounded in the dark stillness. No mistaking that powerful, roaring voice of the Young Lord, Enlil himself. She raised herself fearfully on one elbow, heard Gula talking in a lower voice in the outer courtyard.*

*'Let me speak to her! Let me tell her I love her. Sud!'*

*The majestic confidence was gone out of his still-strong tones. He was almost pleading.*

*'Sud? Will you come out and talk to me?'*

*She slipped from the bed, hesitated, called almost in a whisper, 'I am listening, my lord.'*

*'Sweet Sud. Let me be quick. There is not much time left to me. The Anunnaki have sat in judgment. They have found me guilty. How could they not? An and Nin Mah and Enki will pronounce my sentence. I am afraid of what it may be.'*

*How could the Fifty punish great Enlil?*

*'Listen, Sud. You are carrying my child. For that I ravished you. I am not going to stoop to ask you to forgive me. I need that child. The whole world, all Angal Above and Kigal Below need your child. Marry me, Sud. Be my queen in Nippur, if . . . if I am allowed to stay. If not . . . ' his voice howled in a sob, '. . . love my son. Cherish him.'*

*'My lord!' Her own quick protest brought her speeding to the door.*

*Shame forbade her. She could not bring herself to walk out into that courtyard, face the pulsing energy of the Lord of Air, feel his powerful breath once more on her face, show him the tiny light already held in her own frail body.*

*'One word, Sud. Just one word. Become my Nin Lil, Lady of Air. Be queen in Nippur for me.'*

*A faint and distant sadness. In some as yet unacknowledged part of her mind she knew the appeal was not to her, the young woman Sud. She had been a pretty face at a feast, white limbs dancing in the early stillness, a small, untravelled birth canal, a necessary instrument. She would be giving up her own being, becoming only the complement of his. Nin Lil, a wife for Enlil, the womb he needed for his son.*

*Yet, it was her child too.*

*'Yes, my lord,' she murmured behind the half-open door. 'Whatever the Great Ones decide, whatever your punishment may be, I will be your queen. Wherever you are, I will be with you.'*

*She stood, hearing herself answer, amazed by her own courage, awed at the destiny she was taking on herself.*

*A lengthy pause. As though Lord Air for once was still, unsure of his direction. She still did not come out to meet him.*

*'You must affirm it, Nin Lil. Take me over your threshold. Marry me. I am afraid I have brought you no wedding gifts.'*

*'I carry your gift already, my lord.'*

*An intake of breath.*

*She reached a small, pale hand round the door. He grasped it eagerly and she drew him inside. He took the leap across that ritual barrier that joined him now to her for always. In the shadowed interior Enlil towered over her, not speaking. She tried to smile.*

*Gula's voice called urgently. 'Lord Enlil. There is a message from the court. Nusku bids you know the Council is ready to declare your sentence. You must appear before it.'*

*'Stay true to me, Nin Lil!'*

*Dust spattered against the reed mats shadowing the windows. A gust swept under the door and whirled away. Enlil had gone, without even a kiss. Nin Lil's racing heart urged her to run after him, listen to the sentence.*

*No, she told herself. I am a queen now. All Nippur is mine. I will not run to gape at my lord in the public lawcourt, like some housemaid.*

*She straightened her dress, arranged it carefully to cover both breasts like a married lady, put a beaded headband around her demurely chignoned hair, walked across the courtyard to the reception hall of the Kiur, sat on a boxwood couch. Waited.*

'I know what *I* would have told him! And he judged *me!*'

*Enlil heard his father An pronounce the sentence.*
   'Heam!' *his mother Nin Mah affirmed.* 'Heam,' *Enki avouched.*
   'Heam. So be it,' *murmured around the Ubshu-ukkinna from all the Anunnaki, as if they wondered and feared at their own daring. All eyes were fastened on the Air Lord to see how he would take it.*
   *The young Lord Enlil towered above his brothers and sisters. He raised his eyes past Nanshe, Nidaba, Sataran and Haia on the lower step. Past An and Nin Mah and Enki on the highest platform. Lifted his hands to heaven. A great appeal of despair rang to the dark sky.*
   *'No!* No! *Don't send me to the Netherworld! Let not the Father of the Light be captured by the darkness!' Enlil wept. He scratched his ears, his heart, his liver, his crotch. He tore at his hair.*
   *The Anunnaki trembled and drew nearer to one another for comfort. Haia remained stern-faced, though Nunbarshegunu wrung her hands. An seemed unnaturally calm, showed no emotion for his firstborn son, his unborn grandchild. Mother Nin Mah let generous tears roll down her face, but spoke no word to change the President's decision.*
   *Hail spattered them on a gust of wind. Enki smiled, in a little secret grin, but the lightning crackling across the heavens sparkled on it, made his eyes flash with triumph.*
   *Enlil rounded on him.* 'This is your revenge! Always the crafty, devious Water Man! You're jealous because I have more than you. You couldn't take the Earth from me, and so you have plotted to spoil it. You'd rob the world of the Lord of Air and Space, shut me up in the Netherworld. You would deprive the Above of the light that's coming.' *He burst out sobbing.* 'Don't let my son be born in the Netherworld! Please!'
   'The light, I thought, was in the maiden Sud,' *Enki observed.* 'There is no sentence on her. You have already given her a punishment she never deserved. She doesn't go to the Netherworld. She stays with us.'
   'But I have married the girl! She's taken me over her threshold. She is already Nin Lil. Let us both stay Above!'
   *A beam of triumph on Nunbarshegunu's face. The Anunnaki*

*stirred indecisively. But An's voice was deep and firm.*

'We have discussed the possibility of marriage. Of course we have, if only to cover the maiden's shame. But your impiety struck at roots far deeper than that. You were no greenhorn among the Sons of An to patch things up so easily. You made yourself Guardian of the Earth. You yourself forbade violence in the land of Sumer. You kept the wolves and bears, the scorpions and vipers out in the wilderness. You stopped the Anunnaki quarrelling. But now you are the one who has brought violence in. You broke the sacred trust we gave you. Both Earth and Sky reject you now.'

*A flash of lightning more brilliant than all the rest, and then the roar of thunder.*

'You will all live to enjoy the glorious light, and I who made it shall not,' wept Enlil.

*Nin Mah bent towards her son, as though her body yearned to comfort him.* 'Can the Netherworld hold you in, my son? The Lady of Earth and the Lord of Sky could not.'

'I might return?' *His eyes twisted this way and that between Nin Mah and Enki.* 'But you have banished me . . .'

'To the mercy of her to whom you gave the Netherworld,' *An pronounced grimly.*

'Ereshkigal!'

'Just so. My sister,' *Enki said,* 'whom you never tried to save, though you watched Kur seize her. Well, she has power now. She rules in Kur as you ruled here, till now.'

'Now I see it all. You always were jealous. You will take the Earth in my place while she has the Greater Earth Below. Enki and Ereshkigal. You *planned* this!' *he hurled at An.*

'Silence!' *The Bull of the Sky was rousing.* 'Go! Go as bravely as your brother went.'

'But he came back!'

'Then see if you too can win your return.'

'I have no ship,' *said Enlil at last, in a frightened gust of a voice.* 'I don't know the way to the Netherworld.'

'Follow me.' *The Lord of Wisdom rose, flowed down the steps to his half-brother.* 'I sailed to the limits of the world and beyond, to find Kur. I have become wiser since. It wasn't necessary. My people in Eridu built the Abzu for me. There is a well of roaring water there, opening into the Below. So too, there is a doorway into darkness in every city and in every soul.'

'I do not know it.' *The words came small and sullen.* 'Nippur is the city of the Lord of Earth and Air. I am Enlil. How can my *hill be a portal to the Below of Ereshkigal?'*

*'I will show you, brother. The way to the Netherworld was opened here when you raped Nin Lil. You are the doorkeeper of the Below.'*

Blood purpled Enlil's face, for anger or shame no one could say.

*'I think you've always known it. I've seen the foundations of your E-Kur, where the walls are not yet built.'*

A resentful stare.

*'Yes, brother. An's house towers towards the Sky. Mine plumbs the deep waters. But yours digs under Earth. Why have you built a secret temple underneath, a mirror of this house above? You have filled up its rooms with rubble, but it is under our feet now. It is not for nothing that you call this house E-Kur. You claim more than the Earth and Air, don't you, Lord Kurgal? Let us see if Ereshkigal will recognise your Lordship.'*

Enki had taken him by the elbow, was guiding him away from the assembly place of Ubshu-ukkinna, across the outer courtyard, leaving behind the sound of the Daughters of An weeping.

# Chapter Twenty-two

*Nin Lil lifted her head. The Healer Gula was standing before her. The woman's usually cheerful and glowing face was salt-streaked with tears. Nin Lil felt a leap of fear, as though the baby had jumped inside her.*

*'Is it. . . ? What have they done with my Lord? Tell me!'*

*Gula's capable hands twisted, for once helpless. 'Child, they have banished him from the Earth and Angal Above. There is only the Netherworld.'*

*Blood seemed to leave Nin Lil's cheeks. She felt it draining from her heart, her brain. The hall, already dim, seemed to darken intolerably. She clutched the arms of the boxwood couch and felt Gula bending over her, her mother Nunbarshegunu crowding behind her. They brought her water, steadied her. The faintness passed. With returning consciousness a new decision possessed Nin Lil.*

*'I must go after him.'*

*'Daughter! You will go nowhere. You are pregnant! How could you travel to the Netherworld?'*

*'He raped you,' said Gula. 'Would you still follow him?'*

*'I bear his child.' Nin Lil rose, a little unsteadily, holding on to the bowed couch arms. 'I hold his light within me. My place is by his side. He has made me his queen.'*

*Nunbarshegunu caught her breath a little too quickly. Then her eagerness subsided. 'Where are the witnesses to your marriage?' But Gula hesitated, shrugged her shoulders. 'Queen? How could you be queen of Nippur without Enlil? And there is a queen already in the Netherworld!'*

*'I trust my Lord,' said Nin Lil with a youthful dignity.*

*'Trust Enlil?' Gula burst out indignantly. 'After what he did to you?'*

*Nin Lil ignored her, looked steadily at her mother. 'What is past, is over. We must make the future now. Where is he?'*

*'Gone,' said Gula with brisk satisfaction, as though she had*

*already forgotten her tears of loss. 'You are too late. Enki has shown Enlil the gate to the Netherworld.'*

*'And where is that?'*

*All the women looked at each other, shook their heads. The hall was dark, save for a few small lamps, like eyes of fire. But as Nin Lil, the newly married Lady Air, walked forward, there seemed to spread around her a subtle radiance as though the light imprisoned in Enlil's body were now caught and held in her scarcely rounded belly. The other Daughters of An·fell silent; a faint surprise and awe made them draw back a little to give her passage. Her feet stirred the cedar shavings sprinkled on the floor, released gusts of perfume where she passed. A little breeze fanned the loose-netted wool of the cloth that barely hid her slim legs. The gold-leaf pendants on her tiara rustled musically as she moved her head. She hesitated before the door, lifted the coronet from her head, gave it to a servant girl. She slipped the jewelled sandals from her small, white feet. She loosened the dress length from her shoulder, let it slip to the ground. Naked, she walked across the twilit courtyard of the Kiur and the sense of light moved with her, growing ever smaller. The Ladies of Nippur watched in astonishment and doubt. Her slow, somnambulant certainty silenced them.*

*At the gatehouse of the Kiur she paused again. On a nail inside was hanging the rain cloak that Enlil's man of the Water Gate had thrown around her when she came running from the Nunbirdu Canal. She gestured to it, and the porter solemnly lifted it down and handed it to her. Nin Lil shuddered as it touched her shoulders again, felt as on that day the protest of her torn vagina, felt her abdomen contract, set her teeth, willed her body into submission, walked on.*

*It was not hard to tell the way to go. The streets of Nippur were lined with silent, shocked Anunnaki and the commoner Guardians, all staring in one direction. Nin Lil, less bold in the open, twilit city, drew the cloak about her, did not walk like a queen down the central thoroughfare, slipped behind the throng. No one recognised her, no one stopped her. She hid the light inside her like a costly jewel.*

*Away from the E-Kur, the streets twisted between houses, some one-storey, sometimes two. Small squares opened suddenly in which the dusk seemed to hang breathless. The alleys beyond were dark. She crossed the Id-Shauru, carved through the heart of the city. She passed under the shadowing foliage of the Anniginna Garden and found herself in a street sloping down to the Water*

Gate. Here a larger crowd had gathered, murmuring.

'Let me through,' she said, in her small, soft voice.

Heads turned. Nusku, Enlil's sukkal, spoke roughly. 'Hold your tongue, girl! If Lord Enlil won't even let me, his chief minister, through, do you suppose he wants some chit of a thing like you bothering him in his last moments?'

'I am Nin Lil,' she said with dignity. 'Your master's queen.'

There was a gasp at that. The dusk that had masked her features hid Nusku's consternation. The news ran like the crackling of fire in thatch round the group.

Nusku bowed hastily. 'Lady Air! But . . . you shouldn't be here, my lady. My lord said . . . You didn't stay for the end of the trial . . . You should keep to your house. The child . . . '

'Let me through,' she said doggedly. 'I would follow my Lord.'

'You cannot! Not even I can go any further than this. Lord Enki took him through the gate . . . ' The sukkal's voice choked.

Now it was Nin Lil who must overcome his resistance, force his consent. She felt a strength she had not believed she possessed.

'The Lord of Nippur has been sentenced to the Netherworld. He has made me your Lady. Let me pass.'

The sukkal touched his brow, his lips, his breast. 'My lady, I dare not.'

She moved her cloak apart. The light between her hips seemed as though it struggled for visibility through banks of cloud. There was a mutter of awe, a flinching back. Like dogs that crouch with flattened ears at their mistress's command, the crowd of Guardians seemed to subside into submission. Nusku faltered.

'I . . . I will call . . . if there is still anyone to hear.'

The people moaned.

Nusku moved down the empty, echoing street.

'My lord?' Silence. The heavy-leaved sarbatu trees behind her made no sound. 'Lord Enlil?' Only the breathing of the waiting crowd could be heard. The air in Nippur did not stir. 'Lord Enki!'

'Who wants me?' Swift footsteps swished over the gravel in the tunnel between the inner and outer gates. Enki's crafty, laughter-lined face peered round at them.

'Go home to your beds,' he grinned. 'There is nothing to see. There will be nothing more to be seen here for a long time.'

'Is he . . . ? Has he really gone?' The desolation in Nusku's voice was for his personal loss, the sukkal who had not been allowed to walk in front of his master on his last journey. For the public loss, of the Lord of Nippur from his city. For the cosmic *catastrophe too huge to be grasped yet, the loss of their Guardian of Earth.*

*'Lord Enki, let me go after my Lord,' said the small, slight girl in front of him.*

*Enki threw a quick, startled glance over her, saw at once by the light she bore who she must be. Astonishment threw his features apart, then he roared with laughter. 'Women!' he cried, slapping his thigh. 'You always amaze me!' He swung round to face the thick darkness hidden within the gateway.*

*'Enlil!' he shouted. 'Can you still hear me? Your . . . wife . . . wants to follow you!'*

*With an almost drunken gesture of exaggeration he flung one bronze-bound leaf of the inner gate wide open. 'Go on, my lady. See if you can catch him. If you and your child can find your way to the Netherworld, who knows what might happen. You may do more good there than I did.' His savage bitterness burst out as Nin Lil slipped through the door and he slammed it shut behind her so that its crash shook the echoes from the half-built walls of Nippur.*

*It was thick darkness behind when she had gone.*

# Chapter Twenty-three

Inanna walked down the steps away from An's bedroom, unusually subdued.

Who had won? Who had lost? What did that mean?

Her bare flesh struck colder now.

Nin Shubur watched her anxiously. 'Are you all right, child?'

'Yes,' Inanna said with difficulty. 'Yes. I think so.'

*Nin Lil went on through the brick-built tunnel between the gates. The faint, unborn light tricked her eyes on the mosaic surface. Suddenly she collided with solid wood. Her hand, flung out to one side, groped at a heavy latticework. A massive copper grille, a gleam of metal, like a sullen fire. Two eyes, more light than colour, watched her through the grille of the gatehouse.*

*'Go back, my lady. The door of the Netherworld is closed to you.'*

*The cloak on her shoulders hung cold as death. Was this Kalkal, the same gatekeeper who had wrapped it round her?*

*'Tell me only one thing, please. Did my Lord Enlil come this way?'*

*The light flashed more brightly in the gatekeeper's eyes. 'This way is barred to you. Lord Enlil has commanded me to stay silent.'*

*Light shone in Nin Lil's own eyes now. 'So I am close behind him. You must have spoken with him just now.'*

*A strange expression passed across the gatekeeper's face, like a flutter of wind. 'I have spoken to him, aye. I have held Enlil in my arms, comforted his grief. I have taken him into my body, into my anus, into my mouth.' He smiled a little, shocking smile.*

*Nin Lil felt a cold tightening of her womb. She steadied herself.*

*'If Enlil is your Lord, then I am your Lady. Open the gate for me.'*

*'I dried the tears on my Lord's face. If you are Nin Lil, the*

Lady you say you are, let me feel your cheek, let me touch your private parts and swear my loyalty on them to Enlil.'

Nin Lil willed herself to stand very still. A pale, cold hand came through the bars. She could not help but shiver as it met her cheek.

'The seed of your Lord, the all-bright seed of Enlil, is in my womb already,' she whispered.

The hand of the gatekeeper cupped her neck, drew her towards the colder metal of his grille.

'Let not my Lord's seed go to the Great Below!' he said urgently. 'Let my seed take its place.'

'Man of the Gate, open the copper bolt, undo the silver lock for me,' she said faintly.

The door from Nippur to the Netherworld would not open for her yet. Arms strong as a gale, light as air, drew her into the darkness of the lodge beside it, into the gatekeeper's bedchamber. Nin Lil closed her eyes. She fixed her heart on the shining child curled small within her. For him, she let her lips be kissed, she let her breasts be fondled.

'My little Lord!' she whispered. 'My son!' as she let the man of the gate penetrate her.

She did not see the light blaze in the gatekeeper's eyes.

When it was done, she stood up, arranged the heavy cloak about her shoulders.

'Thank you,' she said, a little breathlessly. 'Who knows? With this child I have got from you, I may ransom my husband. Your baby shall be Meslamtaea, the Tree That Fruits in the Underworld. Which way did my Lord go from here?'

'Turn back, Nin Lil. Do not carry the bright seed of Enlil into the Great Below.'

'I have paid you what you asked. Now open the gate for me.'

Hands turned the copper key, slid back the silver bolt. The outer door swung silently on profound darkness. Like the Lady she was, she walked through it, on her way to the Netherworld. Her womb, which had seemed so light and joyful carrying her child, weighed heavier already. The gate closed behind her.

# Chapter Twenty-four

*Nin Lil found herself shut out of her own city, disorientated. No sense of space, of the familiar ramp leading down to the busy expanse of the Buranun River. She seemed to be standing instead in a park enclosed within high walls. Ningishzida must have been at work here. How else could these trees have grown up so quickly? She thought of their serpent roots burrowing into the underground, and shuddered.*

*A stream ran singing in the darkness. Because there was no other sign to direct her, she followed it. Along its bank, night-scented flowers breathed as she brushed past them. That glimmer of light within her showed her enough for the next few footsteps, no more. Soft grass under her bare feet. Damp earth. Trees reaching low to catch against her hair. She put her hand up to push away a branch. She wore a tiara of dead leaves now, to replace the gilded jewellery.*

*A greater space here. A sound of water falling. A small, stone, circling wall. She walked across a paving to it, on cold tiles. Her hands gripped rougher stone, not clay from the surface skin of Mother Ki. An older, deeper rock had been hewn for this. With a growing sense of giddiness Nin Lil leaned over the well.*

*Nothing to see. She did not believe she had expected it. What light was growing within her had longer far to go before it could be released. It was not strong enough yet. She must cherish it. Almost reluctantly she felt for a small, sharp pebble, dropped it over the edge. Her hand had shaken. She heard the flake strike the stonework with a tiny clatter, then it must have plummeted. On and on into a deep, dark silence. No splash of meeting water. No hollow echo rose from the well's bottom. The Below had taken it for ever.*

*She whimpered then as, long ago it seemed, she, a virgin, had whimpered in her* itima *chamber of the Kiur, before she had gone to bathe in the Nunbirdu Canal. Yet she had passed through that agony and terror and revulsion into the woman she was now, bearing the Light. She was strong. She could feel fear and not turn back.*

*She felt around the wall and found, as she had expected, an opening, steps. The water ran beside her, companionably. It trickled down the cold and mossy walls. She heard its tiny falls nearby, from one stone to the next. But from where it met the nether waters there came no roar or foaming splash, no ring of cascade. It seemed to slither away into profound silence, as though a monster had opened its throat to swallow all sound and life.*

*The steps became hardly more than a ladder. She felt for footholds in the dark beneath. Her rigid fingers hooked on wet ledges, lowered her weight. She blessed the gleam, however faint, that showed the uneven surface as her body passed over it, going ever downwards.*

*'Enki,' she prayed. 'Be with me in the fall of your waters. Give me wisdom. You have known the Abyss.'*

*So long she lowered herself it began to seem like moving slowly in a dream. So when the standing water snatched her ankle she screamed in terror. The tunnel of stone above her echoed with wild laughter. No one was standing in the night garden to hear it. The echoes exhausted themselves at last. The music of dropping water over steps was far above. Here the chill stream slipped soundlessly over slimy rock, losing itself in the underground river with no more than 'Hush!'*

*She felt her difficult way along its channel.*

*There was a roaring in her ears now. The trickles of water that had slipped beside her feet like accompanying snakes were hurrying on to dive into a dashing river. She sensed its shock against the rocks in front of her, felt its spray on her face. All the light there was, she carried in her. It hardly reached the immensity of foam boiling higher than her head, plunging far beneath her feet. She was on the edge of a cataract hungry to gulp her down to destruction in a moment. Little, plains-bred Nin Lil could only halt before it, deafened by the thunder of the falls. She was on the brink of despair. But a force drove her on like a steady wind that must beat all obstacles down to circle the world. For her child, she paused only to look for a way across. She found none.*

*'Go back, woman. You may not cross the Devouring River.'*
*Two points of light, brighter than specks of foam, sparkled out of the darkness at first.*

*Nin Lil started and gasped, recovered herself. 'Tell me first, has my Lord Enlil come this way?'*

*'My Lord has commanded me to be silent.'*

*'You have answered me. How did he cross the river?'*

*'He wept for grief in my arms. He put his water in my anus, in my mouth. I carried him over the stepping stones of the Netherworld.'*

*'What you have done for him, you must do for me. I am Nin Lil, the Queen.'*

*'If you are the Queen, let me touch your pretty face, let me swear my loyalty to you on your vagina.'*

His hand was wet, as the wind of winter that brings the rain. She felt her womb quiver at his touch.

*'I am with child,'* she murmured. *'The Bright Child, the seed of Enlil your Lord, is in my womb.'*

*'Let not the seed of my Lord be caught by the Great Below. Let my seed go to Ereshkigal in its place. Lie with me as well, my lady.'*

There was no gatehouse, there was no bed. There on the hard, wet rock, with the cataract roaring in her ears and the spray dashing on her face, Nin Lil lay down beneath the man of the river.

His moist breath descended on her mouth. Pinpoints of light pierced her closed eyelids. *'My bright baby!'* she said in her heart. *'I have to get back to the Above! For your sake.'* His cold, fierce member entered her.

The felted cloak was as wet inside as out. She drew it round her with an invisible dignity.

*'I shall call this child Ninazu – Lord Water-Knower, the Physician. Perhaps he will know how to heal as well as to wound.'*

The man of the river drew a sharp breath, seemed to tower over her for an instant.

*'I can pay two ransoms now, for Enlil and myself. Show me the way to go on.'*

*'The river of the Netherworld is very treacherous. Do not attempt to cross it, little Lady.'*

*'I have paid your fee. Carry me.'*

*'Then do not let go of me.'*

He guided her up a treacherous face of rock. Nin Lil panted as she climbed. Appalling fear tightened every muscle in her slight body as her feet slipped on the hanging slime over slick stone. The powerful, wet hand of the man of the river pulled her after him, hauled her unceremoniously on to a ledge at the head of the falls.

'That is your way, my Lady. The road to Ereshkigal.'

Huge boulders glistened faintly, humped as hooded crones, between which the river hurled itself to its last shattering plunge.

'I must cross them?' she asked, in a small, terrified voice.

'This is the way the Anunnaki sent your Lord.'

'Then I must follow him.'

The man of the river picked her up roughly. He leaped through the torrent of spray on to the first, drenched boulder. She nerved herself for the next risk. Clung, with her arms around him, eyes tightly closed. She could not shut out the howl of the waters. A third bound into a streaming maelstrom, with the cataract thundering over her. She held her breath, too shocked to scream. At last the deluge slackened, and he threw her down on a rock. He seemed to part from her on a chill gust, before she dared move.

She lifted her head. She did not yet seem to be on the further side. She crawled to the edge of the rock, peered despairingly out into the gloom ahead, sobbed. All she could hear was the bellow of falls and whirlpools in the chasm beneath her. No sound came from the fearful rocks behind to guide or encourage her. She was utterly alone, still trapped above the torrent.

No, not alone! Was that a sheen of solid stone across the abyss? The tiny, hopeful light filtered through frail flesh to shed a little help around her feet, a patch of pale illumination just in front. It shielded the worst terrors from her eyes. She hardly knew now if she was carrying this light or following it. Together, one being, this bonded mother-and-child leaped out in faith, made their last perilous bid to cross the Devouring Cataract. A cascade of water snatched her breath away, knocked her sideways. She shrieked and clutched at spray-filled air, met the shock of slippery stone. She lay sobbing on the further bank of the Netherworld.

All too soon she found her breath again, stumbled to her feet. Moved deeper into the unknown.

Now caverns were opening, across which she could not see. The walls receded out of sight. Dark emptiness surrounded her. She wandered uncertainly on, till the roar of the cataract in her ears dropped to a far-off rumble. She stood still, listened. Only the drip of water from the roof on to the stone floor. Only a clouded pool of light around her feet. Her womb weighed doubly heavy now. Her body was shaken. Her lips were bruised. The half-healed scars of her vagina had been broken open.

But the floor was shelving down, as if in a great amphitheatre.

'I wished to enter the Netherworld,' she murmured to herself. 'I must go lower yet.'

*It was slow, demanding work. There were no walls to hold, no light ahead. She watched the tiny limit of illumination, enough to show her the next step. At last the facets of wet rock slid under a noiseless expanse of unbroken water. Nin Lil stopped, just before the brink. The tiniest wave might have washed up over the rock and touched her feet. There was no wave. No current seemed to move. No bubble of foam beaded the shore. Impossible to tell how far the lake would reach, how deep. Its darkness seemed to swallow the light and not reflect it back.*

*'Hallo?' she called. And her voice faded away into an emptiness without echoes.*

*Yet something answered her. There was no sound. Only the faintest stirring of the smooth, black water. A curl of ripple formed, crept slowly towards her. Nin Lil moved her feet back from the brim of the lake. The water slid, ever so slightly, up the slope she stood on. Another ripple followed, slowly, purposefully. She watched each oncoming circle of motion, waited for its cause. At last the almost silent dip of blade in water, the trickle of droplets from the lifted pole. A boat, as black as the water it rode on, dulled the surface with a thicker shadow. She sensed a hooded figure, saw two shining eyes. The air stirred around her face with a memory of the Great Above.*

*'Who calls the ferryman of the Great Below?'*

*'Has my Lord Enlil taken passage with you recently?'*

*'I answer no questions. I am commanded to silence.'*

*'Only tell me this. Was my Lord heartbroken to death? Could the firstborn Son of An die?'*

*'What comfort should Kur's ferryman give to the condemned?'*

*'You could have taken him in your arms, let him water your anus, your mouth, brought the seed of life to Kur.'*

*A silence followed. The black boat glided almost imperceptibly nearer to her.*

*'And if I did, what is that to you, woman?'*

*'I am his Lady, Nin Lil. I carry his child.'*

*'If you are the Lady of that Lord, let me touch your face, let me reach my hand between your thighs and swear to serve your child.'*

*In terror now, despite her resolution, she let herself take one step lower. The water swayed just past her feet. A hand reached out that seemed more light than she expected, paused, while the bows swung untethered.*

*His eyes pierced through the darkness. 'Once, you lay on a raft under the sky. Will you enter my boat, in the vault Below?'*

'I am with child!' Her words came fast and frightened. 'I carry the All-Bright Baby, the seed of Lord Air.'

'Oh, Nin Lil! Let not the seed of Enlil go to the halls of Ereshkigal! Let my seed water you in his place. Let what comes of it remain down here.'

'Why should you care?' she faltered. 'Aren't you Ereshkigal's boatman?'

The ferryman stared at her out of the shadowing hood. His shrouded form loomed tall as the greatest Anunnaki. Eyes, too light for colour, burned with a yearning that could illuminate heavens.

Nin Lil felt all the sinews of her being turn to water, gasped, cried out. Her hand moved swiftly to her vagina as if to stop a sudden fall she felt. The boat was rocking wildly. The hands were dragging her aboard. She gasped again. There on the floor of the ferryboat of the Netherworld she made herself open like a flower, breathe out her perfume in the heavy night. 'Child of Light!' she cried in joy and in pain. 'This time it is for you!'

The darkness smothered her. The arms of strength imprisoned her. Her small flesh tore. He penetrated her, watered her, left his seed in her.

She lay exhausted, shaken by sobs. 'His name shall be Ennugi,' she cried defiantly, 'Lord of the Sexual Act. Let this at last ransom my brightest son.'

'Ennugi?' said the ferryman cynically. 'And is he life or death?'

'For my Lord,' she answered, gathering her cloak up fiercely, 'he has proved both.'

The boatman cursed, seized his pole.

The ferry had careered a wild passage across the water under their coupling. Another shore appeared beneath an overhanging roof. The ramp of rock was banked with lights of unnatural fire, blue-edged flames around fierce eyes of red. Shadows of limbs and weapons netted the surface of the stone like spiders' webs.

'Go!' said the ferryman, helping her to disembark and thrusting her up the shore. 'Try to ransom Enlil, and Enlil's son, and yourself too, if you think you are so powerful! Go and offer this rich womb of yours to Ereshkigal.'

# Chapter Twenty-five

Nin Isinna had her revenge at suppertime. Inanna was not seated with the full-grown Daughters of An at the long side of the table. Instead, a small table was set for her at the side of the dining room, with other girls who were learning to be hierodules.

'Is this what I am going to become?' she wondered. 'Just another of An's harem, to amuse him in his old age?' She crumbled her bread listlessly, finding it hard to swallow.

Laughter and conversation flowed among the adults, the adolescents, the servants beyond the door. Loss gnawed at Inanna's heart. It had not been like this at the E-Kishnugal in Ur. There, she had been petted, adored by her laughing mother Nin Gal, her gravely admiring father Nanna. She had joined in fights and quarrels with her brothers Utu and Ishkur. The palace had been filled with her high, clear, childish voice, always commanding attention, always receiving it richly.

Now she felt small, smothered, insignificant.

She looked up and found An's gaze fixed on her. Her heart leaped at the intensity of his stare. But he did not acknowledge her. He did not smile. She tried to smile for him, but her lips only trembled. She lowered her eyes first. Was this part of her punishment? Was she being humiliated?

When the meal was over, An rose first. They all stood respectfully for him. He passed behind her. She felt him stop and lay his hand on her neck. When she dared to look up, the blue eyes were warm.

'Come again tomorrow, mid-morning.'

'Yes, Great-grandfather,' meekly. And her heart was racing between alarm and rising hope.

*The galla seized the young woman. Their hooked hands pinched.*

*Their stinking exhalations filled the pure channels of her nostrils so that she gagged and gasped.*

*'Let me alone! I have come willingly, following my Lord.'*

*'Take her to join him.'*

*'Drag her to the dungeon.'*

*'Report it to the Queen.'*

*'A woman of the Above, come willingly to Ereshkigal!'*

*The demons hustled her, faster than she wanted, over uneven surfaces, through tunnels that seemed lightless till they approached, and then leaped to life in the angry blue flames of the torches. In their brief rush of passage, things swung, like the outer skins of creatures not quite sucked dry of life. Moans came from blank walls of rock. The roof dripped dankly, but a disturbing heat brought out a sweat on her face and between her breasts. Her womb weighed triply heavy now. Looking down, Nin Lil caught a tiny sob. In the lurid glare the pure light she carried was almost lost.*

*'Children,' she whispered. 'Where have I brought you?'*

*Sooner than she might have wished another stern gate towered over her beyond which she could not see. Again, with a rapidity she was not ready for, it opened before her. Neti the gatekeeper drew back one leaf and the torchlight jumped on a bird with vast eagle wings, hammered in copper across the ebony lintel.*

*For all her racing heart and the protest of her limbs at the galla's clutch, Nin Lil looked hard at the porter's face. Was there worse to come yet, from this one? It was difficult to look at him steadily. His countenance was rat-like, but startling as a lion's face she had once seen parting the bushes at the edge of a canal out in the wilderness, hugely shaggy and terrifying. Enlil had forbidden such things to approach the cities now. He had kept the land of Sumer safe. Would he have no power here?*

*Neti's feet were yellowed and taloned like a hawk's, claws greedily shifting and gripping. The body between was all too man-like, naked, male. She tried to find his eyes and they stared out at her through his mane with a derisive smile. The hair of his face was stiff, like a dead beast's. The eyes were cold even in their laughter. Enlil's eyes were grey, as rain on the wind, but in him a buried light had struggled to break through his translucent bonds of flesh. Light like that had blazed for her in the eyes of the first gatekeeper as she went out from Nippur, in the man of the river beside the roaring cataract, in Ereshkigal's dark ferryman. As though, in the moment they lay with her, they had not been Kur's servants at all. With a hope not yet fully understood, she stared* long and keenly at this final doorkeeper. His face was the monstrous face of the Underworld. It showed no pity, no warmth. These eyes were lightless.

'Who shall I say comes to the Queen of Kur? Are you another criminal banished by your Council? Perhaps you have come to offer your services to her, like the demons, or the Anunna of death and disease, of roots and snakes, who have found that their proper home is with her? Or can the Children of An die now, like the beasts?'

She forced her trembling lips to answer like a queen. 'I am one of the Anunnaki of the Above, and more than that now. I am Nin Lil, Lady Air, Queen to Enlil who rules from Nippur at the centre of the world.'

A burst of raucous laughter screamed from all the galla. 'Lord of the World Above!'

'Yes. I know you have him here. Him alone I have followed.'

'The caverns of Kur are vast under your Earth. We are building our Queen a palace. But the demons are too few yet. The Anunna who have come from the Above are not many. Once Ereshkigal has a subject, she does not willingly let him go. Or her.'

Nin Lil felt one of her children leap within her. Her hands flew protectively to her belly, found it already swollen. She looked down. The gatekeeper followed her eyes. All the galla seemed to be staring at her abdomen.

'A birth?' said Neti, with a kind of wonder. 'New life, here? In the realm at the end of the road to the west that welcomes dead things?'

'Four births,' said Nin Lil proudly. 'I know your price. Enki escaped, but had to leave his sister Ereshkigal behind. I am no warrior. I couldn't fight against Kur with weapons and a magur ship. I bring my woman's gift . . .' Her words stumbled on a sob. 'A life for a life. For Enlil, for my son, and for myself, I will pay what Ereshkigal demands.'

'And leave more children in Kur? Oh, very loving, Mother!'

'Even in Kur, can there not be justice, a kind of love, a little healing?'

A ripple of discontent, of unease, growled among the galla.

'We are the demons who spurn your sacrifices.'

'We will not drink your libations.'

'We do not accept gifts.'

'We will never make love.'

'We are the chills that squander the plenty of life.'

111

'We are a bitter venom spat out by the Anunnaki.'

Steps were coming rapidly towards the half-open gate.

'Who made you an entertainer of Ereshkigal's guests, Neti? Report the newcomer's business and wait for Ereshkigal's orders.'

'This is Nin Lil, Sukkal Namtar. Enlil's . . . Queen.' Neti made a cynical bow.

'A pair of them? And such a brief spell for her to enjoy being a great Lady. The Lord of Air cannot be Guardian here.' And indeed the stifling stench of Kur drove out all memory of fresh breezes in the sky above; the close confining walls and roof imprisoned air. 'But Nin Lil is welcome, and what she carries.' Namtar's long, dark face gave no hint of emotion behind it. His eyes took in the truth. She could not tell whether he mocked her.

He ushered her in. The empty courtyard of Enki's time was peopled now. Creatures with bull- and eagle- and man- and crocodile-heads, who stared, intimidating. Ragaba and shatam officials lined up upon the steps, as though to taunt her with the formality of her welcome. The skull-topped mound was covered over now. A palace rose, dark walls losing themselves in even darker shadows. Lapis lazuli so nearly black it hardly held a hint of blue. The house was windowless, severe. Not even the red glow of torches beat from it.

'Welcome to the Ganzir, Nin Lil. Do you still want to enter?' Namtar's face glistened unhealthily with a greenish sweat.

'If my Lord is in there.'

A moan, like the wind trapped underground in a hollow place.

'My Lady is there; that is more important.'

'I will go in.'

He led the way across the silent courtyard. The torches of the galla stayed beyond the skull-tipped fence, shifting restlessly, throwing wild shadows across to the steps ahead. As their flames receded, the same cold, blue glow seemed to emanate from the stones of Ereshkigal's palace. And yet the air around it was oppressively hot.

Nin Lil tried not to meet the insolent stares of Ereshkigal's courtiers. The jackal-headed sentries hardly moved aside for her. She had to follow Namtar through the narrow gap, smell the odour of rotting carrion they breathed, feel their eyes feast on her, control her shrinking flesh.

In the shadowed halls chill struck at last. She had not thought that lapis lazuli could look so dark and lifeless, or basalt glisten so cheerlessly, or cold clay feel so sad. An almost tuneless music *mourned lugubriously to the slow pulse of drums.*

*A squat, shapeless Lady, whose turban with a single pair of horns, upswept like rearing snakes, proclaimed her one of the lesser Anunna, shuffled out of the gloom to meet them. Namtar nodded briefly.*

*'Take us to your mistress, Atu. We have a rare and special visitor. Not since the Princess of the Greater Earth herself was brought to the Netherworld has such a royal Lady descended to grace the halls of Kur.'*

*The fat secretary moved away, then hesitated. Her face had an unhealthy yellow pallor.*

*'Ereshkigal is not well. Not well at all. For several spaces of women's time she thinks . . . And then blood. Always more blood.'*

*A swift surge of triumph shot through Nin Lil. The joyful, cruel superiority of the fertile over those who cannot bear children. She was a prisoner in Kur but not powerless. And then as Namtar the sukkal turned to look at her with those dark, all too intelligent eyes, she realised her own vulnerability, the helplessness of the children in her womb. Her terrified eyes appealed to him. She dragged her stained cloak closer round her now, trying to hide the swollen body that seemed to grow more monstrous with every moment. He twitched it from her in contempt, leaving her naked.*

*'There is no pity in Kur, Nin Lil. What will happen, will happen.'*

*Trembling, she let him lead her.*

*'I think this may cheer my Lady,' said Namtar, sweeping past Atu, who followed with fluttering uncertainty.*

*A ragaba stood at the bull-guarded door. 'Hubishag.' Namtar nodded to him. 'It seems we have got a matched pair.'*

*The green-eyed Lord's stare penetrated her. He lifted his staff, a jagged, broken-headed reed, and let her pass.*

*Chamber women kneeling round the bed raised large, frightened eyes towards the door. No brazier burned, but the central, recumbent figure was mounded over with hides of cows, of does, of she-asses, of tigresses. Their hooves and heads hung still attached and bloody yet. Hair twined like snakes, gleamed with unnatural sweat, tossed restlessly. Ereshkigal groaned.*

*'My Princess!'*

*'I am no fit ruler that can no longer people the country of the dead. I am barren, barren.'*

*'You have taken the Lord of Air himself, my lady. What if he*

*were to impregnate your darkness?'*

Nin Lil gave a little cry, moved forward in protest before she could stop herself. Ereshkigal flung back the covers, reared towards her menacingly. 'Who is this? What have you brought to mock the Queen of Kur?'

And in the darkness of that sad bedchamber the form of Nin Lil, young, still to be a mother, did seem to pulse with light again, growing stronger as she gathered her courage.

'I . . . bring you birth, great Ereshkigal,' she said in a soft, steady voice. 'I am the granddaughter of Nin Tu, who was once Ki. She Who Gives Birth is in my mother's blood and in my father's blood.'

'And I am the daughter of Nammu, the wild waters who gave birth to all of them. Should that not be enough to make me fertile too?' Her gaze was fixed on Nin Lil's swelling form that no cloak could have hidden now.

'Your road into Kur is the Road to Sorrow. If you give birth yourself it will be in weeping. Gula has made me eat the plant that the Daughters of An have from Angal Above. I shall bear the children of Lord Air as easily as a strong wind lifts the pollen from the date flowers to make the palms produce their fruit.'

'What is that to me, in the Below?'

'Often, the wind falls silent in the upper air. Then our children must climb the palms with fans and make a breeze to blow the pollen where no air moves. And so the date harvest still comes.'

'Your Lord of Air is silent here. Enlil is a sulky prisoner.'

'But I am his Lady now. And to the stillness of the Netherworld I have brought the life that moves in me.'

'You mock me?'

'No, Princess Ereshkigal. I will give it you . . . freely.' Again that little cry, the sharp remembrance of arms that pinned, of teeth that bit, of hard flesh wounding her soft parts.

Ereshkigal saw all that, and smiled, relishing it.

'His sons! The great Lord Enlil, made coward by the dark! To buy his freedom in the Above, he made these children, put your children up for sale. I had a brother too, who would not sell himself to buy my freedom.'

'Lord Enki braved great danger to rescue you.'

'And saved himself, rather than his sister!'

'Are you discontented with your realm then, Queen of the Netherworld?'

Ereshkigal gripped the tigerskin, glared at Nin Lil. 'You little— Oh, my belly!'

*The women rushed to bend over her, lowered her back on the pillows, fussed over her as she clutched her abdomen.*

*And pains struck like cobras at the womb of Nin Lil. She gasped and cried out, 'Nin Tu! Help me!' Then drew a deep breath and, though the atmosphere was thick and fetid, power sang through her veins, muscles stretched, eased, drew themselves together like strong, knotted cords. The light burned now in Nin Lil's own eyes and the scared faces of the household women turned up in awe. Namtar even put out a hand to help her as she stepped unsteadily towards the vast bed. Atu was on her other side.*

*'That's it, little lady. Lie down, it won't be long now.'*

*Nin Lil stood beside Ereshkigal's bed, panting a little. 'You have no birthing stool in the Netherworld, it seems. May I lie beside you in your bed, Queen Ereshkigal?'*

*Without waiting for an answer, driven by the necessity of the birth forces bearing down in her, she laid her small, willing body with its immense burden at Ereshkigal's side.*

*'Oh!' she gasped, but more in wonder than in pain.*

*There was a smell of blood already in the blankets, an old, dark blood. The fresh, light water of Nin Lil broke over it. Ereshkigal drew a loud, hissing breath, then twisted fiercely, imprisoned the girl in sinewy arms, snarled in her ear.*

*'Give it to me! Give me a child, here in my bed, between my legs.'*

*The child was coming anyway, slipping sweetly from Nin Lil's stem like a ripe peach dropping from the wood, like a gate opening on a well-oiled hinge.*

*'Meslamtaea,' she breathed. 'Lord Who Fruits from the Good Tree.'*

*'Mine!' Ereshkigal's blood baptised the baby's head. 'I shall call him Nergal. Guardian of War, Plague and Death!'*

*Is the light still in me? Nin Lil whispered to herself. But the baby Atu lifted up was dark.*

*Now she felt herself opening again, like a river flowing. Almost too soft to feel, a second baby was sliding out between the light of Nin Lil's body, between the dark of Ereshkigal's body.*

*'Is it come yet?' she asked faintly.*

*This baby seemed to shine as a waiting-woman lifted it more curiously than tenderly and handed it into Hubishag's arms. For a moment Nin Lil's throat constricted with fright. But it was the blue gleam of the lapis lazuli walls reflected in the slime that cloaked the baby's limbs.*

'*Ninazu – Lord Water-Knower, Medicine-Maker.*'

'*A second birth for me!*' Ereshkigal was like a miser seizing a pile of gold.

Nin Lil lay quiet, feeling the tumult still in her body. '*Don't fight with each other, little boys,*' she said. '*Lie still, my Bright One. Your time will come. Ah!*'

She could not restrain herself as the imperative of her vagina thrust all other thoughts from her mind, possessed her whole body. She gave a scream, though not of pain, as the third child passed through her cervix and the cord slithered after it to be cut by the waiting Atu.

'*Ennugi. Lord of the Sexual Parts.*' Nin Lil's eyes were closed as she murmured the name.

The secretary passed the child, still dripping blood, to Namtar, who took it with a shudder.

'*Mine to keep!*' triumphed Ereshkigal, sitting up and holding out eager arms. '*You were all witnesses. Give my baby to me to hold.*'

Nin Lil lay in silence.

'*You have not done yet,*' said Ereshkigal, watching her over Ennugi's dark and curling hair. '*You are holding something back.*'

'*I have given you your blood price,*' Nin Lil gasped, weary now. '*One for Enlil, one for myself, one—*'

'*For the one that will be most truly Enlil's child.*'

'*Our Child of the Light. He cannot be born in Kur.*'

'*You are wrong, girl. You are all wrong.*'

A desperate wail. '*You will not make me bear him in the Netherworld? I have paid your price,*' Nin Lil said more faintly still.

'*You think you can bargain with Ereshkigal, Queen of Kur?*'

An unbelieving pause. '*I have given you three! You cannot take the fourth from me as well!*' Tears leaped from her eyes more agonisedly than the babies had spurted from her womb. Inside her, the last child stirred.

The stifling arms of Ereshkigal were round her now. The newborn Ennugi cried in fright as the Dark Queen rolled over him.

'*I am Nammu's daughter. There is some part of me in all of you. Know that, Mistress Air. Death goes to Kur; life comes from Kur. Take that wisdom back to the Great Above with you, and reverence it. Send me your last son, once every month. And when his light is gone from Earth, when the night is dark again, as it is now, bow down and worship Ereshkigal, all of you.'*

Even in her exhaustion, Nin Lil felt herself dismissed. *'Now?'*

*'Go. And remember me well.'*

Weak from childbearing, clutching the fragile, restless shape still in her womb, Nin Lil staggered from Ereshkigal's bed. No one helped her this time. The hearts of the Netherworld are cold as stone. She tottered to the door. Hubishag bowed, still holding little Ninazu. Meslamtaea wailed in Atu's arms. Ennugi was lost in the vastness of Ereshkigal's stained bedclothes.

Nin Lil turned her head. *'Goodbye,'* she whispered. *'Forgive me!'*

# Chapter Twenty-six

*The palace of Kur yawned emptily before her. She made for the great door by which she had entered.*

*'Not that way,' said Namtar behind her. 'That is not the road to life.'*

*She turned. The* sukkal's *eyes glowed red. That was all that could be clearly seen of him. The far end of the vast hall where he stood was so dark she sensed rather than saw the dreadful robes drooping from him like cobwebs clogged with dust and bat droppings.*

*Namtar waited, and his very stillness was a command. Nin Lil obeyed. It seemed a long and lonely walk back across that hall, towards the twin points of those eyes. It felt as though she was returning into the core of darkness. And she must escape and make the light. Her body was very small and frail now, save for its one last burden. Perhaps her eyes were clouding, or the strength of the child within her was weakening. What little light it could shed before her was swallowed up in the black-blue lapis lazuli.*

*'Beware!'*

*The word shocked her. She was not aware that she had come so close to the* sukkal. *His warning was timely. There was a chasm at her feet. Its darkness was impenetrable. Heat rose from it, when she longed for the cool twilight of the spaces above. She swayed with weakness, trying to peer down. Steps.*

*She raised her head to Namtar. His bony hand was pointing downward, in silence, unemotional.*

*'I cannot,' she whispered.*

*'You must. It is Ereshkigal's command.'*

*Tread below tread, lowering herself further than ever into the bowels of the Netherworld from which she could not hope to rise. Yet, in the solitude and silence, the light within her filtered through more strongly.*

*'Child,' she murmured. 'What am I condemning you to?'*

*The jar of level floor met her descending foot.*

*An awful silence now. A night of labour, and no sympathetic women to cosset her. A triple birth, and no rejoicing for her. Even the Great Below had turned its back on the bringer of life.*

*The galla had gone. Nin Lil sobbed quite loudly in the shocking stillness. No mocking laughter answered her. She was utterly alone. Weak as she was, how could she ever climb back to the Great Above? How could she cross that river? Or would she have to do battle with a raging Kur to escape, as Enki had done? How much simpler it would be to sink down here, in the solitude of this tunnel, and be the first of the Anunnaki to die.*

*If it had been only herself, she might have given way. But limbs stirred in her womb. Her tired and tender cervix seemed to stretch.*

'Not yet, my precious! Not here!' *she cried in fright.* 'I will get you out. Lie still!'

*The movement subsided. There was only her racing heart. She edged cautiously along the passage.*

*And then a sound. A howl like the wind through winter reed beds.*

'Enlil? *Is it you?*'

*Two eyes, bright with the foretaste of sky and unborn stars, seemed to devour her from behind a grille.*

'Little Sud! Oh, my darling Nin Lil! What are you doing here? I forbade you! Have you come to let me out? Or . . . No! Don't say you're her prisoner too!'

'I don't know. I . . . was sent.'

'The child? Tell me! Is my son safe?'

*Her hands roamed questioningly over the swelling of her abdomen. Her womb was quiet now, heavy. No kick of limbs, no sharp contractions. And yet the light was pooling the floor between her feet.*

'I believe he is living. But I am afraid he will be born in the Below. I have given birth to three sons already for you in Kur.'

*The flash of an exultant smile illuminating that face behind the bars.* 'And Ereshkigal has accepted them?'

*She bowed her head.* 'Kur has them now.'

'You've paid my ransom! Then I must be free!' *He shook the door violently. The lock clanged in its socket; it did not give.*

*Slowly, trembling with the awe of her responsibility, Nin Lil reached up a hand. A key was in the lock. She forced it round. Her groping fingers found heavy bolts at top and bottom. She dragged them back.*

*Enlil burst out from the prison. He swept her into his arms, showered her with kisses.*

*'My little love! The whole world will thank you for this. You've bought my freedom.'*

*She began to laugh then, a weak and helpless laughter that was close to tears. 'I've paid your price? For raping me?'*

*Enlil let go of her suddenly. She almost fell. 'Are you making fun of me? Shall I leave you behind?'*

*'No. You would not.' She stumbled, and was grateful that he caught her. 'I am carrying your son, your little Prince of Light. You won't leave us. I have borne you three sons already. Them, you will leave behind, for this one.'*

*'My sons?' His eyes gleamed at her.*

*'Oh yes, Lord of the Bright Eyes. Did you imagine the Air Lord could disguise himself and deceive his wife? I bore Meslamtaea for the gatekeeper, Ninazu for the man of the Devouring River, Ennugi for the ferryman of the Netherworld. But I am no whore. I am more faithful to you than you will be to me.'*

*He gripped her savagely.*

*'My Lord! The child! Be careful!'*

*She felt him steady himself, fight to control his breathing.*

*'Your pain was necessary. How could the world live without the Lord of Air? How can it grow brighter without our son? You shall be honoured for this.'*

*'And how shall I live with my pain?' she murmured, before she lapsed into silence.*

*They stood together, listening. He, holding her possessively; she, holding the child inside her, frightened for him. She waited to hear the laughter of* galla, *taunting her with hope denied.*

*Nothing. Blank walls of unfeeling rock. A door half-open on Enlil's foul-smelling cell. The silent stairs to Ereshkigal's Ganzir.*

*'Which way?' her small voice asked.*

*'Don't you know? I thought you had come to lead me.' He was looking down at her light-filled body with a new wonder.*

*'Namtar said I couldn't go out by the way I came. It is not the road to life.'*

*Enlil took a few hesitant steps in the other direction and came back. 'That path goes lower.'*

*'I cannot see any other way.'*

*His huge hand folded over hers. It was cold and trembling. She led him on. She was walking quickly. There was an urgency on* her to walk whatever road she had to walk, to face whatever dangers she had to face, before the pains began again.

For a price, Nin Lil led her husband and her imprisoned son deeper into the tunnels of Kur, towards the east. Lower and lower, the roof descending too, so that first Enlil, and then she, had to stoop and at last to crawl.

'The rock is turning to mud,' she breathed. 'I think there is water running.'

For a price, she eased her way across it, lengthening out the distance between her and her first three children.

Sound in her ears now, more than the heavy breath of Enlil behind her. Little life-giving threads of water trickling between her fingers. Her hands sticky with clay. Still a soft darkness round them. Her body, bent to the ground, almost eclipsed the light. But she was moving faster now, sensing the burrow begin to swing upwards. Was that a fresher air on her face, or did she only imagine it because of her enormous need? She could not hold her cervix in much longer.

She was scrabbling her way forward. She was like a foetus herself now, uncurling into its neo-natal form, heading irresistibly towards the birth channel, impelled by the need to be born, the will of the womb to expel.

For a price, Nin Lil fought their way towards the upper regions.

Enlil struggled after her on hands and knees in the confining duct.

No imagination now could have conjured this scent of pine, the fingernails digging into the yielding fibre of roots.

'Yes!' cried Nin Lil. 'Oh, yes!'

The way was widening out. She could almost stand upright, begin to run. Then her little stumbling rush was overtaken as Enlil lifted her off her feet.

'The child is coming,' whispered Nin Lil, clinging to his shoulder.

'Not here! Not yet!'

He charged forward, carrying his wife and her almost-born child. Pale stones began to glimmer in the walls, the texture of sandy soil crumbling as he shouldered past. Sweetness and purity in their lungs, the cool touch of night. Lips of soil that seemed to stretch apart for them. Huge space. A limitless sky. A vast, dark, waiting Earth.

'He is here! Lay me down, Enlil. I have to give birth!'
'Not yet my love. Not yet, my Lady.'

*Her womb was opening. As Enlil swept her upwards, the light was spilling from it over the mountains. She saw his features above her more clearly than ever before. She saw the black and white play of leaf shadows from bushes of sage. Wild grasses lifted their silvered heads to her. There was a mountain stream ahead. Enlil bounded across it and its waters sparkled under her. The vast shadow of the Son of An grew before him as he strode with giant leaps up towards the still-darkened summit. She saw the sharp-edged clarity of rocks and screes.*

*Higher yet, with great racing strides, but the contractions strong in her so that she fought against him.*

*'I cannot hold him in. He will be born!'*

*'You must contain him, my Lady. Only a little longer.'*

*Enlil was almost afire with triumph. The radiance in Nin Lil seemed to bathe them both. The mountains were lightening as Enlil swept up and up, silvering the rocks of the steep valleys, throwing their shadows darker still. The vast, black dome of An was close above now, like a dark bull's hide spread out to receive them.*

*On the highest ridge Enlil halted. He drew a mighty breath, lifted his small light wife, whose body burned like a blue-white lamp flame, up to the highest heaven, laid her down gently and reverently on the aromatic herbs, knelt, watched.*

*Up on the summit of the Earth, high on the mountains of the east, above the limit of the cedars, over the sea that circles Dilmun, Nin Lil opened her small, stretched vagina one last time.*

*All over the world the beasts rose from their slumber, stood silent. The Sons and Daughters of An left the darkness of their houses, lifted their faces to the east.*

*Like a young bull raising its horned head on the high pasture. Like a sharp-prowed, high-sterned* magur *boat gliding from reed beds into a clear lagoon, the boy Nanna came out of his mother. And at his birth, the first moon rose. Out of the sky it filled the world with pure light. As it grew, it flooded the land of Uri, gateway to the mountains of the north, the lands of Shubur and Hamazi and all the swift-streamed valleys of the east, the land of Martu, shifting deserts of the west, the beloved land of Sumer, good garden of the Two Rivers in the south. The Anunnaki saw themselves and the Four Quarters in its radiance as never before, covered their eyes, bowed down, gave thanks. In glistening silver the new moon of the heavens rose, grew stronger, waxed towards brilliant fullness, bathed the world with* radiance. *The Lord of Celestial Light was born.*

But Nin Lil, who had borne this fourth son, who was also her first, without pain, turned on the bed of thyme and wept.

'Is it true? I have mortgaged even you to Ereshkigal? Again and again,' she said, 'my son's boat will rise from the east and go down in the west. With each night its strength will wax and then wane. He will sail his ship over the lagoon. He will herd his cattle across the marshes. But once every thirty nights the waters of Kur will seize him. Light will abandon us. The world will be dark and he must descend to Ereshkigal. The loved child we lose will brighten the Netherworld and not us. Once, only that one night, Meslamtaea, Ninazu and Ennugi will meet him. I shall not see them again.'

On the high mountain, no one heard her weeping. Enlil lifted his hands to the sky and shouted out, 'See, Father An, what I have done. Receive a grandson to make all Angal rejoice!'

To the Earth beneath he roared, 'Nin Mah! Behold your grandchild. Let your creation grow more beautiful every night under his gaze.'

To all the Anunnaki, 'Light! Light has come to the Earth and the Great Above. The brightness will always be with you now.'

'Not always,' protested Nin Lil. 'Ereshkigal will have her time.'

But a great paean of praise was bursting from thousands of throats. Far down in Sumer, the Lords and Ladies of the world lifted delighted hands to the slender crescent shining on the mountaintop like a silver cradle. They gave glory to young Nanna the Moon Lord and Enlil who had fathered him and escaped from Kur.

> *Enlil shines on the throne-dais of his palace.*
> *Like a floating cloud he circles the heavens.*
> *He is the one prince of the Sky,*
> *The only mighty one of Earth,*
> *He is the exalted benefactor of the Anunnaki,*
> *The Great Mountain of the Children of An.*
> *To Enlil, praise!'*

Later, they remembered to thank Nin Lil too.

# Chapter Twenty-seven

Inanna caught Nin Shubur's hand. The springtime night had fallen early below banks of clouds. Only now had the waxing moon ridden clear of them. Its wide, two-horned crescent floated free, brilliant silver against the intense black of the upper waters.

'You can see it's Father's boat, can't you? And all the little stars are his cattle he's herding through the marshes.'

'And the big stars?' Nin Shubur's smile teased her. 'The planets are not mere cattle, are they, Miss Inanna?'

'No.' A wide, proud grin. 'There's mine. Dilibad. The Evening Star. She's so bright, she can shine before any of the others, even while the sky's still blue. She's the strongest of them all, isn't she?'

'Eldest Daughter of the Moon,' said Nin Shubur solemnly. Then laughing, 'The Harlot's Signal!'

Inanna tugged her hand. 'Let's go and see it.'

'See what?'

'My tree, of course. Will it be all right? Do you think it's lonely in that park, on its first night?'

The *sukkal*'s hand stroked the child's hair.

'The tree is very well. There was a thunderstorm this afternoon. It will be well watered in by now.'

'But it will be missing me. I want to touch it, hug it, sing it goodnight.'

'The park is far below. It will be dark and lonely. It's no place for walking now.'

'Why? What would we meet? What walks in Great-grandfather's park after dark, Nin Shubur? I want to see!'

'You are too young. And too bold. Do not ask to see what walks in the shadows yet, Lady Inanna.'

'But my tree is there. If there is danger, you can make spells to protect it, can't you, Nin Shubur? You're a wise woman.'

Nin Shubur looked down at the child's eager, agitated face.

'There, I'll do what I can,' she soothed. 'There can be no harm. We'll take the guards with us. Then you must go quietly to bed.'

The flowering smile rewarded her.

Nin Shubur signed to half a dozen *sag-ursag*, in their ceremonial kilts and studded cloaks, to accompany them. The guardsmen took up flaming torches, but Inanna cried out, 'No! By moonlight. That's the proper way. I want to see what it's *really* like at night.'

Even the shaman woman and the Sky House guards, themselves trained in magic, felt the strangeness of that descent into darkness. They left the wide, moonlit terraces of the E-Anna above them. They walked through narrow alleys between buildings that seemed closer and more sinister than in daylight. The gate loomed tall, still glistening faintly with damp. The trees soughed overhead.

'Open it.'

The *sag-ursag* captain, Ganunmah, turned the great key and the garden door swung soundlessly open.

An owl quickened its flight across a grove of fruit trees. The darting of bats made the stars seem to dance.

'Where is it?' Inanna's breathless cry betrayed her bewilderment. The unfamiliarity of the place, the breadth of the park were doubly new to her in the disorientating moonlight.

Nin Shubur walked steadily forward.

'What was that?' A childish shriek.

'A roll of thunder.'

'I thought . . . it was the clap of an enormous bird's wings! I thought I saw . . .'

'Shall we go back to the E-Anna?'

'No!'

No wind stirred the bushes, yet among them a shadow seemed to move.

Inanna clutched Nin Shubur's hand, formality forgotten.

'Tread carefully, Ladies,' the *sag-ursag* captain warned. 'The world's not as safe now as Enlil kept it in the first days. There may be snakes here.'

'Is it true?' whispered Inanna. 'Is it really more dangerous, even for us?'

'Oh, yes,' her *sukkal* said. 'We do not die, but if we are wounded, we may suffer for ever. But don't be afraid, little one. I have promised the Anunnaki I will look after you.'

# Chapter Twenty-eight

*Enki parted the reed clump. Nin Gikuga was bending over the water with her back to him. Her sturdy buttocks were outlined against a sky powdered with stars. Her hands were busy in a silvery pool. Enki could not resist reaching out his own hands and fondling the shape of those female curves. The Cane Woman screamed, slipped in the mud and fell splashing in the shallow water. She floundered round, prepared to be angry, pushed the wet hair out of her eyes, then saw who it was. She laughed forgivingly.*

*'Oh, it's you, is it? I might have guessed.'*

*'I thought I put Nanshe in charge of the fish. Did I get it wrong? You look extraordinarily fetching swimming in the moonlight.'*

*'You've made me more of a mudworm than a fish, you old lecher.'*

*He extended a hand and pulled her out. She stood dripping on the bank, splashing more water over herself and trying to sluice the mud that smeared her limbs.*

*'Let me help,' suggested Enki.*

*The Water Man's hands flowed over arms and legs, thighs and hips. At first she merely allowed it with soft, rustling laughter. Then she softened for him, began to yield.*

*'Oh, Nin Gikuga, who am I that I should fill the tall cane of the marshes?' But she was lying in his damp embrace now, and he was releasing himself into the hollow of her.*

*'Life,' she said, letting her limbs part easily. 'You give us all life. You make us laugh.'*

*'Nin Gikuga, Lady. I came to be serious tonight. There is another tune I want to play on your pipe. I am a great Son of An. As great as Enlil . . . well, almost. I need a Lady for my palace, my Abzu. Will you come and be my Damgalnunna, the Great Spouse of the Prince?'*

*She laughed again then, like water rippling through the reeds when a coot takes off. She linked her muddy arms around his neck and kissed him.*

*'Oh, Enki, I think not. What should the Lady of Pure Canes do in a brick house? I belong here, in this wilderness of water and reeds. I want to sit with my buffaloes and watch the moon rise. I want to dabble my feet in the water and sing silly songs to the ducks that only you overhear. I am no great Lady. Clever Nidaba is the one who turned her reed into a stylus and taught us all writing. And your daughter Nanshe is perfectly capable of running your Abzu for you as well as her own house in Nina. Come to my reed house in the marshes whenever you like. You don't have to marry me.'*

*He stroked the column of her waist. 'You're very generous. You give us so much.'*

*So Nin Gikuga retired to the place where she was happy. In the heart of the marshes, on the banks of a quiet lake, she had caused her reed house to be built. Bundles of the tallest canes were lashed together, planted in the ground like pillars, bent together to form a roof with seven arches. Mats were woven of rushes in diagonal patterns, fastened between the lower pillars to keep out the wandering pigs and dogs. For the upper walls, more canes were split and woven into a trelliswork of intricate patterns, through which the cool breeze eddied. The roof was generously thatched with heavy bundles of reeds to shed the rain beyond its walls. The floor was laid with mats. Bright fire kept the mosquitoes away. The bed was heaped with sheepskins, pillows filled with goose feathers. Wild boar and duck and barbel fish were grilled for her visitors.*

*No wonder the Water Man often slipped away from the town of Eridu, from the silver and lapis lazuli of the Abzu. His* magur *boat, the* Ibex of the Abzu, *came often nosing through the channels of the marsh after long voyaging and set him ashore at Nin Gikuga's wooden quay, before it sailed on to its own harbour.*

*Here while Nanna the Moon Boy was still in his infancy, Nin Gal, their daughter, was born.*

*'Nin Gal? The Great Lady. Why do you call her that?' Nin Gikuga was laughing, even after childbirth, her happiness doubled in bearing Enki's child. 'You have many daughters, and sons too. Half Sumer is salted with Anunnaki that you have sired. Surely Nanshe, of all your daughters, is the Great Lady?'*

*'Perhaps,' said Enki, stroking the little girl's cheek. His face was dark and thoughtful, in one of those sudden changes of mood*

*she could not follow. She would have drawn him into her arms, surrounded him with her own loving darkness, but the child lay between them.*

*'When the Abzu was built, it spoke ... The Deep Place claimed an unborn girl-child from me. Ereshkigal is ...' and even now he could not pronounce that name without a gasp, '... gone. But she may draw a daughter from me yet.'*

*'And this is the one?' Her arms were round the baby now, protective.*

*'I don't know. Perhaps ... A daughter. Or a daughter's daughter.'*

Inanna's hand tightened on Nin Shubur's. For once, she was silent.

Nin Gal was her mother.

*Enki, the wanderer, had found another love, on the steppe away from the broad rivers and their well-watered gardens. Here, in the brief vegetation of the spring, shepherds came with their flocks to graze them on the newly-green desert. Waters lay trapped in hollows in the sand. Streams swollen by storms carved memorials to themselves in gravelly beds. When the scorching heat of the summer came, the milk of the ewes would dry and the shepherds would pack their tents and their pipes for the trek home. Only the wild beasts would be left.*

*Only the beasts, and those few Anunnaki whose* me *it was to care for them. Sumugan, Lord of the Plain. Nin Sun, Lady of Wild Cows. She was not afraid to live in solitude. But she welcomed Enki's visits like so many other Daughters of An before her.*

*'Don't you want to see your son?' she asked this time, smiling with her large, brown eyes from the doorway of the cowhide tent.*

*'If you insist. But I can never quite lose the notion that the getting of them is more exciting than the result.'*

*'For you, but not for the mother. He is my first.'*

*'Let's look at him, then.' His arm was round her shoulders, warm, encouraging.*

*The baby lay on brightly-coloured rugs that glowed even in the shadowy interior. He was clutching a reed pipe which he waved at his father.*

*'He looks a happy child.'*

*'Dumuzi. My little Damu.' Nin Sun picked him up. All the pride and wonder of motherhood were in her fond face. 'Isn't he*

*the loveliest child you ever saw?'*

*'He's well enough, well enough.' Enki flicked his fingers in front of the boy's eyes almost absent-mindedly, but laughed when the child tried to snatch for them, dropping his toy. 'Well, we must think of something to give him, mustn't we? I can name birth gifts no other father could bring. How would you like him to have the* me *of new life? Damu, the power of the rising sap. Or in the orchards of the south, Dumuzi Ama-Ushumgalanna, the power at the heart of the date cluster. In the pastures upriver, Dumuzi the Herder who brings the calves. Here on the inland steppe, Dumuzi of the Sheepfold, the power of milk and cream, for lambs and kids. Look at that; there's a smear of butter round his mouth already!'*

*Nin Sun took him back, laughing and grateful. 'He's a lucky boy. With* me *like that he shouldn't want for a wife. He'll have the pick of all the Princesses of Sumer. You are generous, my lord.'*

*'Oh, I can be a great deal more generous than that, my sweet. And it's much too hot to be standing about with our clothes on. Put that infant down, damn you! Would you be glad if we made a girl, this time?'*

*'Whatever comes after this one, nothing can match my Damu.'*

*When it was done, and it was sweet for her as well, Enki got up to fetch water from the pitcher for both of them. Nin Sun caught his hand. 'If this is a girl, will you bless her too? Make her glad and gifted?'*

*She saw his face darken, as if the newfound moon had lost itself behind a cloud. He struggled to keep the roughness out of his voice. 'Oh yes. I'm a generous father. I give too easily when a woman asks me. I may have given away one girl's birthright already.'*

'And that was Dumuzi's sister? Geshtinanna, who grew the grapes? But what about me? Me!'

Nin Shubur laughed. 'Soon, my little Queen of the Universe. Soon.'

# Chapter Twenty-nine

*Nin Gal lived a sheltered life, much loved. She was full of merriment. She swam in the lagoons, poled her canoe along the waterways loaded with fodder for the buffaloes. She prudently laid out offerings for the great wild sow who lurked in the thickets. When the sky was dark, she kept in the reed house and sang in the firelight as she wove rush mats. Nin Gikuga grew stiffer, greyer. Some of the laughter that had swept her in the days of her courtship had faded now. Enki came less often. She watched her daughter carefully.*

*Here, in the magical world of black and silver lakes and islands, the young Moon Lord found Nin Gal. After a week of rainstorms he came sailing his canoe over the spreading lake. She was washing her hair, pushing the gentle black buffalo aside with scolding laughter, wading out into the deeper water. He watched her diving, rising, shaking the water out of her tresses in silver spray. He saw and loved her.*

*When he came the next night, leaving his boat and wading nearer to her house through narrow waterways, how could she resist his beauty? How could the daughter of passionate Enki not want to run to meet him, throw herself into his eager arms? She stood in the doorway, with all that youthful longing in her eyes. Yet the child of dutiful Nin Gikuga knew that her mother was watching through the trellised window of the reed house.*

*Nanna came again and again in that long, starry night of the world, and heard her singing in the house. All the desire of her newfound womanhood was in that song. Nin Gal sang to the wild geese rocking on the lake of how she longed to lie in the arms of her beloved anywhere, rather than be wrapped in the finest lambswool and swansdown.*

*His new man's voice broke through her dreams outside her window.*

*'If you truly love me, Nin Gal, as I love you, come out into the marshes tomorrow and meet me. Don't be afraid of the dark.*

*The moon will light you. I want nothing to hurt you. Cut yourself rushes and make leggings to protect those lovely legs from the sharp-edged leaves of the canes. We'll make a feast. We'll gather eggs from the nests of the waterfowl and rinse our hands in the silver waters of the marsh. My moon, your reeds will make it a magic land for both of us. I'd like to bring you wedding gifts, milk and cream for your house. Look, my cows are wading thigh-deep in the swamp. Their milk is rich and sweet. But your mother never smiles for me. Oh, my sweet Nin Gal, if I could only come into your house when Nin Gikuga is away!'*

*'I'm not afraid of the marshes. I'd rather eat birds' eggs with you among the swamp cresses. I'm not afraid of the water snake and the wild boar. The moon will make the channels brilliant beside our feet, light up the pig paths through the reeds. I'll be safe with you.'*

*They met in secret. His boat tossed in a little lagoon to their youthful passion. Afterwards, the Moon Lad herded his cows away, singing exultantly. He talked of marriage. But Enki had been long absent, sailing far beyond Sumer, and Nin Gikuga shook her head and would not even speak about it with her daughter.*

*The world grew dark again. Only a faint and misty light travelled the sky. It hardly lit the dangerous marshes. Ereshkigal was waiting. Once every month, young Nanna must travel the underground road to the caverns of the Netherworld. The Above lost him.*

*This time the darkness seemed blacker than ever before. The Sons and Daughters of An wailed. They beat their breasts, tore their ears and buttocks. They made a feast, sacrificed a kid, poured out dark wine. The Children of Sky and Earth praised Ereshkigal. The dark must have its time. But they begged for their Bright Lad to return.*

*The water was low, at the end of the summer drought. The reed clumps stood dry and thirsty, their tangled roots exposed.*

*In that black night a hooded traveller came to Nin Gikuga's reed house. He peered at Nin Gal more curiously than courtesy might allow as he handed the girl a letter, marked on clay. She glanced indoors in alarm at her mother, nodding beside the cooking fire. Then she beckoned him eagerly indoors and knelt beside the fire, holding the words up to the flames. The stabs of the stylus sang of love, of flowing cream and milk, of invitation, of marriage.*

*'He'll come back?' whispered Nin Gal.*

*The traveller nodded, kept his head in the shadows beyond the probe of firelight. 'Back to you, above all.'*

'But my mother won't allow me to marry him. And I don't know where my father is. I could run away with Nanna across the marshes and live with him always, but I don't want to break my mother's heart. Tell Nanna I won't marry him without my parents' consent.'

'Oh, I think that might be arranged.' *And his eyes sparkled suddenly in the fitful firelight.*

*Nin Gal took a deep breath, coloured, leaned forward and stared hard at the stranger. He drew back into the shadows, let a fold of cloth fall across his face. He nodded at Nin Gikuga, whose head had drooped forward towards her lap. Outside, little waves began to lap against the quay, as though far off in the mountains rain was falling and beginning to replenish the rivers of the delta again. Nin Gal looked from the hooded traveller to her sleepy mother and back again. She smiled a little, delighted smile.*

'If you can do what you say, if you are who I think you are, then tell my Nanna this,' *she whispered.* 'When I see he has filled the rivers for me with the springtime flood, when I see he has caused the grain to grow high in the fields, when I see the fish are leaping in the marshes, and the new reeds shoot green amongst the old in the canebrakes, when the stags bell in the woods and the desert comes alive with vegetation, when there is date honey and wine from the orchards, cress fresh from my garden, long life celebrated in my father's palace, then I will be his bride. I will go up and live with him on his mountain.'

*He bowed towards her, chuckling.* 'Spoken like Enki's daughter. Don't let him have you for nothing! I shall see you reign like an honoured queen with Enlil's boy, my girl.'

*With a swift movement of joy she flung herself across the reed mat, knelt up before the courier, kissed him.* 'Thank you, Father!'

*Nin Gikuga started.* 'Eh, what's that? Has a stick fallen out of the fire? Who . . . ?'

*The traveller leaned forward, let the cloth slip from his head. Blue-black hair touched now with silver. A lined and mobile face. Eyes darting under tufted brows that could not stay serious.*

*But as Nin Gal rose to leave them alone, his arm went round her waist and he held her to him. His face looked up at her, craggy now with the fire beneath it.*

*He breathed,* 'Are you the one? Are you the girl my sister wants?'

★ ★ ★

'And then? And then? It's Utu, isn't it? And then . . . Go on!'

*And so Nin Gal bound her impetuous love. She abided by the moon's seasons, the rhythms of fullness and abstinence, the tides of her blood. When Nanna returned, when the Earth and the waters were at their richest, at the feast of the Spring New Moon, Nin Gal left the marshes.*

*They were married in her father's Abzu at Eridu. That was a merry feast. When the ceremonial was over the couple slept together on a down-filled bed for the first time. And in her season, she loved him passionately. They rose to a moonlight water carnival.* Shagan *canoes raced over the ebony water. The* kugalgal *monsters reared up their weedy shoulders out of the waves and sang a deep, booming song like the sea in conch shells. There was much drinking of strong beer and pushing of girls and boys into the lagoon.*

*Then the couple sailed for Nippur. Enki gave them a* nisag *boat laden with first fruits. There were fattened sheep and long-tailed mice, porcupines and* suhur *carp. At each quay they passed, the Guardian of the city came out to bless them, to kiss Nin Gal and congratulate Nanna.*

*They came to the Air Lord's city and celebrated a great feast with Enlil and Nin Lil.*

*'Nanna,' she whispered in their bed, next morning. 'I am with child.'*

*He hugged her fiercely, murmured in her ear, 'Then come on with me quickly to the mountains. Leave the plain of Sumer. Let my child be born where the hills touch the sky, where the cedars grow huge and dark and the mines sparkle with gems. Where the eagle looks down from the other side of the peak of the Land of the Living and sees the Island of Dilmun. At the Gate of the Morning open your legs, Nin Gal, give birth for us. Come and live with me on the Cedar Mountain beyond Aratta.'*

*They crossed the plain between the Two Rivers. They were towed up the Idiglat to meet the furrowed foothills. Asses carried them up climbing valleys, beside rushing streams that had carved a way for them into the eastward mountains. Nin Gal was heavy now with child. She did not complain. She saw the heights towering over her, lifted her eyes higher still, fixed her heart on the sky. The light of the moon was radiant all round them. The wilderness of rocks stood out sharp-edged. The sky was scattered with constellations. The full moon was the greatest light in all creation. The Anunnaki of Aratta welcomed them joyfully and built a house for them on the slopes of the Cedar Mountain.*

*When her time came, Nin Gal climbed the last, high path, with her women helping her. She laid herself down, still trusting, in the same dark cave of Kur out of which Nin Lil had been carried to give birth to Nanna before her, in the Gateway of the Dawn, between the mountain peaks. This mother was happy, loved, treasured, with Nanna watching over her.*

*Contractions came upon her; she gasped and cried, felt herself flowering, the blood running hot between her legs, light spreading all around her, the air warm on her eyes, a light more wonderful than fire, filling the universe. Heat! Colour!*

*Green on the sage bushes, gold on the eagle's beak, the red blood staining her legs in a triumphal banner, the deep, burning blue of the sky.*

*As she held her son in her arms, the Water Lord's daughter burst into happy tears that made a glory of rainbows in her eyes. But the Air Lord's son, Nanna, bowed down and hid his face in his hands. On the ridge of the Cedar Mountain their baby son Utu opened his eyes and smiled. The Sun Lord was born, not from the sea or the sky, but out of the shadow of Kur itself.*

*The world woke, and saw itself truly for the first time.*

'And then it was me, wasn't it? Ishkur for the storms, and then me!' Inanna was jumping up and down with excitement.

Nin Shubur's smile gleamed like starlight in the shadow of the trees.

*On the high hills above Aratta, in the Land of the Living, where Enlil had planted seven cedars, there was only love and laughter, except for one dark night in thirty.*

*Nin Gal and Nanna had been to pay their respects to Enki in Eridu. Now they were travelling back to the mountains. Where the river wound through the steppe, in the wilderness of the Edin, they stopped to camp. A half-grown* huluppu *tree grew all alone. The black shadows that netted the ground under its leaves dissolved into silver mist as Nanna and Nin Gal lay down beneath it and made love.*

*'There is still a time,' teased Nin Gal, 'when the sun gallops down into the deserts of the west. When the moon is still behind the Mountains of Night or bent low in the reed beds of the marshes. The sky is lonely, your little stars too pale to prick out yet. This is the time when the Daughters of An lie down and*

*reach out empty arms for their lovers. Or the morning twilight before sunrise, when the Sons of An wake from sleep and turn to feel for their beloved. What will shine for them then?'*

'*I will show you, water of my heart.*' *And Nanna rolled himself lovingly over her, held her close, gave her what she wanted.*

*So from Enki and Nin Gikuga, out of Enlil and Nin Lil, through Nanna and Nin Gal, with the rising of the planet Dilibad, at the Gateway of Kur of the east, in the mouth of Kurkisikil, the Shining Place, our Inanna was born.*

*And all the constellations danced for her.*

'*The loveliest little girl in Sky and Earth,*' *said Nin Gal wonderingly.*

*The baby's small face was white, framed in a cloud of blue-black hair. Lids, black-lashed and blue-veined, lay gently over eyes that opened to reveal flashes of blue and silver. Her limbs were round and perfect, her tiny nipples like the first flowerbuds.*

*The weary Anunnaki toiling for Enlil in Nippur lifted their heads in gratitude when her planet signalled the end of labour and the time for food and pleasure. As they trooped to work in the grey-blue stillness of dawn, they looked to her Morning Star for a promise of the new day's life and the cool evening to come again.*

*The Daughter of Love. The Princess of Morning to sparkle before the heat of the sunrise. The Evening Star dancing on the rim of the sky before the moon rode up.*

*A little girl so lovely, so merry, no one could refuse her anything she asked. A child too much loved, perhaps.*

# Chapter Thirty

'What do you mean, too much loved?'

But Nin Shubur had stopped. Inanna, too, felt herself checked abruptly. The darkness was thicker in front of her, solid.

'We're here. I hadn't noticed. It's my *huluppu* tree, isn't it? It is!'

Nin Shubur said nothing.

Inanna reached out her hand and felt for the trunk. The bark yielded too easily, still saturated by its long immersion. As she pressed it, water seeped between her fingers. She craned her head back.

'It looks bigger than I remembered,' she whispered.

'Perhaps it has grown a little today, as you have.'

Inanna put her arms round the tree and hugged it close, laying her face against it. 'My tree. My own!' She stepped away, her smile a ghost in the moonlight. 'There. I've given it life again.'

Heavy drops of rain began to patter through the barely-opened leaves.

'We should not be here in the dark, my lady. The E-Anna is far above us. This park is low-lying and the river still in flood. If the water rises we shall not be able to see it coming.'

'But we'll be all right, won't we? Nothing can really hurt us. We're Children of An. It's only the poor little humans who die, isn't it? Not us. *We'll* be safe.'

The thunder rolled closer, shaking the tops of the branches above them.

'Hurry up, Nin Shubur. You said you could protect it. Go on.'

Nin Shubur moved Inanna away and began to circle the trunk, murmuring a singsong incantation half under her breath.

The mortal *sag-ursag* captain took off his cloak and put it round the little Lady Inanna's shoulders. She reached up impulsively and kissed him. She had always been fond of humans.

'That's enough,' said Nin Shubur. 'We've both done what we can. It's time for sleep.'

At the upper gate Inanna paused to look back.

'Look!' she cried. 'It is my special tree!'

The shower had passed. Through ragged clouds, the Evening Star hung, caught in the broken branches.

*Time passed heavily for the worker Anunnaki, still toiling to build Nippur and net the whole land with waterways and settlements. It was backbreaking work digging the canals out with hoes and pickaxes. Every basketful of clay had to be shouldered out of the cut to build up the bank. As each channel filled with the spill of the Buranun or the Idiglat, it must be annually dredged and repaired. And then there was corn to grow and mill, bread to bake, cloth to weave and pots to fashion, animals to be cared for, fish to catch. Food and houses were needed for the growing families of the Children of An.*

*Once Nanna had been born, moonlight made a brilliant wash across the plains by which to work. Walls gleamed on their bases of hewn stone. Vertical buttresses threw sharp-edged shadows in relief. Groves of palm trees stood out mop-headed against the now starry sky.*

*Then the sun came and the world was filled with colour. There was rejoicing then. The scattered flames and lamps of Gibil the Fire Lord were no longer needed out of doors. Never had the corn fattened so richly in its husks, the fruit dripped sweeter juice. The Anunnaki threw off their sheepskin clothing, let the warmth bathe their skin.*

*But they found the sun could be a fierce friend as well as a cheerful one. The Children of An toiled on. Sweat ran down their backs. Clay crumbled to dust, clogging their pores. The wind stirred up great clouds of red fog that pricked their eyes, hampered their breathing. Even the water tasted stale and gritty. They longed for the twilight time when Inanna's star came out to dance in the cool of the evening; for the night, when the moon came striding across the sky like a herdsman driving his cows.*

*In the dazzling light of the sun the Anunnaki of Nippur could see more clearly, work faster. The E-Kur was still not finished to Enlil's satisfaction. It was no longer possible for workers to squat in shadowed corners where the uncertain twilight made them seem inert as baskets of rubble, as goatskins of water. The new sun oppressed them, beating on bowed backs and stooped heads. The first exhilaration of brilliance and colour was over. They learned to long for night.*

*At last the weary Children of An rebelled. They met in secret council, not in the Ubshu-ukkinna of the E-Kur. An and Enlil, Enki and Nin Mah were not invited.*

*'This is no way for Anunnaki to live!' shouted Kulla, the Brick Lord.*

*'All day we're breaking our backs digging ditches, clearing canals,' complained the Farmer Enkimdu. 'This shouldn't be our work. How can I use the* me *Enki gave me? How can I direct the farms of the land so that everything runs as it should, sweetly and richly? We've got our eyes blinded with sweat and we're too busy working for Enlil and filling our own stomachs to care for the rest of the world. Is this what An intended?'*

*'Enlil spoke the Word. He made us what we are,' suggested the Corn Maiden Ashnan peaceably.*

*Gugun of the Building Tools examined the calluses on his fingers and muttered, 'Enlil has his head puffed up with pride. I don't see him dirtying his smooth hands like the rest of us.'*

*'We could get Ninurta to have a word with his father,' suggested Nindara. 'Enlil thinks the world of his second son. Maybe the lad could sweet-talk him into making life a bit easier, at least while summer's hot and heavy.'*

*'It's all right for some,' growled Gugun. 'Fishing? Do you call that work? You sit and idle your time on the cool water. You don't have to build the big Lord's city under the glare of that sun.'*

*'Well, we could appeal to Enlil, at least. Tell him he expects too much from us. We're supposed to be governed by the assembly of the Anunnaki, not by a single Lord.'*

*'Do you think we haven't tried? Monarchy, that's what he's after. Absolute rule over the lot of us.'*

*'This isn't the way it used to be.'*

*'We banished him once. Even Enlil is not above the law.' Haia had not forgotten the rape of his daughter Sud.*

*Only the Scribe Nidaba cautioned them. 'But he is breaking no law now.'*

*'He's breaking my back!' Enkimdu retorted.*

*'Let's get him out,' said Kulla, picking up a brick.*

*'Let's burn the tools!' said Gugun.*

'What if we set fire to the barn we put up yesterday? That'll show him!'

'Smash the canal banks!'

'Break up the looms!'

They made a bonfire of their tools, the rush baskets they were tired of lugging full of rubble, the wooden brickmoulds, the yoke and harness of the plough ox, the weaver's beam. They broke up the beer vats, but not before they had emptied them. The symbols of their servitude made an angry blaze. But some tools they kept back, the heavy, sharp-edged sort.

The crowd advanced upon the E-Kur. They marched by night, with the light of rushes soaked in bitumen tied to pickaxe handles burning over their heads. They grasped salvaged tools for weapons. They had not had far to look for them; the Anunnaki were hardly parted from them now, the work was so heavy. But the implements sat strangely in their hands that night. They had never been turned against a Son of An. They had the pick hoe Enlil himself had created, the source of all their cultivation and irrigation, and axes, hammers, the deadly five-pronged fishing spear.

Enlil's doorkeeper, terrified, heard them coming, saw the lights reflected as they crossed the bridge over the Id-Shauru in the middle of the city. He slammed the gate of the E-Kur shut and locked it. He ran to warn Nusku the sukkal, sent him to wake Enlil urgently.

Enlil sat up in the darkness of his inner chamber. The noise beat at his gates with the sound of a raging sea. He trembled like a gust of wind that rattles the palm leaves.

'What is it?' cried Nin Lil, swiftly crossing the floor of the outer chamber to peer from the window. 'What do they want? Why should you fear them? You are Enlil, Lord Kurgal.'

But Enlil had grown very pale. 'Do not speak that word! You don't know . . . You didn't suffer her imprisonment . . .'

'Hush!' She ran to him and held his great head on her shoulder. 'It is all over. You served your punishment. You have purified yourself from your sin. You went to Ereshkigal's Netherworld and returned. She cannot have you a second time.' But she keeps my three sons, Nin Lil wept inwardly. And even Nanna she takes from me to go down and serve her once every month.

Her arms went round her husband, strongly, possessively. She was a slight thing beside him, but she had learned her own *strength. She comforted the sobbing Air Lord.*

'I can't face them! What if your father Haia is at the head of them? What should I do?'

'Send Nusku out to reason with them. This is treason. An has given you the Governship of the Earth. As you've said many times, how else can houses be built, fields be farmed, forests felled, canals dug, if not by the Anunnaki themselves? Can a sheep do it?'

*Enlil dried his tears, tried to still his quivering face. He summoned his* sukkal *closer.*

'What shall we do? The darkness is on me. They won't send me back to the Netherworld, will they?'

'The Anunnaki are your brothers and sisters, my lord. Your Word called them all into being.'

'They banished me once. They let Ereshkigal imprison me.'

'For my sake, my lord,' said Nin Lil quietly, 'and for my sons, Ereshkigal let you go. The past is over.'

*A roar of impatience came from the gates. The lurid glow of torches flared outside the walls. Enlil shuddered.*

'You could send for Enki. He's supposed to be Lord of Wisdom,' Nusku suggested cautiously. *His eyes and Nin Lil's went to Enlil's strained face, testing to see how he would take this advice.*

'Oh yes! I can see what you're both thinking. I was banished to the Netherworld. But Enki went there in his magur *boat, as the bold hero, to rescue his sister Ereshkigal. He was too late to succeed, but he fought with Kur and came back victorious over him at least. Everyone honours Enki! I was a criminal!'*

'They honour you, Lord Air. You gave life to all of this.'

'I am the Lord who was tried, sentenced, punished. I had to be rescued from the Netherworld by a woman. They remember that.'

'Well, then? What is your will, my lord?'

*Enlil chewed his nails, like an angry dog biting its paw.* 'Oh, very well. If you can offer no better help.' *The words were wrenched from him.* 'Tell them to get Enki from wherever he is on his watery, vagabond wanderings. Let them see if he can think up anything better to satisfy them.'

'Could you not stop this building?' Nin Lil suggested. 'Be content with what we already have? Your E-Kur, my Kiur, Eshmah the Lofty Shrine, the Anniginna, our Kirishauru Park. Isn't it enough?'

'It's much more than that now,' said Nusku. 'They complain

*that their whole lives are spent grubbing for food, digging irrigation channels, cooking, spinning. They say the Children of An were meant for higher things than toil.'*

*'Let Enki see if he can answer that! In all his journeying to Magan, to Meluhha, to Dilmun, to Harali, has he seen any creature that could do the work in their place?'*

*'I will have him searched for,' said the* sukkal.

*They heard his feet going away down the steps. The soft sound was swallowed up in the growl of the waiting workers. There was a long, threatening while before the shouting died into a ragged silence. They could not hear what Nusku was saying. Enlil sat gripping the arms of his carved chair. He would not go near the window. Nin Lil peered out, looking up first at the light of the half-moon. A lower burst of talking, the ebb and flow of argument. The sound of Anunnaki moving discontentedly away. The angry torchlight receded.*

*'They're going,' said Nin Lil in relief. 'He's persuaded them.'*

*Nusku came back up the stairs, holding himself stiffly to hide his own trembling. 'Mighty Lord, Inspiration of Sumer, your decree will be observed. Couriers have been sent to summon Enki. The Council of the Anunnaki will hear his wisdom on this matter.'*

*'And what can slippery Enki do? Am I condemned again to be a prisoner in my own E-Kur, awaiting deliverance?'*

*'No prisoner, my lord. You are free to walk abroad as always. The whole Earth is yours.'*

*'What kind of Lordship is it, when the lesser Anunnaki must have their say, their rights?'*

*'We are one people,' said Nin Lil. 'All of us, descended from the one Mother.'*

*He turned a look of reproach on her, that was almost hatred.*

*A delegation of Anunnaki went to Eridu, headed by Nidaba the Scribe. Enki's ship, the* Ibex of the Abzu, *was moored at the quay and empty.*

*'At least,' said Nidaba, 'he's at home.'*

*But Isimud met them with folded arms.*

*'My Lord is in his Sea House. He has descended the well. It is more than my post is worth to summon him now. No other Anunnaki has ever seen where that shaft leads. You cannot pursue him down there.'*

*'But this is a crisis! The Children of An are rebelling. Nippur may be sacked if we can't bring Enki to help Enlil.'*

*Isimud allowed one of his faces a cautious grin. 'Aah. Is that so, my lady? How very distressing.'*

*Then Haia the Judge raised his hands to the sky in appeal.*

*'We need his help urgently. We must have Enki, Lord of the Abyss.'*

*'No work has been done in Sumer since we burned our tools.'*

*'We're getting hungry.'*

*'But it's not right that Sons and Daughters of An should have to labour all day in the hot sun.'*

*'We should be fed.'*

*'Clothed.'*

*'Looked up to.'*

*'Honoured.'*

*'Enki must find the answer . . . if anyone can.'*

*'You won't catch* him *working like a navvy, that's for certain!' growled Enbilulu.*

*'Enki has gone where you cannot reach him. He may be asleep by now in the sea-green halls of his mother Nammu, in the Deep of the Ocean.'*

*'How then shall we fetch him?' asked the Cattle Woman Lahar.*

*'Sit down and wait in the shade of the palm trees, if it pleases you,' suggested Isimud. 'You complain of too much work.'*

*'And starve?'*

*'We must go to Nammu,' said Nidaba. 'I shall appeal to our grandmother to help us.'*

*Ripples of hope and alarm ran through the discontented gathering of Anunnaki. Nammu, the first mother of all, of An and Ki, and Enki and Ereshkigal, she none of the lesser Anunnaki had ever truly seen. Safe on the level, fruitful plains of Sumer, high on the mountain pastures of Aratta, the primeval ocean was only a name, a notion. Her dark, heaving waters lapped the universe round. Once Enki and Ereshkigal had dived through her waves, back into the starless void of An, rejoicing in their mother and father.*

*But that was long ago. The universe was ordered now. Cities had been built, farms marked out. Canals criss-crossed the desert, bringing it under cultivation. The waters were controlled. The stars and moon and sun lit up the sky. Impossible to see now that wild, untamable surge of sea that had spawned all life. It was only Enki the wanderer who withdrew from the ordered world he himself had called into being, to find her. And her darker ocean flowed under the Earth where Ereshkigal reigned.*

'I am not afraid to go,' said Nidaba, in answer to their questioning looks. 'We need Enki. She is his mother. She is all our mothers. She must help us.'

# Chapter Thirty-one

*Alla of the Net poled Nidaba in his bitumen-black canoe, down the slow-moving Buranun. The mud was cracked and crazed. The sun beat down relentlessly. On either bank the weary Anunnaki had toiled in the fields, raking and pulverising the clods, harrowing, hoeing, leading what little water there was between the plots ready for sowing the young vegetables, scaring the greedy crows from the seed. Now they sat sullenly in the shade of their huts. Cows, unable to wade shoulder-deep in the cooling waters, sweltered under blankets to keep off the clouds of flies.*

*'There must be help,' said Nidaba to Alla. She sounded frightened now.*

*Past Eridu they left the dry, sparse reed beds of summer behind them. Salt glistened unbearably bright across the sun-dried delta. Anunnaki speared the struggling fish in a finger's depth of water. Kites circled overhead, looking down for carrion.*

*They came at last where the thick, brown ooze of the sluggish river exhausted itself into a turquoise sea. Low red sandbanks ran out on either side, going southwards, disappeared into the shimmering haze.*

*Nidaba stepped out on to sand, cried out as it burned her feet. Alla helped her back into the hot black boat whose tarry sides bubbled and softened under their touch.*

*'Come on,' he said. 'I'll paddle you out a little way further.'*

*'You are brave. The Anunnaki will thank you.'*

*Neither of them said what was in their minds. It was in this Gulf that they had seen the huge tidal wave come bearing down on the land out of the belly of the ocean. A monstrous green dragon spewing the shattered planking of Enki's magur boat and the Water Man himself, still clutching the last of Nin Gikuga's stout reed poles. Kur had belched him out, spat him on those sands, left him for dead. They had hymned it as a victory, but it was not. If Enki, Lord of Wisdom, had so narrowly escaped with his life, could lesser Anunnaki like Nidaba and Alla risk troubling the ocean? Had Nammu his mother joined in the attack or saved him then? Too fathomless her ways in the Deep for circumscribed, task-bearing Guardians to comprehend. And what they did not understand might destroy them.*

*Nidaba stood up, a slender reed of a Lady. A faint sea breeze stirred her pale hair. Alla back-paddled, steadying the canoe. Its sturdy wooden planking seemed frail now, over this darkening blue of depth beneath them. Creatures of the Deep, nameless to the Lord who had fished only the rivers and swamps, floated below like thunderclouds though the sky was an aching emptiness.*

'Grandmother,' *called Nidaba.* 'Great Nammu. We, your children, need your help.'

'What help can she who knows no house, no tools, give to her clever grandchildren?'

*The words had almost no form. They might have been waves washing the side of the canoe, had the sea not been glassy still, the only movement the disturbance of Alla's paddle.*

*When the two Anunnaki perceived that the swishing around them was indeed the voice from the Deep, it came as a shock. They had not expected her to be so immediate, so close. Involuntarily they both glanced back to the beach. The quivering, golden shore was not far off. The sand shelved almost imperceptibly. The shallows could not be far behind them. Yet they both knew themselves to have crossed a boundary. The canoe was afloat in an alien domain from which they could retreat now only with permission.*

'Is Enki with you?' *Nidaba pursued.* 'We've come as emissaries of the Children of An. We need your son.'

'He is asleep.'

'Will you wake him? We want his wisdom.'

'You have Enlil.'

'It's Enlil who's the cause of all our trouble.' *Alla took over.* 'He piles the work on us.'

'He makes it hot and heavy,' *Nidaba explained.* 'An and Ki did not give birth to us for this. The Earth limps and gasps because we have no leisure to take care of it.'

'Enki put the me in our hands. But we don't have the time to direct them. We're so busy looking after ourselves and serving our great Lord.'

'Poor little Sons and Daughters of An!' *The water rumbled under them. Waves shook the boat. Nidaba sat down suddenly.*

*She and Alla looked at each other, seeking help.*

*Thin wisps of cloud veiled the sun mercifully now. The canoe rocked more gently. The sea lapped its sides wordlessly.*

*'Mother Nammu? Will you help us? Can you rouse Enki?'*

*A heavy drop of water fell on her arm, struck her hot skin. She looked up, startled.*

*'It's rain,' said Alla, reaching his paddle forward as if to race for the shore, then stopping, looking at Nidaba for guidance.*

*A rip of thunder streaked across the sky. The ocean darkened. Rain fell in torrents. Alla moved quickly, pulled a felted cloak from under the short decking of the stern, threw it to Nidaba, hunched his own broad shoulders under the cloudburst. The rain poured from his hair.*

*A wave larger than usual rose from the deluge-flattened swell. A dark, glistening shape broke its surface, tossed back weedy hair. Eyes sparkled in the next flash of lightning with a grim humour.*

*'So Enlil is in trouble again, is he?'*

*'Enki!'*

*'Father of all the Waters!'*

*'Pull me aboard.'*

*They helped the dripping Water Man into the canoe. He seemed to shiver, as if shaking off some clinging past, coming awake from some long enchantment. A release, a loss? Nidaba held out the cloak for him to rub himself. He shook his head with a grin. 'You need protecting more than I do.'*

*The rain was thinning. Already a fitful sun was making the wet wood steam. Enki squatted on the bottom boards of Alla's canoe looking from Lord to Lady quizzically.*

*'So Enlil thinks I can help him out?'*

*'Help all of us,' said Nidaba peaceably. 'It's not only the workmen of Nippur who complain, shouldering baskets to build for him. You are the Lord of the* me. *You organised the Earth. You gave us each our duties. Give us the means now to carry out your will.'*

*'Give us food, give us clothes, give us worship, give us servants,' demanded Alla more roughly.*

*'Mmm.' Enki's gnarled fingers knotted on the gunwale, twisted speculatively. 'The Maker, Nudimmud, is it? The Fashioner. I cannot have the Lordship of the Earth, but I must fill it, people it.'*

*'The world will bless you.'*

*'Will it? Will it, my dear? My* lubi, *my* labi, *my pretty*

*Nidaba? Well, we shall see. You shall have what you want. See then how you like it.'*

He leaned dangerously over the rolling canoe. Alla fought to hold it from capsizing.

*'My mother!'* The sea washed along the sides, slopped over the stern. Nidaba tried to withdraw her feet but found no place to retreat. *'Listen for me in the Abzu!'* Enki's voice seemed to echo down into the abyss underwater. He turned to Alla. *'Paddle me ashore. It's obvious even to me it's the power of motherhood we need now.'*

The threshold was crossed a second time. The solid, stable shore appeared. Earth. The veil of growing things, warm-blooded animals. Nidaba looked at it all as if discovering its welcome for the first time. Alla understood more. One part of his heart he left on the trackless plain of the sea, an ache to adventure where only Enki had gone.

Enki stepped out of the canoe when they reached his Sea House in Eridu, the blue and silver Abzu.

He withdrew into the Halankug, his room for thought, and lay down on his bed. The Anunnaki waited outside in the steamy shade of the porch. Then they heard a cry, the sound of the slapping of a thigh. There was the boom of his voice rumbling in the deep well.

*'Nammu! Are you hearing me, Old Mother?'*

Nidaba reached out a trembling hand and held Alla's. Even the flies fell silent. The Abzu shook beneath them.

*'Good! Get your big, wet fingers ready. Now, pinch off for me a piece of your very first clay from the bed of the Deep. I'll detail a pair of Womb Women to help it grow. When the foetus is ready, I'll call Nin Tu, Who Gives Birth. All the Guardians of child-bearing will stand around you, bless the issue of your womb, deliver your baby. Out of the chaos of the waters shall come, as we all did, a newborn thing. But these will be helpless little creatures. They will look as we do. They will eat as we do. But they must not have our strength, our wisdom, our power, certainly not our immortality. They will need careful nursing at first.'*

He allowed Imma-en and Imma-shar to enter the Abzu and work with him over the well shaft. No one else.

At last a spring day came when the Deep moaned. All the waiting Ladies sprang to their feet. Enki called again. *'Mother! Have you got your birth chair ready? Nin Tu is here. She has brought her team.'*

*Nin Mah, who is also called Nin Tu the Birth-Giver, squatted on one side of the deep well with Nin Imma, Shuzidanna, Nin Mada and Nin Shara. Enki was on the other side, attended, not without some ribaldry, by Nin Bara, Nin Mug, Dududuh and Ereshguna.*

*The sea boomed in the hollow far under the floor.*

*'Listen,' said Dududuh. 'Her time has come. She is giving us what we asked. Lower the jar.'*

*Nin Mah lifted the ceremonial headdress of midwifery, set it over her hair.*

*Nin Shara let down an earthenware pot, pointed at the base, narrow and dark at its neck. The rope slipped over the edge of the wall like an umbilical cord. The Ladies of Birth, the Lord of Making, watched with a fascinated awe. The hollow chamber called to them.*

*'Take her. Take him.'*

*Nin Shara hauled up the jar.*

*Nin Mah rose ponderously and went over to receive it. Enki more nimbly was on the other side, peering over. Nin Mah's large, loving hands reached down and came out bearing the soft, wet, scarce-formed clay. Enki let out a long sigh, said nothing.*

*Nin Mah laid the two lumps on the cool Abzu floor. They were smaller than newborn Anunnaki. Their puckered, reddish faces were screwed and sightless, as though they did not want to see the world into which they had been lifted. Nin Mah smoothed their eyelids with her thumb. Their limbs looked weak and crooked for the heavy work that was their reason for being. Enki bent over, shaping them, moulding them. Nin Bara and Ereshguna formed their ears, their mouths, their nostrils. Nin Imma and Nin Mug touched the tiny sexual organs of each, distinguishing the female from the male. Still the children slept, as though still dreaming in that long slumber that had held Enki in his mother's abyss. Shuzidanna washed them. Nin Mada wrapped one of them lovingly in woollen bands. Enki himself swaddled the other.*

*The dim blue twilight of the Sea House darkened further. The rain-sweet air stirred. Nin Lil, Lady Air from Nippur, was standing just outside.*

*'Is it safely come? May I hold her?'*

*Slowly, proudly, Nin Mah carried the baby girl across to her.*

*'Here,' she said. 'Here's our little beauty. The first sweet heifer of her kind.' She placed the baby in Nin Lil's arms, and the Air Queen leaned over the sleeping curl of flesh, breathed into her delicate nostrils.*

*'Woman,'* she pronounced. *'Welcome!'*

*Behind her was the reluctant shadow of Enlil. He took the second child. His powerful breath stirred the blue-black wisps of hair on the pale gold scalp. He filled its small pink mouth with breath, uttered its name.*

*'Man. Created to serve the Anunnaki.'*

# Chapter Thirty-two

'You should not have kissed the captain. You are too free with your servants.'

'I like humans.'

'All the same, there is a difference of rank, of destiny.'

'I'm the Eldest Daughter of the Moon. I can do anything I like.'

'You cannot, my lady. We have more power to hurt these humans than we sometimes realise. Never forget that.'

Inanna leaned back sleepily, feeling the dampness of her hair against the pillows.

'I remember what happened after they made those first humans. Enki invited all of us to a party. It was the biggest feast I'd ever been to.'

A sadness twisted Nin Shubur's face. She leaned over and hugged Inanna fiercely, more elder sister than *sukkal* in that moment. 'Do you remember that night? Do you? Then be careful, Inanna, oh, please be careful!'

The child's eyes grew enormous. 'But I won't be like that, Nin Shubur. I won't ever hurt them. I won't! I won't!'

*The Children of An were celebrating the coming of humans. Soon these little creatures would grow and multiply and fill the Earth. They would be willing servants of the Anunnaki. They would till the fields, tend the animals, spin wool, weave cloth, build small houses for themselves and great ones for the Children of An. They would feed and clothe all their Lords and Ladies, revere them, do what they said.*

*The Anunnaki could order the building of brick ziggurats, like cool airy mountains, and retire to look out from their lofty terraces over a well-watered land. They could roam at leisure over the pastures of the steppes, walk in high cedar forests. They could bless the flocks, the palm groves, the fishing fleets, the breweries, the forges, every activity of humans and animals. The world would go well.*

Enki called all the Anunnaki to join him in a banquet to honour the Ladies of Birth. It would be the last great feast they would need to provide for themselves. He had Nin Kasi brew copious beer in her bubbling sagub vat. Ashnan opened her storehouse and barley tumbled out in abundance. Nindara brought carp and lil fish. Young Dumuzi Ama-Ushumgalanna came loaded with date clusters. For An and Enlil, Enki roasted a pure white kid. For the rest, there were beans and vegetable stew, good bread and fruit, and a very large quantity of beer.

While the evening was young, Inanna danced for them, and a mist of stars swam in the eyes of the older Children of An watching her, even the boy Dumuzi's. But no star was as bright as that little girl twirling at the edge of the water outside the Abzu. All the joy of her cherished childhood was in those carefree movements. Yet she was not so small that she could not tell how her dancing moved her audience, and smile for them.

When it was over, she went to curl up beside Nin Gal's knee. The beer jugs went round, strong emmer brew fermented with date syrup. They toasted Imma-en and Imma-shar, Nammu and Nin Tu, and all the princesses of midwifery. They all became very drunk, sprawled on the darkening terrace of the Sea House under a star-filled heaven.

Nanshe raised her goblet to Enki. 'To Nudimmud, the Fashioner!' and to Nin Mah. 'To Nin Tu, the Lady Who Gives Birth.' The brother and sister had their arms around each other, swaying and singing as they downed more beer. Nin Mah's fat face glowed with achievement and intoxication. Enki's eyes glinted with the silver of the stars and the ruby of flames. The firelight threw leaping shadows on the shifting features of his face, making him look wild and wicked. Inanna stared sleepily from between Nin Gal and Nanna, watching her grandfather with childish wonder.

Nin Mah raised her silver goblet to the moon. Her speech came slurred and exuberant. 'I can do it all! I can turn a wodge of mud into an embryo. I can call on my own mother to give birth to please the Anunnaki. I have delivered humans to you. Mortals! I have brought childbirth. I have brought death. I am giving you beauty. I am giving you ugliness. I can do anything I like!'

Enki shot her a glance fired with jealousy. 'Can you do so? These little helpless scraps of humans we've made? Would you spoil them already? Aren't they weak enough, short-lived enough *for you? Show us what more harm you think you can do to them. And I will show you the power of a wiser Lord. There's nothing you can bring to birth but I can find a place for it in my world. Nothing!'*

*He did not know how wildly he was shouting. The noisy Children of An hushed and turned their heads to listen to the pair.*

*'Kept a bit of it back,' hiccupped Nin Mah, beckoning Enki closer as though confiding a great secret. 'Some of our mother's clay from the Deep itself. Look!'*

*She wrenched the front of her sheepswool gown open and pulled out from between her mountainous breasts a fistful of damp, reddish mud.*

*'What would you like me to make?'*

*Enki said nothing. He did not forbid it. He watched her clumsy fingers with fascination as she pulled and prodded, brought a new human into existence, breathed on it, offered it her milk.*

*The first man-child and woman-child had been small but complete. All the potential they needed for their destiny was present in their limbs and features, in their infant organs. This human was monstrous. His shoulders were twisted crookedly and his fleshless arms dangled and shook uncontrollably.*

*'Is that all that's wrong?' Enki scoffed. 'His eyesight's good, isn't it? Stand him on the city watchtower to spy out strangers and shout who's coming.'*

*So she made a blind woman next, and Enki turned her into a gifted musician.*

*She made a man with twisted ankles, who could not stand, and Enki sat him down cross-legged and gave him the art of a silversmith.*

*She made a shambling moron, a giant with a huge head and a back that seemed to hunch like a third shoulder, driving his neck forward like a bull's. The Anunnaki roared with laughter.*

*'That's simple,' Enki chuckled. 'Give him the heavy stuff. Let him stand at the gateway of a governor's house with a mace in his hand to scare off unwelcome guests. He's ugly enough to frighten a lion! He can earn his bread. Is that the worst you can do?'*

*She made a creature with a weak bladder. The drunken Anunnaki belched hysterically as the thing shed urine on the paving like a frightened puppy. Enki waved his cup, grinning.*

'Send it to herd buffaloes in the swamp. He'll be up to his waist in water all day long. Who can tell what's happening underneath? The water's yellow anyway!' The crowd of Guardians rocked as if this were the greatest wit.

She made a barren woman. Enki brushed a tear from his eye, gave the creature a gift, to be a weaver in the queen's harem, or a ritual harlot in the Lady's house. 'No days off for her!' he crowed. 'No children to spoil her pretty figure.' The words came thick and slurred. ''Seasy. More?'

'This then?' Nin Mah shot a crafty look at Enki. 'What use could you or I find for one of these?'

She made a being that had no sexual organs, neither male nor female, laughed coarsely as she showed him the result. For a moment Enki looked taken aback, as though the shadow of a fear had touched him. He turned to call for more beer, downed it at a gulp.

'A eunuch,' he pronounced carefully. 'Very useful. Can do a man's work even in the women's quarters, and his master won't have a thing to worry about.'

And so the blind got song, the eunuch discretion, all the lame things of life took their livelihood from Enki. Inanna, her senses only a little hazed by wine and sleepiness, saw tragedy, tears, fortitude, courage, saw humans maimed by the will of the Anunnaki limp away to find what joy and success they could in the corners of the world.

'Your turn now,' challenged Enki. 'Have you got any of that clay left over? If I made such a thing, you wouldn't have the wit to provide for it as I did for yours, would you?'

'Lord of Wisdom! Think you're so clever? You couldn't fetch Ereshkigal out of Kur.'

Inanna gasped with fright. Why did it seem that a darkness had blackened the stars? Why did her own warm, small body feel a chill like an icy hand over her heart? Pain and fury crossed Enki's drunken face.

'You'll see! You'll see! Give it to me!'

He took the last of the wet, warm clay, balled it in his hand. He let the two Womb Women hold it only a little time. Then he wrenched it from them. He squeezed and pulled, twisted and bent. There was little of it left. The arms and legs came out spindly and misshapen. The spine curved. The head drooped on its too-thin neck. His sigh passed over its skeletal features, barely touched them. The human hardly breathed. He dropped it on the *earth between them, like a foetus born before its time. The limbs barely twitched.*

*Nin Mah snatched it up, pressed it to her copious bosom. Its grey lips moved weakly, but could not suck.*

*'Give it some beer,' she demanded. A cup was passed. The thing could not drink.*

*'Get up. Walk!' she commanded. He could not. He lay from birth, a child as infirm as an old, old man. His feeble hands could do nothing for himself or others. The world was a stage on to which he could never crawl. An* umuul. *Tears filled Nin Mah's generous eyes, ran down her cheeks. 'I can't. Poor lamb, I can't. What shall we do for him? Curse you!' She rounded on Enki. 'Curse your cleverness! Are you satisfied? Are you wise enough? Are you pleased with your victory? With yourself? You've shamed me, haven't you? Would you like me to give up the* me *of childbearing? Leave Nippur and run away from you all? I could build a house in the desert out of sight of you. I'm good for nothing now, aren't I? Not even birth!'*

*She threw the gasping cripple into Enki's arms and lurched away into the darkness to be sick.*

*The Anunnaki were silenced. Enki's eyes shone strangely. He nursed the helpless creature he had made, did not speak to him, did not weep for him, or for himself.*

*'You are right. It was not wise. It wasn't clever. We are Children of An. When we issue a challenge to each other, it is someone else who suffers.'*

*Nin Mah came back and hugged him, weeping noisily.*

*Enki's eyes glinted up at her apologetically. 'It was you he lacked. Your woman's womb, your woman's making. I'm the one who should be weeping, you old silly! What I make by myself, what all men make alone, is incomplete. If anyone ever raises a hymn to the almighty penis again, remind them of this.' He touched the* umuul's *lifeless face.*

*Inanna sat very still at the edge of the lagoon, grasping a handful of water crowfoot. The rest of the Anunnaki had forgotten her, disturbed by the revelation of their power, fearful of its limitations, its dangers, questioning their rivalries. The little Princess of the Evening Star stared at her great-grandmother, that mountain of maternity, more generous body than brain. She looked to her grandfather Enki, saw a pain she did not understand, a face too wisely disillusioned for comfort.*

*I will do more than either of them, when I'm grown up, she thought. I will love better than any Lady in the world, and I shall triumph over even the cleverest of Lords. I will!*

*And while she smiled at the thought, her small fists clenched on the flowers she held, crushing them.*

# Chapter Thirty-three

A cry shivered through the stillness of the E-Anna in the small hours of the morning. The wakeful Nin Shubur padded across the floor and laid a cool hand on the child's forehead.

'Hush,' she murmured. 'It is only a memory. Let the past lie. It is your future that matters, child.'

*Slowly the little Inanna grew in beauty, while mountains rose and rivers filled and forests grew.*

*But death cut down the humans now, as it had the beasts. The immortality of the Anunnaki was not for them. So, in the little time they had, they must cling together, make children, seize hold of all the pleasures of life, get drunk, shout and sing to drown out the sound of Nergal's wings approaching.*

*Enlil called the Council of the Anunnaki to order with a voice of storm.*

'This time, Brother Enki has overreached himself with his cleverness. All very well to make these useful humans. You have all been exclaiming in delight over this black-headed people of Sumer. You think you can take your ease now and eat the feasts they bring you, and sit with idle hands in the shady houses they have built you. But can't you see that they are getting out of hand? Did we think when we gave them childbirth that they would rush to procreate themselves as fast as this? It's because they are mortal. They are afraid that death will win and they will be wiped out from the face of the Earth. The world is teeming with them. It is not enough for them to work for us. They are busy setting up a racket all day long working at their own affairs too. And at night it is shouting and drinking and singing and lovemaking. I am surrounded by them, till I can't hear myself think! If we let it go on, they will want to lord it over the Earth themselves, and topple the Children of An from their places. I say Enki has made a terrible mistake. We do not need humans. It is time we got rid of them all.'

*An astonished silence fell over the assembly.*

*Kulla found his voice. 'What are you proposing? That we go back to being as we were? The rest of us labouring for you?'*

*'Nippur is complete,' Enlil said smoothly. 'The humans have served their purpose. Irrigation canals net the whole land of Sumer. We have plenty of oxen. Many boats have been built. Surely we can keep things running smoothly without their help, now everything is in position?'*

*'Farms don't run themselves,' Enkimdu objected. 'It's work, work, work, all year round. Sowing, watering, harvesting, repairing tools. You wouldn't know, would you?'*

*'Sheep have to be milked twice a day,' Lahar said. 'Butter churned, cheese pressed.'*

*'Cloth spun, dyed, woven,' the Weaver Uttu pointed out. 'Clothes wear out.'*

*'We are wiser than we were at first,' Enlil smiled, encouraging them. 'We have ploughs, looms, fish traps, the potter's wheel. And we have children of our own to take their turn at working. Let them enjoy the pride of their labour while they are young.'*

*'Pride of labour? I don't remember it being quite like that,' Gugun muttered. 'More like slavery!'*

*'We could thin the humans out a little,' Enki suggested. 'A famine or two?'*

*A tear sparkled on Nin Mah's face. 'Poor little mites. But there has always been giving and taking away. Winter and summer. That's the way of things.'*

*'Is it agreed then?' said An. 'We curb their pride, their noise. We reduce their numbers? Let them see that, if we would, we could wipe them from the face of the Earth with a word. Shall we humble them?'*

*'Heam. Heam,' assented the Anunnaki.*

*They loosed the plague.*

*Ensipazianna was* en *in the city of Larak, both a ruler and a priest. He made a pilgrimage and came barefooted, clad in a single garment of mourning, with dirt on his head, and bowed down in the Sea House at Eridu. He lifted his hands to Enki.*

*Enki chewed his beard, beckoned the* en *closer.*

*The advice of the Lord of Wisdom was carried all over the grieving land. In cities, in the marshes, on the high steppes, along the waterways, all praise of the Anunnaki of Sky and Earth stopped. For one intense moment in human history all the pleas of the world centred on a single Lord: Namtar, Ereshkigal's minister of Plague and Fate.*

*It worked. To the astonishment of the Anunnaki of the Above, the Below relaxed its hold. Suffering men and women stirred in their fouled beds, opened wondering eyes to daylight, came out of fever. The gasping breath of children quietened in sweet sleep. The dead were buried. The living turned to each other with grateful arms and began to procreate again.*

*Ensipazianna made generous thank offerings to the Netherworld first, and then to Enki.*

*But the humans' exuberance at their deliverance contained the seeds of a second downfall. They had learned little. They did not seem to appreciate their precarious hold on life. Soon the land was bellowing like a bull again.*

*Even Enki was irritated that his creation was so slow to learn the lesson of humility, could so readily forget. This time the punishment was drought. All the rainbearing winds and the spring floods were shut up in the heavens. There were no snows to melt and fill the arrow-swift Idiglat. The broad Buranun did not overflow its banks. The black earth dried and cracked. The ground grew brilliant with an unforgiving crust of salt.*

*Enmeduranna, en of Sippar, appealed to Enki. This time the Lord was more reluctant. But at last he sighed, 'Vanity, Enmeduranna, vanity. Never underrate it. The pride of you humans is appalling. And we made you like us, only smaller, shorter-lived. The vanity of the Anunnaki is larger than yours.'*

*Pleas thundered before Ishkur, young Lad of Storm. Feasts of many sheep and goats were brought before him. The beasts were scrawny, but the clouds they made in roasting gathered prophetically over the scorched land. Ishkur was a boy on the threshold of manhood. He could not resist their flattery. If all the inhabited Earth believed that the power of life was in his hands alone, he had to prove them right. His hand released the rain.*

*The recollection of mercy is short-lived. For the third time an ungrateful humankind grew too great for its own good. They filled the cities with their noise and self-importance. Increasingly the Children of An felt driven to withdraw amongst the cedars of the Land of the Living, or to high Angal itself, or to the far-off Island of Dilmun. But even there, echoes of the clamour of self-centred humanity profoundly disturbed them.*

*This time the furious Enlil was not to be appeased.*

*'Are the Children of An so weak we can be blown aside by a puff of steam from a food table? Is our footing so unsure we can be swept away by rivers of poured-out oil? The Below and the Above have both betrayed me. But I shall not be turned. I call*

*upon the Anunnaki to pledge themselves to shut up all the gates of life, lock them fast. Not Sky nor Earth, nor wind nor water must bring them mercy this time.'*

His eyes, defiant, met his mother's. Nin Mah stared back at him in wordless anger. Her large arms lifted from her lap, seemed to reach wider, as though she would embrace this teeming, turbulent, uncaring humanity she had brought to birth, shield it to her bosom, hold it on her strong knees. But Enlil stared her down with the force of his wild, grey eyes. She lowered her own brown pair and reddened under her dust-gold skin. Enki, watching, put out a hand towards his sister. The Anunnaki knew, Nin Mah herself acknowledged it by her silence, that she had long since ceased to rank second among the four Great Ones. Enlil her son had taken her authority from her. It was doubtful if even grave old An was now regarded as the foremost of the family.

'Time was,' muttered Gugun to Kulla, 'when we held this Council to decide what we wanted to do. Seems to me that all we come to the Ubshu-ukkinna for these days is to hear what Enlil's already decided.'

'Ssh,' said Kulla. 'He'll hear you. He's got ears everywhere.'

It seemed that this famine must be the last. All the Anunnaki were sworn to keep their hands tightly closed. Nunbarshegunu deserted the barleyfields. Ashnan stayed indoors and wept. Lahar turned her back on the cattlepens.

Vegetables withered. The corn in the storehouses dwindled, was not replenished. The flesh of the round-faced people of Sumer fell in on their bones. By the fourth year those that were left moved like cripples, their backs bent, their shoulders hunched, their steps short and wavering from weakness. Families failed. A starving mother shut her door against her famished daughter. The daughter peering through the reed blinds saw her mother measure out a miserly handful of parched food. The mother spied in her turn on her daughter's scraps. By the sixth year, more than one child who could not be fed became dreadful food on its parents' table. Those that were left had hardly the strength to breathe.

'Don't ask me!' snapped Enki as Ubartutu, en of Shuruppak, dragged his weakened feet into the Abzu where the water sobbed far down the drying well. 'It's a united front. You can't pick one of us off by flattery this time. Go away.'

But even in the heavy, hopeless heat of the seventh summer there were some humans who, with an obstinate optimism they called faith, renewed their praise, burned incense as though the

Anunnaki they served still cared. They confessed their faults, took the blame for the cruelty of life upon themselves, lifted pure hands.

It was never established how and why the carp escaped. Enki spread his hands apologetically and grinned.

'Look, I'm sorry. It was an accident. Yes, I know, I swore to withhold my goodness like the rest of you. But water is a difficult medium to contain. Fish are slippery creatures. You don't understand the problem. Utu's sun could burn for ten thousand years and he wouldn't dry up all the deep. Fish hide in mud, rivers flow underground.'

'And burst out where they have been forbidden?!' Enlil stormed. 'We said the snow-waters should not pour down the Idiglat and Buranun. The spring carp flood should not come teeming up from the marshes to meet it. Look at them!'

The channels of the Land of the Two Rivers were alive with fish. Brown, green, golden, in every size and shape, they leaped for joy in the pure, cascading water, slithered with incredible speed and agility through the brown flood sweeping the reed beds, spawned, escaped, multiplied, gave themselves up to the nets and spears and the eager hands of the last, hungry survivors. Once again humanity was saved. Enki watched. His eyes danced like the fish. When he saw how it infuriated Enlil they sparkled brighter still.

After that, it would have made little difference if mortals had changed their arrogant ways. Ambitious they were, yes, clamorous with their own desires, insufficiently grateful to the Ladies and Lords who made them, remembering to pay their respects only when they needed something, observing the Anunnaki's festivals as drunken feasts of dance and song for their own merriment instead of as the immortals' homage. All that was true, yes. Yet what angered Enlil most now was not that the swarming humans challenged the supremacy of the Children of An, but that his brother Enki had outwitted him.

It became essential to show him and all the Anunnaki who was ruler. He ordered annihilation.

Inanna, too small to take her seat yet among the Great Fifty, youngest of the Anunnaki children present, edged up to her brother Utu and peered round his elbow. Her eyes grew huge as she saw Enlil rise to his intimidating height to challenge the Council.

'Three times we have waited for the leaf to wither on the tree, for plague, and drought, and total famine to wear them away.

*Three times the order has failed because of a weakness in the Anunnaki themselves. You have allowed yourselves to be softened, flattered, cajoled. I say the day has come for us to prove that we, the immortals, are Lords. No turning back, no tender hearts. No unbrotherly treachery.'* His brilliant gaze went straight to Enki. *'This time a single sweep. They say they want rain? Right. They shall have rain! Rain such as no one has ever seen before. Night upon day, day after night, let the sluice gates of the Above be opened. We are going to wash humanity from the face of the Earth. Let there be a total flood. Not one of them must remain!'*

The Anunnaki sat mute, staring at him with nervous eyes. All the doubts, the hard questions, had been voiced time and again and answered. Only the swiftness, the finality of this was different. Kulla opened his mouth, closed it again. Haia stirred restively, said nothing. The forceful gaze of Enlil swept across them, seemed to flatten them like a field of barley before a gale. They did not know how to resist his power, his charisma.

The form was democracy, the issue autocracy. They could have outvoted him; they did not.

'Swear it!' He pressed his advantage home. 'Swear with your hands on your throats that you, the Anunnaki of the Above, will be cut off from the Land of the Living, go down to serve Ereshkigal, if you betray one word to warn the little humans how to escape.'

They lifted immortal, obedient hands. Even Enki's crabbed and clever claws reached for his throat, a little slower than the others, a little devious. But he made the oath.

'I swear, by the breath of life, by the breath of Enlil, I will tell no human.'

'Heam,' An thundered, leading them all as President. 'So be it.'

And only then, too late, the wailing broke out. Nin Tu, Lady of Birth, weeping for her creation.

Young Inanna, crouched tense on the step below the Fifty, jumped up. In her excitement she had shouted the oath with all the rest. Suddenly she realised what it meant. The feel of death was already on her small, pale hands.

'But what about Duganizi who writes poems about me and my star? Nanna's high priestess Kubatim? That nice old Abbakalla who brings me pomegranates?'

She raced up the steps, clawing at Enlil's knees, tears streaming down her face from kohl-blacked eyes.

161

*'What about Ziusudra the en of Shuruppak who dances in giddy circles for Father Enki?'*

*'Gone,'* said Enlil with deep satisfaction. *'Gone. All gone.'*

# Chapter Thirty-four

*Ziusudra was a crazy man who served a wise Lord. Enki was his personal Guardian. The city of Shuruppak belonged to Nin Lil. Its people had chosen him* en *like his father Ubartutu.*

*The interior of the temple spun: the white blaze of light beyond the rectangular door; the offering table opposite, moulded from solid clay, streaked now with blood and ashes; the pillars more massive than any tree trunk, studded with coloured heads of clay pegs in red and blue and grey, their patterns intricately zigzagging as the bark of palms; a scent of incense smoke fanned by Ziusudra's whirling garments; red eyes of lamps, like crouching jackals. Then it was gone. The temple was gone; Shuruppak was gone. Ziusudra was gone, caught up in a giddy ecstasy on the seventh cloud, nostrils full of the scent of sandalwood smoke, ears booming with the hollow earthenware drums and the voice of the immortal louder than his own heart.*

*'How can you find the energy?'* his wife scolded, skirting past him.

He did not hear her. Even if he had, he would have smiled fondly, waved a dancing hand at her, circled happily.

He was getting old for this, to dance before his Lord. But he did not care. His father Ubartutu had taught him to honour the Anunnaki no matter what, and Ziusudra was a pious son.

Just at first this morning, when the drummers were warming their instruments over the lamp flames to tighten the skins, before the first shiver and tap of the tambourines, he had put out his hand towards the new statue, the Lord of Giddiness. As he let his fingers caress the round alabaster limbs, oh, so reverently, as he bowed before the long, white face, the huge, black eyes, the lapis lazuli curls of beard, he had smiled to himself that soon he would be able to see nothing of this, nothing at all. First the slowly revolving familiarity of the temple. Then the blur of reality beginning to melt and run. Black spots, merging rapidly into total darkness. And beyond that . . .

. . . *Middle-aged limbs, that seemed to ache distantly as though they belonged to someone else. Breath like a storm. Feet hot and sore staggering wildly across cool tiles. The drum beats slowing, still continuing, supporting him. The musicians crouched in the shadows against the wall, faces turned up to him, even those who were blind. Had the immortal possessed them, as he had Ziusudra? Had they known themselves watched with the eye of love, even when they could no longer see?*

He was laughing, panting, linen soaked in swèat collapsing around his portly form. He wiped his shaved head, found himself stumbling towards the brilliant doorway.

His hands, guided by ritual habit, found the ewer of water, sprinkled the life-giving libation. His parched lips gasped the salutations before he drank. Booms like the sea thudded around the walls. He squinted dizzily. Were there other celebrants? Or was the echo of his voice magnifying the blood pounding in his ears?

Sun struck like a mace blow as he crossed the hard, white courtyard. Kuansud his wife must have gone already, a thin, dry, lined woman who had made her own lustrations in a more dignified manner. Ziusudra saw the reed house before him, the dark welcome of its door. Crept like a dog into the shade of his kennel, collapsed.

A servant was standing over him with sweet pomegranate juice, cakes of nuts and honey. Ziusudra waved them away with a feeble gesture. 'Go!' he gasped to the girl weaving her fan above him. 'Leave me.'

No drink or food or earthly luxury could match the vision, the rapture of the dance. Shreds clung to him like the sweat that had not yet cooled. He did not want to wash it from him. Like food that came from the immortals themselves, it was not to be replaced by commoner comforts.

Still, the couch was welcome, the pillow steadying under his head. His breath was slowing. The wellbeing of his soul would be enough to transcend physical pain.

Silence, profound as the sleep of noon. Brilliant points of light, like a million constellations, pricked through the interstices of the reed-mat walls. There were no steps, no voices. The drumbeats had stopped. Ziusudra felt the sudden drop of dread, as though this reed hut were the last building left in the world, and he the sole survivor.

'Reed hut!' Two words fell like raindrops out of a clear sky.

Ziusudra's eyes flew open. The reverent silence was suddenly *full of commotion. The Anunnaki themselves were assaulting his ears. His glance flew round in terror. The giddy whirl of the dance was nothing to this! Clear-edged, as in no dream or trance, a canal flashed between stone-cut quays. Huge figures, great Lords and Ladies, were stepping from proud, high-beaked canoes. Their boatmen picked up thwarts and paddles, strode grim-faced after them. The priest-king raised his eyes. He saw, not the lashed bundles of the cane poles pillaring his doorway, but the mighty walls and platforms of Enlil's own house. This was not Shuruppak, where Enlil's queen was honoured, but the most revered city of all, Nippur. His mouth gaped open.*

*'Put your ear to the wall by my left, idiot! Listen, for your life's sake.' A voice bubbling low, like water escaping over the edge of a reservoir.*

*Another rush of voices, one harsh, commanding. A great portentous 'Heam! We swear!' that shook the city walls.*

*'Did you hear that?'*

*'Yes, wise Nudimmud. No! Not all of it!'*

*'Oh reed hut, reed hut. The man is stupid. We shall lose all yet. If only there were one human in the world to take notice of the Lord of Wisdom's advice. Is that too much to ask? Listen, poor little reed hut, you will soon be gone. A flood will sweep you away, will tear the boats from their moorings, the sheep from their folds, the baskets and all who carry them from the city, the temple's foundations from their engendering clay. Man and woman will be no more.'*

*Ziusudra was shivering with terror. 'What then shall be done, Lord?'*

*The voice murmured hurriedly, that was not the crooning of doves in Ziusudra's own date groves, not the rustle of mice in the matting overhead, rapid as falling water and as hard to catch.*

*'Reed hut, reed hut. If only there were one man wise enough and pious enough to listen. If there were a human hero to build a boat. Such a boat it would need to be. The length and breadth of it should be equal, like a floating barnyard. One whole* iku *should be its floor space. One hundred and twenty cubits the height of its walls. Six decks it should have, and the whole of it sealed most thoroughly with bitumen. All life depends upon it. Into that boat should be gathered . . . Is the man listening, reed hut?'*

*'He hears, my Lord.'*

*'. . . all his family. Every small creature the Anunnaki brought forth from the burrows of the Earth. Sheep, cattle, goats.*

*Even the birds of the air that will find no trees soon to rest in.'*

*'Will the flood be as great as all that, my Lord?'*

*'Greater than mountains, little reed hut!'*

*'What shall I say, my Lord, when they ask me why I am building such a craft?'*

*'If I were that man, reed hut, I would speak the truth. The man who escapes that flood will be no friend to Enlil, who has ordered it. Such a man would be wise to flee the city of Enlil's wife. He might well say he goes to find more sympathy with his personal Guardian . . . in Eridu perhaps? The port of many great voyagers. Though Enki, of course, has sworn his oath to tell no human this.'*

*A silence fell. The reed house creaked uneasily as if a rat gnawed at the planted pillars of its seven arches. A shadow disturbed the doorway.*

*'Are you better yet? I've brought you yoghurt and cucumbers myself. Why did you send the girl away? At your age you should find a more decorous way of honouring the Anunnaki.' His wife Kuansud scolded him with a stern-faced love. He took the bowl of cool food meekly, smiled for her.*

*'You are good to me, my dear. I am more blessed than I deserve. Yes, I think I have come to my senses.'*

*'You still look very pale. Sit down and let me fan you. It's hot.' She fussed around him while he sank gratefully back to the cushions. His legs felt unsurprisingly weak.*

*'How would you like to go on a voyage, my dove? A very long voyage, to the roof of the world?' Ziusudra's voice sounded in his own ears as high-pitched and wavering as an old man's.*

*'Whatever you like, dear. Is there too much mint in the cucumbers? There's my sister in Ur. Perhaps we could call and see her on the way.'*

*'There should be room for passengers.' His words were becoming slurred. 'We might even take a few animals along.' A snore, whistling like a pig, escaped his open mouth. Kuansud caught the falling bowl, tutted as she wiped the trail of yoghurt from his lips with the hem of her scarf.*

*'Dancing! At your age. It'll be the death of you.'*

*A gold and white kitten stalked past her, sat down and lapped the cool leavings of the bowl. He purred proudly and snuggled against Ziusudra's breast to sleep with the assurance of life, a future, the confidence of the young.*

# Chapter Thirty-five

*Ziusudra's office of* en *was not intended to enrich the holder. He had been chosen by his city to manage its worldly and spiritual affairs for the prosperity of its people and the comfort of its Anunnaki. True, his father Ubartutu had been ruler before him, but the role was not always hereditary. An* en *could be removed, his office given to another. Power remained with the people.*

*Ziusudra was not richer than many another man. All that he had, all the careful gains of commerce and thrift, he spent and more. Week after week, armies of labourers toiled in the shipyards, under the eye of a master boatbuilder. If the latter had shaken his head at first over the unorthodox plans, he had now accepted them. Ziusudra might be crazy, but he was paying well. The materials were the best that could be obtained. Timber, hardwood imported from Meluhha, not the fragile reeds of the local canebrakes. A triple layer of pitch, as though bitumen would not always well up out of the ground in the desert round Sippar and Kish, there for the taking to renew a ship's caulking every summer. Who had ever heard of a ship with six wooden floors, making seven decks? Of a vessel whose beam was as broad as her length? She filled half the Buranun.*

*'You'll never steer this cow,' the boatbuilder tried to tell him. 'A child's soggy bulrush raft is going to be easier to manoeuvre than this, and a sight less dangerous for other shipping. You'll be a menace to river traffic, if they ever give you a permit to launch her.'*

*'But will it float?'*

*'Oh yes, she's seaworthy. Not that anyone in his right senses would think of taking her out to sea. I hope I make myself plain, sir. I wouldn't want the responsibility. You'd never turn her, let alone steer her back. You'd have to wait till you could run her aground on another shore. She's no handier than a barge the oxen pull up the canals, and a hundred times the size. Now, if you'd let me build you a* magilum *trader—'*

'Magilum *ships can sink in bad storms.*'

'*Oh, this'll ride out a hurricane if she has to. She won't let you down. Are you taking her far, then? The southern marshes, perhaps? Those big lakes can be treacherous when the wind gets up. Where are you heading for?*'

*All the workers within earshot turned their heads to listen.*

'*My Lord knows,*' *said Ziusudra, crossing his hands devoutly over his breast. He was not physically an adventurous man, though his mind had ranged further than most.*

'*Best hire yourself a good pilot, then, if you can find one mad enough to cast off in her. She'll be ready by autumn.*'

*Still, the job was a challenge, and fed his work force for months. Ziusudra stinted nothing. He emptied the sheepfolds, roasting meat for men accustomed to work for barley flour. In the heat of the day he slaked their thirst with wine, as if it were as common as river water.*

'*The idiot's spending as though there is no tomorrow,*' *observed his friends.*

*Kuansud, his wife, put on a brave face.* '*My husband's a very pious man. You know what he's like. He's taken a vow. I like to look at this as a kind of floating ziggurat. In honour of his Anunnaki.*'

'*Which Anunnaki? Nin Lil? Enlil?*'

'*Oh no! Though Nin Lil might have pity on us. She saved her husband and son from the Netherworld. But not Lord Enlil. He's not the one who walks on water. My husband's Guardian is the Lord of Wisdom.*'

'*Ah.*' *The ladies of Shuruppak nodded their heads knowingly.* '*Enki. That explains a lot.*' *And they went away to exchange acid expressions of sympathy over their sherbet in the summer afternoons.*

*The sky thickened, as though Enlil were drawing his brows together. Ziusudra felt the breath begin to catch in his throat as if there were not enough air. The ship was almost finished. Even while the workmen were tarring the decks and completing the cabins, he began to fill the foremost holds with stores.*

'*You're in a hurry,*' *observed his boatbuilder.* '*The water's too low for a monster like her. Wait for the spring floods, and pray they're bigger than usual.*'

'*I have no time to wait. We have no time.*'

'*I don't see the hurry.*'

'*No,*' *said Ziusudra sadly.* '*No one does.*'

*Should he have told? Should he have gathered the double*

*assembly of Shuruppak and broadcast Enki's warning? Should he have sent couriers across the land of Sumer to alert all the cities? He feared the wrath of Enlil. In Nin Lil's city he raised his tiny standard of defiance, one man's protest against the combined decision of the Children of An. The burden of silence lay heavy on his conscience. The fear of speech bound his tongue. What would Enlil do if he discovered the plan? As Enki had muttered his desperate message to the reed hut, hoping that just one man would listen and believe, so Ziusudra, under an open sky, saw his gigantic boat challenge the heavens, waited for someone else to understand and act. And all the time he watched the sky and feared. Did Enlil need to wait for the end of summer?*

*The humans laughed when it began to rain, ran out of doors into the pitted dust, held up their hands and faces. The air cooled rapidly. In a purple twilight Ziusudra, clad in a rain cape, drove with his own hands the bleating sheep up the slippery gangplanks. His warehouses on the quay were stocked with a strange but carefully selected cargo. The golden cattle of the steppe, the black water buffaloes of the marshes bellowing that they would rather have swum than sailed. Cages of frightened doves. The shy swallows had been hard to catch. The ravens swore. Fox moped. For once even Enki's gift of cunning had not enabled him to escape the snare. The gazelles, the ibex, the wild asses, fought against the ramp up this strange mountain. The conies shivered. The bats hung upside down as though dead.*

*At last the decks were packed. The soaked timbers swelled, the bitumen cooled and hardened. Even on the wide mud beds along the banks of the Buranun the great craft seemed to stir and shift as if she felt the tug of water streaming under her.*

*Last, in a silent town, its people driven unwillingly back under their roofs, Ziusudra led his wife Kuansud by one hand, his daughter Suila by the other, aboard. The yellow and white kitten, half grown now, was tucked under Suila's arm, clawing to get free.*

*Zuisudra held out his hand to the boatbuilder. 'I have paid you all I owe you.' The words caught as if on a lie.*

*'Every talent you promised, down to the last half-bushel basket of flour. And a bit more, I'd say. You're not one to drive a hard bargain. And not behindhand in paying, either.'*

*'I want to leave no debts.' Still he held the man's hand, with an unnecessary warmth. 'She's a beauty, isn't she? Thank you, Puzur-Amurri, from my heart. From my family's heart. She'll ride out . . . anything.'*

*The other man looked up reflectively. Lined eyes that had seen storms off Meluhha, ridden out the shocking afterwaves of earthquakes, threaded the life-saving channel through shark-filled shallows.*

*'Oh aye, she'll float. But will she sail? You never signed a pilot. There's been no sea trial.'*

*'Sometimes we have to trust,' said Ziusudra, beginning to withdraw his hand.*

*'Then . . . since it's my handiwork you're trusting, maybe it should be my hand on the tiller. I've served my time in rougher seas than river haulage.' The rain streamed down his upturned face.*

*A sudden warmth of joy fired Ziusudra's eyes. He clapped his other hand over Puzur-Amurri's. 'Come, man, quick! Fetch your family. Tell them to ask no questions. Hurry.'*

*'I've no family left, sir. My wife died in the last fever.'*

*Puzur-Amurri turned slowly, looked at the city half swamped under pelting clouds. 'A few more hours, sir. A few more hours and I think she'll be afloat.'*

*Still, he broke into a run when he reached the street corner.*

*As if he had been holding his fury in only to heighten the satisfaction of release, Enlil let the storm rip. All the Lords of tempest and wind and rain came to his aid. Ninurta, his favourite son, Ishkur, Kurshunaburuam. Big young men exulting in their power and terror. They slammed the Earth. They battered the face of the world. They pounded buildings of clay into mud, tore up the heavy-clustered date palms and tossed them about.*

*The Anunnaki fled hastily up the cloud-thin Stairs of the Sky to take refuge in the high calm of Angal.*

*The raging rivers ripped willow roots from the banks and babies from their mothers' arms. Boulders swept down the valleys from the mountains. Floods swirled up through the canebrakes and sped across the desert. Snakes raced before the rising waters, bullocks struggled to swim in the whirling current and were overwhelmed.*

*A single* huluppu *tree beside the Buranun was wrenched from the earth; its branches cracked.*

*Families wept and screamed from the flat roofs of their little houses. The deluge silenced them. Those that could, leaped into their tugging boats. Great wind-driven waves smashed the frail reed canoes and surged on laughing. The upper waters from the Above met the annihilation welling from the Below. They levelled out into a vast unbroken ocean.*

*The* huluppu *tree bobbed with the debris on its surge.*

*Seven days and seven nights the sluicegates of the Above stood open, the well cover of the Abzu was not replaced.*

*'It is enough,' said Enlil, flashing his smile of triumph across the heavens. 'It is all over!'*

*At his Word the rain ceased. The winds fell into the calm of death. The storm crackled along the far horizon of the ocean and stayed its hand.*

*In the hush there was only the sound of Nin Tu and all her daughters weeping. Young Inanna tore at her grandfather Enlil's skirt with tearful fury. 'Why did you do it? What do you think you've won? It isn't a victory! There's nothing left!'*

*Her mother Nin Gal, her eyes brilliant with tears like all the rest, signed to her son.*

*Utu, a young man now, had played no part in the slaughter. His sun had hidden its face behind thick clouds. Now, slowly and wearily, he got to his feet. He was aware of his grandfathers, Enlil and Enki, watching him. He lifted the cloud aside like a tent flap.*

*'Very well. Let us see what we have done.'*

*The immortals rose, disturbing – a shade reluctantly – the newfound stillness of An's realm. They came crowding round Utu, and peered down.*

*The sun was spreading over the water, like a primeval dawn. A glory of crimson and gold painted its washes across the lifting swell. In all the perfect circle of pristine water that had once been Sumer, Uri, Shubur, Martu . . . there was no island, no rock, no shore. Sedge floated sadly, dark trails of sodden mats and clothing, carcases. Even fish swilled on the surface, stunned and drowned.*

*And in the centre, one enormous boat, dwarfed to the dimensions of a snail shell in that immensity of wasteful ocean.*

# Chapter Thirty-six

*Inanna started to cry out in excitement. 'It's —!'*

*'Ssh!' Nin Gal placed a warning hand over her daughter's mouth.*

*The Anunnaki turned wondering, questioning eyes to Enlil. He sat sprawled on a couch, arms folded, with the exhausted satisfaction of his will transcendent. Their gaze swung the other way, to Enki. The Water Man cast his eyes down modestly, shrugged his shoulders.*

*The Sons and Daughters of An smiled secretly.*

*They watched in hopeful silence. The ship rocked on over the flattening waves. Aimless its motion, as if abandoned. Only the aftermath of the storm still gave it direction.*

*At last, the first, small, purposeful movement. A hatch broke open in the highest cabin. Utu leaned over and directed a sunbeam into the interior. It lit a human face.*

'Praise be!' said Ziusudra, lifting pious hands. 'To the Anunnaki be glory for ever and ever!'

'I always thought your father taught you more devotion than sense,' snorted Kuansud. 'Well, I suppose I'd better start packing if we're going to land. Help me, Suila. This place is no better than a gigantic pig's nest.'

'There is no land, my dear,' said Ziusudra, swivelling his head in every direction.

'No land? Let me look.' She pushed past him. He hoisted her skinny figure through the opening and let her see for herself.

*She slid back down to the floor of the cabin, pressed her lips together.* 'I knew I should have stayed with my sister in Ur.'

'We are only humans,' said Ziusudra humbly. 'Very probably we cannot see the whole picture. The Anunnaki perceive more than we do. Don't give up hope.' *He squeezed her bony knee. She flounced away from him.*

*The boat drifted on.*

'Is the water getting any lower?' *Kuansud wanted to know.*

'Who can tell, ma'am? What's there to measure it by?' said the boatbuilder. 'I'm blowed if I know where it all came from in the first place.' His voice was cheerful, but he turned away, a pilot who had lost all the landmarks of the world.

He busied himself with what was familiar, so as not to let his mind dwell on the enormity of their predicament. Checking the wedges that held the waterproofed timbers in place. Repairing tattered rigging in case there should ever be a reason to steer the ship. Bailing the filth of the holds where invading waves and terrified beasts had made a Netherworld as foul as Kur.

'Will you take a look at this, sir,' said Puzur-Amurri twelve hours later.

Ziusudra squinted. 'My eyesight's not what it was. But it seems . . . I think I can see between the shine of the waves something long and dull and dark.'

'It looks like the back of a gigantic water buffalo cooling herself in the heat of summer, Father,' exclaimed Suila. 'Except that there are no cattle egrets perching on her. No birds anywhere,' she added sadly, scanning the clear heavens. 'Only those in our hold.'

'Rock,' said Puzur-Amurri, staring ahead with frowning brows. 'The bones of the Earth sticking up out of the deep.'

'Land, you mean?'

'I'll put it to you this way, sir. There's been a south wind hurling us north for seven days. And faster than I've ever run before any gale. If that is rock, then it's all the land there is in the world. The tip of a mountain peak. Would you call that *land*?'

'Can we steer for it?'

'No reefs are safe, sir. But I don't see anything else. She's your ship.'

'I'll take the chance.'

'Good man,' chuckled Enki up in Angal. 'That's the spirit!'

The masts were shattered, but in the gentle breeze of autumn they rigged what patches of sail they could on splintered spars and let the wind and waves wash them slowly towards the barren ridge. Puzur-Amurri said little, heaved the tiller as well as he might. The vast, unwieldy cattle pen swivelled and swirled across the rocking surface leaving an unsteady wake in the growing moonlight. You might have thought the hands of drunken Lords were rolling it from one to the other. The Star of Morning beckoned them on.

Next day, before they reached the rock on which they had all fixed their eyes, there was a jarring shudder. Suila let out a small, frightened cry. Ziusudra's eyes flew to the pilot.

'*I reckoned as much, sir. We're mighty low in the water, with all your beasts on board.*'

'*Are we holed? Will we drown?*' demanded Kuansud.

'*No, ma'am. There'll be some damage. But we're safe enough. Unless it rains some more.*'

*Four pairs of eyes rose to the clean-washed blue of the sky, arched over them in sparkling innocence. The mountain ridge ahead showed no more than a shelf of rock, black and wet, across which the slowly-washing waves still almost met.*

'*Is that all they've left us?*' *asked Kuansud bitterly.*

'*It's a start. If you'll excuse me, my dear, I think we ought to rescue the animals from the lowest hold.*'

*They waited seven days, held fast in a great, empty stillness, across which the muffled bellows and yappings and screeches of the imprisoned animals drifted away unanswered.*

*Enlil, still ignorant of these survivors, ordered a celebration in Angal to toast his victory. There was the required song and dance, but not much merriment. Their food and drink were running low too.*

'*Perhaps there's something else,*' *suggested Suila on the seventh day. She screwed up her eyes to scan the horizon.* '*There might be other mountains, mightn't there? Trees, grass.*'

*Her father put out a gentle hand to hold hers.* '*If they exist, they're too far away for us, my dear. We're stuck fast. But, if you like, we could send messengers that need no ship.*'

'*One of the birds! Wait a moment.*' *She ran down the wooden companionway into the foul darkness of the lower decks.*

'*That hole's getting bigger. I think she's starting to break up,*' *she told them, emerging in a hurry.*

'*Don't worry, miss. I'd say there's a pretty fair chance we're on a falling tide,*' *said Puzur-Amurri, smiling grimly.*

*Suila set down the cage she carried, where a pair of doves mourned against each other's breast. She took out the female tenderly in her cupped hands. She offered the bird to her father.* '*Release her. She's longing to build a nest. I know she is. And when she's found a tree she's bound to come back and fetch her mate.*'

*He stroked his daughter's neck sadly.* '*And you, where will you build your nest? Who is there left to fill it with chicks?*'

*They set free the bird, standing on the steaming deck in the blessed warmth of the sun. She flew straight up into the blue of heaven, spread imprisoned wings, circled overhead, sped for the sunlight and the south.*

*Three days they waited, while the sun grew stronger and the moon caressed them by night. The dove returned, limping on weary wings, collapsed beside her mate with barely fluttering heart.*

*'The upper decks are drying out,' said Suila bravely. 'There must be more land somewhere.'*

*'Not in the south, I fear. Not for a long time. The gardens of Sumer were the creations of our own little floods. They are gone now.' Ziusudra looked wistfully homeward.*

*Next day, Suila released an eager swallow. Even faster than the dove, she streaked away to the west. She flew back at evening out of the scarlet and black sunset, weaving an unsteady path on dark, curved wings that could barely sustain her. Suila caught and cradled her.*

*'Brave bird. Oh poor, brave voyager. Is there nothing out there?'*

*'There is more than there was yesterday,' said Ziusudra, looking around them. He strode the big, square decks, peering over the sides. More of the height of the tarred walls was reared now out of the water, the massive bulk of the boat beginning to tilt drunkenly as the buoyancy left it. A sad and yellowed scum soured the lowest level of rock.*

*'That's not seaweed,' said Ziusudra. 'That was once grass.'*

*At the third attempt they released the raven. On strong, black wings she left for the north. She did not return.*

*'The raven feeds on carrion,' Kuansud sniffed. 'She should find plenty to satisfy her!'*

*Ziusudra kissed his wife. Then Suila kissed the raven's mate and let him go. Puzur-Amurri kissed Suila.*

*There was a grinding thump. The camels roared with rage. The cock let out an earsplitting protest. The stern of the boat fell with a crash several cubits down the slope.*

*'Time to disembark, I think,' said Ziusudra, 'and give thanks.'*

*Kuansud looked up at his face, shook her head. 'I'll never understand you!'*

*They let down the gangplanks, stumbled ashore on unsteady legs, fell down and kissed the muddy earth. They opened the doors, flung wide the cages. All the salvaged creation burst out trumpeting indignation or else was coaxed or carried into the untrustworthy daylight.*

*Some did not get far. With his own hands the* en *butchered oxen, slaughtered lavish heaps of sheep. Suila wept a little, but she was a dutiful daughter. Her heart was far away rejoicing for the ravens. Somewhere there was another land, perhaps animals . . . young men.*

*The tarred timbers from the ship blazed to the cloudless sky. From below the boat they gathered the first, sodden handfuls of juniper, cedar, myrtle to make a pungent smoke. Barley cakes they crumbled as they danced round the fire. Oil and wine were poured out on the highest peak.*

*The Anunnaki saw the smoke, smelt the boiling meat, swarmed forward like hungry flies. Bright Inanna, laughing and weeping with joy, held up a lapis lazuli necklace An had given her.*

*'Every time I wear these jewels, the colour of the Sky, I'm going to remember this awful time and what we did. Those poor little people! What would have happened to us if we had destroyed them all? We won't let Enlil have any of this banquet, will we? He doesn't deserve it. He shouldn't have made us do it.'*

*The Anunnaki came and feasted, as was their right, on the food the humans offered them.*

*The last to notice was Enlil. Drunk with the majesty of his own might as much as with the last of the Anunnaki's wine reserve, he stumbled upon the celebration.*

*'What is this? What is this? You've been hiding food from me!'*

*Then at last he let his proud eyes fall Earthwards. A wilderness of water, as though Nammu had returned and swallowed all her making. No, not quite all, a tiny point of land. A crumbling boat. A muddy, motley herd of animals and fowls floundering above the receding water level. A man with a round and shining face lifted a happy, hopeful smile to the sky. A woman, thin, a little bowed with the enormity of the task in front of her, to set right her flooded habitation. A girl stroking a damp cat and looking round her with a youthful awe. A tanned and wind-lined seaman busy breaking up his own workmanship and feeding the fire with neat, capable movements.*

*'Who are these?' Enlil roared. 'How did they escape? Who did this?'*

*The Anunnaki opened their mouths, looked at one another, shook their heads, averted their eyes from him.*

*Ninurta got up, a huge young blood, and went to his father Enlil.*

*'Who always undermines your will? Who is the traitor to the Children of An? There's only one who's got the cunning to laugh*

*behind your back. Your brother, Enki.'*

Enlil swung round in his wrath, saw the Water Man crouched on a small stool, shrugging his shoulders, spreading his hands.

'You!'

'Be reasonable, old cock. You overplayed yourself as usual. Humanity will prove more of a problem than we meant, I grant you that. But total destruction? Couldn't you have been content with a pride of lionesses to pick off the troublesome ones, a pack of raging wolves to sort out the ringleaders? We've sent famines and pestilences before. They worked for a while. We could have gone on showing patience. Just jogged their memories unpleasantly whenever they got above themselves.'

Inanna stepped out before them. The blue jewels of her collar blazed like the sky.

'I love this Earth. You nearly destroyed it all,' she said clearly. 'I hate you, Grandfather Enlil!'

The Air Lord stared down at the small, defiant figure. The Anunnaki hushed. Even Enki looked alarmed, uncertain. Nin Gal her mother was white as the moon itself. Utu moved closer; his beckoning hand advanced the heat of the heavens.

Enlil reddened. His eyes blazed at her. The girl's did not fall. His proud, unreadable face turned to seek the Sky Lord. An gazed back at him, unhelpfully silent.

'I will show you who is in control. Father An!' With an imperial gesture Enlil held out his hand. 'Come with me.'

The Daughters and Sons of An watched with held breath as the two great Lords left Angal, descended the Stairs of the Sky to the mountain range.

'No!' gasped Inanna. 'Is he going to kill them too? After all they've come through?'

Enlil's great, graceful hands spread wide, descended on the trembling shoulders of the man and woman. They fell to the ground, bowed their heads, covered their eyes.

His voice sang like the wind through treetops.

'By the life's breath of the Above, by the life's breath of Earth, by the Word of An and Enlil, I am giving you an honour no man or woman after this will know. Death shall not have you; the Netherworld shall not seize you. You shall dwell in Dilmun the Blessed, beyond the rising sun. Ziusudra and Kuansud, preserver of the small living things of the Earth, saviour of little humans. A future like our own I grant you both.'

And he breathed the wind of immortal life into their lips.

# Chapter Thirty-seven

Dawn stole up over the sleeping world of Uruk. The light of the unrisen sun crept through the trees of An's park and found the *huluppu*. The creatures of day began to stir and stretch their wings. The living things of the night retreated into dark places to wait their time.

The pearly light of morning fingered its way into the passages of the E-Anna, to Inanna's door.

*Slowly, painfully, the Earth recovered, refilled with people.*

*Enki travelled the world and blessed it. In slow-moving, ox-drawn barges on lowland canals, in chariots drawn by asses over hill passes, on swaying camels in the desert, but most of all by ship. Where he passed, he increased the flocks of sheep and goats and the herds of cattle. He enriched the fields so that the humans piled up mounds of grain. He gave them skill, he gave them art.*

*He voyaged to the mountain land of Meluhha, where the black-skinned people dwell. He gave them the large trees of the highlands, to carve thrones for their palaces. He gave them the thickest reeds, the mightiest bulls, the tallest guards carrying spears. Their* dar *birds were brilliant with carnelian-beaded necks. The sweet calls of their* haia *birds filled their houses. Gold was as plentiful as silver, and tin and bronze as common as copper.*

*To the desert Martu, nomads who build no towns, scorn houses, Enki gave hardy cattle as a gift.*

*He enriched Dilmun, the island beyond the sunrise, with grain and dates. He filled the footsteps of its children with sweet water.*

*The Magan Boat of the Nile he loaded sky-high with goods for Sumer. The* magilum *boats of Meluhha brought gold and silver. Enlil's capital of Nippur would grow rich.*

*The* Ibex of the Abzu *sailed home. It entered the broad river of the Buranun, came in sight of Eridu.*

'Look,' said Enki to his captain Nimgirsig, with a reverent love in his voice. 'Seafaring's a funny business, isn't it? When I'm at home, I can never keep still for long. I must always be planning some new expedition. But when we've been months away . . . burning sun on the water, strange lands, all the chaos of the world to knock into some kind of order . . . to come home to this!'

The rebuilt Sea House rose from the lagoon. The silver and lapis lazuli that encrusted its walls were not more bright and sparkling than the waves that lapped around its island and the foam that beaded its brick foundations. All round it, the marshes teemed with joyful life. Jewelled snakes slipped through the sedges in the welcome damp of its shadow. Carp waved their fan tails in the small gizi reeds. Sparrows chirped on the steps that led down to the water. Fish eagles soared overhead.

The landing steps were flanked with Enki's people. He carried no weapon himself, but his attendants stood ready with ceremonial spears. The abgal in their horned headdresses undulated their hands, singing sea songs of welcome. The Enkum and Ninkum, his spell-knowing officers, intoned the ritual words of thanksgiving and homecoming. The scented smoke drifted from the open portals of the Abzu. Inside was a sacred dimness.

As the cheers of greeting broke out over the water, the kara bent their backs to the oars, burst into their own fast rowing song, brought the proud-stemmed magur boat leaping like a goat across the lagoon, landed in Eridu.

There were human attendants now. The linen-clad incantation priests appeared at the head of the steps. A moan of awe swept over the ranks below, their faces turned seaward. Enki himself, tearing his hungry eyes from the Abzu, revolved slowly.

Behind him, fifty jade and sea-blue heads had risen from the waves. Water cascaded from their scaled and shining necks. Their sharp-toothed mouths seemed to grin. Their eyes flashed sunlight, lidded over with the darkness of the deep. Fifty lahama dragons of the sea did homage to Enki. He raised his ram-headed serpent staff in acknowledgement and stepped ashore.

'Well, how is it going?' he asked Nanshe.

'There is so much to do. They are multiplying in their thousands. And they need to be taught every single thing again. Sumer is a wonderful land. We love its black-headed people. But we Guardians seem to be falling over ourselves sorting out who should be helping them with what.'

*Nindara was busy in the marshes. The nets were full of fish, the traps of turtles, the snares of birds, the baskets of crabs.*

*'Who is in charge of the sea fishing?' he asked.*

*'No one, my lord,' replied Nanshe. 'We have always felt . . . You alone of all the Anunnaki travel the highway of the deep in the Ibex of the Abzu. Beyond your mother, who else is fit to guide humans on the sea road?'*

*'You,' said Enki, with a twinkle in his eye. 'You, my Lady Judge. If you can test the righteousness of human hearts and read the intentions of the Children of An, you can listen to the winds, watch the constellations, scan the secrets of the deep. You shall be more than the Lady of the Sirara that flows past Nina. I make you my Sea Queen.'*

*The translucent fish scales of her dress flushed pink with gratitude as he kissed her.*

*In the central ploughlands, the new farmers yoked oxen, drove furrows through the irrigated soil, stacked mottled barley on the threshing floor, repaired canals. Enkimdu, the Good Farmer, grinned at Enki, raised a hand from the plough he was teaching a boy to guide.*

*The harvest was in, the chequered* innaba *grain made patterns on the barn floors, the cats played games with vermin. Ashnan came out to meet him. The sunlight threw dappled shadows through the reed blinds over her. Her smiling face might have been smeared with honey. She offered him bread, sweet, new-baked.*

*Kulla was happy overseeing the humans in the brick fields. He raised his head and laughed. 'Look at them all! Doesn't it do your heart good to let them have the blisters and backache?'*

*The pickaxes struck the soil like snakes devouring corpses, rooted up the plentiful clay. Water softened it. The brickmakers pressed it into moulds, set them out in vast rows to dry in the sun, or fired them for greater hardness in the raging kilns.*

*Where the cool winds blew over the steppe the sheep grew plump and fertile, the vegetation was sweetly scented. Young, mortal men wandered across the plains watching their animals, lifted their eyes to the traverse of clouds, played reed pipes. At night the sheep stalls were musical with the bleat of ewes and lambs, the dairies clean and purified, the cream and milk running rich into the earthenware pots. Enki clapped his hand on the Shepherd Dumuzi's shoulder. 'It is good, lad. It is very good!'*

*The human shepherds' sisters wove the wool. Thread spun*

*from the distaffs at their sides as they walked and gossiped. The cloth on their looms wove ever more intricate patterns. Inside one weaving shed a modest Lady raised her eyes to meet Enki's. Her face was shadowed from him.*

*'My father.'*

*Enki halted, screwed up his eyes in the dimness of the interior. He looked startled and just a shade abashed. But the merry glint was soon back in his eyes. 'So, little Uttu, you've got them weaving. They should soon be knotting a web that will catch them a husband fit for a Daughter of An.'*

*'A husband, Father?'*

*'Ah, yes ... well ... Weave and flow. Spin and splash. In and out. Water and wool. We're a devious family. In and out of each other all the time. Now you catch us, now you don't.'*

*'Yes, my lord.' She bent her head over the pattern she was teaching two young maidens. Her cheeks were blushing.*

*When it was all in motion, Enki went out into the night, shouted to the greatest of the Anunnaki, 'The land is yours, my brothers and sisters! Come back and bless the cities. Enlil has Nippur. I have Eridu with my Abzu. An himself has come down to settle again on the high hill of Uruk.*

*'Let Dumuzi and Nin Sun, who fill the dining hall of the E-Anna with butter and milk, have their own place too in that district of Kullab. You, Nanna and Nin Gal. Come down from your mountain. Take Ur for your City of the Moon. Tell them to build a ziggurat to the stars. Utu, come out of that* hashur *forest where you're hiding your face. Blaze on Sippar for us, lad.'*

*The mountain folk of Aratta wept when their favourite Inanna left them for the plain.*

*The land of Sumer Enki blessed above all. Here the Guardians of the* me *condescended to take up their homes again. Sumer became a country filled with lasting light, growing in wisdom and prosperity with each sunrise and sunset.*

*But Enki led Enlil up to the peak of the Land of the Living, under the seven great cedars Enlil had planted there. He seized his brother's arm and pointed out over the shimmering lands of civilisation.*

*'Look down. Do you see them all? Our creation? Happy and prosperous. Never again! Never again shall you have reason to fear these humans are becoming too proud, that they will rival the Anunnaki's power and rule the Earth.'*

*He raised his voice to a wild shout.*

'I call the lion and wolf out of the wilderness to run through your farms. I summon the snake and scorpion into the yards where your children play . . . '

The tears were raining down his cheeks now.

'I am twisting the tongues of all the nations so that your people can no longer understand each other's speech. From now on, there will be suspicion between you; there will be strife.'

He spoke the Spell of Enki.

'I give you war!'

# Chapter Thirty-eight

*Only one Daughter of An was discontented with her lot. A child too small to be taken seriously. Inanna, younger sister of the Sun Lord.*

*An infant fury raged in her. She wandered through the newly-furbished palace of Ur. She tore the* ub *lyre and the* mesi *timbrel out of the hands of the singers and smashed them. Her angry fingers untwisted the close-spun skeins of wool, tore it to shreds or knotted it into tangles. She pulled the half-finished cloth from the loom, plunged patiently patterned lengths into the darkest dyes she could find. Listened to the* arabu *bird caged in the garden croak out its oracular warning, screamed back an ominous interpretation.*

*'They will all be sorry!'*

*Nin Gal came in, her face still laughing from conversation with Enki and found the devastation.*

*'Inanna! What is this? Who has done it?' Then she saw her mute, mutinous daughter, hands clenched at her sides. 'Where is your nurse? Where is Lama?'*

*She caught sight of the* tigi *singers cowering by the wall, saw the marks on their faces where Inanna had slapped them.*

*'Leave us!' she commanded swiftly.*

*The ruined hall was empty. Then the mother ran to Inanna. 'Child! What is this? What is wrong?'*

*She wrapped her in loving arms, held her tight to her breast. Inanna burst into tears, clutched her wildly, hiccupped, 'They . . . they've got everything. Utu's got the Sun and now Grandfather's given him Righteousness and Justice as well. I've got nothing!'*

*Nin Gal struggled not to smile. 'Oh, little one. You have the Evening Star, the Morning Star. The workmen lift their beakers of beer to your planet when it signals the end of labour. You promise the bliss of cool day before your brother's sun is up. You are more loved than any other young*

Lady. What more should you want?'

'I want to make people do things. I want the sort of power that Enki has.'

'Ssh!' Nin Gal scolded more sharply. 'You don't know what you're asking, child. Enki is the Lord of Wisdom. We all took our me from him. I know he has plans for you . . . when you are older.'

'I want some now!'

'When the moon is full . . . a woman will meet her beloved.' Nin Gal's voice grew warm with memory. 'Who will guide their love? Who will watch over their coming together? Wait just a little, Inanna. Shine for their loving.'

'Nin Mah makes and unmakes. Life and death. So does Enki. And Enlil. And Ishkur with his storms and Ninurta with his thunder. So do all the great Lords. Even Father. He goes away every month, doesn't he? Down into the dark. If you give me Lovemaking, I want something else, too. I want the whole of life. What is the opposite of love?'

Nin Gal put her daughter a little away from her, stared at her small face. She turned slightly pale. 'I will . . . I will talk to Enki. To An. Wait here.'

Inanna waited alone in the empty, wrecked room of the palace. She was not used to being alone. She wanted to call for the singers to come and play a cheerful dance for her, but the instruments were broken. She saw her nurse, half hidden beyond the door, and called to her.

'Lama!'

The woman came stumbling into the room, bobbed a frightened curtsey.

'Oh, it's all right!' Inanna stamped her foot. 'I'm not going to hit you again. I expect I'm in enough trouble already. Pick up this mess.'

'No. Leave it!'

The nurse's hurried hands had hardly begun to sort the damage. Her face grew more frightened still. She backed to the wall, bowing her head.

Enki was standing in the farther doorway, with An himself towering behind.

'Did you do this?' the Water Man asked Inanna sharply.

'Yes.' Her voice was defiant.

'Why?'

'Because it isn't fair! You've given everything to the rest and kept nothing worth having for me.'

'What have I given away that the smallest of the Daughters of An thinks should have been hers?'

'Everything!' She stamped her foot again, tried to tear her face with her small, soft nails. 'Everything that matters! My mother says you've promised me Courtship and Love when I'm older. But you've already made Nin Tu the Midwife of the World. She'll be the one who gives babies, with her headdress, and her lapis *sila* vessel, and her *ala* bowl to receive the afterbirth.'

'Inanna!' Her mother sounded shocked.

'You are well-informed, for a maiden so small.' Enki raised his eyebrows.

'I watch. I listen.'

'Where you have been forbidden, child!' Nin Gal reproved.

'And Nin Isinna.' Inanna coloured provocatively. 'I know she's been given the *unu*, hasn't she? She's the hierodule of Father An. His sacred harlot. When he's not there, she can speak his will and rock the Sky.'

A rumble of indignation came from the oldest Lord of all. White-haired An seemed to fill the colonnade beyond the chamber with his angry person. Nin Gal moved quickly and soothingly to his side. 'Father An, my apologies. The child will be disciplined.'

Enki could scarcely conceal his laughter. 'And what else do you envy, my child? You begin to amuse me.'

Inanna shot a glance at him through lowered eyelashes. She mistrusted his merriment. She muttered less boldly, 'Nin Mug's been given the Gold Chisel and the Silver Hammer. You've given her the skill of precious metalwork. Every human *en* who puts on a tiara or a diadem will take it from her hand. Nidaba's your Scribe. She's got the Measuring Rod, the lapis lazuli Line over her arm. It's up to her to fix boundaries, borders. That's power over estates and kingdoms. And Nanshe . . . you've given her . . .' Rage seemed to boil up like bitumen over a fire. 'You've given her the Sea!' Her voice ended on a squeak. Her eyes were starry brilliant with tears of disappointment.

'Is that so very important?'

'You know it is. You went there. Following Kur. Following . . .'

'Ereshkigal.'

'You were the only one!' Inanna wailed. 'Nanshe had Judgment and the Fishing of the Sirara already. And now you've made her Fishery Inspector of the Sea too! It isn't fair!'

A silence fell over the older Guardians. Enki's mobile face registered too many emotions to be easily read. Nin Gal looked *grieved and ashamed. Unspoken anger still breathed from An. It was he who broke the stillness at last, with a rare, decisive, not-to-be-argued-with command.*

'Bring her before the Council in the Ubshu-ukkinna. She must be taught respect.' *He left them on a blast of chill air.*

*Enki made a face, held out a grandfatherly hand to Inanna.* 'There. You've upset him, my dear. That business about the hierodule . . . '

'It's true, isn't it?' *She gripped his hand, glad of its clever strength over hers.*

'Yes, but I am afraid few of us Anunnaki are well versed yet in the arts of love. Childbirth, yes. Nin Tu has seen to that. But for our mating . . . ' *He shrugged his shoulders apologetically.* 'Rape and seduction has been our history. Well, not entirely. An once loved Nin Mah, long ago when she was Ki. And now your mother and Nanna . . . ' *Nin Gal blushed, warm and womanly. Enki put one arm round his daughter and kissed her.* 'Look at her, Inanna. Learn what real love is. And when you come to your own flowering, bless all lovers.'

*Inanna pouted.* 'And will there be something else besides that? I haven't seen any boy I like yet.'

*He put his other arm around her.* 'Oh dear. We must see about that. I give you . . . the garment Might of the Young Lad. I give you the crook and staff of Shepherdship!'

'But Dumuzi's got those already.'

'Who cares? Let's give her Dumuzi as well, shall we? Will that satisfy you?'

'I'd rather have a warrior for a husband, like Uncle Ninurta.'

'Then I give you Battle, Onslaught, Oracles of War. You shall break the indestructible, you shall destroy the imperishable, you shall make us all sing to the timbrel of lament.'

'Hush, Father,' *begged Nin Gal.* 'Are you drunk?'

'No,' *said Enki, looking suddenly very weary and letting the woman and the girl both go.* 'Not drunk. Too sober and wise for my own comfort. I have seen what harm the pride of great Lords and Ladies can do.'

*He left them abruptly. He turned in the doorway and looked keenly at Inanna.* 'And I'm afraid it's not up to me what happens to you now, young lady. An is angry.'

*Then he was gone, as a splash of water on the tiles vanishes in the sun.*

# Chapter Thirty-nine

*Inanna was summoned to appear before the Fifty.*

*They sailed upstream, through the great lake to Uruk, and on up the river to Nippur.*

*As they wound through the steppe, beyond the Sky House of Uruk, Nin Gal turned, startled, and looked about her.*

*'The river has changed its course since the Flood. The tree! Our* huluppu *tree! The one we . . . slept under.' Blushing now. 'Where is it?'*

*Nanna's arm went round her. 'Who knows? Stranded in the dry desert? Washed out to sea? Poor* huluppu.*'*

*She smiled up at him. 'I hope it's safe somewhere. It deserved a better fate. That was good loving, wasn't it?'*

*'Like all your love.'*

*As the boat worked upstream, Inanna stared back at the wilderness of the Edin. Young willows clung to the bank of the altered river. Thorn bushes dotted the sand beyond. No sign of a* huluppu *tree. Where was the gift of the Netherworld planted by Enki? Washed away? Trapped under the bank of the river, waiting for a lesser flood to release it? The desert air behind her shimmered, like the flutter of wings, like the slither of serpents, like the flicker of dancing limbs.*

*At Nippur they tied up alongside the other boats and found their own house in the city. Assemblies were festive occasions, reunions of cousins and uncles and aunts not seen for a long time.*

*Then the feasting was suddenly over. Now the Great Four were seated on the dais in the Ubshu-ukkinna corner of the huge courtyard. The Seven were ranged below them. Nanshe and Haia took their places among the judges. Nidaba sat ready with tablet and stylus. With a pang of surprise and jealousy, Inanna saw Utu take his place on the lowest step beside Nidaba. Utu, her domineering brother, already learning to be a judge!*

*She squatted beside her mother, scared and defiant now.*

*But she was disconcerted to find that the rebellion of little*

*Inanna was not the most important item on the Anunnaki's agenda.*

*The arguments roared over her head, Emesh and Enten disputing over the Lordships of Summer and Winter. She looked around at them all in their finery. The Four, the Seven, the Fifty, and all the lesser Guardians gathered to listen. Rank was separating them now. It wasn't just her, this desire to be greater than others.*

*At last, when she had stopped expecting it, it was her turn.*

*She was made to stand out in front of them all, like a naughty, scolded child. She bit her lip and gazed down at the dusty clay of the floor. It would be prudent not to look directly at those powerful faces on the highest dais: An, Nin Mah, Enlil, Enki. Though she was only a child, it was important to keep what little dignity she had. If she saw that massive severity, the disapproval of all her family, she might not be able to keep her face set and defiant. She might not be able to stop the catch of a sob from rising in her throat.*

*It hadn't been fair. The world was still growing. Utu had been given a brighter light to guard than their father. Just because she was the youngest of them here, surely she ought to have a greater future than all the others before her?*

*As she listened to Nin Gal apologetically laying bare the devastation of Inanna's anger, she could not help letting her eyes creep sideways and up to Nin Mah, sitting next to An. She saw the Exalted Lady's broad, brown face, furrowed as if in indignation. Old hearsay stirred. Long, long ago, Ki had let Enlil take her power away. And now newer stories of Nin Isinna, hierodule of An, warming the old man's feet, danced at the edges of Inanna's brain.*

*Can't you see, Great-grandmother? This is for you as well, Inanna begged silently. I won't let them humble me like that.*

*The court had fallen silent. She found, startlingly, that they were all waiting for her.*

*'Well, Inanna?' prompted An, severe and distant. 'What have you to say for yourself?'*

*'It wasn't fair!' was all she could gasp.*

*She was sent away to wait, as Enlil had once waited for a more momentous verdict, walking in the smaller court of the Kiur, out of earshot. She was frightened now. The night seemed darker, the possible punishments more threatening because she had no idea what they might be.*

*'Why don't they come? What are they saying about me behind*

*my back?'* she demanded of her nurse.

*'You'll find out soon enough, little Lady,'* Lama told her.

*Eunuchs stood like statues at the entrance to the Kiur. She must not let them see she was afraid.*

*At last the slap of hurrying feet. A boy came round the corner. The final insult. They had sent Utu to fetch her! But no, this was a different lad. She knew him only slightly. The curly-haired Dumuzi, Enki's son.*

*'The Anunnaki are ready to give you their verdict, Lady.'* He bowed formally, self-conscious with the importance of his duty.

*She found she could not move. Lama pushed her forward.*

*'What . . . what are they going to do to me?'* she asked.

*'It's not for me to say, Lady.'* Then he took her arm and grinned. *'Don't look so scared. It's not as bad as all that.'*

*'I'm not scared!'* The words came quick and sharp. All the same, the feel of his hand round her arm was comforting. She looked at him. He seemed quite friendly, for a boy, and he had called her 'Lady'.

*She let him lead her back to the E-Kur.*

*An himself pronounced the decision of the assembled Fifty. Inanna, standing in the shadowed corner of Ubshu-ukkinna, heard the words like the far-off beat of waves in her ears. She had not been able to imagine what she expected as the punishment for her rebellion. She had not thought it would be such an important thing.*

*'You shamed us all when you made that destruction in your parents' E-Kishnugal. We destined you to love, to bless. You attacked without reason those lower than yourself, the humans you say you love: your nurse, the household musicians. And you sought to rival those for whom you should have had only reverence. You were born of a great lineage. When we spoke your name at your birth we decreed a bright future for you. But you are not content with what we gave. Those who seek greatness, Inanna, will have to live worthily of it, as others of the Anunnaki have had to learn before you.'* All eyes studiously kept from looking at Enlil. *'You have been a spoiled child too long. What your parents' love has failed to do for you, a great-grandfather's discipline must achieve instead. You will come to live with me in Uruk, and I will see that you learn what it truly means to be a Daughter of An.'*

*Inanna waited. Surely there was something more? Some painful penance, some unpleasant punishment. It seemed, after all, a small, bleak thing to leave the Moon City of Ur and live in* the Sky House of E-Anna. Then she saw Nidaba folding her tablet away, and the loss hit her. No loving, laughing Nin Gal. No Nanna rocking her in his arms. Not even Utu to fight with. She turned to her mother, tears already springing to her eyes. She had always had love around her. She had always been treasured.

But as Nin Gal's arms reached out to enfold her, An's hand stayed her.

'Let us begin your education here, young lady. If you are to become that great queen you evidently think you should be, then you must have your own sukkal-mah. Our sukkal is more than a servant, the chief minister of our court. He is the guide who walks before us; she is the word of wisdom in our ear. You, Inanna, will need a very knowing guide; you require a far-seeing wisdom. This assembly has appointed for your sukkal the Lady of the East, Nin Shubur.'

The name meant nothing. Nor the face of the slight young woman stepping out of the ranks of the Anunnaki. The two-horned headdress of a minor Lady, and yet those nearby moved aside for her with respect. Enki was leaning forward to watch with a particular interest.

Feathers on her wrist. A pair of cunningly carved serpents twining around her small silver staff. A shaman.

For a few moments, the two looked at each other. Nin Shubur's high-boned face betrayed less than Inanna's childish one. Then Nin Shubur was walking in front of her, leading her away, just like Enlil's own sukkal Nusku. Inanna bowed to the Great Four, then straightened her back.

Inanna in Uruk. Inanna living in the E-Anna, with old, cold, lonely Father An.

She smiled at him now, making her eyes brilliant as stars. That grey, lined, cloudy face seemed as withdrawn from her as the high cirrus cloud that streaks the paling sky of evening before the constellations prick through. She softened every muscle of her tight, rebellious face, curved her lips for him. She was making herself glow like a small opening poppy, just for him. She must see if she had any power over Father An.

She never moved one step from the lowest platform of the dais where she was standing below the seven judges. But the smile bounded for her up the intervening steps, across the dais, seemed to throw her into An's surprised and empty arms.

The old face stirred. The blue-grey eyes fired with sudden light.

Something of the answering gleam of hope in Inanna's small face warned Enlil. He started to his feet forcefully.

*'Do you laugh, maid Inanna? When the Great Four themselves pronounce sentence on you? It is not for a joke that we are sending you to Uruk! One day you will be old enough to take a husband. You must have learnt to be modest, obedient, dutiful, before then.'*

*'Oh, I will, my lord,' Inanna said in a sweet, humble voice.*

*All the same, she hesitated to try the power of that smile on Enlil. The result might be rather frightening.*

*Better not to catch Enki's knowing eyes either.*

*She turned, and followed Nin Shubur with what dignity she could.*

*It was not easy to pass all the ranks of the Daughters of An, especially the ones she had vented her jealousy on.*

*Nin Mug was here in front of her. Inanna pouted. Had Nin Mug deliberately chosen that beaded headdress, tinkling with golden flowers and carnelian-eyed gazelles that seemed to dance when she moved even slightly? Her breast glittered with a silver and* nar *stone frontal. Her wrists and ankles sported multiple rings as if to display every facet of the metalworker's art. I want regalia like that one day, vowed Inanna. I will have a crown to rival the stars. I will have a sacred breastplate. I will have rings of royalty on my hands. I will hold the measuring rod.*

*Nin Isinna's presence came to her first as a waft of perfume, musk and roses from her neck, sandalwood from her thighs. The bitch-headed Lady. The fine hair of her face shone. Kohl etched her eyes like the lines of bitumen bonding bricks. Her curled coiffure gleamed with fresh oil. Below the neck, the skin of her woman's body was honeyed. The cloudy net of her garments scarcely veiled her limbs. One breast showed, pointed, firm. Inanna felt the childish anger tighten like a whiplash again. Her own small, unformed figure seemed like a reproach. Not yet! Not yet! it seemed to say.*

*Nin Isinna smiled. She knows, Inanna thought in fury. Always there is someone who has been given more than I have. She saw how I smiled at An, and she is not alarmed. She knows I am frightened of him, so she thinks there is no need to be jealous of me. She thinks nothing can steal An away from his hierodule.*

*Well, she will see, Inanna thought. They don't know me yet.*

# Chapter Forty

'Is it still there? Is it all right?' Inanna jumped out of bed. Morning light was already showing beyond the door.

'Hold still!' Nin Shubur came gliding in, laughing. 'There was more rain in the night. But it was not like the great storm. The water is dropping already.'

'Not the flood. My tree! My *huluppu* tree!'

'We put our spells on it, for life and safety, you and I. The rain won't have harmed it. Eat your breakfast and we can go and see.'

All down the hill, the gardens dripped with goodness. Inanna ran towards the *huluppu*, shaking the raindrops from the leaves she passed, so that the tree seemed to dance for her through a mist of tears. It looked less ugly and frightening this morning, only hurt and immature as herself.

'It's better already today,' she cried.

More leaves had uncurled in the night and the rising sun caught their delicate trellis in a halo of gold. The trunk was drying silver-grey, still wet, but whole. The roots dug firmly into the fresh-turned earth.

Inanna clapped her hands. 'We must put a fence round it to keep it safe. I'll come and water it every day in summer. I'll sing to it and love it. It's going to grow to be the best tree in the whole world!'

She circled it, singing.

Small birds sang in the broken branches.

Moths displayed their wings against the bark of its trunk.

Red garden worms burrowed around its roots.

'What have you saved it for, Lady Inanna?'

The Princess of the Morning and Evening Star put her arms round the trunk and hugged it. 'Tree! My *huluppu* tree. We're going to grow together, you and I. And when we're both grown-up, do you know what I'm going to do? I'm going to cut you down and make you into the things I want more than anything else.

'Dear *huluppu*, you're going to be the throne of the greatest Queen of Sky and Earth . . . and the most wonderful bed in the world, for my wedding night!'

# BOOK TWO

# A Bed For The Bride

# Chapter Forty-one

Inanna leaned over the parapet of the E-Anna. A mass of young human bodies was wrestling on the parade ground below her. From this height, they were like squirming tadpoles. Dust was flung up by their splayed, shifting feet. Occasionally there was a cry as a young man was flung on his back.

A huge lad, and still not full-grown, was hurling his companions to the ground in all directions. A single leopardskin was knotted round his hips, barely covering his genitals as he swung. Sun gleamed on his muscular oiled body. His muscles stood out like boulders. His hair was knotted back so that it whipped like a charioteer's lash.

'Gilgamesh! Gilgamesh!' Inanna hardly knew she was shouting it aloud.

The girls of her household looked at each other and smiled. They took up the call. 'Gilgamesh! Go on! Gilgamesh!'

A last body went spinning through the air and struck the hard-packed earth.

Inanna burst out laughing and clapping, and all the girls with her.

Gilgamesh seemed to sense her watching. He swung, legs widely planted, hands on hips, grinning up at her, demanding admiration.

Inanna caught her breath and backed away. Too late. The young giant was beaming hugely. Sweat glistened on his reddened face as he kissed his hands to her. His voice rose, still strong in spite of distance and exertion.

'Lady Inanna! That victory was for you!'

All the beaten young men below turned up their faces then, flushed and exhausted. But they smiled when they saw her watching high above them, their Anunnaki, the Young Lady of the Palace. Their arms rose in a salute.

Laughing breathlessly herself, Inanna snatched a handful

of oleander blossoms from the bushes behind her and threw them out into the still air. They fluttered lazily downwards. The young humans, with Gilgamesh at the forefront, leaped for the delicate petals, but they drifted tantalisingly out of reach.

'He hardly seems like a human,' Inanna sighed.

Nin Shubur snorted. 'The son of a mortal and an Anunnaki Lady! Nin Sun, the Wild Cow Woman . . . My lady, your great-grandfather wants to speak with you.'

'Just a minute.' Inanna's voice floated across the terrace where she was now leaning dangerously far out watching the girdled or naked men going back to their exercises.

'He is waiting now.'

Inanna straightened up and came in from the sunshine, walking a little more languidly than the summons required. She was growing tall and graceful. Her figure was beginning to fill out in womanly curves.

'Is my hair tidy? Should I have it combed up in a "stag"?' she asked, seating herself on her inlaid boxwood stool. 'Fetch my kohl and green eye-paint.'

A slave girl moved to obey; Nin Shubur folded her arms across her breast. 'Lord Enlil has been with him.' Her tone was less deferential than her posture.

Inanna's face stiffened. The confident smile of the young woman who knew herself to be the old man's pet vanished.

'Were they talking about me?'

'I am not one who listens at doors, my lady. Surely Lord An will tell you himself when you go to him.'

Inanna played with the handle of her mirror, but her eyes were watching the *sukkal*'s face. Nin Shubur's expression showed, as it usually did, a glint of humour and affection. The woman was no more than average stature, yet Inanna felt that she was like the doorpost of a fine reed house – a bundle of the tallest, strongest canes, bound together into a pillar, its base set immovably into a foundation hole, its tapering upper ends coiled against the sky. A symbol of stability, welcome, shelter.

Meekly now, more fitting to the child she had so recently been, Inanna asked, 'Should I wear my turban?'

Nin Shubur laughed outright. 'Will you play the sedate lady for Enlil, and not my Lord An's hierodule with your hair loose and curly?'

'How do I know what any of them wants me to be?' Inanna

burst out. 'I have had no life of my own yet.'

Nin Shubur ran to her, cradled the fragrant blue-black hair against her body.

'There, there. Don't cry; you will smudge your kohl. Wear this.'

She set a pleated cap of fine linen on her charge's hair. The gauzy cloth, with a frill around it, haloed Inanna's face like a misty ring round the moon. Nin Shubur sighed and smiled.

'It doesn't matter what you wear, child. You are one of those who carry your treasure chest in your face, and the finest scented trees from the forest might have been grown to shape your body.'

'I'm *not* a child now,' Inanna pouted.

'No.' A brief hug, harder than was strictly proper for a *sukkal* to her mistress. 'And those that should have guarded you did not allow you to remain a child as long as you might.'

Inanna reddened and stood up, allowing Nin Shubur to tweak the drapes of her simple gown into symmetrical folds.

'Let me go and see what they have decided for me this time.'

Nin Shubur led the way ceremoniously. E-Anna was now a vast and quiet complex of buildings. There were fewer males in evidence than was normal in the palace of a great Lord, more pretty women, though there were plenty of virile young humans outside in the city. Inanna's glance flashed at the coloured dresses whisking away through doorways, the tinkle of jewellery, the wake of perfume on the disturbed air. She heard a hint of laughter behind covering hands.

Soft-footed eunuchs accompanied them across cool tiles, fanned heavy air, opened decorative doors.

An was sitting in a private courtyard under the shade of a fig tree. He smiled when he saw her, his old, lined, indulgent face breaking out into spontaneous pleasure at the sight of his favourite great-granddaughter. She was dressed in white, so simple, so fresh, so virginal. Through the cool decorum of her clothes he could see she promised so much more.

Inanna felt an immense relief. Enlil was not there. For all her childish bloodthirstiness, her admiration for her warlike uncle Ninurta, Enlil's Flood had terrified her. Since then, time had gone slowly for the Anunnaki, many generations for humankind. Yet even now, with the sun scorching the desert, the clay houses rebuilt, the black-headed Sumerians filling the land again and serving the Children of An, she could no longer look at it all with the same eyes. It had been washed away once at the Word of Enlil. They could lose it again. Nothing was safe, nothing was sure, nothing was so precious it could not be threatened.

An motioned to the pile of brightly-woven cushions on the ground by his couch. Inanna sank on it and turned up her smiling face to meet his.

He looked ill at ease. His hands played with the bull's-head finials of the couch ends.

'My daughter,' he said. 'My *lubi*, my *labi*.'

She put her hand on his knee, felt the sinews quiver. But he did not draw her closer as he usually did.

'Honeyed mouth of your mother, I have been talking to Enlil.'

'Lord Enlil is wise,' said Inanna carefully.

'It has come to his ears that you take a great deal of interest in the humans of Uruk.'

Inanna looked puzzled, genuinely so. 'But don't you too, Great-grandfather? Ever since the Flood, when I held up my lapis lazuli necklace as a sign that the Sky would always be blue over them, we have smiled on the black-headed people of Sumer. Enmerkar has beautified your E-Anna. Lugalbanda enlarged this district of Kullab, with houses for all our family—'

'And Gilgamesh is Lugalbanda's heir. A human. Is it fitting for a Lady of the Stars to lean over the E-Anna wall and throw him flowers?'

'Gilgamesh is my friend. He calls himself my champion.'

'Gilgamesh is a mortal.'

'His mother was Nin Sun, the Wild Cow Lady!'

'His father was Lugalbanda, the *en*. He is not one of us.'

'He's Utu's friend, Ishkur's friend. Why shouldn't he be my friend, too?'

'Inanna, child! Be still. These things are hard to say. You have only just come into your womanhood. There is a contract. The rite of marriage. Our male *ens* lie with the high priestess, as their Lady. Female *ens* with their high priest, as the Lord. That must be done, for the fertility of the soil, for the increase of crops and herds, for human babies. We all know that. Enmerkar claimed he had lain with you on the Lion Bed. The Lord of Aratta boasted he had enjoyed you on your Adorned Bed. We accept their intention, and open our hands abundantly for them. But what is enacted by humans can only be a shadow of our true marriages.'

Colour was burning in Inanna's face right up to her brow. 'How dare you! Just because I clap Gilgamesh when he wins with the mace and the throw net. Just because I scream for him when he wrestles with his friends. Yes. I like him. I think he's wonderful. He's a hero, like Uncle Ninurta, who beat the Basilisk and conquered the Thunderbird. Gilgamesh ought to have a magical weapon of his own too, like Ninurta's Sharur. If I can help him, I will. But that doesn't mean to say I'd let him into my bed. How dare you suggest it!'

An patted her hand rapidly. He looked agitated. 'There, my little lettuce garden. I told Enlil there was nothing in the stories. We'll find you a fitting husband, don't worry. Only yesterday, Enkimdu—'

'*Enkimdu?*'

'And what's wrong with him, pray? He's a sensible man, the Good Farmer, and kind-hearted. I've no doubt your Star would shine very prettily in his irrigation channel and bring forth a bumper crop for him.'

She stared up in disbelief. 'Enkimdu is old and boring!'

His eyes grew cloudy and sad. 'He is my son. I am older than he is. Kindness may not be exciting. But it is better to live eternity with it than with force.'

'I won't marry him.'

'Oh, I know what you want. But the warrior Lords are all in Ninurta's household. There are none left unmarried for you.'

'Then I shall be a warrior woman myself!'

He gazed at her in a disappointed silence. 'I argued with Enlil. I begged him to let you stay here. You have warmed my old, cold heart these many years. I brought you here as a punishment, yet it has been a blessing to me. But I fear that he is right. Nin Shubur tells me you have just passed a dangerous threshold. Things you coaxed me to laugh at in a child are more threatening in a full-grown woman. You have reached the age when you need a mother's advice.'

The words drifted slowly down into Inanna's brain, like the first flakes of snow. 'You're sending me back to Ur?'

'To Nanna and Nin Gal, yes. I have failed you. I am giving you back as headstrong and self-willed as when you came to Uruk. The Council was wrong to trust you to me.'

'No, Grandfather!' Inanna scrambled to her feet and flung her arms around him. 'Don't say that! It isn't true. I love you!

I've been happy here. You've shown me all sorts of things—'

'Things you were very quick to learn . . . Well, well. You were a sweet pupil and a clever one.'

Her hands were inside his loose garment, feeling the places he had taught her to give him joy. 'Inanna. Inanna,' he murmured, finding himself aroused against his will. 'Not here, not now.'

'If you send me away, it will be nowhere and never again.' Her teeth were nibbling his ear.

The eunuchs' unmoving faces gazed away over the orchards that surrounded Uruk, across the flat, flickering desert. Nin Shubur crossed her arms, tried to control her breathing.

Inanna satisfied him, then tidied his clothing deftly, patted his cheek.

'And what would happen to my beloved *huluppu* tree if I went away? I'm growing it for my throne and my marriage bed, remember.'

'My head gardener shall be charged with it. It will be as well looked after as ever, I promise you.' An strove to steady his breath.

Inanna withdrew from him, suddenly cold. 'You've made up your mind, haven't you? You and Enlil?'

'I am setting you free. As President, I declare that the punishment the Anunnaki gave you for your presumption is at an end.' He made his voice sound virtuous.

'But I *want* to stay!'

'I am very tired.' He signed to the eunuchs, who positioned themselves on either side of the doorway. Nin Shubur moved forward to walk in front of her mistress.

Inanna drew herself up to her full height. She looked very tall, staring down at the slumped figure of the old, pale Sky Lord.

'When?' she asked dully.

'You will be home to celebrate your father's return at the New Moon festival next week.'

# Chapter Forty-two

Ur, the City of the Moon, shining like a cloud palace on its mound above the Buranun.

'How does it feel to be coming home?' asked Nin Shubur.

'Home? I hardly know it. I have spent so long in Uruk with An. It is my parents' city, not mine.'

She gazed at it across the eye-hurting levels of the desert. Canals, fringed with dark orchards, led like veins towards the heart. Fields basked in the sun, trod in life-giving water. As the boat neared the city they could see people busy at their labours. Men, women, children, shouldering baskets, filling them with stones and last year's stubble, clearing out the weeds with hoes, levelling the recently inundated surface ready for sowing.

'My brother seems to have favoured the city. It shines more like the sun than the moon,' observed Inanna.

Ur reared like a golden mountain, dwarfing the two Ladies when they disembarked beneath it. Nanna's ziggurat rose as a gateway to heaven. Millions of bricks gleamed golden in the sun, made more dazzling by the black bitumen that bonded them together. A colossal stepped ramp climbed up to the high first terrace with its towered gateway, on to the second stage square-set upon the pavement of the first, up still to the third smaller square, where a dark cool doorway opened into the lofty dwelling place. To stand at the foot of this stairway, winged by other flights of steps from left and right, was to lose sight of the highest sanctuary, so steep and immensely long was that ladder to the Sky.

'Is this how humans feel before us?' said Inanna, a little uncomfortably.

'Courage, my lady,' Nin Shubur reassured her. 'Your place is in the highest rooms. You are Nanna's daughter.'

Already news of their arrival had flown from the city gate. Humans were running to stare. The palace staff were hurrying into their positions. Flower petals and handfuls of fragrant fir needles were flung over the steps in front of them by chanting women. *Algar* harps, their soundboxes set with miniature drums, plucked and tapped a merry welcome. Beribboned tambourines shivered ecstatically. Deep orisons of the *nuesh* priests, the *lagar* priest, the *en* herself thrummed from the graded ranks on successive stairs. Inanna and Nin Shubur were seated in carved chairs under leafy awnings, carried by sweating porters up that mountain of devotion.

The breeze blew cool on the topmost terrace. Nin Gal embraced her daughter.

'Oh my little star, my budding blossom, you are a child no more! Look at you! Look at her, Utu; she's lovely, isn't she?'

A tall golden youth came forward to stand beside his mother. His face was thoughtful, but his eyes were very bright. He looked his sister up and down reflectively. The pleated dress-cloth, patterned with green and red, covering today both breasts and her left shoulder. The heavy dark hair coiled back in a demure chignon. The linen bonnet shading a brow that gleamed as lustrous as alabaster. He took her hand in his strong warm one.

'I have been blind to much when I visited Uruk. Is this the sister who threw stones with me in the rivers of Aratta? Did we play hide and seek here through the women's *giparu* and the school of the scribes after the Flood? Why have we waited so long to bring her back to Ur, Mother?'

'Are brothers always as courteous?' asked Inanna, blushing a little.

'Are sisters usually as gorgeous?' replied Utu, breaking into a teasing smile.

They laughed, formality forgotten.

'I have something for you,' exclaimed Inanna as Nin Gal's *sukkal* led the way into the cool interior. 'A present from Gilgamesh. A copper axe, the haft set with pearl and lapis lazuli.'

'Gilgamesh? They tell me he's getting a reputation for a mighty champion. When he goes to war the Anunnaki will have to look to their standards!'

'The young men of Uruk adore him. They're bound to choose him for *lugal* one day. He'll be a famous war leader like his father Lugalbanda.'

'Will he make a good *en* as well?' The laughter steadied in

204

Utu's voice. Again that note of maturity, considered judgment.

'I don't know. I hadn't thought about it. A priest-governor for peacetime? Well, I don't think he'd want that. War's what he loves. So would I!'

'Still the same bloodthirsty Inanna. Now I begin to recognise the sister I fought with. Just ten times more beautiful, and so ten times as dangerous.'

'Only to those who annoy me.' She smiled at him sideways.

'I am warned!' With a mock bow he turned away to see that his mother was being served with fruit and cool emmer beer like a dutiful son.

In every town and village there were New Moon festivals. But in the Moon-Lord's own city of Ur they were spectacular. At first Inanna felt her senses assaulted by all the fresh experiences crowding upon her.

Bulls everywhere. Gold bulls, with beards of lapis lazuli. White bulls' horns symbolically crowning pillars. The jet-black bull, roped and garlanded with poppies for sacrifice. Bull-headed priests. Acrobats frisking in hooves and tails. A motley retinue of lions, goats, gazelles, human limbs flashing amid hairy pelts. Carpets of flowers. The smell of bubbling beer. The huge Moon Boat hauled into position for the Lord's appearance.

And then the constant rhythm of tambourines and kettledrums, the thickening smoke of incense, the heat of food and beer, began to cloud her senses. She moved among relatives and court officials half forgotten. At first Nin Shubur was in front of her, marking the passage of a royal Lady. Then, more and more often they became separated by the half-drunk throng.

Nin Gal waited alone, in the highest shrine, priests guarding the door.

'It's funny,' said Inanna fuzzily. 'Uruk is not so very far from Ur. And I have met my family at festivals in Nippur. But I had no idea! I didn't realise we were so quiet at Uruk, in the E-Anna with An. It's as if I'd been asleep for years while everybody else was enjoying life to the full.'

'May you find happiness in your father's city, and more in your own, my lady.' It was another girl's voice answered her, not Nin Shubur's.

Inanna turned, eyes widening, clearing a little in a bright

stare. 'I know you, don't I? You're . . . you're . . .'

'Geshtinanna.' The girl laughed as she bobbed a curtsey to a Lady more senior in rank, if not in years. She was not as beautiful as Inanna, her brown hair twining in curls like the tendrils of vines, her eyes purplish blue. Her voice was the loveliest thing about her, deep and musical.

'Geshtinanna! That's right! Dumuzi's sister.' And the impulsive Inanna threw her arms round the other girl and embraced her. She put Geshtinanna away from her, holding her by the shoulders at arm's length. 'Don't tell me. You're . . . apples? Barley?'

'Grapes,' corrected Geshtinanna, with a merry modesty. 'Officially, I'm Lady of the Vine.'

'Praise to the grape and its Lady!' Inanna cried, seizing two electrum cups from a passing tray and raising them both aloft. 'I'll drink to both.'

'My lady.' Nin Shubur's warning voice was at her elbow. 'The moment is almost here.'

'I'll drink to my father too!' She was about to pour a libation on the terrace floor. But the babble around her was hushing, faces beginning to turn to the east, where the sky was blue-black as Inanna's hair and one big brilliant star hung over the distant trees.

Inanna hiccupped and giggled a little in a lower voice. She caught Geshtinanna's arm. 'I've just thought of something. You and Dumuzi are Enki's children, aren't you? That means you're my aunt!' She found that very funny.

'Yes, I am the daughter of Enki and Nin Sun.' Pride in the Lord of Wisdom shone in Geshtinanna's clever face.

But Inanna had caught another idea. In the near-silence that had fallen on the huge gathering she whispered in Geshtinanna's ear, 'Nin Sun? Then that makes you Gilgamesh's sister too!'

'My lady. Please!' Almost too late, Nin Shubur hurried the fuddled Inanna forward to stand at the foot of the final staircase, facing Utu. Only the plucking of the *algar* harps now, the long-spaced beat of drums like slow heart-throbs. A low and pleading litany from Nanna's priestesses.

Then, out of the darkness of the Netherworld, from some unimaginable depth of waters beneath the foundations of the Earth, light speared above the horizon. Two tips of silver, like bull's horns, growing into a crescent boat, a sharp-prowed *gufa*, sailing the sky. And suddenly, on the highest platform, while all eyes had been watching the horizon, a Lord was standing in his earthly ship, hand raised, wearing the eight-horned tiara of the royal Anunnaki. And a Lady, equally gorgeously robed, glittering in the moonlight, advancing across the ziggurat roof, white arms outstretched to him. Father Nanna had returned to embrace Queen Nin Gal.

Ereshkigal's festival of darkness was over.

A roar of joy went up as the Guardian couple kissed. Cymbals crashed. Animals bellowed. Thousands of voices all over the city burst into hymns of rejoicing, outsinging the millions of frogs.

Utu advanced from the other side of the staircase, embraced Inanna warmly.

'Well, that's that. He's back. Another month begins. Let's get these robes off as soon as we can. I'm sweating like a horse.'

'Won't I meet him now?' In the shadow below the steps Inanna's voice had the wistfulness of a child.

'In the morning.' He grinned widely. 'He and Mother have their . . . *duty* to do before then, you know. Or perhaps you didn't.'

'I know! I have not grown up with Father An without learning something. So what do we do now?'

'I know what *I'm* going to do. But you can't come with me.' He started down the lower flight of steps.

'Where are you going?'

'Into the city. To the tavern. Well-disguised, of course. The barmaids of Ur are not a bad-looking lot.'

'I want to come too.'

'Not likely!' And he was off, bounding away and losing himself in the throng below.

'He is right.' Geshtinanna's voice came companionably out of the warm night air. 'We should not be seen in the tavern, you and I. Let them lift their cups to the Sky and toast the Evening Star and the Lady of Wine, while we enjoy ourselves incognito.'

'Where?'

'Oh, we are in no danger. These humans love our family. They would not touch us, even if they recognised us. More likely they would fall flat on their faces! If you like, we could go down into the city square and watch the carnival. Sometimes they have wrestlers who do it with jars of oil on their heads. Or men dressed as lions, fighting with swords in their paws.'

'Could I? Would you take me?'

'If you'd like.'

'Quick, then. Before Nin Shubur catches me and tells me I can't go.'

They sped like moths down the huge moonlit staircase, past crowds of revelling worshippers who paid no heed to them. Once, as they crossed a level terrace to the head of the next flight, Inanna caught her companion's dress.

'Geshtinanna. I think a man is following us.'

Geshtinanna threw a quick confident glance behind her.

'Indeed he is. That's all right, then. Did you think I would take you into the city entirely unescorted? Dumuzi is coming with us.'

Inanna stopped stock-still. The young man running behind her almost collided with her. She turned to face him.

He was broader in face and shoulders than Utu. His hair was pale and fleecy, his skin gold as butter. Dark eyes, that she knew were brown flecked with honey by daylight, now shone strangely dark by the light of the barely visible moon.

'Dumuzi Ushumgalanna!'

He shrugged and smiled winningly. 'As you like. In my father's marshes I am Dumuzi Abzu. My mother calls me Damu. In Uruk I am Dumuzi the Shepherd. But for you, in the orchards of Ur where the fruit is scenting the air, I will be Ama-Ushumgalanna, Life of the Date Cluster.'

'And you are lending us the shade of your palm leaves for our protection?' She held out a royal hand to him, Nanna's eldest daughter, the Princess of the Night.

'I shall be honoured to give whatever the Lady Inanna asks.'

His hand met over hers. It was not the first time. Centuries ago, when she was younger, he had come to the E-Anna in Uruk, bringing her presents of cheeses and cream. But those visits had stopped abruptly. Tonight his nearness felt like a dawning. She was a new star rising. He was a young ram lamb lifting his eyes to her glory for the first time.

'Show me the night, then,' she said, in a low sweet voice of invitation.

'Willingly, Princess of the Stars.'

When she looked at him, it was his eyes that were full of stars.

His hand was firm and warm over hers. With his other he reached for Geshtinanna. Thus linked, the three of them went down the final stairs into the darkness and the noise below.

# Chapter Forty-three

Inanna was frightened. For all her bold words, her black eye-paint and red nail-lacquer, her delicious knowledge of her blossoming body as her bath women oiled her, she had led a sheltered childhood. An's own enjoyment of his great-granddaughter had jealously kept her out of the reach of others. Outside, in the city of Uruk, Gilgamesh and his companions, a young generation growing up to be warriors, had drilled and swaggered noisily. Women began to complain the streets were not safe and hauled their daughters indoors out of sight. Men made mental calculations of the cost of wars to come and shook their heads. Inanna knew nothing of this. In the calm cool house of the E-Anna, in the Anunnaki's district of Kullab, she was untouchable, save by An himself. She could hang over the walls and enjoy the sight of muscular bodies gleaming with oil, showing off their skill with the javelin, their speed with the knife, their strength in the wrestling holds. She could cheer and scream for her heroes, shower jasmine petals, blow a kiss even. They looked up and bowed, grinning sometimes. It had not seemed serious. She had been a child, An's pet. When kings praised her Star and sang of her lovemaking, it was ritual only. No man had yet possessed her. Only the probing finger of the elderly An had been her education. She knew how to give pleasure to men, knew in part how she herself could be pleased. Her body was a field prepared, lightly-raked, ready for ploughing.

'You have strong fingers! I shall have bruises to boast of tomorrow.' Dumuzi was only half joking as he looked down at Inanna's white grip on his own brown arm.

Inanna was breathing fast. She did not apologise. All round her the New Moon carnival dazzled her senses. Lights blazed in the squares, throwing the alleys into sinister shadow. There were fiery braziers where roasting nuts hopped on the hot pans. Monkeys danced to the shiver of tambourines.

Acrobats cartwheeled. Naked girls wrestled with bears. Pairs, loving or greedy, innocent or cynical, male and female, clung to each other, staggered into corners, slipped laughing into the darkness. They sought a human enactment of the blessing being performed for them in the highest shrine by Nin Gal and Nanna.

Geshtinanna seemed not at all disturbed by it. Her feet in their gold-beaded sandals lifted lightly over sprawling bodies, pools of vomit. She whisked her dress aside from dogs fighting over mutton bones, from men drawing knives to fight over a tavern girl. Inanna, still clutching Dumuzi for reassurance, wondered if Geshtinanna's confidence came from an inner courage or from a total trust in her brother's protection.

'You should cover your head,' Dumuzi teased his sister. 'With curls like yours, you'll get mistaken for a harlot!'

She tossed the light brown tendrils. 'You should talk! You wear more eye-liner than I do, and your nails are redder. I think you sprinkle more perfume in your bath water!'

The light was strangely shadowing: thin moonlight, leaping fires. Inanna had hardly studied Dumuzi Ushumgalanna beside her. He had been a warmth, a strong wall between her and this strange, alarming world, a means to experience excitement without danger. She shivered, suddenly realising how different it would have been to have come only with another girl. Dumuzi felt her tremble, laughed, unclasped her fingers and tucked her arm more firmly under his own. She looked at him sideways, examining him more carefully now.

It was true. Dumuzi had grown into a beautiful young man.

His face looked rosier than she knew it, in the flicker of the pitch-soaked torches. His lips had fallen open and she could hear him breathing hard, though they were not hurrying. Was his mouth as bright as that by nature? Yes, Geshtinanna was right, his skin was scented with sandalwood. But when he had bent his head to give the ritual kiss of greeting upon her breast-ornament, his hair had given off a wholesome country smell. That conventional kiss had meant little to her at the time, back there in the E-Kishnugal, the House That Brings Light. A formality, quickly forgotten in surprise and excitement. Now, reliving it, a shudder ran from her breastbone down through her navel.

Geshtinanna had untucked the end of her dress cloth and

thrown it over her head, disguising her festival headdress of rare shell and gold-leaf flowers, and shielding her face.

'There. Would anyone recognise me now?'

'You could be old Mother Sagburru herself!' Dumuzi laughed. 'Or the Man in the Moon.'

'Sh!' Even the ready-tongued Inanna was scandalised for her father.

'Don't be irreverent,' Geshtinanna scolded. 'This is his night.'

She skimmed up the flight of steps on to the open-air dais outside the council chamber. The old men of the senior assembly, the young warriors of the lower house had paid their formal respects to the Rising Moon long since. Now they were roistering through the city or sitting in the cool night courtyards over a cup of wine. Some few bodies, free citizens or serfs, it was hard to tell, slumped in the shadows against the wall, too tired or drunk to go home.

Geshtinanna stood in the moonlight, taller than the humans below her. Her face was lifted to the stars but still in shadow. She began to sing.

Inanna was no great musician. She loved poetry, the flow and rhythm of words, especially when they flattered her. Now she knew magic in Geshtinanna's voice. Deep and bell-like, it seemed to need no instrument to make the air vibrate. Her song was not loud, but it was haunting, compelling. The babble of human voices halted. Heads turned. Some revellers scrambled unsteadily to their feet as though impelled to show respect. And yet the song was light, full of laughter, even a little risqué.

> Our son-in-law, our son-in-law to be,
> The stars are waning,
> The night will be growing grey if you wait longer.
> You will soon be one of our family, after all,
> You are my betrothed.
> I am drawing the bolt, turning the silver lock.
> Quick! The patrol has passed.
> Run! The path is clear.
> Let us not waste this night,
> Let us not wear our youth away in wishing.

All over the square, noise had hushed, instruments tinkled into silence. The drummers stilled the skins with their hands.

The wrestlers drew apart. Even the animals whimpered and fell quiet.

Dumuzi's arm dropped slowly. His hand slid down Inanna's skin to find her fingers, twined with them, gripped harder. She found her body drawn against his side, felt her flesh begin to mould itself into the contours of his. There was a moment, like the pause between lightning and thunder, as if each was waiting for the other to move. Then Dumuzi's arm was round her shoulders, his hand burning under the cloth of her dress. She felt, as well as heard, his breath hot and quick above the hollow of her neck.

He held her strongly to his side, trembling with controlled passion. She was waiting for him to abandon himself, wanted him to do more. Yet he was not An; this was not the E-Anna. She would not use the arts she had learned as a hierodule to coax and bring him on. This was a young virile man among the Sons of An, and she a girl barely come into her womanhood.

Dumuzi laughed nervously. 'You did not know my sister was a famous chanteuse? But she is reckless. Even with that cloth over her head they must recognise her.'

While he spoke, lifting his hand from her body to brush her hair aside and fondle her ear, a shout broke out.

'It's the Young Lady!'

'Come to bless the festival! The Vine Girl!'

'Hail! Geshtinanna!'

'Bless me, Lady!'

'Let me just touch her skirt. She'll cure me for sure!'

There was a rush of eager, grateful, desperate humans for the steps that flanked the dais. Geshtinanna whisked round, jumped from the high platform just out of reach of the first pleading arms, grabbed Inanna's hand and fled with her. Dumuzi let go of Inanna, placed himself in the rear. For a frantic moment Inanna thought he had stayed behind to face the crowd. But she looked over her shoulder and saw him, a dense protective shadow, running fast in her footsteps.

It was undignified, funny even, three Anunnaki pursued by their human subjects. Protocol reasserted itself more rapidly than Inanna would have believed. Temple guards materialised seemingly out of nowhere and waved them on. Then the *sag-ursag* levelled their spears against the crowd, blocked the thoroughfare that led back to the ziggurat, warned the pursuers to take no step closer.

Far up on the terraces of the E-Kishnugal, harps were playing. No lamps were lit there. The Moon of Nanna himself, newly returned from the Netherworld, was all his people wanted.

The road was turned to silver, the black bitumen bonding in the brickwork more strongly etched. There were shadows of retainers discreetly ready to offer service. But the street and the stairway looked long and lonely.

The three truants had dropped apart from each other. There had been no sin or shame. Flesh must touch, bodies must join this night, or life would not be recreated. It was a matter for rejoicing. Yet they were sobered, coming under the great hill of the ziggurat.

Geshtinanna led the way aside into a more modest house. 'Come in, Inanna. You must be as thirsty as I am, after all that running.'

'But I didn't sing. You were wonderful.'

The Vine Girl laughed, blushing. 'I am not my father's daughter for nothing. It is hard to grow up with Enki and not have a love of words and song and art.'

'And a weakness for adventure that will land us in trouble,' said Dumuzi.

She poured him a beaker of wine, then rumpled his hair fondly. 'And you are our mother's son. The Shepherd Boy from the Wild Cow. No hero. You love your comfort. Sweet grazing, plenty of ewe lambs to mount, a secure sheepfold. I can't imagine you taking Father Enki's *magur* ship and voyaging over unknown oceans to do battle with Kur.'

'Did he really? Is it true what they sing of him? That he risked eternity to rescue Ereshkigal?' Inanna's eyes were wide and brilliant over her cup.

'You know the song. He will not speak of it. But he came back so bitter he cast the Spell of Enki over Enlil's world, they say, and taught the humans war.' She yawned. 'I'm going to bed now. And so should you, Inanna. Dumuzi will take you to your father's gate.'

'I will take Inanna to the end of the Earth, if she demands it,' Dumuzi smiled.

'*Would* you? Would you go over the rim of the world to Ereshkigal's Below, if I wanted you to?'

'I am not Father Enki, or Father Nanna either. Let them have the dark. Our generation is for the sun.'

'I hold the Morning and Evening Star,' she reminded him.

'And it is time to sleep, before morning returns.' Geshtinanna kissed them both affectionately and drifted away.

Dumuzi was still gazing at Inanna as though his sister's passing had been no more than the shadow of a leaf blown across the door.

'Perhaps danger attracts me, after all. The ram safe in his pen looking up at the wide free sky and worshipping what he sees.'

He came towards her. His hands were round her, slipping the draped cloth from her shoulder. It fell to her girdle, leaving her white breasts firmly mounded as marble. He bent to kiss them.

'Inanna. Inanna!'

He was sucking her. Hungry, a small boy burying his sweet-smelling head in his mother. She tried to break away, then clutched his head to her, let go again.

'No, Dumuzi Ushumgalanna. Not yet, not here.' She heard the ache of Great-grandfather An's voice in her own helpless plea. 'I must go home. Nin Shubur will be in a terrible rage with me for going into the town without her. She will tell my mother. What if my father gets to hear of it?'

'What's done is done, Bright Star. You are in trouble already. What can another hour matter? Let me show you how sweet one hour can be.' He was leading her towards his own rooms; the colonnades were discreetly empty of servants.

'No. Let me go now. While I can still say all I did was to look at the carnival in the public square, and listen to Geshtinanna singing.'

He crushed her mouth with a kiss. 'Then say that, anyway. Do I have to teach you how to deceive your mother, young lady? Say what you did. Geshtinanna will vouch for you. Your mother is not going to ask me what I did. Just lie still and let me water your lettuce-bed.'

His hands were unfastening her girdle, separating the cloth from her legs, exploring her passage.

She grabbed the dress from him, snatched it to her with a breathless attempt at dignity.

'No! I mean it! Just because they have painted my face like the high priestess . . . I know people call me the Hierodule of An. But I am a virgin. You must ask my mother; you must ask my father.'

She could see Dumuzi's mind, his inner caution fighting

with his body's desire. As she was struggling with her own.

'Ask Nin Gal? Ask Nanna? You want me to ask them if I can *marry* you!'

She nodded, a child still in that moment, with a woman's painted face. Her eyes were eager, terrible with hope.

He laughed uncertainly, staring at her hard, as if to be sure she was serious.

'Here.' He helped her rearrange her dress clumsily. 'I am much more used to taking these off.' His hands clasped her shoulders, less passionately. 'Sweet sister. My lush garden of early spring. Let me walk you back to the Palace of the Moon. Keep our secret tonight. Let us talk about it in the morning. I will tell no one you came to my house.'

# Chapter Forty-four

Inanna slept late. She woke to a feeling of happiness even before she remembered the reason. It was good to lie there rocking herself with the luxury of desire exciting her body. She felt her eyes shine and her face soften into greater beauty, like a blossom caressed by water. She was water. She was her ancestress Nammu, the Waters Above, she was the Moon's Princess, she was the Morning Star. She stretched and smiled and sighed. She was all water and light.

Nin Shubur sent women to dress her. The *sukkal* was still tight-lipped and coldly angry from the night before. Inanna's eyes were full of stars. She hummed, she floated. This day was newly beautiful for her, as never before.

The early sunshine of Ur was already brilliant. The House That Brings Light deserved its name. The Buranun sparkled. The desert flashed silicate jewels. The date groves were vivid green. She skimmed down the steps to her mother's quarters in sun as hot as her heart, Nin Shubur going like an upright shadow before her. The air clasped Inanna's skin, heavy as a man's hand. Her brother's sun danced before her eyes. She had left her great-grandfather An's house of eunuchs and women. She was a woman, admired by men.

The interior of Nin Gal's rooms seemed to recreate the night. The air was cool and welcome as a jar of spring-chilled wine. The shadows blinded her. Rectangular blazes of light marked the terrace beyond. But Nin Gal chose the semi-darkness of the house rather than the flickering shade of fig trees.

Nin Gal, the Great Lady. But she rose eager as a young girl and ran to embrace her tall daughter. She danced Inanna round as though she had been a small child, and Inanna remembered the songs of her parents' impetuous loving in the reed beds. Enki's daughter, Enlil's son. The hurt of an older generation's heart made sweet and loving in the next. And in her turn?

No! It was only the accusation of Nin Shubur's stiff presence, the sudden chill of this room after the sunshine, the withdrawal of her laughing brother's sign in the sky that could make her think like that, this morning above all.

The shadowed room did not grow lighter, but she felt a presence dawn in it. She saw her mother's joy turn to transfer itself to a newcomer.

Father Nanna was standing in another doorway. He was thinner than Inanna remembered. Her knees bowed with instinctive reverence. He did not seem to smile, though it was hard to be sure in the dim light, but she thought his eyes danced.

'Moon Princess.' His voice was low and loving. 'Star Child. Welcome home!'

And his arms were wide and she was in them. He held her away from him then, and looked at her with pleasure.

'So you have come back to Ur? But not, I think, for long. It should not be difficult to find this gorgeous girl a husband!'

'Father . . .' Inanna burst out, impetuous as her mother. Then, 'No, Father,' modestly looking down, and colouring. Better she did not speak her desire before Dumuzi did. Even now, the Shepherd might be on his way to the palace, freshly dressed and scented, carrying gifts to please her mother, to ask permission to seek her hand. Let her appear the Moon Lord's daughter, the Sky Lord's ward, remote, not easily won.

'Sit down, eat,' urged Nin Gal gaily. 'This is a family festival.'

The fare was simple, though served on silver. To Inanna it was a banquet rare and exotic as a cargo of food brought from the Anunnaki's own gardens in Dilmun. Skimmed milk freshened with cucumber had never tasted so delightful. Butter was smooth on the barley cakes as a man's well-oiled skin. Cheese carried a scent she remembered from Dumuzi's shoulder that almost made her faint. She ate as though it were a sacrament. Her head bent over her lap, her fingers stroked the fine wool moulding itself around her knees. She trembled violently.

'Are you cold? The day is still fresh. Run out into the sun, if you like. You'll find your brother somewhere.' Her mother was instantly concerned.

Inanna shook her head vigorously. 'No. No, I'm very happy here.'

Nanna leaned back and signalled for another beaker of emmer beer. 'On the matter of husbands, there is a good man who has been starstruck by your brilliance already. He has admired you from afar in Uruk, has sometimes met you in An's palace.'

Inanna started, felt the colour leave her face, come rushing back. The Shepherd Dumuzi's mother had a house in the Kullab district of Uruk, surrounded by apple orchards. He had come in from his farm on the steppe to the city, bringing baskets of sweet-smelling cheeses to An's house, the purest fleeces for spinning, his rich thick cream. As a child she had thought little of him. More recently, she had been dazzled by the young warriors of Uruk, like Gilgamesh. But Dumuzi had remembered her. And now, last night . . .

'Who, Father?' she asked, innocently blushing, trying to avoid Nin Shubur's all too seeing eyes.

'Enkimdu.'

Inanna froze. Suddenly the room did indeed strike chill.

'But . . . he's old!'

It was not true. Enkimdu the Farmer was in the prime of life. Granted, he did not have that honeyed sheen of youth that made girls sigh everywhere Dumuzi passed. That sweetness Inanna herself had awoken to only yesterday. But Enkimdu was a strong-muscled, well-set man, square of shoulder, ruddy gold with the healthy glow of ripe corn. His produce of beans and flour was drier than Dumuzi's, perhaps, yet warm and wholesome. A kindly man. An had been correct; he would make a good husband.

Today, even Gilgamesh was forgotten. Enkimdu's only crime was that he was not Dumuzi. The Farmer's eyes were thoughtful, calculating the careful passage of the year, the inundation, ploughing, sowing, reaping of the fields. They did not shine like those of Dumuzi's sheep among the free-ranging flocks of the steppe. His hair hung straight as flax, where Dumuzi's springing curls copied the thrusting rams' horns. Enkimdu's skin was grainy as barley husks on the threshing floor. Dumuzi's was soft as fleece into which she could plunge her fingers, his lips were moist as milk, his . . .

'Slowly, Nanna! You are frightening her. The child has not been with us one whole day, and you are trying to marry her off.'

'No child now, I think.' Nanna raised his beaker to her. 'She will break too many hearts if we leave her unspoken for. Our kind know what they want. Once I saw you, my love, in Nin Gikuga's reed beds, I could never be satisfied until I had you. So Enlil saw Nin Lil walking by the Nunbirdu Canal and had to have her.'

'He paid for that. And Nin Lil more so. Inanna is a young Lady used to palace courtesies. I was a green girl from the marshes. Let Enkimdu come to the city and woo her. There may be others here.'

'Are you thinking of young Dumuzi? Has Geshtinanna been putting in a word for her brother?'

'I have not talked about it with my family. Dumuzi is here for the festival. It's true, he's a very pleasing young man.'

'To too many young women, they say! Enkimdu would be loyal.'

The affectionate argument rocked from one to the other, as if they were discussing the merits of two lion hounds, not the future king of her heart. Inanna felt sick and dizzy.

'I'll go out on the terrace. I have not seen Utu this morning.'

'The mayor of a village nearby has trapped a lion in the bean fields. He writes me that he has put it in a cage and is sending it to me by barge. Utu has gone down to the quay to oversee them bringing it to the game park.'

'I must go and watch.'

She almost ran out of the shadowed room that now seemed stuffy and airless. Nin Shubur, as usual, preceded her, walking with a swift step that anticipated her mistress's eagerness to be gone, yet preserved her dignity. Inanna moved out of sight of the long doors, found the shade of a vine-hung trellis, leaned over the parapet where the vast, flat, water-threaded land stretched away before her, buried her face in her hands. She was still trembling. She felt Nin Shubur move closer. The older woman did not touch her. Unseen by Inanna, she motioned the palace girls with their fans away, the musicians discreetly waiting in the shade to draw further back.

At last Inanna straightened, turned to face her *sukkal*.

'You disapprove, don't you?'

'Of what, my lady?'

'Of me and Dumuzi.'

'Not of the young man, child. It is not for me to choose the

Moon Princess's husband. Only of the manner of your meeting.'

'Will you tell my mother?'

A hesitation. 'You are grown up now. A Lady in your own right. That is why you were sent away from Uruk. To discover your womanhood. You will go back as queen.'

'*Whose* queen?'

'Uruk's queen, child. Do you not understand that? An will give the E-Anna over to you when you are ready. You will not be Dumuzi's or Enkimdu's or any Lord's. Yourself, the Queen.'

Inanna swallowed. 'What are you saying? That I can do whatever I like, that I am mistress of own life?'

Nin Shubur's face saddened. 'No, my lady. That if you are indeed to become a queen, you should act like one.'

Inanna's hand whipped upwards. Nin Shubur did not flinch. Then the Star Woman seemed to shrink from her tall commanding height into a little girl. She threw herself into her *sukkal*'s arms and cried against her shoulder. 'Oh, Nin Shubur. I love him. I love him!'

'Love yourself too, my lady.' Nin Shubur patted her fondly. 'Let him not come where he can hurt you.'

'I want to be hurt by him! I would do anything. I am water, parted by the carp. I am the date cluster, harvested by the saw-knife.'

'You are the Evening Star, the Morning Star, far beyond him.'

'I want to be under him.'

'Do not let him see it, my lady. Let him court you, let him woo you. Be the queen in his heart, his rising star.'

Inanna turned away, leaned out over the fencing again. 'Look! They're bringing the lion!'

A noisy crowd was coming up the road from the quay. Two terrified oxen were hauling a wooden cage on a cart, in which, even from the high terrace of the E-Kishnugal the women could hear the beast roaring its rage.

'Look! There's Utu. And . . .'

'Lord Dumuzi is with him.'

Inanna hung, breathless and fascinated, as the two young Sons of An strode with the confidence of assertive manhood beside the trapped great cat. Two golden virile men exulting over the golden fallen creature. Their stride was free. His muscled length was closely confined within the rough-hewn

221

prison. They sang of victory now, of future hunts, of the child on the cage top opening the shutter that would send him bounding out to meet the ready spears. He howled for freedom lost, his pride of lionesses that hunted the deer for him and dragged the bloody offerings to his feet.

Inanna shuddered. Love had exposed every nerve of her being. The slightest sensation pierced her with new vividness. She looked from the joyful Dumuzi to the anguished lion, from the despairing prisoner to the laughing Lord. She did not know whether to cheer or weep.

Nanna was standing behind her, his hand firm and cool on her shoulder.

'Let the young men make merry while they can. There is a time for shining, a time for darkness.'

She twisted round. She found herself in awe of this father so little known for many years. He was strong, he was loving. She felt the joy between him and her mother. But there was a side of him not seen, that had known things unspoken.

'Father.' Her hands lingered over the pale skin of his chest. 'What is it like in the world Below? Have you really met Ereshkigal?'

He shook his head, smiled with dark, gleaming eyes. She could not be sure if he was denying it or refusing an answer. 'Little Inanna. My Morning Star. May you never know the realms of darkness. You were born to dance in the Above, great-grandchild of An. Uruk with its Sky House is your true city.'

'I am Enki's granddaughter. Should I not know the Deep too?' And even as she spoke it, she thrilled to the knowledge that here in Ur, Eridu loomed up like a great ship on the horizon. In the south Dumuzi the Shepherd was Dumuzi Abzu, Enki's son.

His hand played absently through her hair. 'You do not know what you are asking.'

'Where does Utu go at night?'

'He sleeps, of course. Like a child in his mother's lap.'

Could she trust that smile?

'But you? At the dark of the moon . . .'

'At the dark of the moon Earth and Sky invoke Ereshkigal.'

'But how does she come? Do *you* see her?'

'I stand in her Ganzir. And where there was no light or hope, for a short time something shines.'

'And . . . that is all?'

'That was her bargain with my mother. That, and my three brothers Nin Lil left behind.'

'Can no one free them? Will no one end her power?'

'How could this world stand firm without the powers of both Angal and Kigal? If there were no Below, no Above? Ereshkigal lost the Earth and Sky. Would you take the Netherworld away from her too?'

'Yes!' And she turned again to cheer as the cortège passed under the bull-flanked gate into the leafy park surrounding the ziggurat. Dumuzi lifted his head, shaded his eyes against the sun, waved cheerfully to her.

# Chapter Forty-five

Inanna walked down to the park between her parents, demure as a scholar. She was already taller than her mother. Water had been led through the grounds of the E-Kishnugal to make rivers and pools. Beneath the bright surface, carp and barbel wove shadowy dances. Pelicans waded in the shallows, hanging their hungry pouches over the teeming water. As always, kites soared above, to plunge for a sudden stabbing kill. Sun stunned the frogs, which only croaked occasionally till the twilight drew its awning over the land and they burst into a full orchestra of praise.

Away from the cress-fringed water, the dusty ground was shadowed by *mesu* and scented lemon trees, and everywhere the sturdy, sticky-fruited date palms. Each tree was lovingly tended. Small channels ran from the larger canals, governed by sluicegates. They led the water into circular trenches cut round the base of every tree. Ningishzida, Lord of the Serpent-Twining Roots, could drink and be satisfied.

'You know I have planted a *huluppu* tree in Uruk, that the flood washed down to me,' Inanna told her mother. 'It's my own special tree. I hope An's gardener is looking after it safely for me. When the time comes, I'm going to cut it down to make my throne and my marriage bed.'

'For a great queen and a great lover?' Nin Gal laughed. 'May you be as happy in both as I am. A *huluppu* tree, is it? That's nice. I remember hearing your grandfather planted a *huluppu* in the Edin, long ago. I think your father and I may have found it once. Enki wept when it was lost in the great Flood.'

Shade protected the Children of An. Inanna always had a feeling of strangeness when she saw her father walking in the sunshine. Yet now, as they came out into more open spaces, he merely narrowed his dark eyes.

Fences had been set to make paddocks for wild animals.

Rocks had been brought from distant mountains at great trouble and expense. Wild onagers and ibex scampered over them or stood outlined upon their tiny peaks against the enamelled blue of the sky. The ibex's horns echoed in miniature the sprouting bull's crown thrust towards heaven from the higher mountain of the E-Kishnugal with its blue-bricked topmost sanctuary. A wall of pierced clay brickwork formed a stronger enclosure. From behind it came the shouts of men and the roar of the lion.

'Is it safe?' queried Nin Gal. 'Could he not jump over the wall? I hope Utu's not doing anything silly.'

'Enki's grandchildren are not fools.'

Nanna motioned Inanna to ascend a set of steps to a dais where carved stone couches were set in the shade of palm trees. From here, with a glad cry of surprise, Inanna could look down into the enclosure. A circle of trodden clay. A muddy pool. A thatched reed shelter. The lion had been shackled. His legs were roped together so that his powerful thighs moved in restricted steps like an old stiff man. Still, the knot of young men regarding him from the other side of the water observed circumspection. They watched him warily and with each frustrated, snarling leap their eyes measured the distance to the gate.

The lion limped away into the sparse shade of a clump of *shukur* reeds, slumped down on the damp earth, lay with lolling tongue, his great head heavy on his paws. The sport was over.

A warden on the far side of the pool held up his sharpened cane and seemed to query whether he should goad the beast into activity again. Utu called across, 'Leave him. It will soon be too hot for people or beasts to move. Let him have his siesta.'

The young men strolled towards the gate. Sweat gleamed on them. Some few had drawn a cloth over their heads, but most wore only a short kilted skirt and ropes of beads. Dust reddened their well-oiled skin like streaks of paint. Their sandalled feet flinched sometimes from the touch of hot sand.

No one thought it strange that Inanna blushed and stammered when the troop of young Lords came out through the swinging door that was strongly barred behind them. They came with that over-loud swaggering air that was their own self-conscious acknowledgement of the little known and beautiful girl watching them from the dais.

Nin Gal murmured names in Inanna's ear. Some she had known as boastful, teasing boys, others had always seemed men to her. Utu, Ishkur, Asalluhe, Dumuzi, Ningublaga, Enkimdu. Her eyes rested almost fearfully on the Farmer. And yet his expression, steadier and more modest than the rest, should not have been threatening. The smile he gave her was both friendly and respectful.

Utu led the way to his family, holding Dumuzi by the hand. After that first radiant look at him, Inanna tried to turn her face away from the golden Shepherd, but her eyes would keep drawing back, her gaze was locked in his.

'Yesterday I saw you talking to Geshtinanna. Here is her brother Dumuzi, and my closest friend.'

'Dumuzi Ushumgalanna is known to me already. He is also a friend of An,' she managed to say.

Nanna came down the steps and embraced Enkimdu with kisses on either cheek that marked a signal honour for the slightly older man. He led the Farmer to the platform where Enkimdu made his reverence again to Nin Gal and Inanna.

'Sit down and tell me how the canal-building is going between Badtibira and Larsa. I think hunting and lion-baiting is less to your taste than these other young bloods'.'

'I enjoy my share of pig-sticking in the marshes. That's a sport for grown men. Two cubits at the shoulder, the last boar I speared, and a hide like bronze. Unless you know the spot to strike first time, he'll rip your guts out with his tusks. The sow's as bad. I've seen one bite the buttocks off a man.'

Nanna roared with laughter and clapped him on the knee. 'There, Inanna. You see? It's no boring ox of a husbandman I've found for you. Enkimdu is still quick on his feet and steady of aim. He'll serve you well in bed, you needn't fear.'

'Nanna! The girl is not spoken for yet. Don't embarrass her. Forgive me, Lord Enkimdu. But my daughter is newly come from the cloisters of the E-Anna in Uruk—'

'The cloisters of An are a pretty school for women, I've heard!' Utu broke in. 'Eh, Dumuzi?'

'The Lady Inanna has a reputation as an apt and dutiful pupil.' Dumuzi bowed. The quick, teasing smile seemed a secret between the two of them.

'Has she?' Utu's eyebrows lifted. 'And what do they mean by that?'

Nin Gal rose, a little crossly. 'My grandfather has provided the education a young Lady needs. The Lord who wins

Inanna's hand will be fortunate indeed. It will not be lightly bestowed. Let anyone who has ambitions to address her think carefully what he may have to offer.'

'For such a pearl,' said Dumuzi, 'a man should give no less than all his treasure.'

Enkimdu coloured. The words came less fleetly from his lips. 'For such a harvest, I would open all the rivers of my heart.'

Nanna laughed again. 'Easy words, Enkimdu! Let her see the substance before she decides.'

As the party moved away through the still air of the avenues, where the *dar* birds chattered sleepily overhead, towards the midday meal and the long sleep of afternoon, Inanna edged closer to Dumuzi. Utu saw the movement, made room beside him with a wink. Inanna raised an innocent face. She was almost as tall as Dumuzi.

'Why didn't you bring Gilgamesh with you from Uruk?'

'Gilgamesh?' Dumuzi and Utu looked at each other questioningly.

'Gilgamesh is a human,' said Utu. 'What should he do in the sport of the Anunnaki?'

'Half human,' said Inanna. 'Your brother,' directly to Dumuzi. 'His mother is Nin Sun, isn't she?'

Dumuzi touched his brow, his eyes, his heart in gestures of reverence. 'Nin Sun yes. But my half-brother. Would you compare Lugalbanda with my father Enki?'

'I like the sound of Lugalbanda,' said Inanna, her face softening with remembrance into a smile.

'Inanna!' Utu's voice had an edge of warning. 'Remember who you are. Be benevolent to humans, warlike in their defence, upright in judging them. But never lower yourself to become entangled in their loves.'

'Do you insult my mother?' Dumuzi shouted.

The party of Anunnaki ahead turned round to stare. Utu clasped Dumuzi's wrist.

'No, no! What passed between Nin Sun and Lugalbanda on the high steppe no one truly knows. Some men are specially favoured. Lugalbanda had the protection of the Thunderbird. Ziusudra and his wife won immortal life. They are the exceptions. Let's not argue about it. But Gilgamesh is not Anunnaki. Remember that, Inanna.'

And gazing into Dumuzi's face, what could Inanna do but nod and promise that she would.

So while Nanna favoured Enkimdu, walking with him and talking of raising a corvée from the villages to dredge the central canals, of seasonal festivals, and the risk of red *samana* disease to the barley in a wet growing season, Dumuzi and Inanna strolled together, their warm arms lightly brushing at each swing, sending their blood back to the heart in explosions of fire. Nin Shubur walked ahead, could not see them, would not be able to speak of it.

It was difficult for the pair to converse, surrounded as they were by Utu's friends. But Ishkur burst into loud laughter as they passed the ostrich pen, and Inanna, genuinely amazed, clutched Dumuzi's arm.

'What are they? Is it a feathered serpent? But look at their legs!'

'Those tail feathers should grace your turban, like a chariot ass's headband. Their touch would be softer against your skin than palm fronds . . . but not as sweet.' He bent and murmured in her ear, 'Tonight. At Geshtinanna's house again. Your mother likes her. She can persuade your father.'

'My mother likes *you*,' she breathed, before a mischievous laugh.

They reached the foot of the staircase to the E-Kishnugal and the Ladies and Nanna were borne aloft. The younger men followed more slowly.

Inanna lay sleepless on her bed through the long hot hush of afternoon, her body naked and hungry.

# Chapter Forty-six

'I have to go soon.' Inanna tossed her beaded hair. Her fingers lingered among the purple, lascivious grapes in her lap. She enjoyed their surfaces, guided them seductively into her pursed mouth, fed Dumuzi one. His painful desire for her made her bold, confirmed her in her mind a princess more than her father's rank. Yet, facing Dumuzi's beautiful heady presence, she was aware that she *was* bold, provocative, risky. The danger excited her. She felt that she was indeed Enki's granddaughter.

'Stay.' Dumuzi's hand closed on her arm, tugged at her.

From cushions under the window, Geshtinanna smiled at them fondly. Inanna was her friend and constant companion now. The Vine Girl was a little older than the adolescent Princess of the Palace, but she seemed interested in no man as much as her brother.

'Shall I leave you?'

'No!' Inanna said with sudden sharpness.

Dumuzi laughed, and caressed the hollow of her arm, as though that violent cry had been an admission of his power. Inanna felt a flash of anger. She had discovered in that moment she was indeed more than a little frightened of her feelings for him. Dumuzi was not a man like Utu, with sudden flashes of stern anger. But he knew how to melt a girl with that teasing smile, with the gentle pressure of his playful hands. All the slave girls sighed as he passed. She felt he might coax her to do anything he wanted.

But not for long, she told herself. Soon I shall be grown up. I shall be as mature as he is. I shall have come into my own power.

'Why not? Are you afraid?' asked Dumuzi, setting the word out in the open.

'Nin Shubur is in the anteroom. She is probably telling her stones and feathers, casting spells for the protection of my virginity! She would know.'

'Nin Shubur is your *sukkal*, not your jailer. She should do what you command . . . if you were truly royal.'

'She would! She would do anything for me!'

'Well, then?'

'Nin Shubur is a wise woman. Even if she didn't tell my parents . . .'

'Inanna wishes the world, and Nin Shubur, to think well of her. Do not force her, Dumuzi.'

'I? Force this warrior queen who has conquered my heart? She holds me captive!'

Inanna crowed in triumph, seized his arms in turn. Their faces were too close. He kissed her passionately before Geshtinanna's amused eyes.

'Now! Now! Be kind, Inanna,' he urged softly.

'No,' she moaned. 'You have not yet asked me from my father, from my mother.'

'You own yourself, don't you? Yours is the word that counts. Speak it now.'

'Not yet.'

Dumuzi released her with a thrust more violent than she expected. He threw a furious look at the doorway.

'A *sukkal*! What does a girl in her father's palace want with her own *sukkal*? It's clear you're not ruling a court of your own.'

She fought to steady her breath and retrieve her youthful dignity. 'That is where you are wrong. Why do you think they sent me to An's palace for all this time? I was always marked out for a queen. My *me* are waiting for me to take up. I shall have my own city soon. An is tired. Ever since Ki was taken from him, since he lost Ereshkigal, this world means little to him. He still presides over the Assembly of the Anunnaki, but he leaves the management of the Earth to Enlil and Enki. Uruk will be mine one day. I am going to be a great ruler.'

'Oh!' Dumuzi looked startled.

'Didn't An tell you?'

'No. Why should he? You were still a child when I last met you in the E-Anna. After that, I have had to worship you from afar, disguised among the humans like Gilgamesh. I couldn't tell An that.'

'I am not a child now.'

'Indeed you are not, my lovely . . . Inanna! Is that why An

stopped me coming to the E-Anna? Are the two of you saying I'm not good enough for you? First Daughter of the Moon! High and mighty! Let me tell you, young lady, my branch of our family is as noble as yours. Just because you are descended from Enlil! My father Enki is as great as Nanna. My mother Nin Sun is as good as Nin Gal. My sister Geshtinanna ranks with your grandmother Nin Gikuga. I am just as good as Utu!'

'I know. I know.' She laid her finger on his lips, delightedly savouring the victory his indignation admitted, though his words denied it. 'That is what I am telling you. I am going to be queen in Uruk. And I will need a king.'

He gazed at her with suspicious brown eyes. Ambition, wounded pride, naked desire wrestled in his expression. Then they fell into each other's arms again. This time their laughter was more guarded, less spontaneous. But their clinging bodies knew no such restraint.

'My honey-mouth. I will come to the palace this evening. When Nanna has finished supper I will ask to speak to him.'

'I shall see that the wine is good. Oh, Dumuzi, I love you!'

Geshtinanna rose quietly, took a jug of her own wine and poured a beaker for each of them. She raised hers to them. Her eyes were unexpectedly wet but her lips curved sweetly.

'To happiness, and laughter, and life. May the three of us never be parted.'

To Nin Shubur's amazement, Inanna waved away the cedarwood chair that was hurried forward to carry her up the step ramp to the Palace of the Moon. She threw her arms wide, breathed in the cooling air. The sun was setting in a blaze of scarlet and purple. Forays of bats came swooping out of the trees. The jackals crept from their lairs and howled their brief and haunting homage to the night. The frogs by ones, by dozens, by thousands burst into chorus.

'Nin Shubur, tonight I could fly!'

'But I, my lady, shall feel more like a mortal than a mountain Lady by the time we get to the top. I am out of practice for climbing hills.'

Still the Lady of the East's eyes shone with an affectionate warmth. Inanna's joy was hers, and the first beginnings of relief. Whatever had happened in that private chamber, a turning point had been passed. Now, perhaps, Nanna and Nin Gal would give their consent to this union. She need not wait, vigilant, with no power but the dangerous might of spells, outside a closed door, knowing the peril it was useless to warn Inanna against. She need not dread the knowing grins that passed between Dumuzi's servants. Dumuzi held a stronger magic than hers in his beautiful body, in his boyish brown eyes. Today at least, Geshtinanna had been present.

Inanna sped upward, nimble as an ibex. But even she grew hot and breathless before halfway.

'Shall I summon our bearers?' panted Nin Shubur as they rested.

'No. I am strong. I am powerful. I can do anything! I'm going to get to the *giguna* if it kills me!'

Nin Shubur raised her eyes. Already the shadows were striding across the city and the plain beyond. The vast ziggurat cast its own darkness over them. The stones were still warm to the touch with remembered sunshine. But the lower building Inanna aimed at, perched on the level where the side stairs met the central ramp, was lost in the blackness of its own grove of trees, a hanging garden halfway to heaven.

'Very well then. But I shall not forgive you if you deprive me of my supper.'

They climbed more slowly and silently now. From time to time Inanna broke into a breathless laugh, or hugged herself, or sighed dreamily. At last she could not contain herself.

'He wants to marry me, Nin Shubur! He's going to ask Nin Gal!' She hugged her *sukkal*.

'And time enough he's taken to say it, child. I feared he might break your heart before it happened.'

'Oh, Nin Shubur, you're so boring. I *wanted* him to woo me, to wait, to think he might not win me.'

Nin Shubur's smile was touched with pity. 'As if the whole world couldn't see the stars in your eyes when you look at him.'

'He didn't know he was going to be queen in Uruk, though. All those years he was bringing gifts to An he never realised I was Great-grandfather's heir.'

Nin Shubur shot her a sidelong look of alarm. 'And now, at last, he will ask your parents for your hand?'

Inanna lifted her face to her own rising star. 'He will dress like a Shepherd-King of the steppe. He will put on his formal wig, he will comb his beard like lapis lazuli. He will sprinkle cypress oil on my mother's threshold where the bride must open the door.'

'Dumuzi Ama-Ushumgalanna has a sizeable mountain to climb himself, my lady. He must win your father's consent.'

'Nin Gal will persuade him. Nanna adores my mother. He would do anything for her.'

'And does she not love him as much? Why shouldn't she agree to anything to please her husband?'

'But . . . I want Dumuzi!'

'Your father favours Enkimdu.'

Inanna shook her head violently. 'Oh, Enkimdu is boring too! I don't want to hear any more about him.'

The tall dark walls of the *giguna* were close above them. A nightingale sang from the branches of a cypress tree, a final magic. Inanna mounted the last step, leaned against the enamelled brickwork weakly.

'That's enough. Let them carry us up the last stair. Have them prepare my bath.'

Nin Shubur signalled. At once porters came swiftly out of the shadows. Their uncomplaining strength carried their own weight and Inanna's up the remaining staircase to her mother's apartments. Inanna leaned back, inert and dreaming, gave herself up into the hands of others.

Nin Shubur left Inanna in a haze of soap and steaming copper kettles and cedar perfume. She slipped away to forewarn Nin Gal.

The moon was sailing high when Nanna's family had finished supper. They lounged in the silver light of the terrace, speaking little, lulled by the gentle tap of the long drums and the pluck of the *tigi* harps. Utu had fallen asleep, his bright eyes closed in weariness. Inanna felt the warm night air almost too thick to breathe.

Nanna's minister came soft-footed across the terrace with that *sukkal*'s practised step that spoke both deference and urgency.

'Great Lord, Dumuzi Abzu is at the door. He craves an audience of you and Nin Gal on business of great importance.'

Inanna's heart seemed to bound skywards, but her body sat rigid. She whispered almost soundlessly, 'Please, Father . . .'

Her mother moved in the shadow beside her, stood up, bent over and kissed her daughter's forehead. Her eyes danced with an understanding more sisterly than maternal.

'I think, Inanna, it is time for you to retire to bed.'

# Chapter Forty-seven

'Tell me! Tell me! What did they say?' Inanna twisted in the hands of the girls trying to wrap her in towels as she emerged from her morning bath.

Nin Shubur stood, surveying the scene like a diligent housekeeper, with a small secretive smile on her face.

'It is not for me to tell you, my lady.'

'But you must know! It will be all over the palace by now. I must be the only one who doesn't know the answer to the most important question of my life! The servants will be spreading it through the city before I hear.'

Nin Shubur shook her head slightly in a reproving gesture. The bath chamber was full of slaves, but to Inanna they were almost invisible. One in particular, a dark and glowing girl, listened with intelligent eyes.

'Amanamtagga,' ordered Nin Shubur, 'lay out dresses for the Lady of the Palace.'

The girl's eyelids dropped, swift as nightfall over the burning desert. She glided away to the wardrobe room and came back with her arms draped with dresses for Inanna to choose from. She spread them out over a couch, one flounced and tiered, one richly tasselled with softest lambswool, one in a cloak style to drape both shoulders. Inanna's hands fondled the wool voluptuously, the creamy white, the flecked brown, the dyes of heavenly blue and life-blood scarlet. She stroked silky goat hair between finger and thumb. Then, with a mischievous smile, she picked up a simple white length of sheer linen, bordered with strands of gold embroidered as barley ears.

'This one, I think.'

Her *sukkal* started. 'The linen, my lady? You'd choose to wear the Farmer's flax rather than the Shepherd's wool? This morning?'

Inanna stood tall and graceful as a poplar tree, while the

slave girls circled her, winding the cloth round her scented body, under the right armpit, over the left shoulder, draping it loosely round her back and leading it forward again. Amanamtagga hesitated before she made the final pleat and tuck. Inanna glanced down, sighed impatiently. 'Oh, cover both breasts!' The blue-veined alabaster orbs did not quite vanish from sight. They stood like twin moons veiled by wisps of the thinnest white cloud. Her lips were reddened, the nails of her toes and fingers also. Black borders edged her eyes, antimony gave added lustre. Nin Shubur herself came forward, clasped a necklace of small shell and carnelian beads around her throat, hung the heavy roundel of lapis lazuli and gold, the badge of royalty, between her breasts.

Inanna's eyes met her *sukkal*'s at last, smiling impishly. 'Why not the linen? Dumuzi Abzu said last night, "You own yourself." Let him see that I mean to be truly a queen. He mustn't think he owns me. I shouldn't let it look as if I am his slave. I could still choose the flax, if I liked. But, oh Nin Shubur, I want Dumuzi!'

She had looked like a queen at first, even in that pure white dress. She ended her proud speech with the piteous wail of a little girl.

'Come,' said Nin Shubur compassionately. 'I will lead you to your parents.'

Head high, hands holding the pleats Amanamtagga had so carefully arranged clear of the steps, Inanna made her way to the hall of audience attended like a princess by *sukkal*, eunuchs, priestesses, *sag-ursag* guards. Horns brayed for her. Gongs announced her entry. This was a morning for solemnity. The sun was not yet risen. A purple twilight laid a mystery over the desert and mist trailed along the water channels like flocks of fleecy sheep following their shepherd.

Inanna felt the welcome coolness of the morning, knew it could not last. She lifted her face to her own still bright Morning Star. She paused at her father's doorway, sprinkled water, sprinkled flour, went in.

Her father seemed a larger presence now. No longer the gaunt spare man who had returned from the Netherworld. What did he see, what did he do there, to bring him back so changed after such a brief stay? *Did* he meet Ereshkigal? Did anyone, except her uncles of the underworld . . . and the poor dead mortals?

The audience hall was magnificent. Silver and copper

panels graced its pillars. Marble made a black lake of its floor. Everywhere bulls' horns and the high-beaked profile of ships announced Lord Suen, the Crescent Moon, Nanna, the Full-Faced Orb. Lord Nanna-Suen was the Cattle-Herder of the Sky, the Boatman of the Above. He had fallen in love with the passionate Nin Gal, Enki's daughter, the girl from the watery marshes.

Inanna felt herself gliding across that cool smooth floor towards the dais where the pair sat. She had a sudden urge to cast off her sandals, as if her feet might touch bare stone and find it liquid, sink down into the dark Abzu below. Some temples are built in two directions. Within the foundation pit a substructure of walls mirrors the building above. Clay and rubble have filled the interstices, but the hidden temple is there. It is built downwards into Enki's Abzu as well as upwards into Enlil's Air. Libated water drains away through it to meet the Deep Below.

She was halfway across the floor before she came to with a shock. Deep thoughts for a girl to be having as she goes to learn her bridegroom's name. Her parents' faces were warm and full before her now, pale discs that needed no light from the sun striding up over the horizon outside. She reached the dais and made her reverence before them.

'Child.' Her father's voice was full of love. 'Is there something you want to ask me?'

The audience hall was hushed. Ranks of petitioners, personal Guardians seeking favours for their human protégés. Mortals, come simply to revere, hands crossed on breasts. Nanna's *en* priestess, Nin Gal's priests. All Inanna's retinue behind her.

'Oh my father, Ashimbabbar, the New Light, Frisky Calf of Heaven, Fruit Self-Grown, last evening Dumuzi Ama-Ushumgalanna asked my permission to seek my hand from you and my Lady mother. I gave it willingly.'

She held her breath. Nanna bent a little forward, gravely smiling. His voice echoed through the hall with the same royal formality.

'Nin Egalla, Lady of the Palace, Inanna, our Morning and Evening Star. Dumuzi Abzu, son of Enki, Kuli-Enlil, my father's friend, has asked my daughter's hand in marriage. I have consented gladly. We have kissed him as our son-in-law.'

And all the hall broke into jubilation at his words.

Inanna flew up the steps that separated them, hugged her mother and father, kissed them. 'Oh, I'm so happy! When can I see him? Is he coming back this morning?'

'Slowly, my child. You two have eternity before you. Where is the hurry?'

'Where was the hurry in the canebrake when you called me out of my mother's house to cook duck eggs and embrace with you in the marshes?' laughed her mother. 'We are not a cautious family!'

'All the same, I am sorry for Enkimdu. He is a good man. He would have served you well.'

'Oh Father! How could you wish me plodding in the muddy field behind the oxen when I might be the brilliant star over the steppe where the flocks roam free?'

'The wolf is always near on the steppe. How faithful is your Shepherd?'

'Dumuzi loves me!'

'Dumuzi Abzu is my brother,' Nin Gal said sharply to her husband.

'Even you know that his father is not a Lord to be wholly trusted.'

'Enki is the Guardian of Wisdom. He loves all creation.'

'Ereshkigal's brother.'

'Oh Nanna, Nanna! Enlil took your mother in violence. I was the child of love.'

'But Nin Lil has been loving and loyal to Enlil ever since.'

'As Nin Gal is loving and loyal to Nanna, her honey-man.'

'As Inanna will love her Dumuzi always.'

They smiled at each other, twined arms round waists, their flash of family jealousy forgotten.

'Poor Enkimdu,' sighed Nanna. 'He will be going back to Uruk a sadder man.'

'And you, Inanna, must make that same journey soon. An has been your foster-father for many years. You must ask his blessing on your marriage. Dumuzi can build you a new house, like any other young bridegroom. But the E-Anna itself will be your own before long, young Lady of the Palace.'

'I will make Uruk greatest of all cities.' Inanna's eyes shone with anticipation. 'I shall bring there learning and song and art and splendid buildings. The most colourful festivals, the most skilled women, the bravest warriors. There is one there already who could soon be my *lugal*. Gilgamesh. Have you met him?'

'Nin Sun's mortal son?'

A hiatus, as if an impropriety had been spoken. The humans were shaped like the Children of An, if somewhat smaller. When the Anunnaki chose to walk among them, there was little to tell them apart from their subjects. Only that one vast, world-shaking difference: the Children of An did not die.

Lugalbanda's son was mortal.

'Dumuzi shall build a little house for me in the district of Kullab. Geshtinanna says Nin Sun has a house there already, in an apple orchard. I have never been inside it. Soon we shall possess the whole city!'

'We too, in Ur, must make ready a wedding fit for a Sky Princess.'

'Mother. My *huluppu* tree. It was almost fully grown when I left it. This must be the time at last to cut it down and carve my throne and bed.'

'A single tree, an exile already uprooted once, to support so much majesty, so much love?'

'You're teasing me. But I shall be greater and happier than any Anunnaki before me. You'll see. I shall ask Enki to bestow on me armfuls of *me* as my wedding present. If I am to be queen in place of An, shouldn't I have all the powers that are left to clothe me in splendour?'

'You have the Morning and Evening Star. You have the Eye of Love. You have the door pillars of the Storehouse of Plenty for your symbol. Enki was even rash enough to promise you the Warrior Spear. Is that not enough for you, young lady?'

'No! I want it all! The Above, Earth, the Netherworld. All! All!' She spun around in a circle, flinging her long arms wide, and still they would not reach to express the bursting exultation of her heart. Her face was pure laughing light, her body taut with latent energy beneath the flimsy cloth. At that moment the world seemed indeed too small to contain her.

'Dumuzi is a lucky man,' said Nin Gal softly.

'And a brave one!' Nanna commented more wryly.

And so the lovers met again and were betrothed by the Moon Lord's governing *en* priestess. Dumuzi the Shepherd. Nin Sun's immortal son. The young Lord destined for new life, Guardian of the flocks and their milk. Ushumgalanna, power of the rising sap of the orchards and the heavy date clusters. Damu, his mother's little boy. Dumuzi Abzu, son of the Lord of the Deep.

Inanna saw in him only the sunshine of the upper air, felt her brother Utu's warm energetic presence congratulating his friend. Her eyes were full of stars. Her heart was like a storehouse sweet with corn and dates. They faced each other, like the bound cane pillars of a house, majestic, beautiful. Their arms clasped like bolts, silver on gold. He bent his head to kiss her breast ornament, then raised his eyes to hers. He smiled. His hand travelled down in the archaic gesture to rest on her vulva through the lightly veiling linen, the sacred oath of loyalty to a ruler.

'To Nin Egalla, Princess of the Palace, to Nin Ibgal, Queen of the Big House, to Nin Mesarra, Lady of Myriad Offices, to Inanna, Brightest of all the Stars, I hereby swear my hand, my heart, my life.'

And she, more daringly, for it was not the custom, placed her own hand upon his leaping genital. 'And so I give myself to my Dumuzi always.'

'For ever and ever.'

'For as long as you are faithful to me.'

'To the death that can never have us!'

Two young and lovely Children of An, fearless and joyful in their loving.

Their wedding was set for the New Moon Rising at the next Spring Festival.

# Chapter Forty-eight

Utu was to accompany Inanna to Uruk. He chose to travel by chariot, scorning the slow, cool passage of the ox-drawn boat along the glassy Buranun. Dust and heat seemed to fire his blood when others wilted. The faster pace suited Inanna's mood. Here, on the chariot road of the left-hand bank, she could look out over the purpled, shifting sand dunes, the skein of palm groves marking the lines of water channels like clotted thicknesses in woollen thread.

His team of donkey stallions trotted swiftly, making the fresh morning air move welcomely against Inanna's face. Everything she passed delighted her. In reed beds like these, waist-deep in water, Enlil had pursued Nin Lil. But she, Inanna, would never let herself be caught and raped. With barges like these, drawn by slow-plodding oxen, laden with all the generous produce of Sumer, great Lords like Nanna and Enki made their annual voyage to lay their tribute at Enlil's feet in Nippur. But why should Inanna, Princess of the Star that is above both Earth and Air, bend the knee to any other Anunnaki, when even An himself came close to worshipping her? Small naked muddy children played in the shallows like flickering eels. So, on the bed she would design from her *huluppu* tree, she and Dumuzi—

'Whoa, there!' Utu reined in his team beside an inn. He sprang down in a puff of golden dust and held up his arms to her. 'I could travel all day and not be weary, but you must rest in the shade till the heat goes out of the sun. It would not do for you to arrive in your city red and peeling like a dried-up onion!'

She jumped down into his waiting embrace. For a moment they stood clutching each other at the edge of the road.

'You are very hot,' she said in surprise.

'Why should the Sun Lord not be, little sister? I could warm even the frosty stars of night!'

'I shall soon have the fleece of my Shepherd Dumuzi to warm me. I shall not be cold at night!'

He let her go, and they followed their *sukkals*, who had gone ahead to order a meal and a room for Inanna to rest in the alehouse.

She crumbled barley bread between nervous fingers. She had no appetite. She felt that the sun shone too brightly outside, longed for a kindly grey wisp of cloud that would herald rain. Since she had left the E-Anna she had been made aware of her own growing enchantment. Every passing month left her more rounded, more lovely. She exulted in the power she knew flowed from her like the flood wave inundating fields to stir the sleeping seed. She knew she roused males, old Lords like An, young rams like Dumuzi. She knew, and felt the thrill of triumph.

Yet Utu, her powerful elder brother? Danger, unwelcome this time, soured the beer in front of her. Utu, the Righteous, who judged both Anunnaki and humans. Utu, who carried in his belt the curved saw-edged knife with which, some said, he cut his way out of the Prison of the Night. The inescapably just Utu, to whom oppressed humans could address the cry of despair 'I-Utu!' and the ground would open up to swallow the tyrant. This was a conquest she did not want to make. Nor did she wish to be the conquered.

Thoughts, like faint flashes of lightning before a storm, showed her the tangled unhappiness of her family. Enlil and Nin Lil. Enlil with his own mother to make Ninurta. Enki coupling with Nin Mah, then with their daughter, and with his granddaughter from her, and his great-granddaughter, down to clever Uttu the Weaver. She writhed uncomfortably, perspiring and drooping. Was this her destiny? Was this what it meant to be a child of the great Anunnaki? Not to choose her lover in the sweetness and freedom of youth, but to be trapped in a pattern of conjoined family functions that said the Sky needs Earth, that Grain needs Air, that nothing can be fertile without Water?

'Rest now, if you like, my lady. The room is ready for you.' Nin Shubur, observant and compassionate as ever, was at her side. Did she know the cause of Inanna's pallor? Would Inanna dare ask her *sukkal* for advice?

No. It had only been a moment. A hot and searing moment by the roadside, with the asses pawing restively and her brother's arms steadying her as she stumbled. Nothing more.

She lay on a fresh bed of rushes spread with a clean wool blanket and made herself dream of Dumuzi instead. Only a few more months. Months of tantalising kisses from those full red lips. Months of a young man's eager entreaties to seduction. Months of teasing him in her turn, letting him lead her inexperience so far. Months of hugging to herself all she truly knew, the careful teaching of An's practised hierodules. How she would delight Dumuzi on their wedding night! How she would amaze him. She would help him lift the silver latch and guide him through the door into a life together of eternal bliss. Dumuzi! Damu!

Her smile restored, she fell asleep, till Nin Shubur woke her.

'The sun has cooled, my lady. We can be there by moonlight.'

Uruk. She had needed to go away from it to know that it was home. More than Ur, her father's City of the Moon. More than the scarcely remembered mountains of Aratta. The brickwork rose, Enmerkar's city walls, Lugalbanda's defences. Dark against the softly silvered sky. She loved the night. Pride welled in her as all the human populace of the suburbs lifted their grateful faces to her Star. Their hot and heavy labour was at an end. The cows were milked and tethered for the night. Low light and song flooded from the windows of alehouses. The savour of cooking meals rose like rich incense. In the shade of gardens or on the open rooftops, families enjoyed the night breeze or went to grateful rest. A time for love.

Utu yawned. 'Almost there. I can hardly keep my eyes open.'

Nevertheless, they made a proud entry. Under his whip the chariot team picked up their hooves and trotted smartly across the last bridge. The gates were flung wide with loud shouts of acclamation. Wheels rattled over the paved highway to the E-Anna. An was waiting.

She ran to him, less shy of him than of her father Nanna. A little girl again, a knowing, nubile girl, safe from herself, dangerous to others only. An had taught her how to please men, but had not required of her the final surrender of innocence. The world outside was full of men who spoke of morality, but wanted something else.

'So you are betrothed to be a bride?' said An, when they

had hugged and kissed. 'Well, we shall see, we shall see.'

'Aren't you glad, Great-grandfather? Don't you want me to marry Dumuzi?'

'Want? Want? Of course I don't want you to marry anybody.'

'And all your lessons?' She stroked his cheek teasingly. 'All your hierodules taught me? What was all that for, if not to make me the most loving and lovable bride in Sky and Earth?'

'Hm. I could enjoy you myself, if the Anunnaki would let me. Oh, don't look so shocked. You must have known it. I've fathered more Lords and Ladies than all the rest of them put together. I'm not done yet. I could still show you more in bed than it was proper to teach a child.'

'But I ... love ... Dumuzi.' She planted a kiss between each word, firmly, confidently, trying to re-establish the sovereignty of that small spoiled girl skipping imperiously through the great E-Anna as if she owned it.

'Dumuzi. We shall see. We shall see,' he said again.

'Don't you like him? But they call him the Friend of An, Kuli-An.'

'Oh, yes, the lad's good for *friendship*. Keeps a well-run farm on the edge of the steppe, you know. I like his sister too. In the heat of summer I often go to visit them there, sit under her vine arbour, listen to her sing. Delightful girl.'

'You never told me! Why didn't you take me? I've only just met Geshtinanna again this year in Ur. She's my best friend now.' The world was becoming wider than she had known.

'No need to be jealous. It was not Geshtinanna I wanted to keep you from. But why should an old Lord like me put my little jewel in the way of young robbers? I could have guessed that sheep-eyed Herdsman would turn your head. It has been trial enough lately, hearing you cheer the human Gilgamesh.'

'Is Gilgamesh about? I must see him before I leave and thank him for the wonderful axe he sent me,' Utu broke in.

The two turned from their self-absorbed teasing of each other that was only half playful. At once Inanna was conscious of her new-sprung height, the greater fullness of her body. Even her hair weighed heavier in the womanly chignon behind her head. Looking down at the spare, stooped form of An, who had ruled the Anunnaki, and could still loose the Bull of Heaven, she was pierced with pity for both of them. They could not keep that closeness of great-granddaughter and her foster-father, teacher, lover. They had already lost it. She was in Utu's generation now, on the threshold of his world.

'Good night,' she said, kissing An softly in an unspoken farewell. 'Will you make the ritual of blessing for our betrothal in the morning?'

'We shall see, we shall see,' was all he would say, crossly.

He signed for the swift-handed women who attended him to help him from his chair and guide his unsteady steps towards the lightless *itima* chamber. Inanna thought Nin Isinna, once more his favourite hierodule, looked over her shoulder with a smile of superiority. Inanna felt bereft. She should not have had this uneasy sense of being a loser, here in the great E-Anna, which must soon be her own, in the city of Uruk, where Dumuzi would build her a bride's house, at the time of night when her Star of love was brilliant in the sky and all her married life still before her.

Next morning, they gathered at the clay offering table. The omen priest raised his knife. Blood stained the white kid's fur.

The liver was spotted. The priest grabbed a censer and swung the incense violently, showering the corpse with ashes. He gabbled prayers to avert evil. The ceremony of blessing was aborted.

When the temple functionaries had gone, Inanna turned her anger on An.

'You made this happen! You didn't want me to marry Dumuzi, did you? You don't want me to marry anyone but yourself!'

'Another day, another kid. The time was not lucky,' he mumbled testily. 'Where is the hurry? You two have eternity in front of you, haven't you?'

'But will we stay the same? Will we always be young? Will it be beautiful like this for ever?'

Both of them knew that An, who had embraced his twin and lover Ki with such passion, was no longer the Lord he had been.

'Yet,' said An, with a peevish attempt to placate her, 'there is Uruk, there is the E-Anna. I am very tired, my dear. I was meant for the Sky, not the noisy traffic of Earth. There is no joy in it now for me. I would retreat to the high dome of Angal, I would leave it all . . . if you leave me. Have it! I shall become the Thunderer in the distant heights. Only this.' His scrawny hand grasped her wrist. 'Keep it great, Inanna. Make it very great.'

'How?' She sensed an urgency, as though he kept some hidden legacy he had waited to show her.

His eyes went from side to side. Utu was no longer with them. After the failure of the blessing ritual he had taken himself off with ribald jesting at poor Inanna and gone to enjoy the rest of the morning with Gilgamesh and his friends. An's women crouched against the far walls out of earshot.

'The *me*,' he said. 'Enki's emblems of power.'

Inanna started. Surely the majesty to be challenged was Enlil's in Nippur? An shook his head, as if he guessed her thought.

'No, child. Enlil puffs loud. The Earth praises him. The Anunnaki fear him. By his Word he almost drowned humanity in the Flood. But who is it who saved them? Who manages all things wisely? Who feeds the life that Enlil breathes? Who has all the wisdom of the world in his safekeeping? Who gives and who withholds, as he pleases, all the arts of living?'

*'Enki?'*

'Just so. The Trickster. My late-born son, and cleverest of them all. All the highest *me* of civilisation are kept by him in the treasure house of the Abzu, in Eridu.'

She stared at him. The broad brown tide of the Buranun, which had flowed past them all the way north from Ur to Uruk, was also the highway south to the Eridu Canal. Ships passed both ways, bearing tribute to Enlil and Enki. Could it ever happen that Eridu would yield up its gifts to anyone less than Enlil?

*Not less!*

Fire was in her eyes now, flashing from distant planets. Not less! She was Inanna, the Star of Love. She would be Inanna the Battle-Dancer. The Lady of the Great House. She could be more than Enki, more than An, more than Enlil, even. She would wield all the *me*!

He let her go, patted her hand. 'There, my dear. I see we understand each other. Never let your heart be satisfied with anything less than the highest.'

'I will not. *I will not!*'

She bent and embraced him long and finally. The spoiled day seemed now like an old broken toy pushed aside for a new and more splendid gift.

Noise clattered up the steps to the shaded western terrace. Young men's loud voices, the rattle of weapons jauntily carried. Inanna smiled. She was familiar now with that rivalling commotion that breaks out when young bloods are in earshot of an attractive girl. It seemed to be directed at each other, but it was overloud, competitive, vying for her attention.

They broke into view, made the proper obeisances, kissed An's ceremonial breastplate and bowed more pleasurably to touch their lips to hers. Utu saluted her more familiarly on the mouth. He introduced the rest. Friends from his own city of Sippar, some cousins, Ninurta's sons, from Lagash, the minor Lords of Uruk she already knew, and . . . Gilgamesh.

Dumuzi's half-brother. The colour darkened in his already tanned face. With that mixture of reverence and appreciation that had won Nin Sun's heart for Lugalbanda, he bent to set his lips where all the rest had touched. She felt no sexual thrill, as when Dumuzi greeted her. But an exultation passed through her, a leap of hope. Outside the single family of Ninurta, the Anunnaki were not a warlike breed. Farmers and shepherds, weavers, midwives, builders, scribes. Their genius was to create, more than to destroy.

But she was marked for battle. She would claim the Spear. And fight she must, if Uruk was to be pre-eminent over all other cities, against those cities of Sumer themselves, or against the hostile outer countries, Aratta, Elam, Susa. Her warriors must make all lands bow their proud necks, bring prisoners in thousands, tribute in trains stretching to the far horizon. For such ambition, she would need a general bold as Ninurta, fearsome and pitiless in the fight as his magic Weapon Man Sharur. Brave as Enki voyaging out to do battle with Kur.

And here he was. This gorgeous male, half divine, half quarrelsome human. Taller than other mortal men, he hardly looked out of place in the company of young Sons of An. He stood broad-boned by nature, with muscles hard and bulging from feats on the practice-ground. His eager eyes saw her admiration, took courage and seized the opportunity.

'If I can serve Inanna, Queen of Uruk, then only name the task.'

Her hand rested on his bare shoulder, felt the strength beneath give her strength too.

'I will, Gilgamesh, my soldier, my champion. Friend of my

brother. Brother of my dearest friend.'

'Enough to be called the friend of my Queen alone.'

'I hope to test that friendship soon.'

'Prove me, Lady. I am trained and ready. I have come to my manhood with the rest of my year.'

'I see you have. And this seeing gives me pleasure.'

# Chapter Forty-nine

Inanna stretched luxuriously. Moments before, Nin Shubur's voice had snatched her out of that recurring nightmare. The hopeless people, the silent empty storehouse, a little girl entering alone, finding at the end a lamb's rotting carcass covered in flies. But she was awake now, and already it was almost forgotten. Soft lambswool cushioned her youthful limbs. The floor was scented with cedar shavings. Nin Shubur was holding a tray of honey cakes and sherbet.

Of course, there were palace servants to wait on the Moon Lord's daughter. A *sukkal* is not intended to be a nurse. Nin Shubur loved Inanna. She did this service from choice.

The Mountain Woman bent over her charge, plumped the pillows, raised her to lean comfortably against them. The hour was early, the air cool.

'Was it really Gilgamesh's father who brought me to Uruk? Tell me again,' begged Inanna. 'Tell me about Lugalbanda.'

'You are vain enough already. If you had the *ens* of cities fighting over you while you were just a little girl, what will you do to the hearts of Lords and men now you are a full-grown woman?'

'Go on, Nin Shubur. Tell me about Lugalbanda and Inanna of Aratta. Especially the bit about the Cave of Hurum.'

The indulgent *sukkal* settled herself on the cushions beside Inanna, took a silver comb and a vial of jasmine oil. She began to comb Inanna's long black hair and smooth and perfume her neck and back and swelling breasts. The words crooned from her lips in a singsong. Beside the door, blind Zilulu seated herself upon a stool, took up her harp with its lapis lazuli finial of the moon bull's head. She touched the strings lightly to help Nin Shubur's tale along.

'Once upon a time, when you were younger, the stars did not shine on Sumer as brightly as they do now. The mountains were closer than the plain to the Moon and his children. You were born high in Kurkisikil, the Shining Place, where the seven-mouthed river of life pours out from the underworld.

'From the hills of the east your Sun Brother Utu rose every morning from his mother's lap, cut his way out of the chamber of night with his golden saw. He made the Earth glad.

'Rain Man Ishkur gathered his strength in the clouds over the mountain peaks, caused showers to fall, filled streams, sent waterfalls rushing down the hills, swelled out the red floods of the Idiglat, the copper waters of the Buranun, made the hills of Aratta and the plain of Sumer rejoice.

'Young Inanna was the Morning Star, a child shaking awake the sleeper in the cool of day. At dusk she was the Evening Star, decking herself in her mother's finery, painting her eyes with kohl, reddening her fingertips, sitting in the window hung with jewellery, like a harlot in the alehouse. She invited us all to dance and play with her when work was over.

'Aratta was rich with stone and metal, red cornelian, blue lapis lazuli. Silver of the moon.

'Far down the rivers, in Uruk and Eridu, the cities of clay, there was no stone. Where the rivers spread their level floods, there were no hills to mine. Only the asses journeying far under the sun could bring wealth and jewels and stone down for building. The only gold of Uruk was its sheep and grain. But Aratta had closed its proud fist against the cities of Sumer.

'Then the priest-king Enmerkar, *en* of Uruk, saw that Aratta had what was to be desired. Saw that its brightest jewel was its little Lady. He desired Inanna.

'In Uruk a brick house is ready, the E-Anna, built for An. In Eridu, the Abzu is built. Will the Sky Lord's great-granddaughter come down from the mountains, like An from Above, and bless Sumer? Will she enrich their lowland palaces with the treasures of her mountains? Can this be done?

'Then Enmerkar, *en* of Uruk, gathered a great host of warlike young men, chose seven brothers as their generals, and over all, the eighth, his right-hand man, his dearest friend . . .'

'Lugalbanda!' chorused Inanna with her. She sat up

straight to listen, and her eyes shone with anticipation.

'They travelled north and east, crossed one mountain, crossed two. On the Mountain of Hurum, Lugalbanda fell ill. Fever wracked him. Such pain tore at his bones he could not bear to be moved. One hand hung useless. Enmerkar cradled him in his arms, shook him, tried to rouse him. Lugalbanda could only weep. At last there fell upon him a weakness like death. How his brothers mourned. His comrades could not stay longer. There was not enough food to keep such an army in the mountain wilderness. Aratta lay far ahead. They could not carry a dying man to war.

' "Shall we finish him with the mace and bury him here?" one asked Enmerkar.

'The *en* replied with anger, "Would you knock the valiant Lugalbanda on the head, like a fish in a net? No, let us lay him up there, in that cave above us, with his face to the east. Perhaps the Anunnaki who has struck him down will step aside. Or else let him sleep on till the Lords of the Netherworld rise to claim him."

'Sadly the thing was done. They gathered armfuls of twigs from the pine trees, spread sheepskins over them, made a fragrant bed. The hero did not move as they laid him out, touched his still-warm brow, moistened his lips with water, set his axe and dagger by his side. They left him food and drink, and incense for the Anunnaki.

' "We will take his body up when we return this way, and bury him honourably in Uruk."

'They set a rock at the mouth of the cave to keep out the wolves, and they marched away.

'Only his personal Guardian can tell how long Lugalbanda lay in the sleep near death. He opened his eyes . . .'

'And then? And then?' Inanna was laughing with delight. Nin Shubur could not help but smile.

'Yes, vain miss! He appealed first to Utu, and then . . . he called upon the name of Inanna, pronounced the name of the Morning Star.'

'And Inanna rose for him!' Her eager voice took up the story. 'She came up over the Hill of Hurum. She shone in all her beauty over the top of the rock and lit Lugalbanda's eyes. With her touch she healed him . . . I did, didn't I?'

'So he said. With his awakening strength his hero's courage returned. He called on all the Anunnaki to help, Sun, Moon and Stars. Bright Utu shone on him by day, Nanna by night.

Ishkur sent rain to slake his thirst. Lugalbanda rose from his death couch, thrust the rock aside, walked out into life again.

'Lonely that man now. Mountains to climb alone. Fierce rivers to cross. Only his knife to win him food. Far from home. But Inanna never left him. Every morning and evening her Star shone for him, guided him above the level of the woods to where the Eagle Pine of Enlil stood solitary on the peak.'

'And there the Imdugud birds had their nest.'

'Tell the story yourself, if you like, my lady!'

'No. I'll be quiet. I promise.'

'While the parent birds were out hunting, Lugalbanda found the chicks in their nest of juniper and boxwood. He honoured them royally. He fed them food from his rations, honey cake and salted mutton. He smeared fat on their heads, decorated them with white cedar twigs, painted their eyes with kohl. When the Imdugud birds returned, bearing a wild ox and a great pot of water for their young in their talons, this time there was no hungry screaming from the nest. They roared once. Silence. They roared twice. Silence. They feared their chicks were gone. The hills shook with their grief. Then they swooped down on the nest like a thundercloud to find their children, full of food, honoured like Anunnaki.

'For that, they promised Lugalbanda whatever blessing he asked. They offered him barges loaded with beans and barley and cucumbers and apples. He turned it down. They offered him flint arrows that would never miss their mark. He turned it down. They offered him an invincible helmet and breastplate and throw-net—'

'He turned it down!'

'Yes. He chose . . . speed. To cover the ground as quick as a thought, to run without tiring. And so he caught up with the dust of the army's march. His brothers were overjoyed. But Lugalbanda kept the Thunderbirds' secret. And so the host of Uruk arrived at Aratta.'

'And I was really living there then? With the other *en* and all his *mah* priests, and the *nindingir* priestesses and the *mashmash* priests guarding me?'

'In a chamber, dark as night, in the heart of the sanctuary, from which you only came forth one week in the year. And beside your house was a rushing river. The people of Aratta would not let you go, nor their precious stones either. The siege was long and weary. Aratta's *en* boasted they would never submit as long as you lived among them. Enmerkar knew that someone must go all the long dangerous way back to Kullab to find how the siege could be ended.'

'And Lugalbanda volunteered!'

'The hero stepped closer to his *en*. "Enmerkar. I would speak with you privately." In the hush of evening they paced the royal tent. The Evening Star hung brilliant in the east, lit Lugalbanda's heart. He told his story, how Inanna found and saved him. He will journey now, back across the seven mountain ranges of Anshan, alone. He will bring the answer.'

'And did he? Did he? What did I say? What did I do?' Inanna was jumping up and down like a little girl on her thonged bed, so that its cedar supports creaked and threatened to split apart. She had known this story by heart since childhood, but she was never weary of hearing it. It was especially magical, here in Uruk, in Kullab.

Nin Shubur rose, signalled to the body slaves to bring Inanna's dress and jewellery. Still the story sang from her lips, like a highland stream.

'He set out alone, in spite of the pleas of all his friends that it was too risky. He had found his guiding Star. With the speed of the Thunderbird he crossed the mountains and arrived in Kullab just before midnight.'

'And . . .?'

'Yes. Your priestess seer met him in the E-Anna at night. She listened to his story. She offered up incense. And wise Inanna spoke through her lips telling him what to do. He sped back, over all the mountains, to find the *en* Enmerkar. By the river of Aratta was a tamarisk tree, and under the roots of that tree lived an *urinu* fish. If the tree was felled, and the fish was caught, your power would leave Aratta. The men of Uruk and Kullab caught the magic fish. They killed and ate it. They fed some to your fierce battle standard, Aankara.

'Then they made a box out of the tamarisk tree. What followed was even more dangerous. Again Lugalbanda volunteered.

'Stealthily he climbs into the town. Night is his friend now. In the starlight he slips past the sleepy priestesses guarding Inanna's threshold. It would be death for another to enter that windowless chamber, where the Maiden sits, crowned with gold-leaf flowers, girdled with lapis lazuli lions, with her rod, the *nir* stone sceptre, in her hand. But Lugalbanda trusts the eye of love that shone on him.'

Inanna knelt up and clasped her hands as the slave Amanamtagga tried to wind the fringed cloth of her dress under her armpits.

'I could have killed him for that, couldn't I? I could have ordered the Imdugud to tear him to pieces with his talons.'

Nin Shubur shook her head. 'The Imdugud was Lugalbanda's friend now. Do not be too ready to believe that everyone must obey you. You are not all-powerful.'

The girl pulled a face and fell silent, holding out her arms for the blue-beaded and silver bracelets to be slipped coolly on her warm skin.

Nin Shubur glanced at her expecting an eager prompting, then, since it did not come, finished the story anyway.

'He held out his hand to you. You smiled for him. One glance into the cave had been all you needed. Aratta could not hold you. An army could not take you. For Lugalbanda alone you would abandon the mountain and come down to Sumer.'

Inanna said nothing, but her dark eyes were intent on the *sukkal*'s face now.

'He said you stretched out your hand and stepped down from your niche in the sanctuary. For him, you let yourself be laid in the tamarisk box. For him, you let yourself be launched into the source of the Idiglat. Then Lugalbanda crept away to the camp. The men of Uruk and Kullab marched home and laid a net across the marshes.

'They waited. Day faded. Utu went to his mother's lap. Inanna's planet appeared. And when they hauled in their net dripping from the lake, there was the tamarisk box. And thrashing about in it was an *urinu* fish. Gold and lapis lazuli scales, *nir* stone eyes, a tail and fins of burnished copper spiked with silver. And all the stars of the Sky danced in the spray as she leaped from the box and turned into . . . a little girl!

'And caught in the net were other shining fish that were your Moon Father Nanna and your Reed Mother Nin Gal, Sun Brother Utu. But Rain Man Ishkur stayed behind in the hills. The people of Sumer made Ur the City of the Moon, Sippar the City of the Sun. When they had you safe, they sent grain and wool to Aratta, and when Aratta knew it had lost you, it submitted and sent stone and jewels to Sumer. They made the Abzu in Eridu and the E-Anna of Uruk glorious to welcome you.'

Mischief danced in Inanna's eyes. 'It's funny. I can't

remember *any* of that. Not Aratta, not the cave, not even what Lugalbanda looked like. Nor why we came down to live in Sumer. All I can remember is swimming in a river with Utu, when we were small.'

'Can you forget the hills so easily, my lady? I cannot.' Pain swiftly deepened the creases in the Mountain Woman's face. She lifted her eyes to the doorway.

Low morning sun swept the few shadows of buildings and trees far out towards the desert. Canals glinted like sunbeams. Where they ceased, the vegetation stopped. All else was barren gold. Featureless, treeless, lifeless, it stretched in awesome flatness further than eye could reach. Nin Shubur's soul still refused to accept it. How often clouds towered above the horizon and her spirits leaped to greet the majesty of mountains. Mirages tricked her with the image of blue hills. Yet she did not despair. The hills were truly there. She had known them. She had lived on their heights, till Enlil called her down to serve Inanna. They could never be removed, though she could not see them.

When she looked back, Inanna was frowning. 'Lugalbanda married Nin Sun, didn't he? And then Gilgamesh was born.' She suddenly tore a tassel from the fringed blanket. A scowl darkened her brow, so that she looked for a moment like an infant Thunderbird. 'Then I wasn't the only Lady Lugalbanda fell in love with?'

'He must have been a hero whose soul led him to wander in the high places, away from other men. There, where no humans tread, he met the Daughters of An. It seems they liked what they saw.'

Inanna was dressed, her black hair braided with pearl flowers, her soft skin scented with jasmine oil. Hearing a shout from outside, she went to the balcony and looked out, almost secretively, through the vines.

Gilgamesh was on the parade ground below, hurling throw-sticks. As she watched, he swung his splendid torso.

'Gilgamesh wouldn't have chosen speed, would he? He'd rather have had the weapons or the helmet. So would I.'

The last throw-stick struck the clay target, shattering it. Gilgamesh's head turned up, in that remembered gesture, claiming approval. Without smiling, Inanna raised her hand in acknowledgement.

'So a Lady can marry a human,' she murmured.

# Chapter Fifty

For another week Inanna enjoyed the company of the young men. Ninurta's sons brought their seven sisters, Zazuru, Impae, Uragruntaea, Heulnunna, Heshaga and the twins Zurmu and Zarmu. Geshtinanna called, bringing mules laden with jars of wine to make them all more merry. The girls watched mock battles, cried out at real blood, compared the dyes and embroideries of all their dresses, discussed the men. Inanna found herself awaking all at once to the pleasures of both adolescence and her coming marriage, after the strangely sheltered and yet adult distortion of her cloistered childhood. She was as gay as any of them. But she felt she was curiously older than Ninurta's daughters, seemed to see over their heads a larger vision. She talked more animatedly in the company of men and it was not entirely the wish to rouse the desire of their bodies. Only Geshtinanna seemed to her wiser than she was.

In the fragrant evenings, they listened to the Lady of the Vine singing. Geshtinanna's voice enchanted them. The words were gems of poetry to be treasured.

'Where do you find your poems?' Inanna asked her, finding her one day inscribing verses on fresh wet tablets.

'Where are the true songs always found? In the heart. To sing the *balag* lament you must know grief. To hymn an *alari* love song you must experience desire. I tell what I know.'

'You *wrote* those songs?'

Geshtinanna jumped up and embraced Inanna. 'May you know only the joys of the *ala* harp, sister-in-law. Let me bear the grief of the *balag* for you and Dumuzi.'

'You love him very much, don't you?'

Geshtinanna coloured. 'As a sister should love her brother. Of course! Dearly.'

The girls were walking in the Anunnaki's district of Kullab, once a separate city from Uruk, now its most sacred enclave. The great E-Anna, that some said had descended from the Sky itself, was not the only palace. An was having the more modest Urugal refurbished for himself now that he deemed Inanna ready to assume the highest power. The streets were shady between close-set walls. Only the processional ways were wide to the sun. Leafy gardens billowed with white-flowered *mesu* trees, pomegranates, figs, dappled vine arbours. Here, among warm-scented apple trees, Dumuzi and Geshtinanna had their town house.

If anyone had asked Inanna why she was walking that way with her cousins from Lagash that morning, she would have protested that she was going to visit Geshtinanna. Dumuzi was not in town. Yet why did her hands linger over the tracery of palm trees on the gate that had already been swung open to admit her? Why did she stop to pluck blossom from an apple tree, pressing its petals against her face? Why did her eyes leap with joy when she heard the noise of workmen busy on the ground beyond, that overlooked the river, saw the dust of labour turn the air to golden haze?

Heulnunna nudged her. 'Someone is in a hurry to build a house.'

'Lucky the bride who will sleep under that new roof!'

'She will see the New Year Moon reflected in the Buranun.'

'And the Star of Love, caught in a date palm.'

All Ninurta's seven daughters were round her, laughing knowingly and enviously.

Inanna made herself lower her eyes like a modest bride, felt her disobedient cheeks grow warm.

'I am not here to look at what my Lord Dumuzi is building. It is Lady Geshtinanna I have come to see.'

And the Vine Girl was on the threshold, her face alight with welcome.

'Oh, Inanna, I'm so glad you've come. And the seven sisters. You're just in time. I've a new song today for you to listen to, a dispute between Copper and Silver, arguing which of them is best.'

'But surely Silver?' said Inanna. 'There can be no contest, can there?'

'Oh, in my song it is not so. The axe you make of silver is soft, fit for ceremonial only. Hardened copper can fell a tree. Silver lies in treasure houses and temples, tarnishing in the darkness. Copper is bright with use. If all the palaces disappeared tomorrow, where would you find silver then? In the grave, the gateway to the Netherworld, nowhere else. But copper lives in the light, in the mattock that turns the stubble, in the adze that shapes the plough, in the sickle that harvests the barley. Copper is life. Silver attends the dead.'

Jewels of death?

Inanna put up her hand, touched the silver and lapis lazuli collar clasped round her pale throat. Even after her early morning walk, the metal felt cold. Had this wise friend seen it before she spoke? But why should a friend choose ill-omened words when her brother's wife-to-be comes to her home? She shuddered then. Was it a *kledon* omen? The chance word spoken by a priest unseen inside the temple, seized on and interpreted personally by the passer-by outside who hears it.

Geshtinanna saw her shiver and was instantly concerned.

'Come indoors. Shall I have a fire lit? There was rain last night; the air is still cool. Let me pour wine for you all.'

The rest of the morning passed in song and chatter. Inanna felt herself grow warm and confident again with the wine, with the teasing of the other girls about the new house Dumuzi was building for his bride, with the songs of bridal beds Geshtinanna sang for them.

'Geshtinanna, you are no better than the alewife of a tavern, getting her girls to paint their faces and sit in the windows to catch men,' declared Inanna. 'I am sure you threw Dumuzi and me together. That night I came back to Ur, last New Moon festival, when we gave Nin Shubur the slip and you sang in the city square . . .'

Geshtinanna's face flowered with suppressed laughter. 'I confess it, yes. That was not the accidental impulse of a moment. Our escape was planned, to get you two alone to our house, with only our servants for witnesses. But it was not my idea.'

'Dumuzi! But . . .?'

'Oh, he has watched you, these many years. When you were only a child he used to visit the E-Anna with gifts from the farm.'

'I remember them. He brought me sheep's milk cheeses. Pipes of reed. He taught me to play on them.'

'He says you were special, even then. He never forgot you. As you grew towards womanhood, getting more beautiful every day, An closed the palace to young men like Dumuzi.

He hid you in the women's quarters. But he still came to our farm on the edge of the steppe, to escape the summer heat of the city. He talked of you sometimes. He couldn't help it.'

'And just for that, Dumuzi . . .'

'Oh, no! You were more than a rumour and a memory. In spite of An, all Uruk knew and loved you. I am told you used to hang over the wall watching the humans drill and fight each other, laughing and clapping. Gilgamesh and Dumuzi are brothers, you know. Ama-Ushumgalanna was often there, disguised in a sheepskin kilt, with a cloth over his head. He would be one of that admiring crowd that lifted their faces to salute you. When he heard that you were returning to your mother's house, ripe for marriage, I had no peace till I promised to bring you two together.'

Inanna blushed with pleasure. 'Could he not have come up to the palace, formally, as my suitor?'

'How could he tell you in the palace all that was in his heart? He does not have the gift of song, as I do, to throw my secret thoughts on the air for all to hear. Besides, the need was urgent. You already had other suitors closer to your father's wishes.'

'Enkimdu.'

'Poor Enkimdu. He's a good man. Everybody says so.'

'Your useful copper axe?'

'But our Dumuzi is not the jewel of death. Never think that, Inanna. He is the source of life. He is lambs and date clusters and flowing milk.'

'The wealth of my house,' Inanna said dreamily. 'While the sheepfold stands.'

'Your little sheepfold of love is almost ready. I could tell you . . . No! I won't reveal any more secrets.'

'When her house is built, Inanna will need a bridal bed,' said Impae.

'My bed!' Inanna's hand flew to her mouth. 'Oh! How *could* I have forgotten? My poor *huluppu* tree! I've been almost a week back in Uruk and I haven't once been to look at it. And this is just why I saved it, why I planted it, why I ordered An's gardener to take great care of it while I was gone. Oh, let me show it to you! Then I must cut it down. From its wood I am going to make both my throne and my marriage bed.'

'Oh, show us, show us! This afternoon.' Zurmu and Zarmu clapped their hands in anticipation.

'We ought to have a great ceremony. Who's going to fell it?'

'Dumuzi, of course!' declared Heshaga. 'Who else?'

'No,' said Inanna quickly. 'This is *my* bed. *My* throne. A bride cannot ask her bridegroom to provide the dowry she brings him. Besides, Dumuzi is not in Uruk.'

The Lagash sisters looked at Geshtinanna and smiled.

'Utu, then?'

'Yes. The Sun Lord should shine on my marriage.'

'Is An's blessing on you to be tomorrow, now?'

'If the omens are good.' A shadow of annoyance crossed Inanna's face. 'I'm sure that was An's fault, to spite me for choosing Dumuzi. But he won't hold out, now that he has seen I am determined. It was all that upset which put the *huluppu* tree out of my head. It will go well this time. You will see.'

The morning had whiled away. The midday meal was awaiting them at the palace, and then the afternoon rest. Inanna kissed Geshtinanna farewell. The Wine Girl's eyes twinkled. As she waved to them from her doorway, her gaze kept slipping away down the road towards the city gate.

They were halfway along the Age-edinna Street when a shout broke out from behind them, echoing between the narrow walls like the report of thunder.

'Inanna! Inanna!'

She whipped round. Colour blazed in her face. A troop of young men was coming up the road from the river gate, almost running. Even at that distance the voice had been enough for her to recognise the sheepskinned figure at their head waving to her.

'Is it . . .?' Uragruntaea enquired.

'Yes, it must be!'

'It is, isn't it, Inanna? It's him!'

'He obviously can't wait to get his arms round you!'

Inanna had taken one glad step back down the road. But then she halted, seeing the Shepherd running now past the gate of his own estate they had just left. Her eyes flashed like stars on a rain-clear night.

'The impudence of him! To yell at the Queen of the E-Anna in the open street. Just look at him chasing after me, still in a sheepskin cloak and the sweat of travel. Me, Inanna! Let's teach him a lesson.'

She turned on her heel and began to walk swiftly up the

street to the E-Anna, her mouth twitching with suppressed laughter.

'That's true love, Inanna,' urged Zazuru, hurrying to keep up with her.

'Inanna, my *lubi*! Wait for me!'

She looked over her shoulder. The pack of young men were all running now.

'Am I a straying lamb to be rounded up by his sheepdogs?' And she took to her heels and ran too. Nin Shubur stopped to let her pass, turned back and stood in the middle of the road, confronting the oncomers. The *sag-ursag* readied their spears, a ceremonial gesture, but always enough. The E-Anna gates were already open. Inanna and the seven daughters of Ninurta sped through. At once they were up the first flight of steps and on to the roof of the priestesses' *giparu* overlooking the street. At last Inanna burst into giggles.

'Look at him! Nin Shubur's stopped them. Oh, she is marvellous, my *sukkal*. What would I do without her? She will be very polite, very firm, but she will tell him he cannot hail me in the street like a city harlot, however much he loves me.'

'She hasn't stopped him. He's coming closer. They're letting him through.'

The girls crowded to the low reed fence set in clay that served for a parapet. Dumuzi was striding towards the foot of the outer wall. His reddened face turned up to her.

'My Dancer, swifter than the gazelle, more elusive than the *sagkal* snake!'

'Why did you chase me, like a wolf after a lamb? You are not allowed to take me yet. You do not have the permission of my mother, or my father, or my grandmother Nin Gikuga to get me from my pen.'

'Must you always flaunt your family before me? Well, let me flaunt these before you!' He drew from his leather pouch a fistful of jewels and dangled them under her eyes. A collar of many tiny beads of lapis lazuli, bright as the rainwashed sky. A huge ceremonial breast ornament, more gorgeous than any pendant she had ever worn. Gold, silver, carnelian, more lapis lazuli. They glittered like a rainbow.

'Oh!' She leaned further out, caught in spite of herself. 'Oh, Dumuzi! Are they for me?'

'Of course, queen of all riches. Who else? The day you marry me, these gems and hundreds more shall clasp your throat, shall lie on your breast . . . until my hands unfasten their embrace and place their own around you.'

'May it come soon, man of my heart. May it come soon. Oh, let the omen-kid tomorrow speak that day pure as an *udnua* festival for An's blessing on us.'

'This man with his hands full of gems is building a house, I see. A house in Kullab,' Heulnunna called.

'Who will lie in the chamber of that new house?' Zazuru sang down.

'Tell us her name, Dumuzi Ushumgalanna.'

'Inanna, my heart. Inanna, my Star of Love. Inanna, my Queen of Heaven. She shall lie in my new-built house where no woman before her has slept. On a new bed where no bride before her has lain. We shall make a new thing together. We shall make the oldest delight young as the Moon returning from the Netherworld. In that house I am going to celebrate the perfect marriage with Inanna.'

'Soon!' cried Inanna, unable to contain herself. 'Soon, my Shepherd's staff, my tall poplar, my man with the small gems for my throat and the big gems for my breasts. Very soon!'

She blew a multitude of kisses to him and went down the steps as the gongs were sounding for the midday meal. Nin Shubur reproved her with a look, made her wash her hands in the silver ewer at the door of the dining hall, discreetly rearranged her hair.

There was a guest at the honoured long side of the dining table. Inanna started and saw his eyes drop from hers sadly. Enkimdu the Farmer. An shot her a little savage look, the old man's feeble weapon of defiance.

'My lord.' Inanna greeted Enkimdu formally, let him bow to kiss her breast pendant. He smelt more earthy than Dumuzi's milky sweetness. But his clothes were good. A skirt of white linen from his own flax fields that left his brown chest bare. A leather belt, ringed with copper. More copper bracelets on his arms.

They talked desultorily, with an uneasy politeness. Yet when Enkimdu turned to An, his face grew animated. When he spoke of teams of oxen, of the design of ploughs, of the building of a new millhouse to provide shelter and work for widows and orphan girls, he became almost poetical in his enthusiasm. Inanna listened. She could not dislike this man, but she did not love him.

At the close of the meal he stood to take his leave as Inanna made ready to go to her rooms for the siesta. He bowed over her hand.

'My good wishes for your betrothal blessing tomorrow, Lady Inanna. May all go well this time. I need not tell you I wish I could have been the man to whom you gave your heart. But I cannot wish you or Dumuzi ill. Long life and happiness and fine children to you.'

'You will be a guest at our wedding?'

'More than that. I will heap your feast table with the best of beer and flour and vegetables Sumer can grow.'

'Then travel well, my lord.'

'Inanna . . .' His hand squeezed hers with a moment's urgency.

'My lord.' She tried to withdraw it.

'I wish that it was I who had had the cultivating of your garden. I would have served you more faithfully.'

She took it for a sexual metaphor. 'You presume too much, Lord Enkimdu. Just because you bless the plough! In the south, Dumuzi Ushumgalanna is known as Lord of the Orchards. He can water my tree plentifully!'

His eyes grew dark again. He released her hand. 'That is not what I meant. I did not wish to upset you. But the harm I have seen is already done.'

He left the hall without looking back.

# Chapter Fifty-one

No one disturbed Inanna's rest, but the spring afternoon was cooler, with gathering cloud. When the shadow of the E-Anna had crossed the eastern terrace, she was wide awake. Ninurta's daughters were already gathering. Nin Shubur sent eunuchs to summon the rest.

'Where is it? Is it far?' Impae wanted to know.

'Oh no, between our wall and the river. I had a little enclosure made, a high fence of *sushima* reeds to keep intruders out.'

'A secret garden!'

'No. Not secret, really. Private, rather. This is *my* tree. I didn't want a thing so precious standing in the open where any passer-by could snap off a branch or carve its bark.'

'Is it so special?'

'To me, it is. It came to me out of the storm, carried on a spring flood wave down the Buranun, from somewhere in the Edin north of us. I saved its life.'

'Well, let's see Inanna's marvellous tree.'

The girls set out. A shower had settled the dust. Fragments of blue sky and pearly cloud inlaid the puddles. Shade trees dripped moisture. The garden beyond the side gate breathed out the scents of spring. A hundred different flowers raised their faces among the freshly seeding grass. No one minded the wet skirts clinging to their legs, the water squelching between sole and sandal. Water was too precious, too essential, to be greeted with anything less than gratitude.

A tall pale palisade showed far to the left of the main avenue. Inanna led the way towards it. No gate was visible, only a shock of foliage above its jagged crest.

'A *zirru*,' said Heulnunna. 'That's what they sometimes call your mother, isn't it? Lady Reed Fence.'

'It didn't keep Uncle Nanna out, did it?' giggled Zurmu.

'Sh!' Zarmu nudged her. 'Remember we're Inanna's guests.'

'Why should I mind?' Inanna laughed. 'They love each other. No *zirru* I built would keep Dumuzi out.'

She led them round to the far side, stepping across the channel that carried water from the cisterns under the fence into the little plot. At the gate she paused, looked carefully at the fastening. It was not a massive door. A frame of stout reed poles to which a screen of matting had been nailed. The once fresh and glossy canes were greyed and weathered from a season's rains. But Inanna was looking at the cords that tied it, with a frown.

'What is this? What is this?'

'Is something the matter?' Uragruntaea asked. 'Has someone broken in?'

'Worse than that. No one has been here at all. Look! That's the imprint of my own seal in the clay on the knot. It has never been broken! Every day An's head gardener should have come here to see if it needed to be weeded or watered or pruned. I ordered him not to entrust it to anyone else, to look after it with his own hands. This is not his seal, it's not An's seal. No one has been here, ever. All the months I have been away in Ur, he hasn't come.'

With a gesture of fury she snapped the seal of clay moulded over the fastening her own fingers had tied. Her shaking hands struggled with the stiff cords, then the knot fell free. She motioned to Nin Shubur to lift the latch. The girls, a little awed, though by what they could not say, unless it was Inanna's anger, watched in silence.

Reluctantly, on unoiled hinges, the gate creaked open. A little circle of feathery grass, tangled with thistles and camelthorn. The *huluppu* tree was no longer a battered piece of flotsam. They saw a firm, wide trunk, a crown of grey-green leaves so thick that they seemed not to have suffered from the gardener's neglect. Roots spread to grip the ground. Limbs stretched out to bear a multitude of branches.

'It's all right,' breathed Inanna, her face breaking into relieved laughter. 'It's still alive.'

'How thick and dark its branches look,' murmured Heulnunna. 'As though a thundercloud were caught in them.'

'Did the stem get split in the storm that threw it into the river?' called Impae, who had wandered round to the left side and was peering at the trunk. 'There is a cleft here like a cave.'

'How strangely patterned the roots are,' Heshaga said. 'It is not surprising Ningishzida is Lord of both tree roots and snakes. You could almost think . . .' She screamed. 'It is! It is, Inanna! There's a great snake wound round the bottom of your tree! Look! There! It's horrible!'

But the rest of her shrieks were drowned out in a colossal clap of thunder that shook a thousand leaves from the tree, scattering them like hail around the crimson and black hissing head that was rearing up out of the hollowed earth. All Ninurta's daughters were screaming now. The crown of the tree roared like a startled beast. The branches convulsed. In a storm of whole twigs and branchlets a gigantic bird erupted from the top of the *huluppu* tree. Vast wings, greater than any eagle's, shadowed the spring sky. As if at its bellow, drops of thundery rain splashed the ground. Its head was a snarling lion's. It rose, circling, till its roar rumbled away into the distant clouds. It left the jagged outline of a huge nest, perched in the crutch of splintered branches.

The seven sisters fell to the ground, covering their eyes.

'Imdugud! The Thunderbird! Father, save us!'

Inanna stood, white-faced and rigid, clutching Nin Shubur for support. The *sukkal* too was pale and trembling, her mind racing for answers through her fear.

'My lady, we must go. At once! It is far too dangerous for you to stay here. We have no gifts to appease them.'

The massive Serpent knotted round the roots writhed. Its head moved alarmingly. Inanna watched in fascination its flickering tongue, its slithering coils that seemed as though they might at any moment disengage themselves from the arching roots and stream towards her. But still it clung, rising and falling like a restless sea.

From the dark nest silhouetted against a lowering sky came mewing screams, more high and desperate than the Imdugud's roar.

'The bird has young!' Nin Shubur whispered through almost frozen lips. 'It will return. Oh, my lady, leave now!'

Round the side of the tree, some distance from the others, Impae had risen from her knees, peering in horror through fingers covering her face. She stumbled towards Inanna, threw herself on the older girl's shoulder, weeping with shock. Her sisters were scrambling to their feet, running for the gate and the safety of the well-kept park.

Inanna put an arm round Impae. It made her feel a little

braver, having someone even more terrified to comfort. A hard knot of anger was beginning to form in her heart. This was her tree, her precious *huluppu*. How dare the Imdugud appropriate it for its nest! How dare this basilisk-eyed Serpent claim the roots and hiss so menacingly at her to stop her approaching!

'It's all right, Impae. The Thunderbird has gone. There are only the nestlings left. They can't hurt you. And the Serpent hasn't moved.'

'Inanna! There's something there!' Impae wept, shuddering.

'I know. I know. We will call the guards . . . I'll get Utu . . . Someone will drive them out. They must!'

'No,' moaned Impae. 'You don't understand. You haven't seen her.'

'Her? The Imdugud mother?'

'*No!*' Her voice was almost a whisper now. She tried to peep over her shoulder, then swiftly buried her face again, as though she dared not look. 'In the cleft of the trunk. A face. A white ghost face. A woman's face!'

'What *woman*?' With a hard resolve Inanna pushed Impae away. She started to circle the tree, keeping a careful distance from the hissing coils that swayed to track her every step. Nin Shubur and Impae tried to hold her back, but she shook them off. The trunk, the roots, the leaning branches with their mewling load were between her and the open gate now. The Thunderbird still shadowed the sky, coming lower again, its massive wings spread, its lion-muzzle bent earthwards, watching the tree. Outside, six of the Lagash sisters clung together in silent anguish. No one had called for the guards, but shouts were rising in the distance.

Inanna stood alone. The circle of the reed fence shut her off from the rest of the world. Even Nin Shubur seemed as if in another country, supporting the hysterical Impae on the far side of the tree.

The cleft was there before her. Impae had been right. Like a narrow cave, very black in the silvery trunk. A season ago this bole had been stout, fine timber. When she left it for Ur, the bark had not been split.

Three sharp-fanged heads peered down over their twiggy fortress at the owner of the garden, who was now an intruder. The Serpent's head crept round the arches of the roots to stare accusingly. Inanna tried to ignore her thumping heart, these hostile witnesses, to gaze directly into the darkness at the heart of her tree.

Was that a face? Or a trick of the leaf-hung light? The sky was very dark. Hard to know if the rumbling in the clouds was only a spring thunderstorm or the hovering Imdugud. A sharply-angled face, if face it was. Dark slanting eyes. A fall of hair — or was it shadows? — veiling the gleam of naked skin.

No other sound, between the roar above, the hiss below. Strange, this cold fear. Worse than the understandable terror of Thunderbird or Snake. How could this woman hurt her?

'Is . . . Is someone there?'

'Only if you see me. Only if you hear me.' A beautiful lilting voice with an edge of laughter. Why should it chill Inanna?

'Who . . . are . . . you . . . ?'

'In the beginning, my name was Kiskillilla.'

'The Dark Maid?'

'Oh, not so dark, and definitely not a maiden!'

She seemed to be seeping outward, like resin from the wood. Her form materialised within the cleft, still not wholly separate from Inanna's tree. The pallor of her face had been an illusion of uncertain light in thicker darkness. She was more tawny golden than Inanna. Hard to say if she was beautiful. The arrogance of her stance suggested she did not care. She was completely naked, her hair not bound with any jewels, though a few red berries seemed caught in its waves as if by chance. Her lips curved with a mocking assurance. Her limbs were hard-muscled, her body firm and shapely, hips wide, waist small, breasts proud. She carried herself easily, alert and light-footed as a nomad hunter. Light-footed? Inanna's eyes fell to the rain-streaked earth, found clawed bird talons.

'Kiskillilla? Who refused to lie under her husband on her wedding night and, when he would not let her mount him, left him for the wilderness?'

'Kiskillilla, who bears a hundred demon children every day and bewails the curse on her which says that none of them shall live!'

Was she *laughing*?

'You take revenge. You steal and maim or kill our babies.'

'And lure your husbands into the most foul lewdness.

Cover them in the night with my immodest limbs. Drag them off to the desert to do bestial things. I see you know the stories. Yes, I am Kiskillilla.'

'But . . . why? Why?' The words were almost soundless.

'My poor Inanna. You do not mean: Why did I make my great rebellion? Why do I choose to live as I am? You only mean: Why you? Why in your tree? Why in the wood you want to make your throne and bed?'

'Yes. *Why?*'

'You will not learn the answer to the second questions, because you would not ask the first.'

And, like a fungus withering in the sun, she shrank within the closing cleft. Her wind-tanned flesh blended with the grainy fibres of split wood. Her hair became as shadows. Her voice rustled away like the last of the dropping grey leaves.

'My lady!' An anxious call from Nin Shubur. 'What are you staring at? The Imdugud is coming back! Oh, hurry, my lady!'

Startled, Inanna looked overhead. The cloud of lion-face, of outstretched blade-like pinions, of feathered thighs, of sharp, spread talons was swooping down upon its open nest.

The Serpent swelled inside its dull, blurred skin, its eyes extremely bright.

Inanna fled.

Outside the gate, her hard-held courage failed. She collapsed to her knees, weeping for rage and fright and frustration.

'What is wrong? What is wrong? Why does nothing go right for me? The omen-kid. My *huluppu* tree. It's not fair, Nin Shubur. It's not fair!'

'There, my lady. One week of troubles is not the end of the world. Human queens have been robbed and raped and lost their cities. Anunnaki Ladies have suffered too. All will be well in a little while, you'll see. Let us tell Lord Dumuzi. He seems to have returned to Uruk in the nick of time. Let your bridegroom fight your battles for you.'

'*No!*' The cry was wrung out of Inanna's sobs. Her head went up. 'Don't tell Dumuzi! Don't ask him!'

'But why, child? What other hero should you turn to?'

'It's *my* tree. *My* bed. *My* throne. For me to give to him. Don't you understand?'

Nin Shubur stared down with a long, pitying look. Her hand stroked the blue-black hair. 'Yes, child. I think I do.'

'Shouldn't we... shouldn't someone shut the gate?' Zazuru pleaded. 'In case they escape?'

Inanna looked up at the giant Imdugud hovering low over the enclosure and laughed wildly. 'Imprison *them*? How could An's people not have seen them? How could they have allowed them in? Why did they let them stay?'

'We see what we want to see,' said Nin Shubur. 'The heart has many hiding places for its terrors.'

'Then why me?' asked Inanna fiercely. 'Why am I made to see them?'

'You are a great queen,' said Nin Shubur, touching her gently. 'Granddaughter of Enki, Lord of Wisdom. Granddaughter of Enlil, Lord of Might.'

'Utu is their grandchild too.'

'Your brother and your father both know the darkness. They rise out of it, to bring us light.'

Inanna stood, stiffly, still shaken with the last long shudders of her sobs. 'So I must see the darkness too?'

'Poor child. Too great a heart, for those who love you. Too proud a spirit, for those who oppose you. You will hurt others. You will hurt yourself.'

'Are you turning seer now?'

'I was a wise woman before I came to you, my lady.'

'I am sorry, Nin Shubur. I had no right to forget it.'

'Come away. The guards have found us out. They must have heard our cries.'

'Wait!' Inanna ran back to the hanging reed-mat gate. A frail and common thing. Not one of those creatures within could be held by it. It had not been able to keep them out. Its defence was only against human intruders.

Still she scooped up a handful of dark clay from the puddle at its foot, pressed it into a ball. Then she slammed the gate on the terrors inside, tied the cord, wrapped the clay over the knot. Round her neck hung, as always, her personal cylinder seal, a tiny reel of greenstone incised by a lapidary, a design of tall doorposts framing a reed house, with stars and watchful eyes. She rolled its imprint over the damp clay, left Inanna's seal that no one should dare to break without her authority.

Nin Shubur shook her head sadly.

# Chapter Fifty-two

Inanna swept into the E-Anna. She did not turn aside to her own quarters, but made straight for the private chambers of An. Nin Shubur, who had mistaken her intended direction, hurried to catch up with her.

'My lady, where do you wish to go?'
'To see Father An, of course.'
'He will be resting still. Can't it wait till the evening meal?'
'No. It cannot.'

Doors flew open for her. Torches flared in windowless rooms. Dark passages sprang into life with lamps, as though the clouds had been swept clean from constellations. Inanna scarcely waited for the warning gong, the shout of her name, before she burst into An's private *itima* chamber.

Two young hierodules scrambled from the divan. Inanna felt a pout of annoyance that Nin Isinna sat undisturbed at her entry, fully though alluringly dressed, to one side of the room. The Chief Hierodule of An, Great Physician of the Black-Headed People, rose now, looked challengingly at Inanna. One of the maidens, clad in nothing more than a profusion of jewellery that left her skin rosy in the hot firelight, was no more than a child. Inanna set her more gently aside. A slender ghost of her younger self? Her supplanter? The other, taller, blacker-skinned, backed away. Both girls' hands fluttered over their naked parts.

'Oh, never mind that. I have been An's bed-warmer myself,' Inanna told them. 'I want to talk to him.'

The old man had sat up in bed. He clutched a coverlet round his loins. She knew why. She had seen the flaccid failure of his organ. Saw it leap at her entrance, then collapse again. Some distant part of her mind rejoiced in the knowledge that she had more power to please him, satisfy him. She should not be too hard on him. He and his hierodules had taught her those arts.

Yet there was still her beloved *huluppu* tree.

'You failed me!' she accused him.

'How, sweetheart?'

'Don't think you can soothe me with your honey words. I went to Ur. I trusted it to you. My precious *huluppu* tree. Ages, I have tended it, watched it grow. Ages and ages. I rescued that tree. I saved its life from the spring flood. My *huluppu*.'

'*That* tree!' He almost spat the word.

Inanna's self-assurance of righteous anger faltered for a moment. 'Why do you say, "*That* tree", as though you hated it?'

'You don't know where it came from. Why should you? You were not born then.'

'When?'

A black and bitter look filled the old Lord's eyes. He turned his face away from her. 'When Ki and I were separated. When I was allowed to carry off the Sky. When Enlil seized the Earth. When . . . Ereshkigal became Queen of Kur . . .'

'But why my tree?' Her firm young voice was almost a whisper now.

'When Enki went to find her . . . You know he failed.' She nodded. 'A mighty storm pursued him. More terrible than you can imagine. The whole ocean rose against him. The waters Below took on a monstrous form to hurl him out of the Netherworld. Small stones were flung against him more vicious than icy hail. Large stones assaulted him, crueller than giant sling-stones. Waves smashed his ship like rending lionesses.'

'But he escaped.'

'And lay on the beach near Eridu battered almost to death. When he stood up, clutching the sands of home in his palms, and lifted his face to the life-breathing Sky, he found he was grasping something like a small pale stone . . . A nut. The seed of a tree. This little living stone he carried far inland, into the Edin. He planted it beside the waters of the Buranun.'

'My mother told me. And *that* tree?'

'Yes. It was a *huluppu* tree. Enki believed it was lost in the great Flood. But I think not. A lesser flood tore it from its hiding place and carried it past this house. You caught and held it. My daughter Ereshkigal's gift from Kur.'

She did not heed the pain twisting his face. 'But it is mine now! I planted it. I watered it. I *loved* it. And now it's been invaded! The Imdugud has made a nest in it. The Snake is round its roots. Kiskillilla has cut her home in the heart of it.'

A silence.

'Why didn't you look after it? What was your head gardener doing? I ordered him to take care of it with his own hands!'

'My head gardener was murdered.'

It was Inanna's turn to fall silent.

'The day after you had gone, thieves broke into his house at night. His wife admitted them. They beat him over the head and took all he had. They and the woman have been killed now too.'

'But didn't someone take over the garden from him?'

'He would not have known your orders. No one else would have dared to break your seal.'

'And you said nothing?'

'There are some things an old man would rather forget.'

Inanna looked at him for a long while under frowning brows. 'But someone saw what had happened. Enkimdu. When he left us today after the midday meal he said something to me – "I wish that I had had the cultivating of your garden." *He* knew!'

'Enkimdu the Farmer is more observant of growing things than most.'

'I never took him into my garden. And now he has gone.' A sad sense of something missed came over her as she spoke the words. 'How could you not have seen?' she flared at An again. 'A nesting Thunderbird! A monstrous Serpent! The demon Kiskillilla. Could all of these have taken over my garden for months and *none* of you have noticed?'

'Perhaps. To some the Imdugud are sacred and lucky. Lugalbanda won favours from them.'

'Shall I speak them fair, then? Bring them presents? Build them a statue? Flatter their babies?' Inanna asked bitterly.

'It brought him good.'

'I will drive them out! They shall not have my tree. How can I cut it down for my throne if the Imdugud's young are still in the nest? Do you expect me to lie in my marriage bed with the Snake still twined round its legs?'

'The snake is sacred to Nin Ki and Ningishzida.'

'And Kiskillilla?'

The old man's eyelids dropped. A shadow came down over

his face, like a reed blind unrolled to cover a window. 'The demon woman, who will not be under her husband, should be driven out. Yes.'

'So shall they all,' vowed Inanna. 'So shall they all. They shall not have my *huluppu*.'

'Then find a younger champion,' An told her. 'I am too tired.'

She sped away from him across a rain-spattered courtyard to Utu's rooms. Her brother was out. Inanna beat her fists on the door in helpless rage.

'Is no one going to help me?'

That evening, Inanna wept in her own private chambers, refusing food. Nin Shubur sent Amanamtagga, her body slave. The girl crept almost noiseless as spring rain over the cool tiles. Inanna closed her eyes, turned her face to the wall. Amanamtagga left her tray. When the slight disturbance of the curtains had dropped behind her, Inanna rolled over to look. Pomegranates, with blood-red juice, a breast of goose, cakes of fine flour and pressed figs. She stared morosely at it. She felt a growing hunger for food and action, but she would not eat. Already the story would be all over the city. Ninurta's daughters could not keep silent. Inanna would be mocked.

# Chapter Fifty-three

When in the first dawn the birds began to sing, when the twitter of the *tibu* birds had reached An's snow-white sanctuary on the peak of the E-Anna, Inanna started awake. With a cry of wounded pride and anger she leaped from the bed. At once the slaves heard her move, came hurrying in. Impatiently she let them dress her. She would not wait for them to arrange her hair and put on her face-paint.

She was almost at the door of Utu's bedchamber when he came out. She thought he flushed when he saw her.

'Well, Inanna. Let's hope the omens will be better for your blessing ritual today.'

She could not contain her need. Her face was still flushed from the tears she had shed in the night.

'My *huluppu* tree. You know what has happened to it?'

'I heard something.'

'You heard *something*? It must be all over the city. Can a Thunderbird nest in the gardens of An's palace? Can the demon Kiskillilla come in out of the desert and make her house here? Can the basilisk burrow in the heart of Kullab and the Sun Lord only know *something*? These creatures are defying me!'

'Thunderbirds were Lugalbanda's friends.'

'The Thunderbird was Ninurta's enemy!'

'Some say he flew in their form himself once. He blazons their emblem over his palace in Lagash now. He has made them his.'

'I'm going to tame them too. This Imdugud must learn that I am mistress in Uruk now. She must get out of my tree.'

'And what is this to do with me?'

'Make her!'

Utu paled. 'I? What should the Sun Lord do with Thunderbirds? You have got the wrong man.'

'You could scorch the Snake. Blind Kiskillila's eyes and drive her away. Do something!'

'Snakes love the sun. I have no power to hurt her.'

'And Kiskillila . . . You're afraid! Utu, you are afraid of her!'

He shrugged a little, and made to pass her. 'And if I am? Grandfather Enki gave us wisdom. Use it, Inanna.'

'Grandfather Enlil is a stronger Lord. He gives us might. Use that, Utu, Lord of Justice! Uphold my right.'

'The morning court is waiting for me. I must go to the House of the Rising Sun.'

'Go and pass your judgments,' she said bitterly. 'I need a better man than you to carry them out.'

An's words of blessing echoed over Inanna like the good sweet thunder rumbling round the rim of desert that ends the scorching heat of summer.

'I will give you the E-Anna,

'I will give you the Hieroduleship of the Sky House,

'I will give you the city of Uruk, the brickwork of Kullab.

'Nin Egalla, Lady of the Palace,

'Inanna, Eldest Daughter of the Moon,

'Be exalted for ever!

'Wed your Shepherd at New Year and be happy!'

The old, familiar hands descended on her head, light and loving. So gentle a touch to transfer this majesty. Hard to think now that she had once been terrified of him. The President of all the Anunnaki. He who looses the Bull of Heaven. The Sky Lord. Now all that made him great on Earth would be hers. And she would marry Dumuzi in the spring.

The Shepherd smiled at her with brilliant eyes.

After the bitterness of yesterday, this morning seemed impossibly lovely. The sky a deep and glowing blue, the colour that enchanted the Children of An. The earth fresh springing green, nourished by a winter's rain. All water sparkling, as if Enki had newly scattered his semen on the Buranun to make life come.

The omen-kid had been good. She could hardly believe it, so deep had been her sense of foreboding when she woke. One pure-white baby billy, severed by the priests, his tiny heart fluttering into nothingness, his entrails spread upon the altar, perfect. From where she knelt she could still see the scuff marks on the sandy floor that marked his last rebellious struggle for life.

And Nin Shubur, fastening Inanna's ceremonial jewels on her, clothing her in the garment of royalty, setting the diadem on her head that An himself would replace at the New Year with the Crown of the Steppe, had whispered good news to her.

'My lady, someone has arrived from Nippur for the ceremony. Enlil's representative, to witness An's blessing on your betrothal. His concubine, Nin Mada.'

Inanna had struggled to remember, staring at herself in the mirror Amanamtagga was holding up in front of her. Nin Shubur had painted her eyes in the high priestess's way, 'Let Him Come,' so that they looked huge and brilliant.

'Nin Mada?'

'The snake-charmer.'

And Inanna's mirrored face flowered before her into beautiful life.

'Oh, Nin Shubur, of course! Isn't she the most famous one in all Sumer? Surely she can charm the basilisk in my garden.'

'I have spells of my own I can add to hers,' Nin Shubur said, with the firm set of her mouth she always needed when she spoke of her lost country. 'I was a sorceress queen once. First among the wise women.'

'I know.' Inanna kissed her in a sudden rush of affection.

'Mind your lip-paint, child! You only love me if I get you what you want.'

'I want that Serpent gone. And Kiskillilla. And the Imdugud.'

'One at a time. One at a time. Snakes may be charmed. For the rest, we shall have to see.'

'When, Nin Shubur? When?'

'Nin Mada will not stay long after the feast. Let it be this afternoon.'

'What does she need? Can it be ready in time?'

'Never fear. I have seen to it. You must provide the gifts. Little else is needed but pipes, and incense, and a basket or pot.'

Inanna's outlined eyes grew larger yet. 'It will have to be a very big pot for a Serpent like that!'

Nin Shubur inclined her head. 'As you say, my lady. A large casket.'

And so it was. No basketmaker could have woven a hamper both big and strong enough to bear the crimson and black cable of the Serpent's coils that were as thick as a man's thigh. No potter could have thrown a water jar wide and tall enough to contain that living river of cunning. Two oxen lumbered across the park hauling a cart. When it stopped, the palace porters manoeuvred down a ramp of pine logs a lead-lined sarcophagus.

Inanna had taken off her crown and royal cloak, but she was still a jewelled, painted lady. She stared.

'It is . . . fitting,' she said.

Where, in the treasuries of An, Nin Shubur had found it, or whom it was waiting for, it would be hard to say. The exterior was fashioned of moon-pale soapstone, carved in relief. Up its sides, in over its lips and out again poured the sinuous lengths of brightly patterned snakes. Between their almost fluid curves scuttled the smaller shapes of scorpions. Their eight-clawed bodies lurked low on the sides, or hauled themselves over the rim, or emerged, tails tipped with venom dangerously erect. Move the head slightly and the whole cold stone case appeared alive and crawling.

Inanna swallowed. 'The . . . Serpent will not want for company. Yet it is the right container. You have chosen a case of death for her.'

Nin Mada answered this. A small slight woman, whose limbs seemed made to dance with every movement. Her soft words sang seductively. Large hooded eyes spoke sleep and secrets. Around her neck there hung a set of reed pipes strung with silver, not very different from those the shepherds play upon the steppe, or the fowlers in the marshes. Such pipes the boy Dumuzi had given and taught the little girl Inanna.

'No charmer kills her snake. I will enchant her for you into that coffin, and you may seal the lid. Let her lie three days in the darkness while a cart bears her into the desert. Release her there.'

'Poor Serpent!' said Nin Shubur. 'To exchange Inanna's garden in Kullab for that stony wilderness. It will be a bitter waking.'

'It must be done,' Nin Mada said. 'Serpents are holy. But

the Anunnaki must rule the Earth. We cannot let them queen it over us, usurp our space.'

'Lady Inanna, break your seal,' Nin Shubur told her.

'The Imdugud? . . . Kiskillilla?'

'One difficulty at a time. We cannot touch them today. They will know they have nothing to fear from us, yet.'

All the same, the three Ladies looked warily at the darkness nesting again in the vast crown of the *huluppu* tree. They did not attempt to circle the trunk. Inanna was relieved that she could not see Kiskillilla's cleft.

Nin Mada sat down, cross-legged on the grass. The Snake was still there, unmoving among the roots, its jewel-bright eyes observant. The men heaved the sarcophagus into place in front of Nin Mada, withdrew in relief and stood outside by the cart, making the signs against evil.

'Take the honour due to you, and depart, my lady.' Reluctantly Inanna made the signs she had been shown and scattered jewels in the coffin.

Nin Shubur was quietly busy too, kindling a tiny fire, igniting sticks of aromatics, sprinkling the glowing ash in an ever-lengthening line that girdled the space between the gate and the *huluppu* tree, fencing the *sagkal* in. The Serpent stirred threateningly. There was a catch in the low-hummed chant of Nin Shubur's voice, but she worked on. Nin Mada was readying her pipes.

When the spells were laid, Inanna found herself sitting inside a charmed circle between two sorceresses. With sudden alarm her eyes went to the Serpent's face. The black tongue was flickering nervously, but it had stopped hissing. The brilliant eyes, black-edged as hers, seemed to seek her own with a mute appeal. Or was it mockery? Swiftly her hand went to the breastplate of gold and silver and lapis lazuli. This was all the power she had. What did it count here, in this magic ring, with all the normal world outside?

The pipes began to sing. Inanna had witnessed snakes used for entertainment hundreds of times. She had seen them rise in graceful swaying pillars from reed baskets. Seen dancers coil them round their necks and bellies, kiss them. Watched once, in fascinated horror, a foreign spy thrown into a pit of vipers while the crowd roared. Held her childish breath while priest charmers poured their oracular familiars in jewelled streams into boxes and closed the lid.

Would this Snake come?

The little garden fell silent, save for the rising, haunting music. Inanna was abruptly conscious that the boughs above her were still. What she had thought was the sharp creaking of its twigs in the breeze had been the incessant cry of the Imdugud's chicks. Now, three large-eyed, needle-teethed nestlings leaned over to stare. The Mother Imdugud's head was lost in the foliage.

The Serpent undulated uneasily. The pipes slowed, dreamily, beguilingly. A single rasping hiss spat from the gaping mouth. Inanna's muscles jumped. She wanted to spring up and run. But Nin Mada's music and Nin Shubur's circle would not let her go. She and the Snake were both unwilling prisoners.

But the Serpent was not yet charmed.

The magic played on. Inanna's head began to droop. Nin Shubur placed more incense sticks over the fire. The air was blue and pungent. Inanna's breath came ever slower.

Then, from the corner of her eye, she saw what she had feared most. A shape, like the dark gold shimmer of late-afternoon light on the uncut grass. Bird-taloned feet. And now, free of the enclosing tree, she glimpsed the humps behind the careless stance of Kiskillilla's shoulders that spoke of folded wings.

Wide tawny eyes laughed at the three Ladies. No sleepiness of snake-charm in her face. No awe of magic.

'You are wasting your time.'

The Serpent turned her crimson head, rose up and seemed to salute the demon woman.

'You see? You cannot hold her. You cannot compel her.'

Like a breeze falling, Nin Mada stopped playing, lowered her pipes, looked at Inanna. 'This demon speaks the truth, Nin Egalla. I have no power here. This is the Chief of Serpents, the Mushsagkal, that cannot be charmed.'

Inanna's gaze flew to Nin Shubur, frightened. The spell-knowing *sukkal* was already packing away her flint, her resins, her little chalcedony bowls.

'You can do *nothing* with her?'

'No, my lady. My spells will not suffice.'

'Go, Princess Inanna,' ordered Nin Mada. 'The Serpent knows I am a charmer, that I would never harm her. She may not trust you.'

The two sorceresses were standing now, still calm, but wary. Nin Shubur took a feathered reed head, brushed aside a little of the ring of ash, made an opening. Inanna, feeling like a coward in retreat, took her escape. Nin Shubur made a low reverence to the Serpent and followed her. Nin Mada's pipes made a last tremulous farewell, and then the enclosure was empty of Anunnaki, left to the Serpent who cannot be charmed, to the Dark Maid Kiskillila, to the Thunderbird.

Outside, rage rose in Inanna, beating down her shame of failure and defeat.

'They *shan't* have it! They shan't!' Tears burst from her kohl-blacked eyes and ran down her beautiful face, streaking it like a mourner's. 'There must be someone!'

# Chapter Fifty-four

Gilgamesh. Not till the late afternoon did the name come clearly to her, as if the bird that sang incessantly outside her window had been beating it into her ears through the long siesta.

'Gilgamesh!'

'My lady?' asked Nin Shubur, coming into the room to supervise Inanna's dressing for the evening festivities.

'Gilgamesh, Dumuzi's brother. That's whom I'll ask.'

'To do what, my lady?' Nin Shubur kept her eyes prudently downcast.

'To free my tree, of course! Do you suppose I can think of anything else?'

'I should have thought now you're a bride betrothed to be married, Dumuzi himself might have been first in your thoughts.'

'But don't you see, Nin Shubur?' She jumped up on her knees. 'It is for him. How can I be Dumuzi's bride without my wedding bed? How can I make him king of Uruk if I haven't got my own throne?'

'An has a throne already. And I am sure Lord Dumuzi can provide his bride with a bed.'

'But the bed and throne that *I* will bring must be more wonderful than all the others. Don't you see?'

The *sukkal* looked down at Inanna fondly. 'Oh, yes. I understand. But I do not see how that tree can be felled without great harm and danger.'

'Gilgamesh will get it for me.' She sat back on her heels, nodding her head like a satisfied child.

Nin Shubur's hands, that had started to comb Inanna's hair, stilled. She stared reflectively across the room, through open doors, across the distant plain. 'The young champion? Lugalbanda's heir . . . Well, if it can be done at all by force, he is probably your only hero. He, at least, will relish the dangers. Only . . .'

'Only *what*? Why is there always a "but" in what you say, Queen of the East?'

'Because I am wise?' Nin Shubur turned it into a laugh, beginning to comb again, rapidly. 'Because I see too much? I fear too much. I do not want you hurt.'

'It is that Snake who will be hurt! That Im'dugud bird. That demon.'

'I know. Think, Inanna. The female, in your tree. In the roots. In the crown. In the heart.'

'Gilgamesh will get them out.'

'Gilgamesh will hurt them.'

'So much the better!'

'Inanna. Inanna.'

But the Lady of the Evening Star would not be moved, any more than the basilisk, lurking in the shadows of the *huluppu* in the crimson and black sunset.

A message was sent down into the city, summoning Gilgamesh. His answer came back, vowing his heart and his weapon to his queen's service.

At dawn next day, Inanna went out to meet her champion. Her heart beat fast with the excitement of adventure as she waited for him in the cool grey stillness of the park above the river. Nin Shubur was with her, of course, cloaked against the damp. A few apprehensive guards.

Inanna heard his call to the gate, anticipating the gatekeeper's challenge from half a street away. A loud and ringing voice. Her head went up.

He came bursting through the gate, hardly abashed by the presence of the Daughters of An. He looked very young, with that transient freshness of human youth that makes the hearts of the Anunnaki ache, because it is so brief. Handsome. If she did not have Dumuzi . . .

He was dressed in his armour. He had fastened his mailed coat weighing fifty minas around his chest. From the pride of his step you would have thought he felt it no more than fifty feathers. His heavy battle-axe of bronze he hefted on his shoulder. His helmet shone like a brassy wig with a golden headband, brighter than his hair.

This was a warrior! More manly than the careful, judgment-dealing Utu. A fighter.

Fifty young men of his year crowded behind him, the new

bloods of Uruk, fully-armed and shielded, a little more awed than their hero. But their mettle was up. They wanted something to strike.

Now he was fully grown, Gilgamesh was big, bigger than she had remembered him, in full armour. This was no puny, servile human striding through the long wet grass towards her. At least half an Anunnaki. And his father Lugalbanda had been a hero in his own right. Her face flowered for Gilgamesh.

'My Lady.' He made a deep, flourishing obeisance that did not diminish himself, but made her feel higher still.

'Have you come to prove yourself my champion, Gilgamesh?'

'I have pledged my weapons, and my life, and my heart to your service, High Inanna.'

She felt herself colour a little, charmingly. 'Very good. I have a challenge for you which none of the Sons of An could meet. Do you know what that test is?'

He hesitated. He tried to prevent his eyes sliding sideways to his companions. So that was the way of it. The story was out in the banqueting halls, in the taverns, in the markets of the city. Inanna, the queen-to-be, the bride-to-be, had been challenged even before she reached her throne dais, her bedroom. She was not strong enough. She was not powerful yet. She could be mocked.

'They say dark forces, from the Sky, from the Netherworld, from the wilderness, have invaded your private garden.'

'The Imdugud has built her nest in the crown of my *huluppu* tree. Kiskililla has cut her house in the trunk. The Mushsagkal that cannot be charmed has taken over the roots.'

'Then we must teach them a lesson!'

'You will kill them for me?'

Gilgamesh started. Then he slipped his heavy sword from his belt, swung it lovingly with his brawny arms. 'Show me Inanna's enemies and they shall see how I will serve her.'

And serve yourself, Inanna thought. You would do this just for the danger, for the glory, even without me.

And yet she liked the pride in his eyes, his eagerness to please her.

'I'll get you your tree, Lady,' Gilgamesh vowed boldly. 'One way or the other.'

The sword swung. Lightning sizzled through the park, too close to them for comfort. The Imdugud rose, clattering into the air directly behind them, and circled in the rainy sky screaming like an angry cat. Even Inanna paled.

'I am sorry, Gilgamesh. I had almost forgotten. I cannot demand of you that you kill an Imdugud, can I? Your father . . .'

'My father?' A startled flash in Gilgamesh's eyes. Then he bowed with a stiff, youthful dignity. 'Lugalbanda got the gift of supernatural speed from the Imdugud. He ran from Aratta to Kullab with no provisions, faster than a wild ass, faster than an eagle, for love of you, Lady. So I shall make your enemies depart, with nothing in their hands and at great speed, if you will bless my weapon.'

She smiled magnanimously, luxuriating in her sense of restored power. 'That will be enough.'

He hung his sword back at his side and held his axe out to her instead. It lay between them, a bright, clean thing. She touched her fingers to her lips, then laid them on the blade.

Then, 'Break the seal!' Inanna cried to him. She stepped back into the shelter of the plane trees where her escort was watching. Gilgamesh's companions made a ring round the fence, weapons ready. 'Break my seal!'

The lad's huge hands snapped the newly-impressed clay. He tore the rope from the hasp. He flung open Inanna's gate.

The Imdugud had settled on her nest again, but she raised her neck threateningly now.

The shadows of the trunk shifted. A dark golden face came round, like a fungus blooming over bark.

The darkness in the humped roots twisted, spilled towards him.

Grasping the axe, annealed copper brighter than stone, Gilgamesh strode towards the tree. Its occupants were rearing, overhead, before his feet, beside him, images of nightmare. Confident in his armour, sure of his speed, he did not wait to parry monstrous fangs, or wings, or talons.

His first jarring blow was aimed straight at the trunk of the living *huluppu*.

The nestlings screamed.

Kiskillilla's face, her body unseen yet, shuddered and paled.

The Serpent shot out, a flood of blood-red veined with black, pouring unstoppably from the roots.

Inanna's own mouth was open, but no words came.

A second blow was already on its way to the *huluppu* trunk.

The Mushsagkal launched herself towards Gilgamesh's face like fire leaping across a gap.

Whirling round, the warrior took one step back. The axe swung. Then he brought it down with another mighty stroke that chopped the colossal Serpent in two. Black blood showered through the air, eclipsing the crimson markings.

A howl, long and horrible, shivered across the waking city, curdled the listeners' blood.

It was not the Serpent. She fell to the earth in baleful silence and that gush of dark gore. It was not the Thunderbird, roaring and threshing in the shaken crown.

Kiskillilla was clinging to the wounded trunk now, naked, weeping.

A fourth time Gilgamesh raised his weapon. With a bellow of fury, more like a bull than a lion, the Imdugud mother snatched up her young, one in her teeth, two in her hooked talons. She burst into the upper air, rose now in a dreadful, stifled silence, save for the clap of wings, dwindled into the rainclouds, was lost.

The hero lowered his axe, leaned on it, panting. Still that naked wraith, not wholly woman, not truly bat, was poised before him on clenched, clawed feet.

'Will you leave Inanna's tree?' he muttered. 'Or must I strike you too?'

No mockery now in her voice. Her sobs were stilled. 'My wound is already open,' she said, a small, sharp voice. 'Here. Let me help you!'

Her hands clawed in the cleft, tore out the cunningly wrought heart of the wood, the bed where she had slept. She hurled the splinters at his feet. 'Take it back! You, and Inanna! Be merry with your *huluppu* tree, both of you!'

And with an echo of her old bitter laughter she rose on bony wings and fled, like a small dark cloud over the desert.

# Chapter Fifty-five

Gilgamesh strode back to the gate in the reed fence. He raised his axe two-handed to her in exultation and salute.

'Princess Inanna! Lady of the Palace! The tree is yours!'

Inanna stepped forward, radiance in her face. 'I want it now!'

With a shout of triumph the young men of Uruk burst through the fence and attacked the *huluppu*. Gilgamesh's bloody axe thudded against the wide-set base. Beset now on every side, the tree shuddered, swayed, creaked, split, toppled. The reed fence tore. The crash of the tree shook the earth under their feet. A cheer went up then. All the young warriors were leaping in, gouging up roots that clung to clay, hacking off branches ripped out of the sky. The living tree that had harboured life was reduced to a baulk of sturdy timber, a heap of knotty roots, a stack of serviceable limbs, a mess of shattered twigs and leaves.

At last they stood, running with sweat, their weapon tools glinting in the sunshine. Gilgamesh leaped on top of the severed trunk, his huge legs splayed as though he was glorying over a slain dragon. The fighting youths seemed to have tasted blood in the tree's sap.

Only small familiar kites circled in the cloud-flecked sky now. Only the common sparrows hopped nearer in the settling dust. Only red garden worms burrowed to find damp darkness as the sun stared into the crater where the roots had once driven their mooring stakes.

With the victory complete, Inanna advanced across the now dry grass, releasing a cloud of drowsy moths as she passed. Nin Shubur went before her, and the small train of onlookers followed.

She paused in the gateway and faced Gilgamesh. A leap of understanding passed between them, like two puppies pouncing joyfully upon each other to nip and roll and yap and prove themselves. A laugh blazed in Inanna's face. She had got what she wanted. Gilgamesh was aflame with manhood vindicated; he had achieved her challenge.

Tears stained Nin Shubur's cheeks as she walked around the shattered branches of the Imdugud's nest. She bent beside the prostrate trunk. Her hand caressed its bark. No sign on this upper side of that hidden cleft eaten deep into the heart of the wood, where Kiskillila had carved her home. The carpenter would find it.

She stepped back and caught her breath at the sight of seven white pearls in the tumbled hollow unearthed by the uprooting. Each Serpent egg had been smashed or torn by the picks and axes, the life spilt to the Below.

'Where is the Mushsagkal?' asked Nin Shubur.

'Here!' Luenna, one of Gilgamesh's friends, waved his axe proudly. 'We piled some leafy branches over it to stop the sun from spoiling it before the taxidermist can get to work. Gilgamesh is going to ask Princess Inanna if he can have the skin for his trophy.'

He drew back the sprays of *huluppu* leaves, already wilting in the heat. The ground beneath was darkly stained, glistening with a dried, viscous trail. A length of Serpent lay, still menacing by its girth even in death. The crimson was dulled, the black greying. The inert, decapitated reptile body ended in a sharply-pointed tail.

'Where is her head?' asked Nin Shubur.

'Somewhere in this thicket.' The young men round Luenna began to tear the mound apart, snapping more leaves and twigs, scattering the debris. The severed half was not to be seen. Smears of blood and mucus trailed beyond the pile, grew thinner, faded.

'How much was left attached to the head?'

'Not much. A cubit, maybe.'

'Oh, foolish man, to cheer so soon!'

'It was *dead*!'

'Then where is she now?'

'Be reasonable. This place is chaos. It's got swept up in the leaves. It must be somewhere.'

'Is this her trail?' Nin Shubur wondered, finding flattened grass, a shallow, bloodstained scoop in the sandy earth leading towards the fence.

'What?'

'The Serpent's head!'

'How can anybody tell?' The young man shrugged sulkily. 'There were fifty of us breaking in, attacking the tree. The fence is trampled down.'

Nin Shubur's eyes went to the broken *zirru* and the sweep of park beyond to the river.

'Find her! And treat her with honour!' she said sharply.

With glances of alarm at each other they searched the whole enclosure, the tumbled branches, the stack of chopped-off roots. They even rolled the trunk itself and probed the shadowed cleft they found.

The tree was harmless, the enclosure untenanted. The uninvited inhabitants had fled.

The young men scattered across the park, and came back empty-handed.

'It's gone.' Luenna was paler now. Nin Shubur looked at the happy Inanna. The young men looked to the proud delight of Gilgamesh. They did not want to tell their master and mistress.

'Perhaps it is not important,' said Nin Shubur. 'The Imdugud and her young have flown. Kiskillilla has fled to the desert. Can it matter to Gilgamesh and Lady Inanna if the Serpent has escaped too?'

'Gilgamesh killed it!'

'He tried to. Better he had only chopped the tree. Gilgamesh may live to regret this. When a human is killed, he remains dead. But Nin Ki's Serpent is not finished yet.'

'Gilgamesh is half Anunnaki.'

'That may not be enough.'

Scraps of cloud had wandered over the sun, chilling the sweat on the men's skin. But Inanna and Gilgamesh were warm with the heat of their success.

'Shall I send for carts and ropes now, my Lady? I'll have this *huluppu* tree carried to your carpenter's workshops. You shall get your heart's desire. A Lion Throne for the E-Anna. And a marriage bed for you and Dumuzi.'

'The Lioness has replaced the Bull in Uruk,' Inanna glowed. 'And what shall I give my hero of Kullab as a reward?'

'The skin of that Serpent, Lady.'

'It is yours. Give it to him.'

'At once, my Lady. We've got it safe.' His friends hastily bundled up the colossal length of tail in a cloak. Their eyes sought each other for guidance. Would he want to know where the head was?

Inanna's own brightness seemed to have dimmed a little at his request. 'The Snake from the Netherworld?' she said. 'I could not refuse you, but I would rather you had asked from me something more lively than that. Well, take it. I don't want to see it again. And I shall think about another gift . . . You there!' Field slaves, in rough sheepskin kilts, were coming to cart the tree away. 'When you are taking the timber of the trunk to the carpenter, don't forget the roots and crown. They are not to be chopped up for firewood; this moot, these branches . . .

'No! Gilgamesh, let me keep the skin as well. I think I see a plan for them. You will love me for it. We shall both remember this day, when we were victorious together over the might of the Sky, over the menace of the Netherworld, over the trespasser from the wilderness.'

'If the Above and Earth and the Great Below are your enemies, where are your friends?' Nin Shubur asked.

Inanna swung round. 'You go too far, Nin Shubur! What did you want me to do? Let those demons inhabit my space? Push me out of what is mine?'

'They are loose now,' Nin Shubur said, unrepenting. 'You cannot call them back and make your peace with them.'

'Nor shall I ever need to, while I have Gilgamesh for my champion!'

The carpenter's workshop thudded with the blows of the hammer, buzzed with the busy saw. Inanna herself came every day to oversee the work in the long shadowed shelter where sunbeams struck in from the dazzling courtyard, dancing with golden sawdust.

Her throne. The seat was supported on four crouched lions. The back was surmounted by owls. The sides were like two great doorways to a huge reed hall. The finials were carved to resemble those curled and ornamental corner posts bound from shafts of the tallest canes in bundles thick as a tree bole, tapering to tips that are scrolled and coiled.

'A House of Plenty,' said Nin Shubur approvingly. 'You will be the Lady of the Storehouse for your people.'

The bed was vast and lively. Its base was slatted, cool for their summer nights of love. Round its sides the *pirig* lion chased the *ug* lion, the *ug* lion turned and chased the *pirig* lion. Through vines and palms and pomegranates they raced and pounced. Their sport was endless.

Inanna laughed and threw herself down on it. She stretched out her arms till her longing breasts sprang free of the binding dress cloth.

'So shall Dumuzi and I chase each other, leap on each other, never weary from sunset to sunrise of the game of love. First I, then he, will challenge the other, grapple and bite, pierce and satisfy.'

'You would hunt him to death?' Heulnunna laughed. 'Poor Dumuzi!'

'I will dare any chase with him, if he is the hound.'

'Dumuzi is no warrior, to partner the Battle Dancer.'

'I will teach him. He shall draw sweet blood.'

In the instrument maker's shop another craftsman was at work. The base of the tree, like a many-tentacled creature of the Deep, had been sawn off to leave a wide, round table. Stray roots were trimmed away, though knotty protuberances still made strange, swelling patterns round its rim. The interior was hollowed out, and over it was stretched the cured Serpent's skin, thick and supple as a bull calf's hide. But no calf or lamb would have left the colours it had in life imprinted on the shaved leather as here the angled markings of the Mushsagkal glowed crimson and black like flames through wreaths of smoke.

A *pukku* drum.

The carpenter's little girl was playing with a long and slender spray of branches, trimmed carefully to the exact length, each tip padded and bound with the same snakeskin, the *mikku* stick. Watching them smilingly, she tapped the *pukku* with a single light stroke, then swept its table top in a full-throated roll.

Inanna clapped ecstatically.

'My daughter doesn't want to let that go,' smiled the carpenter.

'I have never seen a *pukku* so big, or a *mikku* so long,' Nin Shubur observed.

'Gilgamesh is mightier than any other human.'

'Is this *pukku* what he wants?'

'He wants war. And I shall be the Queen of Battle soon. We will rule the world from Uruk, Gilgamesh and I.'

'I thought Dumuzi was to be your bridegroom?'

'You see! If I had done what you all suggested, and let Dumuzi cut down my *huluppu*, the glory would be his by now, not mine. It is better to have Gilgamesh as my champion. Gilgamesh is not a Son of An. Gilgamesh can serve me as my *lugal*, as my *en*. He will not rival me.'

'Hmm. And where has Lord Dumuzi gone?'

'To his farm on the steppe,' said Utu unexpectedly. 'I warned him he was not required here. I don't think he would have wanted to hang around anyway. The bloodshed you were demanding is not Dumuzi's style.'

Two rosettes of colour burned in Inanna's cheeks. 'Is Dumuzi a coward?'

'Of course not! He and his dog would fight off a wolf if it attacked his sheep.'

'Well, then. Why do you insult him?'

'I do not. Dumuzi is my friend. Let's not quarrel about the Shepherd, sister. You have your *huluppu*, your throne, your bed. Now be content with your bridegroom.'

'Content? I *love* him!'

Utu stroked her flaming cheeks. 'Oh, Inanna. You're magnificent when you're indignant.'

Dumuzi did not return for the great feast in the E-Anna, when Inanna presented her gifts to Gilgamesh. Tables were spread under the stars in the widest courtyard, so great was the number of Uruk's citizens she had invited. Anunnaki and humans sat down in sight of each other. They toasted Inanna and Gilgamesh in flowing wine and rich dark beer. Kids and sheep were roasted. Geese and carp were plentiful. Mounds of dates and figs and apples were sweet on the tongue. Praise-songs rose from the *tigi* harps and tambourines. The Young Lady and her hero enjoyed each other's company. An nodded between his attentive hierodules. Only Utu stayed sober and thoughtful. Geshtinanna was away with her brother.

The new *pukku* had been set on a clay plinth in the middle of the courtyard, like a circular fortress on its mound. The *mikku* lay beside it, a weapon of music. At the height of the feast Inanna came down from her dais, a star-shaft of white, sparkling with jewels, across the thronged courtyard. The crowds fell back at her approach. She beckoned Gilgamesh forward. His boyish eyes were bright with enthusiasm as they faced each other across the plinth. Even the tall immortal Inanna felt momentarily overpowered by this human, so broad of shoulder, so bullish of head, so confident in his strength of manhood. Only because she knew him to be a mortal's son, and therefore marked for death, could she realise her own power was greater, facing him.

He had given her again what was once her own. He had handed her back her own wedding gift to Dumuzi, her bed. He had restored her treasure for Uruk, E-Anna's new Lion Throne. A giver is more powerful than the one who receives. Now she must give him something back, reverse the balance.

'Gilgamesh. I have chosen your brother to become my husband. I name you tonight my *lugal*.'

The two assemblies of Uruk, elders and fighting men, were on their feet, roaring their confirmation of the choice.

'As symbol that you are to be my king in war, I give you what no other *lugal* has. Take from your Lady this great *pukku*. This is the royal drum that will summon your men to battle. And here in your hand, better than any sceptre or measuring rod, I set this *mikku*, carved from the crown of that same *huluppu* tree from which you drove out the Thunderbird.'

'So shall Inanna's enemies take wing and fly off with screams. So shall the women of your foemen wail like Kiskillilla in the wilderness. So shall all invaders lie dead at your feet like the Snake who would not be charmed. This *pukku* shall thunder loud for you, Inanna.'

The mottled snakeskin threw a scaly gleam back to the dancing Star of Evening. Its spread was vast, seemingly lifeless. The sides of the *pukku*, seven strides round the circumference, even for Gilgamesh, were darkly polished, though knots of root stumps still cast shadows blacker yet.

Only Nin Shubur and a few young men, who knew that the triumph over the Snake had not been complete, looked out now over the reed *zirru* that fenced the terrace and shivered. The night desert kept its secrets.

Gilgamesh grasped the varnished *mikku* stick. He brandished it over his head, more joyfully than any battle mace, brought it down on the resounding skin, struck the deep call to arms.

Goblets clashed on the tables. Feet drummed on the ground. All the young men were jumping up and shouting in unison.

'War! War! Gilgamesh! Gilgamesh! Praise to Inanna, Uruk's Lioness! Love, and war!'

# Chapter Fifty-six

'Congratulations. They are crying your name and Gilgamesh's in the streets louder than they ever shouted for An.'

'You're jealous!' Inanna stared at Dumuzi, at first incredulously and then with delighted laughter.

He flushed under his sunburn. Yes, she admitted to herself, he was disturbingly beautiful. Those lambswool curls of his hair into which she wanted to plunge her hands. The fine weave of his clothes, chosen from a wealth of fleeces to give just the distinctive patterns of cream and brown and black he wanted. Had Geshtinanna spun and woven them? Or his mother Nin Sun, whose house in Uruk Geshtinanna and Dumuzi used, though she herself came seldom into the city from the wide peace of the steppe and her animals? Or were there other women Inanna did not know about, who carried out his wishes?

Jealousy in its turn gnawed at her. Now that she was able to move more freely about Kullab, she could not help but hear all the women, young and old, exclaiming over Dumuzi's beauty, the youth he wore like an opening flower, the sense that he was an unplucked fruit ready to be enjoyed by some lucky Daughter of An.

Inanna, soon to be the Queen of Uruk, made lucky only by Dumuzi's favour to her?

He picked up a pomegranate. 'I leave war to humans. Let Gilgamesh swing his mace and his axe to defend us. Why did Enki and Nin Mah make these little people, if the Anunnaki have to raise sweat on their own brows combating our enemies? He has served you as a good soldier should.'

'Gilgamesh is more like a Lord than you are!' The sudden sharpness in her words surprised her. She had not meant to say that. She wondered instantly if that was what she really thought.

'So you've heard that old story, have you?'

'What story?'

'That he may not be Lugalbanda's son.'

'Not Lugalbanda's?' Like a gift promised and then snatched away. All her life her nurse and Nin Shubur and the court entertainers had sung her the songs of the hero, the opponent of Aratta, the Thunderbird's friend, the Wild Cow Woman's lover, the faithful favourite of Inanna. She had loved the sound of him, the thought of him. She loved him now through his brave son. 'But Gilgamesh... Your mother...'

'Oh, yes. My beast-knowing mother became the wife of Lugalbanda, *en*-king of Uruk. I bear that taint to this day, because I am another of her sons. If I were a fighting Lord I should have had many single combats to prove to the world that it was Enki who was *my* father.'

'Then Gilgamesh's father...?'

'Oh, no! I can see what you're thinking. You'd like that to be true, wouldn't you? Gilgamesh, fully Anunnaki. If you thought that, you'd ditch me for him now, wouldn't you? I can see it in your eyes.'

'No! How dare you!'

'I'm sorry. I hate to disappoint you. If Lugalbanda was not his father, it was no Son of An either. She took the high priest of Kullab.'

'Another human, but one who plays the part of the Lord. Then Gilgamesh is closer to the Children of An than to mortals,' she said slowly.

'They count him two-thirds Anunnaki. But that is still not enough for you, is it? Proud Inanna does not want to be like Nin Sun. I can't see you retired to a hut on the steppe, hiding the shame of your lowly widowhood from the rest of the Anunnaki, once your mortal is dead. You want a palace, a throne, a seat among the seven Igigi. For that, you will have to make do with me!' He sat down on a couch and stretched out, grinning up at her hungrily like a young sheepdog now, confident in her admiration of him.

She would not allow herself to be so easily won over. 'I will have to "make do" with nothing! I am the Lady of the Palace. I don't need a husband for that. I could rule alone. An is giving me the E-Anna and his city. Gilgamesh has given me my tree back for my throne. I can find plenty to serve me, men and Anunnaki. I don't need you or anyone.'

'Oh, you do, my sweet Inanna. My star, my rose. The *huluppu* also made your bed. For that, you certainly need me!'

With all the assurance of his beauty and boyish smile he sprang up, reached out his warm brown arms, took hold of her and pulled her down to the couch with him. She cried out and tried to push him away so hard a lapis lazuli bracelet broke and splinters of blue and silver went spinning through the air. But still he held her stiff body. What angered her most was the knowledge that it was true.

Her Lion Bed. The place she had designed for such sweet sport. Her own lovely body, that she was making more loveable for him every day, as the water bathed it, as the oils perfumed it, as her women massaged it. And Dumuzi's body, so close, so demanding. Firm, yet delightful too, in his own rustic way. Not the trained strength of the warrior Gilgamesh, but the warm natural life of bounding goats and leaping rams. She shuddered deliciously in his arms. If she could only let him take her now . . .

He must not see it. She must not let him know his power over her. He was laughing softly against her cheek.

'You see?'

'Let me go! You presume too much, Dumuzi! It is *my* bed, not yours yet. I will choose who comes to it.'

'I am your betrothed now, my *lubi*.'

'But not my husband yet. I could still change my mind.'

'You are not that brave. The new Lady of the Palace would not break her contract made before witnesses, would she?'

She gasped. It was like finding herself suddenly on the brink of a chasm. She had not thought or planned for such a question. That little ground of dignity which she defended became a vast possibility spread out before her. She was no longer the untaught girl shielded behind the E-Anna walls from the world of attractive Lords and men. She was a woman. She had power. She was a great Lady in her own right. Inanna could choose.

'I might. Yes.'

A momentary hardening of his face. Then that laughing, little-boy look. 'Oh no, you wouldn't. You couldn't live without your Dumuzi.'

So warm, so winning. If only she had not seen that flash of angry possession a moment before.

'I decide, Dumuzi. I, myself. Never forget that. I can do anything I want. I don't need you to rule with me.'

The arms around her tightened, and then seemed to go dead. She held her breath, astonished at her own daring, and looked up at his face. She exulted in the shock in his eyes. She waited for his love to come bounding to the rescue like that eager sheepdog, for him to fling himself on her with disbelief and grief, to beg, to plead with her, to fold her again in his passion. He must admit her his queen. He could not bear to lose her, could he? He could not let her go. He loved her too much.

She saw only disappointment, resentment, the stiffening wound of pride. He sat up, away from her. He folded his arms like a sulky boy.

'So that's it. I should have listened to them. In other cities than this, they call you vain, ambitious. They remember the Anunnaki sent you to Uruk to humble your bad temper. But An was too soft-hearted. You twisted him round your finger. They say that before long you will want to be called the greatest of all the Children of An.'

Inanna's mouth fell open. Dumuzi laughed.

'You see? You think all the world must love you and fall at your feet. Well, it isn't true. I needn't. You'd be turning down what every girl in Sumer would give her maidenhood for.'

'Dumuzi! That's not fair!'

'Have you changed your mind? Are you going to come down off your pedestal and stop playing the queen?'

'Why shouldn't I be the greatest of the Anunnaki one day? Why can't I be as great as Enlil?'

For a moment, doubt narrowed his eyes. Then he shrugged. 'Alone? Or you the Lady, and I your rightful Lord over you, Inanna?'

Her turn to hesitate. She felt him stiffen as he understood the answer.

'I am the . . . Can't you see . . .? Oh, go *away*!'

'For always, *Queen* Inanna? You never really loved me, did you?'

Her eyes pleaded with him for help. Her voice took nothing back.

He rose, still like an unfairly scolded boy, and with what injured dignity he could muster he took himself from her room.

Inanna flung herself down on the couch and beat the cushions for frustration and loss. Nin Shubur found her there. With a brisk order she sent the approaching slaves away.

Amanamtagga withdrew with the rest behind the door, saw Dumuzi halt and look back over his shoulder, as though waiting for Inanna's capitulation. There was no recall. The head slave risked a tender, sympathetic smile, then lowered her long black eyelashes in belated respect.

'What is this? What is this?' scolded Nin Shubur. 'A lovers' quarrel?'

'Worse than that.' Inanna sat up, still trying to sound like a queen through gulping sobs. 'I have sent him away. I don't think I'm going to marry him.'

A little pause. 'You have dismissed the Shepherd?' Then the *sukkal* cradled her mistress's head on her breast like a nurse with her child. 'There, there, my little lady, weep all you want. I am not entirely surprised or sorry. Lord Dumuzi is attractive enough to turn every girl's head, but there are those who say—'

Inanna pushed her away. 'Don't you dare, Nin Shubur! Don't come and report kitchen gossip to me!'

Nin Shubur stood up with dignity, smoothed the folds of her dress, bowed. 'I apologise, Inanna. I did not mean to offend you. Let me remind you instead of the advice of Lord An, of Father Nanna.'

'They never liked him.'

'Oh, Inanna, child, they *like* him. It is difficult not to like Lord Dumuzi. They doubted he would make you happy once your first nights of love had cooled. You are a precious flower to all of us, my lady. We did not want to see your petals bruised. Dumuzi has a reputation of one who takes more love than he gives.'

Inanna plucked the fringes of the cloth thrown over the couch. 'I have my throne ready now. I don't need to share it, do I? I can rule by myself. That's what Dumuzi couldn't stand. He's jealous of my power. I see that now.'

'Your new bed is wide,' Nin Shubur said gently. 'Can you occupy that alone too?'

Inanna hiccuped. 'No! I want someone to love, Nin Shubur! Dumuzi says I expect everyone to fall at my feet. That I'm not as loveable as he is. But it's not true! I did love him! I did! I only wanted him to let me be my true self. Inanna, the Queen, not just Inanna his bride.'

'Oh, child, child.' Inanna was in her *sukkal*'s arms again.

'How could he say that? Of course you know how to love. He didn't mean it. You, of all Ladies, are most dearly loved.' She dabbed Inanna's tears. 'There. Not that you always deserve our love! You often hurt the ones who love you. But we will always forgive you. We shall find you a husband to take good care of you, never fear.'

'Who?' Inanna sniffed. 'Someone who *really* loves me for myself? Who won't be jealous or angry if I'm greater than he is?'

'And will you give yourself to such a man as generously as he does to you?'

'I will. I will. I could have given Dumuzi more than he dreamed of, if he hadn't been so proud and stupid about it. I thought our love was perfect, but it's all spoiled now! I'll never find anyone else like him! Never!'

'No. The man you need will not be like Dumuzi. There are Lords enough, and good ones too. Rest now, little lady. When you wake this evening, perhaps the stars will shine brighter for you.'

'What shall I tell people? What can I say, Nin Shubur? I've lost my bridegroom. Will they laugh at me? Will they think he jilted me? Shall I become an old ugly woman without a husband, sleeping alone?'

'Never, never, Lady Inanna. Say nothing yet. By tomorrow your heart may have whispered a better name.'

'Whose, Nin Shubur? Whose? Do you think I could love anyone after Dumuzi?'

'It is not for me to say that, Lady of the Palace.'

# Chapter Fifty-seven

In those rain-fresh days, the mornings were sweet. High on the E-Anna terraces, Inanna could look out as if from a lofty mountain. Immediately below her lay the Annunaki district of Kullab. There, many Children of An had their houses, like courtiers to the great E-Anna. Gardens cooled them. Trees grew, even on the roofs of the palaces, with dark groves around the *giguna* hall. Water played, shaken by the flocks of birds that flew down from their roosts to bathe in the early morning sun.

Beyond, the city of Uruk was vast: its broad processional way from gate to summit, its open squares and market places reflecting the sun, its narrow lanes and storeyed houses crowding one upon another as the populace grew and streamed to the city like a wealthy flock of sheep packing the fold at evening.

The walls were modest in height, but stretched away around the mound that was growing higher with every century of trodden clay. Clay built this city. In Sumer, the land made by the Two Rivers, there was no stone, no forest trees, no precious metals. All that was rare, exotic, was brought for the temples and the palaces in the heavy barges that thronged the Buranun and its canals. Clay was everywhere, a dusty gold as common and free as air.

War was far from Uruk at this time. The gates stood open for her thriving trade. Irrigation ditches netted the level plain like life-bringing veins. Around the lakes, orchards waved, and the brilliant lushness of vegetable gardens. Villages lay among this green, like drops of honey. Date palms and willows sank vigorous roots along the rivers. Neighbouring cities rode the sea of foliage like mighty ships.

Far on the horizon, with that busy happy land like a shield between, lay the purple rim of desert. And further still, out of sight, the foothills of the mountains.

'Mine,' breathed Inanna, almost to herself. She gripped the terrace wall to give herself courage. 'It will all be mine. I began with the stars, and now I shall have the Earth as well.' There was pain at the back of her throat. Unshed tears burned the ducts of her eyes. She had woken conscious of loss, of an awful shadow behind her waiting to fall. She would not admit it yet.

It was not shadow but warmth that came to stand behind her.

'Good morning, Inanna.'

Utu. So large and strong his hands upon her shoulders. It made her feel a child again. For once, that was a comfort.

He came round to stand beside her, looked at her quizzically. He was holding something behind his back.

'I've brought you a present,' he teased.

'Show me!' She tried to be bright and laughing. She must let no one see how much she was hurt.

He whipped out under her eyes a bunch of long, silky stems, their blue flowers faded into a seeding gold that crumbled at a touch.

'Flax?' she said, in a flat, disappointed voice.

He waggled it under her nose, tickled her chin with it. 'Smile!' In a singsong voice he began to chant.

'The flax from the field, the flax from the furrow,
'The rich strong flax.
'Now you have felled your tree, Lady Inanna,
'I will hoe the flax for you,
'I will bring you the flax from the field.'

Sensing a riddle, she intoned back to him,

'Brother, what should I do with your bunch of flax?
'Who will comb it for me?'

She burst out laughing genuinely as he plucked out of his padded belt a handful of soft fibres.

'Sister mine, I will bring it to you combed.
'Inanna, I will bring it to you combed.'

She must play the game.

'Brother, who will spin it for me?
'Who will spin that flax for me?'

'Wait a minute!' Fumbling deeper in his skirt folds now and producing a spindle wound with slender thread, which twisted giddily as he dangled it before her. 'There!

'Sister mine, I will bring it to you spun.
'Inanna, I will bring it to you spun.'

She clapped her hands to please him.

'Brother, who will braid it for me?

'Who will braid the flax for me?'

'This is getting a bit technical!' With clumsy male fingers he plaited the gossamer strands into a stronger line.

'Sister, I will bring it to you braided.

'Inanna, I will bring it to you braided.'

A smile to tease him now. Years fell away, and they were children, before An and Enlil had sent her away to Uruk.

'Brother, who will warp it for me?

'Who will warp the flax for me?'

Utu laughed triumphantly and signalled across the terrace. Amanamtagga and two other slave women pulled out the wood-framed loom on which the spun strands were already stretched for weaving. Inanna gulped and broke into peals of incredulous mirth.

'Sister, I have brought it to you warped.

'Inanna, I have brought it to you warped,' Utu sang solemnly.

And now the *ala* harps were taking up the tune, the long drums began to tap the rhythm.

'Brother, who will weave it for me?

'Who will weave the flax for me?'

'Sister mine, I will bring it to you woven.

'Inanna, I will bring it to you woven.' The shuttle began to dance.

Her voice sank softer now, sensing the climax of the mystery could not be far off.

'Brother, who will dye it for me?

'Who will dye the flax for me?'

'Sister mine, *I* will bring it to you dyed.

'Inanna, *I* will dye the flax for you.'

Sheets. Blue as the bright enamelled tiles that faced the temple walls. Hemmed with gold, like the sun.

Her heart caught. She stared, and lifted her huge and brilliant eyes to Utu her brother. There, on the terrace, in front of Nin Shubur and Ninurta's seven daughters and half a dozen of Utu's friends, with all the women and eunuchs of her household listening, she sang, her eyes on Utu.

'Brother, who will bed me on your sheets?

'Who will bed me on the flax?'

The harper's fingers paused, waiting for the first note of Utu's answer. Only the rhythm of the drum tapped on, unstoppable as blood. His eyes were locked in hers.

Then Utu seized the bright blue sheet and whirled it round his head so that it tumbled over them both like a royal cloak.

'Your husband will bed with you on the flax, of course!

'Ushumgalanna will bed with you!'

She struggled free of the sheet and threw it from her. 'He will not! He will not! I am not going to marry Dumuzi Ushumgalanna.'

Utu started back. Anxiety caught the breath of the crowd of well-wishers like a sudden wind.

'Who, then, will you marry?'

She snatched the bundle of flax. The straight, true stalks of the fields of the fertile plain.

'I will marry the Farmer! I will marry Enkimdu. He loves me!' And tears burst from her eyes, staining the crumpled sheets at her feet.

A silence fell over the close. Amanamtagga's hand was over her mouth. Ninurta's daughters looked at each other, troubled. Ishkur laughed uneasily.

'What are you saying?' Utu asked. 'What have you done, sister?'

'I will marry the Farmer,' she said, chin up now, her voice determined. 'He asked Father Nanna for me, didn't he? But I chose Dumuzi then. I was wrong. I see it now. Dumuzi does not want me to be happy. I will have Lord Enkimdu. His fields are vast, his granaries are stacked high. He has no need to labour with the hoe. He has all his wide estates ploughed with oxen, canals dug by corvées of villagers, his orchards well-watered. I should have left my *huluppu* tree with him. He would have cared for it.'

'Inanna, Inanna, think of Dumuzi! He can give you far more than Enkimdu can. Why tie yourself to the grubby soil? Think of cream and milk and butter, rich and sweet. Think of his sheep grazing over the steppe like wandering clouds. Think of the sides of the cows swollen with new calves. Dumuzi is rich, too. Where other Lords would pile up dates before your threshold to show their wealth, Dumuzi can heap up *unu* stones and *shuba* gems for you. When Enkimdu brings you baskets of grapes, Dumuzi will bring you bracelets of lapis lazuli.'

'I don't choose to marry the Shepherd with the coarse wool garments. I am not a peasant girl. I don't want to live with sheepskin and leather. This flax you have brought me is

Enkimdu's gift, not Dumuzi's. I shall go clad in finest linen, cool as mist. I shall have white flour on my table from royal barley. I shall eat wheat. I shall . . .' Sobs choked her voice.

Nin Shubur's gentle gestures swept the terrace clean of onlookers. Only Utu remained. His arms went round his younger sister, drew her to his chest.

'Inanna, don't cry. Inanna!' He rocked and stroked and kissed her for a long while as she wept, like a mother with a hurt child. His face, bent over her bowed head, struggled with a different grief.

'Inanna?'

'Yes?' So like a hiccupping infant it brought an aching smile.

'Come away with me. Let us go to the mountains, you and I. Think it over. Leave Dumuzi and Enkimdu and the city of An. Let it be as it was when you and I were children beyond Aratta, playing under cedar trees, paddling in icy rivers, watching the pack-asses go down the hills laden with silver.'

She swayed with the magic of half-lost memories. 'Am I only imagining it? The waterfalls were silver, the skies lapis lazuli. The aromatic herbs under our feet like incense. The fir trees fragrant.' She straightened up. 'I must tell An first. He must send a message to Lord Enkimdu to say I will have him.'

'Inanna! Wait!'

'No. I have made my mind up. Dumuzi doesn't deserve me. Enkimdu loves me so much he will let me do anything I like. Dumuzi wants to rule me. He can't bear to think that I am greater than he is.'

'Then let Dumuzi have his way! Share yourself with us all, Inanna. Be generous!' The plea was almost desperate.

'I have made my own choice. I will marry Enkimdu. I don't need to ask Father if he agrees. He never wanted Dumuzi for a son-in-law.'

'But you will still come with me to the Cedar Mountain?'

She cocked her head on one side, smiled bravely for him. 'Yes. I should like that. Let's start today. I cannot bear to be in Uruk while Dumuzi is here.'

An frowned when they told him. 'Even for a Daughter of the Anunnaki this is capricious! After my ritual blessing on you and Dumuzi, you make me look foolish.'

'But you wanted Enkimdu.'

'Wanted?' He shook his head petulantly. 'I didn't *want* you to marry anyone, Nin Egalla. I wanted you to stay with me. Still, I approve of Enkimdu. He is steadier than that randy young billy goat Dumuzi.'

Why did her disobedient body leap at those words?

'You will tell Enkimdu then?'

'I, tell him? I will summon him to the E-Anna and you may tell him yourself.'

'No!' That little pleading cry. 'I don't want to see him yet. I don't want to talk to anyone. Utu is taking me away to the mountains.'

An's gaze shot to the tall Sun Lord. Utu nodded, his hand protectively on Inanna's shoulder. 'Tell the Farmer, if you must. Dumuzi already knows the worst. There was a quarrel last night. But let it not be spoken of publicly yet. Give us time. I will bring her back to you in a few days.'

'The months are passing. Her wedding is fixed for the New Year Festival.'

'There will be a wedding.' Inanna's voice was steady now. 'I will marry Enkimdu.'

# Chapter Fifty-eight

The day was perfect. It made her want to cry. She should not have been here in this crystal air, under the white gaze of the snow-capped mountains, with this dark desolation in her heart.

The beer was good and cold. At Utu's sign the obsequious tavern keeper came hurrying out with another stone jar dripping moisture and filled their beakers. Inanna tried to protest.

'No, Utu. I've had enough. You're trying to make me drunk.'

The words came furred, and her hand knocked the goblet so that dark frothing beer spilled on the pale deal table. She managed to steady the cup. She was in control, she thought, though her face was warmer than the mountain air beside this rushing torrent would warrant, and she had a growing need to pass water.

'It is not the beer of the hills that makes us drunk,' said Utu. 'It is the scents. Thyme and rosemary, cedar and cypress. Can you find them in the air? Do you remember?'

His hand was over hers, quite loosely. She felt a surge of gratitude. Utu, at least, loved her. He did not begrudge her her glory. The Lord of the Sun had no need to be jealous of anyone. The bitter indignation knotted in her again. She must not let it soften. If she allowed the knot to weaken, the door of her soul might burst open and all the demons of loss and grief come tumbling out to devour her.

'I want to walk up the mountain,' she said thickly. 'I want to smell the cedar forest.'

She stood up, unsteadily. Nin Shubur rose at once from a distant bench in the shade, but Utu signalled her away. He put his arm round his sister. She leaned against him, smiling dreamily. A hundred brown-backed butterflies resting against the trunk of a tamarisk tree broke suddenly into the air in a glory of scarlet and black. To Inanna their flight was piercingly magical.

'Utu, look! Look!'

'Let us follow them, sister,' he murmured in her ear.

Again he signed to their escort to stay back. His *sukkal* and Inanna's, their *sag-ursag* guards looked at each other for guidance, shrugged.

The brother and sister wandered away from the road and the tavern. Paths, scarcely more than deer-trails, led ribbons of sunlight between the black-branched cedars. The ground was soft under their feet with fallen needles, sandy earth. Inanna felt it cushion her feet as though Great-grandmother Ki was offering her flesh to soothe her small hurt descendant.

Utu was kind. Ki was kind. Even the still, scented air seemed like Enlil's benediction. She let tears of wordless gratitude roll down her cheeks. She needed friends.

Utu pulled her closer, let her head rest on his shoulder.

'You're so good to me,' she managed to mumble.

'Am I, Inanna?' The arm around her shoulder was no more insistent, but the voice was deep, stronger, pulling her closer.

It woke a warning of danger in her. Her conscious mind struggled to see the reason, like the pilot of a *nisag* boat through the river mist. The needs of her lower body became more imperative now, as though to pass water would be an exquisite relief that was somehow caught up in the magic of birdsong and the far-off glimpse of sparkling snow.

'Utu,' she laughed. 'Excuse me. I must go behind that tree.'

'All right.' He smiled and let her go.

There was a moment's disappointment, not wholly understood, as she found herself standing unsupported. She moved with careful accuracy into the deeper shadow behind a forest giant.

The trunk of the cedar was generous, hiding her from Utu and the distant guards whose heads had been just in view as they climbed the steep slope. It was very quiet. Outside this wood, in the sunshine, birds sang, cicadas chirped, the river roared over rocks. But here the shadows made a barrier beyond which these noises did not seem to pass. She heard them, but they were in another world.

She fumbled awkwardly with her clothes, heard the sudden hiss of urine released into the matted needles. It foamed and drained away into the accepting earth. Strangely, its passing from her body seemed to have inflamed those parts rather than satisfying them. She reached down her hand to scratch and rub.

'Inanna.'

Low, almost reverent.

Utu was standing a little distance in front of her, staring down at where she still squatted with her hand between her thighs. His face was grave. The smallest speck of sunshine crowned his hair.

She started to scramble to her feet, pulling her dress down. At once he was beside her, holding her arms, tugging her to him.

'Inanna. Inanna!' The need was open in his voice now. The fog of beer and self-pity evaporated from her mind. She knew with piercing clarity what was happening.

'Utu! No!'

His hand drove up her buttocks now, hot and thrusting. His mouth bit hers. And, yes, excitement raced through her. All the years of palace training as a hierodule, all Nin Isinna's coaching, all An's lascivious and yet indulgent pawing, his letting her make a plaything of his body to increase her woman's power, all that fell away, like children's toys. This was a man, with a man's need, a man's strength. She felt her body melting treacherously. The cedar bark was rough behind her, pressing into her bared flesh. She was slipping. Any moment now her clutching hands would bring him falling over her on to the soft needled floor.

'No, Utu! I am a virgin!'

She heard the catch of racing breath. So hot his mouth over her face. So like a furnace his body smothering her against the tree. Slowly the weight shifted.

'A virgin? You? Ten years in the E-Anna with Great-grandfather An?'

'Yes!' Her arm just free enough now to tug the cloth over her bruised breasts. 'Oh, I know what you thought. I have learned everything a bride should know. But I have opened my garden to no one yet. My jewel is my own.'

His smile was dazzling. He held her chin in his warm hand and his blue eyes shone for her as if that made it all the sweeter.

'Poor, stupid Dumuzi. To throw *this* away!'

His touch was gentler this time, that reverence again. He cupped her breasts, bent and kissed them softly. Played with a tendril of her hair. More slowly and tenderly now, so that she knew it was love as well as desire, he gathered her to him again. She found this harder to resist.

'No, Utu. I told you no.' How faint and unconvincing her plea against Utu the Judge.

His lips murmured against her hair. 'What are you saving yourself for, little sister? Dumuzi is gone. Enkimdu is a man of the soil. He's a practical farmer. He will not expect you to come from the E-Anna a chaste schoolgirl. You will do him a favour to let me complete your education. Let the Sun shine in glory on your day of graduation.'

His fingers were busy while he spoke, coaxing, arousing, penetrating. And yet . . . not so very different from An's, after all.

She found the strength to push him away. Gasped out the words she only half believed.

'I am Inanna. Daughter of the Moon. Princess of the Stars. You are Lord of the Day. We are not meant for each other. This is wrong.'

'Wrong, Inanna? How can it be wrong? I am Utu the Righteous, Judge of humans and Anunnaki.'

'And I am Nin Egalla, Lady of the Palace. *I* will decide who enters. I, Inanna.'

'You have been hurt, sister. I want to comfort you.'

Harder still to resist, that. Tears of weakness coursed down her cheeks.

'No one can comfort me. Not ever!'

'My lady?' Nin Shubur's call, distant, inquiring, prudent.

'It's my *sukkal*. She's wondering where we are.'

'Damn!' Utu tore a wedge of bark from the tree, flung it on the ground.

Inanna sighed. She leaned back against the trunk again, dizzy with relief. Utu strode past her, into the blinding light of the open path, to let himself be seen by those below. He looked too angry to speak.

Inanna fought the sudden weariness of her limbs. She adjusted her dress cloth, brushed the cedar spines from her skirt. She walked to join him, felt herself grow stronger under the open sky. She took her brother's hand, even managed a small smile for him.

'Come on. We must go back. Don't let's say anything about this. You are still Utu, the Father of the Wanderer, the Mother of the Homeless, the Guardian of the Orphan, the

Protector of the Widow. I want to go home. I want to go back to Mother in Ur.'

'Running home? What will you say to everybody? You will have to give Dumuzi back his lapis lazuli necklaces. You will have to give back all his silver bracelets. Will you apologise to Nin Sun? What are you going to tell Geshtinanna?' he taunted her.

She drew back her hand then and struck him a stinging blow on the cheek, not caring if the approaching escort saw it.

He gasped and staggered, then caught her wrists, his eyes dancing again.

'I should not have forgotten you were the Lion of Battle too. I must tell Dumuzi he should learn to fight!'

Her eyes locked suddenly in his. He saw the desperate hope. He caught her to him swiftly, the elder brother again, and let her cry.

As the two *sukkals* came with diplomatic slowness up the path, he rocked his sister in his arms. 'It's all right, Little Star. It's all right. We'll get him back for you somehow.'

The face of tragedy turned up to his. 'It's too late. It's spoiled for ever now.'

# Chapter Fifty-nine

'Sit here, child.'

'I am not a child now, Father.' Inanna remained standing.

'Sit down between your mother and myself, Lady Inanna.' Nanna-Suen's mouth bent in a bow. She felt she did not know him well enough to tell whether this was a smile at her precocity or a tight-lipped grimace of disapproval.

She felt something of her height diminish, something of her brightness fade. She obeyed him.

'Now,' he nodded to his *sukkal*. 'Admit Lord Enkimdu.'

Inanna felt a leap of fear. She had known this must happen. She had known that when An sent the message of her broken betrothal to Ur, Nanna would at once begin negotiations for a new marriage. She had chosen Enkimdu herself. Why then did she feel like an exile thrown out to the Tent Lands, travelling the long straight road through fertile barley fields, through date groves, through orchards and villages to the boundary where the irrigation channels ceased, the floods could reach no higher, and the desert began?

She had left Dumuzi Ushumgalanna of the orchards behind her. But it was hard not to smile at least a little for this brown, kindly man advancing across the night-dark tiles of Nanna's audience chamber towards her. His lightly-furrowed face was creased now in a deeper happiness. His hands stretched out to her were carrying gifts. More high officials of his household followed, bearing great jars and baskets. Two were even leading asses, milk-white, with trappings of blue and green and gold. Gilt palm leaves sprouted from the headbands between their ears. She clapped her hands with a momentary delight.

Enkimdu's smile broadened in pleasure. He bowed before Nanna and Nin Gal and Utu and Inanna in turn. He kissed their ceremonial breast pendants. His salute to his bride-to-be was circumspect. Even though Inanna held her breath, wondering how she would feel this time, so close to him, knowing they must lie closer yet, she felt no stir of desire, nor of revulsion either. It was a relief. She had made up her mind. She had put Enkimdu in Dumuzi's place. She would welcome Enkimdu to Dumuzi's bed. It *was* Dumuzi's bed. She would never be able to look at the *pirig* lion and the *ug* lion, sporting together like a puppy dog and bitch, and think of anyone else . . .

She reined back the longing that threatened a disaster of tears. She should be grateful that she had Enkimdu. He would never replace Dumuzi in her heart, only in her bed. And there he would be kind, considerate. She read that in the humble concern with which he looked at her now.

'Lady Inanna,' he said. 'You are giving me the jewel of the Sky. What can a poor farmer offer to rival the Star that rides in the wake of Nanna's Boat?'

'My planet can rise before the Moon. It shines even on the dark night given to Ereshkigal.' She smiled with more assurance now. She had been right. Enkimdu was certainly no poor farmer, but he had no intention of rivalling her.

'So much more hopeless then to give you the treasures you deserve. Take instead this tiny thing as token of my love, my lady.'

He opened his palms and showed her. She bent with curiosity to see. At first she could not make it out.

'A handful of clay?'

He laughed, suddenly like a mischievous boy, for all that he was much older than Dumuzi. 'There. I knew it. I have disappointed you. This clod of a farmer, she says to herself, brings me the mud from his fields. What is that for the start of a high romance?'

He gave a little whistling call and his housekeeper stepped forward and handed Enkimdu a doll of clay, such as children fashion to play with in the mud of puddles after a storm.

Enkimdu put his own fistful of unshaped clay aside and laid the doll at Inanna's feet. 'Did you play with one of these? In the beginning, Mother Nammu bore the first humans from the clay of the Abzu, and Enki and Nin Mah brought them into life. I lay at your feet the race of humankind to serve you in your estates and palaces.'

Before she could speak, he called to the other side, and his bailiff came forward with a basket filled with clay in which barley was sprouting. Enkimdu set this beside his previous gift.

'The furrows of Sumer. The rich brown clay of the flooded fields. All its grain, all its fruit, all its flax are yours, my lady.'

To the right side again. She leaned forward eagerly. A wooden mould, opening to reveal a sun-baked brick on which was stamped her own rosette and doorposts.

'The temples of Sumer, its palaces, the houses, the city walls, the dykes of her canals. All yours.'

And now a young woman scribe holding clay tablets which she had stamped with cuneiform.

'Poetry, law, epics of heroes, cures of the water-wise physicians, hymns to the stars. Immortal wisdom that will make Inanna's name remembered for thousands and thousands of years.'

She clasped her hands before her, laughing, hugging her pleasure.

Now they were unloading gifts for her mother and father. Baskets of beans, jars of emmer beer, honey and oil and wine from his farms. Colourful as jewels, the presents lay heaped around the high dais.

'And this,' he said, suddenly stilled from laughing. 'Take my first and last gift to you, Lady Inanna.' He picked the pat of unshaped clay that had been lying near his feet all this time.

'I dug it this morning, with my own hands, with my own hoe. In the garden of my finest farm, under the white poplar tree. There is a reservoir that feeds my canals, where pelicans come to feed at evening. I have planted apple trees on its banks. The sky in all its glory is reflected in its water at sunset. I have laid an avenue of *mesu* trees all the way from the chariot road. They are coming into blossom now. There is a quay on the big canal, where you can take a boat to visit your mother in Ur. All around, the fields are sweet with beanflowers, blue with flax, gold with barley. The millhouses and breweries and brickyards are busy with slaves. Today, in the first light of morning, while your Star still hung in the sky, I cut this sod. I have left my workmen laying out the foundation. Tomorrow I shall drive in the clay peg that will moor the house above to the Deep below. I am building the house for my new bride, Lady Inanna.'

She reached out her hand, let it hover over the clay still faintly damp. Her eyes rose seriously to his.

'I have my own house, Lord Enkimdu. The E-Anna is mine, from the day I marry.'

He inclined his head, with no apparent annoyance, a businessman confirming a deal. 'I know, Lady. Do not think I would try to strip the Queen of the Palace of her dignity with my poor farmhouse. But let it be a place of love for bride and bridegroom to renew their joy. A country retreat, when the heat and noise of the city grow too great for you.'

And he is my retreat, thought Inanna. My country refuge.

She let her fingerprints descend on the cool, smooth clay, then bent, smiling faintly, and kissed it. She took up the cylinder-seal from her neck and rolled it over the surface, imprinting her mark.

Enkimdu glowed with surprised happiness. 'So you have sealed your sign upon my heart, Lady Inanna.'

Inanna lowered her eyes and sighed. The fun and delight of the morning had gone. A man stood before her, a middle-aged man, warm-hearted, generous. A good Farmer. Her bridegroom. And she could feel nothing for him. Her own heart was as unreceptive to his imprint as cold stone.

Inanna had sent her slaves and companions away for the afternoon siesta. When she did not reappear, Nin Gal had come to her room and sat by her bedside.

'You look pale, my child, and the heat of summer is not on us yet.'

'It's the excitement,' Inanna said, picking at the fringe of the bedcover. 'Lord Enkimdu . . . No, it's not! I'm not hot. Cold, rather. And tired.'

Sadness deepened in Nin Gal's eyes. She bent forward and kissed her daughter. 'If I could give you anything for a wedding gift, it would be the love I had – have – for Nanna. When we were young . . .' She gave a laugh that was young yet. 'In the canebrakes, by my mother's reed house . . .'

Inanna struggled to hold back the tears. Dumuzi and she, running through the moonlit city. Sitting entwined under a grape arbour while Geshtinanna sang. What would she become with Enkimdu? A respectable housewife? An efficient estate manager? A feared queen? Never again a young and ardent lover, a girl with her sweetheart whose step makes her blood race.

'Shall I send my elegist in? Would you like the music of the old laments to release the tears and wash you clean for this new wedding?'

Inanna caught her hand. 'You're very wise, aren't you? Does Father see it too?'

Nin Gal stood up and sighed. 'Nanna is right, of course. Enkimdu is the better man. He will never hurt you.'

'But Dumuzi . . .?' How rare a treat to let herself speak that name. Her voice had hardly shaken.

'Dumuzi Abzu is my brother . . . half-brother. The blood of Enki is passionate, unstoppable as water flooding. Of course I favour him. But my father is Lord of Wisdom too. It is possible to love a man, and know that he is flawed.'

'Then . . . what *would* you advise?'

Nin Gal's hand rested on Inanna's head. 'You cannot lean to a different bridegroom every other day, like a reed when the wind shifts. You are a Daughter of An. A great Lady now. An has given you power early. For many Daughters of An their role is that of consort. Who cares what sphere they might once have guarded? I. Nin Lil. Even Nin Mah, who should be the greatest of us all, has been humbled, first to Enlil, and then to Enki. But some of us still preserve the female glory.'

'Nanshe?'

'And Nidaba is revered for her wisdom, if not for majesty.'

'Ereshkigal?'

A startled look. 'I did not think of her! But you, Inanna, you will grow as great, or greater. And I do not know what a great Guardian should do, whom she should wed. My heart, like yours, says Dumuzi. My head, like yours, tells me that Nanna and An may be right. You wanted power. And now you have it. The Anunnaki will not prevent you. Even now, if you changed your mind, Nanna would give his consent, though with a heavy heart.'

The dark dilated pupils of Inanna's eyes shone up at her. 'Could I? Could I still marry Dumuzi? Would he have me back? Oh, but how could I hurt Enkimdu? He was so nice, Mother. What shall I do?' Her voice was rising, desperate.

Nin Gal gently disengaged her hand. 'Stay there and rest. I will send a singer to you.'

And when the door opened again, softly, slowly, it was Dumuzi's sister, carrying her harp.

The two girls stared across the distance separating them, Inanna startled, Geshtinanna wary. Then joy and friendship burst like the sun from behind a thundercloud and they were in each other's arms.

'Oh, Geshtin! I thought you'd never come again! I thought I'd ruined everything!'

'There, silly.' The older girl patted her, mopped her tears for her. 'Of course I'm back. Did you think a lovers' tiff between you and Dumuzi could break our friendship?'

'It's much worse than a lovers' tiff,' Inanna sniffed. 'I told him I'm not going to marry him. I've broken our betrothal. Now Father has arranged for me to marry Enkimdu.'

'I know.' Geshtinanna's head was bent over her *algar* instrument. A gilt ram's head decorated the soundbox. Horns of ebony spread, supporting the nine strings. Along its sides, small drum-heads waited for her knuckles. The ends were hung with tinkling bells. She tightened the pegs, tested the strings.

'How is Dumuzi?' Inanna asked in a low voice.

'Not well.'

'He's ill? What? Tell me!' Inanna sat up in alarm.

Geshtinanna shook her head, would not look at Inanna. Colour darkened her face.

'Tell me! Who's looking after him? Should I send him Nin Isinna? She's a great physician. She takes care of An—'

'This wound even that Hierodule of the Sky cannot reach. Only one person holds the cure.'

'Then send for them! But where is Dumuzi now? Was it safe to leave him?'

'Listen.' Geshtinanna silenced her with a lift of her hand. 'Your mother sent me to sing to you. This is my song.'

She turned her shoulder to Inanna, so that her face was partly hidden. The *algar* instrument was an orchestra in itself, requiring great skill to control its strings, its drums, its bells. Yet Geshtinanna's clever fingers seemed to pick their own way through its singing forest, while all her heart turned inward to find and voice her chant.

After days of plenty, days of abundance,
After months of pleasure, years of rejoicing,
The Shepherd Dumuzi took it into his heart
To visit his sheepfold on the steppe.
He left his Bride behind.

On the farms the stalls are crowded.

In the pasture the sheep are thick.
On the table is butter and honey,
In their cups is beer and wine.
The Shepherd took his sister's hand.

'Come to the sheepfold. What do you see, my sister?'
And his sister said, unthinking,
'I see a young ram jump on his mother's back and enter her!'
'And what does his mother say?'
'She seems to enjoy it.'

'Look at the goats, my sister. What do you see?'
And she said more fearfully, in the narrow shippen,
'I see the kid jump on to his sister's back,
Mount her and copulate with her.'
'And she, what does his sister say?'
'She cries out with joy!'

'Little sister, if she cries out with joy,
Come here now beside me.
As he has flooded her with his water . . .'

Geshtinanna's voice shook, and the bells quivered urgently.
Inanna sat rigid, staring at her.
 'You too! Dumuzi . . . You?'
 The strings played on, wordlessly.
 'You let him?'
 'Inanna, he loves *you*! He's suffering!'
 Inanna threw herself down on her bed, clawed her cheeks. Geshtinanna came and stood over her, then lay down too, took her friend in her arms. They kissed, and Geshtinanna licked the tears from Inanna's face.
 'Utu . . .' said Inanna.
 'Did you?'
 'No. Geshtin, what does it mean? Must it always be like this? Are the Children of An not free? Are we so closely bound, to our fathers, our grandfathers, our brothers, even our sons? Does guarding the universe require that we copulate with each other? Earth with Sky. Air and Earth. Sky and Water. Water and Hills. On and on? Do we ourselves have no choice?'
 She sat up abruptly.

'I have made up my mind. I am going to be mistress of myself. But you . . . You love Dumuzi, don't you? *Really* love him. You'd sacrifice anything for him.'

Geshtinanna hid her head dumbly against Inanna's breast. Inanna's arm went round her, held her strongly.

'I will decide, Geshtinanna. I will decide. I will be strong enough for all of us. You. Dumuzi. Me. Don't you see? Poor Dumuzi could never be a great ruler. If he is as weak as this, to force his grief on you, because you wouldn't refuse him, I was silly to be afraid of his power. When I was grieving too, I was far stronger than that. What have I got to fear from a little boy like him? Nothing! And what have I got to enjoy?' She turned to Geshtinanna with glowing eyes, made Dumuzi's sister lift up her face and laugh with her.

Geshtinanna sprang out of bed, seized her *algar* harp. She clashed the drums and bells. 'I can tell him? You'll forgive him? You'll marry him?'

'Don't you mind?' said Inanna, leaping up after her and laughing. 'How can you bear to lose him?'

'Mind? If it takes his grief away? I'd die for him!'

'But Enkimdu!' Inanna grabbed her, as though drunk. 'What am I going to do about poor Enkimdu?'

'Oh, never mind about Enkimdu now. Just let me tell Dumuzi you love him!'

And she sped out of the E-Kishnugal past ranks of astonished courtiers, with all the bells of her instrument shouting like a flock of plovers taking wing.

# Chapter Sixty

'What is this, Inanna? What is this you have done, Daughter of the Palace?'

'What, Father?'

Hold on to the sweetness of the morning, the twittering of the *dar* birds, the *mesu* trees whose flowers are like the stars of heaven, the smell of purple-black earth where the gardeners have opened the sluices and led the water in its channels to the troughs around each tree. The last two rows are still unwatered. Is this what she is like? The clay dry and hard, the flowers doomed to droop and wither unless they drink?

'Last night you met young Dumuzi again at Geshtinanna's house.'

'Yes.' A whisper of petals.

'You! Soon to be queen of the E-Anna, running out after dark like a kitchenmaid to meet some buck on a street corner!'

'Lord Enkimdu,' announced Nanna's *sukkal*.

'You shame us all,' the Moon Lord said fiercely. 'You cannot change your mind with every shift of the breeze on the marsh. We have sent Dumuzi back his betrothal jewels. Now you are pledged to Lord Enkimdu.'

He was coming. That kind good-hearted Farmer. Why should her heart sink so? Was this how Nin Shubur, Woman of the Eastern Mountains, felt, gazing out across the endless, level plains of Sumer, where the eye found no relief even to the horizon? All mountains here were artefacts, ziggurats soaring into the sky, laboriously imitating what Mother Nammu had joyously thrown up at the first when she gave birth to Ki and An. So was this marriage to which Inanna was contracted now. A constructed pretence, an imitation of the bond she had with Dumuzi. Her first love was a real mountain, all sparkling snow and stone, with seams of silver at its heart, fragrantly dark with cedar forests, alive with goats and mouflons, rainbowed with flowers, loud with rushing water.

As she held out her hand she read in Enkimdu's eyes that he knew this. His look was sweet and tender as just-ripe figs, his hand firm and grainy. In a moment of age-old wisdom she knew this was the better man. With the piercing clarity of her youth she knew she loved Dumuzi more than anything.

Her breast submitted to Enkimdu's kiss now. She felt herself cherished, respected. Voices boomed like drums over her head. Nanna's, Enkimdu's, discussing wedding settlements, the move to Uruk, Inanna's household in the E-Anna, the palace's wealth, the wisdom of its *sanga*, as administrator.

Emptiness in her heart, like a river at the end of summer, like a neglected farm, like a broken wine pot.

'You will become a great queen, Lady. I shall be proud to serve you. I shall lay the bounty of Sumer at your feet. Its flour and beans, its beer and bread. Furrows shall be dug straight for you. Canals kept clean and in good repair. Your slaves shall sing as they work, widows and orphans praise your goodness. Utu the Just shall visit your land and find no cause for complaint.'

But when the Star of Love steps up into the sky? Nanna's spies had reported accurately. Last night, in seeming secret, Dumuzi had held her again. Dumuzi had kissed her. Dumuzi had . . . She trembled, remembering it.

High Inanna, Princess of the Morning and Evening Star, Lady of Battles, soon to be mistress of the E-Anna. How could she nerve herself to say to her father a second time, 'I will not marry my betrothed'?

Dumbly she watched her mother tuck Enkimdu's arm through her own slight one and lead him off among the scented herb pots of the terrace. She could not hope. Drought dried her heart. What did her passionate reconciliation with Dumuzi mean, as long as Enkimdu walked with his friend Nanna and talked marriage settlements?

And yet she did hope. As when the jackal comes at evening and paws the crusted river bed, discovering a last trickle of precious water underneath.

Enkimdu was standing over her in farewell now, warm, solicitous. That sadness in his tawny eyes. Is it because he will marry her, and knows she does not love him? Or because he sees he must not marry her?

'I have to go to Uruk. I will come back to you next week, queen of my heart!'

'Yes.' A cold, bleak smile.

The Land of the Two Rivers was a gift of the immortals. Alluvial soil, washed down from the far-distant mountains, spread its vast plain ready for the touch of life. Lagoons winked to the blue sky. A wilderness of reed beds held the secret of the marshes. Lush date palms marked the pattern of watercourses laid down by the Anunnaki and continued since by humans. The fields yielded golden wealth. Too precious these cultivated *iku* for pasturage, where every drop of water must be led by human hands for half the year's supply. The fat-tailed sheep of the lowlands fattened in their pens, munching the bran the farmer allowed, to be let loose only at harvest time to graze the stubble.

Out on the steppe, where the riverbeds gushed with snow-melt and the desert was swiftly greened, life was freer. The far-off chime of bells told where Dumuzi's lead goat took the ewes and nannies among the pools and rushes. There was a boundary between this world and the other, known to generations, sacred in the all-seeing eyes of the just Lady Nanshe. Where pasture ended and agriculture began. Where the free met the fenced.

Dumuzi and Enkimdu faced each other across the last canal.

The Shepherd's step was firm, his head was up. He did not look like a man beaten, who has lost the highest prize.

'Enkimdu the Ploughman, is it?'

'As you see, friend.'

'No friend of yours, ditch-digger!'

'Sumer is wide, Shepherd. Enki is generous with the water. I have led the canals as far from the Buranun as the slope of country allows. The land is a garden. You have the steppe, the wild places. Let your sheep and your goats range freely. There is room for us both.'

'Room for only one man in the bed that will be at the heart of Uruk. The new Queen's bed in the E-Anna.'

Stillness of waters at evening. Haze veils the sun. Sadness darkens Enkimdu's eyes.

'Why should I fight with you, Shepherd? Inanna has made her choice.'

'You're right! She has chosen! Shall I tell you whom she has picked? Would you like to hear? Has she sucked your lips, like a girl eating cherries? Has she twisted her fingers in the curled hairs of your chest, painted honey on your nipples and licked it, laughing? Has she slid the fine linen from her shoulders to stand like a shaft of her father's moonlight while your hands slip over her like falling water? Has she done that for you, ox-driver?'

Pain furrows Enkimdu's face. 'I knew she loved you. I knew Father An himself had blessed your betrothal. But not before the first omens fell evilly. Inanna has changed her mind. I have her hand and word.'

Dumuzi laughed loud, even coarsely. The sheep and goats, unchecked, began to stray among the vegetable patches, snatching at cresses and cool green lettuce. Enkimdu's troubled eyes watched their depredations. He did not raise his voice to stop them. Dumuzi watched them too, triumphantly, his crook planted in front of him like a battle standard.

'Your flocks are hungry, Shepherd.'

'And so am I, old man. For the sweet date cluster at the heart of the tree. For the lettuce that needs long watering. For the fertile soil that the barley stalk must shaft.'

'I took Inanna from you with her own consent, by her own choice.'

'And I have won her back by her own choice. You could not hold the Star of Dawn!'

'I have offered her everything. The goodness of all this land, my love and service.'

'I can give her better. Black ewes for your dark flour, white ewes for your white flour. Thick yellow milk for your prime beer, fermented *kisim* for your mellowed beer, honey cheese for your best bread, my small round cheeses for your little beans. When your last year's crops are eaten and the storehouse is empty, I shall have surplus cream, I shall have surplus milk. I have greased her lips, I have wet her breasts, I have bathed her vulva with my milk.'

Tears falling now down the Farmer's honest face. He believes this. He has seen Inanna's eyes.

A voice, almost too broken to be heard.

'Why should we quarrel, Dumuzi Ushumgalanna? We both love her deeply. Why should either of us wish to pain her? We would both die for her. Look, your sheep are eating the lettuce of my garden, your goats are chewing my turnips.

I have not spoken out to stop them. I had so much to give . . .' Sobs shake his throat. 'Well, let them drink from my canal. Why should I grudge them? Let them roam my farm, take what they want.' He spoke wildly now, dashing away his tears and laughing. 'Take everything I have! If it is true she loves you . . . if you will make her happy.'

'You'd give her back to me?' Dumuzi's hand faltered on his staff, as though he had expected a fight.

'Give? *Give* Inanna? The Queen of the Night and Morning? Inanna gives herself!' Just for a moment doubt clouded his reckless, selfless generosity. 'I want to make her happy. I want to lay the world and all the Sky and the Netherworld at her feet. I want to serve and solace her. If I must thresh the husk from my heart to do that, then I must. I cannot force my happiness from her, like a captive woman raped by brigands.'

Dumuzi leaped across the canal, a wild goose flying. He clapped the Farmer on the shoulder with an incredulous laugh.

'I was wrong to say you were no friend. You're the best friend a bridegroom ever had, or bride either. You'll really give her up?'

'I will ask her, rather, what she truly wants. I think I can guess the answer. Nin Gal did you a sister's service. Her music was softer than yours, but she sang the same tune as yours to me. If I hear it for the third time from Inanna's own lips, it will be enough. I will be her loyal subject. I will obey her. I will speak to Father Nanna and have the betrothal annulled. My fields are already hers, Shepherd. May you enjoy them.'

Dumuzi hugged the older man. Youth, victory, desire, like sunshine in his body. 'You'll come to our wedding, King of Ploughmen? Be our honoured guest?'

'Oh yes, I'll come. I shall always be there, if Inanna wants me. I will bring her wheat, I will bring her beans, I will bring her lentils for her wedding banquet. Dull, homely stuff. She'd rather eat your cream; she'll drink your sister's wine. You will make her happy. *Make her happy!*'

'I have won!' shouted Dumuzi to the sky. 'I have won Inanna!'

# Chapter Sixty-one

But before Dumuzi and Inanna could be married, danger struck at the land of Sumer.

In the dawn of the world, Asag, Lord of Plants, had defected to Kur. A bramble-limbed thorn-toed demon, fingers like needled conifers, shock-headed like the *numun* weed to seed much mischief. A warped thing, sprung from the pain of Ki when Enlil tore her away from An. He was her son. Now he was threatening all her children.

The mountains were on the move. Boulders came roaring down from the cliffs following their leader Asag. Lords of Basalt, Diorite, Haematite, Alabaster. Rivers sprang aside out of their way, lost their courses. Villages were threatened. Ahead lay all the outspread valleys, the rich farms. There was havoc to be reaped if they reached the plain, cities to be smashed and plundered.

Far away in Lagash, where Inanna was staying with her seven cousins, no rumour had reached the Anunnaki of what was coming. Inanna's Uncle Ninurta sat awesome on his judgment seat. Lions snarled from under its arms. The dark-shadowing wings of the Thunderbird spread out behind him as though they grew from his own shoulders. His voice was a deep roar. The horns of his tiara seemed to stab at heaven like a bull's crown. On the table beside him, fruit was heaped. His eldest son Shulshaggana, as steward, washed his father's hands with pure water, poured him sweet beer, the royal drink, as though he were An or Enlil.

The people of Lagash feared Ninurta. When they came to his judgment hall with petitions it was Bau, his wife, they appealed to first. This Lady, white-faced, black-haired, was one of those who held the *me* of healing, a Great Physician of the Black-Headed People. She came before her Lord, spoke in a voice of balm, worked all the good she was able.

She was pleading the case of a farmer, whose vineyards

were reverting to desert because his neighbour had not repaired the canal banks and all the water was soaking away into a cucumber garden upstream. The soft rise and fall of her voice reciting the facts was swamped by a mighty shout from the door.

'Hail, Warrior King! Invincible Lightning Bolt!'

All heads turned to the opened door and the brilliant terrace. The grapes in Ninurta's suddenly clenched fist dripped blood.

Sharur, his Weapon Man, stood facing him. A shaft-body strong and straight, fit to be gripped in a powerful hand. A massive macehead, greenish-white, carved with an inhuman face to strike terror into the enemy. He bristled with spikes. His hair was lashing thongs, hard leather and slashing wires of metal.

There were seven cries from Ninurta's daughters. Bau's voice stopped. Inanna only stared. The farmers of Lagash hastily backed away to the sides of the hall. Sharur was summoning Ninurta, Enlil's Ploughman, to cut a bloodier furrow.

His voice taunted his master, as no one else dared speak to him. 'Serpent? Rearing and swaying in front of the rebel country! Sickle? Severing the necks of the insubordinate! Lion? Raising your forepaw to strike the snake! What are you doing, sprawling on your throne dais swilling sweet beer?'

'Where else should Enlil's son be found?'

'Have you turned your back on the highland? Have you not heard what is happening there?'

'There is not a rebellious nation that dares move against Sumer or Uri or Shubur or Martu while Ninurta guards them.'

'No human, master! One of your own sort. An enemy worthy of both of us at last. A real fighter. Asag, my lord. The son of Sky and Earth. He knows not cities. A child who deserted his mother and his father when the immortals were young. Kur has watched over him. Wild beasts have nursed him. The savage wilderness has been his home. Hate of you is in his heart.'

Ninurta was leaning forward, his dark eyes fired with lightning flashes at the prospect of battle.

'I never knew this demon. I was not born when he left the Assembly of the Anunnaki. Didn't he go down to the Netherworld then, to Kur?'

Sharur's voice rang so that the clay pillars of the palace shook. 'Not to remain there. Not by a long way, master. And there is far more mischief on its way. Asag has roused a host of warriors. Even the rocks of the Earth have broken loose and are moving in his army. They will invade our land and make havoc here unless a hero stops them. And who is there among the Children of An but you and I, master?'

'The Anunnaki are no warriors!'

'But you are, Son of Enlil, Raging Floodstorm! The Asag knows. All the Guardians of bitter plants have massed together. The thorny kind, the creeping tangle, deep-rooted trees that spread like dragon's teeth. The flinty shard, the rolling millstone boulders, the smooth, hard statue blocks that could fall on a man and crush him. The mountains are moving, Lord. Their Lords have set their mind on you. Asag is mustering his armies. He seeks an encounter with you, is tossing his horns in pride. He has made plans to strip your titles from you, take your powers for himself. He is already sharing out the towns and villages of the border among his friends.'

Ninurta leaped up from the Thunderbird throne. 'By the Word of Enlil, I'll slay him!'

Sharur bellowed like a bull, 'You cannot! No axe, nor mace, nor spear can pierce or shatter the hardness of his wooden armour.'

'I will overcome him! I am Enlil's son! As Enlil has become greater than An, so I am more powerful than my father!' The Lord of Lagash slapped his thigh. His whole throne shook as though the stone-carved Thunderbird had roared itself.

The echoes of that defiant shout made waves across Sumer. Even the marshes of Eridu quivered at the news. In Nippur, Enlil grew white of face, said to Nusku, 'We must call the Assembly. Let us authorise Ninurta to deal with this. Then perhaps Nin Lil and I should leave the E-Kur and the Kiur, retreat to Dilmun.'

'It is dangerous to make the long sea passage. And Asag holds the mountain passes.'

As soon as the Council was over, the Anunnaki scattered like sheep, southwards. Sumer was a country of farmers, weavers, canal boatmen, scribes. Theirs was not a warrior culture. In times of crisis a *lugal* was chosen, not to be a lifelong ruler but to lead the state to war. No human heroes could fight an enemy like this. Ninurta was the Anunnaki's

Warrior-King. They allowed him the glory uncontested. Only Inanna watched his preparations with a hunger in her eyes that had nothing to do with wedding preparations.

When Ninurta set out to war, it was wise to keep out of his way. He sent his generals Lugalkurdub and Kurshunaburuam on ahead. He rode upriver in his ship *Makarnuntaea*. A storm swept him northwards. On seven gales he travelled so fast he almost kept pace with the sun. The evil wind of dust, the south storm of heat seemed strapped to his girdle. The flood storm strode beside his boat. The tempest whipped up the Idiglat, piled it up in heaps and waterspouts. *Makarnuntaea* rode it fearlessly.

For all the danger, Inanna could not be persuaded to stay indoors the day the army set out. She must be down at the waterside, in all the excitement. From the levee, she watched in awe the battle storm sweeping towards her.

'Ninurta's magnificent, isn't he?' she cried. 'Is this what war is like? I want to ride to battle one day! I'll have a chariot pulled by seven lions. I'll brandish the spear of death in my hand. I'll—'

'You'll come down off the chariot road at once,' said Nin Shubur, grabbing her none too gently by the arm, 'before we're trampled by those oxen or swamped by their bow wave. Riding to war may be all very glorious. Let's wait and see what comes back. The dead, the mangled. Prisoners stumbling under the whip. Defeated people, with the heart beaten out of them. Victors who have learned to like the taste of blood.'

'Uruk should have a *lugal* like Ninurta,' said Inanna, twisting her head to see the smoke and spray of his passing as Nin Shubur hurried her to safety.

'Is Gilgamesh not brave enough for you?'

'Gilgamesh is not an Anunnaki.'

Ninurta's army pressed on up into the mountains. The storm crushed the skulls of birds, sent them limping earthwards with broken wings. It swept soil from the earth so that the wild asses and gazelles were starved, their grass stripped off as though by locusts. Dust rose in vast clouds, came flying through the air, settled behind them in a blanket smothering every hollow. The Earth wrung her hands like a woman in anguish, beat her breast, cried out in pain.

As they neared the hills, tall trees crashed to the ground. Live sparks rained down from heaven, lit raging fires in the brushwood. Fish were battered to death as the rivers rose before Ninurta's army and the streams hurled themselves upwards against the mountains.

They were entering hostile country. The humans cowered in terror. They flung up adobe walls and hid behind them. The land was plunged in darkness, no betraying lamp was lit. Its people cursed the day of Asag's birth.

Ninurta sent out scouts to get intelligence. They found Asag's couriers. The helpless ox-drivers hauling their boats fled like pitiful moths. Ninurta's warriors captured them and smashed their skulls. The rebels were cut off from the conquered cities, their messengers slain.

But still the enemy hid, lay in ambush in the steep valleys, concealed in the forest. Every tree, every rock was a potential killer.

'Go, Sharur,' said Ninurta, fondling his mace. 'Find him for me!'

He grasped the leather thong, swung the terrific weapon round his head three times, let go.

Sharur soared into the mountain air, spread Thunderbird wings, circled like an eagle overhead. His unwinking eyes scanned the upheavals of forest and scree, saw where rocks had been ripped from the parent breast, where tree trunks had tumbled and rolled together, where the plants of the wilderness were marching downhill. On heavy beats of wings his shadow descended towards Ninurta's camp, brought accurate sightings.

As darkness fell, the Evening Star shone bright on this eve of battle. Home in the E-Anna once more, Inanna poured out oil and wine before An.

'Bless Ninurta, Great-grandfather. Make him win.'

'I'm afraid Ninurta must look after himself, and us.'

Over the camp fire the Weapon Man lowered his ruddied head to Ninurta's. His stone mouth spat a taunt.

'Oh Warrior, look out for yourself! You great throw-net of battle! You think yourself a mighty conqueror? Let me see now. You beat the Thunderbird and made him your servant, and the Serpent with Seven Heads. You overthrew Kulianna, the Basilisk, the Gypsum Man. You slew the Lord of Strong Copper, Six-Headed Buck, the Hobble of Heaven. I've seen the heads of Magilum and the Bison and King Date Palm hung at your side. But you have met your match here. Let me embrace you, Viper of Heaven! It may be the last time. Hold your feet on the ground, keep your weapon arm down at your side. You have never gone to a battle as uneven as this one. If you had seen what I have! Giant warriors of stone. A whole forest on the march. Jaws of destruction waiting to gulp you down. Can you fence a prison pen for enemies like these? Will you set up a chapel of reeds for your victory ritual? Will you rinse your little weapons in pure water at the end of tomorrow?'

'I will, Sharur. By Inanna's Star rising above us, I will join this dance of battle. Asag shall tremble at our aura of awe.'

A shudder of almost sexual ecstasy shook the *mittu* Weapon Man. Sharur bowed his macehead, hiding his exultant laugh, lay down at Ninurta's side in a sleep like death before the morning of battle.

# Chapter Sixty-two

Far to the south in Sumer, ignorance darkened the sky like the wings of an Imdugud and brought fear. They saw only smoke to the north, as though the mountains were being consumed by fire. The sun set in blood and rose in a thick cloud. It seemed as if Asag had pulled down the sky upon them. The shattered trunks of tamarisks came whirling down the rivers. A rain of black cinders scattered foreboding over the fields.

Enlil leaned shaking against the wall. Nin Lil watched him, concerned.

'We should have gone to Dilmun. If he should die . . . My son, my Ploughman,' the Air Lord gasped. 'Who will stand at my right hand if I lose him?'

'Ninurta is not your firstborn,' Nin Lil told him sharply. 'There is *my* son, Nanna. Didn't I dare the Netherworld for you and him?'

'But Ninurta! My broad-spreading stormcloud. My cedar rooted in the Abzu.'

'Nin Mah has many sons. We are not short of storm Lords. Did you need to copulate with your own mother to make him? Did you force her, as you forced me?'

'Be quiet, Lady! . . . My sweet. My little saviour. Of course I love Nanna, and his children. But . . .'

'But Ninurta is your favourite! The one who serves the beer at your right hand. That should be the elder son's privilege!'

'Will you be jealous still? Even of Nin Mah? While my son may be crushed under the weight of death this very moment, snatched down to Kur?'

'Where Nanna must go every month!'

The angry interchange was broken off abruptly. There were shouts outside.

From beyond came a swell of mourning like a crowd of doves. The Anunnaki of Enlil's court came running in, stopped short before Lord Enlil and looked behind them again.

The great leaves of cedar strapped with bronze burst open. Sharur strode in, the Weapon Man who knew no ceremony, who taunted Anunnaki. His *mittu* head was smeared with blood, his shaft was dusty. Soot, dying foliage clung to his spikes, tangled in his thongs. He breathed heavily, like pulses of sheet lightning. There was no other sound in the fear-filled room.

Enlil clutched the pillar behind him, tried to stiffen shaking knees to hold him upright. His frozen lips would not shape the question he knew he must ask. The clear, cool voice of Nin Lil spoke for all of them.

'Is your Lord Ninurta dead?'

'No.' A heavy gasp from Sharur that released the breath of all the listeners. 'My master lives. But only just. Lord Enlil, help your son!'

'I?' Surprise and terror shook in Enlil's voice.

Sharur's hoarse laughter struck him like a blow. The Weapon Man shook with cynical merriment. 'Don't worry, Great Enlil. Your son does not expect you to pick up a spear and race to his side. He can fight for all of you.'

'What then does he want?'

'My master gave his long spear battle orders; he wound terror into his weapon bindings. He marched to war as a warrior king should. But Asag is worse than any other demon. He has turned my Lord's own strength against him. He has made the waters gash the mountains in gaping wounds. He has made fires rage through the canebrakes. The sky he has torn down from its vault. An did not prevent it. It chokes the air like bloody wool. No one can breathe. The dust is so thick the sun looms out of the fog like a crimson moon. The dogs have gone mad. They are slavering over their paws, snarling at Asag's armies, "Haven't you killed them all yet?" Will you let the Air Lord's son die of suffocation?'

Enlil leaned trembling against the pillar. All strength seemed to have left him. The eyes of his court were upon him, but he was blind with tears.

A big woman rose from the corner where she had been sitting hunched with her head in her hands. Nin Mah made her heavy, purposeful way towards Enlil, shook him hard.

'Enlil, my firstborn son, you fathered this late-born hero on me. Will you let him die? Be a Guardian! Act!'

'How?'

Nin Mah snorted like a she-camel. 'Did you need to be told what to do when you separated me from your father? When you ripped the Sky apart from the Earth!'

'Call the priestesses!' Enlil moved himself shakily upright. He held out an imperious hand to Nin Lil. She took it coldly. But she was Lady of Air. She, too, would do her ritual duty.

The royal procession ascended to the E-Kur roof. On its highest platform, the sacred space where the Children of An are in touch with Sky and Earth, Enlil, Kurgal, began to breathe, deeply, rhythmically, with an increasing intensity, as the chants strengthened him and the incense smoke began to rise and weave. A cool, strong wind fanned Nin Lil's garments as the ritual took hold. Enlil's net skirt flattened its cords against his thighs. His linen scarf streamed towards the north. Kites wheeled and screamed in the sudden gusts of gale, came spinning earthwards. The grasses waved as the rush of air sped towards the mountains.

As it tore through the fog of battle, the dust eddied and lay still and damp. Pines sang to its music. The rivers cascaded, refreshed. A light, soft rain was carried on the wind and all the perfume of the trampled cedar forest was released. The air was clear.

Ninurta's army lifted their grateful heads to the wet gust. Red dust streaked their sweaty faces like battle paint. Their parched lips gasped the welcome freshness of the breeze. Asag swore, cursed, tore up the earth, hurled clods of mud. But Ninurta's men laughed in his face, flung arrows back, charged forward.

Someone was coming behind the wind. A big firm-footed woman, steady of purpose. A mother, Nin Mah. If you had asked her what she hoped to achieve there on the battlefield, in enemy country, she would have looked at you out of moist brown eyes and said simply, 'He is my son.'

Long that journey, for one who did not ride on the storm. The respite Enlil had sent had long since passed. Bitter the weather now. When at last she drew near the mountains, they were hidden under the blackest of thunderclouds. The winds hurled themselves, first east, then west. Dust and grit from the desert stung her skin, made her shut her eyes. Pellets of dry clay rained down from the hills, followed by hail. The ground was white with ice. There were scant trees for her to cover her head and take shelter. Wild-eyed with fear, families came tumbling down the trails out of the rebel country.

'Do not go up there, Mother,' they told her. 'It's dark as the Netherworld in the middle of the day. The forest has massed together like a wall. Ninurta's Weapon Man is spitting fire and venom at it. The lions are roaring in fury. When a spear is stuck in the ground only for a moment, the hole fills up with blood. It is an awful place.'

'My son is there,' said Nin Mah, drawing her woollen dress more closely round her.

When she neared the hills there was a sudden calm. The sun broke through.

'It is over!' she said to her *sukkal*.

'Praise be! Glory to Lord Ninurta, Enlil's life-breath!'

'If my son has won.'

It grew very silent, very cold.

'My lady,' said the *sukkal* nervously. 'The rivers are failing.'

The rush and hurry of the stream beside them had died to nothing. An icy wind was drying the stones.

'Fill the waterskins,' ordered Nin Mah, 'while there are still some pools.'

Sometimes the air softened, as though with a hint of spring. There was then a grinding roar. Boulders of ice came rolling down the gorges. From caves and hiding places the Anunnaki of the locality came slipping out like half-starved jackals. They chipped cold flakes from it with pickaxes and carried their buckets away.

Nin Mah, her *sukkal* and their servants crouched over a fire that seemed at once too sulky and too bright. They melted the ice slowly and half-filled the waterskins.

The ox-drawn barges were left below them now. Nin Mah could not travel fast. She lurched heavily on a patient ass. The murk of storm hung low over the indigo hills. The air grew warmer, oppressive.

'The snow must be melting up there by now,' said the *sukkal*. 'Why is it not flooding the river?'

Nin Mah looked behind her, to the south, lost in the unnatural darkness. There was pain in her face. 'If there is no fresh water in the riverbeds this spring, how will they irrigate the fields? How will they sow the seed? How will they lead the water across the orchards? The sun must be strong in the south now. Is the Land of the Two Rivers dying of drought?'

'I hear no sound of battle,' said the *sukkal* uneasily. 'Is it really over?'

'I tried to catch my children of the cliffs and ask them what had happened. They stared at me as if I was a basilisk, then turned and ran. They trust nobody here.'

'I'm not surprised.' The *sukkal* looked over his shoulder, and quickly back again. 'Madam. That rock behind me. Don't look directly.'

But Nin Mah gazed beyond the shadows of the camp fire with eyes that nursed her own interior darkness.

'Stone. Rock. Hills. Their Guardians were all my children . . . once . . . *Son!*'

Her voice, sharp with sorrow and long-lost authority, cut the air. Neither the *sukkal* nor any of his party dared look round at the rock.

'*Aaa . . . mmm . . . aaa!*' The answer sang like the lowest bass string of the *ala* lyre. The ground beneath them hummed. The *sukkal* screamed.

Then there was stillness. Only the rustle of dead leaves falling, though it should have been spring.

'Set a double guard,' said Nin Mah, turning to her tent. 'Wake me if anything moves.'

The trees had claws, the boulders eyes. A watchful presence passed them on up the alien country.

Nin Mah knitted her brows. 'Asag must be overcome, or we should not have got this far. But something is very wrong. My son is a Warrior-King. He has won the battle he came to fight. He may even have slain his enemy. But can he know how to wring his trophy out of these stones?'

'Do you, my lady?'

His mistress turned on him her blank, broad face. It was darkened with wind, shining with sweat, eyes hooded. 'I am not Ki any longer. The Earth was taken from me. I have been left the tilth on the surface of the soil, women's bodies, seed sprout and birth. How could I move the core of the mountains?'

But the *sukkal* thought of the deep voice thrumming at her word and shuddered.

They climbed the bare bones that had been a waterfall, the servants pushing and hauling the fat Lady as best they might. Nin Mah turned, panting, and looked down over the grey slopes, no longer rimed with ice.

'The land would weep,' she said sadly. 'But it has no tears

left. Even the Idiglat is dry. Down in the marshes the salt water will be creeping up. There is no fresh tide to cleanse it. The soil is turning bitter. When the spring carp flood should be spreading the rich silt of the mountains over the lowland, mud like thick butter, there is only a bright and poisonous salt. Asag has stolen the rivers. He has won, after all.'

'Lady!' said the *sukkal*. 'What is that?'

A sound like giant drums. A shock that made them grab each other. The screech of slipping stones. The lowland party stared across a huge hollow in the hills. Above it reared the steepest mountains, dark smoky purple, bearded with sunless snow. And across the scree and parched grass at its foot, a scene of hectic activity.

A vast field of boulders, like an army of captured giants, was being systematically moved. A mighty wall was rising, like some colossal dyke. Rocks were hurled through the air, fell with a crash that boomed back from the mountain wall. Lower hills were appearing, raw mineral surfaces, stripped of the dignity of soil and foliage, naked as slaves. Ninurta was taking his revenge on Asag's army, was breaking up the last and cruellest plot the demon had left behind him.

Nin Mah signalled to her retinue. They moved to a ridge overlooking the dried-up waterfall, sat down and watched.

The new hills grew towards them. Like a serpent creeping across the plateau, white, grey, green, black, with flashes of red. Stone-dust flew around it. The chant of Ninurta's warrior men became more distinct.

'My son is coming,' said Nin Mah proudly. 'He has sent his gift before him.'

The dry, cracked soil of the upland plain was coming alive. The surface was darkening rapidly. A network of veins appeared in it, ran to find each other, met and spread. The bare earth glistened. Water was welling, rising, running.

'He has rescued the river flood!' cried the *sukkal*. 'He is driving it back to us!'

Like the surge of a herd of goats, the headwaters were rushing towards them. A dark cresting wave was nearing the waterfall. It struck the boulders in its way, leaped over them, fell with a joyful crash into the empty pool below. Torrents followed. The Idiglat was flowing. All the squandered waters were gathered up out of the mountain bogs where the forces of Kur had trapped them, marshalled between lines of captured rocks, herded over the brink, flung down into the thirsty lowland. In Uri and Shubur and Sumer and Martu astonished farmers lifted their eyes to the north and east.

'Bless Ninurta! The rivers are coming alive!'

Carp frisked, the boatmen ran to loose their moorings, get out their fishing tackle. Canal inspectors hurried to check the levees for damage. Geshtinanna knelt down to watch the water trickling round the roots of her vineyard, plunged her fingers in the good black mud.

'The wine will be sweet this year, after all. Sweet enough to warm Dumuzi.'

Ninurta came striding after the flood. His shoulders were squared against the sky with the pride of achievement. When he saw his mother he started with amazement and then a rush of protective love. 'Great Lady! What are you doing here? What has brought you into the heart of my enemy's country? What if you had been caught in the battle?'

'Is Asag dead?'

'Not dead, but beaten and turned to stone. The green of his fingers ground to dust. His seed scattered and lifeless as stone chippings. I plucked him up as if he was rotten sedge. I threw him about like clay slapped on a wall. He will lead no more armies against us. But you . . . how did a weak woman make such a journey? Weren't you terrified of the Lords of the evil trees that escaped me? Of the rocks that fled from Asag's battle line?'

'I am, as you see, unhurt.'

He flung his arms around her, hugged her joyfully. 'What a woman! My mother! I must give you a new title. Look at them? Do you see what I've done with these rebels? I have made foothills. I have cast up banks so that the criminals themselves shall drive the rivers back to their true courses. These hills are the Hursag. And in your honour I give you a new name. You are the Lady of the Foothills, Nin Hursag. I shall give it all to you. The herds of its meadows, vines of its terraces, the cedar and cypress and *supalu* and box forests for you, the gold and silver of its mines, the copper and tin of its smelting ovens, its goats and wild asses, its orchard fruits. Everything shall be paid to you as tribute. People shall make the ritual *Hi-iblal* in your honour. You are Nin Hursag. You are Dingir Mah, the August Lady, Nin Nagarshaga, the Womb's Carpenter, Aruru, Who Breaks the Waters. Ninurta's mother!'

She returned his embraces, kissed him back.

'You are generous, my son. Just think. I, that had only the wombs of women, the top layer of soil, have been given the foothills for my own. It seems all my sons are munificent to their womenfolk.'

'You deserve it, noble woman.'

She sighed against his shoulder, as though sad or very weary, separated herself from him.

'And these?' Her arm reached out towards the line of stone-faced captives stretching away into the distance. Guardians of Granite, Basalt, Hardhead, Crusher, Dolorite, Waterbearer, Topaz, Jasper, Lampstone . . . On and on her eyes pursued them into the falling twilight, naming them over in her heart. They were all her sons. 'What will you do with them?' she asked at last.

'The time has come to judge them. Sharur is leaning in the corner of my tent. I have rinsed the blood from him. But there is still justice to be meted out, after victory.'

'I do not want to stay to see it.'

And to his amazement, despite all his pleading, the old woman set off on the long, weary journey back to Sumer at the first light of the next day's dawn.

'What was it like?' begged Inanna when her great-grandmother came home. 'What is it like on the battlefield? I wish I could have been there!'

'We meant you to be a light for all lovers, girl,' said Nin Mah, drawing the glowing young woman on to her lap. 'There are some hurts it is better you never see.'

'Enki promised me, when I was a little girl. He swore that once I was grown up he would give me the *me* of battle, as well as love,' protested Inanna. 'I want the *whole* of life.'

# Chapter Sixty-three

'He is here already!' Nin Gal rushed impetuously into Inanna's rooms, her white dress streaming out behind her with her movements, like a shaft of moonlight, like a tasselled reed head whipped sideways in the wind.

Her daughter started, eyes huge in her pale face. Girls crowded round her couch, Nin Shubur hovered; her old nurse Lama was bent over Inanna's feet, preparing her for her bath.

'Oh, let me see! Let me see!'

'Inanna, no! He mustn't catch sight of you watching him.'

'Hide me, all of you. I must see my Dumuzi.' Inanna's voice was high and sharp, as if with anxiety.

Nin Gal and Nin Shubur exchanged glances. The mother's look was almost as excited as her daughter's. Defiant too, knowing this match was her doing, against the advice of Nanna and An. The younger woman, Nin Shubur, was tense, withdrawn, a *sukkal* effacing her own dignity in the babble and tumult of Inanna's friends. Ninurta's seven daughters, and all the slaves and waiting-women were hurrying round to make Inanna ready, themselves aflame with the joy of a wedding.

And so, like a sudden dust storm, the bevy of girls swept up the stairs and out on to the rooftop terrace, hiding Inanna in their midst, yet betraying her presence by the very shrieks and laughter and jostling with which they tried to disguise her.

Four men stood before Nanna's house, their arms and shoulders loaded with gifts. A train of servants followed in their best clothes, all richly laden, many carrying small beasts or leading larger ones as gifts.

'The Farmer, the Fowler, the Fisherman, the Shepherd. It's him! It's him!' cried Heulnunna, leaning precariously over the reed fence that bordered the roof.

Inanna's breath came in gasps, like a frightened animal's. All her autocratic self-possession had disappeared. She had caught the mood of the friends around her, almost hysteria.

'What have they brought? What have they brought?' she heard herself say. As if she had not stipulated these wedding-gifts herself. As if it mattered.

'The Fisherman is carrying magnificent carps,' Impae announced.

'The Farmer is bringing you jars of honey that are making the flies intoxicated, and a great amphora of wine that will get us all drunk,' Zagaru supplied.

'Poor Enkimdu,' Inanna murmured.

'The Fowler has wonderful geese and ducks for your banquet table,' Urugruntaea cried.

'They've seen us!'

Masculine heads turned upwards to the fringe of faces like poppies along the reed wall. Screening her face with her hair, Inanna peeped over Heshaga's shoulder.

Dumuzi, in his bridegroom's jewels and finery, stood flanked by his friends. A yoke straddled his shoulders, from which golden pails slopped the richest of milk. His hands were holding a bowl of butter and cool-wrapped cheeses, already greasing his arms in the afternoon heat.

'Such simple things,' Inanna breathed. 'Cheese, ducks, carp, honey. To stand for all creation, plenty, increase.'

'Fertility,' laughed Zurmu, looking pointedly at Inanna's belly and stabbing her finger at her cousin's groin. 'He will plough your furrow, flood your canebrake, fish your waters, fill your nest.'

'Will he?' She shivered strangely in the close-packed, pushing, warm-faced crowd.

'Where is Lady Inanna? We have brought the gifts she requested. Daughter of Nin Gal, Princess of this house, let me in!' Dumuzi's powerful voice, that sang of herding on the plain, calling the scattered sheep home at evening, rang through the city courts of Ur.

The ranks closed before the bride's face. He must not see her yet.

'Inanna is inside,' Zarmu called down. 'You are too early. She is not ready for her bridegroom, Shepherd.'

'Open the door. Open the door, Inanna!' Dumuzi hammered on the solid leaves of the gate.

Any other day, Nanna's door would have stood open in the daylight for human passers-by to catch a glimpse of the awe within. It would in any case have flown open for Dumuzi Ushumgalanna. Now it stood barred. Impassive-faced as sculptured lions, the door guards held themselves at attention motionless, while the bridegroom's party shouted in vain for entry.

Nin Shubur's voice came quietly through the commotion and merriment on the roof. 'Come down, my lady. It is time to prepare for your bridal bath.'

Inanna's look was swift, aware, part gratitude for the respite, but brilliant too with the flash of resentment of a child called in to bed. She averted her head again, to the row of men's faces turned up to hers. She seemed for a moment to look directly into Dumuzi's eyes, gasped and stepped quickly back.

A little spring cloud wandered across the sun. The light dimmed.

'Is my bath ready?' Inanna asked Amanamtagga happily.

The chief body slave inclined her head. 'The water is warm. The milk and oil and perfume are ready, my lady. You have only to step out of your clothes and we shall be waiting for you.'

Some of her attendants were melting away at once to see to the final preparations. Others were forming up discreetly around her, hands poised already to lift the last of her maidenhood's clothes from her. Her friends were falling quieter. In a sibilant hush their dresses swept the stairs and carried Inanna in their midst back to her private chambers.

Now, still and pale as alabaster but far less cool, she let them strip the everyday jewels from her hair, the bracelets from her arms and ankles, unwind her dress cloth. Hands drew her, passive now as though she were drugged, into the steam of the tiled bathroom.

'Like the Abzu itself,' the words whispered from her lips as she stepped into the dragon-supported bath tub around which *lahamu* figures, with curling sidelocks, poured their streams of sculptured water from chalcedony urns.

This water was real, warm, scented, clouded with asses' milk that stroked her flesh. She let the practised hands soap her, massage her, soothe her, starting deliciously sometimes as they cleansed meticulously her most private parts, giving herself over to their impersonal intimacy, while *tigi* harps sang the songs of purification, priestesses chanted, lustrations were sprinkled over her.

The last of her childhood was rinsed from her with copper pans of the cool floods of the Buranun, Enki's river. Her senses cleared a little.

Soft towels now, and she was led to lie on a couch where expert fingers applied oil, stroked skin, anointed sensitive flesh. Not hard to relax under these ministrations. These moments were fragrant, pampered, delicious now. Easy to forget what was still to come, to live only in this cosseted hour where every mind and pair of hands was bent on tending her and beautifying and sweetening her.

Amanamtagga signed. The other slaves fell back. The old nurse came forward now.

'I've waited a lifetime for this, honey!'

Old hands, but sure as if they had done this every day, oiling her pubic hair between her palms. Stiff fingers, bending to part and coax it into curving horns.

'The Boat is ready for boarding, missie. Your Stag is waiting for his arrow.'

Inanna looked down the length of her naked self, lifting her head and stretching her neck to see the starlight softness of her flesh, the black body hair, like shining lapis lazuli, this doorway opened to the self she could not see.

Silence for a moment in the dressing chamber. Reverence, awe.

'Let us put on your wedding garment now,' said Nin Shubur quietly. 'Then we shall paint your face and arrange your hair.'

They hung her with jewels, but nothing seemed to match the rich gateway she carried with her under the pleated wedding gown.

'Give me the royal robe of queenship,' Inanna ordered.

'You will not go to your husband as Nanna's little princess?' Nin Shubur commented. 'But as Queen of the E-Anna?'

'She is no longer our girl from this day. Dumuzi is climbing his date palm,' Nin Gal laughed. 'Let him see how rich a cluster he has cut!'

They set on her breast the jewel 'Let Him Come. Let Him Come.'

They painted her eyes, supernaturally bright, with kohl.

They reddened her lips and nails.

They dressed her hair and set a diadem on it.

They hung the lapis lazuli egg stones for fertility around her neck.

They placed her cylinder seal in her hand.

'Open the door, Inanna! Open the door!' the girls began to cry.

From deep in the bowels of the palace she heard Dumuzi's staff hammering on the still-closed leaves of Nanna's gate. She knew now the boom of those strokes had been reverberating through the house all the long afternoon, deeper than the music of the harps and drums, more regular than the chants of hymns, more constant than the chatter of friends.

'Open the door! Inanna, open the door!' Their cries were rising in a united chorus.

Straight now, tall, proud. As beautiful, as readied as she would ever be.

'Open the door, Inanna!'

'I must let him in!' Hardly more than a whisper, but a joyful one.

She was not left to move out alone. Hardly had she taken the first step towards the irrevocable opening of her door, of herself, when Nin Shubur was before her. No reproach, no advice now. The Lady Inanna's *sukkal* ceremonially, loyally doing her duty. The Shaman Queen of the East, versed in her own magic, wiser than her mistress, walked obediently ahead of Inanna across the chamber, past the smiling Nin Gal who swiftly kissed her daughter, down the long stairs. The brush and rustle of many skirts followed her.

Across the sunlit court where Nanna, Utu, and all the men of her family bowed and saluted in return to the Star Maiden's dutiful farewell. To the outer door, to her father's threshold.

Here, at last, Nin Shubur stood back and made a reverence.

'Lady,' she said, 'I may accompany you no further than this. If you will marry Lord Dumuzi Ama-Ushumgalanna, it is for you to open the door to him yourself. No one can do this for you.'

The staff thundered outside. The sun was dipping below the shoulder of the ziggurat. The first long shadow of evening stepped into the courtyard.

'I will marry Dumuzi!'

Inanna's own hands grasped the copper bolt and threw open the door to her Shepherd in the ritual act that made her his wife.

# Chapter Sixty-four

He was standing in the shadow of the doorway, a young man golden-brown as a newly-ripened date cluster against the sunlit glory of the late afternoon sky. His ceremonial wig rippled, blue-black; his beard gleamed with oil. She wanted to hold, to lick, to savour, to devour his joy and handsomeness. Dumuzi threw his arms wide, picked up a brimming bowl of cream waiting in the shade and held it to her eager lips.

'Will you drink with me always and always, Lady of the Palace?'

Their faces met above the brim. She never saw what became of cheese, wine, fish, fowl, all the mottled, black, white, bleating, lowing train of gifts that filled the lower court of the ziggurat. She was in Dumuzi's arms, crushed to Dumuzi's lips, and all her family and friends were clapping and cheering.

He held her off now, a laughing, skipping girl this time, in the finery of a proud queen. His turn now to be ceremonious, princely. He led her to a mound in the centre of the second terrace below the dark grove of trees that half hid the *giguna* house. Nanna smiled.

'Take what is yours now, wife of Dumuzi,' the young Shepherd gestured, bowing.

A brown heap, faintly glistening in the declining Sun, waist-high, buzzing with flies. She had not even seen it as she swept past so eagerly on her way to the gate. A momentary, shocked recoil. A farmyard dungheap? Here in her father's house? For her wedding day?

But Utu and Nanna were watching with benign approval. Nin Gal's hands were clasped in girlish expectation. Inanna looked closer.

'*Dates?*'

His laugh was low and warm as the departing sunshine. Her regal certainty was lost now. She blushed, not knowing what she was meant to do. But the breath-held attention of the court around her demanded something. Inanna moved slowly to the pile, hesitated, plunged her hands into the sticky richness, disturbing a multitude of greedy flies. Beneath the soft, sugary coating, her fingers met something solid, hard. Her hands curled and clenched. She drew out a heavy, five-stranded rope of lapis lazuli and gold. She gasped, and heard the echo from all Ninurta's daughters. Then she was delving in, scattering the humble dates, finding treasure, jewels, riches beyond imagining. There were narrow gold rings for her ears, heavy bronze crescents for the lobes, alabaster ornaments for her buttocks, jewelled sandals for her feet, precious beads for nose and navel, for loins and vulva, for every part of her perfect body which Dumuzi would enjoy and adore.

Dumuzi stood and laughed, received her ecstatic hugs, lifted her sticky hands to his mouth and licked them lovingly.

They feasted joyfully that evening.

Dusk stalked across the land, purpling the far-flung patchwork of farms, the distant rim of desert. Firelight and lamps winked below in the town. The first brilliant star of evening stepped out over the open gate of Nanna's house. Inanna's Star.

Nin Gal lifted her face to the sky, caught the Moon Lord's hand. The court was hushed, all faces turning to the heaven in the west. The planet blazed as if, new-faceted, it was displaying its full glory for the first time. A few moments' silence, and then all the harps and tambourines and singers and priests broke into praise.

As the paean ended, Inanna stood, still savouring exaltation. She felt larger than life, lifted up to the Sky, one with that flashing star in all its beauty and power and benevolence to the world.

She heard her own voice, high and happy, peal through the thick, warm twilight.

'Prepare my bed!'

She swung, as the harvester's sickle sweeps an arc to meet the neck of corn. Her hands touched Dumuzi's and grasped them. She found his colder than her own. She held him reassuringly, laughed in his eyes. His were intense now, more darkly brown than gold. She saw the pulse struggling in his throat.

'Come to bed, my love. Don't be afraid. Take what is yours.'

'Inanna. My Queen. My Lion.'

'My grandfathers say I was destined to be the queen of all lovers.' Her smile was for him alone.

'The bed!'

'She has called for the bed!'

'Make ready Inanna's wedding bed!'

The cries were all around them, attendants scurrying hither and thither. Inanna took no notice. She nursed Dumuzi's hands, gazing into his eyes. On the margins of her sight Utu raised his beaker in friendly salute to Dumuzi. The girls were forming up behind her.

'Let me lead you, Lady Inanna.' Nin Shubur's quiet voice, that brooked no contradiction, even by her superiors.

So, hand in hand with Dumuzi Ushumgalanna, like a child that has been given an unimaginably marvellous present, Inanna, in her bridal gown, walked under a canopy of stars to enter her own quarters for the last time as a maiden.

They made Dumuzi halt in her antechamber and led Inanna forward into the intimacy of her dressing room. The door stood open to her bed chamber. Fire passed before her eyes, dazzling her. They were purifying it for the sacred act. The *shubzu* priests passed out of sight with their smoking censers. Attendants were shaking the halfa straw of the mattress soft now, sprinkling fresh cedar oil over the floor.

Hands were stripping the clothes from her sweet scented flesh. They left her clad in jewels, rosettes of gold and pearl netted in her hair, Dumuzi's lapis beads cool around her throat. Her royal breast disc swayed like a wave between sand banks. A stud of gold, engraved like a honey-seeking bee, nestled in her navel. Silver shimmered round arms and thighs. Her nurse's weaving of the black pubic hair stood wide and silky now, an undefended gateway.

Nin Shubur led her, dizzy with wine and ceremony and excitement, to the oddly unfamiliar sleeping chamber where lamps burned softly. The slaves were ranged around the walls, quieter now. Amanamtagga's thin clever face showed serious in the shadows. The deep blue sheets of Utu's giving, hemmed with gold, were spread upon the bed of *huluppu* wood. Here was the tree that Gilgamesh had felled for her. The carved *pirig* lion chased the carved *ug* lion in fantastic curves and twists around the frame. The *ug* lion turned and pounced upon the *pirig* lion. Over and over again.

Where was the Serpent who had coiled around the roots? The Imdugud who nested in its branches? Where was Kiskillilla, the rebellious maid, who would not lie under any man? The carpenters of Sumer were skilful. There was no sign in this timber of the hole at the heart of Inanna's tree where Kiskillilla had made her home.

'Inanna?' Nin Shubur called her to the present. Inanna took hold of the foot of the bed for courage. Gilgamesh had got his resounding *pukku* from the roots. He was wielding the *mikku* sticks from the reclaimed branches. For herself, Inanna had chosen this bed, from the heart of the trunk.

A little awed by its wideness, by its beauty, by this untested experience to come, Inanna stepped slowly forward. The floor was cool and fragrant under her bare feet. Perfume was everywhere tonight. The sheets received her, fine and smooth beneath the expectant tension of her flesh. Eyes were appraising, hands were busy, arranging her hair voluptuously over the pillows, sprinkling the last lustrations of pure water and aromatic oil. A final cup of wine was set to her lips and she drank gratefully. It was spiced and, she guessed, laced with Nin Shubur's spell for consummation. They coated her moist lips with amber, anointed her nipples with honey, retouched her eyelids with antimony. She lay back on the pillows, feeling the bed swing slightly on its slatted base. The ring of faces receded, emptying through the door, like a water-channel when the orchard sluicegate is closed. She was alone with Nin Shubur.

'Well, my lady?' The exiled Queen of the East lifted her eyebrows. She was beautiful herself tonight in her ritual robes, with her two-horned diadem of a minor Lady.

Inanna touched the silver and lapis lazuli disc that lay between her breasts.

'Let Him Come! Let Him Come!'

Nin Shubur's back was turned already on the irrevocable words. She passed out of sight into the antechamber.

The first and last few moments of solitude in all that delirious day. Inanna alone, on a wide bed of her own appointing, awaiting the bridegroom of her choice.

Dumuzi Abzu.

And he was there, filling the doorway, filling the room, filling her heart.

Gloriously naked.

Nin Shubur smiled a little as she led him forward. For all his signs of visible arousal he seemed confused, eager to please, obedient as a shaggy sheepdog. The *sukkal* held him with a gesture at the edge of the bed. The bridegroom stood grinning down at her, just a little embarrassed, as Nin Shubur intoned the blessing over them both. Inanna watched Dumuzi's member start to droop as the chant rolled on. She smiled softly for him, reached up her hand and felt herself grow stronger.

'May the Abzu in Eridu shine in its depths for you.
'May the house of Nanna light the night for you.
'May the great E-Anna tower to the Sky for you.
'May Gibil purify this place with fire.
'As the sun has gone to rest below the desert,
'So may you draw your Lord to lie down.
'May the longing of your Lord to lie beside you
'Be matched by the sweetness of the joy that is waiting for him.
'You have called your beloved husband to your lap.
'Send him from your bed in the morning a great king.
'Give him long life and enduring glory.
'Give him the sceptre of justice and the crown of authority.
'May he govern for you from the sunrise in the eastern mountains
'To the splendour of sunset on the western dunes of Martu.
'May the Upper Sea know him, and the Lower Sea.
'May the cedar and *huluppu* forests acknowledge him.
'May his crook shepherd the humans of Sumer and Akkad.
'May the black-headed people turn to him gratefully as to a sheepfold.
'May he be the ploughman bringing forth plenty from the furrows.
'May he be the herdsman multiplying kids and lambs.
'Under his hand let there be vines, let there be grain.
'May the rivers overflow joyfully across the land.
'May the marshes be alive with the chatter of birds.
'May the new reeds spring green and thick in the old canebrake.
'May fish teem in the lagoons and deer in the woods.
'May the *mashgur* grow high for timber,
'And the orchard trees bow low with fruit.
'Let there be honey and wine, lettuce and cress; let the gardens rejoice.

'Speak the word of long life to the palace,
'The water of life to the Idiglat and the Buranun.
'Queen of Sky and Earth, whose generous love embraces all the living,
'Take your bridegroom to your loins.
'Love him for ever.'

Inanna was hardly aware that harps had been singing in the outer chamber. The kettle drums beat on and stopped. Nin Shubur's hands signed her last magic over the bed. She was gliding towards the door. She was gone.

Dumuzi bent across the pillows, kissed Inanna gently. Wordlessly she lifted her arms around his neck. He knelt upon the bed, was kneeling over her, was all about her, overpowering her. Sinking his power in her so she was all around him. And now joy was rising in her too, making her arch above him, drive, thrust, urge on, demand. All An's careful teaching came to a fierce, frightening, triumphant, obedient, ecstatic consummation in the lock of his arms.

Again and again, while Dumuzi licked the honey from her breasts, nuzzled her navel, burrowed in the Boat of her vulva, found a thousand ways to pleasure her, and she him.

Joy, like a rose opening for the sun, like a deer gulping at a dew pond in the evening cool. Like a woman with her first baby. Like a man with his dearest friend. A million epiphanies and ways to love caught up in one night of closeness.

# Chapter Sixty-five

Sleep at last, when the stars were already pale and wan. When Dumuzi and Inanna woke, the birds in the *giguna* grove were in full chorus. Sunlight must be flooding the world outside. Here in the windowless inner chamber it was dim and cool.

Inanna stretched luxuriously, drew a sharp breath at soreness, found an unfamiliar body beside her own.

Sweat, solid flesh, heavy breathing choked abruptly with a snore. Dumuzi came awake, yawned, grinned at her.

An enormous sadness filled Inanna's heart, black and bitter as the lake of the Netherworld to whose ferryman Nin Lil had once given a child.

She threw herself into Dumuzi's arms. 'Hold me! Hold me!'

But all his kisses, embraces, renewal of lovemaking could not assuage this tide of grief she felt for no good reason.

She pushed him away, sat up, shivered a little as she slipped off her bracelets. Then she knelt over him with a desperate fear in her face.

'Dumuzi Ushumgalanna, have you told me the truth? Are you really Enki's son? If you are not, if you are not as fully Anunnaki as I am, then I have sentenced you to death. You have kissed my mouth. You have laid your hand in my vulva. You have had intercourse with a great Daughter of An!'

'Inanna! My *lubi*, my *labi*! Don't be silly. Last night you made me your king.'

She kissed him passionately, straining him against her heart. 'For how long? Oh, what have I done, my darling? If it is not true, then I have destroyed you.'

Dumuzi climbed stiffly from the bed, cupping his boyish dignity in his hands.

'You think I am less than you? I will show you, Lady. Where is the bathroom in this place? Get up and get ready. We are setting out for Uruk today. If I am to govern as king in the E-Anna, I must talk to An. I have business to see to.'

So wide a bed to lie in alone. So crumpled and stained and cold these sheets now love had left them. The stale smell of extinguished lamps and old scent and semen.

'You are my bridegroom, my consort. You can never really be king of the E-Anna. You are not a Sky Lord.' Even to herself her voice sounded shrewish. Tears welled from her eyes.

Dumuzi came back and knelt beside her, kissed the tears away, hugged her.

'Inanna. I love you,' he said. 'I can be whatever I choose, now I'm married to you. Now, get up and get dressed. We're going to take over the palace.'

# BOOK THREE

# The Power Below

# Chapter Sixty-six

Rain had fallen. Mist steamed from the river's surface as the boat poled its way along the serpent curves of the Buranun. Above them towered the city mound of Uruk, layer upon layer of clay houses crumbling into dust with the passing generations.

Inanna twisted her fingers tighter round Dumuzi's. Now that the desolation of the first waking had passed she could not be close enough to him, must touch him, hug him, kiss him every minute. Each little feast increased her hunger.

'How small and shallow human lives are, while we stay young,' she said, wondering. 'And every time their houses fall they raise ours even higher.'

'You think too much of death,' he told her.

'Ereshkigal's realm, where she keeps Meslamtaea and Ninazu and Ennugi to serve her? They are my uncles. Did you know that? Even great Enlil is afraid of the Netherworld. He gave Ereshkigal his sons.'

'Enki was braver. He went against Kur willingly.'

'And came back empty-handed, fleeing for his life.'

'He has learned to laugh again. And so should you. Is this a day to be solemn, when I'm bringing home my lovely Inanna?'

'*Your* Inanna? Listen to my people!'

All the citizens of Uruk, all the Anunnaki's officials of the district of Kullab had come crowding down to the quays and riverbanks, their hair new-washed, dressed in their feast-day clothes, to cheer the bridal couple. Cries of recognition greeted them through the thinning mist. Songs of welcome leaped from group to group upstream, like fire across thatched houses. Flowers and scented leaves strewed the water where cattle waded. The landing steps of Uruk were lined with priests and priestesses.

Dumuzi handed Inanna ashore, proud and smiling broadly,

Lord in his own right, and more lordly than ever now as Inanna's husband. Looking about her, she started between moods of trembling inexperience, radiant joy, and ambitious desire.

She settled her gold-pinned turban, hung her jewels straight, extended her hand to her young husband.

'Lead me to the E-Anna!'

'Not long ago you were a fresh-faced maiden hanging over the palace wall while I sang to you of the house I was building for my new bride. That little house is ready for you.'

But still his eyes turned up to the E-Anna precinct, vast on the summit.

She tilted her face to his, taunting him laughingly. 'Yes. I have the bigger house. The humans believe it descended from the Sky. The great E-Anna is mine.'

'You are my queen. Honour my new house first, wife of my heart.'

The priestesses were waiting to escort her. Nin Shubur stood ready, a slight, observant figure.

'I saw them building it, when I used to visit Geshtinanna in your mother's home by the crooked apple tree.'

So long ago it seemed, those mornings of intimacy with her friend, the secrets of wooing, bridal preparations shared with Geshtinanna and Ninurta's daughters, the sound of workmen hammering not far away, the shared confidences and love and anguish and hope, all resolved on her wedding day.

'Nin Sun is at home now, waiting for you.'

'The Lady of Wild Cows?' She started. 'I did not think she came to the city.'

'She visits us rarely. Since Lugalbanda died she keeps to her farm on the edge of the steppe. But she is here today, to welcome you!' He felt the weight of her arm as she hung back now.

'Am I some little peasant girl bride, to bow my head humbly in the house of my mother-in-law? Do I have to defer to the Vine Girl as my elder sister? I am Inanna of the Morning and Evening Star, Dumuzi. Have you forgotten that?'

'Are you Sky people so wonderful? Your Lords of Air and Moon and Sun have all passed over the rim of the world and gone to Ereshkigal's land. None of them can prevail against her. Don't despise the Earth Lords, Inanna. Roots and dung and blood take power from the Netherworld.' He laughed at her frowning face and kissed her in front of the cheering crowd. 'Don't worry. My mother doesn't care for pride of status, or she would never have married a human. And you know Geshtinanna would always rank those she loves above herself. You'll be royally treated, even in our humble home. My mother would be content to eat her meal in the corner beside the beer vat, but you will dine at the centre of the long table. We are not going to sit you before a loom and make you earn your bread! We are not going to make you wash the floor like our slave! Tonight you must sleep with me in the little house I have built for us, under the apple blossom.'

Her smile was growing, flowering again under his playful coaxing. 'Just you and I? To love, among the flowers, under the stars? Oh, Dumuzi, yes!'

He had her safe, like a fish in a keep-net that has ceased to struggle.

'But first, you must meet my mother. Your mother, now.'

A Lady who appeared smaller than she truly was, bowing her head modestly under a fringed headcloth. Her face was little painted. Sun and wind had brought their own colour to it. Her eyes were deep and dark, still youthful as a heifer's. Her hands in this unfamiliar city house moved a little nervously. On the wide steppe and in the quiet cow byres they would be wise, life-giving, over wombs and udders. She embraced Inanna, shyly, but with a countrywoman's strength.

'Blessings upon you, on your womb and my son's seed, daughter of this house.'

'My duty and love to you, mother of my husband.'

'Oh, Inanna! This is the happiest day of my life. You really are my sister now!' Geshtinanna sprang forward joyfully to embrace and dance her round.

'Oh, be careful! My turban's falling off! Geshtinanna, I'm a staid married woman since yesterday.'

They collapsed on a couch and sprawled laughing among the cushions.

But Inanna's fingers were indeed plucking at her disordered gown, setting her rich costume straight, glancing at the silent slaves. This family house seemed smaller than she remembered. Through the window apertures she glimpsed the soaring walls of the E-Anna precinct, the Red House, the Mosaic House, the Limestone House, that overshadowed all the other estates. Her palace. Tomorrow she would receive it formally from An. She would truly be Nin Egalla, Lady of the Great House.

'Inanna, don't grow old and stuffy yet,' Geshtinanna teased her. 'Let's stay young and merry together for ever, you and Dumuzi and I.'

'You, to say that,' her mother scolded, smiling. 'She is the oldest in wisdom of all my children, Inanna. A tablet-writing scribe. Did you know she is a great poet, and a famous physician too?'

'I know she is very clever,' said Inanna fondly, stroking Geshtinanna's talented hands. 'She brought Dumuzi and me together.'

'Only because I begged her to,' Dumuzi protested. 'I worshipped you long before she spirited you away that night in the square at Ur. I used to stand below the E-Anna wall with Gilgamesh, looking up at that gorgeous girl and longing for one smile.'

'I have invited Gilgamesh to take supper with us,' Nin Sun said.

A little startled silence, as always when the humans' world extends its boundary and impinges too closely on the Anunnaki's prerogatives.

'Mother!' A warning from Geshtinanna, softened with affection.

'I can see you do not approve. I have grown used to the Anunnaki's disapproval. But you must understand that Gilgamesh is my child as much as you or Dumuzi. Do you wonder that I should wish to entertain him when I come so rarely to your city?'

'But this is Inanna's homecoming, Mother!' Dumuzi stood beside his bride, drawing himself up to his full protective height.

'Have I offended you, Inanna?'

The Star Princess's turn now to let a smile of mischief curl round her rosy lips. 'Oh no, Mother. I count Gilgamesh amongst my truest friends. Yes, Dumuzi. Don't forget it was Gilgamesh who drove the Imdugud from my *huluppu* tree, killed the Serpent, banished . . . Kiskillilla. He felled the tree when my own brother Utu wouldn't help me. I had forgotten that Gilgamesh was now my brother too.'

'Gilgamesh is part human. Do not forget that either!' Dumuzi retorted.

'You're not jealous, my love?'

'Humans should wield their axes for us. That's what we made them for. It's not our work.'

'They tell me Gilgamesh is wielding his axe mightily on the battlefield now.'

'Yes, and by day he's taunting every young man in the city to wrestle with him. No one can beat him. And at night he's breaking into any house where there's a pretty girl to wrestle with.'

'Gilgamesh is my son and my guest,' said Nin Sun softly but firmly.

He was bigger than Inanna remembered, muscular, physical. His huge hands holding hers were vibrant with life. His eyes meeting hers flashed admiration, ambition. She felt her own respond.

'Welcome back to your city, Queen of the Sky. My axe is sharp for your service.'

'If I need a champion again, I know where to find the bravest of men.'

She felt a small delight that Dumuzi was watching them jealously. She felt herself grow greater in this hero's adoration. His face was alight, even before the beer-drinking had started. Looking at her eye to eye, he seemed so full of vitality, so square of shoulder. Could he really be only a human?

As Gilgamesh turned away to greet his family and their friends, Inanna clutched at her sister-in-law.

'Oh, Geshtinanna, what makes him so alive? Is it because he must die one day that I can feel the life beating in his blood so strongly? Will he really die? Must he?'

'Yes.' Sage Geshtinanna's face grew serious. 'Even though they count him two-thirds Anunnaki. The human part makes him mortal. It will bear him down to the Netherworld one day soon. He cannot escape his destiny.'

Inanna shuddered. 'Oh, if only someone would break Ereshkigal's power!'

'Enki ventured against Kur, in the dawn of the world, when Ereshkigal should still have been young. It was already too late.'

Inanna was still. Her eyes followed the boisterous passage of Gilgamesh unabashed among the younger Anunnaki.

'It must be possible. How can hers be a greater power than ours?'

'There are some in your city who would already be glad to see him go to her.'

'Gilgamesh? The hero of Uruk?'

'A hero in war. Their *lugal*. But not a ruler in peace. He has not learned to be an *en*. The *pukku* and *mikku* you gave him, to the people of Uruk they seem the instruments of oppression.'

'My gifts? How could they be?'

'The *pukku* calls the young men to war more often now. Their mothers weep. And the maids of your city . . . well, Dumuzi is right. When he sounds that drum outside their houses at night, there is no father dares refuse him entry. Your *mikku* stick has beaten bloodshed on more delicate membranes.'

Inanna blushed darkly. 'My city must be protected. What else should my champion do but rouse the army of Uruk? I am the Lady of Love. Whatever invasions he makes, he does them in my name.'

'Love, Inanna? Love is giving, love is losing oneself for the joy of the other.'

'What do you know of love?' Inanna snapped at her. 'You are not married!'

Geshtinanna put an arm round her, lightly, with no resentment. 'One night as a bride, Inanna, and you have read the whole book of love?'

Dumuzi and Inanna went to bed that night in their little home among the apple trees, happy as two children playing at houses under a tent of palm leaves.

# Chapter Sixty-seven

An received them like the most august of the Great Ones. He sat on his Heaven throne in his Sky House. He was a tall, gaunt man, and though his spine arched with age Inanna was startled to remember how formidable he was, how austere his presence. Perhaps it was because she was a new Inanna, a married lady now, Dumuzi's wife, no longer the merry great-grandchild who ran pealing with laughter through the halls of the E-Anna, pronounced her imperious will to everyone, made the lonely Sky Lord smile.

But was she not still the nubile princess whom eunuchs had led to his couch, who had learned at the hands of skilled women to pleasure his old, cold flesh, the youngest hierodule of An? Was all that past?

Confused, she turned to Dumuzi standing beside her, whose very warm brown presence seemed to bring the sunshine of the outdoors with him. Had choosing him meant she had put all that other behind her? Had she parted for all time from this pale, blue-veined Lord with the cloud-white hair? The space between them increased the power she felt in that ruler up there. And yet, her youthful, urgent body felt a different power in the vigorous Dumuzi beside her, wanted him, here, now, so that she moved her bare arm to brush his living flesh.

'Welcome, Daughter. Welcome, Son.'

Formality stiffened her. The ranks of Anunnaki and human servitors bordered the steps and the long, gleaming hall rich with polished stone and coloured clay pillars.

'Inanna of the Evening and Morning Star and Dumuzi the Shepherd greet you, Father An. I have brought you a gift.'

'Approach.'

So small she hid it in her hands. Would he understand? Would it make him jealous?

She knelt before him. The fine, netted, white wool of her

dress, laced with gold, spread all around her on the step. She looked like a water lily on a lake, like a bright planet in the night sky. Marriage had made her more glowingly beautiful than ever.

She opened her cupped hands, like petals, and lifted them close for his old eyes to see.

A little, golden bee nestled in that fragrant bud. A stillness held the hall. No other eyes knew what lay between them. Three nights ago she had worn it for the last time on her wedding bed, the stud gleaming with promise in the hollow of her navel. Dumuzi had burrowed his head in the hill of her belly, licked her, found her sweet with honey. The fibre of her being shuddered now, remembering his tongue.

She raised her eyes. Two tears stood unfallen on An's face. He understood.

'I have taken sweetness from your lips many times, Daughter Inanna. You have served me well.'

'No better than all the Anunnaki should serve the greatest of us.'

'No great Lord now. Enlil has taken over.'

'Sky came before Wind, Great Breed-Bull. I shall never forget that.'

'You must not. Stand against him. For my sake be very great, Inanna.' He gripped her hands in his still-powerful, bony ones, and the little bee tumbled from her to him. He kissed it, kissed her palms with a fierce passion, then dropped the golden keepsake into the bosom of the cloth that crossed his breast.

He stood up. *Sukkals* moved to support his elbows, but he gestured them away, petulantly. He raised his hand, palm outward in solemn blessing. Inanna, kneeling, lowered her head, felt her heart beating thunderously.

'By the power of the Sky,
'By the waters of Nammu Above and Below,
'By the storms of Heaven,
'By the Bull that thunders,
'I hand to you Inanna,
'Nin Egalla, Bright Shining One,
'The Heaven-built House of the E-Anna.
'Rule. Be happy.'

The silver key to the Temple of the Sky shone in her hand.

He sank down on the cushions again, an old, exhausted man, curled as a caterpillar.

Inanna rose, her face radiant, hugged him with a resurgent, childish warmth, then swung to face the attentive hall. At her turning all the palace servants from the *en* to the smallest slave boy fell on their faces. Their hands stretched out before her.

'Hail, Mistress of the E-Anna. Hail, Great Inanna!'

The dignitaries of An's court lowered their horned diadems in acknowledgement, touched their breasts and lips and foreheads in obeisance. With a flash of triumph she saw Dumuzi hesitate, then do the same. A rush of warmth and love, generous in victory, flowed from her heart to him. She wanted to hug him, nurse him, kiss this hurt away. She knew it wounded his dignity to see her glorified above him. But she could not be bound by the Shepherd, though she loved his body. She was Inanna, Daughter of the Moon, Grandchild of Enki and Enlil, Great-granddaughter of An himself. Ki and Nammu were in her blood.

Dumuzi was royal too, but not of Enlil's line.

They feasted, a last farewell to An.

'Will you walk on the Earth amongst humans and Anunnaki again?' she asked him, leaning against him on the supper couch.

'Oh, yes. I must preside at the Assembly in the Ubshuukkinna at Nippur. I cannot allow Enlil to usurp *that*. And I am keeping a smaller house for myself here in Uruk. Besides, you will walk high Angal to brighten the stars and visit me, will you not?'

'Indeed I will. Often. I need your wisdom, to rule as you did.' Her tongue traced loving patterns round his ears, in reminiscence of years past. He smiled and let his hand stray down her dress. They saw Dumuzi watching.

An stretched out his other hand and patted Dumuzi's arm. 'Do not fret, Ama-Ushumgalanna. I have taught her well so you can enjoy her. She is the Lady of Love. You must allow her to smile on us all. But I have words of advice for you too. Tomorrow, mid-morning, be under the myrtle tree in my Fountain Garden.'

Inanna's turn to be jealous. The two men, heads bent, paced the garden where water lilies opened in the sun and ornamental carp flickered like ruddy flames.

Inanna was busy interviewing all her palace staff. The capable woman who would be her estate manager, the ranger who would oversee her wild park of deer and fowl, the matron of the millhouse who took in widows and orphans and gave them shelter and employment, the master goldsmith, the lapidary, the overseer of the weavers, and all the many ranks of priesthood and stewards. The list seemed endless. Living a life of childish pleasure and pleasuring An, she had not realised how vast an enterprise the E-Anna was, its land, its trade, its services, its workshops. All must be regulated fairly and smoothly for the good of the country.

'I never knew there was so much to think about,' she said wearily, as Dumuzi came in from the garden slow and thoughtful.

'An is going away now. He asked me to bid you farewell.'

'Can't I kiss him goodbye?' She jumped to her feet.

'He said . . . I think he could not bear it.'

A clap of thunder drowned his words. The sky grew intensely dark. Rain lashed the terraces. Wind bent the palm trees. Hail was flung through the open windows, hard as pebbles.

She clung to Dumuzi in sudden grief, and he held her while the storm passed. Sun warmed the wet earth, bringing a rich, fecund smell. Birds sang again.

Inanna drew a shaking breath. 'So. The Bull has gone back to Angal Above.'

'And you are Queen of Uruk.'

She nuzzled his neck. 'And you are my King. It is all ours, Dumuzi. This is all ours.'

'Uruk must be the pre-eminent city. That is what An wants. That is why he's given it over to you.'

'Even over Nippur?'

'Enlil took Ki away from An. Enlil let Ereshkigal go to Kur and never lifted a hand to help Enki. An has not forgiven that.'

'But I am hardly a woman yet. The youngest of the Igigi. How can I stand against Enlil?'

'You need to be armed with strength. I have talked it over with An.'

'You?'

'Trust me, Inanna. It can be done. But at the moment guile will serve you better than might!'

'What guile? For what?'

'To take the rest of the *me* from Eridu.'

The shock of memory made her start back out of Dumuzi's arms. It was not the first time the lure of this had tugged at her heart. 'Take Enki's *me* out of the Abzu?'

'I believe you could do it, Inanna. And what a wedding present from my father that would be!'

'The emblems of all the highest wisdom and craft and civilisation in the world? Bring them from Eridu to Uruk?'

'Then even Enlil would have to acknowledge your power, as now reluctantly he acknowledges Enki's.'

'But Enki would never give them up. He is the Father of all Wisdom. He handed their gifts to all the Anunnaki at the beginning of time. Don't you remember? That's why I was sent to the E-Anna. Because as a child I lost my temper and stormed that I hadn't been given enough. I angered Enlil and An by my presumption. They sent me here to be disciplined.'

'And you charmed An to be your lover.'

'Only in name. Never the final act.'

'What difference does it make? He loves you like a dotard. You could charm Enki too. Easily. Did you ever know a Lord with such a reputation for susceptibility to you Daughters of An?'

'I thought from the stories it was the Daughters of An who succumbed to him!'

'But his *me*, Inanna, his *me*. If you set your heart on it, you could win them from him. I know you. And I know my father . . . and his weakness for girls and beer.'

She stood separated from him, staring at him, his urgent, demanding face. Her heart beat uncomfortably fast. Visions raced through her head. Winds of ambition seemed to be gathering about her, blowing her off her feet.

'Could I? Could I do it?'

'You can, Inanna.' His hands were hard around her again, his body pressing urgently. 'You can. You can.'

'Oh yes, Dumuzi. Now I'm married to you I could do anything.'

'Do it, Inanna. Please! For me.'

'Yes. Yes.'

Victory, exultation, thunderclaps of power and goodness, refreshing rain. A wonderful harvest would spring from this.

'Eridu, is it?' said Nin Shubur, a little rebelliously, when Inanna told her. 'And you want a *magur* boat big enough to carry cargo. If you won't tell me what you are plotting, my lady, I think I had better take along a few spells of protection to see that all goes well.'

'Oh, Nin Shubur!' Inanna twisted out of her *sukkal*'s hands. The Lady of the East was brushing her mistress's black hair, like a mother with a fretful child, though it was not her duty. 'He's Dumuzi's father and my grandfather. Shouldn't he give us a good wedding gift?'

'Your great-grandfather An has given you the E-Anna. Are you not satisfied yet? And how do you know that what Lord Enki chooses to give you will require a cargo boat?'

'Oh, it will. It will.'

'Why are you hugging yourself and looking so smug? It is not for you to say what the Great Ones give or withhold.'

'I am an Igigi myself now. Never forget it.'

'Child, child. Greatness is in our deeds.'

'You're wrong, Nin Shubur. Greatness is where we direct our power. Whether we do it well or ill, it makes no difference, as long as we do it grandly.'

Nin Shubur let the brush fall. 'When you were a little girl you were sent to the E-Anna for wishing that. Did you learn nothing here?'

'I have learned,' said Inanna, turning slowly and fixing the *sukkal* with a brilliant smile, 'that I can do anything I like, have anything I want, bend anyone I choose, if I truly set my mind and will towards it.'

Nin Shubur bent and retrieved the fallen brush. 'Yes, madam. I will give orders for your journey.'

364

# Chapter Sixty-eight

Inanna lay under the crooked apple tree in the garden of her new house. She sprawled back, rejoicing in the hot sun on her face, the cool, damp earth beneath her. The sky was brilliant after torrential rain, the views enormous.

The waters seemed to have stopped with a benevolent precision, so that homesteads and farms stood out as tiny islands, just wide enough to shelter beasts and fowls. Canoes and reed rafts punted busily from knoll to knoll. Brown children dived and splashed. Dogs barked furiously to defend their shrunken territories. The city people came down the great mound of Uruk to where the trading quays were awash and talked hopefully of rich harvests when the waters had soaked away into the fertile soil.

Dumuzi's shadow fell over Inanna. Against the sunlit sky his face was dark with longing. She moved seductively, letting the green and white dress cloth fall open all along her white legs. Her hands parted it further, showed him the blue-black pubic triangle sleek with juniper oil, opened up the rosy door to pleasure.

'Inanna!'

'Yes,' she crooned, drawing him down. 'Yes, my honey-man.'

In the moment after climax, holding him tight inside her, she exclaimed, 'I am going to Eridu. I will go today.'

'Now? On the flood?'

'What better time? When all the world is awash with water, Enki should be more generous than ever. We shall feast and carouse and overdo ourselves to celebrate.'

'You will have to come back by water. What will happen if Enki realises his loss and comes after you?'

'He is one of the four Great Guardians! He cannot retract his word. Once he has given me the *me*, they will be mine.'

'Enki is very cunning.'

'Nin Shubur has ordered a fast ship with a racing crew. No boat swift enough to catch me will be strong enough to stop us. And the chariot roads beside the canals are underwater or thick with mud. Unless he has forces that can fly he can't overtake me.'

'Inanna, I love your courage. Sometimes I worry that you can't see danger.'

'It was your idea. Yours and An's. You want the *me* for Uruk, don't you?'

'You know I do. I want you to be great. Greatest of all the Anunnaki.'

'So that you, my lord, will be exalted, ruling beside me.'

'Just now, you look like a mud urchin, my *lubi*. Don't you care that you're lying in a puddle of clay? What will your women say when they see your dress?'

'What do I care? This mud is soft, this mud is fertile. Feel it, man of my heart.' She smeared a handful of it over his face.

A *magur* boat, black, bitumen-coated. Its soaring prow rose to a spike like a heron's beak. The stern scrolled like a monkey's tail. The crew were tanned, hard-muscled, balancing their bodies on deft feet so that the narrow craft hardly shifted under their movements. The boat was lean and swift, but long and deep enough to load a sizeable cargo.

Nin Shubur seated herself in the bows. Despite her brave words, Inanna felt a stir of unease that her *sukkal* had not dressed for this state visit in the formality of court dress, but in her more primitive garb of an eastern shaman. Instead of jewels, pouches of fur hung on leather strings. Her feet were bare. Strange spots of red patterned her golden skin.

Inanna frowned and pouted. 'Are you trying to shame the court of Uruk? Where is your diadem?'

'Is not Lord Enki himself one of the most elemental Lords of all? He will not despise old ways, old wisdom.'

'He is Lord of Civilisation, Keeper of the *Me*.'

'I agree that without his artfulness there would be no civilisation. He brought it all into being.'

'Don't let Enlil hear you say that!'

'Lord Enlil spoke the Word that made life possible. Lord Enki is Nudimmud, its Shaper.'

'And I? I am the Princess of Light, the one they all love!'

'Yes, my lady.'

And indeed, as the boat drew out from the White Quay, the

crowds who had come out to exclaim over the floods raised a cheer that floated down the Buranun awaking other shouts of praise, as a wind rushes through an orchard shaking falls of blossom from one tree after another.

The river was vast and shining. The men poled gently, letting the strong current bear them swiftly down towards Eridu.

South of Uruk, the huge expanse of the Buranun, swirling brown as vast herds of deer migrating across the steppe, widened into an unchartable wilderness of water. Lagoons had become lakes. Lakes were bright seas that tricked the eyes with false horizons. Canebrakes stood across their path like impenetrable walls, then opened up to reveal themselves as a thousand islands. Buffalo lowed mournfully, paradoxically unable to cool themselves in the too-deep water. Fish leaped with renewed vigour. Ducks shattered the silence, filling the sky at their approach.

The lake narrowed again into the busy waterway of the Iturungal. Far ahead the city of Ur rose, sharply defined. Inanna lifted her face to that distant Moon Palace on its hill.

'Will you not go on to visit your mother?' Nin Shubur asked.

Inanna shook her head. 'Nin Gal is Enki's daughter. She might question me too closely about what I am doing.'

'Are you ashamed?'

Inanna's head shot up. The men paddled steadily, their faces unmoving as the *lahamu* statues on a temple terrace.

'How dare you! Aren't you proud that you serve Inanna? Shouldn't the child grow greater than its parent? I am Enki's granddaughter. It's my turn now. I will do more than he has ever done.'

'Overcome Kur?' The innocent tone, the deeply-mocking meaning.

A whispering silence now, through which drops tinkled from the paddles and the bow wave churned against the wood like Enki's own bitter laughter.

'Why not?' said Inanna, in a strange, choked voice at last. 'Why not even that?'

The ship drove across the current and entered the Eridu Canal. The men sang now. Swift, rhythmic strokes guided their oars as they bore down on the southernmost city of Sumer, its guardian of the waters, the ancient, holy site of Eridu.

The villages they passed, with their soaring, reed-pillared guest halls, had not been empty. Small, swift canoes had darted ahead of them. In golden reed houses like these, Enki had wooed shy Nin Gikuga, passionate Nin Gal had waited for her lover Nanna. Inanna smiled under the shade of the awning amidships. With every hour that passed on the water, she felt herself more at one with this side of her family. Far behind her now were the high, hand-raised mounds of Enlil's Nippur, An's Uruk, Nanna's Ur. Sky Lords, all of them, aspiring to visible majesty. The power of Enki reached another way, down into the depths of water and the mysteries Below.

A tiny check of fear. Was she not Inanna, Princess of the glittering Morning and Evening Star? Was she out of her element in the realm of the Lord of the Deep?

But love was strongest of all. This battle would be won sweetly.

'News has gone before us,' observed Nin Shubur. 'You have a reception party to meet you.'

The functionaries of the Abzu were lined up on its dazzling quay steps. The wharf itself gleamed underwater. Enki's house glittered with lapis lazuli and silver, so that sky, palace and lagoon mirrored each other in flashes of blue and white. Inanna screwed up her eyes against the trickery of light, felt her senses reel.

Isimud was waiting to greet her, the two-faced *sukkal* of the Master Trickster. Difficult to know which eyes to look at. Difficult to be sure each face wore the same expression. Even as she let him hand her from the boat Inanna could not be certain her foot would touch the limestone step and not find it yielding water.

'My Lord has sent me to give you welcome, Lady Inanna. Enter our humble house of Abzu and let me entertain you.'

'Isn't my grandfather at home?'

'Home?'

And where indeed was home for the Lord of Waters, when rivers shift their course across the plains of sand, when a night's deluge changes land to sea?

'My Lord Enki rests in the hammock of the Deep, as in his mother's womb. This house is Abzu. It seems small, but it is one of the entrances to the Great Below. There, the waters of Nammu know no beginning and no end, are neither salt nor fresh. No sun dries them and no storms replenish them. In her lap the Lord of Wisdom dreams.'

Again the young woman said nothing, felt the smallness of her own knowledge in this place. She caught Nin Shubur watching, that slightest lift of eyebrows, curl of lips, knew herself to be on trial.

Drawing herself up tall, consciously softening her face into a radiant smile, she gave Isimud her hand. 'I thank you for your hospitality. Lead me into the Abzu.'

Up the wide water steps. Past the hero guards with curling sidelocks, naked but for their fringed girdles, pouring libation urns in streams before her feet so that the warm stone steamed around them. Another shock. Living *lahamu?* Here, what was spoken of in song, symbolised in stone, was made actual.

Here, the *me* could become solid things held in the grasp of one's hands.

Cool halls now, reflective as water. No lamps, only the light from high skies finding itself again in deep pools and basins. The sound of water falling, the ripple of harps and the liquid notes of reed pipes.

At the first door Isimud stopped, took from a dark-skinned girl a goblet of dew-clear water.

'Be welcome, Inanna of Uruk. Drink.'

Cold. Unbelievably refreshing. Shocking her hot, dazed body into lively awareness.

'I thank you, Lord Isimud.'

Down now. A reversal of old assumptions that all temples lead skywards. At the next door she was offered a cake of barley bread with butter.

Wholesome, sweet. A taste of childhood simplicity.

'I am honoured. Thank you.'

Now an oval chamber, with a dark well at its centre. A lion-headed bird faced her with gaping stone jaws. The sign of the Imdugud, here. In the dimness she heard rather than saw the stream trickle from its throat.

And here an attendant *lahamu* poured for her not water but rich, dark, heady date wine.

'My Lord will join you presently.'

'You make me very welcome, Lord of Before and Behind.'

'Be seated, Inanna. Lord Enki invites you to enjoy all that he has.'

The chamber was dim and cool. The wetness of the floor suggested the flood had not long since left it. A couch had been spread with soft lambskins. The wine jug was left beside it, standing on the rim of the well. Inanna sat down; her fingers wandered to the stem of the empty goblet.

The jug was swiftly withdrawn from her reach. Isimud was moving for the door, one face still turned towards them. Nin Shubur interposed herself between Inanna and the edge of the well. Then, as Enki's *sukkal* vanished, she emptied the date wine into the depths and replenished the jug from the lion-bird's mouth with water.

'You, at least, must keep a clear head, my lady.'

A long, quiet wait through the time of siesta. Then a commotion in the depth of the well beside her, making Inanna start up on the couch. A rattle of chains and buckets, a scrabbling up ladders and brickwork. Crooked, clever hands grasping the rim, a shock of wet and flying hair, grey and rippling blue-black, a mobile face, ancient in knowledge, but curious as a little child whose eyes are opening on the world for the first time.

He jumped down on to the floor, scattering pools of water, a small and agile figure, not quite straight. and never still.

'Well, Granddaughter?' he cried, wrapping her in a cold, wet embrace and giving her a passionate kiss full on the lips. 'You married Dumuzi Abzu, after all, did you? Was that wise? Was that wise?'

'He is your son, Grandfather!' she protested, blushing and drawing back too late from the watery and enthusiastic encounter. 'Isn't he?'

'What of that? What of that? You may live to regret it.'

'I love Dumuzi Abzu,' she said in a low, firm voice. 'I will always love him.'

A laugh burbled through the hall, caught up in all the waterfalls of sound.

'We shall see. We shall see . . . I will tell you one thing,' peering at her through the dim, water-dappled light. 'If it comes to a contest, I'd back my granddaughter against my son. Starlight and Water, there's a treacherous pair for you. What can a solid Sheep Man do against us, eh?'

'You should say, rather, what could he do with us to help him, Grandfather.'

'So what have you come for?'

Those eyes, grey as winter lakes, looking directly into her own. Isimud had come into the room again behind her. One pair of his eyes, at least, was fixed on her back.

'To ask your blessing on our marriage, my lord.'

'And what gift are you expecting from me?'

Too direct. Too close. No way to keep the invading streams of his wisdom out of her mind.

'Whatever it pleases the Lord of Eridu to give the Lady of Uruk, so that she may be able to humble the pride of Enlil's Nippur.'

A startled shift of emotions across the older man's face. And then another shout of laughter, more uproarious than the first. He slapped his thigh, hard enough to hurt.

'Very good! Very good! You may have won yourself far more than you think by that, my girl. Isimud, is there a good supper cooking? I think we must treat this young Lady with great respect.'

# Chapter Sixty-nine

Beer pooled the table, a darker brown than the Buranun in flood. Enki's head, usually thrust forward in lively curiosity, lolled on its wizened neck. Occasionally he would start up, and the manic brightness flash from his eyes, his raucous laughter set the echoes shaking, as he lifted his beaker to toast his radiant granddaughter again. Each time, she turned the brilliance of her smile upon him, lifted her own, sipped circumspectly. Her eyes glowed at him over the rim.

Now he let his head droop on his arm, but the arm itself groped out and found Inanna's white one. The bent, maker's hand closed round it, appraised the smoothness of its flesh, stroked it, fondled it lasciviously.

'Come to bed, Inanna,' he mumbled. 'We've had enough of this and nothing of the other.'

Inanna smiled through a haze of food and beer. She was not as drunk as he was. She still sat upright. She did not look at her grandfather now but stared ahead of her with a slightly vacant smile of pleasure as his fingers caressed her.

Their *sukkals* were watchful, but almost helpless. What could Isimud do when Enki shouted for more drink but sign to the butler to bring it? The Lord of Wisdom did not accept murmured advice. And Enki was not so drunk that watered beer would not enrage him.

Nin Shubur squatted cross-legged near the end of the table. She ate and drank sparingly. Her shaman's gaze was fixed on Inanna as though by the intensity of her will she could hold her mistress back from folly.

'I haven't had anything yet,' Inanna said, 'that would help me counter Enlil.'

'You'd really do it?' slurred Enki. 'You'd stand up to that mighty wind-bag? You'd have words with his Word?'

'An has gone back to Angal Above. He won't visit us much now. I've never even seen Nammu. The older generation has had its day. It's the young ones' time now,' Inanna enunciated carefully.

'And me too? Your old grandfather. I'm past it as well, am I? Come to bed, girl. I'll show you!'

'Not past some things, Grandfather,' she smiled. 'But tell me. With all your arts, what have you done to bring Enlil down and make the powers of the Below greater than the Above?'

He wagged his finger at her. 'But you are the Star Child.' His look shot up to her face with a sudden shrewdness. 'You belong to the Above yourself.'

She turned to him radiantly. 'My planet dances on the horizon, Grandfather. It is both Below and Above. I can rule all realms. I am the Lady of the Threshold, the Gate of Night, the Gate of Morning. I can hold it all.'

A long, wise, sad look cleared his fuddled features. 'I believe you may be my Daughter of the Future. I believe you may be the one. If you had the courage, if you had the will . . .'

'I could challenge Enlil.'

'You could meet Ereshkigal.'

The murmur of their households was all around them. The silence fell only between them, a deep, enclosed well. Nin Shubur, seated out of earshot of their conversation, saw the tension in Enki's lifted face, the shocked stillness of Inanna's body. The *sukkal* frowned and made rapid signs of protection.

'Yes. I could . . . if I only had the power!'

'You shall have it, my dear.'

Enki staggered to his feet, spilling jugs of cream, platters of fruit, dark emmer beer, fragments of duck-egg shells. He raised his bronze beaker, brimming with beer, splashed a copious libation to Nin Mah, Mother of Earth.

'I swear by my name! I swear by this holy Abzu! I will give you the *me*. Hear me, households of Eridu and Uruk! I am handing over to Inanna all the emblems of power that remain in my treasury.'

The talking hushed. All eyes and mouths gaped at him. Inanna herself had risen to her feet, her own beaker lifted head high.

Enki signed to Isimud grandly.

'My lord!' the sukkal protested, shocked.

'The keys, you fool!'

One face tight-lipped and obedient, one openly appalled, Isimud set activity in motion.

'I am giving you High Priesthood! I give you the Everlasting Exalted Crown! I give you the Throne of the Ruler! I give you Immortal Guardianship!'

And frightened pages came running, bearing the *en*'s palm-leaf headdress, the Great Guardian's eight-horned tiara, the royal diadem and the lion-clawed seat of the governor.

Inanna raised her beaker to Enki and shouted, 'I take them!'

Nin Shubur was on her feet also, her expression a tumult of astonishment, pride, calculation of the future, fear.

Enki toasted his granddaughter a second time.

'I am giving you, in the name of all that is sacred, the Most Noble Sceptre, the Staffs of Royal Office, the Pre-eminent Shrine, the Task of Shepherd, the Kingly Rank of *Lugal*.'

And jewelled regalia were heaped round her feet.

'I take them!'

'I give you Long-Lasting Ladyship, the Cult Office of Pure Lady, the Servant Priesthoods *Ishub, Lumah, Guda*.'

'I accept them, Grandfather!'

'I am giving you Truth, Descent to the Netherworld, Ascent from the Netherworld, the Eunuchs *Kurgarra, Girbadara, Sag-ursag*.'

'I take them all!'

He gave her the Battle Standard, the Overpowering Flood, the Weapons of War. He gave her Sexual Intercourse, the arts of Kissing the Phallus and Prostitution. He gave her Law and Libel, all Artistry and the Chamber of the Cult, the Temple Tavern and the Office of Hierodule of Heaven. He gave her Music, the instruments of *Gusilim, Lilis, Ub, Mesi* and *Ala*. He gave her the Office of Elder, the Renown of the Hero, Wordly Power. He gave her Enmity, and the Fall of Cities. He gave her Truthful Speech and Falsehood, Lamentation and the Merry Heart. He heaped on her the skill of the Metalworker, Scribe, Smith, Leatherworker, Builder, Basket-Weaver, Fuller and Carpenter. He gave her Wisdom, Close Attention, Ritual Purification. Fear, Terror and Strife. Peace, Weariness and Victory. Perceptive Counsel, the Soothing of Troubled Hearts, Good Judgment, Firm Decision. She had the Black Garment and the Colourful Garment, the Adventure of Travel and the Safe Dwelling Place. Hers were the Feeding Pen and the Sheepfold, the

Heaping Up of Live Coals, the Kindling of Fire, the Dousing of Fire. The Lion of Bitter Bite. The Gathered Family. Procreation.

And the young Queen of Love and War took them all from her grandfather.

'I give you . . .' the Water Man's voice faltered.

'The storehouse is empty, my lord,' Isimud said, his two faces as rigid as stone. Then, as the Lord of all Wisdom staggered and fell, he moved swiftly and caught him.

Inanna herself stood swaying slightly, brilliant with success, drunk with the knowledge of power. Good and harm, blessing and cursing, all the variety of joy and sorrow lay under her hand, heaped around her in the wreckage of Enki's feast, a hundred symbols of possibilities at her feet.

Nin Shubur stood before her, a slight figure strangely and shabbily dressed, sober, intense.

'I've got them,' Inanna managed to say. 'He's given me all his *me*!'

'Make him confirm it!' Nin Shubur's whisper insisted.

'He's drunk. He can't hear.' Inanna's own speech came slurred. 'Grandfather, I have taken from your hand the *me* of High Priesthood, the *me* of Immortal Guardianship, the *me* of Sumer's Crown . . .' Her voice rose clearer, stronger, telling the emblems of power over and over till all the list was named. 'Is this your will?'

'Listen to her, Isimud? Isn't she glorious? How's that for a wedding present? Look. No, pay attention! This young Lady's going back to Uruk. In her b-b-boat. See that she gets there safely. D'you hear me?'

'I hear, my lord.' Two of his four eyes looked venom at the watchful Nin Shubur.

The wise woman was already busy. Swift orders of her own were given; carrying-baskets appeared in which the treasures were laid reverently. She called Inanna's own servants to come and bear the baskets away. It was night outside, but the moon lent its light to Inanna's triumph. Flood water and moonshine made a magic landscape through which threaded a thousand channels of escape.

'Upstream,' said Nin Shubur grimly to the hastily summoned crew of the *magur* ship on the steps of the Abzu. 'You will need to break all records from Eridu to Uruk.'

The oarsmen nodded. Brief smiles flashed in their dark faces. They leaped down into the ship. Pride in their boatman's skill held their arms poised and ready. The swift coming and going on the water steps was bringing the loaded baskets of the *me* into the waiting craft. The boat sank lower under its exotic cargo.

Inanna still stood, ghostly in her white gown, a little breeze fluttering it out from her legs. Too uncertain this light to read anything in her face but a soft amazement. The unusual stillness of her figure spoke perhaps of a youthful awe.

'Did I really do it, Nin Shubur?' she whispered, as the last load passed her. 'Are they really mine? Have I taken the *me*?'

The smaller woman's look darted up at her. 'You have taken them, yes. But can you keep them? Can we get them to Uruk before he comes to his senses?'

'We can. We must. Come on, Nin Shubur. I've outwitted him!'

Inanna jumped into the boat, rocking it wildly, so that the captain had to seize her and steady both his mistress and her craft. Nin Shubur followed quickly, but with more care.

The ropes were cast off, the ship pushed out from the Abzu quay. They were afloat in the spreading sea of silver and the men were beginning to pull against the current.

The steps were thick with the muttering people of Enki's court. One single, tall figure in a two-horned diadem stood at the top of the flight, barely discernible against the darkness. One face of Isimud watched their departure, powerless to forbid it. The other turned back into the feasting hall where Enki lay sprawled face downwards among the spilled cups.

Enki had drunk too well of his own hospitality. The first fingers of dawn were in the sky before he lifted his head from the couch where Isimud had laid him.

'Where . . . Ouch!' He nursed his head, then grinned ruefully and turned to the bed space beside him. It was empty. He groped, his brain still struggling with the cobwebs of his hangover. He found it cold. A closer, incredulous inspection showed that side of the sheets unrumpled.

'No woman?' The voice sounded querulous, dissatisfaction coloured with a hint of self-mockery. 'There should have been a woman . . . Shouldn't there? I surely didn't dream her. A girl, lovely as starlight. Gorgeously tall and strong. By the Foothills of Kur! I can remember the scent of her flesh, the
caress of her fingers. Why isn't she here in bed with me? I

must be losing my powers! I must be. . .'

The wise and wizened face sharpened into acute anxiety. He sat up, curled forward as a combing wave, yelled, '*Isimud!*'

He was out of bed before the *sukkal* came hurrying. He was across the antechamber, rushing through the labyrinth of the Abzu to his treasury. Isimud, anticipating his command, had the key in the lock, threw the door open, on emptiness.

Enki clutched at the doorpost for support. His voice was weak, strangled.

'Where is Prostitution, the Art of Lovemaking, the Hierodule of Heaven?'

'Gone, my lord.'

'Where is War? The Sword and Dagger? The Destruction of Cities?'

'You gave them away last night, my lord.'

'Wisdom, Peace, Terror?'

'You gave them all to Inanna.'

'*All*, Isimud?'

'All that you had is hers now.'

'Is she still here in Eridu? No, of course she isn't! Weak-headed, soft-hearted fool that I am!'

'She will be far up the canal towards Uruk by now.'

'Then stop her, damn you!'

'How can we catch her, my lord? She has a swift ship and several hours' start.'

'Do I have to teach my own *sukkal* how to rouse forces of magic? Use any of my creatures you have to, but bring my powers back!'

'Even if it means annihilating the young Lady, my lord? The monsters from the Deep are difficult to control once we let them loose.'

Enki paused. The tirade of helpless fury abated a little. He struck Isimud on the shoulder with a short, bitter laugh.

'Oh yes, she is very charming, my granddaughter. Very seductive. You know my weakness, Isimud. No, the beasts of the Deep must not be allowed to harm one hair of her lovely head. Let her and her *sukkal* escape back to my son if they can. But not her cargo. At any other cost than hurting her, bring the *me* back to the Abzu.'

Isimud bowed. 'I will try, my lord. You must know there is danger either way. If I have the strength to hold your creatures in check, I will. Still, I think it may be a kindness to take your powers back from her, lest the young Lady be tempted to overreach herself.'

Enki glared at him. 'As I did? Is that what you mean? Thinking I could go against Kur to rescue Ereshkigal?'

'That was your quest, my lord. She speaks of challenging Enlil.'

A sulky pout of Enki's mouth, not unlike Inanna's own. 'She can't. The Anunnaki wouldn't allow it. Don't stand there with those two looks on your faces, man! All diplomatic respect on one side, and cynical doubt on the one you think I can't see! What are you waiting for?'

'A war canoe!' Isimud commanded from his backward-facing mouth. 'And . . .' He strode through the open courts to where the red dawn streaked the overspilling lagoon with blood.

'Rise!

'From where the winds stream the foam of towering rollers.

'Come!

'From where the storms shift mighty sandbanks.

'Go!

'Stop Inanna!

'Legions of Nammu, waiting in the dark Below,

'Overtake her!

'Overpower her!

'Rise, *Enkum*!

'Rescue the *me* for Eridu!'

# Chapter Seventy

'Do you know where we are?'

'My Queen, we are approaching the Idal Quay.'

'Is it far to the boundary of Uruk land now?'

'The Idal is only the first of the seven staging quays that will bring us out of Enki's territory and into yours, my Queen. The flood is running strongly against us.'

Inanna looked nervously over her shoulder. Already a red flush of dawn was streaking the stormy black. Even on this cool spring morning the sweat streamed from the boatmen's faces. Their captain steered in towards the brickwork quay, where the earliest workers lifted curious heads from washing, or water-dipping, or chasing the wading cattle from the moored craft to safer grazing.

'Why are you stopping?' asked Inanna.

'My Queen, the men have been paddling since midnight. They must rest for a few moments and eat.'

'So near to Eridu?'

'We will get the Boat of the Sky safe to Uruk. Trust us. No oarsmen can outstrip this crew.'

'No oarsmen, certainly,' Nin Shubur said, studying the horizon behind them. 'But who knows what Father Enki will send?'

'Be quick, then.'

One of the crew leaped ashore, made fast the boat by the bows only. He quickly bought fresh bread and milk. They ate in the watery stillness, always watching astern, ignoring the whispers and stares of the Idal people at this resplendent ship of state and its grim-faced crew.

'Look,' said Nin Shubur. 'I thought it could not be long.' From the south a storm was racing towards them, like a mass of black-maned lions. 'But those are not true clouds.' She clutched the cloth tighter round her head against the battering wind. 'See how their feet churn up the water. The

*Enkum* are upon us, my lady.'

As the pursuers grew nearer, they emerged as running figures whose feet threw back huge surges of waves behind them, pillars of whirling water, furious faces lost in shock-headed clouds. Wild hair, green-black, streamed backwards from them. Some grasped staves in their hands with which they beat the canal into a frenzy. Others held upturned jars from which poured unstoppable deluges. The brimming canal was overspilling. The thunderous knock of the approaching waves threatened to overwhelm the Boat of the Sky long before the creatures reached and seized it.

'Save us, my Queen! They'll swamp us!'

Inanna's crew dropped the remains of their breakfast, seized their paddles, made as if to cast off.

Nin Shubur stayed them with a gesture. 'What is the use? They'd overwhelm us midstream in another moment. Stay where you are. Let us hear what message Isimud brings from his master.'

On the crest of the bow wave a tiny black speck rode. In moments it became a small, black racing canoe, guided by a lone paddler who scarcely needed to pole for the force rushing behind him. One taller figure sat in the stern, arms folded.

The men sat pale and paralysed, shaken only into activity when the first wash of the great breaker set the boat of An rocking and threatened to smash it against the Idal Quay. They struggled to hold it clear of the brickwork as the waves tossed them up and dropped them sickeningly. In spite of a brave attempt to retain her dignity, Inanna clutched the sides in terror.

'Now,' said Nin Shubur. And, sure enough, Isimud lifted his hand and the pillars of falling water shuddered and slowed, though the overflowing canal continued to heave violently.

Isimud's lone canoe was nearing the quay.

'Inanna! This is a warning from your Grandfather Enki, Lord of the Abzu. The commands of the Master of the Deep are not to be disobeyed.'

Words were torn disjointedly from her.

'Last night Father Enki spoke me fair. He loaded me with gifts. I heard no commands of his that I would want to disobey.'

'His orders this morning are simple and just. Your

grandfather loves you. You and your *sukkal* may go on your way to Uruk safely. But you must leave the Boat of the Sky and its precious cargo of *me* with me. I will take them back to the Abzu, where they belong.'

Inanna tried to rise, holding on to the mast. Though she moved more steadily in the sober morning it was not easy to balance on the angry swell. She tried to stand tall, queenly, her face softened in no smile. But the voice she meant to be powerful with indignation was shaken by the violent motion.

'You heard Lord Enki give his word! You and Nin Shubur were witnesses when he gave me his pledge. I did not come to Eridu to steal like a common thief. He *gave* me the *me*! What is the worth of his high name? What is the value of his oath on the Shrine of the Abzu? Is he a deceiver? Can his sacred word to me be broken? You dishonour yourself and him!'

The *Enkum* roared. Torrents of water began to descend again.

Explosions of spray shot from the rhythmic beating of their staves as they advanced nearer towards the quay, tossing their wild seaweed hair. A rising wave ground the ship of Uruk against the wall.

The boatmen yelled. Nin Shubur sang. As though this were the early morning of any normal day, she reached up her hands to the sky and sang of sunshine. A crack of thunder split the air. Spray drenched her cloak. Still her hands and voice lifted.

Gradually, very gradually, the violent dark of the storm lightened to shining white, parted in holes like net. Rose-pink of dawn and blue vivid heaven flowered through. Beheaded, the water spouts quivered, tottered, their lion manes collapsing into the Eridu Canal.

The party from Uruk felt rather than saw the current change. The colossal waves hurling up from Eridu smoothed, flattened, sank, turned back into that brown flood race that had been sweeping southwards. One staff still beat feebly in an unseen hand. The water plucked it sideways, washed it away. Only the seaweed hair was visible now, swirling irresistibly back where it had come from.

Isimud, astonished, watched the *Enkum*'s helpless retreat, as his own helmsman fought to hold the canoe against the changed tide. His forward face glared at Nin Shubur.

'Clever. But it is not enough. Your journey will be long and slow against the force of this current. You won't reach Uruk.'

He signed, and his canoe spun round, sped off in pursuit of the disappearing *Enkum*, swifter than a flying-fish.

'He is right,' said Nin Shubur. 'Something else will be back.'

They had hardly moored to rest briefly at the second quay when they heard a hollow roll like subterranean thunder. Inanna whipped round. This time the bottom of the canal seemed to be rising through the surface.

The overspilling channel behind them was reddening into a battlemented wall. As they watched, this bulwark seemed to rear fifty towers like necks, and from each tower seven horned turrets sprang higher yet. The wall was bearing down upon them, the water before it piling up as if driven before a hurricane. On the highest rampart a tiny black speck rode, clinging like a bat.

'Isimud,' said Nin Shubur, but her eyes searched the chaos of waves beneath him. They could all see the jagged-toothed heads now, repeated seven times fifty above the bore. Arms, shaped like scorpions, sprouted from the towers, each with its own full complement of black legs and claws. All ended in a single, massive, upcurved sting, threateningly arched. The stench of rotting fish carcasses and foul sea sludge billowed ahead of them.

'The *Uru* giants.'

'Nin Shubur,' begged Inanna. 'Can't you stop them?'

The *sukkal*'s eyes narrowed. 'Your case is just. Not wise, perhaps, but just. I will try.'

'Isimud,' screamed Inanna. 'Call off your *Uru* giants!'

The *sukkal* smiled and spoke three words. The fifty monsters growled and sank their hideous necks into the water, revealing the swimming bodies behind. Fifty red horny backs, vaster than hippopotami, each sprouting seven heads, that drooped now to rest half-submerged in the falling water. From each, seven pairs of yellow-green eyes watched balefully. Seven beaks snapped passing fish or driftwood in casual, hungry incisions. Fifty multiples of seven tossed their scorpion limbs threateningly.

'Give up the *me*, Inanna! Let us take your boat to Eridu. You can go free.'

'Never! Enki swore his oath.'

But the *Uru* knew no oaths or honour, did not respect Inanna. Next moment, they attacked without questioning.

Hundreds of jagged jaws surrounded the ship of An. Yellow teeth splintered the gunwale as they dragged it out from the quay. The mooring rope snapped like flax. One of the men screamed and beat a scaly head with his paddle. At once seven maws flew open. Seven slimy black throats gaped. Reek of decay poured over the ship. The paddle was snatched, chewed into pulp, gulped down.

In the moment of horror that followed, Nin Shubur raised her hand. A stream of chant, quiet, monotonous, unstopping as water falling, poured from her almost unmoving lips. Her eyes were fixed above the *Uru*'s multiple heads as though she did not see, did not want to see, would not see, those fearsome faces.

Perched high between two red horns, Isimud leaned down and began a sawing chant of his own. Their rhythms fought.

Inanna watched, fascinated, as the huge solidity of the hideous creatures seemed to thin, rock with the waves, grow slowly, slowly translucent, felt the grip that was tugging the boat into deeper water slacken, smelt the breeze sweeten the air. A thick, crimson turbulence in the canal, sinking, dissolving. A low bubbling murmur.

'*Nammu. Nammu. Nammu . . .*'

The huge belly of the waterway swallowed them down, leaving a vast swirl of dredged-up clay. Isimud fell floundering in the whirlpool, black garment spread like flightless wings around him. He struggled towards his fast approaching canoe, was hauled on board.

'Your *sukkal* has proved her strength,' he spat. 'But there are still five landing stages to pass. She will grow wearier than your oarsmen before I have finished.'

'He is right,' said Nin Shubur when he had gone. 'The burden of magic lies heavy on those who summon it.'

'Then Isimud too must grow tired, mustn't he? Paddle on, boatmen!'

'Isimud has Lord Enki behind him in Eridu. And Enki is Nammu's son. We are still in their element.'

'And I have no power to help you, you mean?'

'You won the *me* with your beauty and love, my lady. That is your strength.'

At Dulma the *lahama* dragons caught them.

They came flying over the surface of the water, glorious as the climbing sun. Scales of turquoise and jade, rimmed with gold scattered aureoles of light. Fire scorched from their mouths. Copper-tipped claws raked steam from the flood. Great wings that should have shadowed the desert let through a throbbing blood-red glare. It was as if the crouching guardians at the greatest temple on earth had sprung to sudden life, furious to avenge impiety. From far away, the light of their onrushing eyes was blinding. The watchers threw up their arms to shield themselves.

Inanna saw in her trembling crew the first signs of mutiny and defeat.

'Shall we unload the *me*, Lady Inanna?'

'Queen of the East, you are still strong. The waters of Nammu haven't touched your hand yet, have they? The waters of Enki haven't caught your feet. Quick! You can save us!'

Nin Shubur raised shrewd eyes in a white face. 'It is not you I am saving, my lady. You are not threatened. It is only the *me* he wants.'

Could she believe that? Watching the sweep of glittering wings towards her, the shining vengeance of the Deep?

'Do what you have to do, Servant of Uruk!'

Nin Shubur slowly lifted both hands, palm downwards, as though struggling against a great weight. In the pitiless light of midday, her skin seemed to glow, honey-gold. Soft words sang, sweeter than the crack of the *lahama* wings. Light flowed from her hands, gentler than the dragons' eyes, turning the surface of the river from turbid brown to clear honey.

The *lahama*'s skimming, sparkling legs caught in it, slowed, lifted with difficulty. Questioning dragonheads bent, probing. The water grew warm; steam spread towards the ship of An. Fire flickered, sizzled, as their hot jaws sucked. Like wasps in rotting fruit they swarmed and buzzed. Wings ceased to beat. Unnoticed in their greed, the rushing stream, still strong with the spate of storms, carried them downstream away from the quay of Dulma and Inanna's boat. They dwindled to a mat of iridescent, absorbed, crouched bodies.

Isimud, chanting vainly against Nin Shubur, floated with them. He shook his far-off fist.

Inanna laughed, shakily, with relief. 'We're winning! Nin Shubur, you're wonderful!'

But the wise woman was bent over, her head in her hands, trembling with exhaustion.

'The day is only half over, my lady. My strength is going. I will do all I can, but I may not be able to hold out until we reach the waters of Uruk.'

Inanna raised her hands to the sun. 'Utu! Where are you? Can't you protect us?'

'Trust in justice,' said Nin Shubur faintly. 'Lord Enki swore. Let that sustain us.'

The boatmen laboured on. Haze trembled over the marshes. Uruk must still lie far ahead. The overburdened canal flowed swiftly against them.

'The wind is rising. Listen!'

'I fear it is not the wind.'

'What then?'

With infinite weariness the Woman of the East turned her head. Her hands were over her ears, but she could not shut out the piercing shriek that was growing behind them, coming nearer, numbing their senses, chilling their hearts.

'The *Kugalgal* have come for us.'

Mouths. Huge, blue-white lips, swelling like blisters. Red tongues mottled with black. A glimpse of bottomless throats. Fat fish-cheeks puffed out with wind, between flood and sky. And an icy blast shot from them, flattening the water, pitting it with hail. Their screams were wilder than winds that bring the blizzards in the mountain ravines and block the passes with snow. Inanna's flesh turned blue. The boatmen's streaming hair blinded them. They struggled with their paddles but the boat was being whipped away from the bank, spun round, out of control. And all the time the shrieking shut out the cries of the captain, Nin Shubur's spells, Inanna's yelled entreaties.

Inanna saw Nin Shubur falter, watched rather than heard the words grow still on her lips. This time the shaman's raised hands fell. The *Kugalgal* screamed triumph. Isimud was borne cross-legged before them, like a black feather in a gale.

'Do something!' screamed Inanna, as the boat swirled helplessly.

Nin Shubur shrugged and took a silver pin from her dress. She sketched shaky sigils in the air. Stabbed once, twice, thrice, and seven times.

A hiss of escaping air, like a punctured goatskin bag which a swimmer has inflated to buoy himself up. The intolerable screeches dropped to a lower, more bearable note, grew less in volume, hushed away. The crew dragged the bows round into the current again, trembling with the relief of control restored.

Nothing. No sign of life. The river hushing past them. Only Isimud falling, falling from the sky.

'Will he be safe?' Inanna wondered.

But Enki's canoe was ready, as always, to rescue him.

'He will be angered now,' said Nin Shubur.

'I did not want to make a rift with Grandfather Enki. I thought we could be allies. He to plot and I to act, if I had his power. Won't he give up?'

'Will *you* never give up the *me*?'

Inanna's mouth set in an obstinate line, though she could barely keep it from trembling.

'I am greater than An now. I am greater than Enki. I must be greater than Enlil too.'

'As you say, my lady!'

Weary to exhaustion now, the boatmen hauled on their paddles through the swift-flowing tide. The fields were deserted. No faces peered from the reed huts they passed. The canal was empty of traffic. It was as though the rumour of terror had gone before them. The boat edged with painful slowness towards the still distant sluicegate into the Buranun. The sun glowed through the haze, dropped ever lower.

'Are we nearly there?'

'Do you see that mound ahead? That's Duashaga. The fifth quay, my lady,' the captain croaked. 'This is the last landing stage before we sight the waters of Uruk.'

'Will we make it, then?'

'Who knows, my lady? The men are paddling their hearts out for you.'

'I will reward them with anything they want: treasure, the joy of my hierodules, feasts, as much beer as they can drink.'

'They are doing this now for love of Uruk and its Lady. For pride in themselves and loyalty to you, pure Inanna.'

'Such men are heroes, Captain.'

A sweating silence fell over them as they hauled level with the silent hill of Duashaga.

'Nothing?' said Nin Shubur uneasily.

Inanna gripped the gunwale, peered astern.

'No. There's nothing following us.'

'Where has that sprung from?' the captain started. 'Look out ahead!' The foremost oarsmen snatched their paddles from the water, held them dripping aloft while they peered down. The boat checked, stopped, began to drift backwards, then was caught and held.

All the boatmen were grasping their paddles high now, staring over the side.

A net of fibres, like water weeds, surrounded the boat. White stalks, silky with golden down, growing, spreading, knotting, even as they looked. Tendrils touched the planking of the boat, began to climb.

Inanna shrank back. 'What is it? Nin Shubur, they're covering the ship! Stop them! Look, one is over the gunwale there. Get it away.'

Already the delicate probing frond was reaching out for her dress. She backed away, but other shoots were swarming over the farther side. The men were hacking at the strands that touched the oars. The fronds were brittle, but when they broke, another seven sprouted. The air was full of cursing and the shouts of horror and despair. The coils were round the mast, rising, thickening.

'He has sent the *Enunun*.'

'Never mind what they're called! Can't you stop them?' Inanna screamed. She bent and seized from the cargo of treasure, stowed so carefully in the low hold of the ship, a frightening blue mask with scarlet lips and staring eyes. She brandished it aloft, held it before her face, boomed through its hollow mouth. 'I hold the *me* of Terror!'

The weeds thickened unceasingly, growing like hair now, humping into the shapes of giant heads, white fibres slickening into ghastly pallid flesh that might soon be faces.

Nin Shubur shook her head slowly. 'It's no good, my lady. You hold the arts of civilisation, even that one. These are creatures from Nammu's Deep, more primitive than you can realise. They do not recognise our laws, despise such conventions.'

'Then what?' Inanna froze, feeling chill, fibrous hands close round her ankles.

'I . . . do not know . . . I will . . . try . . .' Unutterable tiredness clogged Nin Shubur's speech. Her hands would hardly lift. She closed her eyes. For long, frightening moments Inanna thought her *sukkal* had lost consciousness. Then, barely audible, Nin Shubur started to sing.

Astonishingly, a lullaby. A simple, maternal tune. Sweet nonsense words that banish nightmare, lighten shadows, rock the basket, surround the child with love.

> Ua-aua.
> Come, Sleep,
> Lay your hand on his restless eyes,
> Let not his babbling tongue
> Keep him from slumber.
> I will make sweet little cheeses for you . . .

And with each innocent phrase, the creepers flowered in a beauty of white and gold, turned pale and brown, their petals fell, the stems grew sere and withered, crumpled, fell apart. The wind blew the light, lifeless scraps away.

Inanna raised her head at last, when she was sure that the Boat of the Sky was finally cleansed. She was breathing deeply, still sick and faint with the aftermath of shock. She could not forget the sense of violation.

She found herself looking over the side into one of Isimud's faces.

'Go! And tell my grandfather he has lost again! He will always lose to me.'

The two-faced *sukkal* shook his head. He looked saddened rather than angry. 'No, Inanna. You must give up the *me*. They are not meant for you.'

'Is Enki so wise he is fit Guardian of them? When he gave them away just for drinking too much beer?'

'Not just for that. For love of you . . . and your fertile body. My Lord of the Waters is changeable. He can give life and take life.'

'But I will be stronger than he is. I will not be changed!'

'Change you will. And anyone who touches your power you will change.'

'Lord Enlil?'

'That is not for me to say, my lady.'

'Go back, Isimud. You cannot get the *me* from me.'

'Not without hurting you, perhaps. There remains the final gate into the Buranun River, Inanna. It may not be my magic that stops you there.'

'I will pass it.'

'I warn you, Inanna. Do not believe that you can conquer everybody.'

# Chapter Seventy-one

'Isimud is no fool,' said Nin Shubur, watching Enki's *sukkal* float away once more empty-handed. 'Do not believe that everyone who opposes you is your enemy.'

'An wanted me to get the *me* for Uruk.'

'Old Lords may be as rash as young ones.'

The water level dropped without warning. The spate slowed and the canal settled between well-defined banks. On one side emerged the raised towpath, fringed with clumps of reeds and scattered palm groves. On the other, a wider chariot road shaded with trees. Beyond these levees the floodwater still lay spilled across the nearer countryside, taking the colours of the afternoon sky, the mud-brick houses, the crops and date palms. In the distance, far across the desert, they glimpsed a watery shimmer that was not a mirage.

'The Marshes of Uruk,' breathed Inanna. 'We shall soon be in our own waters.'

'If we pass this last gate safely,' said Nin Shubur.

'We will. We must . . . Look. What did I tell you? That's the entrance to the Buranun. The river will take us north into the Uruk Lagoon. With a south wind we can sail straight to the City of the Sky.'

'The sluicegate is shut, my lady. That is why the water is falling.'

'The watchmen have seen us. They'll have it open in moments when they see it's the ship of An. Once we sail through that gate we'll be out in friendly waters.'

'There's more than usual of the canal guard on gate duty. Armed too, all of them. Has there been trouble here too while we've been gone?'

The canal entrance was narrow. Old wooden gates set in weathered sockets separated the wide, copper-coloured sweep of the Buranun from the Eridu Canal. They stood closed now, though the flood was still high in the river. Only insistent spurts of water forced their way through the gaps in the planking. The canal lay darkly shadowed under these sluicegates. The watchmen's faces were dark too, watching the Boat of the Sky approach.

'Halt. Who comes from Eridu?'

'Look at the symbols on their breastplates! There are guards here from Ur and Larsa and Uruk, as well as Eridu. What has been happening?' cried Inanna's *sukkal*, clambering her way quickly to the prow and throwing back her headcloth to reveal her shaman-painted face. 'Ah . . . I might have guessed. So you have got here before us, Isimud.'

The tall servant of Enki bowed, but gestured silently to the captain of the canal guard.

'Do your duty, man.' Other watchmen nudged him. 'Tell them.'

Inanna was leaning forward, hands gripping the thwart, an expression of outrage darkening her face.

'Skipper,' said the captain of the guard to the boat's helmsman. 'I am commanded to say that the Iturungal Gate will not open for you unless I know what cargo you carry.'

'I carry the Queen of Uruk, you fool! Open up the gate. For the sake of the Mother of all Anunnaki. We've been pursued by every monster of the ocean from Eridu to here. Let us through!'

A watchman from Uruk stepped up beside the Eridu captain.

'We know you've got the *me*. You're paddling a black ship with a black reputation now. A curse is on you. You are not permitted to bring that unlucky cargo into Uruk's waters. Unload it right there and you can enter.'

Inanna rose, struggling to assert dignity in the swaying craft.

'Don't you know whom you are speaking to? I am Inanna, Queen of the E-Anna!'

'Majesty!' The men of her own city and her father's bowed. They seemed scared at their own daring, yet dully obstinate with the deeper preoccupation of self-interest.

'With great respect, we have our orders, Lady Inanna,' said the captain of the guard. 'From Dumuzi Ama-Ushumgalanna, *en* of Kullab.'

'Dumuzi! Is my husband here, then?'

'He is ruling from Kullab in your absence, my Queen. He sent us with orders, if we valued our future, to keep the *me* out of Uruk's waters.'

'You're lying! How can I believe such nonsense? Lord Dumuzi would never give that order.' Inanna stepped forward to whisper to Nin Shubur. 'Dumuzi begged me to get the *me* for the E-Anna. It was his idea first. His and An's.'

'Perhaps, when he saw the price, he was no longer willing to pay it. You still were.'

The young Lady's hand closed on her *sukkal*'s shoulder. 'I think you have been paying the price today for all of us.'

'It is not over yet.'

'I am Dumuzi's Queen, Uruk's Queen. Open the gate!' Inanna shouted.

'You cannot pass with the *me*,' declared the Eridu watchmen.

The men of Ur and Uruk looked at each other, began to mutter, to push their leaders forward.

'Lord Dumuzi's got the right of it, my Lady. Begging your pardon, your Ladyship, but you won't know what's been happening while you've been gone,' the lieutenant of the Uruk guard burst out. 'A curse hit us just before dawn. We've had murderous storms such as I've never seen in my lifetime. Floods rushing down from the hills and carrying everything away. Earthquakes. And then horrible salt bores riding all the way up from the sea to hit the other. There's bitter water right across the plain! We've had canal banks torn down, whole families drowned, crops gone, land spoiled. And worse than that. When the waters did start to drop, well . . . some of the things they left behind, I wouldn't like to describe.'

The men sucked in their breath and shook their heads. They were crowded together to give each other courage, not looking directly at her.

'But I have triumphed!' cried Inanna. 'The *Enkum* and the *Lahama* and the *Kugalgal* are all defeated. The *Uru* giants have gone toppling back to Enki. The *Enunun* are overthrown. I have the *me*!'

Her own river watchmen seemed unable to recognise her authority. In the sullen deafness of fear they drew their swords, levelled their spears, held ready their maces, swung their nets.

The crew of the Boat of the Sky were unarmed, except for their paddles and a billhook or two for slashing weeds.

'You would raise weapons against your *Lady*?' hissed Inanna.

'Your Majesty, take pity on your people. Listen to Lord Dumuzi. We daren't let you in . . . Unload the *me*. Please! And we'll open up the Iturungal Gate before you can clap your hands.'

Nin Shubur raised a single finger once and pointed. Words trailed from her tired lips. The sun was beginning to redden the river. The canal lay in shadow, still, brooding. Isimud stretched out his own hand, almost carelessly, across the path of Nin Shubur's spell. He snapped his fingers.

The Eridu watchmen had been momentarily scared by this new magic. They looked from Nin Shubur to Isimud. Then they laughed, as though a threat had been lifted from them. Stolid, human, Inanna's river guard, too, serving their own safety, stood their ground. They fondled their weapons, grinned at each other. They kept their eyes carefully averted from the swelling fury of Inanna.

'Open that gate! In the name of the Stars of Heaven! Or you will all die slowly regretting it. If the *sag-ursag* were here—'

'Unload her, boys.'

Hands seized the boat. The crew struck out with their paddles. At once maces splintered the slender poles. Swords hacked at unarmoured flesh. The Uruk lieutenant leaped into the boat, was about to lay hands on the heaped-up *me*.

'Stop!'

Nin Shubur was in front of him, defending the hold, defying him to strike her shaman's person. Under his nose she snatched up the Crown, the Sceptre, the Colourful Garment, dragged clear the Throne. She pushed Inanna into it, hung her with jewels, threw round her the Priestess's Robe, set in her hand the Measuring Rod and Line.

'Open your eyes, you traitors! This is *Inanna*! Behold your Lady, High Priestess of Uruk, Queen, Star of Lovers. Honour her!'

Inanna shone, more brilliant than the sunset on the water. Out of the pale heavens in the west her own planet leaped into life. Across the wide river, hymns were rising to the Light of Evening.

'*You see?*'

The fearful men lifted their eyes and seemed to take in Inanna truly for the first time.

'Pure Inanna!'

'Hail, Sacred Flame!'

'Great Lady of the Thundering Storm!'

'First Daughter of the Moon!'

Dazzled by her beauty, cowed by her majesty, stricken with remorse now, the frightened guard fell on their faces.

'Pity us! Spare us, Lady!'

'Forgive your cowardly soldiers, Radiant Inanna!'

'It was only my Lord Dumuzi's orders, after the horrors struck . . . Let them through, you fool!'

'Stop them, Eridu!'

But even Enki's men had scrambled to their feet and backed away, overwhelmed by the new glory of Inanna. Not a blow was struck now. The Uruk captain ran to the sluicegate, tried to raise it single-handed. The rest of the watchmen rushed to help him. Isimud, unregarded, dropped his arm.

The strong, brown waters surged through the opened sluice, lifted the Boat of the Sky. The watchmen seized the ropes the sailors tossed to them and hauled the ship forward.

Inanna's bloodstained crew lifted their broken paddles, poled from the narrow, dangerous canal into the flaming waterway of the Buranun.

They were in Inanna's land.

They crept along the shore, where the current drove less swiftly.

Presently a huge lake, its channels tossing between islets of reeds, opened in front of them. In the distance, like a cloud of An's own heaven, rose the fabulous mountain of Uruk, accretion of sand and clay soaring now beyond the lemon-gold spread of marsh, lofty with the temples of Kullab, and topped with the Sky House itself, the E-Anna. The crew hoisted the sail to a soft south wind and the ship spread wings like a swan returning to the nest.

'It's beautiful,' sighed Inanna. 'Do you see that little white chamber on the highest terrace of all, catching the last of the sun?'

'Send word ahead,' Nin Shubur advised the captain. 'Signal that everything is well. May it remain so! Have them lift all the sluicegates to the city before we reach the Nigulla Gate. Let the high water flood the approaches to Uruk. The Boat of the Sky is deep-laden. It must sail fast to the innermost quay. Let everyone, old men and old women, all the young folk and children, come down to the waterside and meet their Lady rejoicing.'

They hailed a swift canoe, and it shot ahead with the message. Inanna sailed past islands and riverside fields enthroned in the ship of An like a heavenly vision dressed in the royal and immortal regalia she had won.

As her ship passed, terrors were forgotten, tragedy overlooked. Village people ran to the towpath, gasped in awe, tossed gifts of food and flowers as she passed.

At the outskirts of the city the Gate of Joy, the Nigulla, stood wide open to the ship. It was crowded with children, clinging, cheering. It was night when they entered their own deep-water canal. The quays were lined with priests singing. The human high priestess spoke blessings over the water. All Uruk's young warriors were crowded on the steps, brilliant with parade armour and weapons in the rising light of the moon. Gilgamesh was at their head. There was blood on his raised sword.

'Light the fires!' he cried. 'You have returned, Mighty Inanna! A sacrifice of bulls greets your victory!'

'Loyal hero,' she laughed, kissing her hand to him. Her face darkened as her eyes went past him to the steps above.

Fire lit the night. The bellowing of oxen and bleating of sheep was drowned in waves of hymns. Drums and tambourines beat in frenzy. *Tigi* harps sang. The people raised high the praise of Inanna. The Boat of the Sky docked at the White Quay.

'Where is Dumuzi? Where is my husband?' But there was no answer.

Inanna took Gilgamesh's hand and stepped ashore. Already Nin Shubur was giving orders in a small, tired voice for the reverent disembarking of the *me*. One after the other, the servants of the E-Anna carried the emblems in their baskets ashore, laid them on the wide Lapis Lazuli Quay, at the foot of the steps that led up to Inanna's house.

The waters lapped only with the rocking of the boat. No winds howled here. No magic threatened. Inanna, glorious with her spoils, lifted her head and drew a deep breath.

'People of Uruk, my household of Kullab. I, your Star Woman of Evening and Morning, have brought you the *me*!'

One by one the symbols were lifted out of their baskets and held up before the wondering crowd.

'I bring you Immortal Guardianship. I bring you Priesthood. I bring the Crown of the Steppe . . .' Over and over, her strong, young voice announced the gifts of Enki to his granddaughter. Priestesses carried them up the great staircase into the precinct.

A hundred gifts, a hundred arts of civilisation. The order and skills of the whole inhabited world. Yet there seemed to be still more at her feet.

'She has brought you the Dress Laid on the Ground. She has brought you the Allure of Women. She has brought you Seduction. She has brought you the Perfect Carrying-out of all the *Me*. She has brought you *tigi* and *lilis* drum harps, *ub*, *mesi* and *ala* lyres, tambourines. Be merry with her, people of Uruk!'

Inanna whirled, as the mocking, masculine voice ended with a clap of hands.

'Isimud?'

But it was not the two-faced *sukkal*. In the half-light behind her, shifting with the dapple of reflected firelight on water, was a smaller, bent figure. The dark, lined face of her grandfather Enki.

'*You!* Here?'

Cold fear now. Not the terror of monsters that brought high courage rising to counter it. Not the magic of Isimud that Nin Shubur's wisdom could always outwit. For all her pride of youth, she knew she could not fight Enki and win. Her throw had been made, back there in the Abzu, in a fog of beer and sexual attraction.

'What's a pretty girl like you doing out of bed in the moonlight?' he chuckled. 'Go up. My son should be waiting.'

'The *me* . . .?'

'I swore, didn't I? In the name of my power, in the name of the holy Abzu. They're yours, girl. Enjoy them! May Uruk prosper. May Eridu be her ally. Have the lot!' His voice cracked. He tottered, then staggered away into thicker shadow.

'*Grandfather!*'

The crowd barred her way. Pressing forward for the beer and meat, they seemed oblivious of their Lady now.

Enki's voice echoed back to her with a yelp of laughter. 'Enjoy them! Enjoy my powers, you and Dumuzi!'

# Chapter Seventy-two

Suddenly the steps were clear again, the atmosphere expectant. Gilgamesh was standing beside her, holding out his hand. Now the ceremony was over, Inanna released her fury on the nearest culprit.

'How could you do it? How dare you order your men to keep their queen out of her own territory? The punishment for treason is death!'

She saw a flame of anger in his face to match her own.

'I? Keep *you* out? Do you think I would have given the victory to Eridu without a fight? Do you suppose I didn't beg to raise an army to come to your rescue?'

She must believe his overwhelming indignation.

'Why . . . then?'

Gilgamesh's cheeks darkened with reflected shame. 'Dumuzi . . . He announced himself *en* in your absence. When the plagues struck, he called the elders into council. I beat the *pukku* to rouse the young men, but they wouldn't listen to us. He was afraid. We all believed the Deep had risen against us. I would have fought them. But Dumuzi said . . . only you could do battle with the Below. Until it was fought and won, it was unsafe to let the *me* enter Uruk's territory.'

'And you accepted that?'

A stiffly formal bow. 'I am a mortal, Lady, as my family so often reminds me. What should I know of the Above and the Below?'

Her hand soft on his arm now, her smile forgiving. 'I do not doubt your courage, Gilgamesh. You shall fight greater battles for me yet. Escort me to the E-Anna.'

Above the steps a chariot waited for her, pulled by pure white asses. She rode the steep processional way through cheering crowds to the summit of the hill. Inside the E-Anna gate she let Gilgamesh hand her down and then dismissed him.

'I have to speak with Dumuzi Ama-Ushumgalanna alone.'

So steady her voice, so brave her bearing. She must not let Gilgamesh see how deep the wound his brother had dealt her.

'Inanna, Lady, forgive me. Dumuzi was never brave. You women go mad about him, but not for his courage. He's not like me. I know he's an Anunnaki, and I'm not. But . . . this was the boy you married. He hasn't changed.'

'Thank you, *Lugal* Gilgamesh. You may leave us now.'

How large and empty these halls seemed today. Frightened servants fluttered like moths in the shadows.

'Where is Lord Dumuzi?'

They shook their heads.

A little feast at a dining table. Two cups, two platters, overturned. Dumuzi's chambers neat and empty. Where, then?

'Nin Shubur?'

Behind her, the *sukkal* was deathly white, swaying on the point of collapse. Her eyes were glazed beyond comprehension.

'Oh, my friend! How could I be so selfish, so ungrateful? I'm sorry! Get her to bed at once, some of you!'

Lonelier than ever now, with no one to lead her. On to her own quarters. Silent as the grave.

'Amanamtagga!'

No tall, long-legged, head slave, gliding with a dancer's swiftness to hear her wishes. Instead, the round-faced Nawirtum, pale and trembling.

'Where is my Lord?'

'I . . . he . . . he has fled the city, my Lady, with a few of the servants. When he heard you were coming, he . . . he was very afraid.'

'Where has he gone?'

'I cannot say, my Lady.'

She must hold back her impatient hand from striking this girl. The door to her innermost chamber was open. The Lion Bed was rumpled. Inanna caught a sob. Those bright blue sheets, those playful lions. Had Dumuzi come here, while she and Nin Shubur had been battling against monsters, to cower in her bed, hiding his face in her pillow, trembling for himself and her? She picked up a golden hair and snatched it to her cheek. The sheets smelt of his body. She threw herself face down on them.

'Inanna?'

Only a whisper. A huddled figure in the corner, behind the door.

'Geshtinanna! Oh, where *is* he? How could he do this to me? Me, Inanna!'

'Forgive him, sister. He is not like you. He's not a warrior, not a hero. He's gentle, loving. Good with lambs and puppies. You love him, Inanna. You know you love him. Don't be angry. Don't spoil it all.'

'*Where is he?*'

'On our farm. At the edge of the Arali marshes. He is terrified of you now.'

'And so he should be! He took my power. He tried to keep me out of my own country.'

'He loves you, Inanna. He loves you.'

'He turned my people against me!'

It was not a full Assembly. An was not there. It was more a family council, grave-faced, concerned, that gathered to hear Inanna's accusation. Enlil, taking the central seat, with Nin Lil beside him, Nanna-Suen, with that white, mobile face so hard to read, Nin Gal, full of grief for her daughter, for the betrayal of love, Utu and his young wife Aia, Nanshe and Haia, always at hand in matters of justice, Nidaba, her golden stylus poised, and Nin Mah, a great, brooding presence like a vast hen. Enki, unsurprisingly, was not there.

'So Enki's son has played you false,' Enlil mused aloud. 'But what did you expect, daughter? His father was always the Trickster.'

Anger flamed in Inanna's face, like a stormy sunset against her black clothes.

'Enki did not win the game. He allowed himself fairly beaten. He came and gave me his blessing in the end.'

'And does that blessing include Dumuzi? Or do you wish to see your bridegroom put to death for treason?' The cool voice of Nanna probed the difficult places of her heart.

The blood left her face. Dumuzi, dead? 'The Anunnaki can't die, can they?'

'He could be banished. Is that what you want?'

Inanna wrung her hands. 'He has betrayed me! He took my power. He tried to shut me out of my city.'

'Do you still love him?' asked Nin Gal.

'Yes . . . No. I . . . want him! Is that love?'

'What is it, Nin Lil? Speak if you wish.' Enlil lifted his

hand for the assembled family to hear his wife.

Nin Lil's voice was softer than her husband's, like a breath of sweet, ripening corn and the scent of meadow flowers. She was less often heard, not always noticed, living in the shadow of Enlil's enormous presence. Her eyes held Inanna's with a slightly apologetic smile.

'Granddaughter. That name may be more important than you realise. Let me tell you an old story. It is not without pain.' Her hand rested lightly on her husband's shoulder, as though she must apologise to him too. 'Long, long ago, when scarcely any of you were born, I was a young maiden here in Nippur. I went, rashly, alone to bathe in the canal at daybreak. Your grandfather Enlil saw me and wanted me. For me, it was too soon. I was small and frightened. He forced me.' Her hand tightened as emotion darkened Enlil's face. 'My father took my complaint to the highest Council of the Anunnaki. They banished Enlil. Yes, exiled the greatest Lord of all. How could the city prosper if its ruler was unclean? We Anunnaki must be beyond reproach.'

'So! Nor must Dumuzi escape justice!' Inanna cried out.

Now it was Nin Lil who held up her hand for silence. Her smile deepened, willing Inanna to understand.

'Hear me out. I did a thing which many since have found hard to comprehend. I followed Enlil. Through three dark gateways down into Kur. I was carrying his child, Nanna. There are many who have reviled me for what I did. They say it could not have been a rape, that I had led Enlil on, that my "No" did not mean "No".

'I followed your grandfather to the Netherworld because I still loved him. His seed was in me. I knew his weakness and, yes, his cruelty now. Who better? But I saw beyond them all his possibilities, for strength well-directed, for generosity. My rape was real, but I forgave it. I stood alongside him. I shared his punishment; I took it on myself to turn my defeat into a victory.

'I did not realise how hard that punishment would be. I was made to bear three other children, and lost them to the Netherworld. But I came out on the eastern side, with Enlil beside me. I paid the price that brought him back to the Earth. And with him I brought my gift to all of you, Nanna-Suen, to whom you owe your birth, Inanna.

'How could the Anunnaki exist without Enlil? If we had lost him, I believe the child would have died in my womb. By my forgiveness, I bought eternity for all of us. That is how much I love him.'

Her head bent now, blushing at her own daring. Enlil's own face was turned away in remembered shame. His hand went up to enfold hers. So small Nin Lil was, delicate-boned. Yet, standing protectively over the seated Lord she seemed the stronger of the two.

The others turned their eyes to Inanna, and watched the struggle in the younger woman's face.

'You give me a hard lesson, Grandmother.'

'I offer you the steep steps to happiness. And for the rest of us, life, love and gratitude.'

'And is it my decision? Can I accept or banish him, as I will?'

'You cannot change him, my love,' said Nin Gal softly. 'If you accept him, it must be his whole self, good and ill.'

The daughter of multifarious Enki.

The male Anunnaki stood silent, sharing something of Enlil's mortification, touched by the smear on Dumuzi's fame. The women watched her, wise, loving, understanding, knowing in their hearts how she must weigh the balance of pain.

Inanna looked slowly around the older generations. Enlil and Nin Lil managing the land from such a fragile, dangerous beginning. Nin Gal and Nanna joyfully faithful in their love across the years. Then to the younger ones. A blush in her own face now, catching sight of Utu. The Righteous Judge, in spite of . . .

She bit her lip, made her impetuous decision.

'I will forgive him. I will take him back.'

And Nin Gal ran across the room to embrace her daughter. 'Oh, my love. I'm so glad. So glad for you.'

The room was full of faces beaming with relief, loud with the Anunnaki's laughter.

# Chapter Seventy-three

Her women dressed her royally, wound a gold-cloth turban round her head and fastened it with a mother-of-pearl flower. Necklaces of tiny kids, lambs, doves tinkled over her collarbones. Her eyes, bright now with eagerness, were outlined with kohl. The scratches and tear-shadows with which she had announced her grief to the world were masked with white face powder. More slaves knelt round her, reddening finger- and toenails. Beneath her rich robes the most private parts of her body had already been prepared to allure. At last they set the sceptre of the Lady of Heaven in her hand, and Inanna rose.

'How do I look? What will he feel when he sees me?'

'If I were Dumuzi, I would fall flat on my face with fear,' said Nin Shubur tartly. 'You look lovely. And the lovelier you are, the more dangerous, in my opinion.'

'You're not jealous, Nin Shubur?'

A strange expression of pain and love crossed the *sukkal*'s face. 'No, my lady. No, and yes. I was summoned from my own land and directed to serve you once. Now, I would not have it any other way. I am not jealous of what you have and I have not. But I am jealous of those who take your love, and hurt you.'

Inanna looked at her for a long, shrewd while. Then she embraced the other woman and kissed her hard.

'My *sukkal*. My spell-knowing queen. You, of all the Above and Below, are faithful to me. Don't think I can't see that. I won't forget.'

Then she burst into glorious laughter, threw her arms wide and danced Nin Shubur round like a young lovestruck girl, for all the pomp and finery of her dress. 'But I love him! I am the Lady of Lovers, and *I love Dumuzi*. I shall have him back, Nin Shubur. I can take him to bed.'

'You can do anything you want, my lady. As you so often tell us.'

\* \* \*

Inanna was afraid that Dumuzi might flee from his farmhouse when he heard that she had left her barge on the last canal, at the boundary of Enkimdu's land and Dumuzi's, and was riding on a white donkey towards the house. Then her heart gave a leap of pure joy. He was running to meet her! His black dog Urgi was bounding beside him. Hurrying behind, their faces taut with anxiety, came his friend, Kuli the Herdsman, and Geshtinanna.

Flowers were scarce in high summer, but Dumuzi had plaited rosettes for Inanna of golden reed stems, studded them at the last moment with fragile poppies. She saw that first, that his hands were full of gold and scarlet, before she saw at last the longed-for features of his face.

Dumuzi fell down on his knees in the dust before her, held up his garlands.

'My Queen! Oh, my loveliest Star! You've come back brighter than ever. Sky and Earth bless your name, night and morning.'

She took the glowing wreaths, hung them over her far less valuable regalia of precious stones and metals.

'*Lubi*. I accept your gifts . . . all you have for me. Their beauty is shorter lived than gold or carnelian, but their touch is warmer.'

Savouring her moment of majesty, her power to hurt voluntarily set aside, she extended her hands, empty now, very slowly towards the breathless Dumuzi. In her head was a chorus of bells and gongs, in her eyes a flock of wild birds rising from the marsh to greet the sun. Her heart was pierced by the light flashing on a million crystals of the desert.

He could not see or hear this. He only felt the touch of her strong, warm fingers over his. Dumuzi was weeping.

'I don't deserve you. I'll never be worthy of you. Only you must believe that I have learned my loss. I must have been mad! To have all that you are, all that you mean, the Queen of Love, and then to try and shut you out. Forgive me, Inanna! As you see, I'm as cowardly as a broken reed. Hold me up, Inanna. You're my strength, you're my courage. Don't leave me again.'

She lifted him, able to smile with the glow of virtuous reconciliation.

'My Lord. My beloved.'

Then in her turn she knelt before him, on the dusty path.

Her hands undid his girdle. The netted kilt fell to the ground leaving him naked and startled. There, in front of all her household and his, she kissed his phallus.

A wave of respect flattened the amazed witnesses like windbent grass. With his face hidden, Kuli the steppe-born Herdsman grinned appreciatively. Then the excitement became too much for Urgi. Dumuzi's sheepdog bounded between the couple, licking the tears that were running down Dumuzi's face.

Geshtinanna ran forward and hugged Inanna hard with delight, but quickly gave way to her brother's outstretched arms.

Nin Sun, Dumuzi's mother, was waiting on the threshold to welcome the entwined couple home, with Urgi still leaping around them.

Even the slaves whom Dumuzi had taken from Inanna's household, the clever Amanamtagga among them, were smiling at Dumuzi in relief and joy.

'Why did you do it?'

Dumuzi flinched in the doorway to the simple bedroom. He looked flushed and vulnerable, his richly-fringed kilt and scarf not quite straight, his eyes still scared.

'Inanna, you weren't there. You didn't see.'

'I was facing things a hundred times worse than you were! Have you any idea what I was fighting for Uruk? You tried to stop me reaching safety! And when I brought home my victory, you weren't there to meet me. The whole city was out to welcome me on the quay. Where were you?'

Her young husband held his head in his hands and shook it slowly, as if dazed. 'I heard the message. And I was even more afraid of what I'd done. But I couldn't believe you'd return. When the storm struck . . . When the Buranun rose up on itself and brought all the horrors of the Deep up from Eridu . . .'

'You cowered in my bed in the E-Anna and hid from it. While your wife was fighting with *Uru* giants!'

'I ordered the priests to make sacrifices. I beat my breast and lamented. I sent pleas for help to An and Enlil.'

Her eyes studied his unmarked face, found no trace of scratches, then roamed longingly over his tanned body, his curled and scented hair.

'So when you heard—'

'My love, when I knew you were really coming back with the *me*, I dared not let myself hope you'd forgive me. I saw how terribly I'd acted.'

'You dared to order the river watchmen to keep me out of Uruk! Me, Inanna! Your queen! Your bride!'

'Not *you*, never you, Inanna. You mustn't think that.' His hand reached out and caught her. He dropped on his knees. 'It was your cargo I dreaded. You have lived with the Lords of Sun and Sky and Moon. I'm Enki's son. I should have remembered. I know the power that can be woken in the Below better than you do. Yes. I fear them.'

'And you didn't come out to fight for me? Couldn't you at least have let Gilgamesh lead his army, if you were afraid?'

'Inanna, Inanna. What threatened us cannot be conquered by Gilgamesh's axe.' He was holding her close, stroking her thigh.

'I know. I owe my rescue to Nin Shubur's spells.'

'Can you imagine how I felt, knowing my bride, my radiant Star, might never come back to me? One month. One magic spring. Then, nothing.'

She felt herself weaken as the tender words flowed over her. The arms, stronger now, enfolded her. His shoulder was warm and hard to lay her head against. The faint, lingering smell of sheep and cows was reassuring. Censure faded. She relaxed her hold on will and courage, felt herself giving way.

'You should have stayed to watch me unload the *me*,' she pouted, more like a disappointed child now than a furious queen.

He was beginning to rock her, at first gently, soothingly, then with a growing urgency that aroused desire.

'Can't you understand? I was more afraid than ever. Afraid that I had done you wrong. Afraid that I had lost you, not to Enki's horrors this time, but to my own folly. Have I, Inanna?'

So young, so vulnerable his face. So humble his voice, broken, on the edge of tears. What could she do but lift her face to his, growing in delight with the rising knowledge of her own strength, her own courage, her own right, her own victory. Sweetly, magnanimously, she drew his lips up to hers, slowly and ceremoniously at first in forgiveness, then she let passion sweep them both.

It was a wonderful night. Not even the consummation of

their wedding exceeded it. They clung to each other, drank from each other, laughed and wept. At one point Inanna rode him exultantly and cried, 'I am the Great Lady of Ladies, am I not? I am the Leader of Lords! I have gathered all the *me* into my treasury. Now I can take what is left in the hands of the others. Earth, the Above, the Below shall all fear me!'

'Yes, Inanna,' he gasped. 'Yes. You're wonderful.'

At other times she lay curled in his arms crying like a baby with the release of tension, while he crooned, and caressed and comforted her.

With morning there was no bitterness, perhaps a sad, slow realisation.

Feeling Dumuzi wake, Inanna turned towards him, held his hand. Said simply, regretfully, 'I wish you had been there to meet me.'

'I thought you were bringing me death,' he grinned, sitting up and throwing off the sheet. 'But instead you have brought the treasures of life. Let's go home and enjoy them!'

They had the treasury of the E-Anna unlocked. They laughed and shouted like children as they saw all Enki's dazzling gifts heaped around them. Dumuzi tried on the Helmet of the Hero, the leather Apron of the Smith, the Eye-Paint of the Prostitute. Inanna screamed with laughter.

'Oh, it suits you! It suits you! Let me kiss you!'

She clutched his beautiful face to hers, first in merriment, then with redoubled passion.

She put on the Black Garment of Mourning, the sly-faced Mask of Slander, blew on the Lamentation Pipes. Dumuzi cowered away from her in mock terror.

Inanna went to the doorway, stood looking down over the city.

'Did you know that he was here that night? Your father Enki. Here in Uruk. Distance was nothing to him between the sea and the steppe.'

'Enki goes where he will. It is difficult to stop him.'

'Our Sumer is a land made fertile by the control of its waters. Now I channel its powers.'

Dumuzi came to stand behind her with his hands on her shoulders.

'Floods break out. Then we are in danger.'

She leaned against him, felt his hands enclose her breasts.

From below there were sudden cries of fear. The two straightened up, looked quickly around them. Then Dumuzi laughed.

'The humans have seen you, my love. In your black gown and evil mask. You have terrified them. Look, they are falling on their faces, begging you to spare them. Take it off, before we have priests intoning rites to lift your curse!'

But Inanna wriggled out of his clasp, stepped forward between the squared pillars of her temple portal, let the city see her, a dark commanding figure against the sunlit white.

'Let them look. Let them fear. Let them know I am Inanna the Terrible. Now watch.'

She tore the mask away from her lovely face, let the black cloth slip to reveal the white and gold, took up the *Ala* Harp, and began to play.

An almost audible sigh of relief and adoration breathed from the townspeople. They lifted hands to their queen, praised her, went on their way with lighter hearts.

'You see? I am Inanna the Loving. I am all things. I can do everything. I hold all power.'

'In Uruk, yes. Even in Eridu, now. But not everywhere. Not in Nippur.'

'And not yet in the Below.'

He laid an urgent finger on her lips. 'Hush! Don't say that, even in jest. It scares me that you still don't know what you should be afraid of.'

'I am Inanna. Lady of War and Love. I fear nothing.'

'You are very strong, my jewel, but not as strong as the Queen of Death.'

'Hold me. Hold me, Dumuzi. I will show you life!'

# Chapter Seventy-four

'The Queen is complete!'

The cry of the *lale*, Uruk's Priestess of Birth, rang out over the city in the twilight before dawn. The hot, heavy, dragging summer was past. The busy winter of rain, of seeding and growth, was upon Sumer.

The cry was taken up in every house of Kullab. The secular city, waking, heard it. The news was carried to Gilgamesh in the *lugal*'s palace. The first canoes poling along the canals carried the news.

'Inanna is whole! She has borne a boy!'

'Praise be to Nin Tu, Great Mother and Midwife!'

'Dumuzi has a son!'

It had been an easy birth, in the manner of the female Anunnaki. Not for her the pain, the fear, the struggle of human women. The little dark-haired boy had come slipping into the world as though his path was greased with butter. There had been one swift pang of parting, that made Inanna gasp, and then he was there between her legs. Yet there was blood on him when Inanna's mother lifted him to show her.

She felt a stab of jealousy as Nin Gal seemed to claim her grandchild, as the midwives Dududuh and Nin Imma cut the cord that bound him to her, washed away the emblems of her mucus and blood. Clean and civilised now, in the gold-embroidered wrapper of a prince, the boy was laid in her hungry arms. She held him at once to her left breast that seemed already to want to spout milk like a fountain.

Soon the little mouth that hardly knew how to suck fell slack. Lids like half-moons closed over still misty eyes.

'From the Anunnaki of Air and Moon and Star, what shall you be, little prince?' Inanna crooned. 'You must be great, because you are Inanna's son. Yet not too great, because your mother is and will always remain the Lion Inanna.'

Dumuzi was standing in the doorway. He looked as radiant as she was.

'Lady, I see you've kept my seed well. That looks like a perfect lamb you've given me. Would you like something in return?'

He was holding his hands behind his back. He brought them out now. Brown, Shepherd's hands that opened and rained gently, into the folds of softest wool between Inanna and her baby, tiny, perfect gifts. A gold pin, headed with Inanna's own rosette, in the heart of which a star of green quartz flashed. A ring for her right hand, gold, thick, heavy, richly wrought. A ring for her left hand, silver, slender, delicate filigree. A cylinder seal of dark blue lapis lazuli, carefully chosen so that it gleamed almost black. She picked it up and held it to the growing light from the doorway. Noiselessly Amanamtagga brought a lamp and held it for her. The seal was carved with the image of a Lady in an eight-horned tiara lifting her goblet to a Lord from whose sides two rivers spouted. Behind the Lord stood a two-faced man, behind the Lady a watchful woman. Inanna raised her head with a proud, glowing smile. Motherhood had caught her in a moment of perfection, like a rose fully opened at last.

'There should be presents for everyone. See that the midwives get jewels and the slaves new dresses, all of them. And a bracelet of coral and silver for Amanamtagga . . . I thought I had brought all the gifts I could ever wish for from Eridu. But here in Uruk you have given me the best of all. Hold him. He's yours.'

She held up the tiny, sleeping child whose breath came sweetly through parted lips. Dududuh and Nin Imma guided him into his father's arms. Dumuzi took him reverently. Inanna saw with a small pang of jealousy and surprise that the Shepherd was no stranger to little newborn things. His arms were sure, enfolding, more experienced by far than her own. His head bent over the boy with a fond, fatuous smile.

'Our little lamb. My son. My Shara.'

Again that stab of indignation. He had usurped her right. He had not consulted her. He had assumed the privilege to choose. But the name was spoken. It could not be called back.

'What do you suppose he will become?'

'Let him live to serve you. As the rest of us do.'

The jewels twinkled in her lap, small pretty toys. He held the little, living boy.

'He's like his father.' Nin Gal, sensing Inanna's discontent, reached out to take him. Dumuzi did not seem to notice her.

'Give him back to me.'

Dumuzi lifted his head, half startled, from the absorption of fatherhood. Nin Gal took Shara from him, and the midwives in their turn laid him, proudly, back in his mother's arms. This, their officious bearing seemed to say, was our doing too.

Inanna leaned back against her pillows, beginning to feel at last the languor of a task achieved. Now that she had the baby in her arms again she could feel more generous towards Dumuzi.

'Are you well, my lord?'

'As full of joy as any shepherd who sees the first increase of his flock and marvels that his pet ewe grows more lovable with every day.'

'And how does the ram feel while his ewe is heavy with lamb?'

'Impatient!'

Her turn to smile, tantalisingly. 'It must have been a hot and stifling summer for you . . . without rain! But the days of childbirth and months of weaning must be respected too.'

A shadow of shocked disappointment crossed his face. 'But you are an Anunnaki! You are not some weak human woman, to keep a child at your breast two years and your husband out of your bed. Human men can take other wives then . . .'

He stopped. The realisation was in both their faces of what he had just said. Dududuh and Nin Imma exchanged glances, as if wondering if it would be more intrusive to stay or to make a conspicuous escape. Nin Gal gestured to them to keep still. The slaves flattened like shadows against the wall or crouched motionless, habituated to make their personalities disappear, to be no more than furniture. Only Amanamtagga watched, alert, her intelligent eyes unable to efface her sense of her own separate being.

'No Lord who has the Lady of the Evening and Morning Star for bride could want another,' Dumuzi added hurriedly. 'Yet, sweetheart, to be married to the Queen of Love, and not enjoy you . . .'

She held out a white, inviting hand towards his brown one. He came hesitantly forward and joined his to hers. She took his fingers tightly, even painfully. The baby slept on in the crook of her other arm. Inanna laughed softly.

'I brought the *me* of all the ways of love and pleasure. Should I deny my honey-man?'

'Then you will let me . . . ?'

She shook her head. She was enjoying her new status. Mother of the Young Prince. It carried with it a strength, a new inviolability. A young girl needs a sweetheart. A bride needs her bridegroom. But the mother holds in her arms at that moment all that she wants.

'No, but you can go with my blessing to the Tavern of the Temple. Ask for the barmaid there, Il-ummiya. She brews good beer, but men say she offers juices that are headier still. I like her. I knew her here, in the E-Anna, when we were both learning the arts of the hierodule. You have my permission to act the rites of love with her alone, at the appearing of my Star, in my precinct, with my name on your lips when your body meets hers.'

'Lady Inanna is generous!' Stiff-lipped, as though by licensing his manhood in this circumscribed way she had taken something of his manhood away as well.

She smiled wickedly. 'Il-ummiya is my friend. She will report to me everything you do. Everything!'

Merry laughter from the midwives. Dumuzi's face reddened.

'No surrogate of yours can ever take the place of the wellspring of love itself, Lady Inanna.'

She softened to the wounding of his fragile dignity, held up her arms. Nin Gal rescued the child.

Inanna crooned, 'My date cluster, the crook of my sheepfold. Thank you. You've given me a perfect son. You've let me become a full woman in all her glory. I feel like the sun at midday, the moon at its full.'

'You must come back to me soon,' he breathed into her fragrant hair. 'There can be no one but you. Give the child to a wet-nurse. Don't suckle him yourself. Let me back into your bed. Be the bride again for me, Inanna, Inanna!'

'We have for ever, you and I. Over and over we shall remake our wedding night. Kings and priestesses shall act it out in our honour in brick-built palaces. Couples in reed huts and mud hovels, sweethearts meeting in the marsh or in starlit gardens shall cry out the names of Dumuzi and Inanna when they join.'

But when her second son was born, she brought him forth in unexpected pain. Inanna lamented. She called him Lulal,

Water Scorpion. Through the tears that streaked her face she said to Dumuzi, 'Listen to him! He is like the Serpent of the Rivers. His cry is the cry of the Flood!'

She stood before Enlil, two small sons at her side. These boys were growing with almost human swiftness. Not for Inanna the Anunnaki's ages-long span of motherhood. She was meant to be always attended by adoring young men.

'Shara and Lulal. I present my sons to you, Father An, Father Enlil, Mother Nin Mah, Father Enki. I petition you to pronounce for each of them a destiny and a city.'

An sat on his President's throne, almost as insubstantial these days as a cloud. Inanna felt little sense of his presence. When she looked at him the pale-blue eyes were gazing towards her, but the distance now seemed as great as though he were still in Angal Above. No sign of the intimacy, the laughter, the shared pleasures they had enjoyed in the E-Anna.

Nin Mah she had never lived close to. That mountainous Woman. Great Mother of the Anunnaki. The Birth-Giver. Just for the short, sacred space of childbirth she had come nearer to the aura of this Lady. But it had not lasted long. She herself was the Lion Inanna, Lady of War, Lady of Lovemaking. She must be free again, the Young Lady again, always the victory still to be won, the consummation still to be made. She should be untrammelled by motherhood.

Enki watched her with a knowing smile. He made her uneasy. She could never be sure if he had forgiven her for the theft of the *me*. No, it had not been a theft! An impetuous gift. She held on to that hope. That a rash, drunken, sexually excited Enki would acknowledge the audacity in his granddaughter he could see nowhere else, and admire her for it. She flashed a sidelong smile at him now, brilliant with laughter and understanding. He winked back.

It was Enlil whose presence dominated the Council. No humour there. Even when she was a child he had seen the possibility for rebellion and challenge in her. It irked her that even now, though she was one of the seven Igigi, she must speak meekly and reverently before him.

He towered above the rest. Grey, not with age but gravity, chill even in the heat of summer. Both Anunnaki and humans tensed at the first encounter, then found themselves responding with gratitude.

'They are beautiful children. I remember when my own first son, your father Nanna, lit up the world with the Moon at his birth. They must give you great joy.'

Such courtesy, such condescension. So much left unsaid. She bit her lip to stifle an angry protest. Nanna had not been Enlil's first son. Meslamtaea, Ninazu, Ennugi. All buried in the Netherworld. Their memory buried too, the memory of Enlil's sin, the Anunnaki's punishment. By closing over that doorway into the Below, he made certain his pre-eminence in the Great Above. Father Nanna still made a yearly voyage of tribute to Enlil's Nippur, his *nisag* boat laden with the first fruits of Ur, to bring back his father's blessing.

Nanna was the Moon Lord and Utu the Sun Lord. Enlil was reminding Inanna that a wheel was turning in the heavens. Her sons could never outshine his.

Well, he misunderstood her. She was Inanna, Lady of the First and Last Star. She did not need or want husband or children to surpass her.

'Bring them to me.'

His mouth breathed on Shara and then on Lulal. His Word spoke, that had established the world.

'Shara, I give to you the city of Umma and its house, Sigkurshagga. Be to your mother and all of your family gentle in peace, bold in war.'

The boy held Inanna's hand, turned his eager face up to hers. It reminded her of the day Dumuzi had dressed up in the Eye-Paint of the Prostitute. A face of sensitive, feminine beauty. She loved the touch of his hands, had already taught him how to dress her hair, stroke her body with soft oil, paint her fingernails. He was a clever lad, Geshtinanna's favourite nephew, who went with his aunt to the sheep farm on the steppe and sat at her feet, chin cupped in hands, memorising the poems that flowed from her lips as she worked her loom.

He answered in a high, clear voice. 'Thank you, Great-grandfather. I shall try to be good to you and all my family.'

'Lulal, come here.'

The second boy was darker and more frowning. A warmer welcome for him in Lagash, city of warlike Ninurta.

'Lulal. For you, Badtibira, city between the rivers, and its house E-Mushkalamma. Grow up to guide its elders well. Uphold its kings. Be the war leader who stands at Inanna's side. Let not our land be left unguarded.'

'I shall serve you with both weapons and hymns, Great-grandfather Enlil.'

She let go of their hands, felt years, ages fall away from her as their tutors took them from her. She kissed them merrily, called for a feast to celebrate their going. But she was glad, glad that she need no longer be a mother. She could renew her youth. She could become a girl again. The courtly rites between husband and wife could give way to the wild impetuousness of courtship again. She would be like Nin Gal running to a moonlight tryst with Nanna in the reed beds. She would be Nin Lil dancing naked on the banks of the canal. She would be – a daring thought, this – a reincarnation of that far-off memory of Princess Ereshkigal darting through the sky, still virgin, before Kur saw and captured her.

Back in Uruk, when the feasting was over, she ran light-hearted from her bedroom through the night-dark palace, brushing away the shuffling attendance of sleepy servants.

Without Nin Shubur to precede her she danced without announcement into Dumuzi's own princely bedchamber.

'Sweetheart! My Lion Bed is cold without you. Come to my lair, or let me curl up in yours.'

Silence. No startled grunt. No warmth of sleeping body.

She snatched a lamp and held it over the empty bed.

'Inanna!' He was standing in the doorway tousled, as if he had just staggered from sleep. Gorgeously naked.

'Where have you been?'

'Celebrating with Gilgamesh.'

'Like that?'

'I'd had enough. Came home.' His voice was furred with drink.

'I know how Gilgamesh spends his nights.'

'In honour of you, Inanna. That's what the humans say when they do it. Inanna and Dumuzi! Come on. Let's show them how it should really be done!'

Her need was too urgent for argument. She let herself fall with him on to the bed.

# Chapter Seventy-five

'I must visit An,' said Inanna, 'and see that things are well with him in Angal.'

'Kiss me,' said Dumuzi, when she was ready to leave. 'I hate it when you leave me. Come back to me soon.'

'No more treachery,' Inanna chided him. 'No more river watchmen ordered to keep me out of my own land.'

His face flushed under the deep brown tan. 'You have not forgiven me, have you? You can trust me. I shall be as faithful to you as your own head slave. You can command me to do anything you like.'

She pressed herself around him, let her tongue explore his mouth. 'Then I command you, Lord Dumuzi: love me, now.'

In all her state she ascended the shining stairs to Angal Above, walked in the night fields where Nanna herded the stars like cattle. She found her great-grandfather An in the far reaches of his realm, and sat at his feet like a little girl again, telling him the joys and tribulations of her marriage. She was away longer than she intended.

Dumuzi wandered restlessly in the vast, empty halls of the E-Anna, through Inanna's White Palace, visited his own house in Kullab by the crooked apple tree. His eyes roved reflectively over the women of the household Inanna had left behind, appraised the graceful limbs and sympathetic eyes of Amanamtagga. A shudder of familiar desire ran through him, firing, then chilling him even in the thundery heat. He averted his eyes firmly. The image stayed.

Huge drops of rain spattered the dust outside. He picked up a letter tablet impressed with Geshtinanna's seal.

*'Come home. Inanna's flocks are suffering for want of their shepherd.'*

But Inanna's people were here, in Uruk, in Kullab. He was the visible presence of the Great Anunnaki in Inanna's absence. He was the Shepherd-King. Should he leave it to the human warleader, Gilgamesh?

Yet, when the evenings grew long and he was bored, he would go down into the city and drink with human companions and throw dice. After a while, Gilgamesh would leave the game and beat his *pukku* in the street outside any house that had a desirable daughter.

The storm broke in the middle of the night. Hail scoured the courtyards. Thunder crashed so fiercely that clay tiles fell from the walls and smashed into rubble. Tributaries rose, swirling the muddy Buranun seawards. Canal banks broke. Mud, flood water forced their way through every breach, devastating the growing crops. When broken branches, uprooted trees, crumbling houses blocked the water's way, it piled itself up in orange waves and carved new courses through the fields. In Lagash, Ninurta and Ishkur roared with laughter, goading the Lion to battle with the Bull in the thick clouds that curtained the lower sky.

Far, far away, the high clear stars, among which Inanna stroked An's feet and listened to old tales of the love of Sky and Earth, before Enlil was born.

She returned down the Steps of the Sky to find a ruin not matched since the Flood that had swept humanity away and brought the uprooted *huluppu* tree floating past Uruk's walls. Old men and women were weeping for wasted lives and work. Temple choristers sang of the loss of life from which their high calling had saved them, and raised bitter lamentations for their families, washed away from the low-lying plain.

But worse had followed.

'What is this? What is this?' Inanna said to Nin Shubur as they set foot in Sumer. 'Why is there smoke like a shroud over my land?'

In the days after the suffocating deluge nothing had grown. Then, out of the sea of liquid mud, something emerged and spread. The *numun* plant.

A brown plaster of sediment covered the farmland. It had flattened and smothered all living things. Yet it was fertile, rich with the accumulation of mineral wealth from the mountains, with layers of rotted vegetation of the plain. Nourished by this moist placenta, the *numun* plant broke through everywhere. Soft green shoots, that groped their leafy way across the earth, lengthening with astonishing rapidity. They twined round fallen trees, swept up and over walls, knotted, multiplied. Where they rooted, nothing else could grow. The time of storms was past and the long, fierce days of sun hardened their curved thorns into daggers, made their stems brown and brittle. There came a day when a tiny trail of smoke climbed from a *numun* patch above a drained canal. Then little petals of flame, and all at once, conflagration.

The fire swept from patch to patch, running along the trailing fuses of briars, exploded in sparks and roaring incandescence. It engulfed the farms the flood had spared, threatened whole towns. The survivors, weak and hungry, battled frantically to make fire breaks. They tore at the *numun* plants with their bare hands. But the roots were deep and tenacious in the packed, dried clay. The proliferating tangles defeated every effort to bundle them up. Fire covered the land. When Inanna came hurrying home, the flames were at the base of Uruk's brickwork, threatening to crack the foundations apart.

When she saw the destruction of her land, the queen wailed and screamed. 'What is to be done, Nin Shubur? Do you have spells to stop this?'

'I cannot be over the whole country at once,' said Nin Shubur, spreading her fingers in a little wave-like motion, so that the flames fell back from the walls and smoked bitterly at its base.

The terrified people peered over the city rampart, afraid of the fire, and saw their Lady approaching. Sun flashed on Gilgamesh's helmet.

'Save Uruk, Inanna, if you can!' he croaked in a voice hoarse from coughing.

'Fight it!' she shouted at him. 'Are you a coward too?'

'Do you think we haven't tried? It's all we can do to keep it out of the city. This *numun* plant is an enemy no man can crush. When you chop one with an axe, seven shoots spring up to take its place, and what we cut off burns all the fiercer.'

'An!' called Inanna. 'An! Help us! Help the city you once loved. Send rain from heaven to douse the flames!'

But the sky was vast and distant now, no raincloud wandered across it.

'Enki! Make the rivers rise! For the love of Sumer, which you once blessed!'

The rivers lay low and still in the summer heat, their beds cracked.

Nin Shubur was hurrying here and there calming the flames. But smoke was blackening the air all across the plain. The soot thickened into a living presence. A dark Raven of Death flew down and perched on Inanna's shoulder.

Then out of the murk Dumuzi appeared, staggering, his arms covered with bloody scratches.

Inanna turned upon him, eyes blazing, hair black and flying.

'Again! I go away to Angal and I return to find my land devastated. Is this how you care for Sumer?'

His eyes filmed over with weariness. His tongue seemed clotted as he struggled to speak. 'I have . . . brought . . . from our sheep farm . . . these thongs of sinew . . . blessed . . . that will bind even a plant as vicious as this. Look.'

He bent and roped the smoking heaps that Nin Shubur was wrestling to tame. Regardless of burns and scratches he heaved them up in his arms, staggered with them to the hollow crater of a dried-up reservoir. The *numun* briars fought and struggled against seizure with a wicked life of their own, but the gut and muscle of a sacrificed lamb held out against them. The *numun* screamed in fury. He flung them in. Then back to the task. Each armful wounded him, but he moved steadily, doggedly, at his labour. Inanna watched, amazed, the Raven black-eyed on her shoulder. Soon Gilgamesh and the young men of the city gave a great cheer of hope.

'Open up the gate! Let's help the Shepherd!' And they were all running out into the countryside to accept his leadership. They worked through day and night to tame the fire-rouser, with no weapon but what Dumuzi's flock had provided. Rebel nations opposing Gilgamesh's warband had not inflicted such lacerating wounds on Sumer. But the sheep of the steppe had not given their lives in vain. Enkimdu and all his farmers came, working behind the fighting men, racing to hoe up the roots before they could shoot again. Dumuzi roped and dragged the smoking debris to the pit. They toiled for five days, for ten days, for a month before the land was cleared and safe. Even then Inanna set the Raven to watch over the burning pit and warn her if anything should escape.

When it was done, they were wearied and blackened, even

Inanna. In the hollows the hoes had left, the first food plants were beginning to show again. The craftsmen returned to the city and set to work.

'I feel fouled,' said Inanna. 'We had such plenty and we almost lost it all. We must hold lustration rites to cleanse the land.'

The fuller prepared her garments for her, clean as autumn snows. The potter made new cups and bowls, for the service of washing. The carpenter fashioned a spindle of fresh-cut wood and presented it to her. Dumuzi himself brought the fleeces of six-month lambs, white and unspotted, and laid them before her. She smiled at him lovingly, took his scarred hands, traced her lips up his arms, over all his wounds.

'Poor Dumuzi. You were more than loyal this time. I should not have left you so long. You were right. When we're together it is all joy and fruitfulness, but apart, there is only pain and death.'

'You don't blame me for what happened?'

'My lamb! My honey-bee!'

She laughed indulgently and took his head in her hands. He knelt before her and buried his face in the softness of her lap.

'Never leave me again. I have no wish to be a hero, even to please you. Let us be king and queen together, or shepherd and dairymaid, anything you like. Only let's be together, always.'

She stretched, feeling gloriously cleansed and revived after the ritual washing, the heady incense, the taste of wine and blood. She felt stronger than ever now, with another victory behind her, the oxen ploughing the fields, the new harvest seeded. Life was returning, renewing. She would always bring her people hope.

'There is one journey I have not taken. The hardest of all. I am mistress of the *me*. An has retired to Angal. Father Enki has admitted my superiority now. But there is still Enlil. The Anunnaki will never acknowledge me exalted above all the rest unless I do what he could not!'

'You can't challenge Enlil. The *me* are not enough. No power on Earth is greater than his Word.'

'No. I must defeat him in the place where his authority is only a name.'

'Inanna! No!'

'In the Netherworld the Lord of Air was powerless. In the country of the dead the Breath of Life was silenced. Only a woman could buy his way out of there, with the children of her womb. I shall go to the realm that makes Enlil's face pale yet when he hears of it. I have taken the powers of the Above from An, the *me* of the Earth from Enki. I must take the authority of the Below from Ereshkigal.'

Her eyes glittered with the desire of enormous dreams. Dumuzi's terrified face turned up to hers. His hands clung to her skirt like a boy to his mother's.

'Don't do it! Don't even think of it! No, Inanna. No, no! You will kill us all. If you destroy yourself, you destroy all Sumer. You will destroy me!'

Her gaze went past him, down the thronged hall of the E-Anna, and rested on the huge, resplendent figure of Gilgamesh at the head of his young warrior troop.

'Who knows? If I can defeat death, perhaps even Gilgamesh may live for ever.'

Her hand slid round Dumuzi's neck, nursed him to her breast, rocked him.

'Do not be frightened, little lamb. I am Inanna. I am the First and Last Light of the World. Daughter of the Moon that passes from the Great Above to the Great Below each month. Sister of the Sun who slips over the edge of the world each evening. Grandchild of Enki who went against Kur and almost won. I am greater than Enki. I shall succeed.'

# Chapter Seventy-six

Gilgamesh gripped Inanna's hand, lessening more than the physical distance between human and Anunnaki.

'Can you do it, Lion of Uruk? Can you take the power of life and death from Ereshkigal?'

'And if I did?' It was enjoyable to feel the power in her own smile, to know how much this man longed for her to succeed, how much he depended on her. 'Do you think I should make all mortals like the Anunnaki?'

'Only me. I am your brother!' Eyes burning with the desire for life. The thrill of adventure rose in her to meet his spirit. Gilgamesh excited her in a different way from Dumuzi.

'Yes, Gilgamesh.' She softened for him. 'If I succeed, you shall be the first to take immortal life from me.'

That leaping victory smile.

'You will succeed! You are the Lady of Life, the Lady of Lovemaking!'

'Am I not also the Lady of War and Death?'

'Only to your enemies.'

She wanted something more from him, wanted him to weep and protest and hold her in his arms as Dumuzi had done. To plead she must not go alone into such danger, must not risk her irreplaceable loveliness. To swear he could not live if he lost her.

Gilgamesh the warrior said nothing of this. Longing was naked in his face, not for her body, though she must be more desirable than any other woman, but for the hope she held out to him. The prize of immortality.

I want you, Gilgamesh, she murmured to herself. You must want me.

The hands round hers were strong, warm and hard, threatening the armour of her own courage. Eyes, brilliant with unexpected tears, flashed for him. If she wept now, would he fold her to that chest?

'If I carry off what we both want from the Netherworld, what will you offer me for it when I return?'

'Loyalty. My weapons.'

No, Gilgamesh. For the power over death you will give me more than that.

'You must tell me, Father, everything you know of Kur.'

A shudder passed over Nanna's face, as when the moon is held in the surface of a marsh lake and a night breeze shakes the surface. His eyes were shadows in his pale countenance. Light was always dim in the E-Kishnugal.

'I was the boy who escaped. I was allowed the freedom of the Above. I can walk in the day as well as in the night.'

'But you return Below. In the dark of the month we invoke Ereshkigal. That is the women's time. What do you see then?'

'I meet your uncles. Meslamtaea. The world calls him Nergal now, the Bringer of Death. Ninazu, the Medicine-Knower. Ennugi.'

'But Ereshkigal, the Dark Queen herself? Tell me about her.'

'I cannot help you. My mother sealed a bargain with her. I will not break it, even for you.'

The pale lids closed down over the night-dark eyes. Inanna gripped the edge of her stool in impatience.

'Does anyone see her? Except the Anunna who fled to her, the Lords of death?'

'And life, child. Ninazu heals as well. Ningishzida is at the root of all living trees thrusting upwards out of the pit.'

'Ereshkigal takes humans and never gives them back. Someone should reverse the balance, take power away from her.'

'Enki tried once, and failed. I forbid you to go, Inanna.'

Utu was out of doors, staring down at his own face in a fish-pond. He lifted his head when he heard her coming, but the warmth of his smile could not disguise his gravity.

'The order of the Above and the Below is fixed, Inanna. You cannot overturn it. No more can I. I do what I must, part of the bargain with Ereshkigal our family carries. I have to judge the shades of those who have gone to the Netherworld, while thieves and murderers have their chance to creep in the darkness here. Kur is a sad place, Inanna. A half-life for them. There are pitiless *galla* who whip the dead to work. Husbands have been torn from the arms of their wives, babies from their mothers' laps. The rich lose all their comforts. Do not go there. It is not for you.'

'I was born in Kurkisikil, at the very door of Kur.'

'That is the gate of the Rising Sun and the Morning Star. Do not walk its western road, Inanna. You are Queen of the Above. Let that be enough.'

'Ereshkigal will fear me more, because I am a woman. Nin Lil was braver than all of you. She brought Enlil out.'

'She paid a heavy price.'

'We understand the dark of the month, Nin Lil and I. You men cannot. Life flows out from us then, back to the Below. Your seed cannot come into us to make new life. Then, we are wise.'

'Then, the rituals are made to Ereshkigal. Be careful, Inanna. You would be entering her power.'

'I shall take that power. You tell me Kur is a source of life as well as the land of death. Well, I will bring you up riches, I will bring back abundance. What if I opened up all the gates of Kur?'

'That is more dangerous than you think.' His hand caught her wrist urgently. 'Those gates may shut behind you. Nammu's waters may overwhelm you with chaos.'

'You see? It is the women you fear. Even you, Utu.' She kissed him lightly on the forehead, and he snatched her to him, held her close for a long while, then let her go. He stood back, his face glowing, but stern.

'If it goes wrong, I cannot help you. I am the Lord of Justice. I keep the laws. If you insist on entering Kur like a rebel, like an invader, I would have no power to rescue you.'

Her chin went up. 'I know that, brother. I shall not ask you. Once I asked you to rescue my *huluppu* tree, to drive out the Imdugud and Kiskillilla and the Mushsagkal. You refused me then, too.'

'Inanna. Little sister. You cannot banish all darkness from the world. Gilgamesh drove those dark ones out for you. You got your throne and bed, he got his *pukku* and *mikku*. Have they made you both happy?'

She blushed. 'That's unkind. Yes. Of course I'm happy with Dumuzi. And I'm a great Lady on my throne in Sumer. All the people love me now. That bad time is over. And Gilgamesh is happy too. He's a hero, isn't he?'

He said to her softly, 'Do you never expect to hear, as I do, the cry "I-Utu!" appealing to me for justice against Gilgamesh?'

She tossed her head. 'I hear the shouts of the crowds when he has won another victory for Uruk and me. Now it is my turn to win a victory for Gilgamesh. For him, I will conquer death.'

She came sailing, starting a thrill of remembered danger, into the lagoon of the blue and silver Abzu, with her question.

'Death?' asked Enki, raising crooked eyebrows. 'What has an Anunnaki to fear from death or life, from darkness or light? We are changeable, but we are immortal, aren't we?'

'*You* feared the Below. You've told me horrific stories about your battle with Kur. How your *magur* boat barely escaped destruction before you were in sight of land. How you were cast up naked and battered on the sea coast of Sumer.'

A stormcloud darkened his face. 'You do not know what you are talking about! I wasn't afraid of death. I knew I wouldn't die. I feared . . . changing. I feared the thing I was too late to change.'

'Ereshkigal?'

After all the ages that had intervened, tears still sprang too readily to his bloodshot eyes.

'Child, child. You will never understand. You have never loved anyone as I loved Ereshkigal. As I love—'

'I love Dumuzi.'

He stared at her then gave a bark of rude laughter. 'You? You only know the meaning of lovemaking! You've never *loved* anyone but yourself.'

'That's not true! I forgave him for betraying me. I took him back.'

'Only because there was no one else you wanted. You needed your randy Shepherd. Lust, girl. Covetousness. Sex.'

'Lovemaking is my art! You gave it to me. I could have had thousands of other men!'

'Who? Poor old Enkimdu? Gilgamesh?'

By the flash of her eyes he saw that his second shot had gone home. 'So that's the way of it? The half-human hero? You'd fancy him above all the Anunnaki Lords? You're trying to buy immortality for *him*?'

'Dumuzi is my husband,' she said through furiously tight

423

lips. 'Dumuzi is my bridegroom. Dumuzi is my lover.'

'As things are, Dumuzi can't die. My son and Nin Sun's. But Gilgamesh had a human father. Stick to the one you've got, girl. Dance for us in the Above. Delight us all. Delight *me*, if you like. I've forgotten how long it was since I took a pretty granddaughter to bed. Don't meddle with what is Below.'

All doors were being closed behind her by the men she loved. There remained the most difficult journey. She must voyage to Nippur, as so many Anunnaki had gone to pay homage to Enlil. She would stay in her own palace, Baradorgarra, and dress in her royal regalia to visit the E-Kur. She must throw down her challenge to him with her own lips. But she must do it diplomatically, with seeming reverence. Until she returned from the Below, she was not yet greater than Enlil. He might find a way to prevent her. Yet he must understand what her expedition meant.

'You are pale,' said Nin Shubur. 'Are you well? Shall I go to the E-Kur and cancel your audience with Lord Enlil?'

'Not so pale as Enlil will be when he hears why I have come. Lead me to the E-Kur, Nin Shubur. Announce my name.'

She was carried in a sandalwood chair across the city. Even in Nippur, where through all ages the Daughters of An had thronged to meet in Council, people gasped at Inanna's radiant beauty. She seemed not to age. She was still the Young Lady. Marriage had brought a brilliance of joy to her face, a voluptuous roundness to her body, a confidence that she was cherished and adored. Dumuzi was utterly hers now, Uruk was great. When she stepped up into her window in the evening the people hailed her as the most gorgeous of harlots displaying her gifts in the tavern. She smiled indulgently alike on married couples safe in bed and on secret assignations. She appointed a time for labouring folk to rest. When her Star rose in the cool of the morning they blessed her for offering them life and a new day. She was generous to slave girls, protected women.

Enlil frowned as he digested her announcement. Nin Lil looked dreadfully worried.

'You mean to enter the Below?'

Inanna bowed her head meekly, took a deep breath for her rehearsed story. 'Each spring, over and over, the Bull of

Heaven is slain. They say he is Ereshkigal's mate. In the Sky, the Lion fights the Bull. And always the Lion wins. Out of the sight of all of us, in the Great Below, Ereshkigal mourns her slain Bull, Gugalanna. I have set my mind to descend to Kur, to mourn with my sister-queen.'

Enlil's head went up with a shrewd glance that saw more than she wished. 'You are the Lion, Inanna. What is carved around your bed, on the arms of your throne?'

Blood was hot in her cheeks. 'I am An's child, too. He brought me up in the E-Anna. He is called the Breed-Bull. He can let loose the Bull of Heaven. I am Mistress of the E-Anna. My Star shines on the threshold of night and day. I can bridge those two worlds, can't I?'

'The Bull and the Lion, as you say, are eternally opposed. What will happen if they no longer fight? Will the rainstorms cease, and this land wither and die?'

'I . . . do not know.'

'Or will you take their fight into the Netherworld? You overcame An and took his Sky House. Do you want to overcome Ereshkigal and take her Ganzir?'

Too near the truth. She must bow her head, look meek and helpless.

'Could I hope to succeed where Father Enki failed? Here on Earth I laugh with those who love. In the realm of the dead, let me weep with those who mourn.'

A long, studied silence. Nin Lil broke it.

'Inanna. You are my loveliest granddaughter, full of life. Listen to me. I have seen Ereshkigal. I have felt her terrible arms around me. She has my children. Do not go.'

'Grandmother, what if I were to set them free?'

The words were out. She could not catch them back.

A sigh of breath expelled from Enlil. 'I thought so. You *are* ambitious still. Well, let the Dark teach you what the Light has not. Yes, Inanna, Great Queen of the E-Anna, Mistress of all the *Me*. Go to the Great Below, if you have set your heart on it. Enter Kur. Attend the funeral rites of Gugalanna. And plead to any other Anunnaki you think can help you that yours may not be that corpse on the bier.'

'I cannot die!'

'They say my sons hold the *me* of Death. I say Death holds my sons.'

'I am a new generation!'

\* \* \*

She would not say farewell to An, too frail and distant now to help her. He had passed on to her his own lost ambitions. He, more than anyone, would understand.

Ki fondled Inanna's hair, under her almost blind eyes, Mother of all the Anunnaki, except for Enki and Ereshkigal.

'Life, birth, creation, hope. It is all here on Earth. Why must you leave it, dearie?'

'Because there is a place without life, without hope, where your creation is swallowed up by destruction. Because I can hear the Below calling to me, Great Mother.'

# Chapter Seventy-seven

'You do not look as if you were going to a funeral,' observed Nin Shubur.

Inanna stood in front of the *giguna* in all her glory. Against the background of dark trees whose roots were set in the high stairhead terrace, she shone like a star.

On her head was the *Shugurra*, the Crown of the Steppe. Beneath it she had black curls of hair bewitchingly arranged. Her eyes looked huge and alluring with the cosmetic 'Let Him Come'. Small lapis lazuli beads circled her throat like new-fledged bluebirds. Over her proud breasts fell the heavier ropes of *numug* egg stones. She had called for the *pala* robe of royalty, many-pleated, many-tiered. The rich folds of it draped both shoulders. A magnificent ring of tooled gold clasped her wrist. Over her fast-beating heart, on its star-silver chain, was bound the dazzling breast ornament 'Come, Man, Come'. The precious metal was still clouded with Dumuzi's passionate kiss.

'Give me the Rod.'

The Sign of the Ruler, the lapis lazuli measuring-rod and line. It was the *en*'s task to build the country up, to set foundations deep, to lay the corners square, to make the walls sure. To create, to make secure.

With an impetuous movement she hugged her *sukkal*, though not so warmly as to disturb her finery. 'I wish you could come all the way with me, Nin Shubur. I wish you could walk in front of me, down into the dark Ganzir and announce my name to Ereshkigal's *sukkal*. It will seem lonely without you.'

Nin Shubur's own arms tightened for a moment round her mistress. Then she stepped respectfully back. 'I wish so too, child. You are going against my advice, beyond my seeing. I at least am wise enough to know the limitations of my power. I should be an ant under Ereshkigal's heel. My spells would vanish like dust before Nergal's curse. You believe you have the strength to overturn their laws. Well, show me, make me believe . . . No, my lady, I will not weep today. I have already shed all the tears I have, and to no good. I may weep longer for you in the future.'

'Do not talk of mourning. Shout of victory, celebration. I am Inanna, Lady of Life. Why should I fear Ereshkigal's power?'

'Because you are also half in love with Death, my lady. You have conquered everything else, made everyone love you. You want to seduce even Death to be your lover.'

Inanna looked at her *sukkal* doubtfully, not wholly sure what she meant.

'Let us start now,' said Inanna, finding it suddenly an effort to speak bravely. 'Let us begin the journey to the Gates of the Netherworld. You can come with me that far.'

'As far as my small power runs.'

Three steps towards the stairhead.

'*Inanna!*'

This was what she had most feared. Dumuzi lurching, dishevelled, half-drunk with beer and grief.

'Don't leave me, Inanna! Don't go!'

Dressed in filthy rags that left him almost naked. His body scratched and smeared with ash. Eyes red with weeping, cheeks red with drinking. Bald patches on his head where he had torn out his hair.

She drew herself up, tall, royal, commanding. She must not run and cradle him in her arms, as if he had been Shara, as if he had been Lulal. No! Do not remember that parting from her sons.

'Dumuzi Ama-Ushumgalanna. King of Uruk. I am leaving you the care of my city. Of all my houses, in Kullab, Badtibira, Zabalam, in Adab and Nippur, Kish and Akkad. I am trusting to you the treasures of the *me*. Only these signs of my authority I shall take to the Netherworld. Act like a priest. Rule like a Shepherd. We have said our goodbyes. Do not disgrace me . . . *Do not forget me.*'

As though cloth tore from cloth, before those loved, brown hands could reach out and hold her, she ripped herself away from the Sky House, swept down the steps from the *giguna*, across the lowest courts, on down into the hushed and nervous city. She left Dumuzi weeping.

Even the protective chants of her own priestesses on the steps seemed subdued.

The royal barge was waiting at the White Quay, draped splendidly in purple and gold. Her loyal boatmen stood with their paddles raised in solemn salute. When she and Nin Shubur had seated themselves under the awning, the captain called out once and the blades struck gems from the water. The men were quiet at first, poling through silent crowds that lined the banks. They seemed not to know what songs it would be appropriate to sing. Then, as they forged upstream, out between the open fields, the bow-oar raised the chant.

> The heron's winging to the reed bed,
> The oxen turning to their stall.

The others took up the rhythm.

> The alewife sets the tankards brimming,
> The labourer wipes the sweat away.
> Up to the window of the tavern,
> Inanna steps in all her glory.
> Hail to the Star of Evening,
> Who lights the time for play and love.

An old familiar song, Inanna, the Evening Star. Why should it make her shudder with foreboding that they sang it now in the early morning, when the moorhen's chicks were scattering over the ripples after their mother, and the little boys were setting out in their canoes to gather reeds for cattle fodder, when farming folk were trudging to work with hoes over their shoulders? Why did the flattering words lodge in the pit of her belly like the foretaste of a funeral banquet?

'Strange,' Inanna mused, 'that we must climb to reach the Netherworld.'

Sumer was flat and sandy, mud, where the water mixed with it, desert where it did not. Only the Two Rivers, with all their tributaries, canals, marshes and lagoons, made of it a fertile paradise. In all its eye-aching flatness, no stone, no rock, no hill, except where the layered clay bricks of centuries had built up, one upon the crumbling other, to make a city mound. No place for cave mouths here.

They left Inanna's royal barge, as once Ninurta had left his battle fleet, to journey upwards into the foothills of the Hursag.

'It is beautiful, this Earth I am leaving,' said Inanna, looking about her in wonder.

Pine forests made a dark rest for the eyes after the brilliant summer heat of the plain. Sheep grazed on level grass beside rushing streams in low-cliffed valleys. The air was blessed with the scent of rosemary, tarragon, wild lavender.

The mountains grew higher, biting away more of the blue sky where lammergeyers soared. The gorge grew taller, stonier, narrowing to shut out the sun. Where spray darkened the rocks it did not dry.

The river tumbled more steeply, leaping huge boulders that seemed poised for another fall, as if they had been left behind in the rush of a winter flood. Inanna turned to look back, and all her escort with her. Dizzyingly far below, as if already in a different world, lay a sector of sunlit plain. Its summer patchwork of gold and green faded into a misty violet, lost all definition long before the far-stretched limit of the horizon. The sky throbbed with heat.

Here, poised like the lammergeyer chicks in their rocky nest, they felt the air still hot, but the breeze came fresh and heady, the colours struck the eye vividly in the patches between shadows. The sound of water, though only streamlets among the stones now, seemed loud, insistent between echoing cliffs.

'As though all life had been concentrated by a magician into a single jewel that you could hold in the hollow of your hand,' observed Nin Shubur, catching her breath.

The *sag-ursag* were forced to crowd more closely around Inanna here. Some strode ahead finding the upward way, others massed behind her, while some young men leaped like goats across the boulders on either side. Gilgamesh had wanted to lead a detachment of his own elite warrior troop to guard her but Inanna had chosen the cult soldiers of her temple.

'Their training is more suited to the kind of warfare I am going to. And where I am descending, no one can venture but I alone. No one can protect me but my own courage.'

'Do not go alone, Inanna. Let me come with you.'

And her heart had leaped with a thrill of triumph to see the fear naked in Gilgamesh's eyes. Fear for her. Fear and desire now.

'You cannot enter the Netherworld and leave again, because you are human.'

'I am half an Anunnaki! Yes, I fear the Netherworld because I am mortal. You, you are my Lady. But there are Anunnaki held in the Netherworld too. Even Ereshkigal herself, in the beginning. Come back safely, Inanna. Come back with life for me!'

She had held his face and kissed him, with a little laugh of pleasure. She knew by the trembling closeness of his muscled body how much she moved him, how much he wanted her, how much he longed to crush her in his arms, both hurt and protect her. One day, she thought ... Perhaps ... If Dumuzi ever fails me again ... It made her feel rich and satisfied to know that she could still have Gilgamesh. But Gilgamesh was mortal. His life was short.

They came quite suddenly over the lip of a steeper fall into a little circular meadow. All round it was a wall of rock. Not high. The bluish, snow-streaked mountains were still far above them. This meadow was foamy with seeding grassheads, flecked with many bright, late flowers. The rock wall was dark, purplish-sable. As their eyes narrowed from the sunlit circle they saw that some of the shadows in this wall were deeper, totally black, did not give off even a subdued gleam of light.

'Caves,' said the *sag-ursag* captain, grasping his feathered spear, newly alert and watchful. 'Careful. They may not all be empty, my Lady.'

Over the faces of the guards behind him ran ripples of readiness, for a lion, a leopard, for more fearsome dwellers that only magic and ritual might contain.

Tall clefts of darkness. Low arches of stone. Mouths of the mountain.

Nin Shubur, the spell-knowing shaman-queen, watched Inanna carefully, her body tense now. Inanna, Queen of lowland Uruk, Princess of high Aratta, stood in the sunshine she was about to leave. Her face was rosy with climbing, and she panted from her voluptuous lips, making her seem at once like an eager little girl and a woman in the grip of lovemaking. The waves of blue-black hair were damp upon her forehead, the kohl a little smudged. But the *Shugurra* crown still towered majestically as she held her head high. Her jewels blazed. The lapis measuring-rod and line trembled with her hurried breathing, not with any sense of fear. It quivered like a blue, mottled snake holding its head up, ready, if need be, to strike. The precious breastplate flashed in the sun, both an invitation and a challenge.

'You look very lovely,' said Nin Shubur, simply. 'Very queenly. Very brave.'

Some of the colour left Inanna's face.

'Nin Shubur, you know what you have to do. I am trusting my life to you. In all the Above, no one but you has been so faithful to me. You have been my wise woman counselling me. You have been my warrior woman fighting monsters at my side. Be my watchward now. If I do not return in three days, you must wail for me like a mother searching for her lost child. Set up a lament for me in the ruins like a jackal howling. Hammer the drum for me in all the assembly places of the Anunnaki. Claw at your eyes, your mouth, your legs, your belly. Dress in the rags of a beggar. March round their houses till they let you in. Beseech the great Lords to help me.'

'What use is the counsel of a wise woman if you will not listen to it? Who do you think can help you once you have passed that gate?'

'Go first to the E-Kur. Enlil is the most powerful. Surely his Word of Life will reach me.'

'Enlil fears Kur more than you do, my lady. He has reason.'

'Then go to Nanna. My father knows this western road better than I do.'

'Your father remembers how narrow a path led him out of the Netherworld into the Above. How hardly won. How nearly he was trapped there like his brothers. It is Ereshkigal's power that draws him back still.'

'Then petition Enki! Surely the Water Man will find some way to penetrate the depths.'

'You robbed him of the *me*.'

That small shock of realisation stilled Inanna. Then she tossed her head, so that the gorgeous crown quivered in the sunlight.

'No matter! Why should I talk of not returning? I am a warrior too. I am more crafty than Enki. I am the greatest of all the Anunnaki!'

'That is how I shall remember you, my Lady, my love.'

A locking of eyes.

'Nin Shubur!' Inanna moved swiftly to embrace her. A timeless moment. Then she let her go.

There were avenues of stones in the grass, confusingly laid.

'Which one?'

Nin Shubur did not answer, still looked at her hard.

A wave of deeper colour passed quickly over Inanna's face. Her gaze grew brilliant. Then she tightened her grasp on the measuring rod more firmly, and stood very still.

Without a sign or order from their captain, the *sag-ursag* guards assumed the same rigidity. They stood to attention, eyes fixed before them. No chant breathed from their lips. But their minds, too, trained to smooth the path of their Lady, went out to help hers.

Inanna stood, the Queen of the Above, in a court of flowers. She was like a woman who listens. The circling vultures wheeled silently. Even the river was hushed, lost in the summer grass. Then Inanna began to walk steadily through the stones towards the mountain wall. The gorgeous skirt of her royal robe brushed the petals from all the wild flowers she passed. They tumbled into the dry, gold grass, leaving only brittle seedheads.

When she entered the black shadow at the foot of the wall it could not dim her. She seemed, if anything, to shine even brighter. The watchers, still motionless, their faces intent on her going, found themselves blinking.

She did not hesitate now, did not turn her face back for a last look at all she was leaving. As though her ear were tuned to a voice that was calling her, she began to clamber up the litter of stones, over grass, to the lip of one of the caves. It was not the largest, by no means the tallest, an almost circular hole. As though she might be a girl-baby climbing back into the womb-way of her Mother.

Only a pale blur now, the gold and jewels muted to the white of a moth's wing, but standing upright, defiant under the first arch of that unguessable tunnel. They heard her voice strong, clear, ringing with life.

'Gatekeeper of E-Galkurzagin, Lustrous Door of the Mountain, open up for me!'

Her thunderous knocking startled them.

'Neti! Doorkeeper of Kur! Open this lock!'

And then a smaller, girlish plea.

'I, I have come alone. Let me in!'

# Chapter Seventy-eight

A deep cold voice echoed from behind the door with a dismal slowness. 'Who comes to the gate of Kur?'

A hard darkness in front of her, felt rather than seen. Inanna nursed her bruised knuckles. Impossible to see how high the great door towered, what wood, what metal bindings, what symbols guarded it. She felt her voice ragged in her throat from that first brave shout.

She must hold on to queenship, Ladyship, standing alone and unescorted.

'I am Inanna, the Queen of the Above, Bringer of Life, from the Place of Sunrise.'

She had not expected hollow laughter.

'If you are indeed Inanna, Queen of the Above, Bringer of Life, from the Place where the Sun Rises, what are you doing here? This is the gate of the Road to the West, from which no mortal traveller comes back.'

'I am not a mortal. I have come to weep with my sister-queen, with Ereshkigal. Even now she is mourning for her slain Bull, Gugalanna. I should like to grieve with her; I would comfort her. Let another beaker be set at the funeral feast. Pour beer for me.'

The door quivered a little. A sense of pinpoint eyes staring out from lower than her own face. Rodent-sharp features, imagined as much as glimpsed. Inanna tensed her fists, willing herself not to flinch back.

'Wait there!' said Neti. A rude command, with none of the smooth obsequiousness of the court officials in Sumer. 'I must ask my Queen. I am sure she will be most interested to get your message.'

The door was bolted in her face. The gatekeeper's steps flapped away in the gloom beyond.

Was this how Enlil had felt? Great Enlil, who had separated Earth from Sky, himself banished to the

Netherworld where breath is stopped. But even the guardians of Kur had recognised his authority. The keeper of the Nergal Gate, the man of the Devouring River, the ferryman. All had helped Enlil to trick Nin Lil, to lie with her in their disguise. In their name, he had laid his hand on her private parts, sworn fealty to her unborn son, to Nanna.

*And I am Nanna's daughter, Enlil's granddaughter.*

Would the creatures of the Underworld recognise Inanna's own authority?

Far, far away out of earshot, Neti entered the blue-black Ganzir of Ereshkigal.

'My Queen, you have a visitor. A maid as tall as the starry heavens, as shapely and buxom as the Earth. She stands as strong as the foundations of a city wall. She is not a mortal. She has not come to you weeping and wailing like the newly-dead. Though she says she has come as a mourner at Gugalanna's funeral, she is dressed as if for a coronation. On her head is the *Shugurra*, across her forehead her hair has been arranged in curls like a hierodule. Round her neck are small lapis lazuli Beads. Over her heart hangs a double strand of *numug* Stones. She is wrapped about with the royal *pala* Robe and her eyes are painted with Harlot's Invitation. On her chest shines the breast ornament 'Come, Man, Come'. The Golden Ring is on her wrist, the Measuring Rod is in her hand. She carries the seven *me* of Ladyship, Priesthood, Queenship. These are the *me* she took from your brother Enki.'

A sound of grinding teeth. The chair in which Ereshkigal crouched creaked under her grip. For a long time the doorkeeper waited for her answer, and around her throne seven Anunna of the Below listened. Wild hair hid the Dark Queen's face.

Then Ereshkigal struck the slack flesh of her thigh with a resounding thwack. The voice that had once sung across the Sky filled the tunnels of the Netherworld with bitter directions.

'Shut the seven gates of Kur, Chief Doorkeeper. Close them in her face. Then open them, one at a time, just the merest crack. As she slips through each one, this is what you must do . . .'

The challenge snaked into a whisper.

'Oh, very willingly, Lady of Wisdom. You shall have her enter as you want.'

Inanna heard him coming back from far away, heard the doors boom shut, the bolts rasp home, footsteps nearing, and then another closure. The outermost gate was already locked against her.

Ereshkigal was saying 'No' to her. Death to Life.

Behind her, so very close behind, were sunlight, flowers, swelling seeds, friends.

The bolts of the gate to the E-Kurgalanna, the Lustrous Hall of the Mountain, began to jar, to scrape. The black door shuddered like a thing in pain, jerked reluctantly apart.

The gap was narrow, the darkness beyond impenetrable. But the word was not the expected 'No'.

'Well, come on, come on! Do you really want to enter Kur?'

No, she did not want to take this step, to go where there was no light, no hope, only lost love.

'*You look very lovely. Very queenly. Very brave.*'

With Nin Shubur's words to strengthen her, she drew herself up tall, proud, powerful in vitality and beauty. Inanna stepped through the Gate of the West, on the road to Ereshkigal's Ganzir.

Hands seized her at once. Bodies she could not see pressed around her, jostled her.

'Keep back!'

She clutched her Robe about her, held up the Rod. She was besieged by a babble of chatter she could not understand. She felt a draught of cold air across her hair. The weight of the *Shugurra* was snatched from her head.

She struggled to make her voice fearsome and not fretful.

'What is this? What is this? What have you done? I am Inanna, Queen of the Above, come from the Place where the Sun Rises. Give me back my Crown of the Steppe, I command you!'

The chattering stilled to little panting squeaks. The bodies stayed close around her. One voice, cold, slow, spoke over their heads.

'Be quiet, Inanna! The laws of the Netherworld are set. This is not your realm. It is not for you to question its laws once you have entered.'

Her heart showed her her grandfather drunk over his

supper table, his bare head lying in a pool of beer. It was his Crown she had taken and now lost.

And yet the darkness was not as intense as she had thought. A faint, silvery radiance made a growing sense of what was all around her. Walls hewn from bare rock, yet darkly polished as if dipped in glaze. Lines etched in gold upon them, scenes too dense and distant to comprehend. Worse scenes moving around her. Saucer eyes catching the little light, black open nostrils, big mouths that grinned. These demons were little more than half her height, so that they snuffled round her breasts, her buttocks, her belly, too close.

There was only one thing to do, to march on, if it were possible, with as regal an air as if she still wore her Crown. Within the royal Robe her flesh shrank from the twittering mob that paid no respect to her dignity. To press on through them was like wading through a fouled canal.

Next moment her heart beat suddenly higher, for as she began the long descent into the unseen, the light moved with her. And now she knew, as she had never known in the Above, that she carried the Light. For all the hymns that praised her, for all her ambition, she had not truly understood what she was doing here. She was Inanna, she was bringing light and life to the Netherworld. It was already happening.

Yet even her own glow tricked her eyesight. Here was the second gate. She had almost walked into it, so dark, so dull, so massive. Only the copper hinges gave back a dim starshine.

Suddenly, unnervingly, she found she was alone. The demons with the saucer eyes had vanished. Neti had gone. Trembling just a little she raised her hand and knocked imperiously.

'It is I, Inanna, on my way to the Ganzir. Let me in.'

A little silence, long enough to make her doubt.

Again that stiff, mean opening of the door. Barely a width to allow her through, so that the gilded Robe caught on the edge and she must pull it free. Too careless her grasp on the Measuring Rod in her other hand. She was scarcely in when the Rod was grabbed and whisked away from her, passed from black beak to black beak across the flock of ragged-feathered heads that had surrounded her. She saw their eyes flash triumph.

Too much breath now, coming too strongly from her chest

so that her voice was rough with fear as well as indignation.

'What is this? What have you done? Give me back my lapis Measuring Rod and Line!'

'Keep quiet, Inanna! The laws of the Underworld are fixed. It is not for you to question them in our territory.'

Nothing to grip now, nothing to hold before her as a symbol of authority. Her hand, bereaved, went to the Breastplate and found it warm with the living flesh beneath it. It had been warmer still when Dumuzi had crushed her to him in a last embrace, had bent his head and kissed it, weeping.

The marks of the ruler had gone, but the power to take them from Enki had been in her will, in her love of life, in her own self, long before the *me* were hers to hold. She was still Inanna, the rightful Queen of the Above.

She took another step down into Ereshkigal's domain.

Stalagmites, moulded into luminous white and green curves like neglected skulls. Clay slippery underfoot.

At the third gate she was prepared, ready to fight them off with her bare, living hands. But they took her from behind. Soft, spidery legs scrabbled through her hair, found the nape of her neck. Shivering with horror, she tried to escape their insistent stroking. But the softness of bodies and the brush of fleshless limbs was all around her. As she twisted away, retching, she left the small lapis lazuli choker in their grasp.

Her throat felt cold and naked. What use were her huge alluring eyes? These were no mortal men, no loving Lords of the Above to charm with her smile and the promise of her flesh. They were taking her power away.

If only Gilgamesh could have been amongst these sexless creatures with his axe!

Gilgamesh was in the upper air.

Gilgamesh was mortal.

She hardly needed to say, 'My Beads! Why have you taken my lapis Beads?' to know the answer.

'Quiet, Inanna! The ways of the Netherworld are set in perfection. It is not for you to question them, where you have no control.'

On down, then, because there was no other way.

Light of the day was far behind her now. Three doors had closed above her. Nin Shubur would be sitting in the grass outside, her cloth wrapped round her head against the chill of sunset. What spells was she casting?

At the fourth gate, the middle door of seven, she would play their charade with a high courage. She knocked boldly. 'I am Inanna, on my way from the Land of Sunrise to the Netherworld. Open this gate!'

And the gate opened on a rushing river.

So fierce the torrent that she gasped and almost slipped on the wet stone. So the legends were true! Enlil had come this way, and Nin Lil following. And they had returned to the Above. Hold fast to that.

She was hardly aware that the heavy ropes of *numug* stones had been whipped over her head and away. Yet when she had recovered her balance she groped for the source of that feeling of lightness, and found them gone.

'My *numug* Egg Stones! Restore them to me!'

A man stood with his arms folded, his face lowered, his back to the leaping torrent that her own silver light caught in constellations of spray.

'I am strong!' she thought. 'I am shining. I am still alive!'

But she had lost the symbols of birth on the Road of the Dead.

What would happen without her in the bedrooms and byres of Sumer?

'Be silent, Inanna!' Neti's chill voice came from somewhere unseen at the man of the river's side. 'You are in the heart of the Netherworld now. Its laws cannot be changed for you.'

The man moved towards her. When Nin Lil had stood here, on this rock, it had been Enlil in this disguise whose arms had embraced her. Those eyes before hers had been bright with yearning for the woman he needed.

This man needed nothing from Inanna. His face was approaching now, higher than her own. She looked up into eyes that were hollow, lifeless. Nothing of her lit any spark in them. His arms reached out and took her, unutterably cold against her flesh. She shrank within herself, saw her light almost eclipsed. A little whimper escaped her. This man would never desire anyone. Stiff with terror, she felt herself lifted from the rock. Around her unwilling body, muscles, like moving metal, tightened to carry her. Without ceremony, without emotion, he bore her through the hurtling flood that would have dashed her to destruction without him. How could he hold the Lady of Lovemaking so close and feel *nothing*? He dropped her, dripping and humiliated, on the stone of the further shore.

Hard to be proud and defiant, alone here in the darkness. Even drawing herself up to her full height, she felt as insignificant as a lost child. There was no one to see her, no one to be impressed by her courage, her authority. The halls were now so wide her light seemed weak and small. She wandered through them. Jackal-headed statues stared down from guardian plinths, dwarfing even the tall Inanna. She walked through vast archways shadowed by Imduguds' wings, between the feet of massive bulls. She feared she might lose herself for ever in this emptiness, with no guide even to mock her. But she was mistaken.

The fifth door shone more proudly, studded with copper nails. Her knock sounded small and dull, her voice a reedy pipe.

'It is I, Inanna, Queen of the Above.'

But the Above was immensely far away, almost beyond her power to imagine now. Highest of all, in the farthest reaches of Angal, An was probably asleep, forgetful of her.

She almost cried when the door opened a crack to her. It was impossible to go back now. But a crushing sense of the darkness still Below was coming very close.

Inevitable, too, the next loss.

She clutched the Breastplate to her. 'No! No!'

But they took it away from her. Women, wild-haired, sharp-faced, bird-footed, with wings like tattered cloaks. They smiled slyly as they half turned. Then, even in the tremulous light of a single star, she recognised the face in front of her. Kiskillilla. Tawny, challenging eyes that did not drop when she stared into them. No Gilgamesh with his axe to drive her out this time. Inanna turned her head aside. Kiskillilla on her right. And to her left? Kiskillilla. Kiskillilla. Kiskillilla . . . Inanna felt her very self invaded, derided.

'Give me back my Breastplate!' Though her face was almost too frozen to speak.

Wild laughter. Kiskillilla respected nothing and no one. Like a dust storm, her multiple images whirled Inanna's treasure away.

Neti's voice behind her again. 'It is too late to protest, Inanna. You have invited yourself to the Below. Its ways are unalterable.'

The demon women came spiralling back, seeming to scrape her flesh as they whisked round her, shrieking with laughter.

They spun her giddily, snatched at her hair, her elbows, her skirt, her shoulders. They carried her with them.

Down, down. Past mounds of jewels covered in slime and fungus, past weapons brittle with rust, choked with verdigris. Rich robes of *ens* and priests hung on hooks, reduced to mouldy rags by moths and rot. Her foot struck something, so that she stumbled. A child's rush cradle, that fell apart, riddled with rats. Tiny bones tumbled to the floor with a small, rattling cry and rolled away into silence.

The sixth gate, and her heart knocking like a funeral drum.

'I am Inanna, from the Place of Sunrise. Let me in!'

No ceremony. The gold Ring tugged brutally from her arm. The stink of corrupt flesh from bear snouts. The grin of crocodiles. The greedy grasp of monkey paws. What were bruises to them here where so many were hurt?

'Why are you taking my Ring? I am bringing life! I am Inanna!'

'Silence! You have come to the Gates of Death. Our Dark Queen is stronger than you are, Inanna. Respect her laws.'

She smelt the mouths around her still, but they did not close in again. She heard their waiting breath.

For a while she stood uncertain, holding her Robe tight around her for security, her eyes probing the darkness ahead. Then she saw, by a slight disturbance, what it was. A vast, black pool. As a little wave sucked at her feet she felt the last of her hope and courage draining away. She did not want to cross that lagoon.

Neti's voice pursued her. It had grown almost eager.

'Well, you have managed to reach the Water of Kur, Inanna. The funeral you asked for is on the other side. They are waiting for you. Will you cross?'

She thought of Enki, fleeing from the fury of Kur. She thought of Enlil and Nin Lil, abandoning their sons to Ereshkigal's eternal keeping. She thought of all the human dead, brought into being under her Star of Lovemaking, condemned in a few years to this.

'I am Inanna, from the Land of Sunrise, Queen of all Sky and Earth. *I, the Life-Bringer, will cross the Water of Kur.*'

# Chapter Seventy-nine

Would Inanna have wished to see under the ferryman's hood, beneath his cloak? She turned her gaze away from the hands that raised the dripping pole, lest she should find green decay, white bones, corruption, nothingness.

It swayed no more than a cradle, this boat on the Water of Kur. After all, it was disturbingly easy to cross, like that Devouring Torrent in the tunnels above. In silence, save for the drip, drip of water falling into blackness. Then the slightest shock, and they were at the other shore.

Unfriendly stone. No well-cut quay. No deputation of Ereshkigal to meet her. She looked for guidance. No word from inside the deeply-shrouding hood. The ferryman did not move to touch or help her. He simply waited.

Inanna stood up, feeling her youth and physicality fragile and light upon her, without the weight of jewels and regalia. She drew a breath, deeper than the physical effort required, lifted up the hem of her queenly dress and stepped up on to a ledge of raw, rough rock beneath a low roof.

Her body clenched in tight knots, awaiting the last assault of demons. Silence. Solitude.

Then a voice laughed, its origin lost in a multitude of echoes. She whirled round. The ferryboat was rocking far out in the middle of the pool, beyond reach.

From close beside her Neti's voice mocked her. 'No, Inanna. The Water was not the final gate. Are you too proud to recognise it?'

Scarcely room to move a few steps on the narrow ledge. The pool was threateningly close beneath her. The ferryboat had gone. It was impossible to stand upright. And then she saw it.

She must crouch on hands and knees, like an infant, like a dog. She must reach in her arm and scratch at this low door because there was no space to strike it loudly.

She bowed her bared head and knelt down.

'I am Inanna, Queen of the Above, at the Seventh Gate of the Netherworld. Unbar it for me.'

No time to wish it might not open.

Crawling like a baby into the hole revealed in front of her. Her sandals were pulled from her feet as she dragged them over crevices of stone. Was it only the rock that had ripped them away? The Robe hampered her. Here, in the passage that would admit only her bare body, clawing hands reached forward and tore the royal *pala* from her flesh. They ripped it away, left Inanna naked.

She could not see or feel or smell these demons, and their very fleshlessness terrified her more than the others.

'What is this? What is this? Why have you taken my royal Robe?'

'Be silent, Inanna, in the Place of Sunset. The ways of the Netherworld are supreme. Do not protest at them. You descended to the Below of your own will. You crossed the Water of Kur. You must come to the Land of the Dead as the Unborn.'

The Netherworld drew her back into its womb, to the blue-black Ganzir.

Her sore hands reached, searching, forward, found dim-lit space. She was through!

She tried to stand upright, but the roof still would not let her. She must bow her shoulders. Inanna entered Ereshkigal's palace, not up soaring flights of steps as to the E-Anna, not past ranks of priests and priestesses chanting praise, bevies of her hierodules and *sag-ursag* gorgeously arrayed, but bent almost double under a slimy roof, naked and shivering, spat on and derided by Ereshkigal's court.

Hands pushed her out into a gloomy yard. Before the towering portals, guards stood, white-faced, cold-eyed, their corpse-like cheeks hung about with unwashed grey locks.

At last she could start to straighten up.

'Bow, Sky Woman!'

A whip cracked. For a moment a protest was on Inanna's lips. But the horror of this place was heavy upon her now. There was no one with a heart to appeal to here. The air hung cold and damp. Her little starlight, that had shone so radiantly in the higher levels, did not have the power to penetrate this gloom. She felt the *me* of the Netherworld binding her like metal shackles. She knew with a chilling terror that here she would lack the strength to grasp them.

In dumb obedience she bowed her back. Her blue-black hair tumbled over her face. Her arms hung limp before her. She saw her full breasts sag, felt sweat smudge her face-paint.

'Hurry! Hurry!' Neti had a sharp reed. He was prodding her like a reluctant cow. 'The cup you asked to drink from is waiting for you.'

No noise of mourning from the Ganzir's interior. No funeral dirge, no solemn drum, no shrieks of women, no chants of lamentation priests. Only a dull silence through which she stumbled and felt herself the only warm, living thing.

Goosepimples studded her flesh, though the air was humid. Disrespectful hands forced her head lower as she passed them. She felt their claws, and the first sting of returning courage countered their indignity. Under the portal now, a blank, black rectangle of gleaming basalt. A weight of condemnatory silence hung over her in the antechamber.

Within, there was the glow of blue light. The hollow core of the Ganzir, the Lustrous Mountain Hall, seat of the power of the Great Below. Ereshkigal's judgment hall.

Naked and stooped almost to the ground, Inanna was made to enter before her great-aunt's throne.

They were tall, these Anunna of the Great Below. Shadowy-robed, shadowy-faced, deliberate in their movements as though they had never known any reason to dance with joy.

One figure came forward. By the two bony horns on his crown she judged him to be Namtar, Ereshkigal's *sukkal*. His voice was rougher than Neti's, but with the same tone of mockery.

'Inanna, Queen of the Above, Queen of Earth, born in the Land of Sunrise, Mistress of all the *Me*, Lady of Sexual Intercourse, Princess of the Brightest Planet. Inanna has come to Kur of the West, to the Place of Death, to weep with you, most dread of queens.'

This was the moment Inanna had dreamed of through centuries of childhood stories.

The darkness inhabiting the throne rose, towered, took a step forward to the brink of the dais.

The eyes of the two queens met.

Inanna wept then. Wept for that princess torn from the Sky, wept for her uncles denied the light, wept for the wedding beds that were cold, for the births that had been in vain, wept for eternities of mourning, wept for the annihilation of hope in that terrible face. Wept at last for herself.

Yet she *was* Inanna. No one else had ever had so much right to enter Kur as the Queen of all the *Me*.

She was the Maiden on the night between childhood and consummation, eternally Bride. Always the hope of the future in front of her, and of all lovers. Always the gift of the body promised, the trust of the heart, the quickening of the womb, the laughter of sweethearts.

The roll of the war drum, the Dance of Battle, the final spear thrust.

Star of the Evening, Star of the Morning. First in the Sky, the Invitation of Night. Last in the Dawn, Seal of Return. Dancer on the horizon where the Above touches the Below. Lady of Thresholds.

As Ereshkigal leaned forward, the throne of Kur was empty. Inanna flung herself towards it.

She got no further than the first step. Ereshkigal raised one withered claw. The seven judges of the Underworld surrounded Inanna.

A voice harsh as a vulture's. 'Well, sister? What can you plead now? You stole the *me* of the Above from my brother. You took the E-Anna from my father. Have you come to Kur to get the *me* of the Below as well? Would you seize E-Galkurzagin from me, rule even the Waters of Nammu?'

'I am the Light. I bring the hope of Life. I am the Lady of all Fertility. The Lion Guardian.'

'And I am Death. *Look at me!* There is no East without a West. There is no birthing without dying. If there are Anunnaki of the Above, there must be Anunna of the Below. The Waters of Nammu flow in a circle, beyond the Sky, beneath the Netherworld. She spins us round and round, from our beginning to our end.'

'And from our end to our beginning!'

'*Silence!*'

The Lady of War, Inanna, whose chariot was harnessed to seven lions, cowered before the bull-throated roar.

'There will be no more dawns for you.'

'What have I done?'

'Tell her. Open her eyes before we close them finally.'

The Anunna's voices boomed like gongs. Nergal, Lord of

Plague and Death; Ningishzida, the Serpent Lord; Ninazu, Master Who Knows the Waters; and all the wax-fleshed ring of Lords and Ladies around her.

'She used the arts of the harlot to take the Sky House from An.'

'She has conspired against Great Enlil, who rules in the House of Kur.'

'She looked with anger upon her bridegroom, Dumuzi Abzu.'

'She took the *me* from Enki, from the Abzu of the Deep.'

'She attacked the Serpent, destroyed the Imdugud's nest, drove Kiskillila out.'

'She gave the *pukku* and the *mikku* to Gilgamesh, to oppress her city.'

'She promises love and joy; she brings hate and strife.'

'Not *only* that! Not *only* that! There *is* joy. There *is* lovemaking. I am Inanna! I hold all the *me*. I am both Love and War!'

'And so are we of the Below, both life and death.'

'The sun passes through the Netherworld when it is night Above.'

'The moon returns to us each month.'

'The River of Kur is flesh-destroying in the West, a seven-mouthed source of abundant life and plenty in the East.'

'The Lord of Serpents nourishes the roots of every tree.'

'Ninazu heals as well as slays.'

'Then I am one of you! I am your sister!'

'You have no place among us, Inanna. We can do all things necessary. We do not need you.'

'*Can you make love?*'

A scream of indrawn breath from Ereshkigal. As one, in a terrible awed silence, the seven judges turned their shrouded faces to their Lady. Inanna's own eyes followed them.

No merciful headcloth hid Ereshkigal's features. Writhing blue flames leaped from her shoulders, throwing her curved beak-face into cratered hills and shadows. Bony wings sagged from her shoulders, more like some carapaced insect than a sky-free bird. Talons gripped the edge of the dais with bare claws. The body was a woman's, naked, as if it should have been proud with promise like Inanna's, but it was yellowed, shrivelled, so that its nudity was like a taunt of Inanna's own fate flung in her face.

The Queen of Kur wore no jewels. Her eyes glittered as a

vulture's with the look of death.

Life shone out of Inanna's huge dark eyes and saw herself in Death.

No pity for her young kinswoman in Ereshkigal's stare. No tears for all the joy that was about to be lost.

'You! You are all the same, you Anunnaki of the Above. You take, and take, and take, and call it giving. You take our Darkness, take our Silence, take our Pain, take our Death. Well, Inanna, Eldest Daughter of the Moon, Darkness, and Silence, and Pain, and Death shall take you now ... You have spoken, my judges! She has sought to break the power of the Netherworld. I hold her guilty!'

'*Heam!*' Seven confirmations dropped like lead.

A bloodless arm lifted, curved. Black nails glinted in the wizard-light. She struck suddenly. Claws ripped across Inanna's lovely face. Blood spurted freshly. The hurt was terrible. The young Lady opened her lips to scream ...

The victim hung, upright but still.

From their horseshoe ring around her, the Anunna's shadowed eyes stared. Inanna's glorious body, that had glowed moon-gold and rose in the Above, drained to a ghastly pallor. Full lips that were shaped for kissing Dumuzi, had shouted battle cries to Gilgamesh, turned blue and frozen. All the fluids of life leaked from her resistless anus and vagina in a stinking stream. The cold flesh crumpled, collapsed on the lowest step.

Inanna was dead.

'Hang it,' said Ereshkigal, 'from that hook on the wall in front of me.'

They dragged her, like the carcass of a butchered ewe lamb, across the dark, stained floor. They hacked off her magnificent hair, hoisted her rudely up, drove the hook through her neck so that her blind face fell forward bowed to Ereshkigal.

'Now,' said the Mistress of the Below, seating herself again on her bull-footed throne, 'leave her to rot.'

# Chapter Eighty

A night passed outside the Gate to the Underworld. Nin Shubur watched. Cloud hid the stars. Even the moon could not shine here. Nin Shubur moved small pebbles, feathers, sticks, in patterns over the damp grass, muttering to herself. As night fell, the *sag-ursag* put up bivouacs and invited Nin Shubur to rest in one, but she shook her head. The men lit a fire and crouched round it, talking in low voices, or rolled in their sheepskin cloaks and slept.

Dawn came, grey and weary. Inanna did not return.

Then the sun broke through and the day was beautiful again. Nin Shubur rose stiffly, walked to the river and washed.

'It is too soon to expect her yet,' she said. 'The way down to the Ganzir must be long.'

She slept a little in the shade, then she resumed her watching. The shadows of evening fell early between the sentinel mountains. Another night passed.

At the end of the long second day Nin Shubur said, 'Climbing back from the Netherworld will be harder for her than going down. She cannot come till tomorrow.'

The third night was very quiet. Few slept. A wolf came soft-padded down to the river to drink. She smelt the intruders, turned to stare at them with eyes like yellow moons. Black blood dripped from her hindquarters on to the grass.

'She is on heat,' murmured Nin Shubur.

As if in confirmation, a big he-wolf came more heavily down the bank. The guards grasped their spears, readied. Nin Shubur's hand poised over her pebbles. The he-wolf sniffed the ground in front of him. He trotted on past the bitch incuriously, without turning his head, and sloped away into the shadows. The she-wolf threw up her muzzle to the stars and howled.

Nin Shubur shuddered. 'Is desire dying already?' She lifted her head to the cave mouth above the meadow, the shape of its darkness only a memory now. 'What are you doing, my lovely Lioness? Have you crossed the Water yet?'

On the third day the *sag-ursag* were restless, went hunting, came back with a hare dripping blood. They cut it open, still living, and found three leverets inside already dead. Nin Shubur refused all food, crossed and stood at the lip of the hollow, where the river leaped over in a waterfall even in summer. Far, far below lay the plains of Sumer, the tumbled foothills of the Hursag, the first great city mounds swimming like islands in a sea of haze.

'What will we do if she does not come back to us?' she whispered. 'What will become of this Earth if the Star of Love goes dark? Will the ram ever mount the ewe again, or the bull his cows? Husband and wife will lie apart and the voices of children will cease in the land. The Life-Bringer has gone down into Kur. Sky and Earth are left a desert.'

But still she walked back to the cave, hurrying now. She saw the grim-faced captain of the *sag-ursag* watching her and cried out to him, 'The *me* of the Netherworld will be a heavy burden, even for a Lioness as strong as our Inanna. Her journey back to the light must be weary and long.'

The sun did not slow its stride across the sky. It passed over the cave mouth without halting, on, down below the rim of the western mountains. Nin Shubur stared after it, at the glory it had left behind.

'Where are you now, Lord Utu? Are you entering Kur of the West? Will they let you see your sister? Could you help her? . . . No, you will not delay your march through the Underworld. You will see, you will judge the dead. You will keep its laws.'

When the third day ended, she wept at last, all the full reservoir of tears she had held in her heart since Inanna announced her intention.

'Oh, my little one. What has become of you? Who has got you? My gosling, stretching her newfledged wings over the marshes. My wild kid, eager to leap the mountain ravines. Where is the lust for life, where is the courage, where is your high heart now?' And she began to tear at her hair.

The *sag-ursag*, too, put dirt on their faces, began to intone the rites for the dead. Nin Shubur jumped up and hurled her shaman stones at them.

'Are you men or hedgehogs? Will you curl yourselves into a ball for fear, when Inanna is caught in Kur? It's time to run like hares to the cities. We must rouse the great Lords!'

They were on their feet now, eager to do anything that might still be done for the Lady they loved.

'Can you march as quickly as we can?' said the captain.

'If I could fly, I would!'

They broke out of the foothills in the first light of dawn. The demon army of Asag could not have looked more terrible. Blood, ashes, earth streaked their faces and limbs. Howls burst from their throats like jackals. The ruined temples of the mountain valleys heard them in silence. Villagers hurried back into their houses and barred the doors.

The horror of a fear realised was in the eyes of Inanna's boatmen when the mourning party came hurrying down to the bank without her. Swiftly their arms poled the unhappy boat down the small, summer streams, into the larger canals, sped down the Buranun.

The great hill of Nippur rose in all its pride, the premier city in Sumer.

'This is the House of Enlil who separated Sky Lord from Earth Lady, took Earth for his own. He himself allotted the Below to Ereshkigal. He made the Anunnaki build the E-Kur for him. Surely Enlil has power to help Inanna.'

Nin Shubur beat the drum, marched round his house like a woman possessed. The *sag-ursag* followed her. One side of their uniforms was ripped away, one half of their hair torn out. Nusku came hurrying out.

'What is this, Nin Shubur? Why are you acting like a madwoman, disturbing my Lord's siesta?'

'I must speak to Lord Enlil!'

'Come in, then. Nin Lil is afraid something evil has happened to Inanna.'

'Something evil has happened to us all!'

She threw herself before Enlil in his audience chamber.

'Approach. Speak.'

The Lady held up her hand, pleading to Sky and Earth. 'Lord Air, Master of the E-Kur, you who have been to Kur and carried back your wife and son to us. Help Inanna. Do not let Death have her in the Netherworld. Let not the bright silver of the stars become the dust of decay. Let not her clear blue lapis be shattered into stoneworker's waste. Let not the living boxwood become splinters on the carpenter's floor. She is the Hierodule of Heaven. Don't let her beauty die!'

Enlil gripped the arms of his throne, shouted angrily, 'You know what you are asking, woman! You are a shaman. You do not have the excuse of ignorance. I did not go down to Kur willingly, as Inanna did. I went as a punishment, not in pride. I paid a great price to return. She went alone. What has she to leave behind her in her place? Alone, she must stay there. She wanted the *me* of the Great Above. She took them! She wanted the *me* of the Great Below. Well, she has felt them now. And she will stay under their grip. She who chose the Dark City must remain there.'

'You will not help her?'

'I cannot help her.' And he fell back on his chair, quivering with rage and the forced confession of impotence.

'But you are Kurgal! You rule E-Kur. You *gave* the Netherworld to Ereshkigal!'

'And so it stays. An, she and I. Sky, Netherworld and Earth between. Eternally fixed.'

'Then poor Inanna . . . ?'

The silence was only broken by Nin Lil's weeping.

On then south, to Nanna's city of Ur. The E-Kishnugal, blue-enamelled on its high mound, a place that knew love. And now a house of grief. The news had reached Inanna's parents even before Nin Shubur's straining boatmen could bring her. No need to circle this ziggurat and beat the drum. She was hurried up to the private quarters before Nin Gal and Nanna.

'So, Queen of the East, you bring us bitter information. You, to whom we trusted our dearest daughter, you from the Land of Sunrise, you led her to the West, where your spells lose all their power.'

Nin Shubur fell down, covered her face.

'I am her *sukkal*! No one directs Inanna. She is the Battle Maiden, our Lion, Mistress of First Star in the Sky. Oh, Father Nanna, do not be angry with her. Let her not be put to death in the Netherworld. Let her brightness not be covered in grime. Let her not be ground like stonedust, sawn into shavings. Let her lapis lazuli shine, the boxwood sprout again. Do not let the Hierodule of Heaven, the Lady of Life, die.'

Nanna's white face was solemn, pitted with grief. But his voice was cold and stern.

'I was brought out of the pit of the Netherworld in Nin

Lil's womb. With her great sacrifice I was born to bring the first light to the world. One day in the month I go down. I see what might have held me. I look about, and shudder. I saw my own children born in the Land of the Rising Light, Utu, Inanna. I gave them the Dawn as their birthright. She craved the Going Down. All she longed for in the Above was given her, by An, by Enki, by all of us. It was not enough. Now she has got what she desired, the Great Below. What she would have taken for herself keeps her now.'

'But you go to Ereshkigal's city. Plead with her to release Inanna!'

'What have I to give for her ransom? Ereshkigal has my three brothers. My Light was dearly bought.'

'I . . . I would go,' Nin Shubur cried through her tears. 'I, the Queen of the East, would give myself to Kur, if I could. But I would be nothing. At the first step on that Road Beyond Sunset, all my little power would be extinguished. And what am I, to buy Inanna's life?'

Nin Gal moved forward, cradled the weeping *sukkal*. 'Hush, hush, Lady. You are my daughter's faithful friend. Don't despair. Go on at once to my father. Enki is Lord of the Deep itself. Perhaps he can help her. Hurry, if you love her!'

Close, those two hills of Ur and Eridu, cities of Moon and Water. The boatmen cut the river like racing carp. Nin Shubur shivered, approaching the wide lagoon, the blue and silver shrine. Memories of monsters, the two-faced *sukkal* chasing Inanna's *magur* ship, a great Lord tricked and robbed of power. Was this Inanna's last resort? Did her life, and all the unborn lives of the world's lost fertility, hang now on Enki?

No sign of mourning here. No drums or wailing soured the peace of the marshes. The steps were sunlit, Isimud smiling on one face, thoughtful on the other as he came out to greet her. Cool beer was poured for her.

'I must see Enki. Is he at home? Say he is here! Say he is not on a voyage away from Sumer, is not in the Deep with his mother Nammu. I must see him now!'

Isimud held up a hand for silence. 'Enki is asleep.'

'Rouse him! For the love of all that lives, bring him here!'

'Do you command the Lord of the Deep, now?'

How could she tell if Isimud was mocking her?

The wait was not very long; it seemed unbearable. Swift, shuffling footsteps made her lift her head eagerly.

Enki's shrewd eyes danced with the prospect of another contest when he saw his granddaughter's *sukkal* in Eridu again. Sleep had wiped from his mind the rumour of Inanna's fatal mission. Then he saw Nin Shubur's clawed eyes, the one-ply beggar's rags, her thighs bared and mutilated. A terrible fear passed over his face and was overtaken by a recollection more awful still. A nightmare from the past ripped open like a wound.

'What has happened? What has Inanna done? Was she such a fool, after all? Did she really do what we all forbade her? Has she gone to the Great Below, to seize the *me* from Ereshkigal, as she took mine from me?'

Nin Shubur abandoned her formal pose of courtly *sukkal*, arm lifted in the gesture of supplication. She threw herself on the ground, clutched his ankles.

'Enki. Father. Save her! Save Inanna, your silver Star! Do not let her be blackened in the Underworld. Your precious lapis stone. Let her not be ground to powder. Your sweet box tree, shall the axes smash her? The heavenly hierodule who made love to the Sky Lord himself, how shall we let her die? The Earth is dying!'

Enki's hands grasped her, hurting her with the strength of his own emotion. 'Inanna, Queen of all the Living, sweet Priestess of the Stars. Say she is not caught in Kur. What happened, Nin Shubur? Ai! Ai! All that beauty, all that spirit, all that boldness, all that passion. Say we have not lost that. Say the Above is not beggared of life.'

'She is gone.' They wept together. 'Our Inanna is lost in Kur. She did not come back.'

'Then the light is dimmed indeed. The joy is gone from the Sky. All sunsets are loveless now, all dawns without pity. The taverns will stay dark and the beds cold. Young men will pass young women in the street and no snake will rise for them. Grey, grey, without laughter or love, our lives after this.'

'The Anunnaki will live on to mourn her for eternity. But the beasts and humans will fail and die.'

'Fool! Fool! Once, I could have taken Ereshkigal's place . . . Now, it is too late to help her.'

# Chapter Eighty-one

'You can do nothing?'

All hope was dying.

'Once . . . I . . . My heart was high as Inanna's then. I ventured out . . . I tried . . .'

'You barely escaped with your life, the old songs say.' He did not answer. His eyes were wells darker than she had ever seen them before. In the stillness of the Abzu was the roar of waves breaking far underground.

Then Enki smote his thigh and gave a great leap, startling Nin Shubur.

'By An and Enlil! By the River of Kur and the Hills of Sunrise! I will still fight for her . . . Isimud!' he roared. 'When did that tart last give me a manicure? Find me a nail-scraper!'

Nin Shubur started. '*What is that?* What is that you have under your fingernails, Lord Enki?' Her whole body was tense, her wise shaman's eyes staring at the wizened Lord's hands as if they held the key to life.

He grinned, a fierce, gum-baring leer. His head, with its streaming locks, its clever mobile face that seemed too large for the sinewy neck which supported it, thrust forward into hers.

'Ha! You are a knowing woman, Nin Shubur. Life came out of Kur, out of the Lustrous Mountain. Hold on to that!'

'I was born in the Land of Sunrise,' said Nin Shubur slowly, as if in a dream, 'where the light rises. But Inanna went down into the West.'

'It is all one,' Enki said with a fierce intensity. 'Believe that. Go on believing it, Inanna's friend.'

The *sukkal* clenched her fists, trying to still her trembling. 'Then there is hope?'

The grey eyes softened a little, grew bluer in the misty lapis light. 'I see I cannot fool you. Yes. After all, what is a Star in the Pit of Darkness if not a sign of hope? But you know more of the ways of the cosmos than is good for your comfort. It is only a small hope.'

Nin Shubur's hands were clasped over her heart now. 'Then do what you can.'

Still his eyes peered at her face, uncomfortably close. His crooked eyebrows lifted. 'You know what we are doing, Woman of the East? Our lovely Inanna has attempted a great folly. She has tried to overturn the creation of An and Ki, the Word of Enlil, my order. *We . . .*' He conquered the false, painful note, and his voice grated. 'We gave the Netherworld to Ereshkigal. It was necessary. *She* is necessary.'

'I know,' Nin Shubur whispered.

'Then you know too that if it were possible to rescue Inanna, to give us joy Above, there would be a heavy price to pay in the Below.'

'*Let us pay it*,' begged Nin Shubur.

He studied her for a long, reflective moment. 'I like you. Any other Lady, knowing my reputation, would have fluttered her kohl-black eyelashes, stuck out her breasts at me, tried to coax me into this with promising lips. But you . . . you are thinking only of Inanna, aren't you?'

'Aren't you too?'

'*No!*' The crack of his voice made her jump. 'No. I am thinking of who may suffer if she goes free . . . Well! Very likely it cannot be done. We shall see, we shall see.'

'The nail-scraper, my lord.' Isimud, who had been waiting patiently at his shoulder, handed him a small, silver tool. Enki's eyes flashed up again to meet Nin Shubur's curious gaze.

'Yes, wise Lady. What I have under my fingernails is worth staring at.' His bony hands were still supple, articulate, restless with the love of making. The nails were painted a brilliant red, hiding what lay ingrained beneath.

'You are Nudimmud the Fashioner,' she said. 'Mother Nammu's son.'

'And you are too wise for my deviousness. Your mind runs on ahead.'

'It would plunge deep today. Deeper than the ocean.'

He followed her look to the central well, the sacred navel of Abzu, House of the Deep. The silver scraper was poised in his left hand. He nodded solemnly.

'You are right. I have been with my mother. I will not tell

you what we do. But under my nails, out of the Abzu, I have brought back to Earth the merest fragment of primordial clay.'

He dug out the tiny slivers of dirt with infinite care and precision from under the nails of his right hand. Nin Shubur leaned forward, possessed by awe.

'*That?* That is the substance from which she made humanity? All the people who now fill the Earth and serve us?'

'Just so.'

'But . . . what will you make, Lord Nudimmud? Mortals have no power in the Netherworld. For them, the way Below is the Road of No Return. No human being could rescue Inanna.'

Watching his hands already busy pinching, shaping.

'No human being. Not male or female. How could I do that, without Nin Tu, Lady of Birth? You know about the contest? She and I, drunk as a couple of sailors on shore-leave, to prove which one of us was the best.'

'I have heard it sung.'

'Then you know the outcome. What either of us makes alone is an aberration, a monstrosity.'

The creature was earth-coloured, tiny, with spindly legs, its body little more graceful than a pellet of clay. Yet already it was taking on substance, swelling, beginning to stir its legs.

'The *kurgarra*. Not much to look at, is it? Not very threatening. Not very mighty. Its power lies in what it is not, what it does not have. No sexual organs.' He laughed uproariously, with an edge of bitterness. 'That's rich, isn't it? From Enki! My gift to the world! Well . . .' He stroked the little creature's back. 'Go well, *kurgarra*. What has no power of birth need not fear death. You will blow like dust under the gates of the Netherworld, and those who guard those gates, to drive all human life into the net of death, will see only a speck of inanimate clay. No threat.'

From under the red nails of his left hand he skewered another pinch of dirt, pressed it together, formed it, gave it a stunted body. A thing with rudimentary wings, small feelers, half blind but sensitive in darkness.

'The *galatur*,' he said. 'My little friends. My little impotent monstrosities. My elegist, who can have no kin to mourn. My myrmidon who has no need to be castrated. Slip like flies through the cracks of the doors on the Road to the West. Go and share in a grief you can never experience. *Weep with Ereshkigal.*'

Into the claws of the *kurgarra* he placed three crumbs, taken from the damp, stone table beside the well.

'The Bread of Life.'

Between the shell-like wings of the *galatur* a tiny sac of web in which he poured three drops from that same two-spouted jug that had filled the Idiglat and Buranun.

'The Water of Life.'

He waved the signs of passage over their heads with flowing hands. Nin Shubur added her spells of protection, watched the creatures crawl, small and defenceless, over the rim of the well and drop from sight.

She placed her own hand on the coping curiously. 'I should have known. We need not have climbed the Mountains of the West. The gate is here as well.'

His gaze tested her. 'That gate is everywhere. In Nippur, Uruk, Ur, Eridu. Down any common drain in any house you could pour a libation and it would reach its destination. The ways to the Deep are many. We each find our own. What is harder to find, and bitter for those of us who have trodden it, is the Road of Return.'

'What must I do, then? Where shall I watch for her?'

He gave her a tired grin, a shadow of his old, lecherous self. 'I could offer you a share of a broad bed here, in the Abzu itself. I had hoped once that Inanna . . . No! Don't look so shocked. You're as sexless as a *galatur* yourself. Or . . . maybe not? Go on with you, before I change my mind. Wait for her where you last saw her. At the source of the river, where the mountains turn to the west. Set your face to the east this time, and hope. Make spells for the dead. But you will need to make spells for the living too, if she is released to us.'

# Chapter Eighty-two

Voiceless, powerless, immortal Inanna must still suffer the pains of her own disintegration. She would scream and weep, but she cannot. She feels the festering flesh of her lips creeping with worms and dripping the juices of dissolution. She does indeed hear screaming and weeping in the Ganzir, but it comes from somewhere else. Someone is giving voice to her own anguish. The Young Lady must suffer it dumbly.

The gates of the Netherworld had been closed behind Inanna. No one but the human dead and the Anunna of the Below were welcome here. Mortals, once in, must not be allowed to escape.

No doors were slammed in the faces of the *galatur* and the *kurgarra*.

Supple as lizards, inconspicuous as flies, the creatures slipped under six gates. Neti paid no attention to their noiseless creeping. It did not occur to the saucer-eyed demons to seize them, where so many creatures of decay crawled. The black-beaked crows did not see them in the gloom. They flew the spray of the Devouring River, heroic in their obedience to Enki. They danced in the dust of the desert women and crept among the shuffling feet of the shades of the human dead.

Only the ferryman turned his shadowed hood in their direction as they clung to the stern of his boat. His sigh breathed on the black waters, as though barely condensing into a voice, like mist. 'Who can find the nadir of Kur, where the setting turns to the rising?'

They were neutral, sexless, carrying in their own bodies no threat to the Land of Death. What they brought, between the *kurgarra*'s legs, on the *galatur*'s back, was strangely simple. Crumbs of fresh bread, drops of clean water.

The seventh, low door, that Inanna had had to crawl through, was huge for them. They flew out of the tunnel.

The dusk of Ereshkigal's Ganzir, its portals lost in gloom, was welcome to them. They crept in past the guards with only a tiny disturbance of the shadows.

No doorkeeper demanded their names. No *sukkal* announced their entry. They followed the sound of groaning and wailing, as though to the cell of a tortured prisoner.

Shades of humanity wept often in Ganzir. Women shrieked for the children they had lost. Men cursed the pitiless *galla* who dragged them away from the pleasures of the world. But no grief ever shivered the blue-black palace like the mourning of the Queen of Death herself.

She lay sprawled across her throne in an abandonment of suffering. Her hair was wildly flowing, like neglected leeks. Her nails, like copper rakes, drew fresh blood to add to the hardened crust that streaked her face. No skirt hid the knotted-veined thighs, where purple snakes seemed to struggle around a darker hole. The blood that crept from this was black, unwholesome. Ereshkigal was bewailing the babies she could never bear alive.

Her miscarriage, who had robbed the world of so many babies, who snatched so many mothers into Kur, was, in her own body, agony. She rocked herself, nursing the searing fire of emptying, biting her lip to fight the pain of tearing away.

'Oh, my insides! Oh, my outside!'

The tiny creatures settled down on the edge of the highest step, in front of her. Made as they were, immune to the joys of coupling and fertility, carapaced against the ecstasy of birth and the devastation of miscarriage, you might have thought them as emotionless as *galla*. But their little voices piped, like the rasp of young reeds.

'*Oh, your insides! Oh, your outside!*'

Ereshkigal's screwed-up eyelids shot open. A glance brilliant with suspicion pierced the room. Shrewd, with the intelligence of unimaginable ages, it found the specks of Enki's creation at her feet.

Another spasm clenched her abdomen. She shrieked aloud.

'Oh, my belly! Oh, my back!'

The *galatur* and *kurgarra* crept a step nearer.

'*Oh, your belly! Oh, your back!*'

Stillness, tension held Ereshkigal as the agonising cramps receded. She stared down at these visitants with dawning incredulity. Strangers, no servants of hers, their names unknown and yet they had come to sit with her of their own free will, shared her grief, mourned as she mourned, wept with her, did not curse her.

Tentatively, she shuddered out another sigh.

'Aahh! My liver! Aahh! My lights!'

And the sob came back to her, redoubled.

'*Aahh! Your liver! Aahh! Your lights!*'

She prised herself upright, clenching her teeth, and gazed down at them. The chamber was stilled now. The Anunna of the Below were gone about their duties. Only Namtar and a few white-faced slaves watched this scene in a prudent, fearful silence. Silence except for the buzz of bloated flies around a rotting corpse hung on a hook from the far wall, a dreadful, swarming plague that hid a sight more hideous.

'Who are you?' Her voice deeper and stronger with the force of command than its earlier, self-pitying shriek. 'Who are you, who come uninvited to the Below to share my grief? In all the ages since Kur snatched me from the Sky, no one has ever mourned with me here except for fear of my curses. The only true tears for me I ever saw in the Netherworld were my brother Enki's. And he . . . fled me.

'Ask me what you want. Know that Ereshkigal can be very generous. Out of Kur flows the River of Abundance, as well as the Water of Death. If you are Children of An I will let you return with a blessing. No other Anunna has ever come to Kur only for pity of me. If you are mortals enchanted into this form, I could let you go back to live out long lives. More than that! I will offer you the Water Gift. The rivers of Sumer shall always flood your fields with fertility— *Aah . . .*'

Terrible tears burst from her eyes. The *kurgarra* and *galatur* groaned.

'I cannot carry a baby, and this is how I suffer with every aborting. But you . . . you shall have the fertility Above that finds no soil in the Below.'

The *kurgarra* and the *galatur* answered in their rasping voices, 'We do not want the Water Gift, we thank you.'

Her eyebrows drew closer together. She leaned low towards them. 'What, then, will you have? What if I gave you the Grain Gift? If you lend your dying seed to the darkness Below, it will sprout a hundredfold in the fields Above. You shall never go hungry.'

They lowered their eyelids.

The tiny crumbs of life, the tiny drops of life they carried seemed to weigh like enormous, conspicuous burdens on them. Surely Ereshkigal, who searches every soul, must notice. But she gave no sign that she knew what they had brought to Kur.

'We do not want your Grain Gift, gracious Lady.'

'Yet I have promised.' She forced her wracked body straighter again, sat on her chair like a queen. 'I must give you a gift. What would you take? All Kur is around you. Name what you want, and I will let you go out with it. Hear me, my household; I have sworn to them.'

The *kurgarra* looked at the *galatur*. The *galatur* looked at the *kurgarra*. They said in unison, 'We ask only that corpse which hangs from the hook on the wall.' The Dark Queen stiffened. Her eyes blazed with the shock of realisation.

'That is Inanna's corpse! You cannot have that!'

They bowed their little faces meekly. 'Mighty Ereshkigal. Lady of the dread power of the Netherworld. Your Majesty has spoken. The Ganzir of Kur has witnessed. Whether that dreadful thing is a queen's body or not, that is the thing we want. We are less than nothing. You are all-powerful. We wish you to redeem your promise with that corpse.'

'This is a plot of the Above! You have presumed too far on Ereshkigal's goodness! You are in the House of Death.' Namtar took a furious step forward.

Ereshkigal held up one black-clawed hand. 'Wait, Namtar! It is you who presume too much. I am the sovereign of Kur. What I have said, I have said. The stars do not go back upon their orbits. What is done can never be undone. I know that. An and Ki know it. Enlil and Nin Lil know it. Now let our Inanna begin to learn.

'Very well then. Take what you want, crafty little mourners. Do whatever it is my brother has sent you to do. *Live with the consequences.*'

'Guards!' Namtar struck a gong on the wall.

The deep, melancholy booming brought a tall *galla*, scorpion-faced, with six other horny-clad soldiers following him. Ereshkigal, moving her body with an effort through redoubled spasms of pain, gestured and spat her command.

'Take that . . . thing . . . down!'

The flies rose from the corpse with a crescendo of anger, swarmed like a stormcloud around the *galla*'s heads. They left a sickening sight. The lovely, tinted flesh of Inanna had turned green and putrid. The maggots had burrowed in it so that it hung in ragged ribbons. Bones dangled impotently that had danced in delight after battle victory. The face that had smiled over thousands of sexual unions was a nightmare of death and decay.

The *kurgarra* and *galatur* wept for the ruin of Inanna as they had wailed for the pain of the Princess Ereshkigal.

'Well? What can you do with the face of this foulness, spies from the world Above?' asked Ereshkigal. 'I have no doubt that Enki is behind this. Has he fashioned some cunning plan? Or does he want to show the Above all it has lost?'

She strained towards the corpse, levering herself almost eagerly on the arms of the bull throne. From the tension in her own ravaged body you might have thought she held her breath now with an impossible doubt. As though the salvation of this rotting beauty might in some way signal the first streak of the dawn of her own release.

The *kurgarra* bent its fragile, furred legs, sprinkled the little crumbs of bread over the Maiden's slime-green flesh. The bloated lips did not move.

The *galatur* unfolded its wings, shook from the tiny sac a spray of three clear drops. The Water of Life fell on the oozing fluids of Inanna's remains.

The Ganzir was wholly silent. The blowflies had all disappeared. Ereshkigal gave a stifled sob.

'It cannot be done,' muttered Namtar with satisfaction.

The first hint came with the scent of violets, of dog roses, asphodel, pine needles. As though a breeze from the high mountains of the East had wandered backwards into the heart of the primeval mountain from which all life once came.

A spring of flowers. And then a glow, as if the sun passed through the Netherworld illumining all it saw, revealing past acts, and travelled on. The sickly green of rotting flesh healed over with a smooth, gold skin, touched with the rose of sky at dawn. The round throat throbbed with breath. The breasts swelled firm and young, the nipples budded red. The pubic hair sprang thick and curling. The thighs were sleek, like marble where the moon's rays touch. Her hair, swift gleams of blue in the Ganzir's lamps, half hid her dreaming face. The heavy, black lashes stirred.

Inanna opened star-bright eyes upon the Netherworld. Stretched, yawned and smiled.

She gasped, remembering. Found Ereshkigal watching her.

# Chapter Eighty-three

Inanna rose, slowly, with a terrible doubt. It seemed impossible that limbs which had known such agony could feel so whole and rested, that sinews, stretched to tearing, straightened bone with such a sense of ease and strength. Her gaze was fixed on Ereshkigal's haunted face, as though she feared some trick was still in store.

The Dark Queen rose with her. Every movement, which in Inanna was a glorying in her restored youth, was for Ereshkigal an anguish of grinding bone, of muscles pulled askew, the protest of organs that had failed their original function. Her face bore witness to both pain and anxiety.

They were of equal height. Though the Queen of the Dark City was crouched forward, supporting herself on the standing bulls of her throne, Inanna stood three steps lower. They were both bare-footed, naked, Inanna gloriously so, Ereshkigal contemptuous of all eyes that saw her in the gloom of the Ganzir. Their eyes sought each other's and met, like two champions in the front line of battle.

'You have good friends,' said Ereshkigal. 'Those who love you, even in your pride and folly.'

'I am the Lady of Love.'

'Of Lovemaking. That is a sweet-sounding word, but not at all the same thing.'

'How could you know?'

Ereshkigal gripped her chair arms convulsively. Dark blood crept down her legs.

'You may not love me, but you should fear me, girl. I doubt Inanna the Battle Maiden loves anyone but herself. You do not deserve the love you are given.'

'I love Dumuzi!'

'*Ha!*' The snort of derision and triumph burst from the Queen's nostrils.

'I . . .' Inanna faltered.

More *galla* were crowding into the room. The susurration of their scorpion armour scraped against the silence. Namtar beckoned them in. They flowed around the dusky walls, stood roused, with spears and maces at the ready.

Inanna licked her lips, as though her mouth were suddenly dry.

'You have brought me back to life. Why?'

'Not I. My brother's creatures. There!'

The younger Lady looked down. At her feet the *galatur* and *kurgarra* chirruped in agitation, seeing the stares of the *galla* fixed upon them now.

Her eyes still on Ereshkigal's face, Inanna bent her knees and scooped up the little elegist, the little myrmidon into the seeming safety of her hands. Ereshkigal laughed bitterly.

'You could not take them one step towards deliverance by your own power. It is they who have rescued *you*, sister. They bought your life with words of love. To me, yes, even to me! You may say it was feigned. You may laugh with Enki one day over how you cheated me. No matter. I shall be repaid. Their pity was no more feigned than those words of love you babbled on your wedding bed to Dumuzi.'

'I *do* love Dumuzi! With all my being!' Inanna protested.

'Love? Love gives life. It restores, sets free. Love suffers for the beloved.'

'*And I love Dumuzi*,' she almost wept.

'Go! Back to your dawning. Back to the Earth, where young folk couple and children are born, and kings make war.'

'I . . . am free? You would let me go?'

A sign from Namtar. A dreadful procession formed up. At its head was the Chief *Galla*. His helmet hid all but the burning hollows of his eyes. In his hand was a saw-edged scimitar, at his hip a huge seven-headed mace. In front of Inanna jostled *galla* small as *shukur* reeds, rearing like snakes, but fluttering their bat wings. Behind her towered *galla* tall as *dubban* reeds, jackal-headed with threatening jaws, claw-footed as vultures. Inanna was almost lost, like a pale lily in a muddy marsh.

'Go,' said Ereshkigal. 'Go, and honour my laws of the Netherworld.'

With a mocking skirl of drums the procession moved forward. They came out to the unearthly blue glow of the Ganzir yard.

'Halt, Inanna, on your way to the East!'

A hollow, mournful voice. Seven judges of the Netherworld stood ranged before her. An impenetrable line of Anunna. She looked at their compassionless faces. Nergal, Lord of Death and Plague; Ningishzida, of Trees and Serpents; Nin Azimua, his cavernous-eyed wife; Ninazu and Ennugi, her unknown uncles; Uggae, dread judge of mortals; Atu, the woman who kept the records of the dead.

'You have tricked me!' Terror fluttered her heart in her chest. 'You will not let me go!'

'Ereshkigal has sworn,' Atu rebuked her.

'The laws of the Netherworld are just. They may not be broken,' Nergal pronounced.

'How then shall I leave? How can I reach the Place of Sunrise?'

'How have all your family passed through the realms of death and found the light again?' Nin Azimua's voice was soft but insistent, like a teacher who thinks the logic is self-evident, whose patience may soon wear thin. 'Like them, you will give us someone else as your substitute.'

'Who?'

'It must be someone you love.'

'Part of your soul.'

'Flesh of your blood.'

'Joy of your heart.'

'These little creatures that you carry won your life with words of love.'

'You, when you return Above, will bring the words of death.'

Inanna stood, dazzling with starlight, amongst the frightful *galla*. The Netherworld was bright with her presence. The Anunna of death and darkness did not look away. Pinpoints of life were reflected in their shining eyes. She looked at them in doubt and horror. One hand cupped the *galatur*, the other the *kurgarra*, small messengers of hope who had no more life to give. They had brought about a great resurrection. She was whole, she was alive.

'I must go up to Earth. The world is waiting for me. The people of Sumer will be mourning without their Lady of the Evening Star. The armies of Sumer will be defeated without their Lion Inanna. The Anunnaki themselves will be weeping for me.'

'The laws of the Netherworld cannot be broken.'

'Whom will you choose?' Ninazu was the questioner, himself left in Kur so that Nanna could be born in the Above.

'How can I say that? You are cruel, cruel!'

'You were warned. You endangered both the Below and the Above with your pride.'

'I must return,' she sobbed.

'No one is stopping you.'

Their ranks parted for her. She crawled through the first, low door, stood upright on the other side. The *galla* gave her her *pala* Robe.

The Water of Kur was running merrily, silvered by her presence. Petals of apple blossom and almond flowers floated on its current. She crossed it on a raft of young rushes.

At the second gate the Kiskillilla women, laughing, restored the Breastplate 'Come, Man, Come'.

At the third gate hands placed the gold Ring on her wrist. Symbols of stars and moon and sun shone in the rocks on either hand.

Still the *galla* did not leave her side. They pressed around her like a thicket of reeds whose roots cannot be parted.

She was carried across a bubbling stream she did not recognise, where fish were leaping. At the fourth gate the double necklace of *numug* Egg Stones was hung around her.

At the fifth gate, the small lapis lazuli Beads closed round her throat.

The *galla* swept her upwards over paths soft with moss and pine needles. No pity in their faces. The *galla* cannot be bribed. They eat no sprinkled flour, drink no libated wine or water. Rich offerings to the Netherworld cannot move them.

At the sixth door the shining Measuring Rod and Line were placed in her hand, the precious lapis lazuli insignia of a governor who makes walls straight, foundations firm.

The *galla* have no children, have never loved another's soul or body. They steal the bride from her young husband, the baby from his father's knee.

Before the great outer door they halted with shrieks and growls of growing excitement. Inanna trembled. The first, golden light of day was creeping under the solid gate. Neti himself came forward, carrying the Shugurra Crown high in his hands. He bowed obsequiously.

'Your Ladyship! Radiant Queen of the Sky. Mistress of all the *me* Above, but not of the *me* Below. I see the funeral is over. Gugalanna must rise again. My Queen Ereshkigal will bed with him. Life will stir. The baby will be lost. Gugalanna will be slain by the Lion. The grief is endless. Will you come back to weep with her next time?'

Inanna turned pale, flushed darkly red. 'I am going back to my own, where I am loved and praised. I shall shine in E-Anna. I shall rule all lands. I shall make the flocks and their herders fertile again. I must live!'

'Oh, you shall. *You* shall live, Inanna, Lady of the Star of Love.' He looked questioningly at the leading *galla*.

'Yes-s-s!' The hiss of anticipation spewed spittle on the copper helmet. The Chief *Galla* lifted his scimitar.

Neti raised the Crown in his dark-haired hands. Inanna had to stoop. He set the weight of the great tiara on her shining hair. She straightened her neck, felt all the *me* of Queenship, Priesthood, Ladyship clothe her in splendour again, smelt the soiled touch of death and decay clinging upon it still, grew very solemn and tense.

Neti hauled back the unwilling bolts. Daylight flooded the tunnels of the Netherworld. A wail, of pain, or the lust for pain, broke from the *galla*'s scaly throats.

The largest turned to Inanna with burning eyes. 'Remember your pledge, mistress, as pure Ereshkigal kept hers to you. Betray whomever you love to us, but keep faith with Death.'

The sunlight dazzled her. She could not speak or see. A vision of mountains soaring into a lapis sky scarred itself on her sight and was overwhelmed by the reverse image of darkness. Through her free-springing tears she stumbled into the open. The *galla* held her up, jostling round her. Grass was under her feet, the sun hot on her skin.

'*Aahh!*' Their hiss of satisfaction should have warned her.

'Mistress! My Lady! Inanna, my love, my *lubi!*' The voice of Nin Shubur was broken between joy and horror.

'Nin Shubur? No! *Not you!*'

But the *galla* had seized her already. The Lady of the East. Inanna's shaman, friend and *sukkal*, guardian and counsellor. The woman Inanna most loved.

# Chapter Eighty-four

A woman in mourning. No fine, pleated wool draped Nin Shubur. Soiled rags hung about her, torn by her broken fingernails. Their jagged edges had scratched her mouth and the corners of her eyes, so that she wept red. Even her modest thighs and buttocks had their wounds naked to the gaze through the holes in her dress.

'Walk on, Inanna,' said the Chief *Galla*. 'We have found what we came for.'

'You cannot take Nin Shubur,' wept Inanna. 'Look at her! In all the world of Anunnaki and mortals she has proved herself my most faithful friend. When I am rash, she gives me wise advice. When I was foolhardy, she fought like a tigress at my side. She did not fail me. When Kur caught me, she ran to raise the lament for me. She beat the mourning drum where the Anunnaki meet. She circled Enlil's E-Kur, begging for help. She ran to Ur and pleaded with Father Nanna. She came to Eridu, and prayed to Enki for me. Through her love, the *kurgarra* and *galatur* came to rescue me. She has given me life. I will never give her up to you!'

Her arm was firm round her *sukkal*'s shoulders. Nin Shubur did not look up at her. She begged the *galla* instead, 'Do not listen to her. Take me in place of Inanna. I will descend to Kur for her sake, gladly!'

An expression of disgust and contempt came over the Chief *Galla*'s eyes. 'What sport is this? The Anunnaki of the Above ought to be dragged to the Netherworld in fear and trembling. This woman will come *willingly*?'

'I am offering myself,' said Nin Shubur. 'The Earth needs Inanna. It can live without me.'

The *Galla* pushed her away from Inanna, so that she stumbled.

'These are false tears, Inanna! You weep for her now, but you would still let her go, to save yourself. You'll dance for freedom. You'll exult on the backs of your seven lions in Angal.'

'No, no, you are wrong!' Inanna clutched the trembling *sukkal*. 'You shan't have her.'

'But you must give a life to Kur,' ordered the Chief *Galla*. 'Is there someone that you love more than this?'

Around the edges of the grassy hollow the *sag-ursag* were standing paralysed with horror. They knew too much. Sacred guards of Inanna's house, they would have died willingly defending her from any invasion of sacrilegious humans. But the *galla* of Kur were an enemy whose very existence filled them with dread. Sworn to the service of the Above, they knew in their hearts, felt in their nerveless hands, that no spear or sword could serve them here against the power of the Below.

The *galla* crowded round Inanna and Nin Shubur. It was the Chief *Galla* who walked in front, in the place of her *sukkal*. He held his scimitar raised as his staff of rank. His eyes darted through holes in the copper helmet, a malignant light on the sweet mountain valleys through which they descended.

Inanna walked pale and stiff behind him. Yet the countryside seemed to stir with life where she passed. Soft showers of rain were making the streams run faster. Lambs were quickening already in the ewes' wombs.

The swift-marching column came out at last by the Buranun and seized Inanna's boat. Past Babylon and Kish and Nippur they drove it, like a lightning-blasted tree trunk on the crest of a flood. They turned east to Umma, in the middle of the plain.

'Where are you taking me?' asked Inanna, through lips grown numb with fear.

'To the city of your son, of course.'

Inanna's lips seemed frozen into silence. Nin Shubur took her hand.

No word of Inanna's escape had reached the ploughlands. The *galla* passed like a crowd of mosquitoes through the still stunned and grieving land of Umma. They jumped from the boat and swarmed through the gates, striking the keepers rigid with horror, the stuff of nightmares made walking reality in the middle of bright day. They came up to its highest house, the Sigkurshaga.

Shara was already weeping before they caught him. The

boy who had played at dressing his hair and painting his face like the harlots in Inanna's service was now a mess of dirt and blood, of tangled hair and torn scalp. He lifted his ravaged face and saw her coming with her terrible retinue.

'Mother? . . . Is it really you? How did you get out of Kur? And what have you brought with you? Who are these horrible creatures? Why are you letting them touch you, foul you, my darling mother?'

He threw himself in the dust at her feet, clasped her ankles, kissed her living, precious flesh.

'What are they doing to you? What do they want?'

The *galla* seized him with cries of greed and satisfaction.

'Walk on, Inanna. We shall take Shara in your place.'

She threw herself between them, flung wide her arms trying to hold them off. But the *galla* were all around the pair, behind her, grasping him, hauling him away from her.

'You shall not take Shara! You shan't! He is my precious, my firstborn. Look how he loves me. He was the most beautiful of all the young Lords, but see how he has mutilated himself for grief over me. How can I let him go with you? This is the lad who sings songs to soothe me when I'm angry. His hands brush my hair like the wings of doves. I've taught him how to cut the Lioness's claws more delicately than my manicurist. There is no lad like him.'

'But you must give us what you love. That was your pledge. Or shall we take you back to Ereshkigal yourself and say you have changed your mind?'

'No! Enlil could not be bound by the Netherworld, and nor must I. The Earth needs me. I will keep my word. But not my Shara. Look how he's weeping for me. Not my loving Shara!'

'Your day is running out, Lady of Dawn. You must decide soon. Ereshkigal's price must be paid.'

'Let us go on,' she said. 'I don't know who. There must be someone.'

Now the knowledge of their passing was spreading like the rumour of plague. Children screamed at the sight of the *galla*'s predatory shapes. Farm folk fled indoors. They were barring their houses against the demons who heed no bolts. Only the beasts lifted their heads in startled eagerness, sensing Inanna's return. The land between the Two Rivers hung between hope of life restored and fear of the officers of death.

They were nearing Badtibira. The proud city reared out of the plain. At the quay, Inanna clung to the gunwale, but the *galla* forced her out.

'Do not delay, Inanna. Ereshkigal will be growing impatient. The Netherworld must have its due.'

'Why have you brought me here?' she whispered, though she knew the place too well.

'To Badtibira? This is the city of your younger son, isn't it? What else did you expect?'

The guards on this gate were more warlike. They sprang to arms when they saw the *galla* advancing up the hill. They grew very pale when they made out the cohort of death surrounding their Lady. Grimly they grasped their weapons, prepared to die. But the demons pushed past them, laughing through skeletal teeth, and the human weapons brushed against their unearthly armour, harmless as grass stalks.

Inanna shuddered with dread as they reached the steps of the E-Mushkalamma. At the head of the first flight her son Lulal was standing, legs sternly apart, his boy's battleaxe in his hands.

His face was red with blood already, but it was his own. His too-large mailcoat hung unfastened over filthy rags. His eyes were wild with weeping. He looked like a lad already half dead and determined to die.

When he caught sight of Inanna, beautiful as the Morning Star, but surrounded by a flood of foulness, he rushed to meet her, leaping down three steps at a time with flying strides. He threw himself on the gritty stones at her feet, beat his bruised fists on the ground.

'Mother! Mother! Why wasn't I there to save you? They said you were trapped in Kur. How did you get out? Why have the *galla* got you? Let me die fighting them! I'll set you free!'

'There is only one way you can free her, little Anunna,' hissed the Chief *Galla*, and all the demons of the Netherworld seized Lulal.

'Walk on, Inanna. Go home to your own city now. The choice has been made.'

'No!' Inanna's ringing cry startled the doves and rooks from the walls. 'You shall not take Lulal. I bore him in pain and grief. It shall not be for nothing! He has sworn to be my general, the sword in my right hand, the shield on my left. Look at his eyes. This loving son would lay down his life for me. You cannot take him!'

'We have come precisely to take what you love like yourself. The laws of the Netherworld are perfect, Inanna. You cannot cheat them.'

'Let me go, Mother. I'd dare anything for you. I'll go to Kur.'

'No! Not you, Lulal. Not my young hero.'

'Who, then, Inanna?'

'*Do not take my sons!*'

'It shall be your choice.'

South, downstream now, through the dust and heat of summer noon. The land slept. Dazed fish rose to the surface of the river and flicked their tails, as if they felt a freshening as Inanna passed. But she was not free yet.

The great mound of Uruk shimmered like a mirage through the haze. As they approached, a twisting wind came whirling across the desert. A purple dustcloud hid the horror that was approaching. Through its choking veil the weary Inanna looked up, scanning the darkened brickwork for a glimpse of Gilgamesh. It was the hour of siesta. Even the sentries of Uruk stood motionless, silent as the shades of the dead in Kur. The Chief *Galla* waved his scimitar slowly. The soldiers' heads drooped under the weighty hand of magic. They saw, without recognising, their queen return like a prisoner to her city gate. No word of welcome rang. No joyful paean of praise was raised for Inanna. No voice cried out a challenge. No weapon was lifted in her defence. The procession passed through the open gate and the guards stood mute as the lions of stone. The *galla* marched into Uruk, singing in an evil delight, like the sawing of flies.

They passed through still streets, into the high district of Kullab itself. Here, dust had been washed from its paving bricks. The air was gold with sunshine. The green of leafy gardens softened the metallic heat. The *galla* turned aside from the broad road to the E-Anna. One richly-wrought gate swung, well-oiled, giving no warning. Like a whirlwind that twists across the desert, levelling a trail of destruction but leaving all else calm, the detachment of Kur swept Inanna through the apple orchard to the one, old, crooked tree beside which Dumuzi had built the house for his new bride. Under the shade of this gnarled and leaning apple tree the young

Inanna had made generous love to her Dumuzi. Leaning in the crook of its roots the sweethearts had laid their plans to seize the *me* from Eridu.

'No! No!' Inanna cried out.

The *galla* dragged her on.

'No!' murmured Nin Shubur.

A chair was set under that tree of love. A shocking familiarity. The Lion Throne. Those gilded guardians with lapis lazuli eyes, carved from the trunk of the *huluppu* tree from which Kiskillila had been chased. They opened their mouths to roar defiance at the Above. Their clawed feet gripped the Earth to possess it. Inanna's throne.

And on it sat a magnificent man. Dumuzi Ushumgalanna, Inanna's husband, the Shepherd King of Uruk. He had taken from Inanna's treasury all the regalia of royal *me* that still remained. The *en*'s Palm-Leaf Crown. The Crooked Staff. The Many-Coloured Garment. A gold dagger was bound at his hip. An alabaster cup was in his hand. Wine reddened his mouth. The handsome lines of his face were painted with kohl and rouge. His skin shone with scented oil. At his feet crouched Inanna's young women, stroking his thighs under the majesty of his triple skirt. Music of harps and tambourines flowed from the shade of a nearby willow tree, a love song.

Our darling is Dumuzi of the date clusters.
The *me* of all the world are in his hands.
He gives us fruitfulness, he gives us joy, he gives us plenty.
Dumuzi is King of Kullab, supreme in all of Sumer.

The tambourine clashed. Dumuzi tightened his arm around the one, beautiful, naked girl in his lap, twined upon him in the most intimate of embraces. The dancer's limbs, the slender, intelligent face of Inanna's head slave, Amanamtagga.

A woman screamed. The harps twanged and faltered. Dumuzi turned his flushed and golden face. His brown eyes, sleepy with pleasure, clouded, darkened, grew suddenly brilliant with shock.

Inanna's own face was thrown back, as if appealing silently to the blank, blue sky. But her lovely eyes were closed. From under her thick, black lashes burst tears, painful as blood.

# Chapter Eighty-five

The long, lean limbs were desperately untwining from Dumuzi's. The clever, frightened face lifted. A fall of black hair shrouded it too late as Amanamtagga cowered, her hands flying to cover her sex.

The Chief *Galla* clashed his scimitar against his breastplate, shrieked out in a hoarse exultation, 'Oh, Ereshkigal! Are you feeling this?'

Dumuzi still sat on Inanna's throne, rigid as a gaudily-painted statue. A pipe of lapis lazuli, ringed with mother-of-pearl, lay beside him. The golden-brown of his face, like ripening dates, turned back a season to an unready green. The red stripes of the festival garment could not so easily lose their colour. They could not transform themselves into the dirt of a mourner's rags. The cloth glowed too bright against the gilded *huluppu* wood, where the afternoon sun glanced down through the leaves of the apple tree, on the day when he thought her dead in Kur.

Still Amanamtagga crouched, terrified.

The other slave girls at Dumuzi's feet were trying to shift away. They were wanting to leap up and run, but they dared not take their eyes from the slowly advancing *galla*.

'Seize him!' shouted the Chief *Galla*. 'That one!'

Inanna opened her terrible eyes. In the act of surging forward the *galla*, who love only pain, paused and turned their avid faces towards her. She spoke no word. A towering, awful figure of love betrayed, of hope chilled, she looked upon her young, lusty husband. His strong limbs were sleek with oil, that had once held her to his breast. The hollows of his neck where she had kissed and bitten in passion, were sweet with sandalwood perfume for a human woman. Those hands, now rich with rings, she had lifted to her face, had guided to her vulva. Those lips, moist with wine, had sucked her nipples. He looked the same, beautiful Dumuzi she had always desired, who had tormented her sleep until she made him her bridegroom. But this was not the Dumuzi she had dreamed of marrying. Had he ever been?

The *galla*, revelling in her speechless rage and loss, had hold of Dumuzi by the thighs. They were dragging him off the throne. The women of the court screamed; they broke and ran. The royal guards of Kullab clutched the hafts of their ceremonial weapons as if they were talismans against evil. They knew no blow could be struck against the *galla* of the Netherworld. With grim fortitude they awaited Inanna's orders. Nin Shubur was murmuring words of consolation. No one listened.

But Dumuzi could not accept the inevitability of what was happening. He fought.

'Take your filthy hands from me! Who are you? Who is this ghost who looks like my wife Inanna? She is lost in the Netherworld. I am the true King now! Let me go, I tell you! Guards! Guards! Strike these traitors dead!'

Inanna stood, pale as the apparition he thought she was, with blood-streaked face.

The *galla* snapped Dumuzi's little lapis pipe, smashed his wine cup, struck him a stinging blow across the cheekbone, kicked Amanamtagga aside.

He covered his face, cringing away, but they were behind him too. He babbled through terror, 'Inanna! Inanna! Stop them! Are you her shade come back from the Netherworld to torment me? I am Inanna's widower. I am the rightful Lord of Sky and Earth. Her Lion Throne is mine. I order you all back!'

They pulled him upright, shoved him back on the throne, howling with laughter. They tugged him off again by his ankles, so that he crashed to the ground. They tore off his colourful garment. They smacked him with cords and started to hobble his feet. Still the Chief *Galla* stared at Inanna out of his helmet eyeholes with that fierce expectation.

'Come, World Queen, Star Queen. What do you say? We have your pretty husband. What am I to say to Ereshkigal, your elder sister, Queen of the Dark City? You know her bargain. Your life for another life, your other self. Dumuzi, your honey-man? Dumuzi, your bridegroom? Shall we take him down to Kur in your place? You must speak the word that will take his life away. Or have you changed your mind? Is it *your* crown we shall strip from your head again, *your* robe we shall tear from your back, *your* sandals we shall unstrap from your feet?'

The small *galla* were dancing about her, grabbing mockingly again at her beads, her skirt, even the heavy wig of her hair.

They tormented Inanna, like flies around the carcase of a slain ewe lamb, hung on a hook beside the still-threshing body of a young ram. The bigger demons were punching and pushing and stripping the struggling Dumuzi.

'Hear me!' At last the deep, commanding voice of Inanna broke from her swelling chest, harsh with pain.

The *galla* paused in their bullying, still gripping their victim. Their beaked and snouted faces were eager to hear what she would speak. They had no fear that they would return to Ereshkigal without a prisoner. Even in the Above, the laws of the Netherworld formed an unbreakable part of creation. It was Enlil's Word, Enki's order, the cosmos spoken and fixed in its nature, power allotted to its rightful Guardians, a necessary whole.

'Well, speak then, Inanna.' The Chief *Galla*'s claws were gripping Dumuzi's shoulders.

'Inanna!' A weak despairing plea from the Shepherd. 'Is it really you? Have you brought up the *me* of the Below? *Then save me!*'

She fastened on him her black, glittering eyes. They seemed to stare straight at him, straight through him, as if there should be another Dumuzi she longed to see and could not find. She did not weep for that lost lad yet.

'Hear me, great An in far Angal! Hear me, Enlil and Nin Lil in your E-Kur! Hear me, all you Anunnaki of Above and Below. You, Ereshkigal, listen to my verdict!

'I was the Dancer, the Hierodule of Heaven, the Champion of Battle on Earth. While I was gone, no lambs, no human babies were kindled. Yet this, the Shepherd, took my slave. While I was a prisoner, Sumer was defenceless. No Lion roared against its enemies. Yet he put on my *en*'s crown, sat on my Lion Throne. He laughed and drank wine.

'Dumuzi the Shepherd, I say you are no king, you are no Lord, you are not fit to be Inanna's bridegroom. The word I speak to you is death.'

Her voice was bitter with wrath. Her look was pitiless to herself and her lover. She raised her hand against him.

'Take him! Take Dumuzi Ushumgalanna to Ereshkigal!'

The *galla* gave a great shriek of satisfaction that made the leaves of all the trees in the orchard tremble. Fear loosed Dumuzi's bowels. The demons were all around him, buffeting him, grabbing his jewels, tossing them from one to the other, knotting cords round his feet.

'*Utu!*'

The appeal shot up like an arrow from a beleaguered tower.

'Silence, Shepherd! Keep your wails for the Netherworld. You will find plenty of mourners to echo them there. Utu himself may come to judge you. But he knows better than to try and get you out, once Ereshkigal has you.'

The demon guards knocked him about with the curving backs of their copper axes, so that blood sprang where the sharp corners gouged his naked flesh.

'Utu!' he screamed as they started to drag him towards the gate. 'I am your brother-in-law! Hear me! Don't you remember the day I brought cream to the House That Brings Light? I brought presents to Nin Gal's home, wedding gifts to Ur. I've made love in the lap of your sister, like a butter churn leaping on a dairymaid's knee . . .' His voice was fading as they neared the street. 'Utu! They call you the Just! The Merciful! Help me now! Let me escape these demons! Don't let them have me!'

Inanna stood, more rigid than a cedar tree, her soul darker than the innermost chamber of the Anunnaki's houses, where no light entered. She did not feel the sun blaze. It did not light her eyes. Her hand stayed lifted against the place where Dumuzi had sat on the Lion Throne, though the *galla* had dragged him away. Her gaze seemed locked on the place of her betrayal.

'Utu . . . !'

The squeaks and hissing, the growls and roars from the *galla* made her shudder as if awaking from a terrible dream. She turned slowly. You might have thought she had no part in the scene around her, did not comprehend it.

'My lady,' breathed Nin Shubur. 'Utu has heard him!'

Someone was standing beyond the gate. A young man soiled with the ashes of mourning, like all but one of Inanna's family. Behind him, the sun was dazzling her.

Utu lifted his hand.

The demons from the gloomy caverns of the Below were shielding their eyes, howling with pain. Inanna blinked dully, stared through the blinding glory.

Dumuzi's golden body, streaked with blood, was slithering through the *galla*'s talons. Like the rope they had been lashing round him, he twisted, narrowed, lengthened. The downy skin she had licked and caressed slid into patterned scales as dappled as the sunlight through apple leaves. The large, brown, terrified eyes grew small and glittering. His gasping mouth became lipless, shot out a flickering, black tongue. His struggling hands and feet took refuge in slippery, muscular coils. A *sagkal* snake poured through its captors' snatching hands, spilled through the dry grass of the orchard, shot under the gate, down the gutters of the city streets, streaked out into the desert.

# Chapter Eighty-six

'Inanna! Inanna!' Utu was standing before her, holding her, hugging her. Inanna stood, as though drained of all life, almost of feeling. None of the terrible sounds of the city moved her. Not the screams of the people, newly awakened from sleep, seeing the furious *galla* galloping through the streets in pursuit of Dumuzi. Not the incredulous joy, mixed with half-understood horror, of Utu at his sister's return. Not the low, angry orders of Nin Shubur, clearing the garden of its shameful evidence. Not the quiet, insistent sobbing of Amanamtagga.

'I was dead, and he was dressed for a festival. I came back to Earth, and he and my slave were making love.' Then she turned to Utu at last with a fierce urgency. 'Is he safe? Will he escape? Can the *galla* catch him?'

Utu was rocking her in his arms. Tears streaked his ash-soiled face. He checked for a moment, looking down at her closely.

'I didn't know, when he called out, how much he had hurt you. What do you want, Inanna? What do you want to happen?'

'I hate him! He's broken my heart. I've sentenced him to the Netherworld . . . I love him!' She beat her fists on her brother's chest, till he caught them up to his lips and kissed them.

'I won't say "I told you so", Inanna. It's enough that we've got you back. But the case is serious. If the *galla* of Ereshkigal are after him, I may not be able to protect him for long.'

'What shall I do? What shall I do without him?'

His arms were round her, silently.

There was a commotion at the gate. They heard running feet, the clash of armour. Inanna looked up to find Gilgamesh bounding towards them, followed by half a dozen of his young blades, hastily buckling on weapons and breastplates.

'Inanna! Lion of Uruk! You've won! You've beaten the Netherworld! You've taken Ereshkigal's powers!' Gilgamesh raised his sword in a flashing salute.

'No.' She stepped away from Utu, so that the two Anunnaki, grave and tall, faced the humans. 'I was delivered from the Netherworld, thanks to Nin Shubur and Father Enki. I barely escaped with my life. I do not have those powers.'

It seemed a trivial thing to confess now, the failure of her expedition. Nothing compared with the price she had had to pay . . . was having to pay . . . would have to pay through all her future of eternity. She had lost Dumuzi.

She hardly registered the bitter pain that crossed Gilgamesh's face. For him, the loss of hope was different. The snatching away of his dream of immortality.

'No power?'

'I . . . am not Queen . . . of the Below.'

But the Queen of the Below must have Dumuzi now.

'Then I must die!'

And Inanna must live.

She came to her own chamber in the E-Anna with a deadened heart. Too soon. Nawirtum and two other slaves were hastily changing the sheets.

Inanna clutched the foot of the bed, too full to shout in anger.

'Even here? Here, in my own Lion Bed?'

Long, straight, black hairs upon the rumpled pillow. No springing curls of her own.

'Dumuzi, Dumuzi. What have you done to my *huluppu* tree?' she whispered.

Growing in the garden of Uruk it had been invaded. In her own palace it had not been safe.

A Son of An, wandering wild-eyed in the desert towards the first, low rise of the steppe. His feet shuffle through purplish sand and he looks down surprised to see beneath the skin such common bones as ankles, metatarsals, toes. Behind him, the dragging twin tracks of his heels merge into one long, sinuous trail. But further back, the wind has blown dust across the shifting, not quite level plain and wiped it out. Dust devils swirl and the thirsty Lord looks over his shoulder with a nameless fear and shudders. He knows that back there is something more dreadful than these whirling pillars of grit. He cannot remember what.

On Dumuzi staggered with knees that had lost their strength. Evening unrolled its tents of violet and crimson and lime over his head. He lifted his face to the first cool touch that might herald the fall of dew. A star rose, even before the sun's colours had left the Earth, more brilliant than all the rest to come after. Dilibad, the Evening Star, stared down at the fugitive. Dumuzi screamed and covered his face.

'What's that?' A woman's voice, sharp with enquiry. A dog broke into frantic barking.

Dumuzi lowered his hands, trembled, and recovered part of his senses.

He had walked out of the desert. The ground sloped gently uphill. For some time now he had been forcing his legs to rise without realising it. The soil was sandy, but tufts of scrub and grass loomed as darker shadows in the uneven starlight. From up above him a soft glow of lamplight made a welcome of a doorway. After the echo of the woman and the dog had died away, there was the distant murmur of sheep folded for the night.

All the horrors of the past days were hooded over, like a corpse buried by a sudden shift of sand. Childhood came flooding back like a river released. This hill, that ridge against the stars, this rush-fringed hollow where the sheep could be watered even in summer, that farmhouse whose wide-eaved thatch would shelter him from storm and sun. This dog bounding downhill to meet him, the urgent barking renewed to frenzy, and the whirlwind of shaggy black hair, four sandy paws, flinging itself into Dumuzi's outspread arms. Urgi, his black sheepdog, his friend and fellow herder. He was home.

Geshtinanna came hurrying from the house, but more wary. In one hand she carried a stout shepherd's crook.

'Who's there? Who comes to us at nightfall? Urgi! Is it a friend, then?'

'Sister!' he croaked, as the world turned blacker than the night itself. He pitched face forward at her feet.

It was a terrible night. The unknowing sheep crooned in the fold as if it was any other darkness. Urgi crouched as close to his master as he could come, panting happily, then stretched himself out on the rush-strewn floor and fell into a deep sleep of satisfaction. But Geshtinanna sat beside her unconscious brother, cleansing his wounds and wondering at those evil gashes. When he cried out in terror she wiped the sweat from his brow and held his hand. He did not wake. She did not sleep.

Not till the sun was well up in the sky did Dumuzi open his eyes. His first urgent look was to the uncovered window. The stars had paled to invisibility, even the lingering brilliance of the Morning Star. Geshtinanna heard without understanding his deep sigh of relief, saw him turn and look at her with bewilderment. A little boy lost and afraid.

She gathered him in her arms, kissed his racked face.

'What is it, Ushumgalanna? What is it, little Damu? Tell me, and let me see what I can do.'

His hand gripped the cloth over her breast. 'I had a dream! Oh, Geshtinanna, such a terrible dream! You're wise. You can read clay tablets, write poems, know medicine. Tell me the meaning of my dream.'

She tried to ease his grasping fingers and speak playfully. 'My brother is Lord in Uruk. He has all the priests of the E-Anna and his own E-Mush in Kullab. He even has the painted priestesses of Inanna! Why should he need his countrified sister, his Wine Girl? Surely the wisdom of palaces and temples is better than mine?'

Then she bent forward with a sudden urgency. 'Oh, my dear! It's Inanna, isn't it? I'm so sorry! How could I be so cruel? How could I tease you? Oh, my love, my poor little brother! You have finally lost her to the Netherworld! Is that what you've come to tell me? Did she really go down to Kur? Is it all over so soon? Has Ereshkigal won the victory for ever?

'Oh, Inanna, Inanna! My friend, my love! What shall we do without you? How will our flocks thrive, how will the lambs be born? Will there be no more love, no more children, no more joy, ever again?' She was rocking to and fro, hugging herself now, keening a lament for her sister-in-law.

Dumuzi fell back on the pillow, his face stiff and pale. 'Inanna? I don't know . . .' He passed his hand over his forehead with a dazed air. 'I can't remember . . . I only remember the nightmare.'

'Tell me!' She caught his straying hand, stroked it with her own. 'Tell me your dream, Damu. Let me see what my little wisdom can do.'

Urgi crept closer, pushed against the bed, making it sway on its netted thongs. Dumuzi fondled the dog's ears, put his arm round the rough, hairy neck for comfort. There was no comfort in the Shepherd's eyes as they looked across the farmhouse room to the vivid rectangle of light that faced across the desert to the far, unseen mound of Uruk.

'I dreamed destruction,' he said in a low, hollow voice. A long shudder racked him, and then the words came more clearly. 'Such a terrible dream. It has followed me like a mother's curse. When I lay down in the desert I dreamed it. When I slept in the marshes I dreamed it. It is a dream of little things, but the horror of it is very great. I can't tell you! Now, even here, in my own bed where I slept as a child, even here . . .' He sobbed in Geshtinanna's lap while she nursed him.

'Tell me,' she murmured, stroking his tawny curls. 'Let this poison out. Tell your wise sister. Tell your Geshtinanna who knows the meaning of dreams. Perhaps you are mistaken.'

The words, muffled against her skirt, crept out of him.

'The crabs of the river will mourn for me. The frogs of the marshes will set up a lament for me. My mother will weep for me.

'This is my dream. I was in the marshes. Thick reeds sprang up all around me. A single reed was trembling, shaking its head over me.

'I saw a twin reed growing, two canes from a single shoot. One was broken and taken away, and then the other. It's not much, it's not much, I know! But it seemed awful.

'Then I was in a grove, with a terror of tall trees all around me.

'Last, I was here. I saw water poured on the hearth of my home. The fire went out. The cover of my milk churn was knocked off; my seal was broken. The cup from which I drink milk fell from its peg. My Shepherd's crook disappeared out of my hand.

'Outside, there was an eagle snatching a lamb from the sheepfold. A falcon had seized a sparrow from the reed fence. Sister, our goats were staggering about, dragging their beautiful beards in the dust. Our sheep were in distress; they were pawing up the ground with bent legs.

'This house . . . *this house.*' His voice shook with the desolation of grief. 'The churn lay broken on its side. No milk would be poured from it again. The cup was shattered in the fall. I . . . was . . . gone. My sheepfold was given over to the winds.'

Tears were running down Geshtinanna's face as she cradled him.

'Oh, my brother. Don't tell me such a dream. Don't tell me! I wish I had never learned to read, that I had no wisdom.'

'Is there no hope, Geshtin? Is it so bad?'

'I wish I could lie to you, Damu. I wish we had not been so close that we can have no secrets from each other. But we are the twin reeds that you saw, growing from a single stock. The thick rushes round about you are evil demons. The single reed shaking its head is our mother who will mourn over us. One of the double reeds is taken, and then the other. So shall we be snatched away. The terror of tall trees is the big *galla* . . .

'Oh, Dumuzi, are they coming? Is this what Inanna has loosed on us when she opened the gates of the Netherworld? . . . They will surround the sheepfold. When they have finished with us, our hearth will be cold, our sheepfold will be a desolation. When the cover is knocked from your milk churn, when your drinking cup is smashed, you will fall from the lap of the mother who loves you, for ever. They will burn your Shepherd's crook on the fire. The *galla* will tear your face, like the eagle's talons piercing the lamb. No wall can protect you. As the falcon seizes its prey from a fence of canes, the *galla* will climb over it and seize you. My hair will whirl around in grief like the beards of the goats dragged in the dust. I will tear my cheeks for you like the sheep scratching up the earth. But the cup is shattered, the churn has fallen.

'Oh, Dumuzi, Dumuzi. When the *galla* come for you, when they handcuff and fetter you, how can my grief keep you from death?'

# Chapter Eighty-seven

'How long?' The terrible voice of Inanna echoed through her judgment hall.

Outside, the sun stared down unblinking. More than the hush of summer heat stunned the city's people into silence. Awe lay over Uruk, over Kullab, over every city where Inanna was honoured, Zabalam, Hursag-kalamma, even as far as Babylon.

Difficult to say which woman was more dreadful to look at: Inanna with her hair wild as snakes, her face deeply scratched, ashes on her breast, her black clothes torn, or the slave Amanamtagga, her face as blotched with weeping as her body was bruised and bleeding from the torturers' work.

'Since . . . the day you voyaged to Eridu to get the *me*, my Lady.'

Inanna's bare hands wrestled with the lion heads on her chair.

'While I was risking my life for Uruk! So many years? You are lying!'

The whip descended without the Lady needing to command again. Amanamtagga screamed.

'It is true, my Lady! It is true!' she wept. 'You must believe me.'

'Close the doors!' shouted Inanna in a voice of thunder.

The great bronze hinges turned. The tall leaves of cedarwood crashed shut. Darkness deepened in the hall as fearful slaves hurried to light more torches. Thin wafers of sunlight sliced the dusty shadows, more blue than gold. The humans in the courts beyond, already too frightened to approach closer, groaned and wailed.

'Now, speak the truth!'

'It is the truth, my Lady. My Lord Dumuzi was very frightened when you went to Eridu. When Enki's plagues appeared in the very heart of Sumer we thought . . . he thought you would never come back again. He got very drunk. He sat on his *en*'s throne beside your Lion chair. He caught me as I was passing. He dragged me to sit beside him—'

'HERE?'

Amanamtagga gasped, could not let out the indrawn breath in words. Then the whip descended again. Even before it landed she shrieked out, 'I could not help it! He made me! He made me wear your palm-leaf crown . . .'

'You? In my Lion Bed, *on this Lion Throne*? A human!'

The royal chair, cut by craftsmen from the *huluppu* trunk, where Gilgamesh had thrown Kiskillilla out of her hollow home and she had left it, still laughing, for the wilderness. The lion-sporting bed of the lovers' wedding night, carved from the same, spoiled timber.

'Dumuzi forced me,' sobbed the broken girl.

She could not see that her words lashed Inanna as cruelly as the leather thongs ripped her own back. Honour was stripped from the Young Lady. Her *me* of lovemaking was nothing. The bitter truth, if it was the reality, made of the greatest queen an empty shell, like a hollow statue, with no power. Vitality, sexual attraction, the ladyship of Dumuzi's heart had been in this bloodied, weeping human. The truth was shocking. Shut out of earshot below, the people of Uruk, Inanna's people, already knew too much. Inanna groaned and tore her dress further.

'You treacherous slanderer! When I came upon you yesterday you were not screaming in protest as you do now! He was not forcing you! You bored like a worm into an apple. You seduced him! You took advantage of his drinking, his grief. All these years, you have been robbing me of him. *Me, Inanna!* You tricked out of him the greatest love he should have kept for me. When I bore children, I lent him generously to the tavern hierodule. But you are not a priestess. You were not my surrogate. You desecrated our marriage. You, a human!'

'Dumuzi wanted me!' Amanamtagga wept uselessly.

And sounded her own death knell.

'Listen!' Dumuzi started up on the bed, shaking with terror. 'It's them! They're coming for me!'

Geshtinanna was on her feet, listening too.

A voice floated down the hillside towards them, high and

urgent. 'Geshtinanna! What's happening? Come quickly!'

'Oh, it's only Geshtindudue,' she tried to reassure her brother. 'You remember? My friend who grows vines on the land next to mine.'

'Geshtinanna!' The cry was almost a scream.

'Something is wrong. What has she seen?' Dumuzi begged his sister. 'It's the *galla*! If they lost my track over the desert, they will find me another way by boat. They're carrying neck stocks to shackle my head. They had handcuffs to fetter my wrists. They've brought whips and nets. They'll catch me now. Run! Find out how close they are! Get up the hill as fast as you can. Spy out over the desert. Look down the canal.'

She started to run for the door.

'*No!*' His voice caught her back. 'Not like that! Scratch your face. Tear your dress and bare your legs. Show them blood on your thighs. Make them think you're in mourning for me. They mustn't guess you've seen me alive!'

Her strong hands wrenched the fine-spun wool apart. Her face had darkened. 'I should have been in deep mourning for Inanna if I'd known. So all her family must have been, once she descended to the Netherworld. You haven't told me what happened to her. *This* is because of her, isn't it? Her doing, willing or unwilling . . . or Ereshkigal's. Oh, poor Inanna!'

Her nails ripped her flesh from her crotch to her knees. The furrows stood white, then sprang to life with trails of blood. She tore her cheeks and clawed her eyes. Then, in a whirl of rags, she ran through the door.

Geshtindudue was stumbling over the outcrops of rock above the farm.

'Oh, Geshtinanna! Thank Utu, you're here! Something on the canal . . . Something terrible! Oh, come and see!'

The two girls ran, gasping with urgency, to the top of the ridge. Below lay the boundary where the garden land of Uruk stretched its irrigation canals to the edge of the steppe. The water gleamed in the quivering sunlight, fingers of light reaching out from Inanna's city to touch the pasture land. On the last canal where Enkimdu the Farmer had made his peace with Dumuzi and given Inanna up, rode a dark, beaked boat. Its prow was a copper spike, its sides were black with pitch. The things of nightmare, spewed from the Netherworld like poisonous gases bubbling out of a marsh, were its crew. Geshtindudue stuffed her fist in her mouth to shut in a scream.

'What are they? Why are they coming here? It's the *galla*!' she whimpered.

Geshtinanna took her friend's arm. Only by the warmth of the Vine-Grower's skin did she know how cold her own was. 'Go back home,' she said. 'This doesn't concern you. Quickly, before they see you with me. There's nothing you can do. Inanna has loosed them. Ereshkigal will be waiting for their prey. It concerns our family alone.'

'Are you sure? I don't like to leave you. Come with me, Geshtinanna. Don't let them find you. You can escape too!'

Geshtinanna turned her head, looked down at the thatch of the farmhouse, the wide, sheltering roof.

'I have no hiding place,' she said. 'The *galla* would find me.'

A frightened call came up on the breeze. 'Can you see them?' Short and hoarse, as though he was afraid to make a sound, but could not bear to wait for news.

Geshtindudue threw a terrified look at his sister. 'It's Dumuzi! It is, isn't it? He's come back. It's him the *galla* are after, isn't it?'

Geshtinanna pushed her away. 'Go! Run! You've seen the blood on my face, you've seen my torn clothes. If anyone asks you, Dumuzi's dead! Go and raise a lament for both of us.'

One doubtful, hesitating look from the other girl, then she hugged and kissed the torn face of her friend. 'Oh, Geshtinanna, the power of righteousness be with you both, the gift of healing!' She turned and fled.

'They're coming!' Geshtinanna called back to Dumuzi as clearly as she dared. The ridge was above her now, the boat hidden. 'You must hide. Quick as you can. They'll find this farm soon.'

She was stumbling down the hill, her usual free, long strides seeming too short and clumsy this morning. Scarcely seeing where she was going she staggered through the door. A stitch stabbed her side, her lungs rasped painfully for breath. She leaned against the doorpost. 'Oh, hurry, hurry!'

A shock of altered perception. In the dim, cool living-space of the farmhouse, where the sunlight fell only in scattered, golden drops through matting or window slit, another man was standing.

'Oh!' Her hand flew to her lips, then she laughed in relief. 'It's you, Kuli! Oh, thank heaven! But you must help Dumuzi. You must get him away.'

'I'll do what I can,' the young Herdsman promised. 'I know a little of what's afoot. No, don't tell me more. If the *galla* are coming, I don't want to be found here.'

'We can't hide you on this farm,' Geshtinanna said to her brother. 'You must flee into the steppe. Where, where . . . ? You know that deep hollow by the marshes? Where we drive the sheep when our own pool runs dry in the very worst droughts? Even in summer the grass is long there, the reed clusters are thick. The place is a maze of ditches. Go to the swamp of Arali. If you can find safety anywhere on Earth, it would be a hiding place there.'

'Can I reach it before they sight the farm?' Dumuzi's face, grey in the shadowed room, looked towards the brightness of the open door, torn between panic and hope.

'You must try! Take him, Kuli! Come back and tell me when he is safe . . . No! Wait for that till the *galla* have gone. If I . . . If I am still here, come back then.'

'Can I trust you both? You mustn't tell *anybody* where I've gone. Kuli? Geshtinanna? Promise!'

'We would both die for you,' Geshtinanna said. 'If we reveal your hiding place, let us be torn to pieces. Urgi himself bite my throat out, if I tell where his Shepherd is hiding.'

'I swear,' said Kuli. 'For goodness sake, come on, man! . . . All right, then! May no one betray your secret. May the royal dogs of your palace, the wild dogs of the steppe, or your own black Urgi eat me down to the bones if I breathe one word. Will that do?'

Kuli went swiftly to the door, looked up at the ridge over which the *galla* must come. He looked scared too. He licked his dry lips. 'No sign yet. How far away were they, Geshtinanna?'

'I didn't stay to watch them disembark at the end of the canal. One look was enough for me. You're right, Dumuzi, they have stocks, they have fetters. They're coming to take you like a prisoner of war, like a captured slave.'

'I was Inanna's prisoner! She condemned me!'

'Go!' begged Geshtinanna. 'Don't stay and argue. You'll break my heart. Run, now!'

The two young men looked at each other, grasped each other's hand. No time to kiss the urgent Geshtinanna. No last hug, no tears of farewell. One fearful glance at the empty skyline. They broke over the threshold.

They had hardly run six strides before a furious barking

burst from the rear of the farm. Urgi came bounding round the corner, a splendour of flying black fur and eager red tongue. Dumuzi turned in a confusion of surprise and terror.

'No, Urgi! No, old friend. You can't come! Back! Get back. Stay!'

The willing, obedient dog sat down, swished his tail in the dust. But when the young men began to rush off again, the dog could not contain himself. He leaped to his feet. Geshtinanna lunged forward, grabbed his thick, black ruff. 'No, Urgi,' she begged. 'Stay with me. You can't protect him now from what's coming, and your presence could kill him.'

The dog whined and strained. Geshtinanna held him back with all her strength. She watched Dumuzi and Kuli race away.

Down the slope of the steppe, around the lower ridge. Their heads dropped out of sight. Geshtinanna stood alone in the doorway of the house, the mournful dog still in her grip.

# Chapter Eighty-eight

Now Geshtinanna went down on her knees and wept the tears she could not shed before, not for Dumuzi but for what she knew she had to do for him. Her arms went round the big dog's neck. He licked her tears.

'Oh, Urgi, Urgi. You love him, don't you? As I do? We'd die for him willingly, you and I, wouldn't we?'

She was moving now, pulling him little by little to the outbuilding at the side of the house.

'You want to save him, don't you? And I know what will happen if I let you go. Your big, generous, loving heart will have only one thought in it: to follow Dumuzi. You will track his scent. You will lead the *galla* to the swamps of Arali. They will find his hiding place. You wouldn't want that, Urgi, would you? You wouldn't want the *galla* to find him?'

The dog whimpered and struggled a little, but she held him fast. She had him inside the toolshed now and kicked the door shut behind her. She leaned against it, fighting for breath.

'I could tie you up, old friend. But when you hear what is going to happen, you might pull the posts from the ground to come to my rescue. I cannot promise not to scream. And if they hear you barking, they will come and loose you, and you will lead them to Dumuzi.'

She took the pruning knife from the hook on the beam over her head. Her thumb tested the blade. It was sharp, well-greased.

'So. Every spring I cut back my vines with Geshtindudue. Every autumn I harvest the grapes and make rich wine. Should I go the same road as I am sending you, Urgi? Is it time for the grapes to fall? I don't know. What would happen if I cut my throat? Can a Lady die? We thought it was only humans who were mortal. But it seems that Inanna was caught in the Netherworld, and must go back there unless she sends another prisoner. Is that what death is, even for a

Daughter of An, to be trapped in the Below? But out of Kur comes the seven-mouthed river, all the abundance of the Land of the Living, grain, wine . . . life . . .'

A cry shrilled on the hill above, as wild and chilling as jackals greeting nightfall, though it was nearly noon. The blood left Geshtinanna's heart. Urgi gave a short, challenging bark. It was his last. With the force of her well-muscled arm, Geshtinanna drove the knife down across the sheepdog's throat. Breath whistled in astonishment before blood drowned it. His eyes were wide and yellow, fixed on hers. And then tears blinded her. She sank down hugging the dying dog, covering her already scratched body with his blood that overran hers.

'My time will come,' she whispered. 'Soon.'

Calmer now, because she knew precisely what she must do, she staggered out into the open with the corpse in her arms. The half-severed head hung awkwardly. The stiff, black legs caught in the rents of her skirt. She must not see through the dazzle of tears and sunshine the blackness swarming down from the ridge. She must not hear the shrieks louder than the scream of hawks overhead. There was a heap of stones, a table. She must gather dry grass, branches of thorn, light a fire. It might not be done before the demons fell upon her, but it must seem to them that this was her sole purpose. It was a kind of truth. She had sacrificed Dumuzi's dog for his life.

She did not reach the altar. They were all around her. The small ones were clinging to her sides. The big ones opened their wings over her with a terrifying clap of bony webs. The sky darkened. She could not help crying out in fright and disgust. Her flesh shrank from their touch, but there was nowhere to flee. The stench of their breath, of their sweat, was worse than the stinking camelthorn, or the corner of the wall where men urinate. She did not want to fill her nostrils with it but she was gasping it in. There was nothing to appeal to in their eyes, avid for pain. Those lipless mouths would never speak words of mercy, never sing songs for children, never kiss a spouse. They were not Children of An. They did not drink libated water, or eat sprinkled flour. Skulls hung from their necks. At their hips were maces that could crush more. Over their shoulders they carried nets.

'Take me, if you must,' she managed to gasp. 'I don't want to live. Dumuzi is dead. Inanna has condemned him to the

Netherworld. I have sacrificed his dog to Ereshkigal. Let me follow too.'

They snatched the dog from her arms and flung him away. They pushed her rudely from one to the other, like a doll of straw. They slapped her face. Their voices, harsh as the scream of a hunting owl, pierced her brain with the words she had dreaded to hear.

'We do not want you!'
'What are you to us?'
'We want Dumuzi.'
'Inanna has named him.'
'Ereshkigal has set her price.'
'We must have Dumuzi.'
'*Where is he?*'
'I do not know!'

A claw, armoured in black shell, scored her face across the stinging wounds of her own nails. Fresh blood sprang. The pain of its venom made her scream.

'I cannot tell you!'

They spat in her face, and the poison blinded her eyes. They snatched at her dress. The good cloth, already torn, was ripped away leaving her naked and shivering in the noonday heat.

They dragged her to the farmhouse, threw the contents of the cooking pot over the floor. Two of the bigger *galla* had brought something from the shed, chattering with glee. They broke lumps of black bitumen into the clay pot. They hoisted it over the fire.

Geshtinanna sat, her hands bound behind her, her legs in stocks. Through stinging eyes she watched the pot on the fire with a dumb terror. What did they mean to do? Could she be that strong? Could she hold out against the pain?

'Now!' said the Chief *Galla*, clashing his talons together. 'Will you speak? Tell us where Dumuzi is hiding.'

'He is not here,' she managed to whisper.

'Oh, very good! We are not fools! We can see that for ourselves. *Where did he go?*'

She shook her head, dumb now with a doubled fear. Afraid that any denial might betray some hint of the truth.

The Chief *Galla* drew closer, smiled horrifyingly with saw-edged, yellow teeth.

'The Below is the Kur of abundance. You are called a wise woman, Lady Geshtinanna. You know that. All life goes to it.

All life comes from it. We can give you far more than you can imagine, for that single, useful word.'

Silence. That a *galla* should speak pleasantly to her frightened her more than his brutality. The world was becoming unstable.

'We would give you the Water Gift.' Her face did not move. 'Don't you know what it means?' he snapped. 'In Sumer? Never to go short of water? Never to see your flocks staggering from thirst? Never to find skeletons of your kids in the desert? Never to have your grapes wither before their time in your precious vineyards? *Never*.'

'*No*.' Dry lips formed the word but no sound came.

The pitch began to bubble over the fire.

'The Grain Gift, then? I have Ereshkigal's authority. Always food. Always plenty. More than you could ever eat. Barns piled high with living gold. You could trade it for anything you want in the world. This quiet farm could be the centre of a great civilisation. With the wealth, you could found schools, employ scribes, patronise musicians. Your name would be praised in the hymns of poetesses, carved for all time in stone.'

Her lids sagged wearily over her eyes. When would it be over? She hardly had the strength to shake her head.

He kicked the shackles from her legs, bruising the bones. Small *galla* with pinching fingers pulled her legs apart. The big *galla* were carrying the pot towards her. Black, smoking pitch was pouring over the rim, reversing the flow of life, descending towards the sacred well-mouth of her vulva.

She screamed then, over and over again. It could not have been long before the mercy that sets bounds, even to the limits of an immortal's endurance, decreed enough and the darkness engulfed her brain too. Yet as long as Anunnaki live she would remember this pain.

She screamed. She did not speak.

The Chief *Galla* threw himself down on the couch so that it cracked. He bit his talons into sharper points. A little *galla* sat down beside him, another on the opposite side.

'We are wasting our time, Horror of Aksak, Dread of Uruk. Women are weak in body, strong in heart. Where, since the beginning of time, would you find a sister who would betray her brother's hiding place? They love the beasts!'

The *galla* cackled with hideous laughter.

'Come on,' said the other *galla*, plucking at his chief's

weapon belt. 'There is no more sport here . . . But didn't she scream! Let's see if we can get richer pickings from his best friend.'

'Dumuzi Abzu came this way,' said the Chief *Galla*, rising to his feet with a sudden crack of his carapace. 'The tracks of the snake led out across the desert, before the wind whipped them away.'

'Damn Ishkur for it! Inanna's Storm Brother should have been more helpful to us than that.'

'Where is the pleasure, if the hunt is too easy? Ereshkigal will not be mocked. The power of the Netherworld must find him out. There is no hiding place on Earth the *galla* cannot track him to.'

'And a little torture is a relish to the taste of blood and the meat of fear.'

They went on to Kuli's house. But before they left, they rocked Dumuzi's milk churn, making it roll and spin between them with shouts of laughter. They swung his drinking cup violently on its peg, like a too-ripe apple. The Chief *Galla* himself tested the Shepherd's crook across his knee, stood it upright again, let it reluctantly go, as one who is saving up a particular pleasure. They gathered in a ring around the unconscious Geshtinanna and chuckled knowingly.

Kuli was coming over the brow of the rise when he saw them. He checked and turned to run. The *galla* were too quick for him. On scorpion legs, on hook-fringed bat wings, they shot over his head, around his sides, in front of him, behind him. He stood taller than them, a handsome outdoor Son of An, but trembling in a sea of ugliness, like a palm tree in a hurricane of wind-whipped sand.

'No! No! Get back! Don't touch me!' he pleaded.

'Where is Dumuzi?' The shout was bullying. The Chief *Galla* himself had Kuli by the elbow, jostled him.

'Who? What Dumuzi? I don't know!'

Spears pricked his other side. He was being pushed back into a wall of *galla* who swung their maces hopefully.

'No! No! What do you want? What can I tell you?'

'Come, sit down,' suggested the Chief *Galla*, surprisingly pleasant, in a sudden switch that left his followers snarling behind closed teeth.

He offered Kuli the Water Gift. The Herdsman raised his eyes, wide as his bull's, in a white face. He looked at the dry, sandy steppe, at the chewed thorn bushes, at the too-bright eyes of the *galla*. He accepted it.

'Yes!' he nodded, in a gasp that was hardly audible. 'Dumuzi was here.'

'*Where is he now?*'

Kuli shook his head, struggling against friendship, against the fear of things darker than pain.

'We will offer you the Grain Gift . . .'

Wealth. He could be a ruler in glory, like Dumuzi himself. And if he did not . . . The *galla* were creeping nearer and nearer.

He nodded again with a speechless agony.

'*Where?*' The question cracked round his ears so that he started back on to the spears behind him. He screamed and fell forward and the *galla* shrieked with mirth.

'In the grass!' he gabbled. 'Dumuzi is hiding in the grass!'

The Chief *Galla* moved his great, copper head and stared all around, at the desert below, at the plateau behind. 'What grass could hide so big a Lord? I cannot see him. Do not mock the *galla* of Ereshkigal, Cowman.'

'I will show you!' Kuli jumped to his feet. The *galla* beat their weapons together, startling the cattle, who galloped in all directions in panic.

'Lead on,' said the Chief *Galla*. 'Death is the torrent that sweeps all friendships apart. This is going to be interesting.'

'I do not know the exact place,' confessed Kuli in a rush of shame and self-preservation. 'I can take you to where I left him. But I can't tell you where he may be lying by now.'

'Show us the scent,' the Chief *Galla* smiled. 'We will find him.'

They began to march across the steppe with Kuli a prisoner between their ranks, swifter and swifter, till they broke into a loping run.

# Chapter Eighty-nine

'I must witness this,' Inanna, stony-faced, said to Nin Shubur.

'Can't you give her a lesser punishment? Isn't it enough that you have condemned your own husband to the Netherworld?' the *sukkal* replied.

'Silence! What could she say now to remove one brick of the kiln she built to burn her own body? She condemned herself with her own mouth. You heard her! With the same lips that sucked Dumuzi's . . .'

The *sukkal* walked with a grave dignity down the great staircases of the E-Anna, across vast courtyards to the lowest plinth, close above the crowding city of lesser halls and houses. A murmuring sea of faces thronged the streets and spaces around the precinct wall. Inanna's court and household were gathered on the lowest terrace. Though the sun blazed, a sense of thunder hung in the air, electrifying as Inanna came into view. She was dressed dramatically in the garb of mourning. The radiance of her beauty was deliberately dirtied and scarred. Her eyes blazed from purple hollows of weeping. Blood reddened her arms and legs, which the ragged one-ply garment of widowhood did not hide. The people moaned and wailed, in sorrow and communal repentance. Inanna was angry, and it weighed on them all.

The black-haired Amanamtagga, stripped naked, flung herself prostrate in the dust at Inanna's approach.

'Oh, mistress of loving kindness, forgive me! If I ever did you any good service, remember that and spare me! By the radiance of your planet Dilibad, look favourably on me!'

Inanna came on, like a dark cloud before the wind.

Nin Shubur stopped just short of the young woman and her guards. She murmured to the mistress behind her, 'Where is she from? Was she taken in war, or born into An's household, or sold by her parents?'

'What does it matter now? She was a slave,' said Inanna, as if her lips were frozen, Inanna, who had always been loved as the protector of young women. 'Does she need a history?'

A shadow of longing passed over the face of the exiled Queen of the East. Visions of lost mountains, waterfalls, cedar forests, passed through her mind. Her gaze fell on the crouched, pleading wreck that had been the wise Amanamtagga. Torn nails on hands that had dressed Inanna every day. Dishevelled black hair that had curtained the human's weary face as she crouched silently outside her mistress's bedchamber door, waiting for the silence that told her it was safe to sleep. Nin Shubur could not cross the final space to lay a hand on the petrified slave's head. She could only will her look to fall like a comforting touch.

Ishtaran was there on behalf of the Anunnaki, to see justice done.

'This is your slave,' he said, 'your possession. She sat on your throne. She lay in your bed. She betrayed her sacred trust. The law is clear. The decision is yours.'

Even the birds seemed stilled to listen.

'*Mercy!*' The small, choked, helpless gasp from Amanamtagga, face downward in the dust.

'Death!' A single, bitter word that told of shrivelled hope, of the leaves of the tree of love turned black by frost, of withered joy.

A moan, louder with the lust for spectacle, sobbed from the listening crowd at her cry.

Inanna herself seized the girl by the forelock, dragged her to the edge of the plinth.

Nin Shubur wrung her hands. 'Wouldn't it be more merciful to throw her from the highest terrace? She might die more quickly and certainly then.'

'It is not I who will execute her. Her blood is not on my hands.'

The *sag-ursag* were hoisting the struggling Amanamtagga on to the terrace wall at the top of the lowest steps. Inanna cried out to the uplifted faces of the crowd.

'My people! The betrayer of Uruk's Lady is yours. Let the weaver kill her with his beam. Let the shepherd strike her with his crook. The elegist can batter her to death with her timbrel, the potter shatter her with his kiln-fired jar.'

Out of the pushing throng, Gilgamesh himself brandished

in one hand a copper dagger glinting in the sun; in the other, his great stone-headed mace.

'Throw her to us, Queen of Stars!' he roared. 'There isn't a loyal citizen of Uruk that won't strike a blow at her for love of you and your honour. Give us your traitor!'

'Take her, and destroy her!'

The limp bundle of Amanamtagga's body, like a tattered reed mat torn from a rotten roof, twisted through the air earthwards. Nin Shubur held her breath, closed her eyes. The roar of the crowd told her there would be nothing left to see but the eager, shoving, competing press of city folk raising the tools of their trade to crush the evidence of Dumuzi's betrayal.

When she opened her eyes again she turned to find her mistress pale, sweating, her face almost green with sickness, but her look staring, staring at the swarm of the dark-headed people of Sumer finishing her awful work. Nin Shubur caught her by the elbow, motioned to the shocked household women to guide her into the shade of the lowest cloister.

For a day and a night Inanna hid herself and wept with a terrible grief.

To north and south the plateau stretched away, sparse grazing for the cattle. West was the high desert of Martu, distantly blue as wood smoke. But here at their feet as the demons came over the sandy rise was a wide depression where the winter streams had drained down to make a spreading marsh. It was a green place still. Huge clumps of reeds rose taller than a Lord's head. Weedy ditches, haunted by the cries of plovers, threaded through it, merging into silvery meres. Further from its banks the sweet pastures of spring had dried into tall, gold hay.

Sheep roamed dry-footed on this higher ground, leaving the longer grass, nibbling the short and broken blades. Fine cattle, golden and black, waded in mud, tore with their great soft lips at the taller tufts of fodder.

The marsh was vast, the hiding places many thousands.

The *galla*'s hands nipped Kuli's arms with a suspicion of treachery. 'Where? Exactly?'

'In the long grass. Across there, where the first rock comes to the surface in that low cliff. Do you see that band of copper ore? Look, where it's catching the sun. That's where I left him. The grass is long at the foot of that bluff. It hides several hollows.'

They were running him towards it. The rock flashed in the sunlight with its promise of magic metal. Claws were parting the tall, dry stalks, finding the thick, juicier grass behind it, the earth still damp below the overhanging cliff. There were many shallow depressions under the rock wall. No cowering Dumuzi.

Wordlessly, with slow menace, the *galla* turned their eyes towards Kuli.

'He was here! He was here! Look, you can see the print of his bare feet! You must believe me!'

The confused impressions of Dumuzi's presence trailed away on to drier earth.

'*He is not here now.*'

'He . . . he was in a panic. He was afraid you would track him too easily in the grass. He could have jumped up again after I left him. I don't know where he is now.'

The small *galla* were already snuffling like pigs over the dry ground. They cast about and yelped at the scent of their prey. They rushed through the grass, flattened the hay and sent the sheep bounding away over the plateau like gale-driven clouds. They did not find Dumuzi in the pasture, but at the edge of the marsh a broad splay of feet had trodden in yielding mud, sunk deeper and deeper, like a man running, floundering.

'*Where was he going?*'

'How do I know? He may be hiding in the rushes at the edge of the water. You were close behind us at the farmhouse. He hadn't time to go far. He was terrified you would overtake him in the open. He must be somewhere here.'

The demons tore up rushes with their claws, ploughed up black mud into a stinking swamp. The cattle lowed in agitation, struggled to the shore and galloped off. Coots' nests were broken, herons driven off, grebes clattered into the sky. The muddy waters crept in over the churned clawprints. Dumuzi was not in the rushes of the margin.

'*I think you know.*'

The tall Chief *Galla* moved closer to Kuli. 'You must know. If your little plan had succeeded, as it never could, if the *galla* troop of Ereshkigal had gone back to Inanna empty-handed, you and that sentimental fool Geshtinanna would have had to know where Dumuzi was. You would have wanted to get the news to him, bring him food and comfort.

His trail appears to be lost in the water, *but you know where it leads, don't you?*'

Talons like copper shackles round his upper arm. Helmeted eyes burning with a single purpose. No subterfuge, no tears can turn the *galla* from their prey. They never weary in pursuit.

'I . . . advised him . . . to reach the taller reeds. One of the islands. But there are hundreds. How can I know which one?'

At a sign from the Chief *Galla* the bigger demons took off on leather wings, beating the water into a cringing flurry of wavelets like an evil wind. They swooped on islets anchored in mud or floating stacks of rotting roots. Their copper axes slashed the tall canes. As the reed clumps fell, a merciless light spread over the meres. At each stroke Kuli's heart leaped to his throat, dreading to hear a sudden cry of anguish, a howl of triumph. The Chief *Galla* watched him.

'We shall get him. We would hunt him through eternity, if we had to, and not eat or sleep or stop. Oh, we shall find him. But it is not respectful to great Ereshkigal to keep her waiting when you know the answer.'

'You can see for yourself! He could be in a thousand hiding places.'

*'But he is only in one.'*

Kuli's breathing was loud in the waiting pause. The frightened wildfowl clamoured, netting the sky above. When their cries died away, they left the dull beating of the demon's wings, the crack of falling canes. Kuli licked his lips again, his will pinioned by the Chief *Galla*'s gaze.

'Geshtinanna said . . .' Fire blazed in the Chief *Galla*'s eyes with the triumph of truth. 'She told him . . . to duck his head down in the ditches of Arali. He was terrified. He trusts his sister absolutely. She is wise. He knows she loves him. She would die for him. He would have done exactly what she said. *He trusts her.*'

'*Aahh!* Arali? And where *precisely* is that?'

'This . . .' The words came thick and clotted as if his tongue was swollen. 'This is the swamp of Arali. All this.' He gestured weakly with his head.

'*But?*'

'But . . . yes. The Ditch of Arali. It's what we call . . . When we were children, we played here, Dumuzi, Geshtinanna, Geshtindudue and I. There is a stream . . . over on the far side . . . It flows out from the marsh over the lip of the steppe. It feeds the first canal that leads across the plain to Uruk. It is called the Ditch of Arali.'

'Show me this ditch!'

It seemed a long, heavy walk, the mud of the margin clogging his feet. The *galla* did not seem to hurry him now. They marched with a measured stride, their splayed claws lightly depressing the swamp as though there was less weight in their hollow, heartless bodies than in Kuli's. The still ruination of the mere, with its felled reed clumps, began to move with music. Little streams rippled and bubbled beside them. It became necessary to stride over running water, then to leap it. The marsh was in movement, the ground dipping away to reveal a vista of distant farmland, the first foliage of civilisation.

'So he was afraid to die alone, the poor little Lord of Kullab. Even though Inanna has sentenced him to Kur, he must still come where he can lie and look out over the land of Uruk towards her house.'

'He *loved* her.'

'And Inanna loves him! That is the beauty of it, Herdsman. Without that, where would our satisfaction be?'

'You are cruel.'

'Oh yes, we try to be.'

A broad, clear, flowing stream. An island divided it. Reeds, tall and ripe with summer fullness, made a wall about it. A dangerous place for a hunter. A wild boar might make his lair in such a thicket. The *galla* surrounded it. The wet shells of the small demons' armour glistened blackly. The big *galla* rose into the air, hung overhead.

Then a shriek pierced the sky.

'He is here!'

'Seize him.'

The winged *galla* swooped. The canes were snapped and flattened in the rushing dive. A man's voice screamed. The small demons were wading through flying water, brandishing spears and axes, chattering with frenzied relish. Black nets coiled through the air, spread out and fell. The big *galla* cursed the smaller ones under their feet. Axes flashed in the sun.

Dumuzi was dragged out of the wreckage between two bat-winged *galla* with all the others exulting in a pushing throng round them. He was pale and weeping. They dragged him waist-deep through the running river to the shore where they threw him at the Chief *Galla*'s feet.

'Your prize for Ereshkigal, Dread of Uruk.'

Dumuzi raised his streaming eyes, saw Kuli's face.

'Curse you! Geshtinanna would have died to save my life. But you I called my friend have betrayed me. If my sister bears a child and it wanders in the street, I call on every human and Anunnaki to protect it. If your child wanders from home, may it be lost for ever, may you never set eyes on it again. May it be cursed!'

But Geshtinanna would bear no children now.

The *galla* surrounded him. They whirled him round and round, whipping a cord that fastened his limbs to his body. They drove a spike through it, twisted it ever tighter. They locked fetters on his hands, they fastened a bar on his neck. He bowed with the weight of it and they flogged his back. They hauled up his head by the hair, struck him violently in the stomach. Bellowing with pain he struggled to force his tied hands towards the clear, blue sky.

'Utu! Can't you see this! Where is your justice? Where's your fairness? Save me! I'm your brother. I married Inanna. She made love to me! For the honour of our family, rescue me!'

In Uruk, Inanna lifted her head, saw through her tears Utu, with his back to her, staring out to the shimmering horizon.

A wind blew. Cleared of its towering canes, the whole mere around Dumuzi broke into dazzling waves.

For the second time the *galla* yelped and covered their eyes.

They did not see Dumuzi's bowed back grow longer, striped, supple, stretching the demons' bonds to breaking point. Thick, muscled legs fined down to slender, delicate bones, slipping their pointed hooves out of the loosened cords. A startled head with upcurved horns flashed terrified, black eyes around. The gazelle gave one great leap over the heads of the small *galla* and sped away over the border of the marsh.

The *galla* rubbed their smarting eyes and looked about them. With a howl of fury they went after him. The panic-driven animal bounded blindly down the slope on to the plain, heading for the distant shelter of trees and bushes. All afternoon he ran, and staggered at last into the gardens of Kubireshi.

But muscles and magic were failing with the daylight. Back

in the shape of a man, Dumuzi crouched in a date-palm grove. The demons were close behind. They swooped down and almost caught him. With a desperate shout to Utu, he changed his shape again and took flight into the blinding sunset.

'That is enough!' An thundered to his great-grandson. 'You have had one day to save him. The laws of the Netherworld cannot be mocked.'

'But he is my brother-in-law!'

'You are a judge. You know the rules. The Above must keep its bargain with the Below.'

'Inanna is weeping blood.'

'Aah! I told her she should not have married him.'

'Is it nothing to you either, what Geshtinanna is suffering?'

The Sky Lord twisted reluctantly on his couch. 'Oh, very well, then! If the *galla* find him, if he calls to you again . . . Once more. But this must be the last time!'

# Chapter Ninety

As night fell, Dumuzi staggered, once more on man-wearied feet, towards the light of a house.

A fearsome figure, he staggered over the threshold. An old woman struggled to rise from the fireside, her body too stiff for the force of her fright.

'Old Mother Belili.' He held out a beseeching hand to her. 'Don't make a sound. Please don't scream. Can't you recognise me?'

She shook her head vigorously. The apple quivered in her scraggy throat.

'I know what you're thinking. These wounds. These bruises. I'm not a brigand. I'm not a criminal come to rob you. I'm a Son of An! I'm Inanna's husband. It's Dumuzi Ushumgalanna.'

Still she stared at him with frightened, uncomprehending eyes. Her hands twisted her skirt.

'Believe me! I know you, Old Belili. It's me, Dumuzi. Help me. Obey me. Pour out some water for me to drink, quickly. Give me meal to eat. I am a Lord!'

Her shaking hands obeyed. Cool water from the clay pot flowed into a cup. Fine wheatmeal was spread on a platter before him. He grabbed them with hungry hands. Even more than the needs of the body, his soul craved this reassurance that he was still a Lord, still acknowledged and honoured, not yet extinguished like the shade of a mortal in the Netherworld.

'Water and flour are the offerings we make for the dead,' Old Belili mumbled.

He started, stared at her, horrified.

Then he cast a rapid look behind him. The door was partly closed.

'Let me sleep here, Belili. I'm very weary.'

'Since you are a Lord,' she snorted, 'I can't say no.'

He lay down on the worn blanket she showed him, but he could not sleep. Old age and weariness dulled the edge of Mother Belili's fear. She snored.

When the sun was creeping up towards the horizon, the old woman rose and went outside. The *galla* were coming up the slope. She stood stock-still, a peasant's futile anger in her face.

'You are not surprised to see us, old woman? Could it be you were expecting us?' The Chief *Galla* smiled, but looked into her care-wrinkled face searchingly. 'You don't shake? You aren't going to scream and run?'

'What's the use?' she spat at him. 'You'd only break into my house. You'll take what you want. I've lived too long. I know your kind. I can't stop you. I've lost children, and grandchildren too, to the Netherworld before this. You always get what you come for.'

'He *is* here, isn't he? Lord Dumuzi, Ama-Ushumgalanna.'

'I'm a poor mortal. I can't interfere between the Anunnaki and the *galla*. It will be my turn soon enough.'

'Don't expect gratitude, Old Belili. Don't think because you let us pass without a struggle we shall grant you a few more years.'

'I've known better than to waste my breath begging for pity from the Netherworld.'

From the house behind her came a despairing cry. Belili watched dry-eyed as the prisoner Dumuzi was dragged from her threshold into the blinding sun.

'One last time, Utu! Only help me this once . . .'

'Seize him! Hold him tight!' yelled the Chief *Galla*. 'Don't you dare let him make fools of us again!'

They were fencing Dumuzi in, swinging the net, twisting the rope. The bigger ones hurled sticks at him. He kicked and fought.

The sun was rising. The light fired the crystals of the desert.

In the pastures of An Above, Utu raised his hand.

Out of the mêlée streaked the *sagkal* snake. In a tiny puff of sand it vanished across the steppe. Pandemonium broke out. The Chief *Galla* hurled curses at his troop and they jostled each other, trampling across the trail of the snake.

From Angal, two Lords, one old, one young, looked down, watching the fear-crazed reptile searching for its final refuge.

* * *

A blank mud wall, bristling with reed stakes, on which were impaled several skulls. The gates shut fast, even in daylight, on the sinister booty within.

'Let me in! Girgire! Let me in!'

'Get away, Shepherd! Do you want to bring the hunt of the Netherworld down on us too?'

'You must help me, Girgire! Bilulu! For pity's sake!'

A woman swore. 'You heard what my son said. Better Inanna's flock without its Shepherd. More pickings for the likes of us.'

A stone struck his head, another hit his shoulder.

Dumuzi lifted his hand to wipe the blood away. He stared dully at its familiarity. Four fingers, a thumb. He gave a little sob of despair, a Son of An on the open steppe, without disguise.

Geshtinanna forced herself to walk through the biting pain. The sheep bleated impatiently from the fold. She must let them out to pasture. The third long, bitter day stretched out ahead of her. How could she herd them, mutilated as she was? The farm seemed friendless, too quiet without the leaping, shaggy warmth of Urgi. But the ewes must be milked, the pans of milk set for the cream to rise. The sun was already up and the work had to be done. Perhaps Geshtindudue would come . . . But no, she had ordered her friend to keep away.

Kuli shared her secret. Kuli would help her. He would tell her that Dumuzi was safe. He would take charge of everything.

She opened the hurdle of the sheepfold. The ewes pressed towards her. She gasped as they touched her abdomen. Biting her lip, she fondled their curly heads, their twisting horns. For a while she leaned against the stout reed fence, letting the warmth of the morning sun comfort her.

Then she saw him. The tawny curls that were no sheepskin. The fear-filled eyes that pleaded for help where she had no help left to give. The wounded chest and wrists. Fresh blood on his head. Dumuzi was cowering in a corner of his own sheepfold.

Geshtinanna cried then. Raising her weeping face to heaven she shrieked, careless of who heard her. Her grief soared to the sky. She bowed her body and mourned over the earth. Her wail was flung to the far horizon like an outspread garment.

What difference could it make now who might answer her? She ripped at her eyes, her mouth, her legs. Then she was out of the fold, slammed the hurdle shut and limped off up the slope.

'Geshtinanna?' his cry bleated after her among the lambs. She did not turn back.

When the *galla* caught her for the second time, she was squatting on the shearing floor, combing the brown and white wool from a fleece.

'Show us where your brother is. We know he came this way. The brigand Girgire and his mother told us. Let us get hold of that *snake*.'

She shook her head and sighed, got up and walked away. They followed her. Snapping their jaws and hissing, they trailed her to the vegetable garden and watched her pick up her hoe and attack the ground. They gathered round to stare at what she would uncover.

After a while the Chief *Galla* said in a voice like jagged tin, 'You are making fools of us, girl. He is not here, is he?'

Wordlessly she dropped her hoe, wandered to the drying shed where the skins of butchered sheep were pegged out before curing. She traced her fingers over them, testing the oil, the texture, pulled out the pins. With a grimace of pain she bent and rolled them into a bundle, fastened it with twine. She tried to lift it, only to let it fall.

The *galla* were swarming along the beams, searching the rafters under the thatch, the leather sacks, the storage jars. Grain, wine, oil spilled out over the floor in a savage flow of entrails.

Her head hanging now, her hair hiding her face, Geshtinanna stumbled downhill towards the house. The *galla* jostled closer, breath panting with a rising excitement of anticipation as she lifted the mattress from her bed, staggered to the door, emptied its contents of chaff outside. Their eyes fixed on the empty cover in her hands.

The Chief *Galla* struck her across the face, a blinding blow. 'That is enough! When you taunt us, you mock Ereshkigal! No one escapes the *galla*. You know the price of silence!'

She leaned against the doorpost with closed eyes.

'She has shown us where he is not,' whined the little *galla*. 'What else is left?'

Geshtinanna felt, but did not see, all of them swing to face the reed fence of Dumuzi's sheepfold.

'Where should the Shepherd be,' the Chief *Galla* asked softly, 'but with his flock?'

With brays of glee, as if they had been waiting for this all morning, had known where the end must come, had been playing with him, putting off the sweet taste of his final capture, the *galla* hurled themselves at the fence. They did not wait to enter by the gate. They pushed and elbowed each other for a place on the wall. They attacked from all sides. The big *galla* swooped over in a darkness of wings. The little *galla* clawed and scrabbled and tumbled in head first. The Chief *Galla* threw wide the wicker gate and cut the throats of the lambs and kids as they fled past him.

'Get up, Dumuzi,' they shouted at the prostrate Lord lying with his head in his hands. 'It is time to rise. Husband of Inanna! Son of Nin Sun! Brother of Geshtinanna! What woman is there to help you now?'

A dark dustcloud blew across the face of the sun.

'Utu!' Dumuzi cried out. 'Save me! For the love of Inanna!'

But the sky was full of flying grit.

The first *galla* seized Dumuzi and struck him in the face with a piercing claw. The next hit him a blow on the side of his head with his own Shepherd's crook. They dragged him into the house. They threw his crook on the fire. Before his eyes the third *galla* smashed the cover from his churn and kicked it over on the floor. The milk spilled white on the red earth. The fourth swung the cup mockingly on its peg then sent it crashing to the ground in fragments. The fifth jumped on the overturned churn, cracking and crushing it smaller and smaller.

The sixth kicked Dumuzi. 'Lord! You will have no crown on your head now; you will go bareheaded. You will not want the royal coloured garment today; you will walk naked. You cannot carry a ruler's sceptre where you are going. You must descend with nothing. Where did you get those sandals? Let me strip them from your feet, your little hairy puppies. You must go barefoot to Ereshkigal.'

The *galla* bound him; his wrists stayed bound. They put a captive's stock on his neck; his head stayed trapped.

'*Utu!*' he pleaded.

The Sun Lord, standing beside Inanna in Uruk again, flinched. He turned his eyes away from the distant steppe in grieving silence.

'Can you do *nothing* to save him?'

'You yourself sentenced him. I have tried everything that I can.'

Dust hid the steppe now. A stormwind without rain moaned through the dry grass. In the darkened halls of the E-Anna Inanna waited, speaking to no one, refusing food. Her eyes stared unwearying out of her pale face across the plain towards the unseen sheep runs.

In the depth of Kur, Ereshkigal clutched at her belly and uttered one sharp, fierce cry.

For a long time Geshtinanna stood with the grit stinging her face. The milk from the broken churn had soaked away. The shards of the cup had been trampled into the earth. Water had been thrown on the grey ashes of the Shepherd's crook. Her hearth was cold.

Outside, the creamy wool of the lambs was black with blood. The once lively kids lay still and stiff. They did not twitch their legs. The rest of the flock had fled and scattered. The wind was mourning through an empty sheepfold.

Dumuzi was taken.

# Chapter Ninety-one

When Dumuzi's mother heard the news she broke into a heart-rent keening.

> Oh, my son, my Damu!
> My little crumb, worth five loaves,
> Worth ten loaves of another woman's baking!
> You are a calf stillborn.
> The *galla* have forced my legs apart,
> Torn you from my belly!
> You were a boy still,
> Eternity before you.
> Your cup is smashed,
> The milk is poured out.
> Your sheepfold has become a wasteland.

Geshtinanna's own grief was too deep even for the laments that custom required, but she keened too, to open the sluicegates of Nin Sun's heartbreak, to cleanse her with weeping.

Then she flew on to the E-Anna. Inanna was in mourning like a widow. Geshtinanna ran across the floor that separated them and took her sister-in-law in her arms.

'Oh, Inanna, Inanna! Undo this! Say the word.'

'I cannot. I swore an oath to Ereshkigal. I took the *me* of the Sky House from An, the *me* of Earth from Enki. I cannot take the powers of the Netherworld from Ereshkigal. What Enlil allotted in the first separation stays fixed. There is Above and there is Below. They are not the same.'

'I think they are. I think that you and Ereshkigal . . .' A shudder seemed to run through Geshtinanna, as if she was starting from a trance. 'What was I saying?'

'That *I* am Queen of the Dark City? But I am not! I am not! I have no power Below.'

'Come with me before it is too late.' Geshtinanna tugged her friend's hand. 'Help me find Dumuzi, wherever he is now on the road to the Netherworld. Look in his eyes one last time. See if your heart will change. You love him! Reverse your decision.'

'No! It cannot be done.'

'At least let us see if they have left us his body. If we find it, then you are his widow, I am his sister. Let us lament over our lost love, let us weep together. Come with me, Inanna. You are breaking your heart as well as mine.'

'If you can show me his body, I will bury him royally. I will raise shrines for him in Badtibira, in Arali, in Girsu. I will set up a wail for him on the steppe. I will weep for him like a frog in the marshes.'

'Is that *all*? Well, I, if I were you, I would take his place!'

'That is easily said.'

Geshtinanna let Inanna go.

'We are wasting time. The *galla* are swift and merciless. They never rest. If there is any chance of finding Dumuzi before the gates of the Netherworld close behind him, we must go. We must be as tireless as they are.'

'How can we find him now? We don't know where they have taken him.'

Geshtinanna swallowed a lump in her throat as she thought of the eager Urgi, Dumuzi's black sheepdog. His tail would wag no more. The red tongue was still. She had not been allowed to bury him or burn him. The vultures had descended out of the pitiless sky and torn him apart. He could not help her track his master now.

'The *galla* moored their black barge at the end of the Ditch of Arali. Let's follow the water down to the river. Somewhere, we may still find word of him.'

Three grieving women set out at once. What did they hope?

Nin Sun had departed from the Anunnaki's rules, had married the human Lugalbanda. She had seen him die and laid him to rest. She had mourned bitterly, but she had accepted the world's order.

Geshtinanna would not accept it.

Inanna had gone to the Netherworld, and the Earth's fertility had failed.

They found the broken lair where Dumuzi had hidden among the canebrakes. They stood appalled at the devastation of the *galla*'s malice. Inanna paled.

'Light was born out of Kur. Out of Kur comes all that is green and fresh and lovely. Why, then, is the way back to it marked with such bitterness? I still feel their claws upon me. I still smell their breath. Geshtinanna, the road to the Netherworld is terrible. Its guardians are fearsome.'

'Then you can't send Dumuzi there. You must not.'

'It cannot be changed.'

'I will change it!'

That night a howling storm arose, wind without rain. The three women crouched in the tent Inanna's escort had raised for them. It was a scant shelter only, while the darkness lasted. They did not sleep.

'What is that rag, hanging on the thorns across the river?' Nin Sun asked.

'I think you know,' Geshtinanna answered quietly.

A man's torn kilt, buffeted by the wind, shredded against the spines of camelthorn.

'Whose is that belt, lying at the water's edge opposite?' Inanna's deeper voice questioned.

'There was only one Son of An fled for his life this way.'

Rotten branches of willow trees, clumps of cane roots torn from their marshy hold swirled past in the growing darkness.

'There is something pale,' whispered Geshtinanna, 'in the middle of the stream.'

The three women were on their feet, out in the driving wind. Was that a face, like the moon's disc, turned helplessly to them? Were those arms, lifting above the pluck of the current pleadingly?

'My Damu!' shrieked Nin Sun, rushing to the brink. She would have plunged in, into the boat-wrecking surge of waves that had been the quiet watercourse of Arali. But Geshtinanna held her back. The phantom hands clutched again towards the leaning women. They caught no living grasp.

Inanna shrieked aloud. 'Dumuzi! Dumuzi!'

The wind howled like the *galla*'s laughter. The river grew black, the debris passed. There were no voices but the sound of the storm, no faces but their own.

'We must follow downriver,' said Geshtinanna, 'the moment it is light.'

At the first hint of dawn, Inanna and Geshtinanna set out. They left Nin Sun behind, mourning among the reeds of the upper watercourses. She would not leave the place where her son was taken, as if only there could he return to her.

'I must perform the rites that give some comfort to the dead,' she said.

'He is not dead yet,' said Geshtinanna. 'I will seek him on the road of the living while there is still time.'

'I had to climb mountains to find the gate of Kur,' said Inanna. 'My Wild Bull, my beloved Aurochs of the hills. Perhaps that is where he has been taken. When the people who love me die, when my young men fall, when my maidens sicken, the humans sing that the Bison takes them:

> The Bison with fierce-speckled eyes,
> The Bison whose teeth crush.
> He carries them into the hills.
> Where his hooves strike, camp beds are left empty,
> The jackal sleeps in their tents.
> Where his horns toss, the folds lose their shepherd,
> The raven watches them.
> The reed pipes, now the wind blows through them.
> The songs of Dumuzi, only the north wind will sing.

'Search for him in the hills if you will,' Geshtinanna said. 'You! I think you do not want to face him. I will go where my heart tells me. I will follow this river even if it empties itself into the heart of Kur.'

'You have not been to the Below. You do not know.'

'I am the scholar who is willing to learn anything. For Dumuzi.'

Inanna stared at her friend with an angry defiance, then swung her dishevelled hair and made off up the bank, leaving the river for the wilderness of sand and rock and scrub. Her escort trudged after her, weary and dejected, but still obedient. Geshtinanna watched them go with a heavy heart.

'Inanna! What can I say if I find him?'

Inanna turned, standing tall on the ridge above the river. The cry was wrenched from her. 'You will not find him. I shall never see him again! Dumuzi has started on a journey no one can stop.'

'*You* can!'

The vultures, swaying above them, mocked her plea. Inanna strode on.

A sandy bluff swung the river in a wide curve and sent it

falling below the camp where Geshtinanna had left her
mother. From the steppe she heard Nin Sun lamenting.

The cow has been robbed of her calf.
The baby has been taken from the mother who gave birth to
  him.
I will give away treasure, like the stars of heaven,
To the one who can show me where the Bridegroom is now.
I hear the hue and cry of evil coming nearer!
Son, protect me!
Show your beloved face to me!
Son, I am searching for you.

   A shiver shook Geshtinanna's body as the wind came back
from the walls of the valley.

> Wild Cow on the riverbank,
> Turn your face this way.
> Woman of Arali,
> Look at me.

   A cry of anguish. 'Son! Alas, my Damu! Let me follow you.
Let me walk with you the Road of No Return.'
   Nin Sun was wading across the river now, scrambling up
the further slopes, her face set always towards the west.
   'Mother!' cried Geshtinanna. 'Come back!'

I will set my steps towards the still-light mountains,
To him who lies in blood and water, my little sleeping lad,
To him no ritual washings can ever heal.
I will walk the road that makes an end of all who tread it.
I will follow in the traces of dead kings.
In the landing places of the anointed ones on their way to
  the Netherworld
I will lay down my head tonight.

   The wind, infinitely sad, blew back his answer.

You cannot lie where I lie, in the track of the south wind, in
  the track of the north wind,
Beaten by the small hailstones that destroy harvests,
Battered by the big hailstones that sink great ships,
Where the lightning flashes and the hurricane whirls.

You cannot eat the rotten food I must eat now.
You cannot drink the foul water I must drink now.
You must not walk the road I am on.
I am not of the Above, I am not of Earth, leave me!

'Dumuzi!' breathed Geshtinanna. 'Dumuzi! Where are you?'

But the voice came from downstream now, below her.

'Where is my leech? Is that my clever sister? *Help me!*'

'I am here! Dumuzi, my love, my brother! I will always be here. But how can I reach you?'

The wind fell silent. The river flowed on over stones. Geshtinanna ran upstream, where her mother was wandering the slopes above the Arali, clutching her head. She looked to the endless plateau over which Inanna had gone. She looked down the valley where the river poured away into a thickening mist.

'Oh, wait!' she cried. 'Hold on just a little while longer, Dumuzi! Tell the *galla* I am coming after you. Tell them I will bring them Inanna's mercy!'

With a terror that the demons might even now be dragging him through the Netherworld gate, she broke into a long-legged run, heedless that she was breaking open the scars of torture. Swift as an onager she sped after the tall, striding figure of Inanna.

'Inanna, wait! I have heard Dumuzi's voice. Inanna, it is not too late yet!'

Inanna's party disappeared over the ridge of the skyline.

'Oh, what shall I do?' cried Geshtinanna.

She stood irresolute, listening, in the airless heat. Dumuzi's pleas had died away with the wind. With a sob, she rushed back to the stream and started to run along the bank into a dusty twilight.

# Chapter Ninety-two

Malicious hands threw Dumuzi into the pitch-black barge. Claws tightened the fetters on his ankles, twisted the wooden stock round his neck. The barge slipped away from the quay among the rushes, gathered speed on the current. The water was low. The sun was veiled by dustclouds to a lurid red. The reed beds at the water's edge, the leaning willows seemed to have no shadow. Dumuzi looked down terrified. Had he a shadow? Was he a shade already? The boat was sliding into an ochre nothingness ahead.

Dun ghosts haunted the towpath. As the boat glided by, Dumuzi forced bound hands towards them, cried out pleadingly.

'Are you going downstream to Eridu? Please! Take a message for me to my father Enki. Tell him Dumuzi has been taken by the *galla*. Beg him to rescue me, as he saved Inanna!'

Their voices echoed hollowly in the misty air. 'Do not give us any messages for the living.'

'I am a girl taken from my mother's side.'

'I am a boy stolen from my father's house.'

'We walk the Road of No Return.'

Even the ember of the red sun was going. Brown twilight stretched ahead like a dirty tunnel. Shapes, fainter now, loomed on the raised bank alongside him.

'Is someone there?' cried Dumuzi. 'Are you going upstream? Find Nin Sun! I heard my mother calling my name. She is searching for me. Tell her where I am. She is the Woman of the Wild Cows, a life-bringing Lady. She will protect me! Find Geshtinanna. My sister is a skilled physician. Get help for me!'

'We will not take instructions from you.'

'You are almost at Tummal now.'

'The shrine on the Road That Destroys the One Who Walks It.'

'The Tomb of Tears.'

'We shall meet you there.'

The *galla* hissed delight, pulled strongly on the paddles. The barge drove down the turbid river with the sound of weeping.

Geshtinanna followed on the towpath. She walked as swiftly as she could. She was prepared to be frightened, and the open-eyed acceptance of what she was going into made the most harmless encounter potentially terrifying. Palm trees reared over her like many-headed dragons. Broken reeds swung across the path like demons' flails.

'I know Inanna and Nin Shubur climbed a track to the mountains and found the open mouth of Kur. This riverbank, down past the Dyke of Tummal, must be another way into Kur. Do all roads lead to death?' she thought with growing horror.

She, too, passed wraiths, faceless, on soundless feet.

'Have you seen my brother? Have you met Dumuzi?'

Their spectral voices held no hope or interest.

'I am a man who has lost all joy. Do not ask me about any other man.'

'I am a woman who has no family now. Do not ask me about your family.'

She met a little boy wandering as if lost. She tried to take his hand but it slipped away from hers like wasted water.

'You? Even you have they taken? Do not cry, little one!'

But the child was not crying. His face was dull, unmoved.

'Come and sit in my lap,' she coaxed. 'Shall I sing to you? If I had my harp I could hang it on this tree and let the wind play through its strings.'

'They sing sadder songs in Kur. I don't want your harp.'

And he went on ahead of her, not running, but gliding like a small snake.

Her heart was growing colder now, the muscles setting in her face as though they would never smile again. There seemed no light, no hope. She did not know if she was already in the Below.

A tall figure stood at a crossroads on the chariot track. Geshtinanna hesitated. Somewhere down that side road, perhaps only a little way from the water, there should be a village. Warmth, firelight, nourishing food, frothing beer, living people. A terrible longing for the company of other

Anunnaki, warm-blooded humans, even the comforting pressure of a flock of sheep, tugged unbearably at her heart. Dumuzi had become a name, a task stamped in cuneiform on a dry clay tablet. She could no longer feel the passionate love that had sent her down this friendless way. Yet still she had felt something, she told herself. As long as she could suffer the pain of the life she was leaving, she was still alive, she still had choice. She could go on with her quest. She would find and rescue this Son of An, this Dumuzi, though she could hardly remember why.

A shock brought the blood pounding welcomely in her head. The robe and the pendant of that tall, still figure at the crossroads had a familiarity that penetrated the numbness round her. She wore those marks herself. Her hand went to the symbol on the leather thong round her own neck. She felt fingers touch skin, the beat of the pulse in the hollow of her throat. She was alive. Was this doctor one of the living too?

'Learned doctor, physician to the black-headed people. Why are you standing on this chariot road? Has there been an accident? Is anyone hurt? *Is someone dying?*'

He swung slowly, bringing his hollow eyes to bear on hers. She felt a shudder chill her, but she could not turn away.

'I was sent to stop you. Do not go on.'

'I am a physician too. Let me pass.'

'Why are your cheeks still flushed? Why are your eyes still bright, Geshtinanna of the Vines? Alas, the Shepherd! Alas, the sacrificed Wild Bull!'

Then fear snapped the fetters of her indifference. She could indeed feel, was overwhelmed with a tide of disbelief and despair.

'Is it too late? Is Dumuzi dead? Has he entered Kur? Let me pass! I must get him out! If I have to batter down the gates of the Netherworld and let the shades of the dead loose on the Earth, I must reach Dumuzi! I must overturn Inanna's order! Let me through!'

She pushed against him. But there was no one there. Only the road on and on into a fog that was growing ever warmer. She was running now, no wind in the lifeless air, but the rush of her own going sending her tangled hair streaming behind her. No sound but the beat of her own flying feet. Nothing but mist and dull water and heavy reeds.

The vapour was stinging now, not droplets of water but another dust-storm flinging grit against her sweating face. No bubbling water beside her but an empty rivercourse. The cracks grew wider and thirstier as she looked. The reeds were losing all their young green, withering and splitting. Fire burst out among the clumps. Black smoke swirled all around her.

'Dumuzi! Dumuzi!'

Red glare of flames. Black fog of smoke. The scorching dust. Blindly now, tears drying as they fell, feet burned, throat parched.

'Dumuzi! Where are you? Speak to me if you can!'

A groan answered her.

Her bare toe stubbed on a block of stone. A quay on the waterless river. A blank, mud wall towered suddenly in front of her. This was not the Buranun. She would never reach Eridu and the Abzu by this road. Enki her father, the Lord of Wisdom, would not be waiting at the end of this journey to laugh with her. This waterless channel disappeared under a high, black gate.

Suddenly she was not alone, and loneliness now would have seemed like a blessing. There was a chattering as though the liquid sound of the river had dried and risen into the air in a bodiless rustle. Then it took loathsome form. The *galla* were all around her, touching her. Her still-living flesh contracted with the vivid memory of pain. Her pounding heart knew once again how pitiless these demons were, how no appeal could move them. She hardly dared to look through their crowding ranks, though she knew there was something below them, on the riverbed. At the last instant she felt she could not bear to see Dumuzi in their hands and know the risk that she would have no power to save him.

Yet her decision was made. Her will was fixed like the marks of a stylus baked into clay. She turned her head, craned her neck past the metallic headpieces, the leathery grimaces.

He sat imprisoned in the forlorn, beached barge in the empty river. Naked, bruised, bound, his neck yoked. His beloved face was ravaged with weeping.

'Dumuzi . . .?'

The *galla* drew back, as though relishing this spectacle. She watched the shiver run through her brother even to his bowed head. So slowly he lifted his hopeless eyes to hers.

'*Geshtin?*'

'My little Damu! My brother. If our mother could see you now!'

'I have no mother. I have no father. The Anunnaki have abandoned me.'

'You have me!'

She leaped from the quay and flung herself on her knees before him. The Chief *Galla*'s claws ripped her shoulder.

'He is ours, Vine Girl. He won't drink your wine any more.'

She struggled to shake the demon off. 'Be careful! I come from Inanna. You have not yet passed the gate into Ereshkigal's territory. The Queen of all the Above may yet have a word to say to you.'

'Geshtin!' Dumuzi buried his face in her lap. Only a single gasp betrayed how much his need hurt her. 'Enki has taken Inanna's side against me. Nin Sun will never find me on the steppe. You are all the mother I have. Stay with me. Save me!'

'Hush, little brother, precious Damu.' She put her arms around him, held his head to her breast, rocked him, sang to him. 'My little boy, my Dumuzi of the sheepfolds, I will be your mother, I will be your father. The day that dawns for you will also dawn for me. The night that falls on you shall fall on me as well. The road you tread, my feet shall know it too. The river that carries Dumuzi must also bear Geshtinanna.'

'What are you saying? Don't you know where they're taking me? The stale food of the dead, you cannot eat it. The foul water of Kur, you cannot drink it. I am dying, Geshtinanna. I am going to Kur!'

'I know. I know. I could not prevent your punishment. I tried, Dumuzi. Believe me, I tried. But if I cannot repeal your sentence, I can share it. As a sister should share all that she has with her beloved little brother. I have shared my life with you, Dumuzi. Let me share your death.'

The jabber of the demons was like enraged monkeys.

'What is this treason?'

'What are you talking about, girl?'

'He's Inanna's prisoner!'

'He is Ereshkigal's right!'

She lifted her head to them, proudly, gladly, the muscles unlocking in her face, her smile warm and glowing. She rose to her feet in a long, graceful movement, holding Dumuzi's weeping face still clasped to her side. Strong, protective, alive with love like a steady flame, she faced the *galla*.

'Take Geshtinanna. Ereshkigal shall have her prisoner. Kur will not lose its ransom. I will come with you. I will pay Inanna's dues to death. I will take Dumuzi's place.'

'You?' The Chief *Galla* gave an incredulous crow of derision. 'You, for Dumuzi?'

Geshtinanna drew herself up with dignity. 'I am Inanna's closest friend. That was the bargain with Ereshkigal, wasn't it? Blood of Inanna's heart. A part of her soul. I will pay your price for love.'

# Chapter Ninety-three

A malicious smile cracked the Chief *Galla*'s horny face below the helmet.

'Oh, sweetly generous. Look how he's hoping. Too late, my girl. His sentence was spoken. Only Inanna could change it.'

The demons pushed her back.

The gates were opening. She saw the sharp-faced porter, Neti, peer from behind one leaf. All places are one to him. The mouth of Kur is always ready.

But the noise of the *galla* was stilling. Neti was bowing and standing aside. A tall, fearsome figure loomed in the doorway wearing the two-horned crown of Ereshkigal's *sukkal*. Namtar, the Plague Lord. His face shone with a green pallor. Phosphorescence played around his pitted limbs. The stench of sickness hung on his kilt. Black rats peeped eagerly around his sandals, squeaking their desire.

'Enter, Ereshkigal's guest,' he bowed to Dumuzi. 'Inanna's dance sends us many of her partners from the battlefield. But it is a sweeter thing for her to send us a victim from her bed. And a rarer pleasure still that Kur should be given a Son of An.'

'I am not for you! Geshtinanna, tell him!' Dumuzi clutched his sister.

'There,' she comforted him with a maternal arm.

She could not hold him. The *galla* were buffeting the Shepherd, dragging him out of the barge by force, hauling him on to the bank before the half-open gate. She struggled to reach him as he wrestled against the horror of the darkness. She saw the Chief *Galla* strike him casually across the eyes, temporarily blinding him.

But Namtar held up a hand. Black lips froze even the demons' officer. 'You misunderstand, Captain. He is not your plaything. Dumuzi is a Lord, Enki's own son. Nephew of Queen Ereshkigal herself. This is the surrogate for the Maid Inanna. Her bridegroom. Her lover. Treat him with more respect.'

He bowed lower this time, released the fetters from Dumuzi's ankles with his own hands. The Chief *Galla*'s fist signalled with a bad grace and demons struck the bonds from their prisoner's wrists, unlocked the neck stock. Still, as they snatched them away maliciously, they left rope burns and bruises. Namtar extended a pallid hand, steadying the half-fainting Dumuzi.

'Welcome to Kur, Ereshkigal's kinsman. Inanna came too late for the funeral of the Bull of Heaven. Now the women of Earth will have all the time in the world to bewail Inanna's bridegroom.'

'No! I am not the one you should take! Tell him, Geshtinanna!'

She fought her way to his side. It was hard to hold his shaking body. In spite of herself, Dumuzi's fear communicated itself to his sister. She was the Lady of song and merrymaking, the Vine Girl, giver of wine and festivity. How could she go into that silent tunnel, this cold, dark, emptiness that held no love or joy?

'As the wine is stored away from the sun,' she found the strength to say, 'as the clay is sealed over the mouth of the jar, let me descend for him into the belly of Kur. You may close the seven gates of the Netherworld behind me. I will take Dumuzi's place. I am Dumuzi's sister. I am Inanna's dearest friend. Ereshkigal must accept me.'

Namtar studied her with a deep attention. The *galla* chattered with thwarted malice. What sport in a prisoner who surrenders herself willingly? Namtar turned slowly to Dumuzi and raised his eyebrows.

'Listen to her!' burst out the Shepherd. 'She comes from Inanna. Geshtinanna is wise. You must do what she says. You must believe her!'

'And you . . . you would let her do this?'

A poppy red suffused Dumuzi's face, chased away by the bloodless white of asphodel. 'I . . . Inanna needs me,' he muttered.

'Is this true?' Namtar turned on Geshtinanna. 'Is it true Inanna forgives him? She has sentenced you instead?'

'I . . . she . . .'

'I cannot hear you.'

'I saw her face . . . Her heart was breaking . . .'

'Say it more clearly, Wine Girl.'

Geshtinanna struggled with the truth. 'I wanted to throw myself before her. I would have begged to take Dumuzi's place. I couldn't overtake her and still follow the barge. Can't you release him?'

'Your word is not enough, Enki's daughter.'

'Then at least let me share Dumuzi's punishment. Don't separate us!'

They clutched each other's hands, brother and sister, young Lord and Lady.

Namtar raised his blanched face to the sky. The cloud of dust was turning golden, as if the sun was endeavouring to peer through. Against the ever fiercer glare of light the way to Kur stood even blacker.

Namtar said suavely, 'I think we know what Ereshkigal wants.' He held out a courteous hand to Dumuzi and beckoned him forward. 'Follow me, Lord Ushumgalanna. Enki's son will rejoice the heart of Ereshkigal for the many sons she has lost. Inanna's bridegroom will compensate her for the husband she yearly mourns. Inanna will weep bitterly on Earth for this. But the Netherworld will laugh.'

'*Geshtinanna!*'

They were dragging him away from her, towards that gate that Neti was making yawn ever wider. Her brother's hand was slipping through hers. She tried to hold on to it, struggled to go with him. The *galla* struck their hands apart, forced her back.

'Save me, Geshtin!'

She gasped, white-faced, 'Keep courage, Dumuzi! I will hold faith with you. I will run to Inanna. I will beg her to pardon you. Tell Ereshkigal she has a niece, not a royal ruler, not a high priestess, not a heavenly hierodule. But loving, wise . . . and merry.' The word bubbled defiantly through a gush of tears. 'I would sing her songs. I would sit at her feet in the dark blue palace of the Ganzir and recite old stories. Tell her I will come instead of you.'

She must not see him go. She turned away and heard the gate clang behind her, leaving a heavy silence. The sun burned through the dust. The sky was a hammering blue. Frogs gasped into silence in the cracked mud. Before her scarcely comprehending eyes the barge of the *galla* split slowly apart. Wounds opened in the waterless timber. Pitch

525

bubbled at their lips. The limestone blocks of the quay began to scorch her feet.

# Chapter Ninety-four

Inanna was approaching a house, mud-brick, squat, behind a sharp-spiked fence. The confused sound of sheep and goats came from the compound.

'I know the reputation of that place,' advised Nin Shubur. 'The mother is a matriarch, respected and feared, a wise woman. Bilulu of Edinlilla.'

'Could she have sheltered Dumuzi from the *galla*, if he came this way?'

'None of us have spells strong enough against Ereshkigal's troops, my lady. Besides, it is best to avoid this house. The son Girgire is a brigand. The sheep that fill their pens are not their own.'

The flash of hope faded from Inanna's face.

'Those beasts sound frightened . . . What is this blood on the ground?'

A dark libation, staining the sandy soil beside the gate. A trail of footsteps, dragging away towards Dumuzi's farm, spattered with blood. Less visible, a single, sinuous line coming in from the distant steppe, the slot of a snake.

'He was here!' Inanna dropped to her knees. 'Dumuzi was here . . . and they stoned him!'

The evidence was in her hand. The rock stained with his blood, impressed with his golden hair. She pressed it fiercely to her face.

'Dumuzi fled to these people for help. And they wounded him! They drove him away!'

'What else did you do to him yourself, my lady?'

Inanna stood up, blood leaving her face. Her eyes were terrible. The smaller woman did not flinch.

'*Where are they?*'

'What does it matter, Inanna? It would have made no difference. You marked him for death.'

'Break down the gate!'

The captain rapped on the strong-planked outer door. There was no answer. The soldiers broke it down. Inside, a frightened, bloodstained flock of sheep and goats huddled against the wall. Inanna went among them, running her hands through their matted wool.

'Dumuzi! Dumuzi! Who did this to you? Who has hurt you?'

The soldiers returned from searching the house.

'There is no one here, my Lady, except this snivelling lad.'

They threw the young man at her feet. He shuddered convulsively.

'Where is your mistress? Where is Old Bilulu? Where is Girgire the brigand?'

'In . . . in Edinlilla, my . . . my Lady. In the alehouse. Father went out to celebrate.'

'*Celebrate!* The theft of my flocks? *The death of Dumuzi?*'

'Y . . . yes, my Lady!'

'Take me to that inn!'

Shaking with terror, the boy ran ahead. The *sag-ursag* loped after him. Inanna's long strides kept pace.

The alehouse stood at the roadside, at the entrance to the town. *Sarbatu* trees shaded a dusty forecourt set with tables. Drinkers jumped up from their benches and backed away at Inanna's entrance. One man of middle years, bow-legged, sharp-eyed, put down his beaker and reached for his dagger. The lad clung to his side.

'Where is Bilulu?' demanded Inanna.

Girgire bowed to her, with more than a trace of mockery. The *sag-ursag* stiffened to avenge the insult, but the brigand turned and walked ahead of them. At the threshold he grinned and beckoned them instead round the corner of the inn to a courtyard sheltered from the desert wind. A few sparse palms shaded it. The alewife's carefully tended patch of herbs and vegetables welcomed the eye with green foliage. Radishes showed red and leeks white out of the hard-packed earth.

An old woman was sitting on a low stool. This was not a lean, careworn peasant, like Mother Belili. The matriarch Old Bilulu was vast, impassive, like a queen in her small, desert state. Her clothes were richly embroidered, hanging in voluminous folds around her fat flesh. Rings flashed on her fingers and ankles. Beads swung from the headdress around her heavy face. The unkempt lad from the farm dashed forward and squatted at her feet, clinging to her skirt. From this seeming shelter, he turned his sharp face quickly towards them, like a fox.

Inanna tensed and her eyes flashed. Bilulu made a motion of rising, heaving her body with difficulty from the stool.

'Help me!' she snapped, holding out a commanding hand.

With a not quite mutinous scowl the young man got to his feet again and hauled her urgently upright.

'Inanna, is it? An's hierodule. Be welcome to the poor town of Edinlilla, Dumuzi's widow.'

'Widow?' Inanna pounced upon the word. 'Then Dumuzi is taken? You stoned him! You let the *galla* have him!'

The old woman gave a short, mirthless laugh. 'Who can stop the *galla*? All the world knows what price you paid to Ereshkigal for your life. You sold your husband's immortality for your own.'

'How dare you! What do you know about it? The world will see the price I exact for what happened at your farm! What price did you pay for my sheep I saw in your pen? What price do you pay to the families of the shepherds you kill?'

The younger man cackled insanely. Bilulu laid a warning hand on his shoulder and leaned her weight on him, so that he staggered and tried to shake himself free.

'My grandson, Sirru-Edinlilla. An unlovely boy. And not a quarter the wisdom of his father or me.'

Girgire was behind them now. Watchful, suspicious.

'*Tell me!*' Inanna forced the words on Bilulu. 'Tell me, did you see them taking Dumuzi? Did they bring him this way?'

'What should the *galla* want with an inn? Why should they stop for food and drink?'

'*Did you see them?*'

The mountainous flesh of Bilulu quivered. In any other woman it would have been a shrug.

'There might have been a black barge on the river. What is that to me? What if I saw a young man bound with fetters? What was he to us?'

Inanna struck the old woman forcibly across the face. She snatched out a handful of hair.

'*You saw Dumuzi!* You saw my husband on the road to death and you didn't try to help him?'

'Inanna! What could she do?' Nin Shubur tried to pacify her. 'You ordered it.'

But Inanna raged against the sentence of her own lips. She jumped up on to a bench and raised her hand.

'Kill them!' she ordered the *sag-ursag*. The soldiers started, readied their weapons in well-drilled obedience, then hesitated.

'Kill them, my Lady?' queried their captain. 'All the family? The old woman? The lad?'

'They are brigands, murderers! Yes, kill them! The old one, her son, her . . . No. Leave that young jackal. I have plans for him!'

Her guards seized the three. Sirru was trembling more than the others, even after Inanna had pronounced his reprieve.

The *sag-ursag* dragged them out of the alehouse, back to their lonely farm. Girgire stood expressionless, his head thrown back defiantly. His eyes were still bright as he looked round at his empire of pillage, the full storehouses, the frightened sheep churning up the sand. Old Bilulu smiled a little secretive smile, as though the future might still hold something, as though the *galla* could not take her.

Inanna stood threateningly close and stared into her face.

'Now! I shall make you give in death what you would not offer my Dumuzi in life. Once you are dead, I shall have you skinned. I will peg out your hide in a hollow of the steppe. When the watercourses run dry in the summer drought, the dew of the desert will gather on your skin. The drink you would not give to Dumuzi when he passed, you shall offer to every traveller.'

The woman paled then, shuddered. The flesh seemed to fall in on her with the consciousness at last of her own mortality. She shivered in the skin that clung so closely to her flesh.

'My lady!' Nin Shubur cried out.

But Inanna had turned on the son.

'You, Girgire! You lifted your hand against my husband, you stoned and showed no pity, you would not lift that bloodstained mace against the *galla* and try to rescue Dumuzi from them. You, I shall kill too. Here, your uneasy spirit shall become an *udug* ranging the steppe, a *lama* watching over the desert road. In life, you led my people to their death. In death, your spirit must guide them and show their feet the path to safety.'

'You cannot command the dead!'

'Nin Shubur is wiser than Old Bilulu. Whether you want to or not, your spirit will have no strength to resist her spells. Or would you rather I called the *galla* to drag you to the Netherworld like Dumuzi, to Ereshkigal's judgment hall?'

'No! Don't let the demons have me!'

'If it pleases me that you roam unquiet in the desert, it need not concern them.'

'What of this one?' said Nin Shubur softly, standing by the shaking, hangdog youth.

Inanna looked him up and down. Lovely though she was, she moved, in that terrible mood of judgment, like Ereshkigal stooping from her throne to pronounce condemnation. Red lips, praised in a thousand hymns of love, smiled.

'Sirru shall be my acolyte. Cut off his hair, above and below. He who let Dumuzi pass without the gift of bread must spend his days alone, unless a traveller comes. He shall libate water to the spirit of his father. He shall sprinkle flour on the skin of his dead grandmother. He shall make this house of death into a lodging for pilgrims. He who cut off the heads of others must wash the feet of wayfarers. Who stole the sheep and the grain must feed the traveller. Let him set up a shrine on the steppe. Let him make a sacrifice to Lord Dumuzi's memory every day of his life.'

She swung away. Slow, difficult tears forced their way from her eyes, burned down her cheeks. Still the *sag-ursag* waited.

'My lady!' Nin Shubur pleaded.

'Do it!'

Two screams, no louder than the eagles hunting the air. More swiftly and finally than Dumuzi's, Bilulu and Girgire's lives met their end. The old woman lay in her own courtyard, like a too early harvest of grapes. The *sag-ursag* got out their knives and began their grisly task.

Nin-Shubur, pale but obedient, bent over the corpse of Girgire. She opened his mouth, unstopped his ears, blew in his nostrils. Feathers slipped through her fingers, fragments of flies. Words flew, netted the air. More of the *sag-ursag* gathered round her, drummed and chanted back the words she offered, reinforced her power. The spirit of the brigand rose from the open orifices like locusts swarming from the earth, skeined the air like rising wildfowl, hovered over the place like bees that have lost their home.

'Until the Queen of the Dark City calls you down to her,'

crooned Nin Shubur, 'be here the pilot of the lost, the guide of the benighted. Give in death the blessing you denied in life.'

They were carrying Bilulu's bloodied skin away, readying tent pegs, mallets. Sirru was sobbing, noisier in his surviving than his father and grandmother in their dying. Inanna stood with her back to the work of carnage, her fists clenched, her eyes vainly searching the steppe beyond, the distant, winding river. She was still standing, staring motionless, when Geshtinanna came running up and found the shocking scene.

'Inanna!'

Nin Shubur raised weary eyes, shook her head sadly. Geshtinanna rushed across the place of bloodshed, seized Inanna's arm and whirled her round.

'What is this, Inanna? Can you never see? Blood for blood! Pain for pain! How can this help Dumuzi? How would this have helped you when you were caught in Kur? The *kurgarra* and the *galatur* spoke words of love to free you!'

Inanna turned, her face heavy, drunken with vengeance. Momentarily it seemed to be the bloated, self-satisfied visage of Old Bilulu. Geshtinanna fell back a little, let go of her.

'They should weep for him. The whole Earth shall weep for him!' Inanna bellowed her suffering.

'Inanna, Inanna, it may not be necessary. That's what I came running to tell you. Listen to me!'

'What can you say to help? How can anyone help us now? What I have done, I have done.'

Geshtinanna fell on her knees, pleading. 'No, Inanna. It can still be changed. Only give me permission.'

'What do you want to do, my tablet-knowing sister? Dumuzi is gone. What is there left to hope?' The words, too, were thick, as if after wine.

'I have seen Dumuzi. I have touched him. Yes! At the very gate of the Netherworld. He was pleading to me. Inanna, they took him away. They wouldn't let me in without your word. Only speak it, and I will follow him to the heart of Kur itself. I will take his place. Please. You promised a life to Ereshkigal, a life you loved. If I was ever dear to you and to Dumuzi, if love means anything at all, then grant me this, I beg you. It is only your word the *galla* wait for. Give *me* to Ereshkigal instead of Dumuzi.'

# Chapter Ninety-five

Inanna stared, like a queen who hears a courier deliver his message in a foreign tongue and waits for the interpretation to follow. Then a lump moved in her throat. The light of intelligent life returned to her eyes.

'You?'

Geshtinanna held up a beseeching hand. 'Yes. Let me, Inanna. When we were young together, the three of us, we swore undying love. Let me make good my promise. I would follow my brother. I would be wherever he is suffering now. I would share that. I would take it on me. Let him come back to love you. Be happy with him again, Inanna. Forgive Dumuzi.'

'But you? You don't know what you are asking. You have not been to the Netherworld, Geshtin. It is dark, it is dreary, it is silent, it is cold. The *galla* will not let you sing your songs there. They won't let you pour your red wine. There is no loving touch or kindness. The shades of mortals mourn alone, with no one to comfort them. It is an awful place.'

Geshtinanna's eager face grew whiter, but her resolve did not waver. 'So much the more fearful for Dumuzi, then. He needs love. He needs the warmth of the sun. He needs your arms.'

'You would suffer eternity in Kur for him?'

'That is what love is.'

Inanna held her friend, pulled her into her arms, weeping. 'Oh, Geshtinanna. I didn't think there was any way I could have him back. I thought I had killed my heart when I banished him. Even if I went to the gates of the Netherworld again, Ereshkigal would not have let me in to suffer with him.'

'Nor would she me,' Geshtinanna said very quietly. 'It must be either me or him. Dumuzi and I cannot go together. We shall pass by each other on the road, that is all.'

But Inanna rushed on, not stopping to understand what Geshtinanna was saying, not hearing the full extent of her loss. 'Oh, but I can't let you do it. I shouldn't. Yet in Uruk and Zabalam and Badtibira, all the women and girls were wailing for him. The whole Earth is mourning Dumuzi. They are gathering poppies red as his blood. They are sprinkling water, baking loaves for the dead.'

'Then turn his funeral into a wedding, Inanna. Take him back.'

'By losing my dearest friend? Oh, Geshtinanna, Geshtinanna. What shall I do?'

'Follow your heart.'

'But you are breaking it! I didn't think I would ever feel loss again. I thought I had no more tears to weep. I have already sentenced my husband to the Netherworld. Should I condemn my best friend too?'

'Not both of us, only one. I have made the choice for you. Let all three of us be happy. I, even in the grip of Kur, I shall rejoice for you both if you will let me do this. Take Dumuzi back to your bed.'

'Geshtin. Geshtin, how can you be so good, so loving, while I hurt those I touch?'

'You give us joy too, Inanna.' Geshtinanna hugged her fiercely. 'Your love is dangerous. You wound us often. But your loving is glorious too. People will always praise you. We wouldn't live without your fire.'

'What shall I do? What shall I do?' Tall Inanna rocked the lesser Lady in her strong arms, crooning over the brown curls of her hair. 'I can't let you sacrifice yourself . . . No.' She laid her finger on the Wine Girl's lips. 'Geshtinanna, I know! Listen to me!' She pushed her friend away from her a little now and looked eagerly into her eyes. 'This is what I will do. This is my decision. You, half the year you shall take Dumuzi's place in the Netherworld. As the grapes fall and the vines wither, so we shall have to live without you, and remember you in your wine and your songs. But when the spring is over, when the grain harvest is cut and the long, hard, summer drought is on us, then I must sleep alone in my Lion Bed. All the waters of love will run dry, and Dumuzi will go back to the Netherworld to serve out half his sentence. I sent him away, because he was proud and selfish. You will take his place because you are humble and loving.'

A pause. A few shaking breaths. Geshtinanna forced a

smile on her usually merry face. She blinked away the tears of a too-full heart.

'Thank you. It is not what I asked you for. I can still feel Dumuzi's horror even now. But if I can save him anything . . . if I can make you both happy for six months of the year, then that must be enough.'

'And you will still see Dumuzi,' Inanna exclaimed. 'Not one last terrible parting. Twice a year you will be able to meet each other, one on the way down to darkness, the other towards the light.'

'Yes,' whispered Geshtinanna. 'We must pass each other.'

A stillness fell over Bilulu's yard.

'How shall we tell Ereshkigal? Will she let you do it?'

'Take me to the gate of Kur where you left Dumuzi. Show me. Now!'


The snow-melt of spring was over. The carp flood had fallen. Now water whispered in the sandy riverbeds and fell silent. Heat burned the land. Even the cloudless sky seemed oppressive, copper-hued. Inanna's retinue came out at last to civilisation and the still-broad spread of the Buranun.

Geshtinanna stared around her uneasily. 'I don't remember this . . . There was a mist. It all looked strange.'

'But at the end of the road, you said, there was the Gate of Kur.'

'The river ran dry. The boat was grounded.'

'The grief in my heart could burn up all this water.'

On south, with no news of the *galla*'s passing. They sent out parties of *sag-ursag* to search every tributary and canal.

'What if we never find him?' Geshtinanna licked her dry lips.

'We must! We must! The doors to the Netherworld are everywhere.'

But the mouth of Kur was closed to them.

'The ghosts I passed whispered of the Dyke of Tummal.'

'The chariot road to the Tomb of Tears on the way to Eridu?'

They pressed on, with a silent hope. At every shrine of mourning they passed, the priests shook their heads unhelpfully.

They entered the territory of the southernmost city. The high, hot summer hit them like a mace. The green reeds of the marshes were dying to rustling canes. The rivers were falling lower and lower to leave shelving shores of hard-baked mud. But still the glittering water threaded the distance, without end.

The last city mound loomed up from the horizon, like a giant ship riding on its lagoon.

Nin Shubur raised her head and wiped the sweat away. 'Why don't you go to Enki, my lady? To the Mouth of the Abzu. Say there what is in your heart.'

'You want to speak to the Below? Haven't you had enough trouble yet?' Enki hid his concern under a petulant pout.

'Dumuzi is your son, Grandfather. Don't you want to save him?'

'Geshtinanna is my daughter,' he reminded her tartly.

Their footsteps echoed over the shimmering floor of the Abzu as they walked towards the well.

Outside, Nin Shubur and Geshtinanna sat on the steps above the lagoon in the shade of a colonnade. The air was sleepy with the croak of frogs. The edge of the marsh lay cracked and hardened where the low water had left it. Nin Shubur threw little pellets of mud into the water, making a pattern of stars with the splashes. Geshtinanna hugged her knees and rested her bowed head on them.

The low murmur of chants came through a whine of flies. Incense sharpened the air.

From the shadowy Abzu behind them came a deep, rolling roar. It shattered the ripples of Nin Shubur's pattern. The two women stiffened, raised their heads to listen. The voices within were indistinct, dying away into silence.

After a while Inanna came out, pale, walking a little unsteadily. Enki was frowning behind her.

'How can I tell? She has heard you. Don't expect me to know what she wants.'

Geshtinanna jumped up and went to Inanna. 'What does she say? Will she agree?'

'The Deep shook beneath us. That is all I know.'

'She cannot keep him!'

Their eyes met in a shared anguish. Nin Shubur was still squatting on the ground, some little way off. Her palms were resting on her knees, her eyes closed. They heard now, as they had not noticed before, the steady murmuring of spells from her scarcely moving lips.

Through the slightly humid heat of the morning, a large fly

buzzed its zigzag way between them. The noise drilled the air insistently. With an oddly shocking cessation of sound it settled on Inanna's arm, hairy black and iridescent green, gross, insolent.

With a movement of disgust Inanna brushed it away.

'No! Wait!' Geshtinanna moved to catch her hand, too late. Nin Shubur's voice had stopped. Her eyes were open, startled.

Behind Inanna, Enki raised his eyebrows, shook his head.

'*Oh!*' The bitterness of Geshtinanna's disappointment could not be contained in that single cry.

Inanna brushed violently at the place on her arm where the fly's feet had danced drunkenly. She looked frightened.

'Why? What is wrong with you all?'

'That fly. It was no ordinary insect . . . Did you not think it had the look of the *galatur*, of the *kurgarra*, who crept under the gates of the Netherworld to bring you back?'

Inanna lifted her shocked face. Her cry pierced the sky. 'Fly! Come back! I will give you all the treasure in the world, mountains of honey, whatever you want! Come *back*!'

In a whir of rainbow wings, like the sun seen through tears, the fly was rising, reeling in the vast sky. It disappeared, there was no telling in what direction.

Now, only the gnats and mosquitoes danced over stagnant water.

# Chapter Ninety-six

Gilgamesh stood before Inanna, Dumuzi's mortal brother. It was hard for her to remember that he was human. He looked so big, so arrogant, as though he went about always in padded armour. Whenever he moved she seemed to hear the clash of weapons.

In his face today was something very close to desperation. She saw a greyness under his sunburn. Was that how she looked to him, clad in her deep mourning, without her husband?

'Is there to be no hope for a man like me?'

'I risked my life for you in the Netherworld, Gilgamesh. And I lost a jewel more beloved than that.'

'You came back from the Netherworld, but I shall die and not come back.'

'Dumuzi is still Below.'

'That was your choice! Dumuzi, Geshtinanna. Your word speaks life or death now, even to the Anunnaki. Can't you say the word of life for me?'

'I ... do not ... rule ... in the Below.' Bitter as Ereshkigal's voice.

Gilgamesh bowed and backed away from her throne. She could see it irked him that he could not turn on his heel and stride out of her presence.

The doors swung open on the star-filled evening, letting in a sweet reek of cooking smoke. They heard his voice shouting to his young men.

The *pukku* began to beat savagely.

'Wash me.'

Nin Shubur looked up swiftly, as if to check that she had understood Inanna's intention accurately.

'Yes. Whatever I feel, I cannot stay in mourning for ever, even if my heart is bleeding. Gilgamesh is doing whatever he

538

likes. The people of Sumer need their Lion. I must sit in my judgment hall again. The land has been suffering without me too long.'

'At once, my lady.'

Nin Shubur was almost as eager as Inanna to get the household of the E-Anna into its normal motion again. Soon Inanna was in the tiled bathroom. Showers of clear, warm water were pouring over her from copper ewers. From the bowl sculpted like a duck, the cake of fragrant soap lathered her limbs. The ritual dirt of mourning spread a grey film over the surface of the water round her feet. It was gone, it was rinsed away with the fresh torrents that were cleansing her. Oil sleeked her skin, bringing the scented breath of high forests into the hammering heat of the plain.

'Dress me in my queen's robe. Let them see clearly what they nearly lost.'

But as she stepped from her bath and slaves hurried to wrap her round with soft towels, Inanna looked about her with a puzzled air, a slight disturbance of discontent. Something was missing.

'Where is . . . ?'

A hush of chatter. A suspension of breath. She saw it in their frightened faces even before the ray of truth lit the innermost place of her mind.

Amanamtagga, her body slave, was dead. She would not come back.

For all her furious denunciation, Inanna had never truly equated that rival woman in Dumuzi's lap with the tall, many-skilled slave who had overseen her bedchamber, her dressing room, her bath house. Since before Inanna's marriage, Amanamtagga had dressed her hair, ordered the care of her dresses and jewellery. Amanamtagga's own hands had massaged her after the bath. Inanna had loaded her with presents.

Now there was a sense of loss, of darkness, as when a sudden storm has stripped the blossom from a tree and left no fruit to ripen. And yet, for all Inanna's generosity to her servants, Amanamtagga had hardly mattered to her as a person while she worked in the palace. She had seemed, rather, a well-made, animate tool. It was Dumuzi who had come and recognised her as another woman, valued her, and so destroyed her.

Or had he only wanted her body?

'Nawirtum, massage me, if you please,' Inanna said sharply.

These hands were cool, skilful, though not as understanding as Amanamtagga's. Inanna lay face downward on the couch, trying to recall Nawirtum's features, the colour of her skin, the shape of her body. Could she, too, attract a young man?

'Nin Shubur!'

The woman, more friend than court official, moved forward from the cushion where she was squatting. Inanna raised eyes brilliant with tears.

'What if I do find Dumuzi? If the Below ever gives him back to me? It will never be the same between us again, will it?'

Nin Shubur took her hand, motioned the slaves away.

'You will see, my love. Wait till he returns. Wait and see.'

'Geshtinanna loves him more than I do, doesn't she?'

'There is love and there is loving. Lord Dumuzi needs both.'

'I would give him such loving, if only I could find him!'

'Sh, sh, my *labi*.'

# Chapter Ninety-seven

The summer dragged away.

One afternoon, unable to rest, Inanna stole out alone to her garden in the siesta time. The palace slept. There was no watchful Amanamtagga to see her leave her bed. The plump Nawirtum had not stirred. Nin Shubur was resting in her own chamber.

She wandered down through the park of the E-Anna in the aching silence, nursing her grief. The gardens rose from the banks of the Buranun to the slopes of the city mound. Kullab stood above her now. Here in this park she had planted her *huluppu* tree. Here, she and Dumuzi had met as lovers. Here . . .

How cruelly brief, those days before her wedding. How much had changed since they had wandered in this park with Utu and his friends and Geshtinanna and all the daughters of Ninurta. She had whispered blushing conversations with her newly-betrothed, had touched her fingertips secretly to his. Such tiny thrills of discovery, stolen ecstasies almost as great as the intimacy of marriage.

Now she walked, solitary, along these same avenues of exotic trees. She smiled wanly, with a start of newly remembered surprise, at giraffes and parrots, the delicacy of flamingos. The caged lions first pleased and then distressed her. She stroked her hands over the woodwork of their hutches, as if the golden timber was living hair.

'My beauties. My proud and fearless sisters. Shall you be prey for sport? Will small boys kneel upon this roof and lift the shutter while huntsmen stand around with sharpened spears? Shall you bound out into the daylight and the freedom, and the flung weapons fell you?'

She turned to find the solace of a well-filled pool, a reservoir that even the burning months of summer had not drunk dry. Pink lilies opened faces to the sun, showed their gold hearts. Succulent leaves shadowed the fish beneath. Delicate rushes tasselled the fringes of the pond. She let her hand sweep over them like the push of a breeze.

A carp jumped, tail flaming red for a moment uppermost, then dived for safety as the reflections moved. Inanna looked quickly over her shoulder. Had Nin Shubur followed her? No. Someone else, like the shadow of a palm trunk, almost behind her.

'Who are you? What do you want?' Imperiously, slightly annoyed.

He bowed. A youngish man, dark-faced, supple, slim. He wore the rough sheepskin of an outdoor worker. But his hands were slender, fine though somewhat dirty. She knew she should remember his face.

'Your head gardener, my Lady. Shukalletuda. Excuse me. I did not expect to find you here. I came to feed the fish.'

Memory returned. This was the man who had failed to guard her tree, who had let Kiskillilla and the Imdugud and the Mushsagkal in. She saw by the flash in his eyes that he realised it too, now.

'It was not my fault your *huluppu* tree was attacked! I was new. Lord An didn't tell me.'

She sighed. 'That was a long time ago. Gilgamesh saved my tree for me, to make . . .' The ready tears betrayed her.

'I'm sorry, my Lady. I'll come back later.' The breadcrumbs slithered in the flat basket as he turned to go.

'No. Feed them while I watch.' Too brightly, to cover painful memories.

'If you're sure, my Lady?'

His tiny gifts made a shower on the air, barely penetrated the viscous surface. The plump fish hesitated, then swam out from the lily leaves, rose from the muddy depths, opened gaping lips to gulp the meal down. Inanna laughed, surprising herself for a moment out of the misery of guilt and loss, the anger of self-defence and justification.

'I don't remember this pool. Did you make it?'

Shukalletuda steadied his voice. 'There was a small one here before I came. But what you see now is mostly mine. I sent to Shubur and Uri and even Dilmun for flowering water plants. I planted the *mesu* trees to give blossom in spring and shade in summer. I . . .' Then he fell silent, as if embarrassed by the rush of his own enthusiasm.

'It's beautiful. I have always loved this garden.'

'But . . . what I'm really good at is dates. Yes, believe me. Oh, I know you see palm trees in every garden in Sumer. But I truly believe I can boast, you won't taste dates anywhere in the world as succulent as the ones here. I learned the secret from my father in Ur. Your own father's gardener. It's the watering, you see, and the hoeing around the roots. People think date palms don't need much water.' His eyes were eager to impress her. She felt herself smiling, She knew the dangerous power of that radiance.

'Yes. I remember those dates. They were very good.' She tried to speak like a good *sanga*, manageress of her estate. 'I am glad there is still some sweetness in the world.' She fought to hold the sob.

'I . . . If I can please my Lady . . .' He backed away respectfully. She saw his eyes, bewitched and golden-brown as his own dates, full of desire.

'Thank you.'

She walked away from him quickly. She wished she had woken Nin Shubur.

With each step around the base of the mound the view altered. The desert stretched before her now, flattened as if under a giant hand, oppressed by the heat of summer. There, on that waterless steppe, Dumuzi . . .

'*No!*' The cry was wrenched from her soul. 'I didn't mean it! I didn't! I love you, Dumuzi. Come back! Come back!'

She watched the wind coming across the treetops towards her. She saw the restless sand of the desert scooped up. It was dancing like a whirling woman. The wind was screaming.

Pitiless crystals stung her face, stabbed at her eyes, raked her hair. Inanna gasped and snatched up a fold of cloth to cover her face.

Someone was gripping her arm. Shukalletuda tugged her round, sheltering her. He was standing in front of her, with his back to the storm, his naked shoulders taking the force of the sand.

The whirlwind passed. Dust clogged the delicate leaves of the flowering plants.

'Forgive me, my Lady. That was a nasty squall to catch you in the open.'

His hands seemed proprietorial now, slow to let her go, as if she were one of his beautiful date trees, no longer his Lady.

She shook the cloth from her head, and the sand in its folds pattered to the ground around her, golden as Kiskillilla's skin. Her eyes went up, and the sun pierced her from the desert like a knife, reopening the wound. She stepped back abruptly from Shukalletuda's hold.

'You should plant trees here,' she ordered. 'I do not want to see the desert. Set a screen between my garden and the steppe. A row of *sarbatu* trees, for shade and protection. Do it today!'

'At once, my Lady. Next time you visit this garden, I shall see that you have what you want.'

'Inanna?'

'Look! She's there!'

Inanna glanced behind her. Two women were hurrying through an orchard grove to where she and Shukalletuda stood in the merciless sun. Nin Shubur and Geshtinanna. Patterns of leaf shadows chased over their faces, telling of anxiety and relief.

Nin Shubur came almost running, and started to brush the sand from Inanna's dress like a mother with a small girl.

'My Lady! What are you doing out here alone? I woke up and found you were missing. Not one of those idle slaves could tell me when you'd gone, or where. If Amanamtagga . . . Oh, my dear, I'm sorry!'

Shukalletuda bowed and backed away.

Geshtinanna came up and cradled Inanna against her shoulder. 'Don't weep, my love. We'll find him. We'll find the gate to the Netherworld.'

'When? When, Geshtinanna? Is Ereshkigal mocking me? Will she keep him imprisoned for ever?'

Geshtinanna rocked her without speaking for a while. 'It has been nearly half a year,' she said at last. 'If Ereshkigal heard your word, the gates must open soon. Soon, soon, Inanna. We shall see Dumuzi again.'

Nin Shubur's eyes were fixed on Geshtinanna's face now, in sympathy.

Inanna rushed on, 'Where? Where can we find him? I have searched the whole land of Sumer. He is nowhere, *nowhere*!'

Nin Shubur caught her breath. A drone of sound circled their heads in the dusty, afternoon air. She held out her small, skilled hand, palm upward.

'Be our honoured guest, fly from the Netherworld.'

But the fly skimmed past her and landed on Inanna's hand.

She had to make an effort to keep her flesh from trembling as the fly staggered a few steps sideways on her skin. The suck of its feet made her shiver with an almost sexual ecstasy.

'What does it want? Ask it!' When Inanna did not reply, Geshtinanna lowered her own head and said softly, 'Excellent fly, wearer of the jet and emerald garment, messenger of the many-jewelled eyes, you have seen our grief. What have you come to say to us?'

'Pots and piss!' The fly lurched so that its proboscis pressed into Inanna's flesh. Geshtinanna had hold of her arm, but she would not have moved.

'We cannot understand you, master of eloquence. Speak clearly for us,' Nin Shubur pleaded.

The fly sawed the air with a tuneless, drunken singing.

> Root and fruit and barley ear,
> Froth and fungus, make good cheer.
> Sick and spittle, song and sleep,
> Where the beer swills, drown him deep.

'Who?'

The fly's huge eye swivelled, looking at all of them and more besides.

> Where Nin Kasi dances round,
> Where her spoon turns underground,
> When the butcher slays the sheep,
> Then the brewer's vat is deep.

Inanna could not speak for the excitement that was constricting her throat, the fear that in the next moment the fly would be gone leaving only this tantalising hint upon the air.

Geshtinanna whispered for her. 'The barley harvest is long over, gracious singer. The beer has been brewed. If he was hidden in any brewster's kitchen or brewer's cellar, we would have searched him out by now. Are you mocking us? *Where is Dumuzi?*'

> Red this beer, very fitting,
> Life renewing, demons flitting,
> Kur's a mountain, Kur's a flood.
> Seek Dumuzi in the . . .

The iridescent wings quivered into stillness. One hairy leg

rubbed against another. Nin Shubur was imploring it in a strange tongue, but the fly rose lazily into the air and danced away, lost in the dazzling dust motes of the sky.

'Come back! I will give you all the riches of Uruk! Where? *Where?*' Inanna cried in desperation.

Geshtinanna's grasp was warm on her arm. The Wine Girl's face was flowering into a beauty of happiness, as though at last she had been given what she most longed for.

'It's all right, Inanna. He's coming. It's true after all. Dumuzi's time is almost here. I know the place!'

# Chapter Ninety-eight

'What are you doing, Mother?' As if she had not come expecting it. As if she did not know the time of year.

'What does it look like? I'm brewing beer.'

'Oh, wise Mother. You hold the answer. The barley and the emmer wheat were harvested long ago. We could have searched all those breweries of Sumer in vain. They were brewing that beer at the end of winter, when . . .'

'She took my Damu away.'

'Don't weep any more, Mother.'

All summer Nin Sun had never ceased to mourn. She squatted now outside the fragile hut of reeds she had raised to shelter herself from the sun. Her black cloth was wrapped about her body and head, partly hiding her face. Her strong, brown hands were busy with a knife. Over the fire in front of her a clay pot bubbled, sending out clouds of heady steam. The knife flashed down, severing the crimson tubers. Nin Sun tossed the fragments into the pot.

'And now the summer is almost over, and I'm brewing the blood beer, as I've done every year. I used to make it for Dumuzi. He loved it.'

Geshtinanna shivered suddenly. She looked up then at the burning sky that had spread its unvarying tent for six weary months. There was not a cloud in sight, but a thundery grey thickened the atmosphere over Uruk, hiding from sight that mound in the monotony of the vast river plain. She stood up slowly, shook the dust from her skirt where she had crouched to greet her mother. The sun was hot on her bare right shoulder. How long before they felt the benediction of the rain? She looked across the dry grasslands of Arali towards her vineyard on the edge of the steppe.

'My grapes have ripened. It's time to harvest them.' She bent and kissed her mother's creased forehead. 'May your beer be good. Make it very strong this year. Make it nourishing. May the pouring of it bring you your heart's desire.'

'Are you going so soon?'

'So soon . . . yes.' Geshtinanna lifted her thoughtful face and looked around her more slowly, dwelling on every detail of this sunlit world. The sheep, fewer in number since the spring slaughter, beginning to grow heavy with lamb now. The dwindling patch of green rushes round each dried-up pool. The breeze flattening the feathered grassheads. The silver of willows and black of date palms marking the distant watercourses of the plain. Close at hand were all the loved miniatures of daily life: strings of golden onions, a half-finished cloth on the loom, a pottery cup of milk, her mother's red-stained hands.

She bent and folded Nin Sun in a long, loving kiss. 'I will be back,' she said. 'One day, I shall come back.'

Inanna stroked her hand voluptuously, as though she still felt the thrill of the fly's suckered feet stepping across her skin. She stared out of the window at the gathering clouds, then turned back in an agony of restlessness and hugged Geshtinanna.

'Oh, Geshtin! Geshtin! Did ever a Daughter of An have such a friend as you. Will he really come? Can that beer revive him? Will he live again, as he did before? Oh, how can I wait? What shall I wear? Where should I meet him?'

'There is still much pain between you that cannot be undone, cannot be unsaid.' The Wine Girl found her face stiff and heavy. Speech was an effort now. Feeling seemed to be withering even before she set foot on the road to the Netherworld. Rain was coming. The storm that would gladden the hearts of everyone after the summer could only chill her. 'Try to go back to the beginning. Be the Maid Inanna again. Be the Daughter of the Moon, the pure Morning Star. Dumuzi's bride.'

'Here!' The light was brilliant in Inanna's eyes. She touched the Lion Bed. The precious, carved wood of the *huluppu* tree, where the *pirug* lion chased the *ug* lion, and the *ug* lion swerved and turned, bounding after his partner again. The wood that Kiskillilla had cut into to make her home in the land of Sumer, in the heart of Kullab, in the very core of Inanna's tree. The tree among whose roots the Serpent had been severed to make a *pukku* out of them for Gilgamesh, from whose branches the Imdugud and her chicks had been driven off to give him the *mikku* stick. The bed that matched the Lion Throne in splendour. Dumuzi had learned his lesson. She would be Queen for him and all the Earth again.

Geshtinanna was by the door. Pale, quiet, without a song.

Inanna seized an embroidered pillow, hugged it to her breast. 'Oh, here, yes, yes! It shall be our wedding night all over again. It will be new! It will be perfect this time!'

Still Geshtinanna stood just beyond the threshold, in the shadow of the first day of winter.

Nin Shubur coughed gently. Inanna raised her glorious face, cheeks glowing, eyes like stars. She ran and hugged her friend.

'Geshtin, we love him, don't we? You and I. It's for love we're doing this. You are descending to Kur and I am taking him back.'

'Yes, Inanna. We are doing it because we love him.'

They kissed strongly. Geshtinanna walked away, down the long, dim halls of the E-Anna. Priests bowed in respect. Slaves drew back from the touch of her skirt with a more superstitious dread. The *sag-ursag* saluted her.

Behind her, Inanna's voice rang through the palace with a joyful cry, 'Prepare my bath! Bring all the sweet perfumes of the mountains, my most intimate jewels! Make me ravishing for Dumuzi, my lover!'


On into the outer air and the thickening darkness. Clouds lowered over the Vine Girl's head, oppressing her, making her stoop. Wind whipped the loosely-wrapped cloth from her, screaming in her ears, tearing it free, leaving her naked. Hanging hair, hiding her lowered face. Dust under her feet, solidifying into clay, into rock.

Water.

When had the rain begun? She looked up through a curtain of tears, through a winter downpour. Ghost-white, the wet limbs coming towards her, the only gleam of light in this black tunnel.

'*Dumuzi?*'

'Who asks?' A voice like the wind through a hollow reed.

'I am Geshtin. Dumuzi, is it really you?'

'If you are Geshtinanna, you must not walk the Road of No Return.'

'I am walking it.'

'You cannot eat the mouldy bread of the dead; you cannot drink their foul water.'

'I will eat it, I will drink it, for you, Dumuzi.'

He was close now.

'*Geshtin?*'

'Damu! I'm here!'

Her eager hands were reaching out. Touching his. His chill flesh beginning to pulse with warmth as her own grew colder.

Sliding away now. Light dwindling fainter and fainter behind her, going higher.

A hopeless darkness.

A metal bolt scraped. A gate clanged mournfully open. The stench of rottenness made her stumble.

'Welcome to the Netherworld, Inanna's sister. Come in, Lady. There is nothing that we can strip from you! You have given it all away already, haven't you?'

Even at the end of summer there was still a trickle of water in the river. Nin Sun did not watch it. She moved with the same steady industry as a woman who knows her time of childbearing is near and is determined to see that everything is ready. She will not yet allow herself to imagine what may be ahead for her.

Just once she turned her face to her daughter's farm and muttered, 'She should have had time. She will have the last of the grape harvest in by now, the juice pressed and fermenting. Geshtinanna's a clever girl. She knows her wine jars must be capped for storing.'

So the wind-tanned Woman of the Wild Cows, who had once been Lugalbanda's queen, went to the clamp at the side of the house, pulled aside the clods of earth with soiled hands, dug out more of the blood-red roots. Again she took them to the mat and set to work, chopping, tossing, stirring, brewing. Her face was bathed in sweat, her eyes dimmed by steam.

'*Alas, my mother!*'

Was that a drop of thundery rain hissing on the white-hot heap of burning canes?

'*My hands hurt.*'

The knife poised over the chopping mat.

'*My back hurts.*'

Trembling, her own hands fell, but the tuber stayed uncut.

'*My neck hurts.*'

She scrambled to her feet, shaking all over now. Was the air growing dark, or was her sight beginning to dim with old age? She stumbled to the fire, drew out a ladleful of the dark red liquid, poured it into a clay beaker.

The cup was warm within her hands, warm as the lifeblood of the newly slain. She lifted her head, and the first wind running before the coming storm blew the black cloth back from her hair. An eagle screamed.

Through the rising excitement of the grasses, through the dust devils dancing round her ankles, she made her way, surer now, beginning to laugh, to the side of the Arali stream. So slender the thread of life between its banks. Not deep enough to bear the *galla*'s barge.

With hands that hardly quivered, with a priestess's incantation, with a Queen Mother's homage to the heir, with the lullabies of a nursing mother, with a milking song, she poured the steady flow of beer, thick, red and foaming, into the silver river.

The water thickened, began to run in veins, outlined the grey stones it skirted like muscled flesh. A gale was stirring the surface now. Dry reeds were flying through the air like golden hair. The rain came driving across the steppe in a striding column. The thunder roared like a lion.

Dumuzi was standing, whole and laughing, rain dripping from his curls, his arms flung wide.

'Oh, my mother! My wise brewster! You were always the one who gave life to me. I'm alive! I'm back!'

Inanna lay on Utu's blue sheets. She was scented with cedar oil, sweet with the touch of honey. Costly amber gleamed round her lips. Her hair was piled and looped in intricate waves of lapis lazuli. Moonlight bathed the Lion Bed, catching the sparkle of silver ornaments in nose and ears, the stud of the gold butterfly in her navel, the blue and gold beads round her firm-fleshed legs. Her nipples and eyes were painted. Her nails were coral. All else was moon-white flesh, veined with the blue of planets.

Nin Shubur stood, holding the edge of the curtain ready, a little smile on her lips. She surveyed the beauty on the Lion Bed with an almost maternal pride. Music from *tigi* strings and *ala* harps rose from the court below like the scent of blossom expressed in sound, backed by the percussive drumming of the rain. Thunder rumbled in the distance, and Inanna laughed and roared herself.

'Now?' asked Nin Shubur.

'Now! Now!'

The woollen curtain lifted. A naked Lord was standing on the threshold. In his hand he held up a giant cluster of golden-brown dates, lustrous in the gleam of the lamps. At the sight of Inanna his wavering penis leaped erect. Inanna laughed with delight. She held out eager arms towards him.

'Come, my honey-man, come! Quickly!'

Rainwater was pouring down the sides of the house. The moon dimmed. Only the lamps shone on like stars. Nin Shubur's voice was a flowing river of benediction. 'May the king pass long days in the sweet place. May the Idiglat and Buranun rise in a high flood under him . . .'

But Inanna already had Dumuzi in her arms, was rolling him over, grasping him with her strong legs, mounting him, smothering his half-formed words of entreaty with passionate kisses.

Nin Shubur withdrew, turned a bland, discreet face to the eager eyes of the waiting maids and body slaves. From the room behind her came a double shout of ecstasy.

# BOOK FOUR

# The Last Enemy

# Chapter Ninety-nine

The New Year Festival in Uruk, in honour of Inanna.
Inanna . . . Nin Mesarra, Lady of Myriad Offices . . . Nin Ibgal, Lady of the Big House.

Titles were heaped upon her. Wealth flowed to her city. Corn was emptied out of its granaries and stored in clay-domed clamps so that the barns could be filled with a more precious harvest of jewels and metals pouring up from the landing quays. She had gathered all the *me*. She had gone to the Netherworld and returned. She had restored Dumuzi. Gilgamesh her *lugal* had beaten all rebel invaders. She was a roaring Lion. Columns of captives came to serve her city.

Morning and evening the people praised her with hymns.

Now she sat enthroned under the colonnade while a multicoloured procession streamed in front of her.

All the gradations of priests marching with *algar* instruments, silver-inlaid, and the beat of tambourines and kettledrums.

'I will hail Inanna, Great Queen of the Above!'

Men with their right arms clothed, women with their left shoulders bared, their buttocks playfully painted, reversal of the normal order at the pivot of the year.

'I will hail Inanna, Eldest Daughter of the Moon.'

*Kurgarra* in chariots, bloodied and scarred from festival combat fought before her eyes, their ranks thinned by the newly-dead, slain in the games.

'Our Queen, the Evening Star Inanna, is exalted to the boundaries of the Sky!'

Small virgins and crones, with their hair curled like harlots. *Sag-ursag* guardsmen, locks plaited with ribbons, wearing the sheepskin cloaks of an older order.

'I will hail the Pure One, the Awe-Bearing Queen of the Anunnaki!'

She turned, half intoxicated with the praise they piled upon her, dazzled with the splendour and colour of the day. Dumuzi sat beside her. A breeze from the far-off steppe fanned Inanna's face. Her hand went out and closed over Dumuzi's warm, brown one.

'My love, my *lubi*. When this is over, let's go away again to your sheep farm. Let's run from the dragons of summer in the plain. We shall walk by marsh pools with a new sheepdog at our heels. We shall picnic in cool tents while you pipe to your sheep. In the evening we shall drink Geshtinanna's wine and sing the songs she taught us under the stars.'

Dumuzi shifted on his seat. 'Have you forgotten already? I shall not walk the Earth with you in any summer, ever again.'

'Oh, my love, my dearest. Don't think about it. Let's be happy while we can.'

'Don't you think about Geshtinanna? I miss her. I don't want a new dog. I miss Urgi. I think Queen Inanna will not be happy in a shepherd's hut. There are few to praise you like this on the steppe.'

The Lady looked at the clowns and tumblers following the E-Anna soldiers. She waved her hands to them in acknowledgement.

'I was not city-born. The farms are mine as well as this. I have walked the Sky. I know both the solitary places and the towns.'

'You are Queen of the E-Anna. My place is beside you as your king.'

'Your place is beside me as my lover!' laughed Inanna, slipping her arm round his waist so that the two of them were entwined. 'Gilgamesh can look after the city. Look at him, Dumuzi. There he comes. He is my Big Man, my warlike *lugal*, our royal hero. He is planning to enlarge the walls for me. We can go away and leave our champion here.'

'Gilgamesh is not a true Lord,' muttered Dumuzi.

'But more lordly than many Anunnaki,' Inanna said, clapping her hands as the huge hero marched by at the head of the city's young fighting men.

Feasting and drinking, song and athletic competitions filled the day till the festival was over and the moon sailed, round and silver, and the sun strengthened towards early summer, the time when Dumuzi must return Below.

Impermanence was an unwelcome guest at the banquet. Dumuzi and Inanna loved more passionately because they knew the time was brief now. Gilgamesh and his still more human companions felt the long shadow of darkness over their young lives, like an eclipse of the moon.

Perhaps that was why the beakers of strong beer rattled more loudly on the tabletops, most of all down the long side of the board where the hosts and their highest guests sat. What was there, after all, between the two half-brothers, Dumuzi and Gilgamesh, if even a Lord could die? If the blood of Enki could not save his son from the Netherworld, how could the blood of Gilgamesh's mortal father, already dead? Better to get drunk and see the gorgeous Inanna swimming through the fog of beer like a brilliant star on a misty winter night.

Inanna would never die again. Oh no, Gilgamesh thought, clenching the electrum goblet in his powerful fist. Oh no! She went once to the Netherworld, threw down her proud challenge and bought her way out with her husband's life. Look at her now, as lovely as ever. She will never age like the rest of us. Yet there is something more awesome about her now. The rippling hair could make you think of black snakes. Those voluptuous lips red as if they had just kissed blood. The turn of that white, muscled arm. You could imagine she would fling a spear as straight as I can. And yet, yet, yet . . . He had only to look down where the fine linen stuff hardly veiled the cleavage between her pillared legs. The hang of the birth-beads between her swelling breasts. The deep, erotic voice. When she lifted the dark flames of her eyes he was caught, conquered. He was fired with desire to take her, to take any woman if he could not touch her. He looked at the flushed, excited faces round the tables. She had them all. They were in love with her glory.

'Oh, Inanna,' he breathed, hardly knowing that he murmured aloud. 'I am your city's hero. Why not me?'

She turned upon him a radiant smile of welcome. She said nothing, but her lips parted over the perfect gate of shell-white teeth, where the small, pink tongue licked and played in lascivious promise.

Gilgamesh almost fainted, felt his lower body strain towards melting. He found himself leaning on Ishkur for support.

'Hold up, man! It's not bedtime yet. Inanna hasn't had bulls slain for her champions only to have you stagger away from the board before they're eaten.'

'She brews a seductive beer,' he muttered thickly. Better to pretend to this Son of An that it was beer that was weakening his faculties and not this all-conquering desire.

'There's a rumour that Ebih is rising against us. They say the voice of Kur is behind it. Inanna has raided one nest too many.'

Dumuzi heard them. He got to his feet, walked out on to the chilly terrace. The rainswept night showed patchy stars. He turned to stare to the north-east, as if his eyes could see beyond the sweep of flood plain, faintly pricked with firelight, to the greater darkness of the wall of hills, the boundary of this known world and the other. No one among his mortal drinking companions, not even his half-brother, dared to question him about his going into the Netherworld. What had happened between Dumuzi and Inanna was too terrible for humans to contemplate. It had increased their love for the Shepherd, because he shared now, in some sort, their experience, the fate that awaited them all at the end of the Road of No Return. Women had always loved him. Now they mourned passionately for him. For Inanna they felt something different: awe of her power, dependence on her word of love that alone could bring him back from the Below, over and over again. Praise to Inanna, the Pure Bride! But each summer . . . Soon. Soon.

Gilgamesh's hand descended on Dumuzi's shoulder.

'Did you hear that? This is Earth! What business has rebel Kur coming out of the dark into the light of Sumer? If they challenge us, I'll take our army against them!'

Dumuzi turned slightly, eyes filled with horror that did not seem to see his brother. 'You do not know. You haven't been to the Below. Utu knows. Enki knows. Enlil knows. We are not as strong as you think we are, we Anunnaki. Ninurta was overwhelmed with emotion when Nin Mah went looking for him alone in the enemy territory.'

'But our Lion Inanna is worth ten of them!'

'You still say that? Man! Ereshkigal killed her! And now Geshtinanna and I must take her place.'

'Dumuzi.' Gilgamesh hugged him. 'Inanna brought you back, didn't she? And our sweet Geshtinanna in her turn? There's a heroine for you. What have you got to be so bitter about? When the Netherworld takes *me*, it will be for ever.' His voice cracked on a harsh note that belied his cheerful rallying.

'None of us can change that. Inanna tried. And I am paying the price. You are a mortal.'

'I won't accept that!'

The girl screamed. There, on the flat rooftop of the mud-built house, Gilgamesh could see her flickering silhouette if he squinted up against the wheeling stars. He laughed almost soundlessly, baring his teeth like a panting dog. She wanted it! Oh yes, he could sense the raw excitement, the pleasure made greater for them both by her struggles to resist. This would be another to notch on his *mikku* stick. The count was great tonight. Wounds on wood, wounds on women. All down to him. He was the conqueror, *lugal* under Inanna's standard.

His friends of the evening, humans and Lords, were fewer now, fallen in a stupefied heap, or sick over the canals, or wandering home to sleep. Ishkur was with him. Ishkur was always aggressive in drink. Utu never came on these night raids. Utu was a prig, too puffed up with his role as Lord of Justice.

Dumuzi was besotted with Inanna.

Gilgamesh hammered on the *pukku* and the *huluppu* drum bellowed like a bull in pain. The hero of Uruk laughed. A lesser warrior would have given the massive wooden cylinder to a servant to carry. But his own chest was broad, his shoulders strong. His fists loved the grasp of the *mikku* stick, enjoyed the singing throb of hide and timber against his taut body. He crashed it again. Why didn't the parents answer him?

'Open up! Kick the door in, somebody. Don't you know the roar of the *pukku* of Gilgamesh? You're honoured tonight. I want your daughter. That one! I can see her on the roof. Pusar, is it? Bring her down, or shall I just leap up your stairs and have her under Inanna's planet?'

The bolts drew back, showing a darkened room. The father's scared face peered out into the lane. The terrified mother's was in shadow behind him.

'Sir, our daughter is a virgin. She was betrothed before this, but her young man fell in your last battle. We are in mourning, sir. He was one of your own band. Sheshkalla. Spare her tonight, sir. Let her keep the funeral rites for her man.'

'A virgin? In tears? Stand aside! I'll soon cheer her up.

Sheshkalla, eh? She's in luck, then. I'm a better man than Sheshkalla ever was. Look at that!' He hardly needed to lift his kilt aside to show the thrusting cock.

The roof was silent now, but he sensed that Pusar had not been alone in her mourning.

'How many of them, eh?' His arm, warm with familiarity, embraced the father's shoulders. 'More daughters, friends? Are they all up there? Shall I go and find them, or will you fetch them down?'

'I forbid you, sir.' The quavering bravery of the older man's voice was all he had, helpless as his hands that wrung themselves together over his deerskin apron.

'Well, then, hear this!' The *mikku* rattled a roll of ruin around the living room, shattering pots and bowls, overturning stools, scattering flour. A final crash on the *pukku*. Gilgamesh heaved it off him, thrust it at Ishkur.

'Look after that. You can beat a victory roll when you hear me shout.'

'Sir! I beg you! Our roof is overlooked!'

Stamp of leathered feet on the outer staircase. More screams, thin and delicate as the lesser stars. A huge and heavy darkness hid them. Out of its bestial sounds a final roar of achievement burst, swallowing the hopeless trickle of weeping.

The *pukku* crashed again in Ishkur's exultant hands. All down the lane, families shivered behind closed doors. Adolescent girls looked wide-eyed at their fathers. The fathers lowered their eyelids, bowed their heads.

'Gilgamesh fights to protect you, doesn't he?' their sons would demand as they reeled home in the early morning. 'Gilgamesh is the hero of Uruk. He deserves all he can get.'

'Inanna came back from the grave for us,' murmured Pusar's mother, washing the blood from her sobbing daughter's thighs. 'There, my love. It's time to ask how the Maid of the Sky House will use her power for her women.'

# Chapter One Hundred

In the high, hot summer, Inanna returned to Uruk alone, newly grieving for the loss of Dumuzi.

In her absence, Gilgamesh had thrown himself into work, enlarging the defences of Uruk. He laid forced labour on the citizens and serfs, driving them almost as hard as Enlil had once made the Anunnaki work to build Nippur.

Inanna frowned, riding the barge home to Uruk. She stood forward of the awning, balancing gracefully, for all her height, a woman grieving, but still voluptuous.

These walls would be magnificent. Seven sages of Inanna's household had laid their foundations. They shone like copper in the level sun, layer upon layer of desert-coloured brick, walling the mounded city of Uruk and Kullab. Imagination, colossal as the man, had dreamed their soaring height. Strength and inflexible will were driving the people to accomplish it. Corvées of labourers swarmed up ramps and scaffolding. Women toiled under baskets of rubble and bitumen. Even children heaved waterskins. Asses stumbled among the debris with panniers of bricks, stamped with Inanna's own rosette. Fires rose, shimmering the heated air, to soften pitch. Vast brickyards were slowly emptying their regiments of moulded clay. Vertical buttresses cast edges of shadow to break the glare for admiring eyes. The first length of the new rampart walks was showing, made of fire-hardened brick. Gilgamesh's soldiers meant to tread them often.

Once E-Anna had dominated the city. The Sky House had connected Angal to Earth. This was the place of stepping down. The people could lift their eyes and see what gave their lives importance lifted above all other occupations. Around had been gardens, lesser halls, flowing down to human habitations, bright canals, estates of the temple and palace, humbler farms, spreading away in a sea of barley and beans.

No fortifications were needed then, other than the awesome presence of An.

Now, this interruption, dominating the view. Between the fertile fields and the benevolent Anunnaki, this man had interposed a human statement. 'I am the *en* Gilgamesh, your prince. I am the *lugal*, the hero-warrior. I expect war. Look to me for protection, and not to your Lady.'

Inanna knew these walls could not have grown so very much higher in her absence. She was seeing them with new eyes.

'Gilgamesh would rival the Anunnaki.'

Nin Shubur sat, shading her eyes with her hand. The sun drove the lines deeper into her wise face.

'Gilgamesh is at least half a Lord. Some say two-thirds.'

'Gilgamesh is mortal. You know the rules.'

'Does even a single drop of human blood cancel out his claim to immortality? And what is immortality to Dumuzi now?'

Inanna could not hear that name without heat in her cheeks, pain in her heart.

'Dumuzi will come back. He will! With the autumn. He has not gone for ever.'

'And one day Gilgamesh will die, and not come back. I think his pride imagines these walls cannot fall, and while they stand they make a kind of armour for his life.'

'He is using my people for his life-blood. Look at them running in veins, unable to stop, in case the heart of Gilgamesh should cease to beat.'

'Doesn't it please you that your city is growing so great, so strong? It looks a warlike place.'

'You think I kill for pleasure?'

'I've seen the blood-flame in your eyes too much lately.'

'When my land is attacked! I give life. I protect it too. I will not see what I have quickened spilt.'

'Many of Sumer's young men fall on the battlefield.'

'Sumer's women are saved, Sumer's children are spared.'

'I think Gilgamesh will need many wars to justify these walls.'

When there was no enemy army, Gilgamesh fought his own comrades in violent wrestling matches.

'This cannot go on.'

Pusar's father, Ur-Baba, faced the assembly of the elders of

Uruk. Uneasy looks passed from the older family men to each other.

'You know what I mean. Do I have to spell it out to you? I'm not the only one here who's had a daughter violated. Is there a bride in the city who's allowed to go to her husband a virgin? No! Gilgamesh must always get in first. He claims it's the *en*'s right.'

'Sons' blood is as precious as daughters',' Abbagina said.

A sighing groan rippled through the seated lines like a wave washing across a reservoir. Some eyes dimmed with tears. Imagination showed them the loss of their hopes.

'We are a rich city. We don't need these wars for booty.'

'There's so much trade coming in, we've had to tip the grain out of the barns to make room for the silver.'

'I've lost two sons because . . . that bully . . . wanted to dress up in armour and play at wars. For nothing. For nothing!'

'Too much hot blood in one big body.'

'I put it to this Council. We take away his *en*ship,' Ur-Baba proposed, determined to force the point.

But a superstitious dread changed the faces before him. Eyes shifted more questioningly now. Their shared grief and indignation were being undermined by self-preservation.

'He protected us from the Martu.'

'Inanna favours him.'

'The walls are half-built. However much we may curse at his forced labour, they're there now. That's a challenge other cities can't ignore. They know we want to be top dog. What if we throw Gilgamesh out and they march against us? Are bricks and bitumen alone enough to keep them off?'

'What would Inanna say?'

'What if she turns her back on Kullab?'

'She'd never desert us!'

'She handed her husband over.'

'Will you bow your necks like slaves?' Ur-Baba expostulated. 'Will you let him trample over us like beetles? Will you go home to your wives tonight and get more daughters for him to rape?'

'There must be another way.'

'Great Enlil himself was a wild young man,' Dudugula, the *sanga* of the E-Anna estate, said thoughtfully. 'Didn't he rape Nin Lil when she was just a small virgin? But the Moon Lord came of it. Enlil forced the Anunnaki to work on the brickwork of Nippur till they revolted. That's when we humans were made, to do the work for the Anunnaki.'

'How does that help us? My daughter Pusar isn't pregnant with another Nanna. *We* can't sentence Gilgamesh to the Netherworld. We're not Lords.'

'Easy, easy, Ur-Baba. A new man may still be the answer. He'll need to be more than an ordinary human, though. And you're right. We haven't time to wait for a baby to grow, however Sky-bright. Not while the *pukku* and *mikku* are beating through the streets of Uruk day and night.'

'To rape our daughters.'

'And kill our sons.'

'Well, then?'

Dudugula stroked his beard. 'We could make petitions to Inanna. She has children too.'

'Do you think she'd side against him?'

'Nin Mah is the Mother of all of them. If we could touch her . . .'

'She's the one who shaped the clay from the Abzu to give us human bodies.'

'She's the Lady of Birth.'

'But what *is* this birth you're talking about?'

'Something to stop Gilgamesh before he destroys a whole generation.'

'Lay it before Nin Mah, then. Trust her.'

'We're Inanna's people.'

'Inanna's Lady of Love and War.'

A halt in the argument. A lowering of voices. Inanna was Gilgamesh's Lady. His walls honoured her city. His wars promoted her power.

'Inanna is Queen of Lovemaking. Is birth her sphere?'

'But *this* birth? What could help us?'

Bar-Namtar spoke, high priestess of Dumuzi's household, who said little in public debate, but whose rare, quiet voice was listened to.

'Uruk was once An's city. He still loves it. Inanna should beg him to intercede with the Great Lady for us. We need a rival to Gilgamesh himself. There is no one else of his stature to check or counsel him. He listens to no voice but the sound of his *pukku* and *mikku* stirring his blood to greater excesses. We need a hero, with strength as great as his own, to teach him a lesson. Someone he can respect but, if possible, with a more loving heart.' Her voice died away into an atmosphere

of scepticism, consideration, a grudging hope, enthusiasm.
'No son of ours can sway him.'
'The young fools follow him to their deaths when he beats that *pukku*.'
'Would An hear us nowadays? He never answers.'
'Will the Great Lady help us?'
'She used to be a generous Mother.'
'Well, then, it's up to Inanna to protect her people.'

# Chapter One Hundred and One

Inanna hesitated. 'My people want me to oppose Gilgamesh?'

'That's what they are saying. Couldn't you hear the cacophony?' Nin Shubur smiled. 'It is like the days just before the Flood, when we could get no peace. Is your heart so dull these days you haven't even been listening to what your city is asking?'

'I? Not care for my city? Of course I do!' She rose, with that swift, decisive grace, and carried the matter across the furthest reaches of Angal, accompanied by crowds of Anunnaki. An sat cross-legged, reproachfully watching her coming.

'I thought you'd forgotten me.'

'Forget you, Great-grandfather? Never. But Dumuzi—'

'So the worm's bored his way back into the fruit, has he?'

'Great-grandfather, I love him.'

'Then what do you need me for?'

'A birth.'

'Me? A birth? Isn't that you women's department? Or Enki's?'

She caressed his shoulders. 'You could speak to Nin Mah. She would soften for you. For Uruk, Great-grandfather. We need a new creature. A strong but tender being. Like and yet unlike Gilgamesh.'

'So your soldier has proved too rough, even for you, Lion Inanna?' An let his favourite help him reluctantly to his feet. 'The people of Uruk need a saviour, do they? A new creation. Well then, we must go to her, and see if she will help. Though sometimes I think Ki is not a wife, a mother, a Lady any more, but a solid lump of her own clay and stone.'

The following Anunnaki tried to avoid looking at one another as the Sky Lord drifted rather than walked across the far blue slopes of Angal and stepped down the Stairs to the green-brown Earth.

'Ki? Nin Mah . . .' All her other names, of soil and motherhood and making, he let fall from his loving lips. 'Antum, Nin Tu, Aruru, Urash, Dingir Mah . . .'

'Mmm.' She rolled and murmured. The Anunnaki felt a stirring under their feet. Their mother was waking from the nurturing sleep that fed them all in her primeval dreams. 'Who's there?'

She opened vast, brown eyes. The cloth fell from one swelling breast. She had aged less than An. Milk spurted freely with every movement of her shoulder. She heaved herself up on one elbow and looked around, smiled sleepily.

'So many children. What, my loves? Is it a party, that you've all come to see your old mother together?'

Inanna bent over her. 'Great-grandmother, An is here.'

That look, the twin of his. Pain, love, the memory of a lost closeness in the irrecapturable eternity before creation, before that closeness had bred the birth of Enlil, before he separated them, so that all creation could grow. Enlil had taken her himself, while An returned to Nammu, to sire Ereshkigal and Enki. So many separations, so many splittings off of Sky from Earth, Above, Below, Anunnaki and humans, life and death.

'You'll want something,' she grinned knowledgeably, coming more awake now. 'You always do. Greedy creatures. Greedy little Children of An. It's a good job you can never suck me dry.'

They smiled shamefacedly.

'Yes, Great Mother,' Inanna said, more respect in her bearing than she ordinarily showed. 'An has a request to make for our city.'

Nin Mah turned slowly on her side. The watching Anunnaki waited for her to hold out a great, earthy hand, for An's frail one, through which the light shone, to descend towards hers. But their flesh did not touch. Only the blue and brown eyes leaped to find each other.

'Well, Lady?' That boyish smile.

'Well, my lord?'

He squatted beside her. 'I don't often beg. I, the President of the Anunnaki. I am not just a tutelary guardian, to bring the pleas of humans before the Council. But hear this. For my beloved city, for Uruk, for graceful Kullab. Make us a creature to stop the headlong folly of Gilgamesh before he destroys them all.'

'You gave your Sky House to this lovely girl. Has she loved

so fiercely that she's a destroyer too?'

An lowered his head, as much to hide from the passion kindling in Inanna's eyes as in acquiescence to his wife's judgment.

For all her bulk and age she stood upright with a slow grace.

'Well then, let's see what we can do to put it right. It's been a long time since Enki and I mixed clay and water to make humanity, and then pitted our wits against each other to see how we could spoil it.'

The Anunnaki stood aside for their ancestress. They followed her as she walked with huge steps across the foothills, trod over the yielding marshes. In a remote lagoon she bent with difficulty, panting a little. With ritual incantations, a wordless humming like the song of the millions of wide-eyed frogs around her, puffing out their cheeks like hers, she rinsed and lifted her hands nine times. The early morning light turned the thick, brown water she scooped into falling silver. Enki was at her shoulder now.

'Let it come. Let it come! Don't let's make a botch of this one, my creating sister. No beer this time. I'll treat you later, when we see what you've made.'

He placed the clay of the Abzu in her hands. There, in the wild marshland far from any city, Nin Mah made a new creature. No gasping baby. A thing that was not quite a man or a beast. Her wet thumbs distinguished body, head, arms, legs. Her nails scored the clay already drying in the sun, gave it the semblance of rough hair all over. As Enlil breathed life into her shaping, the thing grew rapidly. Large as a man, even larger than most. Almost the girth and height of Gilgamesh. She let it suck from her right breast. Then her huge, strong arms flung the creature like a toy across the river plains of Sumer to fall in the loneliest part of the surrounding steppe.

The creature lay, stunned as much by the suddenness of his coming into being and his separation from love as by the force of the fall. As the winter sun warmed him, and the breath sent into him by Enlil began to be expelled, his clay chest moved, softened into flesh and lungs, hardened into ribs of bone. Hairy legs flexed. Man-like, he stood. Long hair, like a woman's, flowed past his shoulders. Pelt like a monkey's covered his limbs. He might have been Lord Sumugan, running among the wild cattle dressed like one of them. But he was not a Lord, and he was not a dumb beast. The name pronounced by Enlil as he left Nin Mah's hand rang in his head, muttered from his lips.

'*Enkidu* . . . ?'

No other human on the steppe answered him.

He ran with the gazelles, unaware of his destiny. At sunset he crowded with the wild creatures at the drinking hole. Pelicans waded in the crimson water. Wild mouflons whitened the shore like flowers of bog grass. The vast sky, black, golden, flame, was netted with crying ducks and the creak of geese wings.

'Enkidu . . .' the creature said again.

The deer lifted shy faces, gazed at him trustingly. They could not reply.

He ate grass with them. He drank bog water with them. The does stood still while he sucked their udders. He looked less than human. He possessed the silence and the freedom of the steppe like a Son of An. He loved his fellow creatures. He had never seen a human man or woman.

# Chapter One Hundred and Two

The magic never failed.

Next winter, the red blood-beer was brewed by Nin Sun's loving hands. Next winter, the grapes were cut and they wept gold and purple tears for their Wine Lady. Geshtinanna disappeared.

That day came when a long-awaited step sounded lightly outside, brushing the newly reviving grass, releasing the scents of the wet garden. Inanna was wildly beautiful. Tears of passion sparkled on her skin like her scattered jewels. A gauzy wool gown draped her against the cooling breeze, but it could be flung off in a moment. She left aside the insignia of royalty, for the theft of which Dumuzi had died. Only the marks of love stood out on her scented body, boundary stones of silver and lapis at throat, wrist, thighs, stelae of gold set up on the sacred hills of breasts and pubes. Her hair was a river of blackness more inviting than the waters of Kur. A man might drown more sweetly in it.

Again that moment, when the door swung open and Dumuzi was on the threshold. All the hours of preparation, the days of anticipation, the months of grief, culminated in this, the desperate love in her returning Dumuzi's face.

She was generous. She held out arms, largely-muscled now, maturer, strong with desire and pity. Nin Sun wept to have her Damu back from Kur, but Inanna was radiant. This blazing light of love must be the vision that sustained him through his season of darkness; the running liquids of her body should compensate for the grey dust of the Netherworld. She was very skilled, tireless, insatiable, joyous. When Dumuzi had exhausted his longing upon her, he could still thrill her with the merest touch, on through the night into the sweet bird-babble of the morning.

Gilgamesh watched the first stages of their reunion. He

came more often to the E-Anna, now Inanna was queen. He was more sober in the presence of his Anunnaki family than rioting through the streets of Uruk. He drank his sister's wine, thoughtfully, respectfully, with frequent shudders when he tried to imagine where she had gone. Inanna observed this, lying against Dumuzi's shoulder, dropping the bloomed, purple grapes into her mouth.

'This is a feast, King Gilgamesh. You are not merry.'

'Your pardon!' He grinned and raised his goblet to her. She leaned across Dumuzi's knees towards him, took the stem of his electrum beaker in her jewelled hand, guided it to his lips, less steadily than he might have done alone, and laughed as the red wine dribbled down his beard. Then her head bent closer, so that the scented heap of her hair was under his face. She, too, sipped, letting more notes of laughter fall at the awkwardness of the movement.

'So, we are brother and sister. We have pledged our love.'

Her body was laid across her bridegroom, a warm and heavy weight. Dumuzi did not move to caress her, but his eyes filmed over with a trance of ecstasy. She knew his whole being sang with the touch of her skin against his, the pressure of her contours. But she let her head rest now in Gilgamesh's lap, looking up at him with a merry face, helpless as a child.

She watched the warrior's body, usually so eager for action, freeze at her intimate touch. Her gorgeous head was resting lightly against his member. Only his woollen kilt separated them. She made the slightest movement, stroking it. She saw a constriction rise in his throat, threatening to choke him. He looked desperately for help to his half-brother. Dumuzi seemed drunk with beer and wine, with relief at escape, with the weight of horror he had just emerged from. No one questioned him. He still could not bear to speak of it.

But Inanna was smiling at Gilgamesh as though her young husband beneath her was no more than the bright woven cushions packed with lambswool.

What did she mean? What could the Lady of Love herself want from her brother-in-law? It was dangerous to misunderstand Inanna.

Yet he was her hero, the champion of her city. No man on Earth was like Gilgamesh. He was more than human.

But mortal. And to profane a Lady was to die.

Dumuzi and Geshtinanna were Anunnaki, and they died.

Lugalbanda had married a Lady.

Inanna moved her head slightly, making Gilgamesh gasp. The discreet servants withdrew. Nin Sun had already retired, exhausted first by mourning and then by celebration.

The three sat on, the woman reclining across the laps of the two males, smiling secretly with the confidence of power. Both men were still, Dumuzi numbed with drowsiness, with the promise of fulfilment like a warm blanket covering him, Gilgamesh alarmingly awake, his senses sharpened like weapons. Desire, terror, the hunger for violent action, the soldier's caution strained to anticipate the fatal wound. He did not know how to move.

It was Inanna who ended it, sliding in a flurry of perfumed cloth to stand on the floor, tugging Dumuzi to his feet and twining one arm under his shoulders. He leaned against his wife gratefully, blissful in half-sleep, his sex beginning to stir. But Inanna bent, put her left arm round Gilgamesh's neck, kissed him with a lingering sweetness. He felt her tongue press into his mouth, could hardly restrain himself from jumping up and seizing her.

Her eyes danced as she drew herself away from contact with him in a trailing, seemingly reluctant slowness. The sense of her touch clung to his skin like cobwebs. He was standing now. She could see the hunger in his eyes.

She smiled widely, turned with Dumuzi on her shoulder like a Siamese twin.

'May your bed be blessed as Dumuzi's is, my heroic brother.'

'*Heam!*' he breathed. 'So be it.'

A sudden, serious dart of her glance, as if she sought to understand him. His eyes challenged hers.

'Come on,' she laughed, as Dumuzi stumbled. 'It's only a short step to my bed. Then we can both fall down.'

Was Gilgamesh wrong to think that he and Inanna were both shaking with the force of that encounter of eyes? The Lady and her *en*.

How had Lugalbanda felt when he stood by Nin Sun's bed and let his kilt drop?

She was gone, and now he really was trembling. He emptied the wine jug into his mouth without bothering to refill his beaker.

His fists clenched, beat on the low table. 'I am two-thirds a

Lord! I am the champion of Uruk. I am worth more than Dumuzi!'

A hunter came to the lonely drinking hole in the watery gold of a rainy sunset. Silhouettes of deer raised their antlers, like the leafless branches of trees, and bison their moon-curved horns. The mournful howl of jackals saluted the going down of the sun. Grasshoppers fell into silence and the frogs took up the chorus. A hairy figure came through the shyly shifting herd of gazelles.

Mashduku the hunter stiffened. The raised bow with its notched arrow stilled like a carving.

The figure crouched and bent his head to lap like a beast. Then he cupped some water in his hand and threw it over his face, shook the drops away from his eyes. He seemed to stand straighter and stare around.

Slowly, with muscles that fought to stop himself from shaking, the hunter brought his bow level with his face. He had only to draw back the powerful string. The hairy man, if man it was, was in his sights.

The creature was huge. No ape from Dilmun or Meluhha had a physique like this. Now that the gazelles had stepped aside he stood alone, feet in the shallow silvery grey of the water, massive shoulders and head outlined against the bleached sky. Darkness and hair shrouded his face. Across the mere, no features could be discerned. Yet the hunter, trembling, felt that this unarmed monster gazed across the water at him. If he saw the aimed weapon, if he knew what it was, he did not move.

The hunter's arm seemed frozen. The power to kill seemed to turn back along the arrow's shaft, threatened to strike his own heart. Shivering with uncontrollable dread, he let the bow drop a little. The string loosened.

Some shift in the breeze must have carried his scent across the water. The herd wheeled cautiously, though not in panic. They flowed away over the ridge out of sight. The bison rose and lumbered after.

Their huge companion turned away last, as though he was their herdsman, though he had no stick, no dog, gave them no commands. Like a guardian spirit, he went up over the low skyline and vanished too beneath the gathering clouds.

Darkness was falling fast. Mashduku scrambled to his feet.

He ran for his camp with loping strides. As he passed each trap he had set, he pulled out the mangled game, despatched those that still struggled. With shaking hands he set the nooses, the hidden holes again, wondering what they might snare next time.

In the dark between sunset and moonrise, only Inanna's planet led the way. He was very glad to be crouched in his tent, with the thongs tied tight and the desert silent all around him.

Gilgamesh woke, conscious almost at once that a woman was standing by his bedside. A mixture of dread and the shock of realised ambition stopped his breath. He lay, conscious of his own taut body, of the space beside him in the bed, of the subtle perfume.

That perfume . . . rosemary, thyme, the sweet-sour smell of herb-flavoured cheeses.

He knew that smell, the homely, motherly scent of Nin Sun, Lady of Wild Cows.

He rolled over, tension relaxed, with relief, disappointment? Nin Sun bent and touched his forehead.

'You're alone. That's good. I was afraid for you.'

'I can look after myself. I'm *en* of Uruk, now. I'm a big boy, Mother.'

'Too big, perhaps, for your own safety.'

His mind was racing. But she hadn't been there. She hadn't seen Inanna sprawled uninhibitedly across his lap. She hadn't watched the shared goblet of wine, the probing kiss. She hadn't heard Inanna's provocative laughter.

'You married a human. And I am half a Lord.'

'Son, I am not Inanna. I was not ambitious and nor was Lugalbanda. When the Imdugud offered him any gift he wanted, he turned down riches, power, and chose only speed. He saved his people, ran like a courier, ruled like a good shepherd.'

'And I am not such a man?'

'Nor is Inanna such a Lady, to retire to a farmhouse on the steppe, and be content with a small city house. No.'

'Can a mortal say no to a Lady? *This* Lady?'

'I have lost one son to the Netherworld because of her.'

'Dumuzi is back.'

'If I grieve more quietly for my daughter, it is only because I know she is stronger.'

'Inanna wouldn't need to sentence me to the Netherworld. Dumuzi was a fool. He didn't value what he had.'

'You? I hear the cries about you from Uruk, as do all the Anunnaki. Could you really keep your eyes and your hands off any other girl, if Inanna favoured you?'

A cold sense of danger crept into the chamber, as if the *galla* stood around. Involuntarily Gilgamesh clutched his mother's wrist. 'But she is a great Lady. A powerful queen. She holds the *me*. If we had a quarrel, if she sent me down to the Netherworld, couldn't she bring me back? Couldn't she give me life, if she truly loved me?'

'Gilgamesh. My little boy. I saved your life with difficulty, when you were just a baby, not a Lord, not even Lugalbanda's son. I had slept with the priest. You were a child between two worlds. Soldiers, fearing the king's anger, threw you from a tower, but I called to an eagle who caught you between his wings and carried you to an orchard. A gardener reared you until I knew that Lugalbanda would take you for his own. And then he died, and you fled to Kish this time, till you reached your manhood. Your life has been precarious and precious. Don't risk it a third time.'

'But if Inanna took me while Dumuzi was gone, wouldn't that make me fully a Lord?'

The hand stroked his head in the darkness. 'Son, be what you are. It is my fault. I am sorry. I have failed even Enki's children. Although they are Anunnaki, they have each lost half their immortality. They are prisoners to Kur, one because I raised him too weak, the other because she is too strong. You, you are mortal. Don't think you can change that. If Inanna sends you to the Netherworld, you will remain there.'

He held her tighter. 'What is it like? Is it as terrible as they say? Why is this poor, short life all we're allowed that's bright and loving? Can nothing save me from the Below? Isn't there anyone who can give me eternal life?'

'Only the Great Guardians can do that, and they have done it only once. For Ziusudra and his wife, who escaped the Flood and saved the human race.'

'Then there *is* hope!'

'No!' Her voice was sharp with panic. 'No, don't think it! You are mortal, Gilgamesh. When you die, that will be the end.'

He flung himself back on his pillows. 'I won't submit to it.

Enki escaped from Kur. Inanna escaped from Kur. Surely I can conquer death?'

She cradled him fiercely. 'Live while you can, my son. Love what is allowed. Enjoy your kingship. Drink wine, make friends. Marry a wife, get children. Don't hope for more. Above all, respect Inanna. You are not Dumuzi. What she once takes away from you, she can never give back.'

Yet when Nin Sun had gone, how could he not lie awake and dream the daring vision of himself and the Lady of all the *Me*?

# Chapter One Hundred and Three

Mashduku the hunter woke with profound disquiet. He could feel the pall of nightmare hanging over the day ahead. Something had happened on the steppe. Something had arrived that had not been there before. It was a lonely place to run with only a bow and arrows. Yet he must get a living.

There were traps to be checked. He came slowly to the first pit. Though the bag hung light and empty on his shoulder, he would rather have found the place undisturbed, no footprints in the faintly damp clay, the covering reeds he had laid across to conceal the pit unbroken. He dreaded to find the pit full. He did not know what he would do if he had trapped the thing he feared. He could not imagine that he might kill and skin it. His own strongly beating heart felt suddenly mortal, his own weathered skin insufficient protection.

When he came through the little patch of scrub, where animals sometimes wandered to graze the shoots or scratch their hides, he was not expecting what he saw. He rounded a bush of camelthorn and thought for a moment he had mistaken the place. The land had shifted; his skills were sliding from him; he was lost.

Then he understood. Someone had been here before him. Where Mashduku had dug a pit big enough to contain a buck, the earth had been clawed back, refilling the hole. Frost was caught in the roughened soil. Where he had laid branches and rushes carefully over the mouth, closing it with lying lips, his camouflage had been flung aside.

Someone had challenged the hunter. He could have run then, back from this loneliest range of the steppe to the safe familiarity of his home and his family. Never mind the empty game bag. But a terrible curiosity had hold of him.

He moved from trap to trap. The careful stakes with their nooses, set across the trail to a hare's form, had been snapped in pieces, torn up, hurled across the ground with a savagery their little power did not seem to deserve. The incomer had found them all.

The long day wore away. Shaking already, Mashduku found his steps, as if drawn by the compulsion of a spell, taking him to the same drinking hole as before. This time he crouched, well-hidden, and did not lift his bow.

The creature came. After the dread of the day, evidence piled on evidence, it was a relief to find he seemed somewhat smaller than Mashduku's imagination had painted him, more like a human. Still he was large, wild, immeasurably powerful.

The wild beasts drank, undisturbed, moved off into the twilight. It was time to go and find his own shelter. Yet, watching the hairy herdsman lope after his charges, Mashduku found himself drawn still further into dangerous ground. Like a shadowy, swift-running fox, he sped around the bulrushes to the far side of the pool and the trampled clay. He bent with the hunter's experience. His fingers traced the great impressions in the mud, the print of a bare, leathery pad, the press of five, curved toes, the fuzz of the hair that matted this foot. There could be no mistaking. This was a human foot, however strange and furred.

The moon would rise later tonight. The darkness after nightfall would last longer.

He was too afraid to set his traps a third time. The memory of the fury with which the pegs had been broken, the earth flung back, made him unwilling to provoke this retaliation again. Yet, he was a hunter, he had to feed his family. With the courage of the remaining sunlight he turned another way until he spied a herd of antelope. The land was open. The deer ranged widely where the grass had sprung up in the newly-wet desert. One arrow, well-aimed, should be enough. An arrow ill-placed would bring disaster.

The herd was alone. No lioness padded across the distance. Even the vultures were silent. Why then did his fingers tremble as he drew back the string and let fly the arrow? It struck the doe's shoulder, but missed the vital entry spot that would have driven it straight to her heart. She leaped in the air, soundless, but with a violence as shocking as a scream. The herd sprang into flight in instant alarm. A flood-tide of russet and dun and black flowed past his eyes and raced away like cloud-shadow. He set off after them, running hard. Was the doe wounded enough? Would she limp and tire? Were there stragglers, young, old, pregnant, injured, that he could cut down? He floundered up over the windswept undulations, down into sandy hollows, tracking the flurried footprints. The hard determination of the chase was all he thought about.

Their smell came to him over the sand-piled ridge. The smell of hide and sweat and over-pressed bodies. He hauled himself up towards it.

This time the head and shoulders seemed more massive than he could imagine. They rose above the dunes in front of him with a terrifying nearness.

Now it was Mashduku's turn to make that check that was like a shout of alarm. He could not make himself turn and run. Like the stake of one of his own discovered traps, he stood exposed. For a terrible moment they stared at each other, the glaring black eyes of the Wildman, the startled tawny gaze of the hunter. Behind the stranger's shoulder, the deer jostled together, frightened but trusting their newfound protector. Under that accusation the bow slipped from the nerveless fingers of Mashduku. The sun was low in front of him, making it hard for him to see. Then the beast beat with his great, furred paws against his matted chest. Lips, shockingly human beneath their hair, stretched wide. A roar, shaped by a tongue no other animal of the steppe could boast, rang with the only word he had ever known.

'*En . . . ki . . . du!*'

His stance declared him victorious. His friends were safe behind him. His eyes dismissed Mashduku. The hunter turned, scrabbling for his bow in the hot sand, retreated, fled.

Like a beaten dog he crept home from his camp next day. It was not the weight of the game he had caught which slowed him. That hardly needed the wooden sled he towed behind him. It was a kind of shame, as if a door to the wilderness had been barred in his face and he was now an outcast. If the steppe was closed to him, what would he do in the civilised world? How would he get his living? Even so, retreating, he cast anxious glances behind, as if the long-dead, sun-dried flesh of his catch could still drop telltale blood to accuse him.

Fields began to embrace him. Familiar clumps of trees marked the way to the village. His father's roof was welcoming. His wife met him outside, but her cries of distress at the smallness of his bag were quickly silenced by his face.

His children's eyes widened, sensing calamity in the air. There was barley gruel, fermented milk, a bowl of dates. Naati his wife did not think it wise to prepare a celebratory stew. There were few enough hides and little enough meat to trade for cereals and oil as it was.

His father sat by the winter fire of dung and rushes, dribbling gruel into his beard. He saw more in the half-invisible flames than in his son's face. But when the meal was finished and the children put to bed, he lifted his wrinkled face to Mashduku.

'My hands are shaking. That's cold and old age. You're in the prime of life, boy, and you can cover the distance from the hunting grounds to home faster than I ever could. Your blood should be hot enough tonight. But you're shivering like a girl on her wedding night. What's got into you? Found a viper in your shoe?'

'I've seen worse than the horned asp. Worse than a wild boar starting up in front of my face.'

'We've all got tales to tell round the fire. What's yours? Have you wrestled barehanded with a lion? Did you have to fight off a pair of wolves? There's never been a hunter didn't like to spin his yarn to make the young ones gasp. What's your story?'

'No hunter's tale of our old enemies. This wasn't tusks or fangs or claws of anything you ever saw.'

'Has the desert spawned a new demon? Or have you met Lord Sumugan himself?'

'I . . . don't know what it was. But I can't go back there.'

'What sort of talk is that? No son of mine is going to hang his bow on the wall and let his old father starve because he's too frightened to face up to a wild beast!'

'This . . . thing . . . is not a beast. He's covered in his own hair, head to toe, but I've seen the prints of his feet. I've tracked him. I've looked into his face. He runs with the gazelles, and he's a friend of the bison, but he's a man.'

'So what are you scared of? You've got knife and arrows. You're telling me you're afraid of some poor boy that's been abandoned and brought up by wild things? You should pity the dumb creature.'

'You haven't seen him! You haven't heard him roar. He's bigger than any man I've ever set eyes on. He's as strong as a workman Lord. I couldn't talk to him. He drops on all fours and eats grass like the deer. He laps up water out of the drinking place like a bull. But he's no shy, dumb thing. He found the pits I dug and he filled them in. He found the snares I'd set and he tore them up. When I chased after a herd of gazelles, he barred my way. You can't imagine what he was like, close to, the way he looked at me! I couldn't have taken one step nearer if I'd been armed to the teeth like Gilgamesh himself. He won't allow me back there. I'll never kill another creature while he's free.'

The old man stared into the crumbling ash as if he might find the answer in its fantastic architecture of burned-through reeds. His own hands still trembled on his knees, unregarded now.

'If this is a new creature, and as fearsome as you say, and you're afraid to tackle him, you must go where there's a bigger than life-size hero. To Uruk.'

'Me? To the big city?'

The old man bared his gums in a grin. 'You've shot a leopard that was guarding her young. And you'd run away from the painted city women?'

'The steppe's my place. But that's closed to me now.'

'So you'd better take your story to our Big Man, Gilgamesh. That's a hero larger than life, by all accounts. He's never been beaten yet. They say Inanna still smiles on him. If you want to kill game again and save us all from starving, he's your answer. Let him fight this . . .'

'Enkidu.'

Almost as fearfully as if he were stepping into the barge of the Netherworld, Mashduku the hunter set his face towards Inanna's city.

# Chapter One Hundred and Four

Wind blew refreshingly across the rampart walk. Inanna and Gilgamesh walked briskly, both of them enjoying the hint of ice in the air, the brilliance of the visibility. If goosepimples rose on Inanna's rounded flesh, she laughed and walked faster. Gilgamesh's body beside her radiated warmth. There would be warm wine, hot bread dripping with butter and honey as soon as they cared to descend. Dumuzi was already waiting by the fire.

'Well, what do you think of my walls? Is there any of the Anunnaki in Sumer as honoured as you are in Uruk?'

'I think you honour yourself, King Gilgamesh.' She inclined towards him, knowing the radiance of her beauty, the warmth of her nearness, the overwhelming effect her bodily presence must have on any man, mortal or Lord. Knowing that, she smiled.

'If I must die, I will be remembered!' Trembling with a passion that was only half to do with his desire for Inanna, Gilgamesh felt himself drowning in those soft, dark eyes.

A palace servant came soft-footed along the brick wall behind them. He made his presence felt by the very stillness of his waiting.

Inanna kissed Gilgamesh with a sister's privilege. The servant's face turned, studiously looking out over the last, yellow lines of the vineyards from which the crop had been cut.

'Well?' The bark might have been relief or anger at the interruption.

'Sir, a man from the steppe has arrived. Some trapper or hunter. He seems to have a strange tale to tell. He is appealing for help which he thinks only *Lugal* Gilgamesh can give.'

Praise was like warm coals to Gilgamesh. 'Some quarrel between neighbours about hunting rights? Some family lawsuit? These peasant folk like to think I'm their grandfather, not their battle leader.'

Inanna slipped her hand into the crook of his arm. 'You are my *en*, now. Their *en*. Priest, intercessor, governor in peace as well as war. Not just my young *lugal*.'

'I'm a warrior, first and always.'

'I think this man brings a challenge more to the liking of Gilgamesh than the usual whine for justice, sir.'

'What? No. Don't spoil it by telling us. Will you go down and hear this with me, Lady?'

'Shouldn't I frighten the poor human more than whatever terror has brought him to you?'

'Anyone who throws himself before Gilgamesh needn't be terrified of the Lady of Love.'

'Be careful, Gilgamesh. You will never be as awesome as an Anunnaki.'

She saw once more the anger of frustrated ambition crease his face. Still, some fellow feeling leaped across the gap between them. Dumuzi had stolen her power behind her back, in her moment of greatest danger, when she hung in death. Gilgamesh would always challenge her to her face. She loved him the more for that. He believed himself lordly, worthy to become a Lord. Was there no way she could share with him something of her power, her Anunnaki future? If she were as great as Enlil, who had granted Ziusudra and Kuansud immortality, could she do it then?

The small, lithe man waiting in the antechamber of Gilgamesh's palace did not know what wild things he had stirred up in the hearts of Uruk's leaders.

They came indoors, shivering and laughing with the sudden realisation of how cold they had been.

'There'll be ice on the steppe this morning,' said Gilgamesh, rubbing his hands. 'Better to be humans, with thick walls round us, and fires and fermented drink, than live like the beasts out of doors with only a hide between them and the wind.'

Inanna slid gracefully on to a couch beside Dumuzi and kissed him sweetly. She smiled with a tacit superiority that spoke her free to range Sky and Earth by day or night, any time of year. She was not bound by the weakness and limitations of humanity.

'Let the peasant in.' Gilgamesh seated himself and signed for hot wine to be poured. 'Let's hope his story's a good one.

Winter's the time for curious hearth tales.'

Mashduku the hunter was led in. His deerskin wraps looked out of place among the pleated linen of the house servants and the bright, dyed wool of the aristocrats. His hands twisted nervously in his kilt. His eyes darted from side to side with the hunter's caution.

When he approached the three, he went down on his knees, and spoke huskily. '*Lugal* Gilgamesh . . . Madam? Sir?'

Gilgamesh reached out a hand to rest on Inanna's thigh, almost defying Dumuzi. 'This is your Queen, above all the *en*'s on Earth. Great Inanna.'

The man threw himself face downwards, shielding his eyes. 'Pure Inanna! Spare me! I didn't know! Forgive an unwashed human!'

Inanna threw a triumphant look at Gilgamesh. 'You are excused, mortal. We shall leave you to Gilgamesh's care.'

Like a girl playing at hide-and-seek she pulled Dumuzi away with her through a curtain. Gilgamesh felt the loss of the warmth beside him.

'Your tale, man. What have you come for? Make it a good one!'

The man struggled for self-possession. 'Yes, *Lugal* Gilgamesh. I appeal to you. I'm a poor man but a skilled trapper. Look. I've brought this skin of a striped badger. You won't see many of those in Sumer. Take it, sir. It's the last I'll ever bring back from the steppe unless you help us.'

He unfolded his tale of the hairy Wildman of the wilderness running with the deer. He described the bristling enormity of anger that had defended the wild things, the broken traps and filled pits, the fierce, black eyes that told of a human soul peering out through an animal body.

Gilgamesh rose to his feet. The challenge warmed him like the hot wine in his belly.

'By the horns of the Moon, I like your adventure! I'll fight your Wildman for you. I'll kill anything that stands between the subjects of Gilgamesh and their prey.'

'Bless you, sir. Only you could do it. This Wildman's a monster. He thinks he's king of the steppe now. If you'd heard the way he beat on his chest and bellowed "Enkidu"!'

The curtain parted. The trembling Mashduku tried to hold himself steady as Inanna came back into the room, still smiling.

She leaned over with a lazy grace and took hold of the

sleeve on Gilgamesh's arm. 'No, Gilgamesh. I have a better plan. I want to see this Wildman, this hairy human who can run with the gazelles, this piece of masculinity that even the bison acknowledge as their leader. Don't kill him. I don't wish to see him brought back to Uruk hanging from a pole. I would rather see the soul the hunter speaks of in those black eyes.'

'How can we avoid a fight if we meet, man to man? If he speaks no human language, how will he understand my call to surrender? It has to be a fight to the death.'

'You'd prefer that, wouldn't you? There is no need for you to meet him, man to man. Not yet. My way is sweeter, and more powerful. Man to woman! Take one of my hierodules. I can name you one of uncommon beauty and courage. Take her to the steppe, where the Wildman eats his grass and drinks his bog water. She will show him what he can never find between the furred flanks of the does. The marvel of her breasts will wake in him longings deeper than the udders of bison can rouse. She will entice him from his savagery and lead him here to us.'

Gilgamesh hesitated. His face clouded, like a small boy who has lost a new-given toy. Then he slapped his thigh and tried to speak brightly. 'Very well. If that pleases you. But, by the Imdugud's nest, when you and the rest of the city have had your fill of him, when you've stared at him, and poked him, and put him through his paces, I'm still going to do battle with the savage in front of the lot of you.'

Inanna smiled more widely, red lips stretched over pearled teeth. 'We shall see which of you is the more savage, then, *Lugal* Gilgamesh.' The spiced wine was treacherously exciting her blood as she looked at him.

Shamhara, the sacred prostitute, was eighteen and highly skilled. No pregnancy had interrupted the service of her city's moons. Her body was ripening with the Lady's own fulfilment. Breasts stood like enormously irised eyes, the bright pupils of her nipples highlighted with knowledge. Beneath the colourful, flimsy skirt, her vigorous pubic hair made an arrow pointing the way to a portal already opened to make the entrance easy. The warmth of her eyes promised a welcome inside.

Inanna looked her over approvingly. She held out an affectionate hand. 'Child. No, woman. You are hardly less lovely than I am, but less terrible. When the incense rises, evening after evening, you make the sacrament of life. You teach men gentleness and joy. You lay yourself open to their passion and violence, and direct it to the Above. All women should bless you for what you teach their males.' But the Lady's eyes had left Shamhara's reverently inclined face, and met Gilgamesh's over the hierodule's head. Gilgamesh, womaniser, rapist, hero, ruler, stared back at her with a mutinous obstinacy.

The Hierodule of Heaven herself, lovely Inanna, opened her legs a little, almost unconsciously. Gilgamesh's eyes grew stormy with longing, terror, hope. There was a serious difference between what was offered by a hierodule and what the city's women surrendered to him by force. Did his stiff-backed pride want to pay this price?

'I am ready, Inanna,' Shamhara said with a quiet confidence. 'In your name, I will meet this man.'

'You'd lay your treasure before this savage? You'd go with a beast?'

'With this Enkidu. He owns a name, spoken with Enlil's breath. He has a human soul, sir.'

'What if he rapes and kills you?' Gilgamesh asked.

'He cannot rape what I shall freely offer. And I have laid my life before Inanna already.'

'Pah! There's no fight in any of you women. Look at Geshtinanna. Falling over herself to give half her life away for her brother. Take a knife at least, and slit his belly if you get the chance.'

Inanna stirred warningly. 'I have used weapons, Gilgamesh, as well as you. Easy to kill, harder to create a life. Both are my province. Shamhara displays a power you, a man, will never know.'

'Bring him here,' Gilgamesh ordered the hierodule brusquely. 'At least I can have some fun with him before he dies!'

The young woman smiled at him out of her exquisitely painted face. Bells tinkled softly on her wrists. 'I shall carry out Inanna's will, sir.'

# Chapter One Hundred and Five

It was a three-day journey to the steppe. Shamhara, the city girl, in her ritual clothing, let a white ass carry her beyond sight of Uruk's mound as the E-Anna vanished below the skyline. The hunter could have run faster, but Shamhara would not hurry her mount. She rode, head bent a little, smiling at the ground or to herself. Four times a day she made her prayers, sprinkling a little flour, pouring a few drops of water. She did not stare forward with anxiety or excitement. She did not look back.

They passed the last of the outlying villages. They stayed one night at Mashduku's house, where the children gazed at their exotic visitor, their fingers in their mouths, and the hunter's wife was overcome with nervousness. But his father smiled and nodded and when Shamhara came to sit on a cushion before the fire, he laid a slightly shaking hand upon her knee. The courtesan smiled without speaking. Presently she moved over and stroked his head, massaged his neck and shoulders with her smooth, skilled hands. No more. He dropped asleep before she had finished.

The dawn was cold without frost, a wind picking up bits of chaff and dust and tossing them here and there. Over the colourful stripes of her dress, blood-red and ochre, the prostitute draped her ankle-length cloak of lambswool flounces. Gold-petalled flowers made a bonnet over her oiled wig. Her face was painted more boldly than a butterfly's wing. She had reddened her nails and nipples.

Into the land of the dun deer and the sand-coloured fox this peacock-bright beauty allowed herself to be led.

It was not quick or easy. They found a place by the drinking hole, and Mashduku cut her a couch of dry reeds. She sat patiently, not quite alert, not quite relaxed, ready. The hunter's tension was more wearying. The sun, hot even at winter noon, fell on them both. She drew the soft cloak over her head to shade herself. Dust clung to its fluff. Reeds scored a pattern under her thighs. She went to find a trickle of fresher water and came back again.

They waited in silence. Dusk gathered early. A few antelope, with backward curving horns, came down to drink. Wading birds swooped, skidded to a standstill in a flurry of spray, paddled stiff-legged for a while, slept. The hunter touched Shamhara's arm.

'He will not come now,' he murmured.

Stiffly, she stood upright. 'I should like to sleep.'

He had made a shelter of canes and thatched it with branches. More rushes became her bed. Like a muddy wild sow in the marsh, the soft-scented creature lay down her head and closed her eyes. The hunter watched, dozed, woke again. He did not touch her.

A second day, warmer, the breeze almost still. Just enough wind to bend the reed flowers lightly and send the lamb-white clouds wandering across the sky. The courtesan smiled, and let the cloak slip from her shoulders. Mashduku watched the skyline. The long, still, sunny day ended in a rosy sunset that sent a path of gold across the pool. Hundreds of gazelles began to appear over the opposite slope, delicate black hooves stepping silently, fragile legs flickering with nervous movement, eyes large and lovely in their striped faces.

He was coming behind them, blacker than they were, hair tumbling shaggily to his waist. In the warm, gold light his pelt seemed less thick now, a hint of paler skin beneath the covering down. His hands were on the rumps of two of the does, companionable, protective. He came through the herd, waded a little way out into the gilded water, bent and drank.

'It's him! Now! Strip off. Get his thing up.' Fear made the hunter gabble, but a lifetime's training kept his anxiety to a rustling whisper.

She did not need to be taught her vocation. She stood, with an easy, almost liquid movement, like a lily flowering. The cloak was already round her feet. One moment she was white and red and yellow, then the dress slipped from her shoulder and she stood like the autumn moon that hangs between gold and silver. She came, slow, almost dancing, to the water's edge. The deer all round raised their heads; their shining eyes stared over the water at her. Enkidu straightened slowly, let his hands fall, still dripping, to his sides. She took three steps out into the sunset shallows, laughing a little at the shock of the cold. Like him she stooped, squatted rather, but did not drink. Her lotus hands cupped the copper water, poured it on the hillock of her pubic hair, cleansed her vulva. She was standing again, legs parted, fingers searching, opening the lips of her labia. Her face was half hidden under the luxuriance of wig and flowered wreath.

Enkidu gazed. The days since his creation were few. But he seemed to hold a lifetime, an unmothered childhood of longing in that hungry look. A tide rose in him that was at once a hot flood of pleasure and an unbearable pain. The sun was nothing. The deer were a world away. The pool was no more than a dewdrop between them. He flung himself across the water, scattering it more wildly than a landing goose. She waited, laughing lightly.

He had not expected the perfume of her, the supple oiliness of her skin. He had not expected to be met and welcomed, coaxed, guided in. To be wrapped in her, rolling in lapping waves, tumbling on dusty ground, finding the soft wool flounces under him and losing them again. Discovering a deep, furred darkness, rivers like milk, passages soft as the skin of newborn fawns. A murmur of love.

Praise to Inanna breathed through tumbling hair.

'Enkidu!' he said. 'Enkidu.' It was the only word he knew.

She taught him. She taught him love, she taught him sex, she taught him motherhood, she taught him friendship. She taught him the names of things, sleeping in a hut, the eating of bread, the feel of clothes, the sharing of a cup. Everything she did was a grace to him, everything she said was a precious lesson. She rewarded him richly, richly. No ruler in Uruk at the New Moon feast was better served by Inanna's high priestess. She was a sacred woman. She made Enkidu a man.

Six days and seven nights they lay together, loved together. Then grey dawn broke. Enkidu woke, shuffled out of the hierodule's arms and went to the door of their hut.

Mashduku was sitting outside cross-legged, with his bow on his knees, a watchful guardian. Enkidu looked at him, almost with surprise, and away across the pool. The deer were coming down to drink in the early morning, a dark wave of bodies, just beginning to take russet colour. A grebe launched itself into the air, starting a skein of others. The morning was cool and blue and clean. An older longing stirred in the heart of Enkidu, for an innocence, a freedom he had almost forgotten. The black eyes of the gazelles seemed to reproach him. He began to walk towards them, upright now, a little awkwardly, no longer swinging his arms to the ground in that loping run.

The gazelles stiffened. Their neck muscles tightened with a timid mistrust. Their eyes grew wider still. Soft ears twitched nervously.

Shamhara stood at the door of their bower, with a wise pity on her kohl-lined face.

He was halfway round the marsh, murmuring thickly, 'There, there, easy now. I'm here. I won't hurt you.' Words that Shamhara's voice had whispered against his throat.

They spun. Like the sudden twist of a dust devil lifting dead leaves, they whirled away across the level plain. He started to run, he raced, he galloped. His two hands brushed the ground. He was trying to bound on all fours. His voice croaked, rasped, panted the unfamiliar words.

'Come back! It's me, Enkidu! Wait for me, my friends!'

But they fled him, swifter than his lungs had breath to follow, more tirelessly than his straightened legs had strength to bear him. His old skills had left him. His old companions would not recognise him. His new manhood had no power to compensate. He lost them. They flowed over the sandy swells like a flood of melting snow-water that surges above the banks and across the dry fields and is gone. The endless wake of hundreds of hoofprints stretched away into the path of the sun.

Enkidu sat down in the friendless wilderness, in the fear-flung tracks of his vanished friends. He sobbed the terrible tears of the realisation of what he was.

Loneliness was too great to bear alone. He limped back, his great, strong frame held upright, but his head hanging with a half-understood shame. Shamhara had cut his hair. She had trimmed and combed the matted fuzz of his body covering. Needles of wind pierced through to the skin. His sex was hidden from him under the briefest of doeskin aprons. Yet he was conscious of its enormity, of the price that had been paid to clothe it. He felt a groan rise in his throat, heard it bellow its pain to the sky.

'*Inanna!*'

It was not the roar of an animal now.

He met Mashduku halfway. The hunter had tracked him, as he tracked the deer. They met on the shifting dunes, among the sparse grass sprung with the rains, gone in the summer.

*'Where is she?'*

It was the family man's turn to be wordless. His sunlined face showed caution, but little fear of the other now. He hunched one shoulder and motioned Enkidu to follow him. They trudged apart, not speaking, the lean hunter leading the tamed monster like a dancing bear.

Shamhara was sitting in the sunshine, her hands together. Her head was bent and words were whispering from her lips. She raised her head, more slowly than necessary, and let the liquid darkness of her eyes open for him.

She was, if possible, lovelier than ever. Groomed to perfection. Sweetened in every part. She did not smile or move. A dark solemnity was all she offered today. But what she was, she laid before him, defenceless, unafraid, unashamed.

'You!' he screamed at her. 'You have done this to me! You have robbed me! You have fouled me! May you be cursed. May men leap on you and use you, whether you will or not. May you grow raddled and ugly, and whine for food while they abuse you. May . . .' He crumpled at her feet, overcome with weeping.

She touched his cheekbone, lifting away a tear, raised his hand to her face, let him feel the wetness. For a long time she held his hand, lightly but warmly. He could not help but smell her scent, feel her softness. He groaned his terrible anger. But still he lay, curled like an infant shrinking from the world, and let her hold him. There was no one else to love him.

At last rage relaxed, muscles drooped in exhaustion, eyelids dropped. The fires of fury had consumed themselves into a dull grey ash.

Shamhara bent and kissed him lingeringly. She stroked his newly trimmed hair.

'We are what we were made to become, you and I. Come. It is time to go to Uruk and meet Inanna and Gilgamesh.'

# Chapter One Hundred and Six

Bar-Namtar the priestess bowed her head in the Limestone House.

> My Lady, as this incense rises,
> Hear my plea for your people.
> Lion, rouse yourself!
> Listen to the yelping of your she-cubs.
> The doors of your house stand open.
> See what is happening in your city.
> Judge what Gilgamesh is doing.
> My Lady, avenge your young women!

'What? No! What is it?' Gilgamesh thrashed about so that even the broad bed seemed too narrow to contain his fighting limbs and heaving body. He woke in a sweat, though the last hours of the night were midwinter cold. Darkness and the disturbance of his dream were heavy on him.

'I must ask Geshtinanna about it . . . ask Geshtinanna . . .' And he bit his thumb and fell asleep again.

He dreamed almost the same scene again. This time he woke to the grey-white of early morning. Cold river mist crept up from the Buranun and mingled with the cloudy breath of the canals. A thick frost lay on the ground.

'Geshtinanna?' he said again, rubbing the sleep from his eyes. 'Geshtinanna . . .' But knowledge, cold as the morning, was creeping into his heart. The laughing Wine Girl, his dream-knowing sister, was no more. Kur had taken her. While Dumuzi lay in the E-Anna, cuddled warm against Inanna, Geshtinanna would be sitting at the feet of Ereshkigal in the dim, dusty chill of the Ganzir.

Was his dream a nightmare? Hard to say. Strange and alarming things had happened that shook his very belief in what he was. There had been physical struggle, but the challenge drove deeper than that, like a pick under a foundation. And yet, there had been moments of tenderness too in his dream, a sweetness almost more disturbing in its unexpected source than the violence before it.

'Oh Geshtin,' he muttered, swinging himself out of bed and dressing quickly to cover his cold-taut skin. 'Where is wisdom now you're underground?'

The skill of interpreting dreams ran in the female line. Nanshe, above all, could have told him. But the Lady of the Sirara, who judges among the Anunnaki and looks into secret places, was far away in her waterbound citadel in the southern marshes.

'Yet, there's Mother!' A sudden, joyful realisation that Nin Sun was here in Uruk itself, in her small town house. The shy, loving Lady of Wild Cows, whose heart had seemed to be happiest on the steppe after Lugalbanda died, hardly left the city now, in winter. It was as though she could not bear to stay away from Dumuzi in the half of the year when the sun shone for him again. Too soon the spring would pass, and the rains fail, and she would wander the barren pastures again weeping for his return.

She ached for Geshtinanna with a more private grieving.

Would she weep like this one day for her mortal son, who would never return from the realm of the dead?

Gilgamesh balled his fist at the unacceptable thought and crashed it against the wall. A clay rosette, blue and red, shivered from the frieze above him and shattered on the floor. The blow brought a slave running to see what was wanted.

'Get me some breakfast! I'm going out.'

Nin Sun looked like the chrysalis of a moth, wrapped in white woollen layers. She would not emerge with a bright flutter of wings. She did not have the flamboyance of her children. She sat beside her brazier, as though even the closeness of Dumuzi across the gardens of Kullab was enough. Later, he would emerge, bright as the enamelled panels of the palace when the rains have washed the dust away and the sun comes out. He would come and sit at her feet, and lay his head in her lap, and she would stroke his hair and sing to keep the horrors of the dark away.

But now this other son, this huge, martial, noisy half-human. Not at all like modest Lugalbanda, but grasping for greatness, laying hold of what he wanted, as though life was a river in flood, carrying it all past him too fast and he must snatch everything he could.

She raised her face and smiled at him. 'You're early, Gilgamesh, in spite of the frost. They say you give the nights no peace, and now this morning your bed has hardly had time to work out its hours of service under you.'

'I had a bad dream. No, two dreams. Or the same one twice, but altered. No, well, I'm not sure whether it was bad or not. It shook me, though. I can't shift it out of my head. You know something about dreams, don't you? I'd ask Geshtinanna, but . . .'

A cloud behind her eyes. A shudder of remembered horror. The last interpretation of dreams that Geshtinanna did was for Dumuzi, before they tortured her, before they caught him.

It was a waste of breath to try and comfort her. The pain had happened. The grief was real. Better to look to the future, Gilgamesh's future.

'Could you? Shall I tell you?'

She patted the seat beside her and waved the servants away. 'Tell on. I am not the stylus-wielding scholar your sister is. But dreams are an older wisdom. We don't need tablets of clay when there are pictures in the fire. What's brought you hurrying across Uruk to me, instead of out of doors practising the mace and the javelin?'

He squatted at her feet and held out his hands to the coals. Even in this lowly position he could not look like a little boy, as Dumuzi did. He was a man, a big man, a great man. That mattered to him.

'It started like a dream for a king. I was in a good mood. I'd feasted and drunk well, and had a couple of women. I was taking a turn out on the palace court to get a breath of air. All my mates were round me. There was a sky like you've never seen before. All the stars flashing and burning, as far as you could see. Inanna's was there, of course, like the battle standard in front of the host of heaven. Then one star moved. It wasn't Inanna's. I didn't know the name of it. I don't think I've ever seen it up there before. But it came slipping and sliding down the Stairs of the Sky, getting brighter and brighter as it rolled. It was coming straight at me, but I couldn't move. Then it crashed down in the courtyard right beside where I was standing. The whole palace shuddered.

'It stood there, a great, shining rock as big as me, getting colder and darker all the time. I knew I had to shift it. I tried to lift it, but I couldn't. I put my head against it like a bull, and gripped my arms round it, but it wouldn't budge. And all the time people were coming up to stare at it. The whole city was gathered round to have a good look.

'When I let go, I thought my mates were going to have a try, though I could have told them they'd be wasting their breath. Instead of that, do you know what they did? All the top heroes of Uruk, my mates who've never been beaten in battle? They knelt down on the bricks and kissed the foot of that stone. Then I . . .'

She touched his hair and waited while he struggled with himself.

'I . . . bent over that stone again. And it wasn't a big, male rock that I was wrestling with. It was . . . a thing of soft light, and . . . supple . . . and shining. I . . . I knew it was a rock, but I was loving it like a woman.'

The words were hard to say, for Gilgamesh, who had possessed so many women, and loved none of them. Nin Sun did not speak or move, waited for the end of the story.

'Well, in the end we all got together and heaved the thing up between us. We carried it here, and put it down in front of you. And you put your hand on it, and held out your other hand to me, so that we were standing, one on each side of you, like a pair of sons.'

Her face was sad and wise. 'I have lost a son; I have lost a daughter. It seems the Anunnaki are giving me another child. A companion is coming for you, Gilgamesh. Someone stronger than you have ever met before. A friend worthy of you. Someone you will love as you have not loved till now.'

His eyes flashed with delight. 'Then it's a good dream! A hero, a comrade to fight beside me? To share the beer, the brawls, the women with?'

'He will share your fate, yes.'

He was starting to scramble to his feet. 'There was a second dream. Almost the same as the first. I was walking down the street in Uruk, and I came into the Market Square. There was this axe lying on the ground, shining in the sun, all by itself. It didn't seem to belong to anyone. There was a crowd gathered round it. They were all staring down at it, but nobody would touch it. I pushed my way through and went up to it.

'It . . . wasn't like any axe I've ever seen. I don't know why.

It was a two-headed one, but it wasn't that. I . . . had that same feeling. I bent over it . . . It . . . It was like stooping over a woman on a bed. I picked it up, and hung it on my side, and came here. All the time, I could feel it swinging against my leg. And you did the same with the axe as you did with the stone that fell from the sky. You made it equal to me.'

She was less like a mother now. More withdrawn and stern, a Lady of oracles. 'You cannot escape your destiny. It is coming. The Anunnaki have decreed this.'

The journey from Uruk was slow. As they approached civilisation, Shamhara tore off one half of her colourful dress to give Enkidu, then wrapped the rest more tightly round her own shapely form and pulled the fleecy cloak closer. They came to the edge of habitation and parted from Mashduku at a village of shepherds.

It was a dangerous entrance to the inhabited world. When the villagers saw the hairy creature, even though Shamhara had trimmed him and given him clothing, they snatched up clubs and knives, fearing in his evident wildness a threat to their flocks of sheep and goats.

The courtesan held his hand firmly. Her grace and beauty, the aura of temple and palace she carried with her, overawed them. Grudgingly at first, and then their curiosity getting the better of them, they let the strangely assorted pair in and made them welcome at their headman's board.

Now Enkidu must learn to eat more than the camp food that Mashduku had provided. This two-legged beast, who had sucked milk from the udders of wild cows, must learn to toss back beakers of strong beer. By the time his belly was tight with hot bread and stew and he had downed seven cups of barley beer, his bowels and bladder felt full, his face was red and shining. This was a different Enkidu.

'Where did you find him, mistress? What's he good for?' They crowded round and laughed at the fuddled savage.

The head shepherd's daughter brought a jar of sesame oil and began to rub the creature's fur. As her fingers worked, the matted covering moved aside revealing more sensitive skin.

'He's a man, all right!' she laughed, blushing a little as her hands worked down his body. He stretched and sighed loudly. His penis started to rise, but then spilled urine. The girl jumped up with a cry of disgust. But her father took over.

'And a man can't eat and drink what he's had without needing a leak.'

He helped his guest outside and stopped him against a wall, stood alongside him and showed him what to do.

They civilised him. They gave him more clothes. They taught him to use a weapon. Soon he was taking a javelin and guarding the flocks by night for them when a man-eating lion was reported to be on the prowl.

The lion came. Enkidu, alone while his hosts slept, caught it. In the morning it was caged and roaring, ready to be presented to the king in Uruk. No commoner may kill a lion.

He killed a whole pack of wolves.

'You are almost like a Lord,' said Shamhara when she saw this. 'Gilgamesh will be glad to meet you.'

He trotted beside her mount happily enough, and they went another day's journey.

The villages were growing more frequent. Large farms spread around courtyarded villas where cypress trees made dark spears among the ragged palms. Oleanders flowered. Willows bent trailing hair over widening channels fresh and brimming with winter rain. Wealth and order were increasing all around them. Enkidu adjusted his red and yellow striped cloth and pulled himself up straighter as he walked the chariot road beside Shamhara's white ass. At the eve of the second day they reached an inn. The beer was good here. As they sat on the bench outside drinking, Enkidu soon got merry.

A man was coming along the road towards them, bound for the same hostelry. He was walking swiftly, though one foot was making him limp. He would soon be in hailing distance.

'Lady Hierodule,' said Enkidu, still shy of human contact. 'Who's this stranger following us? Ask him why he's in such a hurry, when he's obviously got a bad foot.'

The courtesan smiled. It was no trouble to her to make friends with a strange man. She had skills to fend off the unwelcome too. She was a young woman whom no one had profaned.

'Sir, you're in a hurry,' she called out. 'My friend would like to know why you don't treat that bad foot of yours more kindly. If my ass were lame, I wouldn't drive it the way you're forcing yourself to cover the ground.'

'Time enough to rest when my business is done,' he

gasped, curt but polite. He came up to them and leaned on the doorpost gratefully. 'You're right. My shoe's a mess of blood. But I need to be in the Town Hall of Uruk before another day's out. There's a niece of mine. She's getting married tomorrow evening.'

'Then you should wear a happier smile than this,' scolded Shamhara. She poured him some beer from their jug. 'The bride's uncle! You'll want to dance at her wedding, bad foot or not.'

'I'm not going there to dance. A wedding in Uruk is no time for a family celebration these days. You look like a city girl yourself. Where have you been that you don't know that?'

'I am an E-Anna servant. A hierodule of Inanna,' she said warningly.

'I thought as much. Your lot are favoured. You've got the *sag-ursag* and the Lady herself to protect you. Who protects the city's girls? You tell me that!'

'Protect them from what?' asked Enkidu, shyness forgotten.

The man half turned to him, too taken up with his own rage to make more than a flicker of surprise at the other's appearance. Indeed, Enkidu was looking less of a Wildman, more a sturdy countryman now.

'I can see you're not town-bred. You've some excuse for not knowing. Though I'd have thought it was over the whole countryside by now. From Gilgamesh! That's who. Our *en*, our *lugal*. He who's supposed to protect the people. Well, he's fought off invaders, I suppose. I'll give him that. But he's had his price, and more. And our women have paid it. There's not one bride in Uruk goes to bed on her wedding night a virgin now. Gilgamesh, bloody Gilgamesh, must always stick his cock in first. That's why I'm in such a hurry. We've had enough. I'm going to tell the council of Uruk it has to stop, right here, tomorrow! Never mind if Gilgamesh is the darling of the Lady of Lovemaking herself! That shouldn't give him the right to fall on our girls like a wolf on a flock of ewe lambs.'

Shamhara's hand closed over Enkidu's. The grip was suddenly tight. A warning? A challenge?

But Enkidu's face had grown pale behind his dusty beard. His eyes shone wild.

'Like a wolf on a flock of ewe-lambs? Like a wolf . . .'

He jumped up. Shamhara was beside him.

'In the morning, my friend.' She stroked his shuddering body. 'Yes! Tomorrow.'

# Chapter One Hundred and Seven

In Uruk, Ku-Ishhara the bride crouched in an upper room of her father's house. This should have been her day of joy. It was a love match. The children had grown up together. When Shu-Enlil went off to war, Ku-Ishhara had had a cylinder seal made showing her own Lady leading Shu-Enlil before An and pleading for his protection.

No one would protect her now.

All the women, mother, aunts, cousins, knew what would happen. No one would talk about it. Ku-Ishhara tried to send her mind ahead to the new, bright morning that would be coming. She would sleep with Shu-Enlil at last, in this marriage bed that her friends had made ready. She would be in his arms. He would kiss her face over and over again. She could weep all she wanted . . .

It was no good. She could not make her mind leap over what lay between now, this fast declining day, and tomorrow. She hunched, tenser than any foetus, in a cold, curled ball of fear and outrage. Her face had never been painted so beautifully. Her hair had never been dressed with such expensive oils. She had never been swathed and pinned into such a richly embroidered and fringed red dress. She was the bride. But not Shu-Enlil's woman. Not yet.

There! A great roar from the community house across the square. The men were bursting into the open and the dusk.

Ku-Ishhara raised her heavy, burning eyelids then. Yes! Dilibad, Inanna's planet, was there, like a brilliant lamp in the grey-blue rectangle of the doorway to the roof. She held up her left hand, palm outward, in a pleading gesture.

At the other end of the market square the young men were cheerful enough. They were friends of the bridegroom and members of Gilgamesh's elite troop. Their *lugal* was drinking with them. In Uruk, the bridegroom had more reason than most to put back strong beer as the evening approached. His friends had more reason than most to shake the walls of the community house with noisy singing. Better to pretend that what was about to happen would be done with their consent. After all, they had been at orgies with Gilgamesh themselves, hadn't they? There had been women for them as well.

So Shu-Enlil got unsteadily to his feet when Gilgamesh rose. The big warrior towered over his fellows. His shoulders outstrapped theirs.

Gilgamesh strode down the steps into the clay-paved square. His thumbs were loosening the padded girdle at his waist. He'd have to be careful. Girth of bone and muscle was well enough, but he was in danger of getting a beer belly. He would need a few hours on the exercise ground tomorrow morning to get him back in shape after today's carousing. A satisfied grin spread over his sweating face. The night was just beginning. He'd got some exercise yet to take in that house across the way. And when he'd had enough, well, back here to drink the rest of the night away, and make his conquest better in the telling.

Shu-Enlil could have what was left, of the night, of the girl in her bloodied bed.

There was a crowd in the square. Well, why not? It was a wedding, wasn't it? Look at them carrying Shu-Enlil shoulder-high across the plaza, as if he was any bridegroom in any other town. They'd hung flowers round his neck. There were flowers round Gilgamesh's neck too. He'd put fine clothes on. The girl ought to feel honoured.

He paced with the confidence of a king across the paving to where the mass of the crowd was densest. He took it for granted that they would part at his approach, as the moon-curved prow of a boat on the Buranun cleaves the yielding water. They were Uruk. Gilgamesh was Uruk's ruler.

There seemed a dark excitement among them in the evening dusk. Eyes glowed as they stared, as if they caught the light of the stars. He sensed a ripple of tension, of apprehension, even a kind of eagerness, different from the sullen rage he was accustomed to shoulder aside. Who was this — what was her name? — this Ku-Ishhara then? Why was it different tonight?

He raised his head to look at the upper storey. The roof terrace was empty, but he could see a press of young women at the windows and inside the upper door.

'I'm coming to get the bride!' he bellowed. 'Send her down to unbolt the door!'

They were all his women, once they let him over their threshold. He passed them on to his men afterwards, like a general handing out booty after he has won a battle.

He saw the commotion of panic among their whirling dresses, like a flock of frightened doves. The evidence of their fear broadened his smile.

He was almost at the door. The crowd had backed away. They lined the square now, like the spectators at a wrestling match. Only one man stood between him and the bride's door.

A shock. Even Gilgamesh broke the rhythm of his stride and stopped.

This man was huge. As huge, a wandering part of Gilgamesh's mind told him, as I am. Well, no. As the stranger — for strange he most definitely was — stared back at him, massive legs planted like a bull's, unmoving, Gilgamesh could see that the other was a little shorter. Yet he had an uncomfortable feeling that the giant was more strongly boned.

The creature did not speak. He lowered his head a little, and his breath snorted through wide-flared nostrils. Big fists were loosely clenched, swinging at the end of powerful arms. His skin was unnaturally hairy. The long locks of his head had been knotted at the back of his neck. He had thrown off his cloth skirt, and now only a brief leather apron covered his genitals. His forearms were bound with studded leather. His great, splayed feet were bare.

Gilgamesh, in his best clothes for the wedding, felt suddenly effete. He did not like the feeling.

'Get out of my way, whoever you are! Do you know who I am, ape-man? *Gilgamesh!*'

That should have brought a full-throated cheer, 'Hail, Gilgamesh!' from all his citizens.

The young voices of his own band sang out dutifully. The crowd was silent.

With astonishment, fuzzed somewhat by the beer he had drunk, Gilgamesh's gaze swivelled around the square. What was this rising sense of anticipation, people pressed back to the margins of the houses as if in fear, yet standing on tiptoe to peer over each other's shoulders or nudging and whispering to their neighbours, still not taking their eyes off the scene in front of Ku-Ishhara's house? Even the girls in the bride's house had come out now to hang over the parapet fence and stare. Was the red-dressed bride squatting alone in her bedroom?

Gilgamesh took another step towards the door. He had come unarmed, except for the weapon he had carried from birth. Enkidu did not move at first. And then . . . One foot braced itself against the doorpost of Ku-Ishhara's house. The message was clear.

'By the thunder of Ishkur, who are you that defies a king in his own citadel?'

'En-ki-du.' The voice croaked strangely.

'Well then, *Enkidu*, I'll show you how the champion of Uruk treats rebels. In the name of Inanna!'

He hurled himself forward. For all his size he was light on his feet and near the peak of training. Arms thicker than pythons whipped out to surround and squash his opponent. But Enkidu was quick as a buck to spring in the air and sidestep. Now they closed and grappled. Heads lowered, skulls crashing against each other. Neck sinews strained and rage snorted. Gilgamesh's wrap was torn away. With astonishment he saw shreds of sheepswool caught in Enkidu's teeth. Then he went smashing back against the doorpost. The house shook and his vision spun with rainbows. But he was maddened now. Gone beyond the limits of his knowing were the staring crowd, the vainly cheering young men, the breathless bridesmaids overhead. All that filled his consciousness was the grim and heaving bulk of this hairy Enkidu, that set and singleminded face, the power of those arms.

Aah! Breath whistled in a shriek, as a rib cracked. He found the strength of fury, backed with a barely remembered skill in his booted foot. Enkidu's turn to hurtle back against the house, so that even the kiln-hardened bricks cracked and fell.

Like an eagle-winged lion guarding the gate of a temple, Enkidu crouched, his monstrous head reared. Then his splendid body leaped through the air back into the fray. His hands were wild-cat clawed; blood reddened his eyes. In a growing darkness of panic Gilgamesh fought a physical struggle with this untaught, savage fury and at the same time an internal battle to recall all the conscious training of his boyhood.

The king of the city fought the creature from the steppe. As night thickened and the citizens gathered round with torches, the combatants no longer remembered why or over whom they fought. Their minds, like their arms, were locked solely against the other. The battle must be won, this opponent beaten, for its own sake. Each must assert his own self.

Ku-Ishhara crept out on to the roof behind the others and peeped fearfully over. Shu-Enlil did not lift his eyes to see her. What was happening here in the square enthralled them all. Few noticed even Inanna herself, with Nin Shubur silent beside her and Dumuzi behind, come down the steps from Kullab to watch intently.

It seemed to take hours. They were scratched and bruised, bleeding from mouth and ears. The battle shifted, swayed on the open paving with only the scrape and grunt of their wrestling, then crashed back again into the shadow of the house and the echoing thud of wood and bricks.

Dumuzi's eyes went searchingly to Inanna's face. It was hard to read in the flickering torchlight and the uncertain stars. Her lips looked black, in a pale oval. They moved, like fluttering moths. 'Gilgamesh? Gilgamesh?' A whisper, too faint to be a cheer. There was no laughter of excitement in her strained bearing. It was hard to keep the jealousy out of his voice. 'You want him to win, don't you? Your human hero!'

'No!'

The doorpost shattered. The girls screamed from the roof.

One figure reeled from the darkness of the porch, alone now, stumbled into the glare of torches, collapsed and fell. A moment of horror. Eyes fixed on the place of shadow and ruin he had left.

Then Enkidu came halting out, still barely upright. One giant hip moved awkwardly.

The warband of Uruk raised a great groan. But Enkidu did not raise his fist in victory. He came to the fallen mound of his opponent. Still, as earth.

A sigh from the women in the doorways. Enkidu stood, one foot planted beside the beaten Gilgamesh, the wounded leg resting more lightly. He bent over, breathing heavily. He touched the forehead of this man who, a few hours ago, had been a total stranger, whose damaged body now he felt he knew better than the hierodule's.

'Gilgamesh?'

The *lugal* did not stir. Enkidu turned his face away. The square was hushed to stillness.

At last, the darkness heaved. The beaten champion moaned. Painfully, Gilgamesh struggled to his knees. A hairy hand reached down and helped him to stand swaying upright.

Then, in the tense silence, Enkidu went down on his knees before Gilgamesh. The same dark hand, lit by the dull red glow, laid itself in the hollow of Gilgamesh's thigh. A gesture of submission.

'*Lugal* Gilgamesh. There is no man on Earth like you. The Wild Cow of the Grasslands has borne a splendid bull. Enlil has spoken for you the name of Shepherd, and me the Sheepdog. Let me serve you.'

'No!' whispered Inanna again. 'No!'

So quiet the king now, outlined in darkness. Then his hand moved to cover Enkidu's.

A night chill crept over Ku-Ishhara. 'He will come for me now! He will be furious!'

But Gilgamesh was helping the wounded Enkidu to his feet. They leaned against each other for support, laughed a little together, through the roughened panting of their breath. They hugged each other in a new way.

The torches flared around them, escorting them, running ahead. Gilgamesh led Enkidu to his private quarters.

# Chapter One Hundred and Eight

Inanna moved through the lower halls of her E-Anna. A breath of spring was in the air, making her restless. Ranged on the smooth tiles facing her image, their backs to the blue sky and the budding *mesu* trees, were lines of reverent statues. Past rulers, life-size, hands crossed on breast, eyes calm, black-lined around wide whites, lost in the contemplation of her Ladyship. Small statuettes of commoner people, husband and wife, smiling a little as they stood side by side. The gilded figure of a princess-priestess, one hand lifted in an attitude of prayer.

Ordinarily they soothed Inanna. They were evidence of generation upon generation of fidelity. They spoke of a people so in love with the Children of An, so dependent on them that the weekly festivals, even the four daily sacrifices at which food was offered to the Anunnaki, were not enough. They, some part of them, must be always here, in the sacred place, in the holy presence. The statue worshipped on, while the living worshipper – and in time the dead – performed human duties elsewhere.

But now *this* statue. She paused and ran her hand over the new arrival. It was, of course, occupying the central place. Gilgamesh had set his own likeness, towering tall, facing the clay offering table and the niche beyond, where her own alabaster image gleamed under a canopy of stars and roses.

She looked from one to the other of these sculptors' artistry. The living reality of Gilgamesh's face was not there to meet her own.

She was aware that her hand was still resting on the flank of the stone hero's body, and that Dumuzi was watching. She began to move it again, tracing lightly the lion's-tail girdle, the sunburst mass of hair, the flanks like a bull's, the tumbling beard.

This diorite Gilgamesh did not lift his hands in supplication. Each carved fist grasped a serpent, strangling it.

'Gilgamesh is too proud to stand before me empty-handed and ask for my help. He has to be the one to offer gifts to me.'

'Perhaps he is reminding himself, and you, of your help in past battles. Besides, look around you. There's hardly a harp, a vase, a frieze that doesn't show processions of your people bringing you every gift you could possibly imagine. Why turn your nose up at Gilgamesh's?'

She snatched her hand away from the new statue, as though the cool stone burned her. 'Because it is not the living man! Look at these kings, these priestesses, these merchants and manageresses. In life, they could never get enough of me. They wanted to be in my presence day and night. When they commissioned these statues, they left a part of their souls with me. Do you honestly think that that's what Gilgamesh means? It is a mockery, an excuse, to leave his statue here, when the man does not come to me himself any longer.'

'He is the *en*. He keeps your festivals.'

'Oh yes! When the city of Uruk turns out, when there are crowds in festival clothes, when he can march at the head of the procession with the drums and trumpets, when my white, still statue doesn't answer back and all the noise is on his side! Does he come to our private chambers? Does he walk in the garden with us?'

'He has Enkidu now.'

'Yes. Enkidu. Better than a wife, isn't he? What wife would go on lion hunts with him? What wife would pass the night away drinking and singing with him? What wife would wrestle with him, so closely matched?'

'You might have.' The words were more than a little bitter.

He spoke aloud too clearly what she had tried not to allow herself to think. The rush of colour to her face made her look a young girl again. To cover her confusion she seized his arm, twined it round her and kissed his cheek.

'I am already a married woman. Why should I need another husband? A human!'

'Gilgamesh is more than half a Lord.'

'You know that is not enough.'

'If you thought that lying with him would give him immortal life, you'd do it, wouldn't you? But you're afraid you'll kill him, too.'

His hurt, sheepdog eyes carried that perpetual accusation. She took his life away. Year after year he must go to the

Netherworld. Year after year she would welcome him back to her bed with triumph and joy and wonderful lovemaking. But she would not lift his punishment. The sentence was fixed. He could never possess her absolutely now.

'You come back. The question doesn't arise.'

'But if it did? When I'm gone?'

He was probing an old wound. However much it hurt him, perhaps because it hurt him, he must ask this question, to which he did not want to know the answer.

She moved in front of him, let her breasts brush his bare chest, clasped her hands behind his neck and kissed his mouth more passionately.

'I still have you. Always, always, you'll come back to me. Why should I break my heart over your brother and then lose him to Ereshkigal for ever? Why should I let her have that victory over me? She takes enough from me already.'

'But if you could find a way to give him immortality, wouldn't it be a different story?'

'Dumuzi, Dumuzi. There can never be another lover like you. All the women of Sumer sigh over you.'

'Then why are you jealous of Enkidu?'

She flung his hands away. 'I am not! I am not! Let him keep his boyfriend. The city has been quieter since they found each other. The girls have a breathing space. The walls will soon be finished.'

'And so shall I!'

'Poor boy, poor boy!' She stroked away the sweat that was beginning to bead his face. 'Your death was necessary, to save me for the world. What will Gilgamesh's serve?'

'You love him though, don't you? You'd like to marry him.' Dumuzi struck the figure of the almost naked hero so hard that it almost toppled. Inanna gasped and grabbed it.

'His statue! Your image!' he shouted. 'What is the reality of you two?'

The fortifications of Uruk were finished. Seven ranks of priests blessed their completion. Turrets frowned over gateways. The tough shell of inner and outer walls was packed with hard rubble. Water spouts stretched serpent necks ready to spit the winter rain beyond the reach of the clay-faced walls.

The brickwork was grim, gigantic, businesslike. Gilgamesh marched around it well pleased. Incense smoked. The blood of bulls bathed the work in strength. Horns brayed and priests intoned prayers. Young soldiers stepped out in their parade armour. Once, humans climbed to the E-Anna to serve the Anunnaki. Now Inanna's personnel processed down to the boundaries of the mound to support the might of a human.

The hand of summer lay heavy on the land again. Enkidu pined on the lowland plain. Gilgamesh, too, was restless. The violent wrestling with young men, the rape of young women were things of the past since Enkidu came. The two sweated the days away and caroused at night. Life was slipping away, this single unrepeatable span of human days.

One hot afternoon Gilgamesh came upon Enkidu in a summerhouse at the end of the siesta. There were tears glinting among the Wildman's facial hair.

'What's up? Weeping like a girl?'

'I'm no longer the man I was. I'm losing my strength. My muscles are running away to grease in this city.'

'It's this cursed summer. It takes Dumuzi, and beats the heart out of all of us. Only this morning I was walking by the river. I saw dead bodies floating in the water, rotting on the mud. The stench was awful. When I gave you a wife, she died, this time last year, with her baby. I thought to myself, shall we all come to this?'

'I feel as though I'm suffering a living death already.'

Gilgamesh smote his thigh. 'I won't endure it! Aren't I the champion of Inanna? Haven't I wrestled barehanded with bulls and leopards in her honour? Haven't I cowed all the kings of Sumer? Listen. We'll put some muscle back on these bones of ours. If I must die, I'm going to make a greater name for myself yet, before they take me.'

Enkidu raised heat-weary eyes from where he sat cross-legged in the doorway of the summerhouse, trying to shield himself from the sun and yet get some sense of refreshment from the watered grass and the myrtle bushes and pools of Gilgamesh's palace garden.

'What's left? Who would dare fight you in all the Land of the Two Rivers now?'

Gilgamesh leaned over him, one sweating hand darkening the wood of the doorpost. 'Then, friend Enkidu, we must look beyond Sumer, mustn't we? We must go where ordinary humans are afraid to venture. We must seek out someone that no mortal has ever dared to challenge.'

An animal caution haunted Enkidu's eyes. 'Who might that be?'

Gilgamesh smiled. 'Once, when I was young and green, Inanna called on me. The Maid of Uruk, the Young Lady herself! She needed my help. She had a *huluppu* tree she'd raised in the years after the Flood. But the Imdugud had taken it over and built its nest in the branches. The Mushsagkal had laid her eggs in the roots. Kiskillilla had cut herself a house in the trunk. I drove them out for Inanna. I smashed that nest. I hacked the Serpent in two. I threw the demon of the desert back where she belongs. My axe cut down that *huluppu* tree and I presented it to the Lady. Her craftsmen made it into a throne and a bed. That was the bed she married Dumuzi on. That was the throne he'd stolen from her when she sentenced him to death.'

'And she rewarded you.'

'Oh yes. My *pukku* and *mikku*. Yes, she gave me those.'

'They say you used to frighten all Uruk with them, before I came. It was all brawling and women.'

Gilgamesh started and straightened up. 'I want something better for myself now. I mean to carve my name in the place of the Anunnaki. And I know the tree I want for mine, as she knew hers. It will not be easy to win, as hers was not. But I swear I will take it.'

'Are magic *huluppu* trees and Imduguds and serpents so common in Uruk, then? Why are we lounging around your garden as though all the adventures are over?'

'No *huluppu* tree for me. And not in Uruk. No. I have set my heart on the highest tree of all, the mightiest of Enlil's own seven cedars, that grow in the Land of the Living, on the mountains east of the sunrise.'

Enkidu scrambled to his feet in a paroxysm of alarm. Gilgamesh was beaming like the noonday sun.

'Don't say that! Have you any idea what you're suggesting?'

'I didn't intend it to be a challenge for weaklings.'

'But the Land of the Living is under the protection of Lord Utu. Enlil planted those cedars there himself. The forest is guarded by the monster Huwawa. Those trees can't be touched!'

'If I can overcome the Imdugud, Ninurta's creature, if I can butcher Ningishzida's Serpent, why should Enlil's Huwawa scare me? And Utu is Inanna's own brother. I'd be carving my name on that tree to exalt her, as well as myself.'

'You don't know! You're a town man. I was born on the steppe, I've run with the wild creatures. I know the tales they bring. That forest is vast and dangerous. You could walk ten thousand hours and not cross half of it. And if you found Huwawa, and the grove you're talking of, well then ... Listen to me, Gilgamesh. He's worse than anything you've ever seen in nightmare. He's not a human inside a rough skin, like me. His roar's like the noise of a flood storm breaking down houses. He spits fire. Even his breath is deadly. Don't go there! Think up some other quest.'

'Are you scared, then? Shall I have to leave you behind? I thought you were pining for action?'

The hairy one trembled, like a scolded dog. 'You know that I'll go where you go. I'll fight where you fight. I'll die the death you die.'

'Nobly said! That's what I wanted to hear. If we can't have immortality like the Anunnaki, at least we'll leave this glory behind us, eh?'

'I shall go, if you go. I won't let you do this alone. But I still plead with you, my master, the only friend I've ever had, don't attempt this. Evil will come of it.'

'Evil? I'm *en* and *lugal*. What's evil and what's good, but what I choose to call them? They say my *pukku*'s evil, do they? My *mikku*? Because I beat them to stir up the young bloods to war? Because I've stuck my stick into any girl I wanted? Why not? I'm Gilgamesh. I'm their king.'

'So you'll leave the city in peace now, and make war against the Anunnaki?'

'One tree, Enkidu. One mighty cedar tree. My name, carved on it for eternity. That's all I want.'

'I think it's more than that.'

The elders gathered in the respite of nightfall, in the marketplace under the stars.

'We know what you're planning. We advise against it. The rashness of youth will be your undoing and ours.'

Gilgamesh's teeth flashed moon-white. 'I am not as young as I was. You've always advised against my adventures, old men. You've counselled peace, and then I've won the war. You'd like to turn me into a coward and a slave of others, a fat, scented *en*. I'm still your warleader. I was made for battle. I'm Inanna's champion.'

The *mikku* beat the *pukku* to call the young men to the square next morning. Gilgamesh looked them over with a proud, glad eye. Some were his own age, though fewer now. Battles had claimed their dues. Some were very young, flesh still firming on their slender bones. Some had never fought in earnest. Their faces were disciplined or eager, frightened of showing fear or resigned. Many of the eyes carried the same love he saw in Enkidu's. They were his men, his boys.

'Well, you've all heard what the plan is. I can promise you glory at the end of it. Which of you wants to miss out on that? We're not marching against another city's army, this time. One mighty grove of cedars on the peak of the Land of the Living, the last country before the paradise of Dilmun. One terrible guardian to overcome, this Huwawa.

'If I were to take all of you, we should be falling over each other's feet. It will be no place for cowards. I beat the *pukku*, which you were bound to obey. But I'm in a good mood today. If anyone wants to turn back, he can fall out now. I won't hold it against you. If you want to run back to your mothers and sisters, now's the time. I'll let you go. But I won't forgive you if you desert me halfway. Make up your minds. Who's coming to challenge Huwawa with me?'

Their mothers could not cry out. Their lovers could only silently beg. Many young men took the chance he offered them, out of simple fear, out of awe of the place, because they doubted their own youth and inexperience, or because they had fought and survived too many battles already. The band that raised their spears to Gilgamesh was loyal, high-hearted, massing closer together in a hot, heady comradeship.

'Fifty's enough,' beamed Gilgamesh. '*I love you, boys!*'

Inanna summoned him to her audience chamber. She looked paler than usual. Her hair hung damply on her forehead.

'Do not go, Gilgamesh. You're only a man. Don't throw your short life away.'

His head went up proudly. 'You! You say that? Didn't Sky and Earth plead with you to stay at home? But you went to the Great Below. You defied them all.'

'And lost what I most dearly love.'

'I have no wife. If I die, no woman is going to break her heart over me as they do for Dumuzi. And there's no one else's death can hurt me . . . except Enkidu's.'

'Aah!'

'He's as sick of peace as I am. We must have war and fame. You coveted the *me* of the Netherworld.'

'I did not get them. And you are not of the Anunnaki.'

'You're throwing that in my face again? That you're immortal, and I'm not? And even so, you'll try to stop me getting glory that will make the name of Gilgamesh live on for ever. Well, you won't succeed!'

She rose from her Lion Throne suddenly, dismissing him.

'The Anunnaki thought Enkidu would tame you, and give my people peace. But it seems the savage has turned you against your Lady.'

'You! You've turned your face away from *me*! You refuse to give me the thing you know I long for more than anything else.'

Inanna's eyes brimmed with bitter tears. 'I *died* trying to get that! Dumuzi and Geshtinanna are suffering for it still.'

'Died? You'll live for ever. My life is running out.'

'I cannot help that.'

# Chapter One Hundred and Nine

Gilgamesh got the armourers busy. He had them make for himself and Enkidu colossal swords. The blades were two talents each and the pommels alone weighed another half a talent. At three talents, their mighty axes stretched strong muscles. And then there was armour.

For the fifty young men who were to accompany them, willow and apple and box were cut to make hafts for their weapons. Copper blades were annealed to harden them.

Gilgamesh knew how to act the prudent general as well as the rash adventurer. He took Enkidu to visit Nin Sun, bearing the proper gifts: a white kid and oil and fine flour. She looked at them wisely.

'You want something from your Anunnaki mother.'

'Yes. You've got influence. Utu is the one you need to talk to. The Land of the Living is his particular concern. Couldn't you sweeten him up? After all, I'm doing this for Uruk. Inanna's name will be all the greater for this expedition. She challenged Enlil herself, didn't she? They are still close, those two, Utu and Inanna.'

A thread of anger tightened behind Nin Sun's eyes. 'What good has that branch of the family ever done ours? I welcomed Inanna into my house like a daughter. I wish now she had married the Farmer Enkimdu. I should have had Dumuzi safe still. I shouldn't have had my Geshtinanna torn away from me to work her stylus in the Netherworld.'

'Then be my advocate. Let's assert our power over all that lot.'

'Gilgamesh, I am often afraid of the children I have borne. You dare too much: Dumuzi, to marry Inanna. Geshtinanna, to snatch Ereshkigal's sentence from him. Now you, to attempt this. When Inanna challenged the Netherworld, it was not she who paid the final price. You are a hero, I don't doubt that. You may succeed in this folly. But who will pay for it? I warn you, someone will.'

'Our swords are made, Mother. The axes are sharpened. I'm going.'

She sighed, then straightened her back with a conscious effort. 'Very well, then. I will do what I can. Wait here.'

When she came back she was dressed like a Lady of the Anunnaki, and a queen. She wore a tiara bound with horns. She had a collar of rows of gold leaf about her throat. The ceremonial breastplate was bound over the gold-threaded dress that draped both shoulders and fell to her jewelled ankles. Her face was painted like a high priestess.

Gilgamesh felt in his stomach a small quiver of awe he did not often experience in his mother's presence. She kissed him formally, as he bent his face to her breastplate, then she embraced Enkidu with a more tender warmth.

'Motherless lad, my adopted son. I know you've done what you can to tame this wild bull of mine. It's you they call the savage, but my heart says otherwise. We have run with the creatures of the steppe, you and I. We know their gentleness, their friendship. Be a friend to Gilgamesh now. Don't leave him. Look after him. My blessing go with you.'

Leaving them, taking only a small retinue of her household, she mounted the outer stairs to the roof. On the highest point she would lay the offering and set fire to it. She would raise her hands to the sun. She would formally invite Utu to grant her a hearing.

The men waited, hearing the muted bursts of chanting, catching the faintest trail of incense and burning flesh spreading on the still air, filtering into the house.

Gilgamesh paced up and down. 'It's no different to having a weapon honed by a master armourer. She knows her business. It's a necessary line of defence.'

But Enkidu stood with his hand lifted, face rapt and listening, like one of the white-eyed statues of Nin Sun's admirers.

'. . . Hear my request, Utu!'

They heard a male voice answer her. 'What can I do for you this morning, Great-aunt?'

'Bright Lord, you know what my son is planning. Stay your hand to let them pass. Let them not meet their death in the Land of the Living. I shall talk to Aia; I shall beg your bride to remind you daily of my plea.'

'Enlil put the Cedar Mountain under my protection.

Would you have me be a false shepherd?'

'My son is Inanna's *en*. What help did Enlil give her when she was in the Netherworld?'

There was a silence. When the voices resumed, they were further off, rising and falling, as if in argument. Gilgamesh gripped Enkidu's arm, listening in vain.

There was a sharp whiff of extinguished incense. Nin Sun's figure blotted out the sun in the upper doorway. She blinked water from her eyes, as if she had just lowered them from the sky. She came down the steps and into the shady room, a woman once strong but growing frail inside the splendour of court regalia. Gilgamesh went swiftly towards her and enfolded her in a hug. But she kissed him quickly and slipped out of his arms. It was to Enkidu she went.

'I did not bear you, but you have no mother of your own to watch over you. Take this. I, my priestesses, my hierodules, my votive virgins have done what we can to protect you.' She hung a plain, calfskin pouch around his neck. Impulsively he kissed her hand. Then he touched the pouch, questioningly, but did not open it. 'Now, you must protect my son,' she continued. 'I have lost two children to Kur already. Bring Gilgamesh home to me alive.'

'You shall have him back,' he said. 'If I die for it.'

She turned to Gilgamesh, smiled somewhat wearily and held out her hand. 'Son, I have done what I could. Utu gives you a stern warning. The cedars of the Land of the Living belong to the Anunnaki. You are taking on more than your match in strength. I told him no one could dissuade you from this folly. I begged him to spare a mother's tears.

'He told me I was not the first. Inanna had spoken for you already. He has promised me this much. He will rein in the demons of the winds who protect the road to the Land of the Living. You will not meet your death on the ranges nor in the ravines. He will allow you to cross the mountains and enter his forest. The rest is up to you.

'I am very afraid. I fear it is no kindness to bind the lesser guardians and leave the greater one loose.'

'Bless him. Utu reads my heart. If I must die, at least it will be as Inanna did, facing the uttermost challenge.'

Breastplates shone. Knapsacks were packed with food for the march. The fresh wood of their weapons smelled sweetly.

Lu-Shara the Elder stood by the seven-bolted gate of the

city. It stood open in the broad, bright daylight. But the flow of merchants and porters and laden donkeys had ceased. The whole city seemed to have gathered to watch the young men depart. Beyond, the country people had come out to stare from the banks of the waterways.

Gilgamesh lifted his head. Inanna had not come down with the rest of her household to bid him farewell. She stood on the highest terrace of the E-Anna, watching.

He waved his copper sword high and shouted to her, 'The *lugal* of Uruk salutes you, Lion Inanna! I will bring Enlil's Huwawa back for you with a ring through his nose!'

She raised her hand in reply, more solemnly than she had done as a child.

Gilgamesh turned to embrace his sister Geshtinanna. He marched across the square, and took his place at the head of his troop. Lu-Shara stepped forward and placed a wreath of myrtle around his neck.

'We, the council of the elders of Uruk, have given you our best advice. You chose to ignore it. Nevertheless, you are our king. Uruk is strong because of you. Come back to us safe. Don't leave us leaderless. Be prudent enough to let Enkidu guide you. He knows the ways of the wild. Let him walk in front of you on the path through the forest. Listen to his warnings.'

Gilgamesh slapped Enkidu on the shoulder cheerfully. 'Do you hear what they're saying, comrade? You're the one with brains and I'm the brawn. There's promotion for the savage! Well, Nin Mah and Enki made you for me. I won't despise their gift.'

The drum rolled. Curled trumpets bleated. The fighting men marched out of the city. At the foot of the ramp that led to the base of the mound, Gilgamesh turned and looked back. Viewed from below like this, the walls were enormous. It seemed impossible now that little humans, with two small hands, should have completed such labour, brick upon brick, course after course, mile upon mile, to make this mighty splendour. It circled Inanna's city, Inanna's house, a strong defence. And she herself was still standing there, a distant, white figure high above the crowd that was pouring out of the gate to watch him go.

Catching that blazing, beautiful sight of the city and all that had given meaning to his life, a sudden rush of unaccustomed tears filled Gilgamesh's eyes.

'To the east, and fame!' he cried. 'March!'

They covered the ground faster than stallions on the steppe. They crossed the copper Buranun and the arrow-swift Idiglat and reached the foothills of the east. Still they pressed on, over one mountain range, over two, over seven.

'Where are the ice and storms we were threatened with?' laughed young Amu. 'This is too easy!'

'Utu has tied the wind demons up in the caves. You won't die here.'

In a month and a half they came to the gate of the forest.

No wind stirred its dark branches. Straight pines and spreading cedars locked their boughs in a sunless canopy. The ground beneath was silent with a mat of dead needles, through which nothing grew. Across their path and as far as eye could see on either side stretched a dense hedge of tangled thorns.

'The Land of the Living?' Gilgamesh laughed shortly. 'There's not a bird stirring!'

Enkidu was casting about for a way through. 'Look. Here's a gate.'

Two slender trunks of timber, with a hurdle fastened across them. As they came nearer, they saw it was not a rough lattice of branches, but a delicately carved filigree of trailing flowers through which birds flew.

Gilgamesh reached out his hand, then, uncharacteristically, hesitated. The same uncertainty stilled them all. If it had been a towering portal of stout planks, hung on pivots of bronze between big stone pillars, they would have yelled with glee as they charged it. But this thing was so frail, so beautiful.

'That wouldn't keep out a determined sheep,' murmured Amu.

'Then beware Huwawa's sheepdog!' came a terrifying roar behind them.

They whirled around, making a defensive ring, shields ready, weapons lifted. The woods still rang with the echoes of the shout, but there was no one to be seen.

'Master, let me.' Enkidu stepped out of the shield wall, went down on hands and knees. In a little while he signalled that he had found a trail going downhill away from the gate. With a hunter's infinite caution he tracked it, the soldiers, less expertly, following him.

Enkidu held up his hand and crawled back. He was pale, but his eyes were sparkling.

'Sir,' he whispered, 'don't hesitate. It's clear this watchman had no news of our coming. He's an ogre of a man, but the heat has been his undoing. He's got seven massive coats of mail down there. If he'd had them on, the keenest axe in Uruk wouldn't have been able to touch him. As it is, he's just dragging the first one on him now, as fast as he can. If you're quick, you'll kill him.'

'Watchman of the Land of the Living, defend yourself against a human!' With a bellow like a bull Gilgamesh flung himself down through the bushes into the dell. The ogre spun, snatched up a club, roaring with laughter. But when he found the axe of the champion of Uruk hurtling towards him, his face showed fear. His eyes slid with a desperate glance to the huge heap of armour that could have enclosed his sweating flesh sevenfold. Only one coat of leather and bronze, insecurely fastened, stood between him and the blows launched by Gilgamesh's colossal arms. That glance itself was almost his undoing. The edge of the axe half-severed the shaft of his mace and he stumbled over a briar root with the force of the blow.

Now they were fighting in earnest, almost evenly matched. The watchman was bigger than Gilgamesh, but soft with long idleness. The ring of Uruk's soldiers drew closer round the contestants.

No help was needed. To Enkidu's enormous relief the ogre spun, blood spurting from his throat. The mace catapulted through the air, almost decapitating Amu. Gilgamesh stood, one foot on the conquered watchman's chest, strength flowing freely in his victorious limbs. Enkidu rushed up and hugged his friend and master.

'You were right. It can be done. If we stay bold, if we're quick and seize our chances, even the defences of the Anunnaki can't hold against us.'

'Well, the gatekeeper is down. Now for the gate.'

Emboldened now, they marched back. What had seemed too frail to be trusted, as if it must hold some treacherous magic, seemed now no more than a pretty piece of craftsmanship. Gilgamesh strolled up, would have flung it aside with a flick of his hand on the thong that secured it.

But Enkidu was quicker still to be there in front of him.

'Allow me, sir. I promised Nin Sun and all the elders of

Uruk I would go in front of you into the unknown.'

One hairy hand reached out, gripped the peeled wood.

He screamed. Answering cries of fear echoed round him. Then nothing. The men stared. No flash of fire. No opening pit. No thunderbolt from the Sky. Enkidu stood, apparently unharmed, his hand still clasped around the opened gate. They saw he was trembling. He whimpered like a terrified dog.

'What is it, man?' Gilgamesh asked. 'You're not hurt, are you?'

'*My hand!*'

'There's nothing wrong with it.'

'I can't move it!'

With breath-held caution Gilgamesh reached out. One warm hand touched the other's cold wrist. Applying careful strength, watching to avoid his own flesh touching that malign wood, Gilgamesh forced Enkidu's curved hand upward and prised it off the bar.

With a long shudder of relief Enkidu backed away. But when Gilgamesh let go of his wrist the bent hand stayed paralysed.

'The mark of death is on me! I've lost my strength.'

'Don't be a coward, man. We expected wounds.' He had bruises and cuts of his own to show.

'But where is the doctor for this?'

The king took him by the elbow and led him through the gap Enkidu himself had forced.

'There! Two defences passed, with no great damage.'

The fifty men followed soberly, pupils widening in alarm as they edged through the narrow opening.

'Now.' Gilgamesh seated Enkidu under a tree. 'The best physicians are the women of Uruk. Geshtinanna herself is the most skilful in the land.'

'Uruk is far away,' moaned Enkidu.

'Not as far as you think.' The other touched the leather pouch that swung at Enkidu's neck.

His eyes flared wide with hope. He raised his good hand, trembling, then carried the stiff, clawed fingers up to join it. His eyes searching Gilgamesh's, as though he could read the answer there, he forced the numb digits into the soft opening. He felt fine, light powder, the grittiness of tiny crystals . . .

He felt! He gave a great cry of gratitude.

Gilgamesh grinned, clapped him across the back, disguising his own relief.

'You see! We have help on our side. We can't be beaten.'

'Are these the cedars we're after?' Young Amu was staring at a massive trunk.

Gilgamesh came and looked it over. 'If it were timber alone I was after, that would be a fine specimen. A king among cedars, and only the first outlier of this forest. What must the trees be like up ahead? No, young friend. I've set my heart on something far rarer than this one. Nothing will satisfy me but to set my mark on the tree at the very heart of this Land of the Living, on Enlil's cedar itself.'

'There is your way,' said Enkidu. 'Huwawa has been here.'

A track had been crushed through the forest, as though an elephant train had passed. Colossal footprints had forced their weight into the earth. Incipient trees had been cracked and flattened on either edge. Stout lateral branches had been snapped aside. The track led straight, a hot, hard ribbon of sunlight up to the burning skyline.

The march through the forest was as long as across the plain and over the mountains. It led over rolling ridges, plunged into dark valleys, rose up more precipitous slopes whose limits they could not see. At first the woods on either side were dark and silent. It was hard even for Enkidu to find game to feed them. Then, as the summer days wore on, the land rose higher, the air struck sparkling and cooler. The forest thinned till there was green grass between the trees. Hares sprang away. Deer vanished behind shadowy trunks. Birds swooped and sang. The harp song of running water lulled them into laughter.

'Now we're getting somewhere,' said Gilgamesh, 'where each tree has had a chance to grow to its full majesty. Look at the girth of them!'

The specimens became fewer, but more and more magnificent.

At last they jumped across a running brook. A cone-shaped mountain rose before them. Here, finally, the giant forest trees ran out, like a skirt that stops at the waist. Above stretched clear green slopes. Only on a platform just below the summit, like the wooded *giguna* on a ziggurat, seven massive cedars stood before a rampart of rocks. Their topmost branches swept the sky. Their shade darkened the mountain peak, heavy as a thundercloud at the end of a drought. Even from here they were unmatchable.

Gilgamesh lifted his joined hands to the sky, shook them in triumph.

'There! There's my tree! My royal cedar. My Tree of Life!'

Enkidu touched his arm. They smiled at each other.

'It can't be more than another day's journey, can it? Will you camp here, sir, and make the assault tomorrow?'

Yet at twilight, as he gathered twigs from the last pines for his leader's bed, he began to tremble.

'Are you sick, old friend? Have you caught the fever?'

'You haven't seen Huwawa. You don't realise the evil you are stirring up.'

'Sleep, man, you'll get your courage back when the sun rises in the morning.'

But in the middle of the night it was Gilgamesh himself who cried out in sudden fear. Enkidu was beside him in a moment. 'Master! What's wrong?'

Gilgamesh clung to him, the hair of Enkidu's arms as comforting in the dark as the wool of his mother's sleeve.

'A dream! It was enough to shake the heart of the bravest man. I dreamed a wild bull attacked me on the open steppe. I thought he would run me through. With the utmost difficulty I grappled his horns and sent him crashing to the ground. But the terror of that encounter has still got me.'

'You think *I'm* afraid of phantoms? This is a good dream, surely? It was Huwawa coming at you like a wild bull, and you threw him down!'

'Yes! Yes. I see it now.' Gilgamesh gasped his way back to reality. 'Of course that was it. Praise be!'

Yet, as Gilgamesh settled down to sleep again, Enkidu sat cross-legged watching over him. His shaggy head was lifted to that far, dark summit of the Land of the Living, barely outlined against the misty stars. One light blazed through, as vibrant over the mountain as it had been over the city. Dilibad, Inanna's planet. Enkidu shivered.

# Chapter One Hundred and Ten

Still they climbed on, another day's journey. They passed beyond the earthly tree line. Only the cedars of the Anunnaki could grow above this. Short, sweet, green grass made pasture for wild mouflons, who gazed at the newcomers with reflective, gold-flecked eyes, then leaped away, more in delight of their springing limbs than in fear. The air was intensely blue, not hazed with dust. In the primeval silence the men walked quietly, not speaking.

'That grove on the summit must be further off than I thought,' panted Gilgamesh.

Slowly the realisation of what they were approaching sank in.

'Those trees!' said Enkidu, 'we could pick out all seven of them yesterday, and yet they're still at least another day's march off. They must be enormous!'

One was beginning to stand out among the seven. Gilgamesh eyed it, without comment. His hand hefted the giant axe slung at his side. His throat began to constrict with the daring of his own ambition.

They camped again. Brushwood gave them a scant shelter. The stars were dancing more brightly, larger here. Again Enkidu's troubled sleep was broken by Gilgamesh's shouting. This time more of the fifty woke and listened in alarm.

'Enkidu! Enkidu! Was it you? Who woke me? Who saved me?'

'Hush, my friend. All's well. I'm here. Enkidu's here.'

'Aah! Then I'm awake? I'm really alive?'

'Safe here, with your comrades round you.'

The hero's grasp was fierce on his friend's arm, but Enkidu suffered it. He waited till Gilgamesh's breathing had steadied enough to tell his dream.

'It was even more terrifying than the last one. Not a bull charging at me, that a fighter could grasp and wrestle. This time . . .' He could not help a shudder. 'A whole mountain attacked me. It fell on me. I tried to run. I couldn't escape it. My legs were buried. I was trapped. Then a light shone on me, unbearably bright. Out of the light a man appeared, more handsome than any human. He reached out his hand and pulled me out from under the avalanche, as though it was nothing to him. He gave me cool water to bring me round and set me down again where the ground was firm under my feet and the earth wasn't shaking . . . What does it mean, Enkidu? What are we up against?'

'Courage, son of Lugalbanda. Dawn is coming. Look, there's the last valley between us and the final pitch. Since you're awake, let's pick up our gear and walk down there. On the way, I'll tell you what I think . . .

'The mountain that fell on you is Huwawa, who will come at you like an earthquake. But the man of light is surely Utu. He will help you. Huwawa will fall, but the Lord will set you up on your feet as the victor.'

'Is that what you think? Are you sure?'

'What else could it mean?' The Wildman's eyes gazed up at the vast darkness of the shadow under the cedar trees.

'Stop here. Dig a well and find some water to make a libation. I'm going to climb to that rock like a table.'

The men waited in the valley bottom while the *en* of Uruk lifted his hands to the sky. They could not hear what he asked.

'Utu, are you listening to me? Give me victory. When my enemy falls on me, strengthen my hand and foot to stand against him. And what of Enkidu, who will be fighting beside me? You've given me fearful dreams, both warning and promise. What about the Wildman, my friend? Will you give him a dream too?'

The sun fell on the water the men had uncovered, on the burning rock and the scattered flour.

'Well, what news is there?' Inanna asked her brother, trying to disguise her eagerness.

Utu let his lips brush her bare shoulder.

'Dreams. Dreams.'

Inanna threw him off impatiently. 'Can they live? Tell me the worst!'

The Sun Lord smiled. 'You have heard Enkidu's interpretation.'

But Inanna wrapped her dress back over her shoulder and stared at him suspiciously.

'What dream will you send our Wildman?'

Her brother laughed, as he caught her in the crook of his arm, and shook his head.

That third night, Enkidu yelped and shivered like a stray dog caught far from home in an icy blast of hail. When he woke in darkness he cowered and hid his face in his arms. He did not dare to look up at the stars. He told no one his dream. But when Gilgamesh awoke with a shout, Enkidu forced himself to uncover his eyes. He hunched nearer to comfort and be comforted.

'Did you touch me, Enkidu? Why am I shaking like an autumn leaf? Has a Child of An passed by us? We're on Enlil's ground. I can't move my legs! Has he paralysed me now?'

'Did you dream again? Tell me, if you want to.'

'Yes. Yes, I dreamed again. I can't tell you the horror I felt this time in that nightmare. Words aren't enough. They're like pictures on a cup that has poison inside. This time Heaven itself roared at me. Earth bellowed back. I was a tiny speck between them. Daylight vanished. There was darkness without stars. Then lightning flashed, fire blazing all round me. I was in the middle of thunderclouds, raining death. Then even that terrible light was gone. The fire went out. And all around me was a rain of choking ash.

'Let's go back to that valley, Enkidu! Let's appeal to Utu again!'

Enkidu took his elbow, put his arms round him, pulled him close. 'My friend, my friend. The fire attacking you is surely Huwawa. He will do his worst against you, but his fire will go out. His body will collapse to earth like a rain of ash. That is surely the meaning of your dream.'

'Is it? Is it really? And you? Didn't you dream anything?'

But Enkidu hugged him strongly and said nothing except, 'See, you can move your legs again. Sleep now. We're almost at the summit. In the morning we'll purify ourselves. And then we'll cut your name on that cedar you've set your heart on.'

'Yes,' murmured Gilgamesh, rocked in Enkidu's arms like a tired child. 'Tomorrow we'll do it, won't we?'

\* \* \*

But in the morning Gilgamesh slept on. The sun rose, yet for a long time heavy darkness remained over the camp of the men of Uruk. They had bivouacked at the foot of the final peak, on the westward side, and the mighty shadow of Enlil's cedar grove lay deep over them. The fifty wrapped themselves in their cloaks and sat waiting, hardly speaking to each other, listening.

'Are those footsteps, making the ground shake?' asked Amu.

'Is that the roar of the wind in the cedars?' another wondered.

'There has been no wind for weeks.' said Enkidu. 'Utu has hold of them.'

Noon passed, and still the trees overshadowed them. Gilgamesh did not wake. More frequently now Enkidu went to stand over him, biting his lip. The king did not roll about, there were no shouts of nightmare. He lay still, in a deep unconsciousness.

'Can we hunt?' asked Luudu, a bachelor of Gilgamesh's age group. 'If it's only a hare for supper.'

'Don't go far,' warned Enkidu. 'Stay in sight of each other.'

The half-dozen who rose to their feet looked up at the cedar grove, like a vast, shadowy temple. They did not need a second telling.

At long last, in the late afternoon, the brilliant edge of the sun rode past the furthest fronds of cedar boughs and a brief sunlight lit the grass where Gilgamesh lay. He stirred slightly and creased his eyelids with a little moan. At once Enkidu was kneeling beside him, shaking his shoulder.

'Gilgamesh. Can you hear me? Are you well?'

Still the great face was closed in sleep, the mouth slack.

Enkidu shook him harder. '*En* of Kullab! How much longer are you going to sleep? The day is almost over. The sun is going down behind us. Once Utu goes to the house of Nin Gal the darkness will be on us even deeper than the shadow of these trees. Huwawa is above us. If you don't get up now, you may never rise again. Your fifty men will lie dead on this slope for ever. Nin Sun will run into the city square to wail that she is childless.'

'What?' Gilgamesh's eyes flew open with sudden awareness. 'Where am I? Is it you, Enkidu? What's wrong?'

'Nothing's wrong yet, master. Except that we are on

forbidden ground, come to do an unholy deed, and darkness is coming.'

Gilgamesh scrambled to his feet, agile for all his bulk. He seized the 'Word of Heroism', his mailcoat, and strapped it round his chest with Enkidu's help. The hunting party came hurrying back with a brace of hares. But no one was thinking of eating now. They checked the fastenings of armour and weapons. In the declining day they seemed the only living creatures, but they spoke in whispers, with many a look at the black mass of trees that hid the rocks of the summit.

'Do you think he's up there?' murmured Amu.

As though in answer, the earth moved under their feet. There came a rumble like summer thunder, far off but deep.

Gilgamesh, resplendent in all his armour, bent to kiss the crumbled soil, to Kigal, the Great Earth.

'By the immortal life of Nin Sun, who bore me, by the human courage of Lugalbanda who made me his son, may I be lifted up now on the knees of Ereshkigal, the Great Princess, as once Nin Sun held me up on her lap for the world to admire.'

'Hail! Gilgamesh!' His troops raised their weapons.

The roar broke louder above them. The cedars shook.

Gilgamesh lifted his axe to the skies. 'By the love of Nin Sun, by the fame of Lugalbanda, I shall not turn back to Uruk till I have vanquished this thing that waits above, whether it is an immortal or not!'

The sunset reddened violently. Enkidu screamed. 'Master! Did you see it?' All the men whipped round, but the flash of lurid light was already fading and the darkness between the trees was impenetrable again.

'What was it? What did you see? *Tell me!*'

Enkidu clung to him. 'Gilgamesh! Huwawa is everything the wild things told me, and worse. If you had seen him, you wouldn't be standing here calmly like a hero. Now that I've seen him myself, I'm terror-stricken, and I'm not a coward. His teeth are curved like a dragon's fangs. His face is horrible as a man-eating leopard's. Didn't you hear his roar? It's a storm flood that could sweep whole villages away before it. There were rays from his forehead . . . like lightning striking the canebrake and destroying it with fire . . . His aura was awful! It would be death to look at steadily.

'Listen, Gilgamesh, this expedition is folly; this is impiety.

Let's go home. Let's turn back to the city while we have the chance. If you go on, then I'll be the one who has to return without you. I'll tell your mother first of your glorious heroism, and she'll shout with laughter. Then I'll have to tell her the bitter news of your death, and hear her break her heart with weeping.'

The two great, warm hands of Gilgamesh enclosed his friend's arms. He looked Enkidu steadily in the eyes. 'I'm going up. No one is going to die for me. I'll protect my people. I'll set my name on the Land of the Living. Our loaded trading boats won't be sunk. Our women won't cut their fine dresses into mourning rags. The watchers on my walls won't be thrown down by our enemies. The houses in our towns and the huts in our villages will stand safe from fire. I, Gilgamesh, will ensure all this.

'Help me, Enkidu. Enki went against Kur, and his *magur* boat was smashed and sunk. But I will go against the Lords of the Above and snatch their Tree of Life from them. We'll look at this monster. We'll defy his dreadful aura. If there is fear there, we'll meet it and overcome it. If we face terror, we won't let it beat us. Eh?'

Still shaking, but his eyes locked in his friend and master's, Enkidu forced himself to say, 'Is this what your heart is still set on? Can't I persuade you? Right then, let's go forward together.'

They marched, every nerve strung warily, up the path towards the seven giant cedars. The light of evening slanted red upon the bark of trunks vaster than the towers of Gilgamesh's walls. A whole shady pleasure garden of Kullab could have been gathered under the branches of one single tree. As they came under its shadow their feet sank deep in the fallen needles of centuries.

'*Look!*' said Amu in a whisper that was nearly a scream.

'No! Don't look at it, whatever you do!' cried Luudu almost at the same moment.

One glance was enough. They saw a flash, redder than any lightning, from a cavernous mouth. Huwawa, rearing himself impossibly high above them, was swaying his mass on huge clawed feet. His matted hair flew, more terrifying than a lion's mane, as he sprang. They glimpsed the ridges of fat on his face, the gaping jaws, like some evil fish cast up by a storm from the depths of the sea. Fire leaped from his eyes, burning with rage through folds of flesh under lowering cliffs of bone, subsiding into holes black as the lair in the mountain behind him. He howled pure enmity against them. The red light sprang from under his forehead again, unbearable. They felt its heat as they flung their shields up. Even Gilgamesh trembled.

He did not turn back.

The path was almost level now, but it had become as difficult to force their muscles on as if they were climbing a vertical rock face. Still they did it, following their leader's footsteps.

Out of that constant roar assaulting their ears, battering their senses like storm waves flinging a ship against a cliff without mercy, thick words emerged that made an ominous sense.

'Bull of Uruk! Man with hair like Utu's sunrays, who wears the garment of heroism! A proud mother bore you; a proud nurse suckled you. Look to your fame. My Lord is merciful. Enlil will be gracious to you. Put your hand on the earth and submit to me. I shall let you go home, little man.'

'By the life of Nin Sun, I will get what the Anunnaki have! By the fame of Lugalbanda, I will never turn back! You? If you beat me, you can have my sister Geshtinanna for a foot-maiden! You can have my sister-in-law Inanna for your concubine! We've come with ropes to bind you. We shall put fetters on your hands. We shall fasten great shackles on your legs. I will lead you captive!'

As the proud rage swept over Gilgamesh, it had become more than his name carved for eternity on the sacred wood that he needed.

'Now, strike, men! Get me that biggest tree! I mean to have a throne and a bed like Inanna's!'

Gilgamesh's axe hit the tallest cedar. The grove shook with the impact of the blow. Sparks flew through the twilight and were answered by a dreadful rush of red from Huwawa's brow. Some screamed as it scorched them. The fifty men were in a circle, desperately hacking at the cedar to keep back their fear. Terror lent fury to their muscles, superhuman speed to their strokes. As Huwawa rushed to defend his treasure, the huge cedar shuddered from crown to roots. The men leaped back as it toppled with an enormous roar through the branches of its fellows and split the ground where it crashed to earth.

# Chapter One Hundred and Eleven

Huwawa howled, as though the axes had severed him. For a moment the awesome rampart of the felled cedar stood between its guardian and the men of Uruk. Then Huwawa sprang. The tempest of his monstrous head reared over the cedar wall, more fearsome than the vast, brown breaker that curls above the canal bank for a second before it smashes down to wreak destruction. Fire shot from his mouth dangerously among the shavings and sawdust. Men shrieked and leaped for unsafe shelter among the broken branches.

'Utu!' yelled Gilgamesh. 'If you love Inanna, help us!'

Inanna, in Uruk, cried out and clutched Utu's hand.

'What is happening?'

He smiled thinly. 'Your hero has overreached himself. We must see what Enlil's creature will do about this now.'

'Save him!' whispered Inanna, feeling the blood leave the taut skin of her face.

What else could Utu do, at the end of the day, among the dark of the still-standing cedars?

He loosed the winds of the eight points of the world from the caves where he had imprisoned them. He unleashed the north wind and the south wind, he loosed the whirlwind and the hurricane. He set free the sandstorm and the icy wind, the thunder-gale and the scorching simoom.

The storm winds raced across the forest lashing the living branches. They hurled themselves upon Huwawa from all directions. They flung the twigs and sawdust in his eyes. They beat his matted hair like whips across his face. Even the boughs of his own grove thrashed him mercilessly. The Uruk troop sheltered as best they could under the prostrate trunk.

And out of the farthest west a great voice called across the sky, '*Now! Seize him!*'

Gilgamesh and Enkidu were on their feet, clambering over

the cedar tree. Its great wall shielded them from the raging blasts. Then they were out in the opened space. They crouched, shielding their faces from flying twigs, and circled Huwawa. His claws were scrabbling at his eyes, masking their horror and blinding their deadly fire with blood.

'Yield, monster!' cried Gilgamesh, struggling to close in with his axe. His net was thrashing in his left hand.

'Stop! I'll submit. I can't fight against Lord Utu! Yes! Gilgamesh, the human, shall be my master. Take Enlil's tree! I'll build houses for you in Uruk with my own hands.'

Huwawa threw himself on the ground, felled like his beloved cedar. Enkidu's and Gilgamesh's nets flew over the ruined heap and bound him fast.

The winds rushed on down the mountain, bowing the forests before them. The sawdust settled.

'Now! Fell all the rest!' called Gilgamesh. And the men set to work.

The seven most magnificent cedars in the world lay cut for timber. Their trunks were hacked away from their roots. Their crowns were lopped. Their boughs, each mightier than a normal tree, were chopped off and bundled up. The exhausted fifty were still busy hauling and rolling their booty down the mountain. Huwawa lay and sobbed.

'Now,' said Gilgamesh, turning his attention at last to his prisoner. 'What are we going to do with you?'

The fire had gone out of Huwawa's eyes. His dragon teeth were chattering harmlessly. With the greatest difficulty they hoisted him to his feet and pushed him back to the rocks. On the naked summit, scarred with the splintered stumps, Huwawa's lair showed as a dark mouth in the rock wall. They pushed him in. They flattened him against the rock as one slaps at a snake in a cellar. Gilgamesh stuck a ring through his snorting nose, like a captured ox. Enkidu twisted rope round his wrists like a taken slave.

Huwawa's teeth rattled. His bound hands tried to clutch at Gilgamesh. 'Let me plead to Lord Utu! He put me here to guard the cedars of great Enlil. Why did he desert me? I have no mother. I have no father. The Land of the Living is all I know. By the Above and Earth and the Netherworld, be a father to me!'

Magnanimous in victory, Gilgamesh held out his hand. 'What can he do, Enkidu? The cedars are felled. I've got what

I came for, and far more. We'll find the first river that tumbles down through the mountains and float our booty back to Uruk. Imagine Inanna's face when she sees what I'm bringing!'

'And what of this beast?'

Gilgamesh raised his eyebrows. 'He pleaded for mercy. He's appealing to Utu. Well then, if he submits, let him go free. Let the trapped bird see if it can find a nest somewhere else. Let the orphan seek some other mountain to call his mother. What's he to us?'

'You'd regret that. If you let this bird go to his nest, and this orphan find a mother, you won't return to your own home and your own mother. Don't trust him. We've stolen his cedars. You may be the strongest hero in the world, but if you have no wisdom, Ereshkigal's *sukkal* will mark you down for death. Namtar will turn this glory into mourning.'

A flash of anger from Huwawa's lips, a crimson ghost of his extinguished fire. 'Why should Gilgamesh listen to you, a hired man? Gilgamesh the king? Gilgamesh the hero? You're only the slave who trails unwillingly behind him, eating his bread and his courage. What right have you to speak so ill of me to your king?'

'I, a slave? I, a coward? I'll show you! Liar!'

The cold starlight pierced the cave, sparkling along the length of Enkidu's suddenly bared sword. With a force of uncharacteristic savagery Enkidu whirled the blade. Huwawa's mouth opened in astonishment and terror. His black throat gaped.

Then, like a majestic stone lion from its pillar, his huge head tumbled at Gilgamesh's feet.

'There!' gasped Enkidu, in rage and shame. 'Now, call me a hireling! Now, call me a coward! Master, I brought you to the Land of the Living and I've saved your life here. Do what you want with me now.' The sun had gone down again, below the rim of Ereshkigal's Kur. Only the stars looked down on the cave mouth, silent, remote. The men were murmuring outside, very weary and shocked now. The stench of Huwawa's blood fouled the floor.

Gilgamesh moved, slowly, with a stiff reluctance. He embraced Enkidu formally, kissed both his cheeks.

'My friend. I never doubted your love or your loyalty. But it was not well done to kill a bound prisoner who had surrendered, the servant of Enlil.'

'You are your city's *en*. I'm only a savage,' Enkidu muttered against Gilgamesh's shoulder. 'Yet I think I'm the wise one. Nin Sun should thank me, Inanna should reward me, when I bring you back to them.'

'Well, it's done now. Open your knapsack, man. Is it big enough to carry your trophy home?'

# Chapter One Hundred and Twelve

'Will he never come back?' said Inanna from the terrace of the Limestone House. She stood staring north-east over the baked, unbroken plain. Dust hazes and mirages made it impossible to see the horizon. Heat sucked up the water led into the thirsty fields for the young corn. Vegetable gardens were watched over like jewels. The sheep were penned in their folds away from the summer crops, champing listlessly on last year's straw, or roamed the desert margins in search of what scrub they could find.

Geshtinanna sat more sensibly in the pillared portico, plucking her harp. The air did not move, except when slave girls fanned it, but there was shade. As the summer dragged on and the air thickened with a thunderous grey, she looked up often at the heavens. The songs of love and laughter with which she tried to cheer Inanna's loneliness could not help but drift into the minor key of lament as her skin waited for the first drops of rain and the change that must come for her.

'He, meaning Gilgamesh?'

Inanna's head spun round. It was not surprising that her face looked flushed, standing there so long in the sun even with the linen bonnet shading it. Then she turned abruptly back to her watching.

'Dumuzi will come with the rain ... I'm sorry, Geshtinanna. I never meant that you should suffer then.'

'Oh, but it would have hurt me far worse to live and sing in the Above while he ...'

'And I wanted to condemn him to eternal darkness. Go on, say it! I, his lover!'

'He hurt you,' she said softly. 'I can see that.' Her fingers found the soothing notes that could calm wrath.

Inanna's hands picked at the bitumen sealing the drain of the parapet. 'Must I hurt everyone I touch?'

'You give love, passion, war. You are dangerous, but you

are wonderful too. Your people would not have you otherwise.'

'But those I love? Those I love most!' She ran and threw herself on her knees beside Geshtinanna, buried her glorious head in the other girl's lap. Geshtinanna stroked the thick waves of blue-black hair, kissed the alabaster forehead unnaturally pale over the flushed cheeks.

'There, there. It will not be long. Autumn is almost here. The rains will break. He will come back.'

'And I shall lose you! Do you realise I know all the horror you are going to? Every day I must imagine what you made me allow you to do. But Gilgamesh?' She raised her great, dark eyes. 'Kur must have him by now. He went to challenge the Above, and his reward will be the Below.'

'Gilgamesh is not for you,' Geshtinanna said, a little sharply. 'I gave you one brother. Let Dumuzi be enough.'

'Half of myself is torn away every year, Geshtin. Couldn't I give something back in Dumuzi's place? Raise Gilgamesh higher?'

'Can't you deny yourself anything you want, Inanna? You and he, must you grab at life and power and fame wherever you see it?'

'We don't have your generous heart. We can't pour ourselves out for others, as you do. But where *is* he?' She got to her feet restlessly and went back to the parapet. 'Geshtin! Something's happened. Someone's coming. Look!'

'Is it a trail of dust on the chariot road? Is it them?' The hero's sister jumped up and ran to join Inanna.

'No. Not dust. A great train of barges on the river, coming from the north.'

Black, linked to black, like necklaces of toadspawn in the spring marshes, boats were coming downstream. Now they could see men standing triumphantly in the bows and stern. Great mounds of cargo weighed the craft down, threatening to ground them in the late summer shallows. As they floated nearer, the watchers now crowding the city's walls and roofs could see that they towed behind their upcurved sterns rafts wider still.

'He's returning?' said Inanna, awestruck. 'Gilgamesh has done it! He's felled all Enlil's grove of cedars. He's bringing them here!'

'Oh, the poor trees,' breathed Geshtinanna, clasping her hands together. 'Those great, proud, Sky-touching trees, reduced to baulks of timber.'

'The cedars from the Land of the Living, the mountain of the Anunnaki. What does it mean, Geshtinanna? You're wise. What has he done? What has he got?'

'Fame,' the Wine Girl said with an edge of bitterness. 'Glory. Pride.'

'Immortality? The Tree of Life?' There was a whisper of impossible hope in Inanna's voice.

'Can it win life, to destroy what will take thousands of years to replace?'

'For greatness, a great price must be paid.'

'Who pays your price?'

Even Inanna was silenced for a moment.

'It *is* Gilgamesh! He's stepping ashore. That must be Enkidu beside him. Listen to the crowd roaring! Oh, Geshtin. What a gorgeous figure! He *must* be more than a man!'

'You have . . . you had . . . a Son of An already. Will you stoop to a mortal after him?'

'Look at him waving!' Inanna snatched off her white bonnet and waved it back.

'He has his arm close round Enkidu. He loves him more than a brother.'

Inanna hung far out over the parapet, watching till the splendid, free-striding warrior passed from sight under the gate.

'Quick! Call a messenger! Gilgamesh must report to the E-Anna immediately to tell me how it all happened. I'll invite him to supper. Nawirtum! My bath, and my festival clothes!'

The soft-footed slave who had taken Amanamtagga's place bowed silently. She sped away to oversee preparations to make her mistress lovelier still.

'Inanna. Be careful. You and Gilgamesh are a dangerous mix.'

'We were made for each other. Mortal he may be, but he understands my soul better than Dumuzi ever did.'

'Dumuzi loves you.'

'I thought so once.'

The colour was flooding Inanna's face again. 'When the rains come, when Dumuzi comes home, the whole world will see how I love him. But he is not here now.'

'You know what Dumuzi is suffering.'

'Yes. What I was suffering while Dumuzi was sitting on my throne!'

* * *

Gilgamesh washed off the dust and sweat of the journey. He and Enkidu soaked themselves in scented baths. Slaves massaged hard-used muscles, combed and oiled hair, laid out rich robes. Gilgamesh walked from his bathroom, refreshed and triumphant, and let his valet wrap him in the layered cloth and tie a padded sash round him. Last of all, he placed on his head a new tiara set with seven golden shafts, like sunrays.

He appeared before Inanna as the setting sun was softening the glitter of her White House with voluptuous pink, like the heart of a rose. In his hands was a white kid, unblemished. Behind him came a procession of servants and soldiers carrying milk, butter, cheese, oil, wine, dates, all that the *en*'s estates could offer for his Lady. She already had a welcome waiting for him. Lamps burned like stars in the shadowy interior. Their scented oil added to the heavy warmth of the evening. Incense-burners made columns of blue smoke among the mosaic flowers of the pillars. Ivory plaques of bulls and leopards, lions and lambs looked down on the living tribute being brought in.

Inanna's kitchens had been busy. When the formalities were concluded, the guests sat down to tables heaped with meat, grape wine and date wine, barley beer and dark emmer beer, pomegranates and figs, honey and butter and fresh bread. Fish had been brought from the marshes by fast runners. Geese and teal lay in nests of their own feathers.

Inanna ate less than usual, but drank deeply. She had placed Gilgamesh opposite her and one of her curly-haired hierodules facing each of Gilgamesh's fifty heroes. Geshtinanna shared dishes with Enkidu. Between each couple were the jars of beer, plentifully refilled, and men and women both drank through copper tubes, mouths pursed around the warm metal, forming two halves of a separated kiss. Eyes met across the table with admiration, with promise.

When the wreckage of food was cleared, and the night was softly dark outside, Inanna rose, a little unsteadily. But she was still mistress of her intention. Her *sukkal* did not need to call for silence. Inanna's presence, with the strength of a sculptor's column, with the transcendence of a shaft of moonlight, was enough to still the noisiest crowd. She carried the authority of natural power. She had the hypnotism of sexual charisma. Men fell to the glance of her eyes as

Huwawa to Gilgamesh's net. Her women watched, admired and sought to imitate.

She raised her silver goblet reserved for wine. Gilgamesh, still seated, saluted her in return.

'*En* of Kullab. *Lugal* of Uruk. Your city and your Lady greet your safe return. Prayers have gone up for you, sacrifices have been made for you throughout this long, slow summer. The Anunnaki have not been allowed to forget your journey. I myself have knelt at my brother's feet and pleaded for you.

'You have told us of journeys and hardships, of watchmen and ogres overthrown, of the mighty cedars of Enlil fallen to the hands of mortals, to glorify this city. Still there is something yet you have not told me. You come wearing a new and wonderful crown. Where did it come from, this tiara with the seven golden shafts? What is its story?'

More than the oppression of heat seemed to thicken the heavy night. Enkidu stirred and growled. Gilgamesh's attention slipped from Inanna's hold. He took his friend's hand and squeezed it lovingly.

'We came, as travellers from the east must, down the first tributaries of the Idiglat, daring the rocks and rapids. We brought our cedar cargo into the arrow-swift river until it met Sumer's plain. Then we let the slow oxen draw us through the canals to join the broad Buranun. We came by way of the city of Nippur. That was a place of danger. We had cut down Enlil's grove. With Utu's help we had taken the cedars of the Lord of all the Anunnaki.'

'I am the Mistress of all the *Me* of the Earth!'

'Praise to Inanna who wields Enki's power! Yet, my Queen, it seemed prudent to us to pay the Lord of Air our respects, to give him homage for what he had allowed us to take.'

'I was carrying the head,' Enkidu said more roughly. 'The beast Huwawa's head, in my sack. I rolled it out on the floor in front of him.'

The women moaned deliciously, imagining the gory horror, fearful of Enlil's response.

'*What did he say?*' Inanna, too, was rapt in the calculation of her rival's reaction.

A darkness of anger was on Gilgamesh's face, a cloud of sulky fear in Enkidu's.

'He cursed us, for the death of Huwawa. He said our faces should be scorched. We should wander where heat blasts all food, where water is withered up. Then he gave a scornful laugh and called for these seven gold *melams* from his treasury. "These are the terrors that will protect you, Gilgamesh," he said, "lest you die too quickly before you learn the bitter truth." '

An uneasy silence lingered. Then Geshtinanna asked, looking across the table at her partner, 'And what of Enkidu? What protection does he have from the wrath of Enlil?'

'I will protect him!' cried Gilgamesh, surrounding Enkidu within one arm like a husband. 'I will defend his life!'

'I think you cannot do it,' said Geshtinanna softly.

The two men, two heroes large as each other but so very different, sat locked in comradeship while the festival company stared at them. Then Inanna flung the wine from her goblet over the table, throwing her arms wide gloriously. Her eyes blazed with triumphant laughter. Her mouth flashed in an exultant smile.

'Gilgamesh! King of Uruk! You are wonderful! What Lord in the Above would have dared do what you have? Only I, the Lion Inanna, have ever challenged Lord Enlil, who sets himself above all the Children of An. I too shall take what I want from him, as you have done! Glory be to Uruk!'

'Uruk! Kullab! Inanna and Gilgamesh!' The goblets clashed.

'Yes! Inanna and Gilgamesh.' The Lady swung her refilled beaker round, let her magnificent gaze both warm and shake everyone it touched. The hall hushed again, hung on her words, sensing a climax coming in the affairs of Uruk, drunk with success and danger and daring and power.

'Gilgamesh,' she said, making the words distinctly, 'now our delight is complete. You have come home to us bringing the cedars from the Land of the Living. I shall reward your daring. Today I am granting you a space within the precinct walls of my E-Anna. Build a new house here with your cedarwood, my *en*, my *lugal*. May your bedchamber lie close to mine, and may you step out from your hall's portico each morning to meet me coming from mine.'

A ringing cheer surged from Gilgamesh's men and the king flushed.

'More than that! You shall ride with me in a chariot of lapis lazuli and gold. Storm demons shall be the stallion mules that draw us. My women shall pour cedar perfume on my threshold and invite you to enter. All kings and rulers and sages and queens on Earth shall bow and kiss your feet. I am Inanna, supreme in the Above! Sheep shall bear twins for you and your goats triplets. Your pack-donkeys shall run faster than battle asses. You shall harness rare horses from the north to your war chariots. Your oxen shall have the strength of wild bison. And you yourself, when you come to my house, you shall be the most favoured of men.' Her hand reached out across the table and clasped his, electrifying. She raised it high, trying to bring him to his feet. Her voice rang through the house, sang to the stars, 'Honour Gilgamesh.'

Pandemonium broke from Gilgamesh's soldiers, from Inanna's prostitutes, from all the Lady's retinue gathered round her banqueting hall. Their shouts swept out into the night and fired the city. News sped through the E-Anna precincts, on down the mound, rousing the night-warm houses.

Only four people in the hall did not join the cheering.

Nin Shubur stood grave and silent.

'Inanna,' pleaded Geshtinanna. 'Dumuzi!'

Enkidu turned and clutched his master with a wild jealousy on his hairy face.

Gilgamesh lurched to his feet, his face aflame. 'I take your honour! Let Uruk sacrifice to Gilgamesh as well as Inanna. I will pronounce laws in the E-Anna in your place. In your judgment seat of the Gipar I will judge. I shall reign as your Lord.'

Inanna grew very still. Her eyes blazed, more brilliant than the *melams* of Gilgamesh's diadem. 'You too? Another man would steal my glory from me? No, Gilgamesh, to receive the beasts that are dedicated to me, I do not grant you. To pronounce laws in the E-Anna, I do not grant you. To sit in judgment in my Gipar, I do not grant you. You are a human being. You must remain so.'

Gilgamesh tore himself free from Enkidu's grasp and gripped the table. 'Lady Inanna, I beg you! I must be more than that. I have loaded your court with gifts. I will pay you anything you want. Herds of oxen and flocks of sheep, silver and precious stones from the mountains. Look, I have brought you a lapis lazuli vase, filled to the brim with perfume. Didn't I fell Enlil's cedars? Give me the reward of immortal power.'

'No. You have given me gifts, as befits the *lugal* of Uruk. And I have heaped favours on you in return. But this I do not grant. I, Inanna, have been to the Netherworld and back. I have wrestled with the Queen of Darkness. I won my way back to the sunlight and all the Earth was reclothed with new life at my rising. You have not done this.'

Inanna was staring at him with enormous eyes, as though she saw again in him the betrayal of Dumuzi, seated on her throne when she came back from the dead. Gilgamesh grew very pale. Words fought in his throat. He reached for Enkidu's hand, found the power of speech at last, more bitter than his assault against Huwawa, than his defiance of Enlil.

'Woman! Did you ask me to marry you then, just to be your toy? My brother married you. What must a man give for that privilege? Look what Dumuzi surrendered! If I am your husband what will I get in return?

'What did he who loved you get from you? You are a back door that doesn't keep out the icy wind. You are an unsafe palace that falls on the heroes inside it. You are an elephant that shakes off its saddlecloth and its rider. You are pitch that dirties the one who must carry it. A waterskin with a hole that wets the porter. A limestone block toppling from the rampart to kill a sentry. Jasper that buys betrayal to the enemy. An ill-fitting sandal that makes its wearer trip and fall.'

'*How dare you!*'

'I dared to go against Utu and Enlil. I will dare you too. Look at your husband! Do you think I will lower myself to become like him? Dumuzi, my brother, who loved you with all the folly of a starstruck boy. Where is he now? Tell me that! Year after year he must go to the Netherworld bewailing his fate, for the rest of eternity. You have broken his life in half, like the mottled *allulu* bird that lurches through your garden crying "*Kappi, kappi.* My wing! My wing!"

'Lions guard you. Seven of the finest draw your chariot. But you hunt them through the wilderness, and dig pits and traps for them. You were given a horse, a marvel in the land of Sumer, and you ill-treated that noble animal with whip and spur, making him gallop from sunrise to sunset just for your sport.

'They say you turned on your chief herdsman, who worshipped you and sacrificed the best of his kids to please you. You bewitched him into a wolf. Now his herdboys chase him away with stones, and his own dogs try to bite his heels.

'They say you fancied Ishullanu, your father's palm gardener. And when he refused you, because he was content with what he had, you turned him into a mole, to dig in darkness.'

'You slander your Lady! These are lies! Be silent, before I have your tongue torn from your mouth!'

'I am not Dumuzi. I'm no bird with a broken wing. I've beaten Enlil. I've cut down the cedars from the Land of the Living. Don't think you can break me like your other lovers! I can be king without you!'

Inanna stood rigid, like a limestone pillar of her own house. Her mouth stretched in a snarl like one of her copper lions. Then, with the force of a clap of thunder that breaks overhead, she overthrew the table, making the men on the other side scatter for safety. Gilgamesh leaped back, still clutching Enkidu. The Wildman hugged him fiercely with a proud gratitude.

'You think I wanted to *marry* you! Get out!' screamed Inanna at them. 'Get out of my house, out of my city, off my Earth!'

# Chapter One Hundred and Thirteen

When Inanna went storming up to Angal she found the sun smiling above a thickening atmosphere that should promise rain. An lolled on fleecy cushions under a vast, pale blue tent, like a nomad patriarch overlooking his herds. Inanna had scant regard for the beauty of the scene, for the remote peace far from the fretful wars and jealousies of humans. Tears of outrage were in her eyes. The pain of Gilgamesh's words was in her heart, all the sharper because some small part at least was true. A different pain because so much of it had been malicious gossip, in the city where she had believed herself adored, because he had not understood how she grieved for Dumuzi, because he could not see how deeply she had been hurt. But above all, fuelling her rage, was the colossal insult of the *en* of Uruk against his Lady of Uruk.

He had wished to supplant her.

Uruk should be trembling now within its stout, brick walls.

She flung herself before her great-grandfather. He saw, with a pang of remembrance of days long past, not a tall and splendid woman, magnificently beautiful even when distraught, but the furious little girl stamping her feet in the palace at Ur because she had not been given what she considered her right. That day he had determined to take her to live with him in Uruk, to school her. Remembering that, he found himself looking round to catch irreverent laughter in Enki's eyes again. But his wise, water-knowing son was far away. Enlil was there instead, lordly, disapproving. Of which of them?

Inanna threw herself at An's feet in a flurry of flounced skirts. He could not but admire the hair streaking back from her neck like angry snakes. He felt the breath of her fury hot on his knees under the net kilt. Almost unconsciously his hands were fondling her head. So long, so long. She had left

643

his failing age for the passionate youth of Dumuzi. She had not been wise.

'Gilgamesh has opposed me. He has insulted me. Me, the protector of his city! I will curse Uruk in its turn. I will break every brick of his walls. Help me, Great-grandfather.'

He stroked her hair, so thick and silky. 'I? I am an old man now. What can I do?'

'Give me the Bull of the Sky, Great-grandfather. Raise it for me.'

He started a little, uncomfortably, though few things surprised him now. 'Why should I do an evil like that? Uruk is my city too.'

She grasped his hands eagerly. 'Then he insults you and all the Children of An when he illspeaks me! I was made to stand, like a wife at a divorce court, while he enumerated every lying tale against me. I was humiliated! There was not a man I have quarrelled with, not a pet I have grown tired of, but he flung it back in my face! I, his Lady! He wants to rule from the E-Anna!'

An stirred again, wanting to back away, like a man standing too close to a furnace. 'My child, my child. Even the Anunnaki are not above question. Is nothing of what he says true? Have you never hurt men and beasts who served you well? Women, too . . .'

'I have protected my women. I have always cared for my people. Shall Gilgamesh be my judge? A mortal? My rival?'

'If you really did not wish to marry him, how can his refusal hurt you?'

She jumped up and ran passionately to her great-grandmother. 'Nin Mah, Great Mother of us all. You understand, don't you?'

The old, maternal hulk of the Exalted Lady shifted more sympathetically than An. She took her great-granddaughter's hands in palms that smelt earthy. 'I think I do, my love. You're a giving woman. You've got all the riches of our kind dammed up inside you. You were willing to give him more than any *en* could dream of, and your city and the land and the people would have grown richer still along with him. How can the farm prosper if the farmer won't lift the sluicegate and let the floodwater through?'

'He calls himself a hero. He is a coward! Because he thinks my flood is dangerous, because it has breached a bank before; he would rather his land should die of thirst, so long as he alone was exalted!' She spun round to An. 'Give me the Bull!'

An's eyebrows rose questioningly to Enlil. The Lord of Nippur's face was set, angry. Inanna would not wait for either of them to answer.

'If you do not do what I ask, I will wreak worse vengeance! I will batter down the doors of the Netherworld. I will let Ereshkigal have her day on Earth. Even Ninurta will not be able to protect you. I will not be your champion. All the shades since the time of human creation will swarm out of Kur! The dead will eat up the land of the living. The Below shall devour the Above!'

'Wild words, wild words.' An shook his head. 'You have been hurt, and you want to hurt others. Have you considered what you are doing if I loose the Bull of the Sky?'

'Yes, of course I have!'

'Lion Inanna, the Bull is Ereshkigal's mate.'

'I know that.'

Again An looked at Enlil. He nodded slightly, with a small smile of satisfaction. The Sky Lord leaned towards Inanna and continued carefully, 'It is almost time for the breaking of the rains. If the Bull comes out, and the Lion does not fight him, what will happen?'

'The heavens will not roar. The clouds will not collide. The rains will not fall.'

'And Uruk? Your people, your city? What will become of them?'

She raised her head proudly. 'Father An, I see you do not know me. My quarrel is with Gilgamesh. With Enkidu,' Enlil moved involuntarily at that name, a spasm of dislike in his face, 'Enkidu who stole Gilgamesh's love for me, who made him believe he could rule like a Child of An. My city is strong. My city is prosperous. I have blessed my people. Their barns are full to overflowing. Their treasuries are piled with traded goods that could buy far more. There is fodder for thousands of cattle and sheep. They have dug reservoirs and filled them, planted shade trees, dredged and repaired every irrigation channel. Not one child in Uruk will starve, though the rains should be shut up for seven years. I only want to show them that Gilgamesh does not have my power.'

The hands of Enlil gripped the sides of his skirt, nothing more threatening. He managed to keep his voice low and level.

'My father, Inanna has been insulted. This Gilgamesh is a

dangerous being. Almost Anunnaki, he presumes too much. Nin Mah,' he inclined his head to his mother, 'made the creature Enkidu to ease the suffering of Uruk. But it has led to . . . this problem. It angered me to know that Utu and Inanna had conspired against me to take the part of Gilgamesh and Enkidu. Now they can see the folly of their youth. You understand now, Inanna, where such overweening pride has led your favourite. It is too late to call back their treason. My cedars are felled, and Huwawa is dead.'

The hot and painful colour mounted in Inanna's face. 'I must admit you were right, Grandfather. This time.' Her head was high, belying the apology.

The two turned to An, he wind-fair, she star-bright. Before the power of their double stare he hesitated, capitulated. 'Very well, very well. Call Ninurta, Ishkur, all the Lords of Storm.'

The Warrior Lords came racing across the plains, their chariots sped by *umu* demons.

'My sons, my grandsons. Stand back. This year, Ereshkigal will have no cause to mourn her husband. I am raising Gugalanna from his byre in Kur. The Bull of the Sky will snort and paw. No one will fight him. Not you, Ninurta, not you, Ishkur, not Inanna.'

'But if we don't—'

'We know, Ishkur! I am not a fool. This battle will not be fought in the Above. The Lion will not bring the Bull down in a rain of blood. The Bull will trample the Earth.'

'Do they know what that means?' Ninurta whistled, and exchanged glances with his sons.

'Those that are rash enough to follow Gilgamesh are about to learn.'

The rest of the Anunnaki, Ladies of grain and weaving, Lords of fisheries and brick-making, watched in an appalled silence as the Warriors of Storm signed their assent. Below, the copper glint of the Buranun trickled through lowered mud banks. The pale green shoots of barley thirsted for the cool drench of rain. The people squatted at their tasks on the rooftops lifting their faces to the sky, waiting.

Inanna went to the stables of Angal, stroked her seven lionesses, checked that they were securely chained. 'Rest easy, my beauties. Eat well. Take your sleep. We shall have another hunt, another battle, one day soon.'

Then she took her place on the Stairs of the Sky to watch what was coming.

He was a great, black bull, powerful at the shoulder as a mountain range. His thighs were polished obsidian, his eyes were red as jasper. His upthrust horns sparkled like limestone. The snort of his nostrils spattered the Anunnaki with rain. Seeing him led like that, the ring through his nose, the ropes like hawsers, Inanna's heart ached for the flash of gold, for the released Lion, for the yell of the charioteers of the Children of An and the rolling, golden wheels, the dancing weapons, the attacking Storm Lords, and herself, spear raised, and all the stars of morning glittering on her forehead.

She felt in her heart the shock and terror of their meeting. The bellow and the roar. The peril of those horns to sweet, white flesh. The stiffening of the nerve. The spear pointed against a rampart of bone. The effort of courage and will to bear that slender blade against the single spot of vulnerability. To lean her weight and find herself rushing towards the encounter, driving in, the spurt of thick, rich blood, the yielding, tottering, swaying mass. The great collapse. The roar of triumph. Did it come from her? And then the steady rain.

And afterwards . . . Dumuzi.

But this year? Trembling a little, with a feeling of unreality, she walked across the topmost step and took the rope from An. He looked unsure too, a little ashamed, as though his children should not be stooping to make war on their humans. But Anunnaki had wrought far worse destructions upon their cities than this. This was only against Gilgamesh.

Gilgamesh and Enkidu.

Her hands were steady on the rope now. The Bull's eyes burned in his lowered head. How much did he understand?

'Inanna!' whispered Nin Gal, but hushed the warning with her own hand.

Inanna loosed the rope. Great Gugalanna swung his head from side to side, then raised it suddenly and bellowed.

The humans lifted their faces and listened. They saw the great, black shadow above them and smiled.

The seven chariot lions roared from behind shut doors. Ninurta's wild-sired stallion asses brayed defiance.

Now the Bull made a rush across the step. The Anunnaki whirled their skirts as they backed hastily away. Then to the other side. He met no resistance. Again that hollow, baffled bellow. Ninurta and his sons grounded their spears but held their shields prepared.

Now Inanna was backing down the steps in front of him, almost dancing. Her arms were weaving an invitation.

'Come on, my darling. Descend, Ereshkigal's mate. Come, Jailer of Life, Bringer of Death. Come and meet the man who is waiting for you. Humiliate him!'

From a safe distance, hushed, the Anunnaki watched them go down the long, shining stairs that led to An's own Sky House, to the roof of the topmost room of the E-Anna. A young priestess in white, dancing before an enormous snorting black bull.

Gilgamesh saw them descending the steps. All the citizens of Uruk stood gripped in terror. The king laughed, a short, savage bark.

'So that's her vengeance. I'll show her. Get out the *pukku* she gave me, Enkidu. Run! Beat it with the *mikku* as hard as you can. Call all the war troop of Uruk to battle!'

# Chapter One Hundred and Fourteen

He came like a destroying cloud, bringing blood not rain. The huge size of him darkened the E-Anna below him, spread his shadow over the whole city. The waters of the Buranun turned sullen, lightless. Masking their terror, the sacred prostitutes of Inanna, her priestesses, her adolescent virgins lined the terraces and staircases in full regalia. Priests beat on tambourines and made the harp praise the Bull. Even the stone lions viewed their old adversary with awe.

For all his enormous bulk, he stepped with delicacy on polished, moon-bowed hooves. His tail, more powerful than any whip, swung from side to side. Inanna danced down the steps before him. Her burning eyes were locked with his. Both moved with an animal grace in a slow weaving trance, full to the brim of their unsubdued souls with power and passion.

Down the sky-thin, shining stair, beyond which the faces of the watching Anunnaki were lost in cloud trails. Inanna's foot touched the highest roof, and her priestesses breathed a dubious welcome. Gugulanna followed her.

The clay shrine shook under him, as with the first tremor of an earthquake. The shiver ran all down through the clustered architecture of the E-Anna precinct. It tossed the leaves in Kullab's gardens. It sent the pots of Uruk's houses rattling. Gilgamesh's gate trembled. Waves lashed the moored boats at the White Quay. On the open ground between the walls and the river, Gilgamesh, Enkidu and their army gripped their weapons tighter for courage as they struggled to regain their balance.

Maidens and mothers, children and men past fighting age crept to courtyard doorways or looked out from the roofs of houses. They feared this epiphany of the immortals' wrath that was descending solid stairs now, crossing the E-Anna's courts, shouldering his way through gateways. But they were afraid also to be caught indoors in their shuddering houses. So fragile is the clay of mud-brick buildings. So fragile the clay of mortal flesh.

The Bull was loose in Uruk. When he burst out of the Lion Gate from the E-Anna, Inanna was no longer leading him. His huge, snorting face drew screams from the first citizens. Files of sacred women with flowers and musical instruments and waving palm branches escorted him in a colourful, dancing file. But he chose his own course.

Down the broad processional way, hooves forcing the shards of its paving into the stone-hard ground. Sparks flew in the darkness under his massive belly. His tail lashed from wall to wall sending a thunderous drum roll down the road ahead of him. He crossed the market square, a huge eclipse of the glaring sunshine. Quaking gatekeepers had the leaves of cedarwood and bronze pulled back to their fullest extent. No one in Uruk wanted to detain the Bull within the walls. The Lady's staff flocked up to the city ramparts to watch what was going to happen.

Inanna, magnificently colourful now in a high priestess's robes and turban, stood on the E-Anna's own walls. Between the splendour of cloth and jewels her face was pale with passion and retribution. The attendants who stayed with her, and Nin Shubur and Geshtinanna, were subdued and apprehensive.

The Bull emerged from the Water Gate, and a roar broke from the throats of all the young men waiting, like the baying of hounds when a great boar charges from the canebrake.

They were coming at him, through the braying rams' horns, the constant pounding of the *pukku* drum. Gilgamesh was running up the ramp. Enkidu was beside him, swinging a mace, with his dagger in his left hand.

The Bull's bellow crashed like colossal thunder. A storm of dung burst from behind him, spattering the city walls. Fire snorted from his nostrils. The foul stench checked the force of the onrush.

'Charge!' yelled Gilgamesh, rallying them. 'What's one Bull against a thousand heroes?'

It was the Bull who charged. With one furious leap he crossed the space towards the stumbling left wing. Too late they saw the ground fissuring before the authority of his hooves. A chasm opened. As he snorted rage, a hundred, two hundred, three hundred men tumbled into it, smothering each other, crushing each other, spearing each other in their fall. The onrush slackened again in horror. The weakest tried to turn.

'Kill! Avenge them!' ordered Gilgamesh at them in a hoarse shout.

As the young men struggled to obey, the hooves descended and the heavy head drove towards the right. The treacherous earth gave way again under the Bull of the Sky. Another three hundred, rank after rank, lurched over each other into the sudden abyss.

The rest backed off, retreating desperately to the river. Only Gilgamesh remained standing in the unbroken centre, with Enkidu a step or two in front, protectively.

A woman's wail trembled from the city wall, plaintive as a ewe lamb in the still, shocked air. Even the parents who had seen their sons fall had locked their hands over their mouths after that first heartrending scream. They waited, dry-throated as an autumn without rain, for the final act.

A third snort, almost casual in its contempt. Fire blazed along the ground. Like a lapidary's tool that opens up a fault in the jewel, a crack of darkness split, widened, gulped suddenly at wildly kicking legs. Enkidu fell in.

Screams then from the watching city. Gilgamesh was on the edge. His friend, his battle-twin, was gone. The king stood paralysed. Then, with the strength of his savage, steppe-wild running, Enkidu braced himself against the closing walls of the chasm and vaulted out. A groan of superstitious horror greeted his appearance. He was like a shade sprung from the Netherworld, dirty, weaponless, grey-faced under the soil of the escaped tomb.

He was face to face with the enraged Gugalanna. Gilgamesh was on the other side of the fissure. Before his friend could stop or help him, Enkidu seized the giant, lyre-curved horns in the moment when they swept down to gore him. His tautly-muscled arms catapulted him into the air. A sea of spittle whitened a vast tract of earth, like salt drying in the fields after a flood. Another drench of dung behind. Gugalanna's tail whipped it into a miasmal fog. Still Enkidu clung on. Then, dancing light-footed along the contorted back, he yelled to Gilgamesh.

'I've lost my weapons, brother. The kill is yours! Between the nape of the neck and the horns is the place.' He was down in the muck and the wildly kicking hooves. Blinded, he seized the cable-like tail and twisted it, and then hung on with superhuman strength. Like an eagle in flight, Gilgamesh sprang across the rift. He was dodging the slashes of the Bull's stone-sharp horns. The black shoulder towered over him. The great neck was crazed with sweat and spittle. Slippery with fear and ordure, his hands were round his copper axe. The mighty blade curved. The stroke that cut the *huluppu* tree, severed the Mushsagkal Serpent, felled Enlil's cedars, now found the place of fatal entry behind the horns of the Bull.

The matchless monster of ebony, the blinding brightness of stone and lapis lazuli horns staggered and reeled through waves of blood. The jasper eyes and scarlet tongue gasped for life. So short a time since the cowherds of An had led him up out of the byre of eastern Kur. And now the shadows of the west were darkening his eyes. His weakened knees stumbled a dance of death. The two heroes stood back. With the awful finality of the drum roll that closes the tomb of a king, his shoulder crashed against the hard-baked earth. From far beneath, Ereshkigal howled.

The legs that had trodden the Stairs of the Sky twitched and were still. The breath that Enlil had given stirred no more in the soft caverns of his muzzle. The foul stink of death choked the hot air.

A thin cheer, ragged with grief and revenge, rose from the citizens of Uruk. Victory for their king and his Wildman friend, too late to save their sons.

Inanna's retinue lined the walls in an appalled silence.

Then Inanna screamed, with a madness of shock and disbelief. She was running down the empty street, distraught as a servant girl panting towards a door that will shut her out at sunset.

For a while she could not see what was happening beyond the gate. Blood was dancing before her eyes. The sun beat down on the closed lanes of the city. From the massive wall ahead of her came the outraged moan of her household.

The Lady, incandescent herself with rage, burst out into the blazing sunlight beyond the darkness of the gate. The Buranun dazzled her like burnished copper. There was a huge blackness on the ground that tricked the eye. Then she saw blood, vivid as an accusation. Bright blood on Gilgamesh's hands as he held up the Bull's heart to the sun.

'Glory be to Utu who gives strength to the king!'

'Praise to brilliant Utu!'

The mutilated corpse of Gugalanna steamed in the sun.

'Where are the lapidaries? Where are the armourers?' yelled Gilgamesh like a man who has banqueted too well. 'Cut those horns off! Let Inanna have them for her perfume flasks.'

With a howl, Inanna doubled back into the gateway, dashed up the stair to the city ramparts. She towered over her human priests. She flung her arms to the sky. Her voice of grief and passion hurled down curses on the heroes that turned the citizens ashen and made the listening Anunnaki murmur in answering pain.

Enkidu was clutching handfuls of the Bull's intestines, like reddened rope. Fire was already smoking. He turned his bloodshot eyes on Inanna. Like a man drunk and blasphemous, when he heard his friend cursed he flung back imprecations of his own.

He dropped the Bull's intestines. His bloodied fists wrenched at the fallen magnificence of the Bull. He tore the colossal thighbone from the right shoulder. The gory mass of hair and meat and bone whirled through the air and struck the astonished Inanna, ringing on the breastplate 'Come, Man, Come'. Her face and chest were smeared with blood. She staggered back, gasping with the force of the impact and the blow to her authority. Beauty, terror, adoration, awe were snatched from her like a kitchen maid's skirt in a backyard fight.

Enkidu's voice, blood-thick but powerful, hurled his hatred after the thighbone. 'You speak so to King Gilgamesh! You're the foul thing that escaped from the Netherworld carrying death! If I could get up on that wall and tear your own shoulder out, I'd do it gladly. I'd tie these guts round your waist and pull the knot tight!'

The tears were tumbling down Inanna's face. She knelt on the rampart walk, keening over the great black wreck of the Bull's forequarter, like a woman over her slaughtered baby.

'Oh, Gugalanna! Oh, hero of Angal! Creation of An! Champion who looked for the golden Lion to come springing at you, and met the bloody blasphemy of human weapons. This is not how I meant it to be. This is not why I danced before you. Forgive me! Avenge me! Oh, my great black Bull! My Gugalanna!'

The priests and priestesses, the prostitutes, the young,

vowed virgins, all knelt around her, lamenting. Their crimped hair matted in the seeping tide of blood. Unconsciously they imitated the age-old wail of Ereshkigal for the untimely fall of her Bull.

But Gilgamesh and Enkidu walked with the uneven steps of the greatly weary, their heads held defiantly high, through the stunned remnant of their army, down to the edge of the glittering Buranun. They waded in and sluiced the blood and slime and filth from their almost naked bodies. The sun burned fiercely through the droplets on their skin. They washed the blood from their weapons.

When they turned, the walls were ominously empty and silent. The sound of a mourning procession was going up the hill to the E-Anna.

Tentatively, like beetles scuttling from under furniture, at once hurrying and afraid, craftsmen were coming out into the open. They gathered round the carcase.

'That's a tremendous pair of horns. Even the elephants of Dilmun couldn't touch them.'

A stoneworker handled them. 'Limestone quartz, veined with lapis lazuli. No wonder they sparkled fit to blind you.'

'And how's that for a hide? Pure black, and not a blemish.'

'Except for a missing leg!'

The lapidaries exchanged glances and set to work. It took a long, hard sawing.

'I never saw a thickness of horn like this. There must be thirty *minas* of lapis apiece in them.'

Gilgamesh reached out his hand. Enkidu's was cold as he said, 'She will hate me now. Purify her city with fire and incense, master. Make amends for both of us. Offer her the heart of the Bull to show respect.'

'It was the heat of battle. She's a warrior herself. She should understand. If we give her the horns and the heart and beat our breasts a bit, it will all blow over.'

The Wildman's loving eyes glowed back at him. Hand in hand, like two guilty boys, they walked at the head of their retinue back into the waiting city, with the dazzling horns carried before them. The Bull's great weapons were reversed in defeat, pointing to the Below.

The people of Uruk crowded the rooftops in silence. They watched from the shadows of the alleys. Gilgamesh, turning his glowing face from side to side, shouted at them. 'What's wrong with you? Maids of Uruk, have I left you alone too long since I found Enkidu? Have you gone cold on me? Then I shall have to warm you up! Give us a shout! Who's the most glorious hero in the inhabited world? Who is the greatest man on Earth?'

And all the young women, cowed by that imperious stare, sang back to him as he required, 'Gilgamesh is our glorious hero! Gilgamesh is the greatest king on Earth!'

The young men who had survived feasted drunkenly that night.

When his master was laid out at last in the safety of slumber, Enkidu staggered to his own couch in the next room. Sleep was lying in ambush for him.

# Chapter One Hundred and Fifteen

Utu stroked Inanna's back in sympathy.

'Is it time now?'

'I honoured him.' She could hardly speak for the dry sobs that choked her.

'The rain is falling. Dumuzi is coming back.'

She caught his hand and held it. 'Help me! From the very first, I gave that man treasures. The *pukku* and *mikku*. I made him my *lugal*, my *en*. I would have given him more than any other mortal!'

'Save it for Dumuzi.'


'You look as though you've got a hangover worse than mine. We may be the greatest warriors in the world, but we're out of training for carousing.' Gilgamesh nursed his head in his hands and examined his friend with bloodshot eyes.

Enkidu did indeed look ill. He stood respectfully in his master's presence but his hand gripped the curved sides of a chair to steady himself.

'Sit down, man. You're swaying like a ship in a gale. You look as if you're about to be seasick too. What's the matter with you? Are you hankering after onager's milk on the steppe again instead of good emmer beer?'

Enkidu retched, then collapsed into the offered seat and caught his friend's hands.

'Master, I thought I'd sleep like the dead last night after what we did. That was a victory! But . . .' His voice trailed into silence and his eyes wandered past Gilgamesh's shoulder, as though he saw beyond the watery horizon. A benign rain was falling, pattering steadily through the autumn leaves. There was a scent of fresh lemons in the air. From somewhere in the kitchen quarters a girl was singing. The Bull was dead. The rain was falling. Life was being renewed.

Enkidu's fists balled, crushing Gilgamesh's fingers. 'We saved the city, you and I. We ought to be honoured like heroes. We fought like the warriors of Angal, Ninurta, Inanna.'

'And so we are heroes, old friend. What's the problem? Uruk will put on a great feast for us. I've told the council. That lot at the E-Anna will do their duty. I'll stand for no sour grapes from them. It was a fair fight. Enough of our side got killed. And I'll tell you something else. The girls of Uruk, I've been letting them off lightly since you came. But I've a mind to celebrate this victory in the old way. Do you want to join me?' He winked with the heavy conviviality of bleared eyelids.

Enkidu snatched his hands away. 'I had enough of that when Inanna tricked me with her harlot. I lost the speech of my friends in the wild.'

'You've got me, though. Isn't that friendship enough for one man in his lifetime? Gilgamesh the king?'

A long, warm moment of silence between them. Enkidu forced a smile. 'For that, yes. It was worth dying for.'

'Dying? Who's talking of dying? We won, man. We won!' Enkidu hung his head. Gilgamesh strove to make his powerful voice gentle. 'There's something really wrong, isn't there? Do you want to tell me?'

The words came quiet but steady from Enkidu's ash-grey face. 'I dreamed. Last night I dreamed I was a prisoner at a law court. There should have been two of us but you weren't there. The judges were An and Enlil and Enki and Utu.'

'No Ladies? Not even Nanshe the Just?'

'No. The crime before them was all our heroic deeds. Killing Huwawa, felling the cedars, slaying the Bull.'

Gilgamesh chewed his moustache. 'We fought them fairly. We risked our lives!'

'Father An asked for the death sentence. One of us must die. And Lord Enlil pointed the finger at me and said, "Enkidu is the one, because he slew Huwawa." '

'I killed the Bull!'

Enkidu shook his head hopelessly. 'Utu spoke up for us at first. He confessed that he'd listened to our requests and accepted our gifts. He'd helped our expedition and strengthened our hands against the Bull of the Sky. But Enlil flew into a terrible rage. "Would you take the side of humans against the Children of An? You talk like a mortal yourself.

This man humiliated your own sister!"

'Then Prince Utu was silent. No one else spoke for me. I saw Father Enki's eyes watching me, very bright. For a moment I hoped. Then I remembered how he's always loved Inanna. He saved the future of all humankind at the time of the Flood, but he wasn't going to save me. An pronounced the sentence of death on me. And they all said "*Heam*".'

The two sat listening numbly to the falling rain. Neither suggested they take the dream to a wise woman to interpret it. The meaning was plain. Now it was Gilgamesh's turn to make a ball of his fist and crash it down upon the chair.

'Why you? I am the king! I am the son of a Lady! I did all this!'

'They love Inanna,' murmured Enkidu. 'In spite of all she's done to them, they still love her. An, Utu, Enki. And Lord Enlil has to defend the pride of the Above. You insulted Inanna. But when she cursed you with the Bull of the Sky, I was the one who flung her bloody oath back in her face.' Tears of despair squeezed painfully from his eyes.

Gilgamesh strode the room like a leopard in a cage. 'Inanna? Let her see! I'll rut the young women of her city like a stag going through a herd of does. I'll show her! Is she going to wave death in front of us to taunt us with our mortality? I'll show her a man's life before I'm finished! Love and War, is it? She's going to see both in plenty, till I drop from exhaustion. Will you join me, Enkidu? We'll go to war on the girls of this city, and by all the priggish Daughters of An, we'll have the lot of them on their backs! Get the *pukku*. Get the *mikku*. Beat them in all the streets. Yesterday it was the men's call to battle; today it's their sisters' duty to bleed.'

Enkidu tried to smile, a bleak, nightmare travesty of mirth. 'Very well, sir. As you say, if our life is short, we might as well live it to the full. Is there some more of that beer?'

They gave the women no mercy. In houses weeping for the six hundred lost to the Bull there were widows, sisters-in-law, mothers even, as well as virgins. Gilgamesh appeared determined to take them all. During days of orgy and nights of drunkenness Enkidu loyally went before his friend and master. The *pukku* beat for their coming. Only the thunder of the rains was louder. If Gilgamesh's fleshly weapon failed, the *mikku* stick pulsed on.

The council of elders had appealed once to the Anunnaki.

Enkidu had been their answer. Now he too had fallen to the charisma of the bright-haired king. The oppression was worse than before. Pure Inanna herself had been mocked, humiliated.

Still, from the high E-Anna came the sound of singing.

'Lord Dumuzi's back, by the sound of it.'

'Uruk's womenfolk won't be celebrating that this year.'

'She won't come down here again.'

'She wouldn't risk meeting Gilgamesh face to face!'

'The young women of Uruk may cry out to her, but she can't help them.'

'It seems like one human's stronger than all the Anunnaki, after all.'

And their eyes turned resentfully to the windowless outer walls of the precinct.

It was a girl of nine who ended it. But not before Gilgamesh had deflowered her, painfully. Gimkuzu, Servant of Wisdom. A child without a mother or father or brother to stand up for her. While other victims wept on their mother's shoulders in the privacy of their courtyard houses, shutting their shame from the world, Gimkuzu had fallen to her king in Inanna's millhouse, where widows and orphans go to find work and protection.

When it was over, she jumped up from the stained fleeces on the floor, ran past the sobbing matron and the outraged overseer into the open street. Her skirt was half torn away; blood streaked her legs. As she flew past, women gasped and veiled their eyes. Men's faces coloured. The girl's hair was wild but her black eyes blazed with righteous indignation.

The market square was a subdued hum of business, an attempt at normal trading. But it was falling ominously still even before Gimkuzu reached it. Enkidu was beating the *pukku* down a side street towards them, with Gilgamesh following unsteadily after. Gimkuzu reached it from another alley. She sped on, out into the open, like a wounded bird.

In the midst of the colourful mats laid out with the wealth of Uruk, the pots, the metalwork, the beads, the sweetmeats, the vegetables, the charms and medicines, she pointed the finger across at her city's king. Her voice rang to the Above with the age-old cry for justice,

'I-UTU!'

The sun shivered in the sky. From beyond the scattered flock of clouds a great voice rolled around the walls.

'*It is indeed time!*'

Enkidu was stepping into the square. He stumbled backwards as a shudder rippled across the surface like a lion waking. Light flashed in a thousand puddles between the heaving potsherds of its paving. Piles of apples and figs went tumbling into chaos. Copper pans clashed. Groans and screams, as merchants and customers clutched each other, bargaining now for life. Darkness ran, like a stylus scoring across a clay tablet, between Gimkuzu and her oppressor. The damp underground subsoil of the chasm steamed in the sun.

The city stilled. The hymns and drumming, that had formed a background of music from the E-Anna unregarded, were noticeable now by their silence.

Gilgamesh clutched Enkidu by the shoulder to steady him.

'Are you all right, friend? That was a close call! I thought I'd lost you again.'

'They've gone,' said Enkidu, staring into the bottomless abyss just in front of him.

'What's gone? The girls of Uruk? Don't worry. I can see one or two still left on the other side of this hole.'

'Your *pukku*. Your *mikku*. The things Inanna gave you. I dropped them.'

'What?' The king shouldered past Enkidu and peered over the edge. Enkidu caught his sleeve and tried to pull him back.

'Master! Be careful!'

'Surely the Bull is dead?' But he stared deep into the underground for a long time, then rubbed his eyes as though to brush away the darkness. He turned back to Enkidu and studied him with a slowly growing disbelief. 'Is it true? The *pukku*, the *mikku*? They're down there? You've lost them?'

'The Netherworld snatched them from me,' said Enkidu hotly.

A ragged, disrespectful cheer broke from the other side of the abyss and the recovering townspeople.

'Praise be to Utu!'

'He's taken the *pukku*!'

'He's broken the *mikku*!'

'He's heard the cry of the weak at last and thrown down the mighty!'

Gimkuzu slowly lowered her accusing arm and began to cry.

Gilgamesh turned on his heel and sat down heavily on the

ground, with his hunched back to the chasm. Tears streaked his own dusty cheeks. He buried his face in his hands, like a boy mourning a lost toy.

Enkidu watched him. Dread and love wrestled together in his face.

# Chapter One Hundred and Sixteen

Inanna was in bed with Dumuzi, as desperate with desire as Gilgamesh himself, but more joyful. She clasped and rolled him, biting his ear. 'Oh my *lubi*, my *labi*. I've missed you so much. If I could only have you for always. If I could devour you each night, and find you whole in the morning.'

An animal wail of pain broke from Dumuzi. 'It was you sentenced me to the Below! It is awful! Must I go back to that again, year after year? Save me from it, Inanna. You must!'

She murmured against his throat, 'Geshtinanna has gone to the Netherworld in your place. Would you leave her there for ever?'

She felt him grow cold and still beneath her. Heard a little hiccup. 'Geshtin. We pass each other on the river road, weeping. Shall we never be together again, she and I?'

'Geshtinanna does not weep for herself, only for you. Oh, Dumuzi, Dumuzi. Why did you do it? Why were you unfaithful to me? Why did you make me angry with you?'

She held him strongly, forced him into her again. His hands played with her hair.

'I don't know. You make the red blood beat so hot in me, in all of us. I couldn't bear your absence. It was like a little Netherworld to me, without life, without love. All women call you their Lady. You live in their flesh, you flower in their secret parts. It was *you* I loved in her, Inanna! In all of them. You must believe me.'

'Too late,' she mourned against his forehead. 'Someone had to go. The world was lifeless without me. You should go like a hero, Dumuzi. Head high, step firm. Don't let the Netherworld see we are afraid.'

'But I am! I am!'

She pushed him away, tossed back her hair and walked

from the dark inner chamber on to the terrace, disturbing sleepy-eyed servant girls.

'The nights are growing colder,' she said, shivering a little as the dark breeze stroked her flesh. She hugged herself voluptuously, smelt the fragrance of her own skin, let the lightly-downed arms brush her cheek. Toes curled against the grittiness of blown sand upon damp paving.

'But next summer will take me again. Over and over!' His voice, high with distress, called from the tumbled comfort of the bed.

'I am a warrior. I have suffered more than you will ever know. I died there. I was hung from a hook on the wall. But I endured. I could not overcome Ereshkigal, but I returned. I am here, she there, equal in strength. If she ever oversteps her boundary, I shall turn her back, as her judges turned on me. I am the Gate Guard of the Above. The Lion Inanna.'

'They say Gilgamesh is stronger than you are now.'

She swung, slowly, unspeaking. Indoors, he could not see the light burning in her eyes, could not feel the hot flush of her body, did not know the hand that gripped her heart and made her gasp with pain.

'*Gilgamesh?*'

'Yes. Inanna, is it true what they are saying? You asked him to marry you?'

A silence impenetrable as darkness. Then a harsh laugh. 'They say I loved Lugalbanda when I was only a little girl. And before that, Enmerkar, and all the kings of Uruk and Aratta. They say I bed with every *en*, in all my cities. I am the Lady of Love. That is my function. But marry Gilgamesh, beyond ritual? No, Dumuzi. You are my bridegroom, no one else.'

The wide-eyed slave girls listened.

'Hold me. Make me forget the darkness and the terror. Inanna! Inanna!'

'My poor little Damu.' She ran back indoors and stroked his hair. 'Don't be afraid. Do you know what I do while you are underground? I weep. I wail. I wander the steppe like a wounded plover, pursued by the shadow of Namtar, groaning, searching for you. I am the widowed bride.'

'If I could believe that!'

'Do you want to make me weep, this night of all nights? When you are gone, Geshtinanna brings her harp and a flagon of wine and tries to make me laugh. She cannot do it.'

'Will Gilgamesh rule as King in the E-Anna next summer? Will he sit on your Lion Throne? Will he have you in this bed?'

'Gilgamesh has lost. Utu has taken away his power. And you are back. My love, my *lubi*.'

They clung together.

The sun had gone down, and in the blue moonlight Gilgamesh haunted the lip of the hole in the market square. The city was quiet, but it was not asleep. Smoke lingered from the evening cooking fires. Drumbeats and songs of mourning came from the houses that death still shadowed. Others gave out more cheerful sounds as though a weight of tyranny had been lifted from them. Higher up, E-Anna was celebrating Dumuzi's return.

'I will not be humiliated!' muttered Gilgamesh. He lay full length on the damp ground and reached his arm into the yawning gap. His bodyguard shifted restlessly and watched the dark alleys. 'I won't have those butterfat citizens say, "He has lost his *pukku*. Utu has taken away his *mikku*. He's a naughty boy." I will get them back. I killed the Bull. I am Gilgamesh!'

His men stepped forward in alarm as Gilgamesh swung himself bodily over the edge and clung there. His vast head, with its springing shock of hair, showed like a lichened boulder while his legs disappeared.

'Sir,' Luudu cried, 'come back! That's too dangerous an expedition even for you.'

Gilgamesh heaved himself back into the shimmering square. His chest was panting with exertion. His eyes flared wildly.

'You're right. Kur is closer than I thought. I've had a glimpse of what lies below. The Netherworld is underneath us. I have just seen what Inanna journeyed into the western mountains for, what Enki set out to sea in his *magur* boat to find. I saw the blue-black walls of the Ganzir, lying in wait for all of us. Under Uruk!'

The men exchanged looks, from the veteran Luudu to the boy Amu. Fear that this might be true showed in the ghostly pallor of their faces. Fear that it might not be true was reserved behind the eyes of the older ones.

Gilgamesh sat down again, like a man who cannot leave the

corpse of a dead friend. 'We know the worst now. I couldn't see them, but they must be there. Ereshkigal has got them!'

'Then let her keep them, sir. There's no getting them back.'

'I will *not* be beaten!'

A scent of pine oil and the soft slap of sandals spoke of someone coming out of the shadows towards them. The men's hands moved to their weapons and then relaxed. A great bulk cast its shadow beside Gilgamesh's. He reached up his hand and caught the other's.

'Enkidu!'

'Still here, master? Supper is ready at the palace. We're waiting to toast the hero who killed the Bull.'

'Hero?' He made a petulant movement. 'The Anunnaki have made me look like a small boy who's been smacked and sent to bed without his supper.'

'They mean that much to you?'

'Inanna gave them to me . . . Yes, don't stare at me! Our fates were bound together from the beginning, hers and mine. I cut down the *huluppu* tree to make her great. I overthrew her enemies. I gave her her bed and throne. The *pukku* and *mikku* were her reward, from the same tree.'

'And both of you are afraid you have lost your power. She to charm men to her bed, and you to force women to yours. And both of you to rouse an army to war.' The words were acid with jealousy.

'Who says we've lost our power? What do you know about us? Because you insulted Inanna? Because Utu's played a trick on me? I'll take the *pukku* and *mikku* back somehow. I'll show them who's king!'

'Then let me get them for you.'

Slowly, staring before him like a sleepwalker, Enkidu walked to the edge. Gilgamesh scrambled up beside him.

'Don't be a fool! I've tried that. I reached my arm in, but I couldn't touch the bottom. I swung my legs over, and there was nothing under me. Then I looked down. In the darkness I saw it, like an evil star in the night below. Blue-black, as the darkest lapis lazuli. Windowless; no fires. Just enough of its own ghastly light to tell what it was. Geshtinanna won't speak of it. Dumuzi turns white when you mention it. But I know. All mortals know what it is, what we have to come to. The Ganzir. The Dark City. Ereshkigal's awful palace.'

'I will go down there for you.'

'It's a trap! The Anunnaki want to kill me. Don't let them fool you.'

'How else could you get your *pukku* and *mikku* back?'

'But the risk?'

'We went to their Land of the Living, and we came back. Inanna went to the Netherworld and she returned. The Anunnaki have marked me for this, not you.' His voice was choked but insistent.

Gilgamesh gathered him in his arms. 'I . . . You know I'd be willing to die in battle, my friend, or fighting any terrible monster. I'd be glad for their mothers to tell my children about my brave death. But to go down into the shadows . . . just to disappear. I can't die in the silence and the dark!'

'I'm only your servant. I can die anywhere in your service.'

'Enkidu! Are you trying to break my heart?'

'If I am your friend, then let me give you what you want.'

'I shouldn't let you do this . . . At least take precautions! Take that festival robe off you. Go naked or in rags. Wash the scented oil off your body; don't let them smell rejoicing. Don't take any weapon in your hand. If you were to hurl one throw-stick, the demons would be on you. Take your sandals off. Go barefoot and silent, as you used to do. I gave you a wife once, and she died with her baby. If you should meet her, pass her by. If you loved her, don't kiss her now. If you hated her, don't hit her. If your little boy should run to you, don't cuddle him or smack him. Walk in silence and fear. Don't let me hear the terrible cry of the Netherworld that tells me its queen has woken, the one that Nin Lil gave her children to. Ereshkigal sleeps on these moonlit nights, naked and terrible. See that nothing wakes her.'

Enkidu twisted out of his friend's embrace, the Wildman of the steppe, dressed in a rich, city robe, oiled and scented, shod in gold-studded leather. His lion-headed staff of office was in his hand.

'So you've had enough of me, Enkidu your lieutenant? I'm to become the savage again, as I was before you found me? Hairy and naked, knowing nothing of civilisation and weapons and family life? Be a brute, you're telling me. Go to your death like the wild dog you are.'

'Enkidu!'

'Do you go to war without your armour? Did you fight the Bull without your axe?'

Enkidu snatched a throw-stick from Amu's astonished

grasp and was over the edge with a monkey-like swing. A swish of pale robes was all they saw of him, a waft of perfume on the air.

He dropped out of sight. They heard the thud of his sandals landing on something hard. Further off they heard cries of surprise, a welcome, a wail. There came a rush of running feet. A missile ricocheting against stone walls.

An inhuman shriek echoed from the caverns of the Below.
'ERESHKIGAL!'

A flash of blinding, blue light made the stars reel.

The square groaned. The houses shook and leaned together, then settled again. When the shouts of alarm had died away and the men at the lip of the abyss had regained their dazzled sight and steadied their pounding hearts, the paving was still shuddering under their feet, like the aftershocks of a woman's orgasm. But the wound in the earth was closed. The gate to the Ganzir was gone. The Netherworld had seized its prey.

# Chapter One Hundred and Seventeen

Enlil was watching the acrobats. Two wrestlers in the masks of a lion and a donkey were attempting to grasp each other's oiled body and hurl it to the ground, while a vulture, female-breasted and pigtailed, sat cross-legged at the drums and a cat and a jackal danced with pipes and lyre.

There was a shouting from the antechamber. Enlil moved his hand and signed to the doorkeepers. They lowered their palm-leaf fans across the entrance, but Nusku the *sukkal* slipped swiftly and smoothly down the pillared hall to investigate. He came back flushed and ruffled as a barnyard cock whose territory has been challenged.

'Lord Enlil, Gilgamesh of Uruk demands . . . begs . . . an audience with you.'

'Are the Guardians of mighty Uruk not strong enough to do what he wants? An and Inanna? It is not so long since he stood here in this very hall and his henchman rolled the bloody head of my watchman on the floor in front of me. Why should I help him?'

'The henchman Enkidu is dead.'

'Aah!' A smile of satisfaction spread across Enlil's features. Nin Lil's glance darted to him and back to Nusku with a dark sorrow.

'Shall I send him away, my lord?'

The lion catapulted through the air and landed heavily on his shoulders. The donkey brayed with glee. Enlil stood up and applauded and tossed the troupe a handful of silver and carnelian beads and a pair of ivory dice. They scrambled for the bounty with squeaks and grunts, then made way for the *ala* players.

Enlil sank back into his chair and rearranged his robe. 'No. Send him in. I am glad to hear that justice still walks the Earth. Utu has been a trifle rebellious in that quarter lately.'

The court of Nippur moved back against the walls to watch

the door swing open. Gilgamesh appeared, his breath still steaming, away from the warmth of the braziers.

Enlil beckoned, and Nusku led the king forward. Gilgamesh bowed, his hand on his heart, the stiff reluctance of pride warring with his urgent need.

Enlil's smile was gracious. 'You are returning to Nippur quickly and in a different mood. How can I help you?'

'Lord Enlil, Source of the Black-Headed People, I appeal to you. My friend Enkidu . . . This is your doing, isn't it? He dreamed his death before he fell into the Netherworld. He said you demanded his life. You are supreme among the immortals. What you have taken away can't you give back?'

'You come from Inanna's city and call me supreme? Your Lady challenged the Netherworld herself.'

The flush darkened in Gilgamesh's face. 'I am appealing to you.'

'All humans must die.'

'But his was not a true death! The Netherworld has kidnapped him. He didn't fall in battle. No monster slew him. Namtar didn't bring sickness to steal him away. Nergal didn't kill him with plague and war. The ground opened in front of him. My *pukku* and *mikku* fell in and Enkidu climbed after them to fetch them back. Kur closed its terrible mouth over his head and swallowed him.'

A horrified mutter rippled down the ranks of courtiers. Nin Lil put out her hand and held Enlil's wrist.

'The Netherworld has spoken. What can I do?'

'They call you Kurgal. We're standing in the E-Kur. What you have built here on Earth is a symbol of what exists in the Above and Below. *You rule Kur.*'

A taut and frightened silence. Enlil was very pale. 'I gave the keys of the Netherworld to Ereshkigal. What is done is done.' Nin Lil's arm was around him now, supporting him.

'Speak the Word of authority. If I can march to the Land of the Living and defeat Huwawa, if I can grapple the Bull of the Sky and throw him down, surely you can overrule Kur.'

Enlil seized on his words. '*My* watchman! My Huwawa! The Bull An sent! You and this . . . *Enkidu*, you defied the Above! Take your retribution now and live with it, *man.*' And he signed for a group of black-skinned dancers from far Meluhha to come running on to the floor and entertain him.

Gilgamesh backed out of Enlil's presence into the cold, winter morning. Luudu and the rest of his escort were sitting playing dice in the anteroom. They scrambled to attention and followed him out of doors. Luudu stood at his elbow, watching his general with concern.

'No go? I didn't think so, somehow. Not after the way old Enkidu rolled that bloody ogre's head under his nose and then tore the shoulder out of their Sky Bull. You could hardly expect him to overlook that, sir.'

'Is there no hope, then?' Gilgamesh hunched in his sheepskin cloak, looking at the frosty sky with sullen defiance.

'Well . . . you wouldn't ask our Lady Inanna, of course? No. I thought not, somehow. Perhaps best not. Still, there's one possibility.'

'Where? If all the Anunnaki have hardened their hearts against us . . . Utu himself has turned his back on me. He punished Enkidu.'

'But there's always been one of the Children of An who strikes me as different from the rest. Not sprung from Mother Earth like all the others. A bit of a freebooter, if you ask me. He's helped our sort since before the Flood.'

Gilgamesh swung round with realisation dawning in his eyes. 'Enki?'

'The same, sir, who helped to fashion us at our birth from clay.'

'And rescued Ziusudra from the Flood!'

'And brought Lady Inanna out from the Netherworld.'

'You're right! By the Imdugud of Ninurta, he's the one. He tricked Ereshkigal into letting Inanna go.'

'Old Enkidu's not a beautiful young Lady, though, is he?' muttered Amu to his neighbour behind Gilgamesh's back.

With the haste of a man of action who cannot be still, Gilgamesh boarded a boat at the Karasarra Quay. Soon they were speeding down the river in his black-prowed warship.

The air was milder in the sweetwater lagoon of Eridu, nearer the coast. Houses rose from their gold reflections in the water, like the temples that are built on their mirror images underground. White egrets and green and russet ducks flashed in the sunlight as they flew from the reeds. Rising fish inscribed perfect circles on the surface of the water.

Enki was not alone. He was walking in his orchard with his grandchildren, Inanna and Utu, and his son Dumuzi. The

younger Anunnaki checked when they saw who was coming.
An embarrassed anger clouded their faces. It was only a little
satisfaction to see the big man stooped and shrunken in
defeat. But Enki hurried hospitably forward as though he was
enjoying his family's discomfiture.

'Gilgamesh of Uruk! Our famous champion. Welcome,
boy. Have you come to pay your respects to the Lord of
Wisdom? A little late in your career, but never mind, never
mind. What can I do for you?'

The words came stiff and difficult as Gilgamesh gazed past
the wrinkled Lord to where Utu hung back behind the
branches of a fig tree. 'I think you know what has happened.
Lady Inanna, Lord Utu, they will have told you. The
Anunnaki have cursed me, and my friend Enkidu has paid the
price. Battle did not fell him like a hero or sickness weaken
him. Kur seized him. Lord Utu there, he opened a gateway to
the Ganzir and my *pukku* and *mikku* dropped in. Enkidu,
who is the bravest and most loving friend a man could have,
went after them. Kur slammed the door on him. The
Netherworld has got him.'

'Bad news. Bad news. It's always best to let the Below keep
what it has, undisturbed. I should know.'

'Yet,' the plea was more difficult still, 'you rescued
Inanna.'

'So I did. So I did. And the whole Earth thanks me for it!'
He turned his loving eyes on his beautiful granddaughter, his
glorious daughter-in-law. 'It wasn't easily done. Others have
wept for it since. Your own mother . . . And Geshtinanna.
Poor, lovely, clever Geshtinanna. Where is she now?'

The orchard was very quiet, except for the croon of doves.
Inanna reached out her hand and took Dumuzi's. They stood
in a painful lock of love, looking at Gilgamesh and not each
other.

They saw Gilgamesh's accusing eyes swing round on them
with the heat of jealousy. 'You! You, Dumuzi! You go to the
Netherworld but you come back. What about us? What about
Enkidu? Why must we go to the Netherworld and never
return? Your father is Enki, a Son of An. Mine was a priest, a
minister to the Anunnaki. I was called son by Lugalbanda,
hero among kings. *Why is there no immortality for me?*'

'You are not a Lord, Gilgamesh, only a human.'

'*What about Enkidu?*'

Enki turned to his grandson and shrugged his shoulders. 'Well, lad? You've heard what the hero says. Can't you do anything about it?'

Slowly Utu stepped out to stand in a shaft of pure light between the trees. Gilgamesh shaded his eyes. The voice was measured, thoughtful. 'The Children of An have always been good friends to you, Gilgamesh. But it was not enough. I cannot reverse the order of creation. Enlil decreed the name of each thing. Nin Mah gave you birth. Enki appointed each creature to its task. The gates of life and death stand east and west of Kur. Ereshkigal holds them both. Yet, as you have seen, shafts may be dug into eternity wherever you stand, wells into wisdom. Like this.'

He raised a shining hand and snapped his fingers. With a startled cry the others saw a dark hole opening at Gilgamesh's feet between the fallen leaves of fruit trees. A breath sighed from the underground and vanished in the clear, blue air. A familiar head, grey now with ashes, rose above the ground. The pale and haggard form of Enkidu clambered out into the winter sunlight.

Inanna first clapped her hands with surprise, then in the next breath gasped with remembered rage. But Dumuzi pulled her roughly aside. He was trembling as much as Gilgamesh. Enkidu was weeping as he faced his master. Gilgamesh ran forward and crushed him in his arms.

'Enkidu! Praise be to all the Anunnaki! A million thanks to Enki and Utu. I'll slaughter a thousand bullocks for them. I'll stand them *gurs* of wine. It's you, old friend. It's really you. You're back. You're alive!'

But Enkidu's hidden face wept on Gilgamesh's shoulder. 'No. You're wrong. You still haven't learned.'

They took him home to Uruk, and the Anunnaki watched them embark with a grave sympathy. Inanna leaning in the protection of Dumuzi's arms even smiled stiffly at Gilgamesh, though not at grey-faced Enkidu. Utu's gaze was more regretful than censorious. Enki's eyes twinkled with interest, like an old man who waits for a child to untangle a riddle. The boat poled more slowly upstream against the current of the Buranun.

Inanna turned her questioning face to Utu. 'He didn't bring what Gilgamesh lost, the *pukku* and *mikku*.'

'I am the Lord of Justice. Would you have me overturn the laws of the Netherworld?'

Brother and sister smiled at each other with a delicate understanding. Dumuzi trembled like a whipped dog.

When they landed at Uruk, Enkidu seemed very tired. Gilgamesh had him put to bed and the richest of meat and broth and beer brought to feed him. But Enkidu turned his face to the wall and would not eat.

Gilgamesh came and sat beside him and took his hand. 'You're cold, friend. You there! Get another brazier! Bring the lionskin from my own bed and wrap it over him.'

Still Enkidu shivered. 'No fire will ever warm me again, sir.'

'Don't be a fool! Our luck has turned. Good old Utu has relented and brought you back. All right, you didn't bring the *pukku* and *mikku* with you. But I'll survive without them. Didn't you see how Inanna was softening to me already? We'll go on some other adventure, get new trophies. We'll become greater heroes than ever before.'

'Gilgamesh! Gilgamesh!'

'Oh, I know. I'm an unfeeling brute. I'm forgetting what you must have been through. I've seen Dumuzi when he comes back from the Below. He's shocked for weeks. It takes all the fire of Inanna's lovemaking to get him warm again. Geshtinanna's braver than he is, but even she is pale and silent when she returns. But you . . .' He leaned forward with avid curiosity. 'You're a man, as I am. You don't need to keep the secrets of the Anunnaki. Can you tell me . . . what is it *like?*'

Enkidu rolled over then and clutched at Gilgamesh with his pale, cold hands. 'I won't tell you! Pray that your life be long, that the day is far off when you need to see what I have seen.'

'*I want to know.*'

'Why should I take your happiness away? Why should I force you to cry?'

'You're my closest friend. If it's so bitter that you must still weep over it, let me weep with you. We'll both of us mourn for the dead.'

Enkidu's fingers slid away from his, as chill as snakes. 'If you weep for the dead, King Gilgamesh, you weep for me.'

'You? But you're back. Kur has released you. You've returned to life.'

'No-o.' The word was a slow wail of despair. 'Lord Utu tried to tell you, but you couldn't understand. All the

Anunnaki know. I am *dead*, Gilgamesh. Kur has me captive for ever. He has only let me out to warn you of the Netherworld.'

'You're here! I can touch you, kiss you! I'll get you warm again. I'll make you laugh.'

'No. Never again. This is not the body you hugged. The flesh that beat against your heart has gone underground. Vermin will gnaw it, like a cast-off garment on a rubbish heap. The body that fought and feasted with yours is crumbling to dust. Like the *sukkal* who walks before Ereshkigal, I've come to show you the road to death.'

Gilgamesh put out a shaking hand and touched the icy flesh, felt it yield too softly. He retched and leaped back with a great cry, overturning the stool. He threw himself in the dust and ashes beside the brazier. His powerful hands beat vainly on the floor. His feet drummed a tattoo.

'Woe to men, then! Woe to those who mock the Anunnaki! Is it true? Is it true? Can we never defy death?'

'No, Gilgamesh. Death is in front of you. I have been allowed back to Earth only to show you how you must die.'

# Chapter One Hundred and Eighteen

'Yes, I have seen the dead.' Enkidu stared at the vaulted ceiling as though it were a cavern of the Netherworld. The light was dying fast.

'I am afraid. I've no trueborn son, only a train of bastards who go by other men's names,' said Gilgamesh soberly. 'I always saw myself as a warrior and a womaniser. I thought I had plenty of time. I could get married and settle down like a citified *en* when I'd had my fill of conquests. Later, but not yet.' He turned to the still figure on the couch urgently. 'Tell me. What happens to a man who has no sons?'

'Dust is his lot. Filth covers him in bedraggled feathers. He crumbles to a skeleton and his manhood leaves him.'

'Yet . . . if a man had time to sire just one son to honour him?'

'He lies in the streets of the Ganzir, outside the walls, and weeps bitterly.'

'Would two be enough?'

'It is sad for all of us, but he has a house of brick and may eat the bread his children leave out for him.'

'Three? Surely three brings happiness?'

'They are spared the foul, stale puddles of the Netherworld that the others must lap like dogs. They may tap the waterskins that hold the pure streams of the Abzu, but they drink it in darkness.'

Gilgamesh's hand moved to the silver jug, then fell back again. It was no use. Enkidu would never eat or drink now in the Above.

'Four?' Obsessively he pestered.

'I have seen moments of gladness in such men's faces, to know they're remembered.'

'Five? It can't be as bad as you say. For a great man, for a hero, surely there must be hope.'

'Yes. Ereshkigal acknowledges the power of procreation.

675

She felt threatened when Inanna came. The family man you describe, he bares his right arm like a scribe, picks up a stylus and is allowed into her palace.'

'Shall I be a petty clerk to the Queen of the Netherworld? Could six sons save me? Surely six would be enough?'

'You would be a courtier in her household. You would oversee her slaves.'

'There is no escape? Not even for seven sons?'

'You might sit in the highest seat and wear fine robes. But you would still be bound to her.'

'I scorned Inanna . . . Is my reward to be *Ereshkigal*? Is there nothing to be done for us, whether we die gloriously in battle or alone on the steppe?'

'Heroic warriors are surrounded by their family. The unburied, who have no one to mourn them, squabble like beggars over the rubbish of the Ganzir. The Netherworld is a city; it has high and low. But no one escapes past its border guards.' His voice failed with weariness.

Gilgamesh sat in a stupor of grief, not noticing the tears trickling down his cheeks. He moved to take Enkidu's hand, but the wasting flesh could not be warmed by human touch. He dropped it, afraid and ashamed.

*'My hand is lame.'*

With the reluctance of dread, Gilgamesh turned his head towards the whisper. Like the stiff claw of a dead hawk, Enkidu's once powerful fingers were hooked in a yellowed impotence.

'I thought . . .' His own voice was hoarse. 'Geshtinanna's physic . . .'

'The Lady Geshtinanna has been taken from us. Did you never guess, when I lost my weapons and faced the Bull unarmed, when I dropped your *pukku*?'

'But you vaulted the Bull like an acrobat, you twisted his tail . . . No, I didn't want to believe the Anunnaki had harmed you.' He forced his arm under the thinning body, knowing it was useless, knowing he could give no comfort.

'I curse that gate to the cedar forest. It looked so beautiful. But if I had known then how it would cripple me I would have taken my axe and smashed its face! If I had stayed whole and strong, if I hadn't dropped your *pukku* and *mikku* . . .'

'Stop it! Stop it!' Gilgamesh was crying more shamelessly than Enkidu was. 'I know. It's for me that you're dying.'

Enkidu collapsed back on to the pillows with a long sigh. The grey light waned. Harps played softly in the background, a consolation on the edge of lament. Servants came soft-footed and set down lamps.

When Enkidu opened his eyes again the sun was in the sky.

'Another day already? Another night gone? Gilgamesh, where is Gilgamesh?' Panic was in his voice.

'Carry him out into the sunshine,' said a soft voice.

The sun dazzled his eyes till they turned his bed away from it. He was in a little courtyard, sheltered from the wind. Lemon trees made shade beside a pool, but Enkidu lay in the full, mild sunlight. There was a scent of perfume more exotic than the lemons. It was an effort for Enkidu to turn his neck, though his head felt light and unreal.

The hierodule had put on her finery. Her face was professionally painted with green and black and red. Her wig was threaded with pearls under its gold-flowered chaplet. Heavy fringes of beads layered her gown. They tinkled and rustled as she swayed. Delicate, reddened toenails peeped from filigree sandals, just as her nipple stood out from her carefully draped gown. But the smile softening her enamelled lips was of genuine compassion.

The touch of her hand made him shudder. So warm, so living.

'Do you remember?'

'Do I remember.' He flung the coverlets off with a passionate strength, then fell back exhausted. 'Shall I ever forget how you trapped me? It's Inanna who's sent you, isn't it? To taunt me! Am I not even allowed to die in peace, in my friend's arms? Where's Gilgamesh?'

She laid a finger on his lips. 'Hush. Yes, I have Inanna's permission to be here. Because Gilgamesh grieves, she grieves, though it is hard for her. We brought you to the city to tame his violence, but that violence only turned another way and assaulted the Anunnaki themselves. You hurt Inanna.'

'And for that I must die? Curse you! Curse you, treacherous Shamhara! Why didn't you leave me on the steppe where I was innocent? Why did you have to foul my body with your temptations? Why did you take away my strength? Damn you! May you be a childless strumpet in the Netherworld for all eternity! May you be an ageing tramp, wandering the streets. May you hold out your wrinkled hands to men for shekels and even drunkards hit you across the face and the man who hasn't had it for a month laugh in your face. May you be robbed of your beauty and brought low, as I am!'

'Enkidu. Poor, frightened love. Can nothing warm you? Is it too late to stir the thing that gives life?'

'Can a dead man do it? You cruel bitch!'

The pool shivered with a searing light. Both man and woman gasped and covered their eyes. A grave voice shocked echoes around the courtyard.

'Enkidu, that is unjust. Shamhara gave you a fortune. Why should you curse her? Without her, would you be lying in this palace, on the magnificent couch of a king? Would the *en* of Uruk himself be not only your master but your beloved friend? Would Gilgamesh sit by your bedside and weep bitter tears over you? Shamhara led you here. You will have a name in history, companion to the hero king, the brother whom Gilgamesh loved. Is that nothing to you?'

The leaves of the lemon tree grew dark again. Gilgamesh was standing under the colonnade, pain and hurt in his face. The too-easy tears of weakness ran from Enkidu's eyes. He made a helpless movement to brush Shamhara's hand.

'I'm sorry. It's true. The best thing to me in life is here, in this palace. You deserve a better reward than I wished you. Stay beautiful. Let kings and nobles rival for your favours. Let them untie their girdles as soon as you walk into the room. May they pour jewels at your feet, black basalt beads and lapis lazuli and gold. May the priests of Inanna lead you to the bedchamber, and wives lie alone while you enjoy their husbands. You did your duty. And you brought me my dearest joy of all.' He forced a painful smile. Gilgamesh was across the courtyard in a moment.

'Enkidu. My brother, my brother. If only gold could buy your life. If the mighty walls of Uruk could keep out death.'

Shamhara let her lips rest lightly on Enkidu's forehead, and stole away to tell Inanna.

Enkidu dreamed, in the loneliness of the night where no friend could reach him. But his waking cry brought the sleepless Gilgamesh running.

'They're coming, Gilgamesh! They're coming for me!'

'What did you see? Shall I send for an exorcist? If any

power of Above or Earth can fight them off, I'll do it, if I beggar my treasury.'

'You can't beat them. The one who was coming towards me in my dream was like the Imdugud. Face sombre as a lion about to snarl. Talons crueller than any eagle. I lay in front of him, weak, lamed in my weapon hand, wasted with hunger. There was nothing I could do. I couldn't even run. He spread his terrifying wings, shut out all the light. He leaped on me and I was choked by his darkness.

'When he released me and I looked down at myself . . .' His voice began to tremble. '*I was no longer a man!* There were bedraggled feathers hanging on me like a moulting crow. The Imdugud fixed his eye on me and led me down to the city of the Dark Queen. I had to follow him, even though I knew that every footfall was a step I would never retrace. Neti closed the door of the Ganzir behind me. That clang was final. Dust is the bread of the Netherworld; cold clay is their meat. They shuffle their wings like black birds; they belong to the darkness. I saw kings serving as kitchen boys to Ereshkigal. Those who had worn great crowns poured water for her. Even the high priests and prophetesses were not exempt. The Lords and Ladies of the Netherworld themselves bow down before her. I saw . . .'

'What, friend?' As though it could matter, as though he could say anything worse.

'Geshtinanna. Your sister. The one who surrendered herself to Kur of her own free choice. She is the scribe of the Netherworld, kneeling before Ereshkigal's throne. She had a tablet in her hand and was reading out the names. She lifted her head and saw me. Such great, sad eyes, that used to dance over the wine cup . . . She sent the Imdugud away. Then . . . she took my hand and led me to the throne, to the feet of that naked Queen. *She read out my name!*'


Gilgamesh burst out on to the steps of his palace trumpeting his grief. 'Elders of Uruk, hear me! The noblest creature in all Sumer is dead. Enkidu my friend, my younger brother! The axe at my side, the bow in my hand, the dirk in my belt, the shield in front of me. Who has stripped my festival robe off me and left me naked? Who has robbed me of him? Enkidu!'

He rushed back into the house like a madman. He flung

himself down beside the stinking couch and his voice grew quiet.

'Enkidu? Are you sleeping?' He touched the disintegrating face. 'My little brother. You were the wild onager bounding up the mountain. You were the panther racing across the plain. We could do everything together. We've climbed impossible crags, we've achieved tremendous journeys. We killed the Bull of the Sky, didn't we? We overthrew Huwawa. Enkidu, why are you still sleeping? Can't you hear me?'

He laid his hand on the Wildman's heart, but only a mass of corruption moved under his palm.

'Sir.' Shamhara sat cross-legged and still in a corner of the terrible room. 'He is gone.'

Gilgamesh raised his heavy, bloodshot eyes like a man kept without sleep by torturers. 'Yes. I know,' he said quietly.

He lifted the white linen cloth at the foot of the bed and drew it gently over the corpse, like a mother veiling an only daughter for her wedding. Then sorrow burst out from him again, uncontainable. Like a lioness robbed of her cubs, like an eagle searching for its vanished prey, he circled the deathbed again and again, beating his breast, tearing off his princely clothes and hurling them on the floor, tugging out handfuls of hair to leave a startling white scalp. Shamhara drew the edge of her headcloth across her face against the stench of death. She murmured a liturgy of mourning through the laments of the professional wailers outside the room. Through the hours of darkness they kept the last vigil for him.

With the first glimpse of inappropriate sunshine and the chatter of birdsong, Gilgamesh got to his feet. He ordered a table of *elammaqu* wood to be made for a bier. A bowl of carnelian filled with honey was set at the head, another of lapis lazuli with butter at the feet.

Gilgamesh stood before his mother, unashamedly crying. 'He lingered twelve days. There was no hope. We could all see it. But he went bitterly. "I wish I had died in battle," he said to me. "I have known fear in war. But I see now that if I had died fighting I should have been blessed. As it is I shall pass into the shadows disgraced."

'I couldn't comfort him. On the twelfth morning, when the first light of the sun was stealing over the roofs, I tiptoed into his room. He looked calmer. I sat down beside him. His eyes were closed, but I talked softly to him. I told him of his great deeds. How he had run with the wild gazelles, their match in speed. How he had known the language of the mighty aurochs and the cunning fox. How we two had wrestled each other, equal in strength and courage. How we had ventured beyond the gate of the Land of the Living to meet Huwawa. How we had rescued each other, and the city, from the Bull of the Sky. Great mountains, great monsters, great heroism, great friendship.

'He lay so quiet I thought for once my words had reached him and lightened the blackness in his soul. He never spoke after that.

'I couldn't leave him, even then. Not till Shamhara shook me and showed me the worms were eating away his face. Then I looked down. Maggots were dropping out of the hand I held. He is dead. They tell me I had sat beside his rotting corpse for seven days.'

'His was a loving heart. A brave heart.'

'I know that. You don't have to tell me.'

'What will you do now, son?'

'I shall bury him with the richest honours, as a hero. And then . . . I am leaving the city.'

'Son, would it not be better to stay here, to marry a queen and have children?'

'Is that all? Is that where you think a man's immortality lies, only in a woman's womb? No! This time, my journey will take me even beyond the gate of sunrise. I will get what the Anunnaki refuse us. I am going to bring back the secret of eternal life.'

# Chapter One Hundred and Nineteen

The call went out through all the land that Enkidu was being buried with the honours of a king. Queens and governors came to kiss the foot of his gilded coffin. All the panoply of royalty was ordered to escort him to the tomb. A solid copper statue set with silver and jewels was commissioned on the palace mound. Long after death Enkidu would stare defiantly across at the E-Anna. Uruk groaned under a heavy service of funeral rites, almost as when the people had laboured to build Gilgamesh's walls.

But at last it was over, and one early morning Gilgamesh stepped from his palace into the still, misty air. His hair was longer and unkempt. No oil sleeked his thick beard. The smell of sweat was rank on his unwashed body. The only garment he wore was a lionskin, a trophy from his heroic past.

His silent courtiers and servants watched him go in an uneasy awe, as one might watch a captured wolf released from its cage. His eyes were wild and the course he took across the outer courtyard was not quite straight. He found the gate, fumbling a little with his hands as though his sight was clouded.

Outside, the first rays of the sun touched the new copper statue. Gilgamesh caressed it, and his eyes grew suddenly intelligent. He laughed harshly. 'A reversal of roles, old friend. Stand here outside my palace in your finery of lapis lazuli and gold. You deserved to be a prince. Let me have the desert you came from. I will become the Wildman. But the creature I stalk no hunter has ever brought home before me. I am too late to help you, my friend, my brother. But I will go on the track of life and win it for myself.'

The lapis lazuli eyes glistened in the sunlight. The carnelian lips were dumb.

The highway that ran between the E-Anna and the palace

was lined with priestesses and Inanna's household. Inanna herself was standing at the edge of her leafy park under the *sarbatu* trees the gardener Shukalletuda had planted for her to stand between her garden and the desert. She saw Gilgamesh coming, his head proudly high.

'You are really going to seek Dilmun? Can I not dissuade you?'

'To get what you would not give me,' he snarled. 'Eternal life.'

She raised her hand in acknowledgement. 'Then I shall ask Utu to protect you in your wanderings.'

'You will not bless me yourself?'

A spasm of pain tightened her face. 'My blessings are for the bed and the battlefield. I offered you victory in both. You rejected that.'

'I won them for myself. It is not enough!'

She shook her head. 'Come back to us wiser, Gilgamesh. Yet come back.' She was trying to smile. Her breath was sweet as perfume. He leaped backwards like a rabid dog from water.

'Don't try and tempt me, like Shamhara with Enkidu. Leave me alone!'

'Yes. Alone, you must walk where you are going. If you return, see that you do not remain alone.'

He strode away from her along the dusty road, watched by silent townspeople.

When Inanna turned away, her hand caressing the bark of the shade trees, Shukalletuda the gardener was behind her. He was startled by the tears on her face.

'My Lady!'

She pushed past him, plunging into the wilder foliage of the park.

Beyond the city gate, Gilgamesh looked back. Luudu and half a dozen of his men were following him at a distance.

'Go back!' he yelled. 'Didn't you hear what Inanna said? I have to do this alone!'

Luudu grounded his spear with a sigh. 'I didn't think it would work. There isn't enough cover in Sumer to hide us from him.'

'He's mad! Isn't he?' asked young Amu behind him. 'He'll never find old Ziusudra and the land of Dilmun, will he?'

'Maybe he will, maybe he won't. But will he ever get

back to us in Sumer if he does?'

They watched the king, barefooted in his lionskin, leaving his city, travelling west.

It was not an easy journey for Gilgamesh. It was not easy for those who crossed his path. Beyond the cultivated gardens of Sumer, wolves roamed the wilderness. Lions guarded the passes to the nomad lands. When he saw the smoke of camp fires or the tents of the herders, he turned away among the dunes and passed them by.

One night he woke sweating from a dream. He had happened upon a wedding party of the Martu. The bride was brilliantly dressed, with silver discs on her forehead. The young friends of the bridegroom were shouting and stamping round the fire. The two clans were full of the joy of life and the promise of children to come. Then Gilgamesh broke in upon them, brandishing an axe in one hand and his sword in the other. He hacked the wedding party to pieces and spilled their blood in the sand.

When he woke, white and shaken, the moon stood over the empty sandhills. Gilgamesh prostrated himself on the sand and called out to Inanna's parent. 'Father Nanna, you herd the stars of night as a loving Guardian. Death is on everything I touch. Guide me through the dangers of this journey. Death lies in wait for me. Let me bring back life!'

When lions and serpents crossed his path, he killed them with his bare hands.

Months later, he came at last to where the twin horns of Mashu towered against the western sky. The sun was going down between their treeless screes. He began to climb the remnant of a river, grey in shadow. Then in the stillness he heard a stone move. He looked up, his hand on his bow. But what he saw froze his weapon arm into immobility. Each peak held its own sentry. Black, gigantic, cased in an armour hard as rock, but shifting, living, setting boulders rolling as if they were runnels of sand. Eight feet scuttled beneath the stony scales of their bodies. Vast wings flexed and spread and folded back again restlessly like watchful vultures. But their powerful span could not hide the curving tail that snaked and arched to point in a scorpion's sting. One on either side of him, they turned their massive faces so that the setting sun caught them in dazzling splendour. The one on the right wore a man's beard as if carved in glittering basalt. The other flashed with the awesome beauty of a woman.

Gilgamesh threw himself down before them. Silence now, except for the little running river and the slipping of smaller stones. It was hard to lift his face from the ground and look up again. Better to pretend it was some trick of the sunset flaming on wind-carved rocks. Such creatures could not walk the Earth, even here.

But he had come to seek the Land of Dilmun, that lies beyond both the sunset and the sunrise, and the only man and woman in the world who held the secret of immortality. He must pass the sentries of the immortals.

Like a king and a hero then, he must pull himself to his feet and bow with courtesy before this pair.

A voice shattered his composure, crashing across the saddle of the pass. 'Wife! What is this, stumbling through the wilderness towards us? It has the features and appendages of a man. But it seems no dried-up strip of human flesh, for all the desert way behind it. It has the radiance of beauty, like the shape of the Anunnaki.'

'Lady's blood is in him,' shouted back the Scorpion Woman. 'This is Nin Sun's lad. They count him two-thirds a Lord, and one-third man. But he is mortal.'

Then the Scorpion Man called down to him, 'If you are Gilgamesh, you are very far from your city. Why have you come on such a difficult and dangerous journey? What do you want from us? Man-eating waters and dangerous passes you must have crossed alone. What is your need that seems so great?'

'I am searching for the way to Dilmun, the earthly garden of the Children of An.'

'No humans walk in Dilmun,' sang the Scorpion Woman. 'Why?'

'I mean no disrespect, Lady of Might and Majesty,' ventured Gilgamesh. 'But you are wrong. There is one human couple. Ziusudra and his wife, who rescued humanity from the Flood. The Anunnaki tell us that Enlil granted them eternal life.'

'And if you could speak with Ziusudra, what would you say?'

'I would ask him to tell me the secret of life. He surely knows.'

The Scorpion Man's voice rolled towards him like another great boulder. 'You cannot make that passage. In all the ages since the Flood, no human has walked the difficult road to where the Anunnaki set Ziusudra and Kuansud. Can a mortal follow the tunnel of darkness by which Utu passes from sunset to sunrise through the bowels of the Earth?'

Gilgamesh began to shake. 'Must I enter the Netherworld after all?'

The answer was grave, not without compassion. 'Twice twelve hours of darkness, without one gleam of light. You would not be allowed to track the radiance of the sun. You must tread that darkness utterly alone. But no, this passage avoids the Ganzir. You would pass through Ereshkigal's territory. But this is her eastern road, to life, not death.'

'Then let me attempt it, my Lord, my Lady. Whether in sorrow or pain, whether in ice or scorching heat, though the only sounds I hear may be sighing and weeping, yet, if this dark road has an end, and the end is Dilmun, I will walk it. Open the gates of the mountains for me, honoured ones.'

The shining eyes of the Scorpion Man looked across the pass at the Scorpion Woman. Their huge tails flicked, arched over their winged backs and struck simultaneously where the stream came bubbling out of the earth at the head of the gully. There was a flash of furnace fire, an incandescence of molten rocks. Then the white heat steadied to gold, and the gold to red, and the red darkened into the black of night. The single, brilliant star of Inanna in the east blazed on a gaping hole going under the mountain.

'Go, child of a Daughter of An, son of a man.'

'Go, Gilgamesh,' said the Scorpion Wife. 'May your feet carry you safely beneath the Earth and bring you home to Uruk.'

'Go. The gateway to Dilmun is open to you.'

He climbed till he passed between the vastness of their guardian presences, unseen now except as a deeper darkness in the night. Utu had entered long before him. There was no trace of light.

'The sun rises every morning and brings a new day. Surely I will come back to Sumer with new life.'

He felt the rocky walls and stumbled on the uneven surface. The Evening Star was left behind him. He struggled the first two difficult hours like a newly-blind man, going always down.

# Chapter One Hundred and Twenty

Inanna's feet touched the Earth in the stillness that was not quite dawn. The Stairs of the Sky were behind her. Father Nanna, herding the constellations, Great-grandfather An resting in his far-off, rose-striped tent, remote from the pain of the world. She was home, in Uruk.

'You look tired,' said Nin Shubur.

'What is there to be glad about now?' she said. 'Without Dumuzi, without Gilgamesh?'

'Come indoors and rest.'

'I would rather walk in the cool of the park.' And indeed, her face was flushed, though the day had hardly begun.

Sensing her mistress's need for space and silence, Nin Shubur followed at a little distance, watching Inanna's skirt grow heavier with the dew that would be swallowed up in moments when the sun rose.

The light was coming now, shocking the eyes, hurled like weapons from walls of golden clay and dazzling limestone. Inanna flinched.

'Stay here,' she said, on a little sob.

'My lady . . .'

But Inanna was running across the blazing space of dried-up grass, leaving Nin Shubur in the shade of the apple grove. The *sukkal* watched her reach the far boundary of *sarbatu* trees, whose shade, planted at Inanna's own order, protected a little space of herb beds. The Young Lady stood between the trees, looking out over the farmland of her city to the distant, burning desert, where Dumuzi had been taken.

Pity wrenched the heart of the Queen of the East. So young, so lovely, after all these millennia, was Inanna still. Impossible to think of her as the mother of two grown sons. She would always be the girl who waited with beating heart for the coming of her Shepherd.

Only now she must carry both desire and pain, rising and

falling in huge fluctuations, like the great river itself. Nin Shubur watched Inanna sink down in the shade of the trees and lay her head at last on the accepting earth.

The *sukkal* squatted herself in the shelter of the fruit trees, to keep watch.

The city was waking. Workers who had breakfasted by the Morning Star were now going about their tasks. The subdued sounds of human voices, of tools and beasts rose from below, or echoed from high E-Anna. The birds sang one joyful chorus and then hushed above her.

Someone was coming across the park between the two women. The young gardener Shukalletuda, casually beheading the dry, gold grass with his hoe as he passed. A headcloth shaded his sharp, dark features. His hands were fine but earthy.

Nin Shubur opened her mouth to call out a warning to him, but, fearing to wake Inanna herself, she caught it back. She saw the man reach the first bed of lettuces and set to work.

The heat advanced in great strides. Flies danced before Nin Shubur's eyes, weaving a net between her closing eyelids.

It seemed only seconds that her head drooped, irresistibly heavy on its slender neck. A great scream split the morning. Nin Shubur was on her feet in a moment, racing across the sunlight, heart thudding as loud as her feet.

What she found was more shocking even than she had imagined.

Inanna crouched, wild-haired and wild-eyed, with her white dress flooded with scarlet.

Blood between her thighs. Blood running down her legs. Blood seeping away into the thirsty earth, as if after all these centuries she had been deflowered for the first time.

'*Who did it?*' she screamed. '*I was asleep. Who was it?*'

'That young man. Shukalletuda! *Guards! Guards!*'

Nin Shubur went running round the ditches of the garden like a wounded bird, but she did not find him. It seemed an age before the *sag-ursag* arrived. They gasped and turned away their faces when they saw their Lady.

'How *could* he? How could any man do it to me?' Horror and incomprehension were in Inanna's cries.

'Find him! Find the criminal and drag him to the E-Anna!' ordered the *sukkal*.

A trembling maid threw her own cloth round her violated mistress, but the blood would not stop running. Geshtinanna came hurrying and tried to comfort her.

'Why did the humans dare to do this?' Inanna could not stop shuddering. 'To me! The Lady of Uruk, their queen, their protector.'

'Hush. Hush, my love. Men are violent, they are greedy. They take what they want.'

'He was my gardener! Once he was terrified of me . . .'

'He will be found, my lady. He will be found and punished.'

'Who?' Inanna laughed harshly. 'Who should be punished for this? This is Gilgamesh's fault. When he rejected me, when he threw the gifts I offered him back in my face he set his *lugal*'s palace above my Sky House. He told the people they did not need their Lady. Where was awe, where was respect, then? There is no more reverence for the Anunnaki.'

They helped Inanna back to the E-Anna, her bloodstained garment blazoning her accusation. The flow seemed unstoppable. There was blood in the wells when the women hauled their early morning buckets to water households and flocks. There was blood running in the groves and the gardens when the men came out to fetch firewood. Blood in the city's drains as Inanna climbed the hill.

The *sag-ursag* found the gardener's house. They tortured Shukalletuda's father within a hair's breadth of his life. But all he could shriek was that his son had fled to another city where his brothers lived. They went through Sumer's towns, wrecking houses, overturning hiding places. He was not to be found among those myriad, wide-eyed faces of the black-headed people, who might have been mocking their insulted Lady. His brothers pleaded that he had fled to the desert to hide among the demons and dust devils.

The soldiers marched out to search for him under the merciless glare of the sun. Only the tantalising face of Kiskillilla peered out from behind the camelthorn and laughed as they went by.

The country faltered towards the rains, its increase stopped, its life-blood spilt. No culprit was ever found to take the punishment for Inanna's shame. There was no *en* in Uruk to avenge her. With burning eyes she sat down to await the return of Gilgamesh.

# Chapter One Hundred and Twenty-one

Four hours and the way was entirely dark. Six hours, and there was silence all around him. Gilgamesh stamped more angrily to drive back the fear of the sounds that might be lying in wait for him. Eight hours, and still the rock bruised his feet dispassionately. He heard nothing, met no one. Ten hours, and he was utterly alone, leaving life and not even approaching death, lost, beyond the reach even of the burrowing worm.

Twelve hours, and the way began to level, the walls to recede, the darkness vaster all about him.

Fourteen hours, and he was tiny, insignificant, wandering on with nothing to guide him now.

Sixteen hours, and he was stumbling, sobbing, no longer caring where he arrived, as long as it was somewhere, anywhere.

'Light!' he cried. 'Is there no more light?'

At eighteen hours a breath of wind touched his face, cool and fresh, as though from northern hills. Gilgamesh wept, and felt the tears chill on his fevered cheeks.

Twenty hours, and he began to feel that the sound of his footsteps was smaller now, shuddering away into an immensity that was starting to stir with infinite other possibilities. He looked up quickly, hardly daring to believe there might be sky and stars again. Thick darkness hung overhead still. Was it the roof of the Netherworld, or the vault of Angal?

At the eleventh double hour he knew the universe was lightening. Now tears of humility and gratitude were pouring down his face. No colour yet, no clarity of outline to anything. But he was back in a world again that would soon have contours, horizons, objects, vegetation.

Twice twelve hours came and the sun rose again on the far side of the world. It found Gilgamesh staggering at the edge of a sea, a dirty, hairy, angry, exhausted savage of a man, in a garden of exquisite, jewelled beauty.

The dazzle of roseate gold from the water showed him bushes heavy with scarlet fruit. He lunged towards them. But his hands met the hard smoothness of carnelian. He tore the precious stones loose and hurled them away. Vines hung temptingly overhead. But the blue sheen of grapes that fell into his hands was lapis lazuli. He shattered them against the copper-hued rocks of the beach.

This was the sight that Siduri the alewife saw, stepping from her inn at the edge of the world in the early morning. A dishevelled, wild-eyed giant in a filthy lionskin, wrecking the garden of the immortals. She dropped her jug and the gold mashing-pestle given her by the Anunnaki and fled indoors to peer out of the window. She thought he was a murderer come to the furthest end of the road that any human can tread.

But Gilgamesh saw the whisk of her long, white veil and turned with a bellow of loneliness and rage. He came pounding after her. She had slammed the gate shut and tugged the great cross-bar into place. He vaulted over it. Now she locked the door inside and barred it. Gilgamesh heard the wood thump into place, shutting him out. He leaped at the window and shook the frame.

'If you bar your gate, I will smash it down! If you lock your door, I'll break it in! Open up your inn, barmaid!'

Siduri shook her head. The fat red cheeks quivered with prudent fear and not with merriment.

'Who are you, who come to the treasure garden of the Anunnaki and smash the precious fruit? Who are you who come like an assassin to the shore of the sea of death which none of the living dares to cross?'

'I am Gilgamesh,' he shouted with contorted face. 'Gilgamesh! Does that name mean anything here? I was a great king, once. I was happy. I was victorious. I had a friend, like no other man on earth. We did everything together. Everything a hero could imagine. We killed the watchman of the forest in the Anunnaki's Land of Cedars. We overthrew Huwawa himself and cut off his head. We killed the Bull of the Sky and strangled lions in the mountain passes. We were heroes! Heroes!' He beat his fists on the windowsill till the blood ran.

Siduri picked up her ladle. She had seen men in grief coming to her beer vats before. Her breathing grew steadier.

'Where is your brave friend now?'

The tears blubbered afresh through the clotted dust of his face. 'Enkidu, whom I loved better than any woman, Enkidu, who shared every danger and hardship with me, Enkidu has gone the way of every human. I thought it couldn't be true. I wouldn't believe it. I watched for him to wake seven nights and days, till the worms started to drop off his nose. Since then . . .'

'You've come a long, hard journey, boy.'

'I am searching for life. The true, immortal life I would have given Enkidu if I could. Barmaid, what have you got in there? Is that the elixir of life? If I drink what you brew, can it keep me safe from death for ever? Will it save me from the Netherworld?'

The lock was turning, the bar was lifting. Warm hands guided him inside. 'Sit down. Drink all you want. Siduri the alewife brews a beer like nothing else. A beaker or two of this and grief floats away like the geese at evening. There now, let me wash your feet. You're a terrible mess. If your wife could see you now!'

'I have no wife.'

'Tsk, tsk.' Her hands stilled over his matted hair. Then she began again, brushing and stroking, washing and wiping, setting a cup of good, dark drink in his trembling hand.

'King Gilgamesh, is it? And a mighty hero? Lad, the race you're running now has no finishing line. You can wear out this gorgeous body of yours, but you'll never find what you've set your heart on. You're a human. Don't start away from the truth, my handsome. Say it over to yourself. "I am human. I am human." There. It isn't so very difficult, is it?'

'I am the son of a Lady!' he yelled at her. 'I want immortal life!'

She sat down on the bench beside him and slid her arm round his waist. She was a small, round woman, older than he was, but still firm and merry. Her eyes shone with wise sympathy and laughter.

'Forget it, lad. Be what you are. A king, a hero, but a mortal. Enjoy it all while it's here. Good food, strong beer. Wrestling and dancing and fighting and drumming. Whatever you like most, you can have it, can't you? Drop this silly lionskin. Get yourself good, bright clothes. Wash this brawny body. You've got slave girls, haven't you? Well, go on, you ought to be revelling in the pleasures of their soft hands massaging your skin, tickling up your private parts, giving you a good time. A fine king like you should be married by now. You want a beautiful, warm wife. A string of fat babies, brave boys and pretty girls. A palace full of your own children. A woman can give you the gift of life a man never can.'

'You too!' He started up and backed away from her in a kind of terror. 'You're like all the others. Is this the trickery of the Anunnaki? Did they send me through such awful loneliness to tell me just this? Gilgamesh may live on only in his deeds and in his children? But Gilgamesh the man must die?'

Siduri sat with her hands knotted in her lap. Her dark eyes stared up at him.

'All men must die.'

'No! It's a lie! Not all. Why do you think I've walked half across the world and through the gates of darkness? You're keeping his secret from me. Where's Ziusudra?' At his name she jumped up and shook her head. 'I'll do anything, brave any danger. Even put to sea like Enki when he sailed against Kur. If you refuse me, I won't go back. I'll roam the steppe and become a wild beast, like Enkidu before the harlot tamed him. Tell me!'

'Gilgamesh, Gilgamesh. There has never been a mortal traveller who made the crossing you talk of. That bay outside, that looks so sweet and golden, it leads out into the sea of death. Yes, you might well turn pale. If you'd dashed on before you saw my inn and sailed out into that, it would have been the end of you. This beer I'm offering you is the drink of life.'

'But not for ever.'

'No. How could it be?'

'Then, how?'

'Don't try it, Gilgamesh. Father Nanna crosses over this sea between death and life every night to bring us the moonrise. But Nanna is a Child of An.'

'And the Anunnaki mock us. Nanna, Utu, Inanna, all of them walking the Sky. Is Ziusudra the only human who has ever crossed it?'

'Well, I don't know if I should be telling you this. But there is a boatman. Sursunabu, Ziusudra's descendant and ferryman.'

'*Is he human?*'

'Ye . . . es.' Her eyes appealed to him, compassionate but warning.

'Where can I find him!'

'In the woods by the shore. But take care. Don't you try and venture out alone on that sea. He knows the secret. Where the stone pillars stand looking out across the water towards Dilmun the Distant, there is the landing place. But listen, Gilgamesh. If he tells you no, then swallow that mouthful now as soon as later. Turn round. Go home. Be happy while the sun and the stars are still shining for you. Nanna and Utu and Inanna have a lot to give you.'

He snatched his axe from his belt and his dagger in the other hand and dashed for the emerald-leaved trees at the edge of the glittering sea.

# Chapter One Hundred and Twenty-two

Inanna stood before the Council of the Children of An in terrible mourning again. The black garment of widowhood hung on her like raven's plumage. Ash streaked the lovely face reddened with emotion. Old, dark blood stood out unwashed on the scratches of her cheeks and arms and legs. Her eyes were unpainted, but the shadows of sleepless grief darkened them.

The Anunnaki drew back from her, as though she were unlucky. They had gathered, as always, at Nippur, in the Ubshu-ukkinna court.

An, in the President's chair, would not meet her eyes. He looked so old, so frail, so insubstantial. White hair blew over his face like ragged clouds. He scorned the heavy, ceremonial wig of blue-black. Indeed he looked almost unwilling to be there at all, sitting uneasily on his seat as though the lightest breeze might blow him into the sky. So long ago, her playful childhood in his palace. 'Has it ended in this?' his embarrassment seemed to say.

And Ki. To Inanna, with all the curious eyes of her family on her shame, the Great Mother now seemed a mountain of earth-coloured flesh she longed to run to and feel those arms close round her, be smothered in that bosom, overwhelmed by that embrace.

She bit her lip, held her head proudly high under its black veil.

Enlil.

He sat, one of the four Great Guardians, beside An and Ki and Enki. He did not occupy the President's chair, but when the Council of the Annunaki met all eyes turned to Enlil first. A very great Lord. It was as though all the winds of the world had gathered themselves to fill his almost transparent skin. Energy radiated from him. Where An seemed light enough to float off into the ethereal blue, Enlil would choose his own direction. He marched with huge, swift strides across the Earth. Humans shook and bowed before the power of his Word. When he smiled and spoke softly, blessings came into being. When he cursed, cities fell.

'Approach, Daughter.'

No husband now to support her with his warm presence. Her brother Utu stood by her instead, as if she had been an unmarried sister, or a divorced woman.

'You know my complaint already. I have been raped.' Her voice was breathy with passion.

She had not realised, till she saw his expression. But the shock of the memory ran through the whole court.

Once, Enlil himself had stood before this Council and heard them sentence him to the Netherworld for rape. He controlled himself now.

'And you know the criminal.'

'Shukalletuda. Nin Shubur is my witness.'

The whole land of Sumer knew the accused's name by now.

'No one has been able to find him. What do you want me to do?'

'Someone must suffer for it. This concerns you all. The Anunnaki have been humiliated. I am the Lady of Lovemaking. I am the Guardian who gives. I cannot be robbed!'

'You have already punished the humans. All Sumer is groaning because of this.'

Nin Lil leaned forward, and An signalled her to speak.

'Let yourself weep clean, wholesome tears, Inanna. Wash away this stain.'

'I will have blood!'

Enlil's face, which had itself frowned dreadful justice on the black-headed people, tightened with disapproval.

'You yourself dishonoured the Anunnaki, Inanna. You offered too much to Gilgamesh. You, a Lady, to so favour a mortal. And he refused you. How can the humans respect us, if we do not safeguard our own rank? You have been too generous to humans, and now they despise you for it.'

'I loved them! Is that a reason for rape?'

All round the forecourt, the Anunnaki of wind and work, of healing and growing, murmured their sympathy. Then heads began to turn. A commotion was breaking out in the lower courts. Those at the back divided their attention, tried to see the cause of the disruption.

Nusku, Enlil's *sukkal*, roared out, 'Who disturbs the Council of the Great Guardians? Who interrupts the mighty Enlil? Is there no reverence now in the land of the black-headed people for their Lord and maker?'

The ranks of the Fifty parted, and a courier rushed in, covered in dust, his kilt torn, panting to find the breath to fill his labouring chest and deliver his speech. He flung himself down on the clay pavement before the four highest seats.

'Pardon, Lord Enlil, Father An. I have run night and day to deliver my message. A word of alarm. A challenge to the land of Sumer, to the Children of An themselves.'

'What challenge could make us afraid?'

The courier scrambled to his knees, stood on his feet. His shoulders still heaved with the exertion of his running.

'My lord, Great Enlil, Mount Ebih has risen against you. Kur is behind it.'

A gasp, like wind suddenly lifting the dried leaves from a courtyard, rustled through the Ubshu-ukkinna. The gathered Anunnaki trembled like the fluttering of bat wings in the dusk. Their faces gleamed pale as moths. Enlil himself, after that first great inhalation of breath, turned his glowing eyes on Inanna.

'Is this your doing too? Is this some treacherous folly you are stirring up in the Below?'

'I? What have I done?'

Even An looked alarmed, clutching the arms of his chair for support and twisting to peer at Enlil.

Lord Wind arose, and all the ranks of the Anunnaki fell back a little before the majesty of his standing presence. His face was thunder, but his limbs quivered with suppressed emotion.

'What has happened? Tell me, man, quickly!'

The courier, dwarfed by the agitated Lord, stammered out his message, trying to preserve the correct dignity of his office.

'Great Master, Mount Ebih, the land that strides along our borders, is in motion. Fire is shooting from its peaks. Its stones are hurtling over our peaceful land. Its people have armed themselves and come rushing down upon your beloved Sumer. Your houses are overthrown; the shrines of the Anunnaki are shattered. Behind the troops of Ebih, Kur is in rebellion. It is attacking us!'

Inanna stood, outwardly calm, but her heart beating

thunderously. Enlil was erect on the dais, a figure of woe and wrath. Dread flashed in the faces in front of her. Too many of them held their own fearful memories, old pain.

She saw Enki, who had struggled to escape the chaos of the primeval ocean. Enlil, a hopeless prisoner in the Ganzir. Nin Lil, leaving three babies in Ereshkigal's bed. Geshtinanna, who must take Dumuzi's place again and again.

She saw herself, struck down by the hand of death, hung like a butchered lamb.

But here in the Ubshu-ukkinna, Inanna still held the central place. Unconsciously she lifted the lapis lazuli rod in her hand as though it were a spear. Her brilliant eyes stared at Enlil in the gathering dust to see what he would do.

He flared back at her. 'Is this how you want to punish Sumer? Have you made a league with Ereshkigal now?'

'I? Is that what you think of me? I am the Lion of Sumer! I would sacrifice my life against her enemies, even now.'

'Ninurta! Where are you?'

'Here, Father. What are your orders?' Hope was vibrating in the warrior's voice.

'Champion of the Anunnaki, Spear of Angal, you who conquered Asag and threw up the wall of the Hursag, lead your army out against these rebels. Let Sharur loose. Crush Kur. Confound them.'

The magic weapon leaped in Ninurta's grasp. Its macehead glowed red with lust.

'Whatever needs to be done against the enemies of Sumer, against the enemies of the Above, you know I will do. I will lead your army. The men of Girsu and Lagash will be proud of such a task.'

Ki, his mountainous mother, stirred in her seat. 'This may not be an army of demons like Asag, my son. What if Kur itself is rising from the Netherworld to overwhelm us?'

Again the horror of the Below shook the Anunnaki of the Above. Faces were fixed on the tall figure of Enlil, their Lord, their leader. Then their eyes turned to Ninurta, his younger son and warlike general.

Inanna's head went up, beautiful and awe-inspiring now. Her veil was thrown back. Her eyes burned like a lioness whose cubs are threatened. A Lady who had walked the Road of No Return and come back from Kur. A woman who had died and was now disturbingly alive. A queen who could condemn her husband to the Netherworld and call him up again. But raped by a human.

How closely matched were Inanna and Ereshkigal, queens of the Above and Below? How strong, as sisters fighting against each other? Angal was fixed Above, the Netherworld was secure Below. Who could take the Earth between?

'Go!' Enlil ordered Ninurta. But his eyes flashed uneasily over Inanna too. 'For the beloved land of Sumer, for the safety of the Anunnaki, you must drive Kur back Below.'

# Chapter One Hundred and Twenty-three

'Sursunabu! Sursunabu! . . . Boatman!'

The beautiful, dangerous sea lapped the stones almost at his feet. Gilgamesh drew back in belated alarm.

'Boatman! Where's the ferry to Dilmun? Come here when I call you!'

The fruit of onyx and jasper and crystal and amethyst tinkled teasingly on the shimmering bushes.

'Sursunabu, you dog! It's King Gilgamesh, demanding a passage!'

He whirled round, sensing rather than hearing a presence behind him.

There were indeed two beings. Tall, taller even than Gilgamesh. Slender but strong, two grey columns. Stone. Carved into a majesty whose shadowed eyes stared out beyond him across the brilliant sea. Stout legs supported well-proportioned bodies. Their feet were bare, splayed, powerful as tree roots. On one, a woman's dress hung from a snake girdle. On the other, a shorter, netted kilt appeared to swing above the knees, petrified in one eternal moment. Their faces were calm, glad, radiant in the sun. Hands clasped over their breasts expectantly. The intensity of their staring eyes over his head forced his own attention round.

The island hovered over the water, seeming to float on it, rather than rise from it. With a painful stab of homesickness he had not felt since he fled from Inanna's city, Gilgamesh remembered Uruk. So the colossal mound heaped up by hands, then centuries upon centuries of occupation, old houses crumbling into new foundations, had raised the hill on which E-Anna stood. So it had quivered in the distance, across the heat-haze of intervening desert. Uruk and Kullab stood up out of a sea of life-giving gardens. Dilmun the Distant was cradled on a sea of death.

Gilgamesh wept with frustration, seeing it at last, unable to reach it.

'Ferryman!'

No slaves or *sukkals* or soldiers came running to his shout here.

In baffled fury Gilgamesh hefted his axe, brought it crashing down upon the female figure. Her head, expressionless, went toppling down the slope into the wicked, clear water.

A shout he hardly registered. What if Siduri was watching from her alehouse? What if she raised her silly protest against anger and waste? A jarring blow to his arms, but the force of its impact severed the male figure at the waist. They would mock him no longer with their trusting, prayerful eyes fixed on the unattainable island of the immortals.

'Stop! Vandal! Thief! Idiot!'

A furious figure like a bristling boar was charging out of the bushes towards him. Gilgamesh planted his feet challengingly, axe in one hand, dirk in the other. His eyes flashed danger.

The man was short, broad-shouldered but spindly-legged. His hands swung empty, his fists balling and opening again. The water of impotent anger sparkled in his eyes.

'What have you done? Fool! What have you done?'

'Who wants to know?' demanded Gilgamesh rudely.

'Who should I be on this last shore of the world? Whose name have you been bellowing? Sursunabu, boatman to Ziusudra and his wife.'

A check. A feeling of infinite weariness approaching, as the end of his long quest glided in sight.

'Sursunabu? The ferryman?'

'I was,' the other said bitterly.

'You are the one who sails across to Dilmun?'

'I did!'

'You can carry me to Ziusudra?'

'I could have.'

'You must!'

'How can I, now?'

'I am Gilgamesh! King of Uruk. I have journeyed over half the world looking for this shore. I saw a man who came from the Netherworld and told me all its horrors. I had to watch him decay before my eyes while the Anunnaki did nothing. I won't walk that road. I can't die! I have to reach the island of

Dilmun, and Ziusudra. I must find the secret of immortal life. Take me!'

'No one can cross that sea now.'

'You're the ferryman! If you value your life-blood, you'll do it!' Gilgamesh sprang like a leopard across the intervening space. His ankle caught in something, and it brought him crashing to the ground. Sursunabu grabbed the fallen dirk and stood over him warily. Gilgamesh still grasped the axe as he staggered to his feet.

There was a line of knotted vines that seemed to be tangled all around his legs. As he bent to pull and snap them apart he found the cord was immensely tough. It was spun of hundreds of strands of copper twisted and twined together like living fibres. It coiled over and over in a heaped confusion and then led single and true down into the water. From the snapped torso of the male image, past the severed head of the female figure, lost underwater now, towards distant Dilmun.

'Gilgamesh the hero, is it? Gilgamesh the king? Gilgamesh the fool!'

'Why? What have you done to me? Are you refusing to take me?' His voice rose dangerously.

The man looked at the cable sorrowfully and the smashed images.

'Why did you do it, sir? Why did you destroy them?'

'Because you didn't answer me!'

'For eternity, they would have stood here. The daymarks to Dilmun. The pillars at the start of the line for the passageway. This is the cable that linked the mortal world to Dilmun the Blessed. How do you think I can ferry my boat across the ring of death now? No hand can touch a drop of that. Sink a pole in it, and you'd draw up a dose of poison. Time was, when there were only Anunnaki on the Earth and it was easy trading between Dilmun and Sumer. Since the Flood, the Annunaki have got more wary of humans. They've poisoned the water, to set a circle round their island. Those images guarded me. Hand over hand, I hauled myself along the cable they held up over the waves from the reef to the island.'

Chill struck, even in the blazing sunshine.

'I didn't see the rope.'

'There's more than that you haven't seen either, *hero-king*!'

'What's to be done? Can we rescue the line?'

'After it's been in those waters? Do you want certain death?'

'Isn't there any hope?' He would not weep yet. The island floated, impossibly close and clear now, it seemed, as the sun rose higher.

Sursunabu gazed at him, with a cautious pity. 'You've got an axe in your hand still. It's done a damage that can't be mended, now or ever. But it might patch up some kind of good.'

'Tell me what.' Hoarse, the submission of obedience, a king to a boatman.

'It will need a mighty stack of punting poles to get us across. Every single one of them can be used only once. One push, to the furthest stretch of your arms, and then drop it and let it float behind. In that poisoned sea, you couldn't lift it up, all dripping wet, and have a second go.'

Gilgamesh shuddered. 'How many must I cut?'

'Say each is five *ninda* long. One hundred and twenty? That should do it. And then you'll need a good knot of bitumen on the upper end, to handle it, and a metal plate for the tip, to hold fast on the seabed for the full length of the thrust.'

'I will do it.'

Sober, humble, Gilgamesh followed Sursunabu into the woods. He did what he was shown. He cut boughs of *urnu* cedar, carefully lopped and whittled them. He dug bitumen, heated and moulded and hardened it on the punting pole's end. He found the boatman's workshop and hammered and wrapped the copper sheets into hard ferrules.

Siduri brought them a pitcher of ale and watched them with pursed lips. Then she shook her head again and again and went away with the empty jug.

Gilgamesh watched her going up the hill. His passionate determination faltered a little. 'Is it all no good?' he asked Sursunabu. 'Is she right? Will I fail?'

'Win or fail, it's all the same to me,' said the boatman. 'I have to get across to Ziusudra, whether or no.'

Three days they laboured.

'The ferry?' asked Gilgamesh, when the last pole was stacked. His voice was small, as though he feared even now some final disappointment.

A pause, enough to punish him. Then Sursunabu laughed. 'In the boathouse over there. She's safe and dry.'

Big, black, more soundly waterproofed with bitumen than

any boat before or since. Thick solid timbers. An inner skin of leather lining all her joints, tarred inside and out and caulked in every crevice.

The hundred and twenty poles were heavy. She settled ominously low in the water.

'Good thing the weather's fair.'

But not quite calm. A little slapping sea that sent the wavelets running prettily along the stiff, black side. Sursunabu held the boat steady as Gilgamesh clambered carefully on board. Then, with a spring like a monkey, the ferryman cleared the dappled strip of shallows and landed lightly in the stern.

His push shot the boat out from the shore and the running swell smacked briskly against the bow. With a cry of fear Gilgamesh flinched back from the spray.

Sursunabu laughed, and began to hoist the sail. 'Not yet . . . hero. We haven't even cleared the bay. That ring of death is three days' sailing yet.'

A thread of white, like the hem of a garment, pleated along a line of rocks. Sursunabu, sober now, lowered the sail. The boat glided forward towards the narrow opening. The ferryman picked one mighty pole and balanced his way past Gilgamesh up into the bows. Like an upraised lance he held it over his head; then he thrust it down. The copper ferrule clattered against the stones close underneath. Sursunabu's shoulders tensed. The muscles bulged on his arms. Slowly, surely, gathering speed every moment, the boat slipped through the rocks into clearer water.

The breeze lifted the hair around Gilgamesh's face. The sun plucked up a throbbing haze from the surface of the water. From his low thwart Dilmun seemed dangerously distant still. Sursunabu was walking back the full length of the ferryboat, grasping the pole, taking the thrust of the seabed through his tautly sinewed arms. At last he reached the stern, let the long pole trail behind to its uttermost extent. The laughing droplets winked from its slanting length into the waiting sea. With a gasp of relief, Sursunabu dropped the pole. The tarry head drifted away astern. In silence Gilgamesh handed him the second pole.

But Sursunabu shook his head. 'You've seen how it's done. I'm sorry, sir. But it's you that got us into this danger. It's only fair that you should be the one that poles us through it.'

# Chapter One Hundred and Twenty-four

'What news of Ebih?'

'The Lagash army will slaughter them. When has Ninurta ever come back from a campaign without winning?'

'The men of Lagash are soft. The troops of Girsu are sheep!'

The proud voices of Uruk's young fighting bands roared round the beer table.

'When did Lord Ninurta last march against anything more threatening than a few boundary shifters from Umma?'

'He threw his net over them pretty quick!'

'He knocked their heads in with his mace!'

'Umma is the land of Inanna's son,' Ishkur said coldly.

An uncomfortable silence.

'It's a long time since Ninurta last had to fight against Kur. But he bound the demon Asag. He threw up the Hursag to make the waters of Sumer run sweet again. Do you think he can't cope with this one?' Ishkur twisted his knife in his fingers, as if he was eager to strike into something more resistant than the seethed beef.

The people of Sumer were appalled when Ninurta's troops from Lagash and Girsu came back beaten. The Lord disembarked from his warship stony-eyed, Sharur scowling viciously at his side. The troops were white-faced, shocked. There were bloody bandages, scorched faces, hair singed from the sides of heads. But wounds to the body seemed less serious than the crippling of their spirit. The Lord of the South Wind strode like thunder up the steps to the E-Kur to report his failure to his father in the dark, autumn halls.

Fear held the city of Nippur. It spread like an evil flood out of its time, when the canal bank has given way. Gales lashed the date palms. Grit, like hail, flattened the barley in the fields. No rain had fallen yet, but the early fires were not enough to warm the shivering limbs of the Sumerians. Kur was advancing. Soon the grey, cold days of dread would give way to a redder sunset of death.

The Anunnaki, peaceful overseers of growth and light, gathered in fear to face the possibility of destruction. Enlil hunched forward on his chair, barely containing his impotent anger.

'One of our number challenged the Netherworld. She walked boldly down to seize the *me* of the Great Below. She brought Ereshkigal off her throne, only for a moment. Now Kur is throwing that insult back in our face. It is rising to take what was ours. Shall we have to retreat up to Angal and leave the Earth to Ereshkigal? Will all our creation be given over to darkness and corruption? Have the gates of the Ganzir opened and the dead come out to overwhelm the living?'

The listening family of the Children of An knew the horror in his voice. Nin Lil stood pale and grieving. The boundaries had been set long ago, the rules fixed, the *me* allotted. The Lord of the E-Kur had given away part of the cosmos's power to Ereshkigal. He had not even been able to demand his own freedom.

Inanna could not contain herself. Her chest was bursting with fury. She had thrown away her weeds of mourning. Beneath her jewelled turban the locks of her hair swung like the thongs of a whip. Her eyes seemed to leap like the stallion ass bounding forward in front of a chariot. Her hand struck her lapis staff against the pavement, threatening to shatter it.

'Are you sparrows, my brothers and sisters? I am a falcon! Are you moths? I am a wasp! Will you stand and shiver when your enemy eats up the land you love? I will hurl them back! If my Uncle Ninurta's army have turned tail and fled before Ebih's army, if even the Lords of Storm quake before this rebel mountain, I will not be terrorised. Yes, I challenged Kur! And I am whole and living! The Netherworld could not hold me, the Lady of Life. We have an understanding, Ereshkigal and I. She for the Great Below, I for the Earth Above. She shall not take one cubit beyond the seven gates of the Ganzir. Here, I live! Here, I give life! Let *me* drive her army back.'

Ishkur gripped his lightning-spear beside her. Nin Gal, her mother, grew pale, said nothing. All the bewildered, trembling Anunnaki turned their half-hoping eyes upon this young, this devastatingly beautiful Lady, this girl-child, as she seemed to them still despite her two grown sons. Shara and Lulal's faces were fired with love and passionate loyalty to their mother's daring.

Ninurta's voice cracked with wounded pride. 'You think you can succeed where I did not? You were always too ambitious, Inanna. Even a Lady of War needs a human army to be the flesh-and-blood fist and muscle against the enemy troops. Can you find courage, where I was given cowardice? Will the men of Uruk die, where the warriors of Lagash ran away? Can you inspire and hold your army when mine slipped like a swarm of locusts through my net?'

Her head went up. Her eyes danced like stars even in the daylight. Her voice was strong with pride.

'I tell the Anunnaki of all the Above, yes, I can. My lion team will not turn back until Kur itself flees inside Neti's gate and the mountain closes its doors on their dead. I had a leader of armies such as Sumer needs. His *pukku* sounded the call to war. His *mikku* drove the warriors out of the arms of their mothers. Gilgamesh is gone. But I, myself, will ride my lions of war! I, Inanna, will lead the young men of Uruk, the young men of Kullab. We will defeat the hordes of Kur.'

# Chapter One Hundred and Twenty-five

The poles towered above even Gilgamesh's head. With the energy of a warrior he strode to the prow and thrust the ferrule firmly in.

Sursunabu watched, crouched closely in the very centre of the boat, furthest from the reach of any careless flick of water.

'Steady now, sir,' he murmured. 'It's a long passage and a dangerous one. Take it easy.'

Foot over foot, stumbling breath-stoppingly across the thwarts, Gilgamesh drove his way from stem to stern. The reef was slipping away, a new wake gilded with sunlight opening out behind them. The second pole dropped with an alarming splash and floated back after the first. Sweat was already standing on Gilgamesh's face.

As he picked up the next pole Sursunabu gave him and made his way forward, the boat glided on further from the rocks, still borne on the memory of his last thrust. He waited poised, till he felt her begin to slow and the waves slap more challengingly against the bow. Then down again, the long pole finding deeper water. His arms stiffened, the boat took off again.

So, length by length, pole after pole, they worked their perilous way out from the boundary of the mortal world towards Dilmun the Blessed. As the stones of the seabed receded into a green-gold twilight, Gilgamesh began to fear that his poles would not be long enough. Each push seemed to bring him bending lower over the bows, dragged his reluctant hands nearer and nearer to the water. What would happen if he could no longer touch bottom? Here, one unguarded moment could end abruptly all the long painful quest for immortality. One burning drop was all it would take.

'You're getting the hang of it nicely, sir,' Sursunabu said after the thirtieth pole, daring to break the silence at last and risk upsetting Gilgamesh's concentration. The king grunted and laboured on towards the stern without interruption of his hard-learned rhythm.

For a time the seabed seemed to level. The afternoon sun beat down. Gilgamesh stripped himself of the stinking lion pelt and let the sweat run freely. The evening came, and he moved with a slow weariness, let the ship glide on for longer and longer between the drives of his aching arms. Inanna's star came out, calm and brilliant, to watch his progress.

The sun rose again, and they were almost becalmed, the sea now a deep and joyful blue. Sursunabu moved to the side and peered down.

'It's getting deeper,' Gilgamesh panted, 'and the poles are almost done.'

But still Dilmun hovered mockingly on the horizon.

'Keep going, sir. I think we'll do it.'

The hundred and twentieth pole. A sudden stagger. 'Sursunabu! Help!' Gilgamesh tumbled forward. The ferrule found no purchase, slipped treacherously out from the boat, drawn sideways in the current. The weary king lost his balance and fell across the gunwale of the upswept prow. It almost saved him. But one hand, too exhausted to release its hold in time and snatch for safety, slid downwards with the escaping pole, touched water.

A howl broke from his lips. 'Inanna! You trickster! Is this your revenge?' he cursed the Morning Star.

It was disappointment, not physical pain. Baffled ambition, the wreckage of hope. To die here after all, and not in battle, no monster rending him, only a tarry punting pole for his final weapon.

No pain. He waited for the poison to burn through his skin, enter his veins, course searingly through his body and strike his heart.

The sea, not cold, not warm, lapped gently round his hand. Both sun and star laughed overhead.

Slowly he pulled himself upright, stared at Sursunabu. 'It was all a trick! There was no poison in the water. This is not the sea of death!'

The boatman shook his head. 'The venom was real enough. You risked both our lives. But we've come beyond the ring of danger, sir. We're in Dilmun's own sweet waters now. This is Enki's sea.'

Blue as the deepest lapis lazuli, silvered with foam. A little breeze beginning to get up as the sun strengthened and

Inanna's planet withdrew to rest.

'But the poles,' Gilgamesh queried. 'They're all gone.'

'Safe enough to hoist a bit of a sail again now, sir.'

Together they ran up a small, lateen sail. The boat leaped and bucked merrily forward. Wholesome spray sparkled over the bows, wetting them while they laughed with relief. In another half a day they covered a distance that would have taken more than a week of hard poling.

Ziusudra saw them coming, with Gilgamesh standing forward of the mast, his hand shading his eyes. He went scampering up the sand to where Kuansud was pounding corn for the day's baking.

'Wife! Is there food in the house? We've got a visitor!'

She smiled indulgently. 'Have the Anunnaki ever come and I've disgraced you with food fit for less than the table of the immortals?'

'No Anunnaki this time, my dear. Though he's a pretty lordly figure, I can tell you. Another human.'

Kuansud dropped her pestle and jumped up. 'You're teasing me again! On Dilmun? After all this time? Since we let Suila and her Puzur-Amurri go back to the land of Sumer and people the Earth again . . .' Her face creased with the old longing for her daughter, for her grandchildren, for humanity.

'Come and see! Come and see!'

In a swirl of white skirts the skinny priest-king seized her by the hand and galloped with her down the beach.

'The cable!' she cried, checking suddenly and holding him back. 'Who's cut the cable?'

At the entrance to the bay an equal pair of stone pillars, more colossal than the ones below Siduri's alehouse, reared from the dark blue water, staring back towards the peopled lands. The sunlight glinted on the copper vines falling slack and uselessly into the waves.

'Oh dear, oh dear,' tutted Ziusudra. 'I fear this is a vain and violent newcomer we may have to deal with.'

'Does he come with the permission of the Anunnaki?'

'How could he cross that sea if they didn't allow it?'

'But will they let him leave?' Her eyes stared anxiously up at her husband's face. His own unhappily met hers.

'Will he want to?'

Their hands sought and found each other, secure in love after all those centuries.

Sursunabu ran down the sail, and the waves washed the boat the last few lengths to the shore. Ziusudra, eager as a boy, ran into the water to haul them up on the beach. Sursunabu jumped out to join him. But Gilgamesh stood with his arms folded, head high, kingly, were it not for his wild and matted hair, his face burned by the deserts he had crossed, the bloodstained lionskin tied round his loins again.

Kuansud's frown deepened, concerned for him, concerned for themselves.

Gilgamesh stepped from the boat, but stumbled undignifiedly as his legs buckled with unaccustomed weakness. Ziusudra caught his arm.

'Steady now, steady. You've come a dreadfully hard, long journey by the look of you.'

'Take me to Ziusudra,' Gilgamesh said thickly. 'If this is the Isle of Dilmun the Blessed, lead me to Ziusudra the king.'

The priest-king laughed uproariously, a man senior to Gilgamesh, but still not old. 'Did you think Ziusudra the Distant and his wife have servants to wait upon them? In the Island of the Immortals? We ourselves are the servants of the Anunnaki here, and glad to live our own immortal lives in their service.'

His wife smiled more quietly, but with that same glad warmth with which the sun had touched the faces of the stone images.

Gilgamesh seemed to shiver. His eyes raked the spare, scrawny form of Ziusudra. Sparse hair without a ceremonial wig; a gown of unbleached linen, not entirely clean; bare feet and calloused hands. His wife in homely brown, banded simply in dull red, with streaks of flour on her breast and knees; a necklace of shells.

'*You* are Ziusudra?' He staggered, as if about to faint.

'The darling of the Anunnaki and their giddy dancer!' He pirouetted a few steps, till he caught a look from Kuansud and sobered down. 'Excuse me. We don't get many visitors . . .'

'None,' said Kuansud firmly. 'Except the Anunnaki.'

'But . . .'

'You're disappointed. What did you expect? A towering tiara? A bodyguard of lions? Seven coats of armour and a *gur* of jewels?'

'A king,' said Gilgamesh weakly. 'Yes. A man more like a king.'

'More like yourself?'

Gilgamesh turned his face away. 'I . . . How can you be Ziusudra? How could you have got what no other human in all the history of the world has laid his hands on? Immortal life! Why you? How?'

'It's a long story. And you should not be standing out in the sun to hear it.'

They guided him up the beach. There was no palace, no temple, no ziggurat. Ziusudra and Kuansud lived in a golden reed house fashioned in the style of the Land of the Two Rivers from time immemorial. Lashed pillars of cane bent into shadowed arches. Split stalks made intricate trelliswork at every window. Mats of Kuansud's weaving hung brilliant on the walls and carpeted the floor. Her pottery stood waiting with water and date wine. Simple, rustic and beautiful. No gold. No courtiers. No pride of weapons. No luxury.

'We have each other,' said Ziusudra, watching his face. 'And the company of the Anunnaki.'

'Why?' was all Gilgamesh could repeat. 'Why you?'

They seated him and served him like a royal guest, with their own hands, since there was no one else.

'Because we listened,' said Ziusudra. 'And we believed.'

He sang the tale of the anger of Enlil, while Kuansud plucked the *tigi* harp.

Their song recalled how harmony ruled the Earth, till Enlil grew jealous, lest humankind might no longer require the Anunnaki. Their numbers and their confidence disturbed the Lord of Air. The Anunnaki, alarmed, sent plagues and famine to thin their ranks. But still they grew greater. Enlil decreed annihilation. The young Lady Inanna threw herself at his feet, pleading for him to spare them. The other Children of An looked on shocked and concerned, while she poured out her love for humankind to her grandfather . . .

'Love? Inanna?'

'Yes. The Young Lady who led your father to your mother's bed, and sang the magic which kindled you between them.

'Enlil had spoken the word of death. The Anunnaki were forbidden to warn us. Only Enki the wise, the compassionate, the cunning, whispered to the reed hut where I lay after serving my Lord. I listened in the darkness, heard the plans of the Anunnaki, and followed his advice. One mighty ship, exact in all its measurements. A cargo of animals and food.

My wife, my daughter and a pilot. We were a world in miniature, cast adrift on the waters. The storm broke, the rain fell, the Buranun and the Idiglat rose and the flood swept over everything . . . everything . . .'

Silence, but for the distant, quiet waves lapping the shore.

'Well, when it was over, and we touched the mountain top, we made a sacrifice and thanked the Anunnaki.'

'*Thanked* them?'

'Inanna came and lifted the necklace An had given her, blue as the sky without clouds or rain. She promised us undying love, to bless and increase us, humans and beasts, as long as she walked the Earth. She tried to keep Enlil from finding us. She failed . . .'

Kuansud's dark eyes rose and met his, remembering. 'We thought our end had come at last, that all our effort, all that epic voyage had been for nothing. That was a terrible meeting.'

'It was Ninurta, his favourite son, who rounded on Enki, and shifted the wrath of Enlil from us to his brother. Then Enki spoke the wisest words I ever wish to hear. "Let the anger of the Anunnaki fall in smaller measure on their descendants. Let the lion and the wolf, famine and pestilence be enough to curb the folly of these humans. Ziusudra and his wife are good people, they dance before the Anunnaki, they make us offerings. They listened to me, and they obeyed. Because of my word to the reed hut they embarked on a colossal folly. Surely such crazy faith as this honours us?"

'Well, we stood trembling, watching the shudders passing over the face of Lord Air. Then Enlil bent and touched our hands. He led us back on board our ship, marooned on its mountain peak. There, he breathed on us both and gave us the gift of immortal life.

'Then, in the world we left, the Lord of the Abzu spoke the Spell of Enki, which tangled human speech. When our descendants filled the lands again that spell set people against people, and brought war. The human race will never again be strong enough to rival the Anunnaki. But us they set down here, in paradise.'

Bees buzzed among noonday flowers, heavy with nectar. Doves crooned in pomegranate trees.

Then Gilgamesh crashed his fist furiously down on his knee.

'What good is your story to me? Where is *my* opportunity?

Am I not as good a man, as good a king, as you were?'

Kuansud's fingers stilled on the harp. Husband and wife looked at each other.

'Come,' said Ziusudra gently. 'When I was a child I trained to serve before the altar. I learned to dance my childish dances, to dream small dreams, to be still a little while before my Lord. Perhaps, when the critical moment came, that was why I was ready.

'Sleep is the younger brother to death. Why don't we make a small trial? If you would fight this colossal monster, see first if you can stave off the little fox. Sit here, unsleeping, for seven nights and the six days between. Can you be faithful in the little thing to earn the greater gift?'

'And if I do?'

'You will win wisdom. Oh yes, King Gilgamesh, the Children of An have a secret waiting to show you.'

'And you *hold that secret*?'

The face was ages old now, wrinkled, compassionate. 'Yes. I know it.'

'Bless me, Great-grandfather.'

'Inanna, Inanna. I was once more to you than this.'

She did not sit curled at his feet like a little girl now. She stood, a strong and splendid woman, a spear grasped in her right hand, a net in her left. A breastplate, rich with gold, curved alarmingly over the thrust of her chest, catching the light with aggressive points of fire. Her feet were bare, even in the autumn chill, her kilt was short. An, hunched before the early fire in a thick woollen gown, looked her up and down sadly and not a little fearfully.

'Don't go, Daughter. Don't risk your precious person. I was not here to talk sense into you before you descended to mock Ereshkigal. I should have pleaded with you not to risk opening up that old wound.'

'Don't blame yourself. All the Anunnaki did your work for you, from Enlil down.'

'And still you defied them.'

'I am living to tell you, yes!'

'Have you brought pride back even from that? Ereshkigal defeated you.'

'I was not defeated! I was born again in Kur. Once Nin Gal bore me in Kurkisikil, in the Shining Land where the sun rises. Then, that second time, I was born in Kur Kigal, the

Great Below of Darkness. Yes, it was terrible. I will not speak of that to anyone. But I came through it. With Enki's help I was reborn. Yes, Ereshkigal struck me down, in her own territory. I bowed my head to her. But, in that very place of death, I found new life. It was her turn to be appalled. I came back to the Above with one resolve. I will rule as absolutely on Earth as she does Below. She shall not send up death to overwhelm Sumer.'

'Alas, child, child. Don't you see? Enlil spoke the destiny of Kur. He ordained death as well as life for mortal creation. Earth must pay its dues to Ereshkigal.'

'And I say life must have its payment too! This is our land, our time. The invaders from Below must turn back!'

'Enki would not be able to save you in a fight like this. My cunning son works subtly, with subterfuge and humour and with the susceptibility of the heart. You will be riding to outright war.'

'And I shall win it! My cause is just. Utu will lift up his hand to bless me. Ishkur will guard my flanks with his storm chariot. Shara and Lulal are my brave generals now.'

'And where is your greatest champion? Can you go to war without Gilgamesh?'

'Will you bless me or not?' The net lashed angrily against the floor.

'No,' he said, dropping his old, tired hands. 'I can't let you go. I dread my daughter Ereshkigal more than you do.'

Her face altered like a disappointed child. 'You'd let me ride into war without your blessing?'

'I am ordering you to stay safe in Uruk.' A weak, flat voice that knew it had no hope of being obeyed.

'There is no safety for you or anyone if I stay!'

'I'm too old to waste my breath. I warned you not to marry Dumuzi, if you remember. I gave in then and blessed you both. Dumuzi may have wished since I had cursed you instead.'

Her face blazed indignation. Then the old habits of fondness overcame her. Smiling persuasively, she dropped to her knees before him, 'At least, kiss me goodbye?'

His hand hovered over her gleaming head with the awful temptation to rest in benediction. She could not see the dread that clouded his features. Instead he leaned forward and kissed her on the lips with surprising passion.

She laughed, startled but pleased with the force of the love she had compelled him to acknowledge. She got to her feet, dominating the small, stuffy room. 'I shall show you a joy that need never tremble. I shall bring back victory. Ereshkigal shall not have the living Earth!'

Then she was gone, and the small house seemed unbearably gloomy and lifeless.

# Chapter One Hundred and Twenty-six

Gilgamesh was no stranger to sentry duty. The day was long spent when the meal and the story-telling were finished. But he sat in the doorway, with a stout reed pillar at his back, and settled himself to begin the most challenging vigil of his life. The unclouded sky drained into a soft, pale grey and the stars pricked through. He would not turn his head to where he knew Inanna's planet watched, first of them all.

The stars multiplied themselves in the waves, over and over.

He tried to peer across this shifting sea back the way he had come, but the horizon was lost in the dark distance as though it had never been. Such a long, hard way, such a long, hard way. If he won the secret, could he carry it back safely?

'He's starting to nod,' whispered Kuansud. 'Give him a shake.'

'Let what will be, be,' warned Ziusudra.

Gilgamesh's feet burned with the memory of deserts and mountains. His arms and back ached with the thrust of all those poles.

Inanna. It was all Inanna's doing. He had rivalled her for the rule of Uruk, for the love of her people's hearts. She had given him the *pukku* and *mikku* long ago, knowing they came from a cursed tree, knowing they would lead him to ruin. At any time she could snatch them away from him into the Netherworld. It had only needed a word from Utu and the ground had opened. She had stolen Enkidu away to mock him with death and decay. She had taunted him that she could come back from the Below, and he could not. Through his friend's hollow eyes his own death stared out at him.

'Enkidu!' he groaned.

He forced his burning gaze round to stare at the planet Dilibad.

Inanna! So beautiful. So pitiless.

He tried to imagine the young Inanna on her knees, pleading with Enlil for mercy on the human race.

'But not on me!'

Her star swam into the hovering mist. Now all the stars were dimming.

Someone was shaking his foot.

'Gilgamesh!'

With a shock he realised that he had almost fallen asleep. It was daylight. Not the soft, blue morning of yesterday, but grey overcast. It seemed to have been raining recently. He did not remember that. With a sense of panic he knew that he must have been close to dropping off. He blessed his Guardian that Ziusudra had saved him in time.

He smiled apologetically, his heart still racing with danger narrowly escaped. 'Thanks! You almost caught me napping there. After one night!'

He struggled upright again. The canes of the doorpost against which he was slumped seemed to have embedded themselves deep in his back. It was painful to disengage himself. He lifted his heavy head. His neck muscles burned. He tried to peer through crusted eyes.

Ziusudra's hand was light on his shoulder now. 'Gently does it. You will be very stiff. It has been a long sleep.'

'Sleep? You lie! I never really closed my eyes. Can't a man lower his lids when there's nothing to look at but darkness and the tricksy stars? I wasn't asleep!'

'You have slept for six and a half nights and six full days.'

'Never!' He was on his feet now, raging like a mad dog. 'Gilgamesh sleep on duty? With the secret of immortal life hanging on the bet? Do you think I'd dare to doze off? Would I throw away *that* for as much as a cat-nap? You're trying to cheat me!'

Kuansud came from the back of the house, carrying in her hands a warm, fresh-baked loaf and a pitcher of milk. She held them out to him, her eyes shining with a grave, wise pity.

'I wanted to rouse you, the first night. But my man wouldn't let me. Breakfast is ready. It has been ready every morning these seven days.' She motioned behind him. A row of loaves was ranged beside the place where he had been sitting. Each was very like the one she held in her hand, yet each in its own particular way unlike the others.

One was still fresh, though lacking the mouthwatering

smell of the new morning's baking. The next had a film of blue mould. On the third the fungus had turned to white. The fourth held only the last remnant of its moisture. The fifth was dry and hard. The sixth had cracked apart.

Gilgamesh stared down at them, at the evidence of his failure. Then up at the clouded sky and shook his fist.

'You did this, Inanna! You tricked me! You bewitched me!'

Ziusudra shook his head. 'No witchcraft, lad. Only your own mortality, your humanity. Sleep is inevitable, sooner or later. You couldn't beat him. He fell on you like a rainstorm and swept you away. So how much more invincible is his big brother, Death?'

Gilgamesh was shaken with dry bitter sobs. 'Is this all your wisdom? Is this the secret you promised me? If I *had* fought sleep off and stayed awake, was there nothing better you could have told me?'

Silence from Ziusudra and Kuansud. They did not look at each other.

Sursunabu was coming up from the beach, slowly, unhappily, as though he was reluctant to be involved in the grief and rage of this scene.

Gilgamesh said, still staring at the seven loaves, 'I have opened my eyes and found a robber in my bedchamber. Death is coming to steal me away.'

Ziusudra's face became more severe, turning to the approaching boatman. 'Sursunabu. The link is broken. You are the last of our line since the Flood who will make this crossing to Dilmun.' Kuansud began to weep silently. 'You let the images of those who serve the Anunnaki be smashed, their life-line severed. You must cut poles again to get you back to the inhabited lands. But that passage must be the last.

'Take this poor creature you have brought here. Make him look more like a man and less like a wild animal. Cut off his long hair. Wash what is left of it in the sea and tie a clean band round it. Throw away that disgusting skin. Kuansud will give you new clothes for him to stay fresh and bright with the goodness of Dilmun until he returns to Uruk. Take care of him, till you have brought him back to his own people.'

'Yes, sir.' No argument, but the voice dull and heavy with the knowledge of this glimpse of paradise denied.

Gilgamesh could not stop weeping, helpless as an exhausted child. As a child too, Sursunabu took him to the water, bathed him, cut his hair, dried him and dressed him.

Days later, when the poles for the voyage home were ready, they went on board. Already the sail was rising, beginning to billow out and dance them away. So bright and beautiful this morning, this island. Gilgamesh shut his eyes.

'Is this really the last time?' Kuansud stood beside her husband, shading her eyes from the dazzle of the waves.

'It must not happen again.'

'We shall never see him again? Sursunabu, or any of them? Our great-great-great . . . well, children of our Suila and her Puzur-Amurri, if you go far enough back.'

He squeezed her hand. 'Do you regret that, my dear? That we lived on, while they went to the Netherworld?'

She turned her head and met his eyes with a long, fond look. The boat was gathering speed.

'Poor lad. So mighty a journey, to the end of the Earth, across the sea of death. And at the end, to go home with nothing.'

'You think I should have told him?'

'If you don't, you will tell no one ever, now.'

A swift grimace of uncertainty. The boat was skimming across the bay.

Then, 'Sursunabu! Sursunabu! Come back one moment!'

The boat put about, the sail slackened and the bow wave fell. Gilgamesh was kneeling up now, gripping the gunwale, hope suddenly refusing to die.

Kuansud was walking down the beach, smiling maternally. 'We are a poor host and hostess! You struggled so far, through so many exhausting dangers, to visit us after all these centuries. And we almost let you leave us without a parting gift.' She nudged her husband.

'Well, yes. I do have something for you.'

Gilgamesh seized a pole and with a mighty heave brought the boat close inshore.

Ziusudra was looking past him, to the last of his pilots, Sursunabu.

'This Sea of Enki has many exits. Take Gilgamesh back by way of the waters of creation. Sail to the Gulf, to that deep place off Eridu.'

'The Mouth of the Abzu?'

Ziusudra inclined his head. 'Just so. That well of sweet waters bubbling through the salt. The deepest hole, where Enki dives to meet his mother Nammu.'

'What will I find there?' Gilgamesh almost croaked.

'The hole is deep. The dive is very dangerous for a mortal. But you have shown you have the courage. At the bottom of the trench, in those sweet waters, is a secret known only to the immortals . . .' They waited. Kuansud laid her hand on his arm. 'A plant. A flower like a rose, with thorns that may wound you.'

'I will suffer anything!'

'Yes,' said Ziusudra softly. 'I think you will.'

Kuansud looked at him with a sharp suspicion. But Gilgamesh tossed his pole in the air, flashing in the sunlight.

'The blessings of the Mother of all Life on you!'

The boat took off again, heading south-west.

They watched it dwindle to a speck, like a cormorant low on the waves. Their arms were round each other, their eyes and hearts far away.

'Will he find it?' Kuansud asked finally. 'Can Gilgamesh possibly succeed?'

'Oh, he'll find it.' Ziusudra's smile was as mischievous as a small boy's. 'But for the other . . . that is in the Anunnaki's hands, not ours.'

# Chapter One Hundred and Twenty-seven

'*You* will lead us to war, my Lady?'

The young men leaped to attention, spears clashing against shields. The dismay that had swept through the Land of the Two Rivers seemed to have reached its high flood mark and begun to turn.

'Yes, I, Inanna. Did you think the troops of Uruk would stay shivering inside his walls just because Gilgamesh is missing? The safety of all Sumer is at stake.'

Luudu, Gilgamesh's lieutenant, looked with awe and astonishment at the Lady standing on the highest step like an alabaster column adorned for a festival. Two spots of colour were burning in her pale face. His glance flew with rising hope to her sons Shara and Lulal, grinning like eager dogs behind her.

'We were ready to die defending the honour of Gilgamesh and the city to the last. But if you will fight for us, Lion Inanna...'

She saw the flame of courage leaping from face to face, love rushing in to warm their hearts again. She was more than a human general. She was their young Guardian, their Queen, their hope. She had been to the Netherworld and back. Kur could not hold her.

'If I lead you, we will do more than defend Uruk. We will carry the battle into the rebel territory and crush Mount Ebih!'

Beyond the river, angry with winter spate, the mountain stretched its seven-peaked range. Anger growled in its belly. Red rays shot with alarming suddenness from its mouth. Its sides were black as bee swarms with the mustering armies that broke across into Sumer whenever they chose, to raid and smash and pillage and come back celebrating.

The troops of Uruk and Kullab, the ranks of Zabalam and

Badtibira and Umma drew up on the level ground. They had to look up at Ebih. They felt in spite of their bravery like a flock of sheep that sees the eagle spread its wings across the sky.

But the sun seemed to have broken free from the vault of the sky and to be burning here on the steppe. Inanna had scorned a chariot.

Seven tawny lions, terrifying the mules of the human army . . .

Inanna, standing balanced astride them, holding the leather thongs, as though there were sturdy bronze under her naked feet and not this rippling, muscle-twitching, supernaturally vital hide, covering taut sinew and pounding blood . . .

The faces of her mortal army turned up in adoration towards her.

'Yield, Ebih!' Her voice, that needed no herald, fanned out on the strong south wind and carried to the distant crags. 'I am Inanna, whom death could not hold. I am Inanna, risen from Kur. Tell Ereshkigal the *me* of the Above are as unshakeable as the *me* of the Below. Withdraw from Sumer or learn humiliation and devastation. Bid your troops fall down on their faces now and honour me. Let me see them wipe their beards in the dust. Or else, find how the heart of Inanna can turn from love to wrath!'

A great shout rose from the ranks of humans behind her. Young men, rejoicing they were Inanna's army, her beloved.

A bellow, harsh with the grinding of rocks, silenced them.

*'Humans are expendable. Kur will always find more warriors. If the earthly dealers of death fail us, we will open the seven gates of the Ganzir. The dead themselves would rise to overwhelm the living.'*

'I know your demons and what defeats them. Life and loving!'

'You will need grimmer weapons than that today, Inanna! Your Anunnaki of the Above are powerless against me, and they know it. Ninurta fled. In Nippur they are fluttering about like moths in a sandstorm. I am going to tear those airy wings to shreds. Ereshkigal is a mightier queen than Inanna. Sumer is mine now!'

The Lady of War scorned to turn to see if the dread of Kur had eclipsed the battle-light in the eyes of her followers.

'Strike them! Show them!' Her spear flashed in the cold light. 'We will teach this proud Kur to fear me!'

'Charge, Uruk! Follow her, Kullab!'

The lions were surging across the river, splintering the diamond surface with a rush of gold.

The human voice of Luudu strove to rival hers in strength and courage. 'On Zabalam! Badtibira!'

'For the Maid! For Inanna! Follow the Lioness!'

Her seven magnificent beasts were across the river, carrying war into the territory of the invaders. Now a thousand lesser eruptions broke the fast-running shallows as Inanna's troops flung themselves after that bounding flurry of gold.

The black mass on the hillside descended swiftly, prickling with hornet stings of arrows and javelins. It grew into the barbarous shapes of hill tribes, among which, like poison in the blood, wound an insidious column of shell-backed demons. Ravens flew over them, darting aside at each roar of the mountain that flung searing rocks to redden and then blacken the air.

To the right, Ishkur drove at the mountain as if he would penetrate its skin of soil. On the left, Shara and Lulal whooped like madmen, flung their nets in a bright doom.

But the human Sumerians in the centre faltered at the steepness of the slope and the colossal terror of the rebel forces pouring down on them. As they closed with the demons, horror gripped them by the bowels.

Inanna was left alone, with the hostile forces swirling all around her. She turned, and saw her army begin to stumble and fall.

'For life and glory, my darlings!'

Luudu, lifting his head to her, felt the crazy laughter of war wiped from his face by amazed awe.

A blue-white flame struck from the forehead of Inanna, eclipsing the red rays of Mount Ebih into lurid darkness. Hot rain lashed from the storm-clouds round her, driving towards the faces of Kur like venomed spittle.

Then he turned back with a cry to fight for his life against a mace-swinging opponent. Only a human, but the blow had been almost deadly. Instead, the hillman died.

Inanna was blazing everywhere along the lines. When the young men of Uruk staggered backwards downhill with weariness under the weight of their attackers, fiery words shot from her scarlet lips rallying them, driving them back into the thick of the fray. When they screamed at the approach of demons, she threw the glory of her body between the living and the horror of death. She was tireless, giving herself for them. Even the sweat of battle on her flushed skin seemed, to the men who saw her bound to their rescue, more beautiful than if she had just stepped from her bath anointed with juniper oil. Her dishevelled hair flying in the wind swung like strong ropes which they could grasp to haul themselves up this mountainous task of conflict.

Slowly, miraculously, the Sumerian tide rose up the slopes of the rebel mountain, sweeping the dark mass of the enemy into an ever tighter enclave. Still men were falling on either side. The red fire on the peaks leaped more fitfully, darker, desperate. It fell to a sullen glow.

Inanna stood on the top of Mount Ebih. Tall and glorious against the lowering sky, rampant as her lions.

'I am Inanna, Mistress of all the Earth! Does Ebih submit?'

A frantic chattering, as harmless as frightened sparrows, rose from the encircled forces. Luudu grinned.

'Oh, Gilgamesh! You should have been here to share this!' His face turned, still expectant, to the summit. The Lords of Battle waited too.

'And Ereshkigal? Does Kur acknowledge defeat? Who rules here?'

Her voice went out on the dusky air, rang in the Above, echoed deep in the Below.

A hollow laugh shook from the lip of the crater where the last of the demons were scuttling over like damaged beetles.

'If this is the rule you want, take it, *sister*! Queen of Life!'

The red fire died from the western peaks as though a gate had closed. All across the slopes the night wind blew the kilts of the dead of either side, their only movement.

'The Earth is mine for ever! I claim the victory!' And Inanna's spear shook to the Sky as the first blazing planet stepped out.

'Victory to Inanna! Glory to the planet Dilibad! Inanna of the Seven Lions! The Maid of Battle!'

The adoring shouts gushed out like strong wine. The Young Lady smiled, radiant but still dangerous.

'Tie the living up. Parade the prisoners in Nippur and Uruk. Skin Ebih like a calf. Peg the trophy out on our lowland. Then take and destroy all that the rebel land has left. Smash the rocks of this mountain like stoneworkers' dust.

'Let the Above and the Below both acknowledge that I have

planted a boundary stone between them here today. Kur shall not pass it again. From now on I will be their Door of the Highlands, their barrier between life and death.'

The thunder of praise and love roared up to her out of the darkness.

'Hail, Inanna! Great Queen of all the World!'

# Chapter One Hundred and Twenty-eight

Blue. The heart-disturbing blue of lapis lazuli. Precious and beautiful as Inanna's necklace, the waters south of Eridu. Calm, flattened under a hot sun, so that only the slenderest threads of silver glinted along the black boat's sides.

'You'll need stones,' said Sursunabu the boatman, 'to get you down that deep.'

Red desert. Low, baked; unremitting sand. Gilgamesh scanned the uninhabited coast.

'There's no stone in Sumer. It's a land of clay. All the building stone for our palaces and temples comes from the mountains.'

'Some people have been here before you, and gone again. There's not much we leave behind us when we're dead, but it may be enough.'

Sursunabu was poling over the sandy shallows to the shore. The waders and waterfowl looked at them uneasily and enlarged their swimming circles, but did not take flight.

'There's not many travellers or hunters have been this way, by the look of it.'

There was a mound, hardly distinguishable from a wind-blown dune. Sursunabu prodded. The pole rang suddenly on a harder surface. Gilgamesh jumped out and waded through the warm water.

The sand-covered wharf was hot to touch. But below the waterline, barnacled blocks made a secret reef. He heaved and grunted, splashed a great deal in the water that tricked his eyes with reflected sunlight and swirling mud. At last he forced free two rectangular stones, larger than common bricks, heavy to carry even for an Anunnaki's son like Gilgamesh. He staggered to the boat with the first.

'Careful, now,' warned Sursunabu. 'Drop that one in, and it will go clean through the bottom boards and send us both to the Abzu.'

Gilgamesh lowered it, panting with the effort, and went back for the second one.

Out in the middle of the Gulf again it was very hot, very silent. Winter had not struck here. Gilgamesh looked round at the uncertain horizon. No sail of tiny pearl-fisher or hefty trader marked the deep shimmer of the sea or the paler blue of the sky.

'We might be the last people left in the world,' he murmured.

'If you find what you're looking for, perhaps you will be, sir.'

Gilgamesh shot a sudden, suspicious look at the boatman. But Sursunabu's face was set, watching his position. At last he nosed the boat into the faint breath of breeze, and dropped the sail.

'Here, as near as I can reckon. This is the best I can do for you. They say there are many ways into Enki's Abzu. In inland cities, they even pour offerings to him down their drains. But I'm a sailor, from a long line of pilots. This is the one we know. No pearl-fisher has ever been known to dive here and touch bottom. Or if they have, they've not come up again.'

For a while Gilgamesh seemed not to have heard him. He was gazing round at the precious blue of the sky and waves, the carnelian shore, the flash of emerald on the neck of a teal, a dolphin leaping in the distance.

'It's a risk, sir,' said Sursunabu, understanding. 'Is it worth it? If you lost it all so soon?'

'Yes!' said Gilgamesh savagely, harshly. 'Yes! It's worth any risk to live as the Anunnaki live, without fear of death. To be able to go to the Netherworld and come back again. To be like Inanna, and not like Enkidu.'

Sursunabu's hand moved in a protective sign. 'Well then,' he said. 'I'll wait . . . And good luck to you.'

He helped Gilgamesh lash the heavy stones to his ankles and plug his nose with rags for the dive. He guided him to the gunwale and stood ready to trim the tilting boat.

Gilgamesh's heels were red with the sand of Sumer. Then the mighty splash of his backward fall washed all sight of him away.

The boat spun and steadied. But its own shadow hid the darkness of Gilgamesh's plunging form.

Down, down, into a deeper, colder darkness. Were these silver fish or bubbles of light passing before his eyes? Nothing for hands to meet or feet to resist. His head was rebelling, shockingly light, wanting to race to the surface and gasp air. But the stones were relentless, carrying him down, down, to where lungs could not breathe, and mind could not think, and hope of return was blackening with every cubit.

'Did you despair in the Netherworld, Inanna,' he thought grimly, 'when they dragged you naked before Ereshkigal's throne?'

Had Enkidu known this horror, too late, plunging into the abyss after the *pukku* and *mikku*?

'Is this a trap of the Anunnaki, to send me to my death?'

No answer.

'Enki!' he begged. 'You were always kind to humans. It's your well I'm dipping into. Seize the rope! Draw me up again!'

Huge piscine craft floated impassively past. Vast tails stirred spirals of shells and sand. Gilgamesh gasped, and almost brought about his own undoing. Water entered his mouth, his agonised lungs. Sweet, fresh-tasting water, in the midst of the sea. He fought not to choke, to hold his rebellious lips from opening again. Not yet, not yet! But this was the deep sea bed, further than any human had ever dived. His nose and ears and brain seemed to be exploding. His fingers scrabbled frantically. It was impossible. How in all the immensity of this darkness could he find the one small certainty that could transform all life?

Two stabbing pains, so close upon each other it was hard for his starved brain to disentangle them. One to his heart, an agony physical as well as spiritual: I have lost! I am lost! I am finished. The Anunnaki have mocked me.

The other to his finger. A hard spine driving into the nerve.

The rose of immortality.

More urgent than a lover with a woman's body, his uncontrolled hands fumbled bruisingly among the petals, leaves, thorns, stem, roots. A firm and bushy clump. A sturdy, healthy plant. Quick, now! With the last of his failing strength he dug and scrabbled, pulled and made himself coax the last, wiry lines of root out of their primeval clay.

He almost swooned, hung on to consciousness just long enough to tuck it in the firm embrace of his girdle.

There were arms round him now, female, archetypically maternal, infinitely strong and secure. This was the breast he had yearned to lie on, even before he left the womb. The wordless song that hovers on the edge of sleep and rings beyond hearing at the moment of ecstasy.

A thorn pierced his loins, stabbing him awake.

'Mother!' scolded a laughing Lord's voice. 'Let him go!'

Nammu released him. Return to life and terrible pain. Hands clawing now for the knife at his belt. He thought his head must explode before he sawed through the strands Sursunabu had knotted round the stones. He hardly knew the moment when that heaviness of the past parted company from him and sank slowly away. He only knew that he was rushing upwards, fragile as a bubble and stretched intolerably to bursting.

He shot into sunlight, but for him it was darkness. Heat hit him, but he was deadly cold.

Sursunabu dragged his huge weight with difficulty on board, forced the water from his lungs, saw the rose tucked in his girdle and the scored skin running wet with pink and silver.

His eyes widened. His hands reached out. Then he blinked the temptation away.

'So?' he said. 'My ancestors gave you what they kept from the rest of us. Will it make you as happy as they are?'

Gilgamesh opened his eyes, as blank as a baby's.

The world seemed just as before. The rocking boat, the afternoon sky, a fish eagle soaring lazily high overhead. He closed his eyes again, breathed, rested.

'You'll be wanting to go home now, sir, I expect. Show everybody what you've found.'

With the flooding return of consciousness, the first emotion was jealous alarm. His hand darted protectively to his girdle, his eyes shot suspicion at Sursunabu. In those few, unguarded moments of rescue, had he been robbed?

The rose was whole and safe. Enormous weakness numbed him. His hand still cupped over the plant, he lay unmoving and let Sursunabu steer him towards the coast.

'This is the plant of age made young,' he murmured after a while. 'I can't eat it yet. There are still long years of manhood ahead of me. I must make a secret garden for it, a safe place to plant it, and water it and see it grow. I'll look after this better than Inanna did with her *huluppu* tree, which the Snake and

Kiskillilla and the Imdugud invaded. No one is going to steal this from me.'

The sea rocked him softly, almost without waves. The breeze was cooling, the clouded haze beginning to be tinged with pink.

'When we get to the head of the Gulf we could make for Eridu, if you like, sir.'

'And offer thanks to Enki? That might be fitting. Later, maybe. Let me get this plant home first, secretly and swiftly.'

They looped the desert coast, avoiding settlements. The vast mouth of the Buranun gaped greenly. On into a waterscape of wide lagoons and narrow channels.

'Keep away from the Iturungal and the trading canals,' ordered Gilgamesh. 'I don't want word of my coming to run ahead of me.'

Sursunabu looked at him sharply. The king was clothed and clean now. But there was a fierce, withdrawn look about him, almost like a holy man. He sat, with his thumbs tenderly telling over the leaves of the sacred plant. Its roots were cupped in fresh water, faintly reddened still with ancient clay. Its petals were scarlet as life-blood, its perfume fragrant. It breathed out a scent of indescribable freshness. Gilgamesh held one glossy green leaf between forefinger and thumb.

'How does it taste, do you think? Delicious, or bitter?' The boatman could see the longing to break off one fragment, to eat, to know. But Gilgamesh held himself under a heroic discipline. 'I'm still young and whole. I don't need it, yet.'

When Inanna had hung like a corpse on the wall of the Ganzir, Enki had sent her the bread and water of life. Gilgamesh had not been able to feed the dying Enkidu with anything to restore him.

'I'm mortally tired, sir,' said Sursunabu at last.

'We'll stop and break bread.'

Then Gilgamesh took a turn at the pole and they slowly worked their way upstream against the sluggish current.

'The river hardly moves,' said Gilgamesh. 'It's not so difficult to counter it.'

'All the same, sir, drop that pole and you'd see us drifting back and out to sea. To go against the stream you must never rest, not for a moment, or your work's soon undone.'

It had been a week now, since the dive. They had lost sight of the glittering coast, of Eridu's mound. The shimmering hill of Ur was a phantom over the reed beds. They followed the meanders through the marshes, upstream towards Uruk. The canebrakes made a narrow line of life on either side. Beyond was level desert.

Near the end of that day, Gilgamesh lifted his eyes and saw a clump of date palms.

'That's enough for today. We must be halfway home. Let's sleep in the shelter of that oasis there.'

They hid the boat in an inlet of the reeds and approached the grove. There was no sign of a house, no tents of a passing caravan. A still and shadowed pool glistened darkly, delectably cool.

Gilgamesh loosed his girdle carefully. He had carried the plant, with its roots still moist, up from the boat. He could hardly bear to let it out of his sight. Now he set it reverently on the ground, as a mother might put down her sleeping baby before she bathes.

With a sigh of relief, he slipped off the white and purple cloth of Kuansud's weaving. His body felt young and strong and free. An enormous weight was lifted from his shoulders. He would always be like this. At the first hint of age sagging his shoulders, slowing his arm, he need only come to this plant, growing in the secret garden he would make for it. He would eat a few leaves, and the deep magic of the Abzu, Nammu's first life-giving source, would enter his blood, renew him with life and strength and youth. *This* is what he was. What he would always be. Gilgamesh the immortal hero king, the ever young.

Sursunabu was already splashing the sweat of the day off him in the dark water, under the heavy fringes of the date palms. Gilgamesh stepped towards it, then gave a great shout of joy. He jumped, he leaped, he sprang. He dived his magnificent body, golden in the sunshine, bronze in the shadow, suddenly white as limestone underwater.

The sun dropped. The shade shifted. The rose of immortal life lay lit with the last light between the shadows of the trees. A tiny treasure, exposed at the edge of the desert.

# Chapter One Hundred and Twenty-nine

'Was such total destruction necessary?' It was Nin Gal who asked, watching the victory parade through Uruk beside Inanna. 'Such humiliation of the rebel land. What good does it do? Where is the love, where is the healing?'

'It had to be so,' said Inanna, turning from the balcony where she had been waving and smiling to the exulting troops that marched across the open square below her. Her face looked almost drunken, flushed, her eyes too brilliant, her smile too wide. At least, it seemed so to the concerned eyes of her mother. 'It was Either/Or. The Anunnaki of the Above or the powers of the Below. I am the Guardian of Angal.'

'You were already the Mistress of all the *Me* of Earth: of Loving and Deceiving, War and Life-making. You are Both/And, my child. When you slew your enemies, when you ground the stones of Mount Ebih into dust, I saw Ereshkigal in you. When I bore you in Kur of the Rising Light long ago, I felt you were another gift come to us out of Ereshkigal's darkness. Enlil thought he had fixed the boundaries of Kur of the east and Kur of the west and that they could not be crossed. I say there is a water between them. The Moon Boat sails it. Enki, too, knows the secrets of E-Nun, the twilight chamber of the Abzu that links two worlds.'

Inanna looked at her long, fighting indignation with love. Then she threw herself on her mother's neck, almost overwhelming the smaller Lady. 'Mother! Mother! How can I be more like you? You know the darkness, but you're always shining with love. Why hasn't the shadow entered your soul too?'

Nin Gal shook her head. 'I don't know. Your father travels the darkness. I hadn't thought about myself. Perhaps it has. Perhaps the shadow is not so terrible if you hold out your hand to it. I can't tell you. Good enough that I'm there to welcome Nanna after the dark of the month and make him laugh again.'

'You make us all laugh,' said Inanna, with tears in her eyes. 'Your home in Ur is happier than mine.'

But there was no trace of doubt in Inanna's bearing when she strode up the steps from the Karkurunna Quay to stand again before the Anunnaki in the court of the E-Kur.

She had dressed herself carefully for this occasion. The turban clasped with the eight horns of Ladyship. The wig, its blue waves curved on her brows. The painted eyes defiantly proclaiming her allure, 'Let Him Come, Let Him Come'. The small lapis lazuli Beads, clasped round her throat where the pulse of life beat so strongly. The great twin Egg Stones pendant between her breasts. The golden pectoral ornament 'Come, Man, Come', holding itself forward to be kissed. The *pala* Robe with all its myriad tufts and flounces. The golden Ring, snake-coiled on her arm. The lapis lazuli Rod and Measuring Line of authority in her hand.

She had fought against Kur and won. She had been to the Netherworld and come back. All the *Me* of the Earth were in her hands, all the *Me* of sexual power were on her voluptuous body. She had been killed, and she was alive. She was the Slayer and the Life-bringer. Where she passed, on the canal from Uruk to Nippur, the earth would bound into life again. Bulls would mount heifers. The fish would chase each other. Young men would embrace girls on every street corner with passionate desire, and the women's bodies answer. Inanna felt her power growing with every swing of her boatmen's oars, with every step as she ascended the E-Kur steps.

Her radiant face flashed triumph at An. Even Enlil seemed to have shrunk somewhat and the hand he held out to Inanna trembled slightly. Ninurta looked older.

'We must congratulate you, Nin Egalla, Nin Mesarra. You have indeed shown yourself worthy to be called Lady of the Palace, Mistress of all the *Me*. You have saved the land of Sumer.'

'And far more than that,' Enki murmured.

'I am Enlil's servant.' The words were formally meek as she bowed, but the voice was not subservient. 'My Lord himself is Kurgal. You appointed the boundaries of the cosmos at the beginning of time. I have enforced your will.'

'We reproached you for your folly when you trespassed into Kur. Now we can only applaud the wisdom and courage which has thrown the invading Kur back where it belongs.'

'Long may death stay away from the land beloved by the Children of An, unless it be the death of our enemies.'

'Come here, Inanna.'

She stepped up the rising platforms towards the thrones of the Great Four.

'An has given you his Sky House on Earth. Enki has allowed you to keep the arts of life you won from him, and heaped still more on you.'

'I am grateful to my great-grandfather and my grandfather.'

'You have two sets of grandparents!'

'I honour Enlil and Nin Lil. What Anunnaki does not?' Still that haughty tone.

He had to look up at her now. She was standing in front of him. She held no weapon in her hand today, but in her bearing it was not difficult to imagine that still more majestic sight. The Young Lady astride the backs of her lions. The inescapable net thrown over the struggling bodies of enemy invaders. The star-keen spear launched against the fiery mountain itself. The heart so high with courage she would not bow even to the Kur which had once put her to death. Never since he was a young Lord banished by the Council had Enlil been able to shake off his own dread of the Netherworld. He lived always in the E-Kur, whose innermost cell was the Kursig, where he must daily face and hold together the duality of all life. He felt more keenly than all the other Children of An the depth of the darkness in which Ereshkigal lived, the urgency of the life Inanna had to restore.

'Twice now we have trembled for your safety.'

'Twice I returned alive, and now victorious. I am the Aurochs of the Anunnaki. I am the Dragon of Angal. I am the Lion Who Is Not Afraid. The High Wall and Bolt of the Door to the Dark Lands.'

She saw him shudder.

'If you had not come back . . . Inanna, never again must we take such a risk. An must give you the blessing you went to this war without. We could not have survived without you. You hold the *Me* of Earth. Now take all the powers of the Above in your safekeeping – *for* your safekeeping . . . and ours.' His eyes, brilliant as her own, searched for her understanding. 'Take my blessing too, and with it my authority.'

He stood, and his hands rested on her shoulders. His warm breath touched her face.

She gasped. For all her pride, she had not expected this, from Enlil himself.

An rose to stand beside Enlil, tall, frail, but still with that dignity as old as creation. He motioned her slightly to kneel and she sank down, lifting her shining face to smile at him. He laid a light, kind hand on her head. She felt a stronger one join it. Wonder drove the laughter from her eyes. This was *Enlil*, not cursing her presumption but blessing her, and more than that, affirming her to act in the Above and on Earth as he once did!

A drift of corn-rich wholesomeness perfumed the air. Nin Lil was before her too. She sensed the warm solidity of Ki.

Only Enki's voice came sharp with wry humour, mocking the solemnity of the moment. 'Oh, yes. Better get it done and over. Give her all she wants. We'll only suffer for it if you keep anything back. When she hurled her wrath against Mount Ebih, her flames were so hot they boiled the fish in the depths of my Abzu!'

The Great Ones blessed her.

'Be exalted, Inanna, over all the Above. Rule in Angal as in your Sky House. Take the authority of our action and armies. What An dreams in Angal, what Enlil's Word speaks to the Earth, you shall incarnate with the reality of life.'

'I take your power! I take the authority from An and Enlil! Do not fear. I will be your roaring Lion. I will be the horned Bison. I will bring the joy of life to trample down death.'

She turned in happy amazement to her gathered family, radiant to everyone in this day of her greatest triumph. What were the cheers of a human army compared to this? She caught the delight in all their faces, in Utu's, in Ishkur's, in Geshtinanna's.

Only one was missing. One aching void in this field of joy, like a severed poppy. Dumuzi.

The breath of rain was in the air. Beyond the E-Kur, couples were already embracing, hardening their bodies against each other. Rams were chasing ewes. Birds babbled in an ecstasy of courtship. All growing things were bursting to push their colours above the soil.

Life and desire pounded in the veins of her splendid body.

Her blood beat all the harder because the year was turning to its fertile season. The end of the drought of summer, and of its terrible loss.

# Chapter One Hundred and Thirty

Very fresh and sweet, and greatly to be desired, was the scent of the rose of immortality. Mushsagkal, the Chief of Serpents, smelt it from her burrow underground.

The men splashed each other and shouted, revelling in their manhood, the boatman to cover the grief of what he had lost, the king for joy at what he had won. Very silent, Mushsagkal the Snake. She flowed into the chequered sunshine and shade under the palm fronds round the pool. Red and black, gloriously patterned, but the tough skin dulled and leathery with age.

If you had stepped closer to watch, where no one watched that evening, you might have noticed that the tapering tail was a little lighter than the flattened head and the thigh-thick, forward body. No scar was visible. That small, defiant sharpening of colour was all that remained to tell of the terrible day in Inanna's garden when Gilgamesh had taken his axe and severed the body of the Mushsagkal for daring to make her home in the roots of the Young Lady's *huluppu* tree.

The tail had grown. The wound was hidden. The Snake had not forgotten.

Was it vengeance? Could she have resisted the temptation if any other pilgrim had staggered to this oasis on the last leg of his triumphant journey home? Why should she? The plant was sweet beyond telling. The level sun fell softly on its petals and coaxed from them perfume to arouse immortal desires.

Over the delicious striations of cool mud, hot sand, Mushsagkal poured her aged body towards that fragrance. Her unclosing eyes had it in their sights now. A small but bushy plant. Each sprig was still beaded with moisture, where Gilgamesh had watered it in its pot. The leaves gleamed faintly in the light, dimly reflecting the deep red petals, or the blood of the sunset. At the heart of each flower, seven perfect, yellow stamens.

Green and red and gold, the colours of life.

Her jaws were widening now, her tongue flickering. No matter that the stems were tough, armoured with thorns.

Gilgamesh dived and swam and sang. He was a man. He would soon be like a Lord. He would live for ever. He would walk up to the E-Anna in his parade armour, past the statue of dear, dead Enkidu. He would flash his teeth in a victorious smile at great Inanna and say, 'I am one of you now!'

Not the slightest noise from the slithering Snake, inexorably crossing the barred shadows.

Gilgamesh ducked Sursunabu for the last time. 'I've won!' he yelled, to the palms, to the sky, to the spluttering boatman, to the far-off city of Uruk, to the Anunnaki themselves in Angal, to the cheated Netherworld.

He waded out of the pool, naked, magnificent.

'Look out, sir!' Sursunabu shouted a warning. 'A snake!'

Gilgamesh checked, rigid. Unarmoured, unclothed even, weaponless. Breath whistled sharply as he glimpsed the reptile, at first only a shadowed coil among the roots of the trees.

Monstrous, heaving. Swallowing some prey.

His huge fists hung empty, flexing. Would he dare to grab this devil and squeeze the life from it with his bare hands?

He ached for his axe, but the Serpent lay between him and his clothes, his weapons, the plant. The plant!

'Look, sir!' whispered Sursunabu. 'It's splitting its skin!'

All down the reptile's mottled back the thick, grey, outer skin was tearing apart, like a moth-eaten curtain too strongly pulled. Out of the imprisonment of age a new and younger *sagkal* poured on to the sunset sand. Scarlet as berries. Black as charcoal. Fire and sap and blood, brilliant and new. Her eyes were burnished gold.

As the men watched in awe, the rejuvenated Mushsagkal raised her knowing head. The unlidded eyes stared up at Gilgamesh. The colours blazed a memory of that other garden. Her voice hissed triumph.

'No, Gilgamesh, *I* have won.'

And all that beauty, all that youth, all that power, all that knowledge, flowed down the hole back to the underworld of Ningishzida, Lord of Roots and Snakes.

A catch of breath, too small for the impossible calamity entering Gilgamesh's mind. Then he started to run forward.

The clothes were there, brightness fading now as the sun went down below the rim of the desert. The weapons, axe and dagger, that should have protected his dearest treasure. The fallen girdle . . .

Dark drops of moisture still pitted the sand. A little indentation, scored with the disturbance of thorns.

Emptiness. A tiny space of sand. A colossal desert in his heart.

Gilgamesh threw back his head and howled, as he had not cried even for Enkidu. He was too stricken with grief to see the Evening Star rise through a haze of dust and grit, as though she wept blood.

'It's gone, has it, sir? Has she taken it? All of it?'

'All! Down to the last thorn.'

His tears were watering the desert now, though nothing would grow.

'All that mourning. All that struggle. Labouring across half the world and killing everything in my way. The Scorpion Pass. The sea of death. The dive that nearly cracked my heart, to the bottom of the Abzu. For her! So the Mushsagkal I thought I had killed can live for ever, while I . . . *die*!'

'Yes, sir,' said Sursunabu after a while. 'We'll all die. Except Ziusudra and his lady.'

'He knew, didn't he?' said Gilgamesh, rounding on him suddenly. 'He knew!'

'He is a wise man.'

'*And I am a fool?*'

'No bigger fool than the rest of us, sir, if you'll pardon me saying so. Though perhaps a bigger heart.'

Comfortless, supperless, utterly spent now, Gilgamesh, surprisingly, slept.

'What will you do now, sir?' asked Sursunabu next morning.

'Return to Uruk. What else is there for me now? I can't waste a moment of what little life she's left me. It's become a thousand times more precious to me, now it's all I've got. What about you?'

'I've lost too. Shut out from Dilmun. I won't be allowed back there again. I'm the last of the pilots. And no children. There's none of our line will ever see Ziusudra and Kuansud again.'

Gilgamesh clapped him on the shoulder. He even forced a smile. 'Hide your boat in the reeds. Let's put the past behind us. Come into Uruk with me. I'll find you a job. We'll live for the present, eh? Make what we can of the future we've got. Leave a little something behind us for folk to remember us by.'

'They'll remember you all right, King Gilgamesh. I doubt that they'll bother with me.'

They finished the slow, hot, quiet journey on foot. They walked without talking, in a companionship of shared pain, king and boatman. They came in sight of Uruk. It grew out of the haze. The shining E-Anna on the peak. The restful darkness of Kullab's gardens. Street upon street of mud-built houses climbing the mound, standing on the shoulders of older dwellings to get nearer to the Anunnaki's. And round it all, like protecting arms, the mighty circle of Gilgamesh's walls.

Sursunabu stopped short on the canal bank in awe. 'Well now! I never saw anything like that in all my life! Human beings built that? Somebody thought it up, made marks on a tablet, got architects to plan it, wrote lists of everything that was wanted, and made all that happen?'

For the first time since the Mushsagkal stole his hope down into nether darkness, a real warmth lit Gilgamesh's eyes.

'The fortifications? Yes, I did it! Come on, now. Take a closer look. I'll take you up on the rampart walk . . .

'Look, there's the foundation. All hewn stone, brought down from Aratta. The Seven Sages laid good magic under that base . . .

'Feel that facing. Kiln-fired bricks, every single one of them, to stand the worst weather. Millions of them, stamped with my sign!'

Heads turned in amusement, but no one recognised the dark-burned stranger in Kuansud's cloth of archaic style, dragging his companion up the broad, brick steps and chattering furiously.

'Take a look round you now. Do you see all this land? There's a *shar* of city buildings, a *shar* of orchards and fields, a *shar* of grazing. To say nothing of the fallow land reserved for Inanna. All mine, as king of Uruk, *en* to Inanna . . .'

But he was weeping now.

The boatman could not touch him, could not comfort him.

'Why didn't I leave the *pukku* in the carpenter's workshop!

His little daughter liked to play with the *mikku* for a toy. If only I'd told her to keep it!'

'You think the immortals have punished you with death, sir? You're no worse than the rest of us. You're just human.'

'Human!' shouted Gilgamesh, beating his fist on the hard, brick rampart. 'In the land of the Young Lady?'

'Sir?' A woman in hierodule's dress came round the nearest turret of the walk and stopped, startled. 'King Gilgamesh! It is you, isn't it? You're back! You're still alive! Oh, sir, I must run and tell Inanna!'

# Chapter One Hundred and Thirty-one

Inanna stood on the blue-tiled floor of her bathroom while slaves poured pitcher after pitcher of scented water over her wonderful body. Even after her triumph she was not easily contented. Again and again she made them rub lather over every part, into every crevice. The hair of her private parts dripped black and silky. Though still more pails, warmly steaming, were brought, and fresh vases of ointment unstoppered, she could still not feel wholly clean.

'The time for blood is over. Will you not be done?' murmured Nin Shubur.

'They raped me, and I protected them. Should I have had to fight my own cause? Why was there no one to defend my honour?'

Her women looked at each other through the steam.

'Dumuzi is still in the Netherworld, my lady.'

'No human hero?'

'The men gave you their best. Gilgamesh has never returned.'

'And I still live on! I have what Gilgamesh wants, what Dumuzi wants, eternal life on Earth.' The bitterness of disappointed love quivered in her voice.

Nin Shubur's own hands took over from the slave Nawirtum, stroking, soothing. 'All over the Earth, the people lift their eyes to your star and bless your name.'

Shivering a little, in spite of the heat, Inanna stepped from the shallow basin into the embrace of soft, woollen towels. Looking down at the water running away over the blue tiles into the drain, she fancied that it was still discoloured.

She swung round slowly, blinking tears away, in the small, fogged chamber.

'I didn't know there was so much blood in me.'

There was a glad shout, from somewhere lower down the terraces. A breathless cry swept the woman past the guards.

Light footsteps came running up the steps, through the outer chamber.

Shamhara the hierodule, who had once tamed Enkidu, stood panting in the open doorway. Her brown eyes were laughing. Her curly hair was tumbled round her shoulders.

'My Lady! Pure Inanna! He's back! He's here! Gilgamesh has returned to Uruk!'

A wave of colour rushed over the open pores of Inanna's already warm body.

'Here? Alive?'

'Alive, but altered. I hardly recognised him. His face is burned almost black, as if he'd struggled months across deserts. He's lean and gaunt, like a vagrant who's gone short of food.'

'Has he found what he wanted? How does he seem?'

'I didn't stop to ask. But his eyes are dark, like those of a man who has lost as well as found.'

You might almost have thought a smile touched Inanna's lips. Then she shook herself and pushed the towel-wrapping slaves away.

'Gilgamesh is a hero. Whatever the outcome of his quest he would surely not come back to me without something.'

She summoned Gilgamesh up to the E-Anna. After the bitterness of her humiliation, she was half afraid he might not come. Gilgamesh had once challenged her here for authority. In his contempt, all Anunnaki, all women, had been insulted, lost their proper respect. Did he know about her greatest triumph? Had he heard how the Anunnaki had exalted her above them all?

'What will you wear?' said Nin Shubur, understanding. 'Shall I lay out the royal Robe?'

'Yes, bring me . . . No! Just my tiara and my jewels.'

The secret signs of Nin Shubur's hands should have warned her. But her women, stunned, followed her orders.

They set the eight-horned Crown of Ladyship on her head, arranged the ceremonial blue-black wig over her shoulders. They looped the lapis lazuli beads around her neck, set the Rod and Measuring Line in her hand. Her eyes and breasts and navel were painted with green, scarlet, gold. For the rest, she was clothed only in her power, awesome, blinding.

She seated herself on her Lion Throne, carved from the heartwood of the *huluppu* tree where Kiskillilla had cut her home. Two young lionesses prowled on golden leashes, like half-grown, sandy kittens. An owl hunched on each side of her, staring, wise. Her people were hushed around her, *sag-ursag*, hierodules, priestesses, priests.

They heard the chatter of a merry voice outside, a deeper one answering it more haltingly. Geshtinanna swept into the audience chamber, laughing for joy, almost dragging her half-brother with her.

They both stopped when they saw Inanna and the grave, still faces of her retinue. Geshtinanna dropped to her knees, as Gilgamesh threw himself down and covered his eyes.

'Come, King Gilgamesh. Why should you fear I will hurt you? See! I am the one who was insulted. I am the one who was raped.'

Slowly, trembling, he got to his feet. She saw how under the golden helmet, shaped to resemble turban and hair, his own newly-trimmed locks were streaked with fresh grey. The magnificent armour of the hero-king was buckled a little slackly over a sparer frame. He had tossed the red cloak over it bravely still.

Geshtinanna held his hand protectively. She led him forward.

'Inanna, Gilgamesh has come back from Dilmun the Distant. Rejoice with us!' Her eyes pleaded for a mercy no one was sure Inanna would grant.

'No human, except the ferrymen of that family, has ever set foot on Dilmun since Enlil breathed eternal life on Ziusudra and Kuansud. And you have returned to tell us the tale?' So sweet and beautiful that smile.

'The immortals spared me.' Was that bitterness in the tightness of his lips?

'Have they rewarded you?'

His eyes were fixed on her feet. He could not lift them to the terrifying loveliness of her body. She felt the healing of her being nearing completion, like a cat relaxing in the sun.

'They let me hold eternal life in my hands for a moment. The Serpent snatched it away and swallowed it all.'

'A-ah!' As though she had not known it, she who walked across Angal. 'Lift your eyes, Gilgamesh. Tell me what you see.'

She thought he dared not obey. But Geshtinanna pressed his hand. Shaking, he raised his mortal gaze to the Lady, and blinked in terror.

'The crown of the immortals,' he said huskily. 'Then . . . great feathered wings that shadow you.' His eyes travelled down her sweet-fleshed legs. 'Two clawed bird's feet.'

Inanna started up, blazing. 'I am Inanna! The Maiden, the

Lioness. The Young Lady of the Evening and Morning Star! I am not Kiskillilla the demon. *I am not Ereshkigal!*'

He had buried his face in his hands now. Geshtinanna's arms were round him. She looked from one to the other, alarmed, concerned.

'I can only say what I saw.'

Inanna was slumped in her *huluppu* chair. Her face was darkened with a conflict of emotions. 'Is that what you see when you look at the Lady of Love and Life? Is that what all men see? A demon? The Queen of Death?'

No answer from the too-mortal man standing in the presence of the Young Lady.

'Fetch my *pala* Robe!'

Slaves ran to cover the white fire of her nakedness.

Geshtinanna said softly, 'Gilgamesh has lost, Inanna. Dumuzi and I will always return from the Netherworld. He never can.'

'Poor Gilgamesh.' Inanna reached out a hand and took her *en*'s. Hers was warm, almost generous. His was cold with shock, stiff. 'You have done much to be proud of. You have built up the walls of Uruk. You took Enlil's cedars. You slew the Bull of the Sky. You found Ziusudra. Do not fear. The world will not forget you. What will you do now?'

'What is there left for me? Marry a wife. Breed children. Beautify your E-Anna. Defend your land.'

She laughed softly and stroked the hair beneath his helmet. Her perfume breathed dizzyingly around him. The gold-edged Robe was merciful, covering the glory that had shaken his senses. No sign of wings or bird claws now; she was all woman. The lion cubs settled down and purred. The owls flapped and settled.

Inanna kissed him gently on the forehead and smiled at Geshtinanna over his head.

'Go well, Gilgamesh. May Uruk be blessed under your rule. Long life and joy to you . . . And a noble death.'

Outside, thunder shook the clouds at the end of summer. The wells were running again with clean, sweet water. The smile faded from Geshtinanna's face, and she stole from the room.

Out on the steppe, Nin Sun lifted her wet face eagerly from the beer she was brewing. In the city, a girl leaned over the parapet of her house and beckoned to her lover. Rain dripped from the E-Anna terraces.

'Let me find you a loving wife, Gilgamesh.'

# Epilogue

'He is going, then?'

A figure more than ordinarily tall stood, veiled from head to foot, in the doorway of the king's chamber. The professional mourners weeping in the antechamber, the lamentation priests inside, the funerary musicians crouched around the walls had seen so many of the great coming to pay their last respects to the dying Gilgamesh that they hardly raised their heads to look at one more woman. True, she showed no sign of dishevelled hair, scratched face, ripped clothing, like the others. Who knew what lay under the light covering of black wool?

Geshtinanna nodded. She moved easily between the Anunnaki and humans. The Wine Girl was always welcome. Now, at the deathbed of her half-brother, folk looked at her with a new respect and remembered that she knew better than any human the paths of the Netherworld.

The wounded king groaned. The two women moved softly forward. The *entu*, leading Uruk's priestesses, raised her eyes and knew at once who had come. Her hand flew without conscious thought in the signs of reverence, to head and eyes and breast. The others caught the movement, and, with a sharp intake of breath, followed it. Inanna made a small but commanding gesture that stopped them from prostrating themselves on the floor.

The tear-stained queen and her kneeling children were too absorbed in grief and duty to notice.

'Send them away,' said Inanna softly.

The *entu* shepherded the palace household outside. She herself remained ceremonially at the door. Two physicians stayed, making themselves as impassive as shadows. The blind musicians played on.

'It's you!' Gilgamesh twisted against the agony of his wound. 'Have you come to gloat that my time is over so soon?'

She laid a soft hand on his forehead. 'Peace, brother. I have given you all I promised. Was there ever a king in Uruk who had a destiny like yours? You did a great wrong to the Anunnaki, but their punishment fell on Enkidu. They let you live. Why are you sad, Gilgamesh? All the light and darkness of human life we have allowed you. You have reigned supreme over my people. You have led my army into battles from which you never retreated. You have a lovely and loyal queen who has brought you a flock of children. We have kept from you one thing only. After years of victory and wealth, you have won your last great battle. You have come home to die of an honourable wound. Be glad, Gilgamesh. What more could you have asked?'

He gripped her hand savagely, even in his weakness. 'What more? You know what more! What my sister has, what my brother has, what you have! What the Mushsagkal stole from me!'

She bent and kissed him then. 'Yes, I remember. The Mushsagkal once stole a tree from me. I, the Lady of Love, wanted that tree for my marriage bed. I, the Lady of Battle, had marked that tree for my throne. You got it for me. You slew the Snake, threw out the demon, sawed off the Imdugud. You gave me my bed and my throne. You were a magnificent young hero then. Do you remember?'

'But the Snake came back to life and grew a tail again. And now she has stolen the rose of immortality. If she keeps it safe, whenever she needs, she can eat and grow young again. While I must grow old just once and die!' His fist was beating on the cedar frame of the bed.

A physician moved, fearful but solicitous, holding a flask in his hands.

Geshtinanna took it from him. 'You may wait outside. I am a doctor. I hold the *me* of healing. What needs to be done for him, what can still be done, I will do.'

For a few moments she was busy with soothing cordial, staunching a flow of blood, strapping a bandage. Inanna stood back and waited, the veil slipping a little from her hair. When Geshtinanna had finished, Gilgamesh turned his face to Inanna, still pleading, weaker now.

'Is there nothing you can do? Is this really the end of me? Will there be nothing left of me after today? Just a shade whimpering in the gloom?'

Inanna met Geshtinanna's eyes. The two women smiled, the Maid of the Evening Star, who had gone down to the Netherworld and brought back life, Geshtinanna, who was Ereshkigal's scribe. Both returned out of the darkness, eternally young.

Then Inanna let the black cloak fall from her. No sign of mourning. She stood in the full splendour of royal and divine regalia. The eyes of the *entu* priestess in the doorway flashed suddenly with knowledge.

'The seven great gates are opening for you in a wall stronger by far than the fortifications of Uruk. Enter your new realm like a king, Gilgamesh.'

They buried him magnificently, in the brilliance of his parade armour, with the golden helmet. Armed with a precious, lapis lazuli-hilted dagger, clad in a sheath of filigree gold. With copper-headed spears reversed in the ground. With ships of silver in full sail and leaf-bladed oars. With a gaming board set with gold and silver pieces.

Soldiers with copper swords lined the way underground. Court women clad in red cloaks put on their New Moon headdresses of gold and pearl-shell flowers. The harper seated herself beside a glorious instrument whose strings were keyed with gold, and from whose frame towered the lapis lazuli head of a bearded bull. The priests set a copper kettle of goodnight drink, laid ready the hundred cups of silver, copper, soapstone, clay that would be needed.

The queen took a chest of clothes with her, the most exquisite garments, chosen quite calmly. Her women had been sewing them for days now. Her cosmetics were laid out carefully in cockle shells. Harder perhaps to take this one beloved son, and leave the others. A little prince. He would have all the same attributes laid beside his father, in miniature. A little hero. He did not scream or cry, but walked like all the others, solemn, even hopeful, to his own small chamber.

The ass-drawn sledge left the queen and her grave goods under the low, brick vault. The heavy, ox-drawn cart bearing the king was manoeuvred more ponderously down the ramp. A little silver ass, a little golden bull, surmounted their rein rings. A glory of carnelian, agate, chalcedony, lapis. The treasure of basketworkers, goldsmiths, potters, leatherworkers.

The incense smoked. The flour was sprinkled. The wine

splashed. The priest ladled the dark brew into the little cups. The second, final draught. Already the men standing sentinel in the passages were drooping over their upright swords. The women lay down like beds of flowers, the edge of their robes falling across the thousands of tiny beads on their breasts.

The *entu* laid the golden saw by Gilgamesh's hand, with which they say Utu cuts his way out of his nightly prison. She whispered the words of hope in his ear. Then she raised her cup. The ranks of *sangu*, *mahhu* and *pashishu* priests followed her. She drank. They drank. And all the household of Gilgamesh, trusting, did the same.

Neti swung open his seven gates of the Ganzir.

Dark. Only the fluttering of ragged, grimy feathers, the shuffle of inhuman feet, the scrape of claws. Far, far behind him, the retinue of a king. The doorkeeper had taken his armour, his helmet, his kilt, his weapons.

'Inanna!' he found himself mourning. 'Is this what they did to you? Did they strip you, humiliate you? Did they make you feel so utterly alone, oppressed, abandoned?'

Only the slap of his bare feet on the damp rock. The snicker of the *galla* alongside him.

'Down there!' the Chief *Galla* ordered.

Like her, he must bend low, on hands and knees, crawl into darkness.

A cold, blue light now. A palace, almost black, rising up into the shadows. A copper fence, like a reed *girru*, its stakes tipped with skulls.

The courtyard was almost empty. Better not to look at those motionless sentinels on the steps. He could not help himself. The lion head, the ox face, the eagle beak, the goat with human hands, the crocodile with man's feet. They swung great maces in their fists or paws. They trod on serpents.

Then Namtar, the *sukkal* of death, seized him by the forelock and dragged him into the Ganzir's black-floored hall, threw him down before Nergal, firstborn son of Enlil, second husband of Ereshkigal.

A red cloak wrapped the Dark Lord round. In either hand he held a demon-headed mace, whose blue lips moved of their own accord, one grinning, one scowling. Their carbuncle eyes flashed angrily on Gilgamesh.

The *galla*'s hands were cruel. Gilgamesh bent, forced down to kiss the Death Lord's feet.

Two arms shot out of the cloak, swift as vipers about to strike. The mottling of plague glistened along their length. The mace heads whirled greedily.

'You have come at last, little man. Blasphemer! You who insulted the Queen of the Netherworld!'

'I have never insulted the Dark Lady! I made all the sacrifices at the dark of the moon,' Gilgamesh gasped.

'Sacrifices!' Nergal spat, a gout of blood. 'What does my Lady of Everlasting Night want with sacrifices, when all her Netherworld is peopled with death?'

'What then?'

'Yourself. The man. A living, willing man, desiring her. A great retinue is following you, Gilgamesh. They honour her. They let the earth close over them, trustingly, willingly, in hope that you, their king, could lead them to eternal safety. Only you had to be dragged here like a prisoner, fettered, protesting.'

'I didn't want to die!'

'What have you seen? What do you fear?'

'You *know*! I passed those desolate ones who eat clay and lap foul puddles. The naked ones in rotting rags. I've seen their feet shrivelled to talons. They flap wings like moulting crows. I have seen the wife taken from her wedding bed, who will never know the warmth of husband or baby. I saw the beaten king sitting in a dark corner, without people or arms or honour.'

'What might you hope to win, Gilgamesh? Why is your court and family following you in faith?'

'What is there here, for any of us?'

The shadow was stooping over him, fury beginning to crease Nergal's brow between the red-fired eyes.

'*Who* is there, Gilgamesh?'

'I served Inanna! I fought for her. I honoured her city. I enlarged E-Anna. I lost her when I lost life and light and stars and lovemaking.'

'You have crossed the River of the Netherworld. Whom will you take for your Queen here, Gilgamesh? Whom will you serve?'

'... *Ereshkigal!*' Head bowed, eyes fighting tears, voice straining to admit respect and disguise bitterness. A king, kneeling in defeat. A hero, conquered.

The shrouded Anunna on either side of the throne stirred in relief.

'*Heam!*' The word of reverence sang like the wind along their lines. Ningishzida. Nin Azimua. Uggae. Nin Ki. Ninazu. Ennugi.

An intensification of blue-white light was growing in front of his bowed face.

An eagle's golden talons.

White calves and thighs.

A pure-formed, alabaster body, proudly breasted.

A glory of rose-red wings.

Lapis lazuli chains of beads looping the pillared neck.

A face he dared not look upon.

The eight-horned tiara.

'Ereshkigal! . . . *Inanna?*'

'*No life above, unless there is death below. No stepping through the gates of morning without a going down into the west. We share the world, Angal Above, Kigal Below. Men die a little death upon Inanna's bed. Men find eternal life here in my darkness. Welcome, Gilgamesh.*'

Friendly hands were reaching out to him on every side.

'Welcome, Gilgamesh.'

'Welcome, brother!'

'*Dumuzi!*'

No longer the boyish, laughing bridegroom hiding jewels under a heap of dates. No longer the Shepherd running for his life through the wilderness of reed beds that could not save him. This was Dumuzi Abzu, King of the Deep Places, Judge of the Netherworld among the great Anunna.

Dumuzi's hands were lifting a horned tiara, gold flashing on the regalia of Lordship.

A dark red robe. A lapis lazuli sceptre. A breastplate of bull-horned silver hung over Gilgamesh's chest. Bewildered, he let them crown and clothe him, turned with embarrassed laughter in his family's hands.

The Lady's voice sang, older than Inanna's, but with the memory that it had once been merry and young, echoing across high Angal.

'She could not give you immortality, King Gilgamesh. It was not hers to grant in the Above. But I, her older sister-self, grant you eternal life in my Below. I appoint you a Judge of the Anunna over your human race. I am crowning you an Immortal Lord.'

Her hands were cooler than Inanna's, but strong and sure. The kiss from paler lips pressed on his astonished mouth. These eyes were dark and steady and true for all eternity.

'Praise be to Ereshkigal, Queen of Darkness!' he stammered.

'Look. Your people are following you, Gilgamesh. Take good care of them.'

Inanna walked through the garden of the small house in Kullab where Dumuzi had brought her as a bride. Here was the crooked apple tree under whose shade Dumuzi had set her Lion Throne the day she came back from the Netherworld and found him playing the false king. Here was the bedchamber where she had lain on her Lion Bed opening her arms, her vagina, her heart to her bridegroom.

In her hand, almost unregarded, she was carrying Gilgamesh's copper axe.

She stopped at the edge of the hill. The Buranun was shimmering with vapour. The city was loud with the lamentations for its king. Its citizens had beggared themselves with offerings to the city of the Netherworld for him.

Down there was the park where she had grown her *huluppu* tree. Where she had run in terror from the Serpent and Kiskillilla and the Imdugud. Where Gilgamesh had swung this selfsame axe and felled the tree for her.

She turned. Here were the workshops along the lowest court of the E-Anna. Here was the carpenter's shed where the *pukku* and *mikku* had been carved.

Sky House and Palace. Dumuzi and Gilgamesh. Two brothers, a Lord and a man.

And the Lady of Love must walk in her garden, alone.

She bent her head under the boughs of the apple trees that shaded a well. She fondled the red-gold, kiln-fired bricks of its coping. The well was very deep, the water dark beyond seeing.

'Mother Nammu,' she breathed. 'I know there are many gates.'

She clung on for just a moment more to the bright past. Fingered the edge of the blade, remembering.

Then she let the axe fall into the echoing depths.

She laid down her head on the edge of the well, and wept.

There was a whistling of reed pipes, a rustling of disturbed branches. Inanna lifted her head, the tears like crystals on her cheeks.

He was coming! Flinging the raindrops from the wet boughs as he ducked under them. Curls springing on his head like ram's fleece. Eyes merry in his wind-brown face. A shepherd's kilt. Bare, sensuous feet. She hardly realised she was on her feet and running towards him.

Young lovers' arms opened in joyful abandon. Bodies straining towards each other. Mouths that scarcely knew whether to pant out the dearest name or close the beloved's with a passionate kiss.

'Dumuzi! *Dumuzi!*'

He was laughing and kissing every part of her body, pulling her down to the moist earth. It was like the first time, the first Lord and Lady, the first man and woman, making love under the apple tree.

*More SF/Fantasy from Headline:*

# WINNER OF THE WORLD FANTASY AWARD

# Dan Simmons

# SONG of KALI

Calcutta – a monstrous city of slums, disease and misery, clasped in the fetid embrace of an ancient cult.

Kali – the dark mother of pain, four-armed and eternal, her song the sound of death and destruction.

Robert Luczak – caught in a vortex of violence that threatens to engulf the entire world in an apocalyptic orgy of death.

The song of Kali has just begun . . .

"*Song of Kali* is as harrowing and ghoulish as anyone could wish. Simmons makes the stuff of nightmare very real indeed."
*Locus*

0 7472 3044 7

*More Fantasy Fiction from Headline:*

# Sheila Gilluly

# GREENBRIAR QUEEN

## A GLORIOUS FANTASY EPIC

**The runes surged at once into flame so that the whole length of the wand was limned with a brilliant glow. In the dim room they watched as a second, spell-image staff materialised out of the air, seemingly, and hovered there above the real wooden stave in Llodin's hands. Two ghostly hands appeared, a mirror of the wizard's own, and seized the light wand. With an abruptness that startled them all, the magic hands moved quickly in the manner of someone breaking a twig, and the spell staff snapped in two. In the gap between the two pieces a piercingly bright gem shone like a star, caught and held there, distant and unattainable.**

The Dark Lord's reign is about to begin, for the age of doom prophesied long ago is now upon the people of Ilyria. The Greenbriar King is dead, his children have vanished, and his treacherous bastard half-brother, Dendron, now holds the throne. But more dangerous by far than Dendron is his wizard adviser, the Fallen, who can free the dread Dark Lord from exile and bring ruin to all the world.

The Fallen needs the blood of Princess Ariadne, the true Greenbriar heir, to weave his spell. But a group of loyal Watchmen would brave sorcerous evil and warriors' swords to protect their future queen. For only she can wield the magic Crystal, Ilyria's final weapon against the Darkness to come . . .

FICTION/FANTASY   0 7472 3454 X

*More Fantasy Fiction from Headline:*

# JENNY JONES

# FLY BY NIGHT

**Volume One of FLIGHT OVER FIRE**

'An extraordinary book. A vivid original. There is something very special about Jenny Jones'
**Michael Moorcock**

Eleanor Knight is a child of her age: spoiled, bored, a stranger to commitment. From another world a desperate rite of summoning calls and she is carried on a whirling nightmare of hawkflight, out of her self-indulgent unhappiness . . . to the wind-lashed coast of the Cavers, worshippers of the Moon Goddess Astret.

The Sun God Lycias and His High Priest Lefevre maintain the Stasis which holds Peraldonia, an ocean away from the Cavers, in a summery land of light and eternal life. But the Stasis has a converse side and it is in ceaseless night that the Cavers eke out a barren existence – the rite of summoning is their final despairing attempt to break Lycias' hold on Time . . .

Disoriented and dismayed Eleanor wants no part of the Cavers' problems, but the Moon Goddess will not be denied. In the outsider's hands rests the fate of a people: the final heart-rending agony of choice will fall to her alone.

'Definitely something out of the ordinary, and something good' Michael Scott Rohan

FICTION/FANTASY  0 7472 3398 5

# A selection of bestsellers from Headline

| | | |
|---|---|---|
| THE PARASITE | Ramsey Campbell | £4.99 ☐ |
| GAMEWORLD | J V Gallagher | £4.99 ☐ |
| SCHEHERAZADE'S NIGHT OUT | Craig Shaw Gardner | £4.99 ☐ |
| THE GIANT OF INISHKERRY | Sheila Gilluly | £4.99 ☐ |
| THE HOODOO MAN | Steve Harris | £5.99 ☐ |
| LIES AND FLAMES | Jenny Jones | £5.99 ☐ |
| THE DOOR TO DECEMBER | Dean Koontz | £5.99 ☐ |
| HIDEAWAY | Dean Koontz | £5.99 ☐ |
| MIDNIGHT'S LAIR | Richard Laymon | £4.99 ☐ |
| HEART-BEAST | Tanith Lee | £4.99 ☐ |
| CHILDREN OF THE NIGHT | Dan Simmons | £4.99 ☐ |
| FARNOR | Roger Taylor | £5.99 ☐ |

*All Headline books are available at your local bookshop or newsagent, or can be ordered direct from the publisher. Just tick the titles you want and fill in the form below. Prices and availability subject to change without notice.*

Headline Book Publishing PLC, Cash Sales Department, Bookpoint, 39 Milton Park, Abingdon, OXON, OX14 4TD, UK. If you have a credit card you may order by telephone — 0235 831700.

Please enclose a cheque or postal order made payable to Bookpoint Ltd to the value of the cover price and allow the following for postage and packing:
UK & BFPO: £1.00 for the first book, 50p for the second book and 30p for each additional book ordered up to a maximum charge of £3.00.
OVERSEAS & EIRE: £2.00 for the first book, £1.00 for the second book and 50p for each additional book.

Name ...................................................................................

Address ................................................................................

............................................................................................

............................................................................................

If you would prefer to pay by credit card, please complete:
Please debit my Visa/Access/Diner's Card/American Express (delete as applicable) card no:

| | | | | | | | | | | | | | | | |
|---|---|---|---|---|---|---|---|---|---|---|---|---|---|---|---|
| | | | | | | | | | | | | | | | |

Signature ............................................................Expiry Date .......